SO RIGHT AND SO WRONG

Before Blythe could protest, Warren's lips found hers while his hand went to her shoulder, and he eased her back in the grass.

"What's wrong, Blythe?" Warren asked.

"I . . . I don't know," she answered. "You see, I've never been kissed like that before."

Lovingly, he captured her lips again, cupping her face with his hand so that she couldn't turn away.

Blythe wanted to scream, cry out. Her eyes were closed, while sweet sensations ran through her, running down her spine into the small of her back, then leaping like liquid fire into her loins. She didn't want him to stop. She never wanted him to stop. Her body was on fire.

Could lips that kissed like this tell lies? Could anything that felt so right be wrong? Blythe had to find out. . . .

About the Author

The granddaughter of an old-time vaudevillian, Mrs. Shiplett was born and raised in Ohio. She is married and lives in the city of Mentor-on-the-Lake. She has four daughters and several grandchildren and enjoys living an active outdoor life.

Tides of Passion

- ☐ **RETURN TO YESTERDAY** by June Lund Shiplett. (121228—$4.99)
- ☐ **JOURNEY TO YESTERDAY** by June Lund Shiplett. (159853—$4.50)
- ☐ **WINDS OF BETRAYAL** by June Lund Shiplett. (150376—$4.99)
- ☐ **THE RAGING WINDS OF HEAVEN** by June Lund Shiplett. (154959—$4.50)
- ☐ **REAP THE BITTER WINDS** by June Lund Shiplett. (150414—$4.50)
- ☐ **THE WILD STORMS OF HEAVEN** by June Lund Shiplett. (126440—$4.99)
- ☐ **SWEET SURRENDER** by Catherine Coulter. (156943—$4.99)
- ☐ **FIRE SONG** by Catherine Coulter. (402383—$4.99)
- ☐ **DEVIL'S EMBRACE** by Catherine Coulter. (141989—$4.99)

Prices slightly higher in Canada

THE GATHERING
OF THE WINDS

June Lund Shiplett

A SIGNET BOOK

SIGNET
Published by the Penguin Group
Penguin Books USA Inc., 375 Hudson Street,
New York, New York 10014, U.S.A.
Penguin Books Ltd, 27 Wrights Lane,
London W8 5TZ, England
Penguin Books Australia Ltd, Ringwood,
Victoria, Australia
Penguin Books Canada Ltd, 10 Alcorn Avenue,
Toronto, Ontario, Canada M4V 3B2
Penguin Books (N.Z.) Ltd, 182–190 Wairau Road,
Auckland 10, New Zealand

Penguin Books Ltd, Registered Offices:
Harmondsworth, Middlesex, England

Published by Signet, an imprint of New American Library,
a division of Penguin Books USA Inc.

First Printing, December, 1988
11 10 9 8 7 6 5 4 3

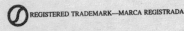 REGISTERED TRADEMARK—MARCA REGISTRADA

Printed in the United States of America

This book is dedicated to my friend and typist Elaine Seely. She came into my life with her computer when I was going down for the third time and rescued me from a horrible mess. God bless her!

1

San Antonio, Texas—May 8, 1835

Warm breezes wafted down from across the tops of the adobe buildings, bringing with them a fine dust that settled quickly on everything around, including Loedicia Chapman's aged hands where she sat on the buckboard, holding the reins, keeping the team of horses under control. She pulled her dark blue bonnet down a little farther onto her forehead to keep the dust from getting in her eyes, then, freeing one hand, used the decorative fan attached to her wrist to fan her face, gulping in a deep breath of air as she glanced back toward the government building at the far side of the plaza, where a fancy carriage was just pulling to a stop. The carriage had gone by so fast, she hadn't even been able to see the driver's face. It wasn't often wealthy strangers rode into San Antonio de Bexar, and the occupants of the shiny black carriage were obviously well off by the looks of the driver, footman, and amount of luggage bulging the boot in back.

With the dust settling, she squinted, trying to avoid the hot sun as she continued to watch the carriage, then she jumped, startled at the sound of her great-grandson's voice close to her ear.

"Who do you think it is, Grandma Dicia?" Braxton asked as he settled onto the seat beside her and took the reins, extricating them gently from her firm hands.

Loedicia smiled as she looked into his gray eyes, so intense for one so young. He'd just turned seventeen in February, and yet, with his tall height, not filled out yet, as she knew it would be when he was finally full grown, he seemed so much older at times. His face was tanned to a deep bronze, making the blond hair beneath his wide-brimmed hat look even whiter from the sun, and so many times he reminded her of his great-grandfather. Even his devilishly teasing temperament.

"So, who do *you* think it is?" she shot back.

"Whoever it is, I bet they expected more of a welcome than what they're getting." He glanced behind them, across the plaza, trying to ignore the bustle of people milling about, and watched the footman descend to the street and hurry to the other side to open the door.

Loedicia turned again, following Braxton's gaze, and both of them watched one of the occupants from the carriage step into view and gaze about hesitantly, his fancy tight-fitting calzoneras, with their silver buttons along the flare bottoms, and elegantly embroidered bolero, both of black velvet, clinging to a muscular body that looked right on the verge of manhood. He appeared to be rather irritated, called something up to the driver, then swept the wide-brimmed hat from his head, tucked it beneath his left arm, and walked toward the building they were in front of to greet a slightly rotund man, who was joining him.

"Evidently he thinks he knows where he is," Braxton said, while they both continued to watch.

Loedicia frowned, squinting a bit harder, wishing her eyesight was better. Damn! It wasn't much fun, growing old. Ah well, she was better off than most. At least the only time she really needed the stupid glass was for reading. And she still had all her front teeth too, even though most were missing in the back. Still, there were moments—like now . . .

"You think he's from the South?" she asked.

Braxton shrugged. "Your guess is as good as mine. Maybe he's one of Santa Anna's men."

"A bit young for that, wouldn't you say?"

"Hell, Grandma, he's gotta be in his twenties, or at least close to it."

"The young man you two are staring at so intently will

be nineteen later this year sometime, according to Juan Seguin," a feminine voice interrupted from below, near the boardwalk. "At least if he's the young man Antonio's told Juan about."

Loedicia and Braxton both whirled around to face the woman who'd spoken, and Braxton reached out to help her up onto the seat beside him.

"You know who he is, Ma?" he asked.

Lizette Kolter settled into the seat beside her son and smoothed the skirt of her dark green dress, then tucked a dark curl back beneath the matching bonnet as she too glanced behind them toward the fancy carriage.

"I ran into Juan a few minutes ago, and he was saying a messenger arrived at the de Leon ranch several days ago telling Antonio that his brother-in-law had died and had left instructions for Antonio to take care of his children for him." She turned back around, looking at her son, then over to her grandmother. "According to Juan, Antonio sent a letter discouraging their coming, only it looks like the letter and the children may have passed each other on the way."

"Maybe it's not them."

"Antonio would only wish." Lizette patted her son's hand. "But there's a huge letter A on the side of that carriage, dear, and Antonio's sister had been married to a gentleman named de Alvarado." She glanced back toward the carriage again and saw a well-dressed Mexican crossing the plaza toward it. "Ah, I see Juan's heading over that way now."

"And we're sitting here staring as if we've never seen a fancy carriage before," Loedicia said, half-whispering, then she drew her eyes from Lizette and started searching the street in front of them. "Now where did that husband of yours get to, Liz?" she asked testily. "Good heavens, when he said he was coming to town, I didn't know he was going to spend half the day."

Lizette's green eyes crinkled at her grandmother's attempt at being cranky. Grandma Dicia was never any good at being a bossy old lady, even though Bain did tease her all the time, saying he'd rather cross tempers with a rattlesnake. But Grandma was right this time. Where was Bain? And Lizette too began to search the crowds, trying to spot her husband among them, yet knowing he was probably with those men again.

Revolution! Revolution! It seemed that all anyone ever talked about anymore was fighting. It was would they, or should they? And if they did, what then?

Suddenly she smiled, forgetting her momentary irritation as she caught sight of Bain making his way down the street, hat off, his deep russet hair catching the sun and turning it to deep burnished fire, in a contrast to the darker clipped beard he still wore after all these years. She'd noticed though the last time she'd trimmed it a few gray hairs had crept in here and there, but then they were both growing older, and as she called to him, she reached up again, straightening her bonnet, hoping the small gray hairs near her own temples weren't visible, as she saw he wasn't alone.

"So, I might have known who was keeping you," she said quickly as she greeted the powerfully built man who stood beside her husband. "I didn't know you were in town, Jim. I thought you were still at Nacogdoches."

Jim Bowie smiled as he always did at the sight of Bain's wife. Some folks said she was fat, most called her plump, but Bain never seemed to notice, or even care, and Jim always thought she was a lovely sight regardless.

"I rarely stay in one spot too long, you should know that, Liz," he answered, then reached up, shaking hands with Braxton, who was almost falling off the seat to reach him. "Seems like this boy of yours gets bigger every time I see him, doesn't he?"

Braxton took a deep breath as he savored the older man's firm handshake, and he opened his mouth to say something, only Jim wasn't through with his flattery.

"And I still wish I'd have known this pretty lady when she was courting age. What do you say, Grandma Dicia, you think we would've made folks sit up and take notice?"

Loedicia's eyes caught Jim's, and a strange warm feeling went through her as she smiled, the soft wrinkles in her face caught up in the warmth of the smile. "You know, I think maybe we would have at that," she answered, then looked quickly at Bain, Jim's red hair, charm and good looks reminding her too much of bygone days, and another man, whose hair had been blond instead of red, but whose eyes had been the same gentian blue. She sighed. "Well, are your meetings over for today?" she asked, changing the subject. "It's so hot, Bain, and I did tell Pretty and Luther we'd be back in time for dinner."

"Don't worry, Grandma, we'll be back way before dark," he assured her, then took Lizette's hand, squeezing it as he looked at Braxton. "You can pull out now, son, and I'll go get my horse and meet you before you can get around the corner," then he turned back to his companion, who was now staring at the same carriage they'd all been watching a few minutes before. Bain followed his gaze.

"Seguin must have been right," Jim said as they both watched Señor Juan Seguin talking animatedly in Spanish to the young man who'd descended from the fancy carriage only a short time before.

Juan was the main government authority in town, and as they all watched curiously, he glanced across the plaza, spotted them, and suddenly raised an arm, motioning for them to wait as he grabbed the young man's arm and hurried him across the dusty plaza, making their way hastily around a number of oxcarts and a buggy or two on the way.

"Aha, thank heavens for small favors, señor," Juan began when he reached them.

Bain had taken a quick glance at the young Mexican, then addressed Juan. "He's Antonio's nephew then, right?"

Juan nodded. "Sí, and I have tried to explain to him and his driver where Antonio's rancho is, only I am afraid I have only confused them." He eyed Bain hesitantly. "Could they follow you, Bain?"

Bain took another quick look at the young man, who'd undoubtedly been brought up to be a gentleman. "Better than that. I'll see him right to de Léon's door. Only I wish there was some way we could warn Don Antonio."

Juan Seguin, who wasn't quite thirty, let his sharp eyes tell Bain he knew what the other man meant. "Ah, sí," he answered. "But I am sure that when the shock is over, he will recover. But let me introduce you, Señores Kolter and Bowie, Antonio de Léon's nephew, Joaquín Luís de Alvarado. Joaquín, this is Señor Bain Kolter and Señor Jim Bowie."

Joaquín's dark green eyes framed by thick dark lashes bored into Bain's as he nodded slightly, then shook hands with both men. "Señores?"

"And my wife, Lizette, her grandmother Loedicia Chapman, and my son Braxton, Señor de Alvarado," Bain said, introducing the rest of them. Now, seeing him more closely, Loedicia was surprised at how nice-looking the young man was, and surprised also to be staring into a lovely pair of dark green eyes rather than of brown. But then, more than one Mexican had mixed blood. Many Europeans had lived out their exiles in just such faraway places as Mexico, she thought as she watched the proud look on the young man's face.

Joaquín straightened, staring hard at these people, who looked anything but prosperous with their weather-beaten wagon, piled high with foodstuffs, and their boots as dusty as those worn by the vaqueros who had ridden herd for his father back home. Well, he thought silently, at least everyone he'd talked to so far spoke well of his uncle. Perhaps all of Texas would not be as uncivilized as what he'd already seen. Although this blond young man did seem to have an air about him, Joaquín thought as he shook hands with Braxton. What was it Tío Antonio had said the last time he'd visited them in Montclava? The settlers of Texas are a breed unto themselves? And they smell faintly of cow dung too, Joaquín thought silently as he smiled, trying to be cordial.

Braxton frowned, his own thoughts wandering far afield as he tried to imagine how this fine young caballero must have lived down in . . . Where was it Juan just mentioned he'd come from? Montclava? Brax glanced over at Mr. Bowie, as Juan went on explaining that Joaquín should have the driver follow the Kolters' wagon, and that Señor Kolter would see that he and his sister arrived safely at Señor de Léon's hacienda, and Brax knew the name Montclava wouldn't sit well with Jim, since he'd lost his wife and children there only a few years earlier in a cholera epidemic.

Most of the time, Brax knew Bowie could keep the past under control, but occasionally a word here or there, a reminder . . . somehow Brax knew this was one of those times he couldn't, and minutes later, after Joaquín had returned to his carriage, and Brax got ready to rein the team out into the dusty streets of San Antonio, he looked back just in time to see Bowie heading for a nearby cantina to wash away the memory of Montclava in a round of drinks.

Braxton frowned as he straightened on the seat, then glanced toward the fancy carriage again, watching it turn to follow as it maneuvered around awkwardly in the plaza, while trying to avoid the other traffic. Then he relaxed as he saw his father mount up, and he turned back around, flicking the reins, easing the buckboard away from the buildings, and on toward the next street, with the others close behind.

For the next two hours, as the procession made its way along the rutted road, heading northwest from San Antonio, the late-afternoon sun forced the women to shade their eyes with their hands, in spite of the bonnets they were wearing, while the conversation on the wagon was centered on the occupants of the carriage behind them, and the speculation as to how Don Antonio de Léon, one of the wealthiest ranchers in the area, and a widower who'd never had any children of his own, was going to accept his life being interrupted by their arrival.

When they finally reached the cutoff that led south toward the de Léon ranch, Bain rode up alongside the buckboard.

"I promised Juan I'd see they reached de Léon safe and sound, Liz, remember?" he said.

She nodded. "Just so you don't forget dinner's waiting."

"I won't." He whirled his horse around. "I'll be as quick as I can," and he cantered back to the dust-covered black carriage and told the driver to follow him. As he rode down the left fork in the road, leading the carriage, he waved, they waved back, then Brax flicked the reins again, and the buckboard continued moving northwest.

As Bain preceded the carriage along the dusty road, the monotony of the landscape relieved here and there by the rolling, tree-lined hills, he figured he'd no doubt have to head for home cross-country later, if he wanted to get there before dark. The sun was already dipping lower in the sky, and he pulled his hat down a bit more to keep it from tanning his face any more than it already was, then patted his horse's neck affectionately, wishing as he often had the past few years that he was still riding his old black Morgan horse, Amigo. However, animals didn't last as long as people, and he had to be content now riding the stallion's namesake, even though he was a sorrel.

It wasn't quite half an hour later when Joaquín, sitting uncomfortably inside, felt the carriage slow down, and he stuck his head out the window just in time to catch sight of the stone pillars marking the entrance to the de Léon rancho. Well, at least it looked impressive, he thought, and settled back on the seat, sighing, then glanced at his young sister sitting across from him, her arm resting on a small trunk and some boxes beside her on the seat. She'd been furious there hadn't been room in the carriage's boot to hold the rest of her things, and was still pouting because Joaquín refused to bring some of the servants and another carriage, or a wagon at the least.

Her dark eyes glared at him as they had the whole trip, and he knew there probably wasn't another fourteen-year-old around who was as stubborn and ornery as Catalina could be when she made up her mind she'd been wronged.

"I still think it was stupid, having to ride with our trunks," she complained to him in Spanish as she glanced at the seat beside Joaquín, where his silver-trimmed saddle lay. "And there was no reason you couldn't have ridden. But no, I have to endure that smelly old saddle of yours the whole way, as well as being poked in the side by handles and boxes."

"It was only a few hundred miles."

"Only? You, dear brother, are a tyrant! It was a miserable ride and you know it. Not a decent place to stay on the way, and being forced to sleep on the ground. It's a wonder we weren't robbed by bandits, or worse, even killed."

"So at least it would have shut your mouth for you, wouldn't it?" he answered, then watched her fan snap to attention in disgust as she turned her head, the black mantilla covering her ebony hair catching on one of the dangly earrings gracing her ears. Madre de Dios! he thought as he watched her fuming while she tried to untangle it, what a horrible wife she was going to make for someone someday when she grew up, and he settled back on the seat, trying to get more comfortable, wondering if the young man he'd met earlier, Señor Kolter's son, had a sister, and if she was as obnoxious.

Once more Joaquín felt the carriage begin to slow down, and again he leaned toward the window, only this time his eyes narrowed curiously as he caught sight of abode walls stretching for what looked like hundreds of yards on each side of a wooden gate that lay just ahead, and within minutes he could hear shouts of welcome, in both Spanish and English, from various people.

"Well, it looks like we've arrived at last," he said as he watched Catalina finally free her earring after a long bumpy battle, then tilt her nose in the air. "That won't do you any good, you know," he went on. "Tío Antonio has no idea what it is to cater to the whims of a spoiled little muchacha, so your airs and insults will probably be lost on him."

"You, are impossible, Joaquín," she retorted furiously. "I am not having a tantrum." She reached up, patting her hair, then smoothed the skirt of her black silk traveling suit, which unfortunately had picked up stains during the long journey. "I am merely trying to look dignified, if that is at all possible."

The carriage suddenly stopped, and Catalina's face paled as she stared at her brother, suddenly losing the animosity that had filled her eyes only moments before.

"I do not want to get out," she said hesitantly as she stared at Joaquín, and her brother smiled.

Poor Catalina, she'd been so used to having her own way. "Do not worry, my little cougar cub," he assured her affectionately. "Tío Antonio will no doubt love you, temper and all."

Catalina threw him a disgusted look, just as the footman, who'd been sitting beside the driver, opened the door, and Joaquín caught a glimpse of Señor Kolter shaking hands with a man Joaquín recognized only too well.

He hadn't seen his uncle for at least eight or nine years, since Antonio de Léon rarely journeyed south, but even so, he'd kept in touch with the family most of that time, although Joaquín knew his father and Tío Antonio had had a falling-out a couple of years back over the political situation in Texas. Joaquín's father had been a Federalist, and Tío Antonio was neither a Federalist nor a Conservative, calling himself a Texan. He was a Texan who happened to have been born in Mexico, so he often said. The idea was ludicrous. Joaquín's father had said Don Antonio always referred to Texas in his letters as if he were speaking of another country entirely, and now, as Joaquín studied his uncle from inside the carriage while the footman helped Catalina down, he frowned, wondering if they were going to be able to get along.

Don Antonio finished shaking Bain's hand, then turned toward the carriage, trying not to let his consternation at having his wishes ignored show, then he stepped forward at the sight of the lovely young señorita the footman was helping to alight.

"Catalina?" he said, startled as he stared at her. He'd completely forgotten that children grow up, and he hadn't been expecting her to be so close to womanhood. "Cielos santos!" he exclaimed in their native tongue. "I had no idea you were almost grown already."

He kissed her hand, his gaze moving to inspect her face, the lips hidden somewhat behind a filigreed fan, leaving him only the dark eyes, high cheekbones, and small tapered nose to access, before turning to the young man who was stepping down from the carriage behind her.

"Joaquín! Ah, what a delight to see you, my boy!" Antonio stepped back and surveyed Joaquín for a moment. "Only I should not call you a boy, should I? You are taller than I am already."

Joaquín wanted to dislike his uncle for many reasons, but as he looked into the man's smiling face, and caught the genuine air of pleasant surprise in his eyes, he knew it was going to be hopeless. At thirty-three, Don Antonio was not only charming and considerate, but in spite of the fact that he'd always been somewhat shorter and heavier than most other men, he carried himself with an air of importance that emphasized his dark good looks. His face was clean-shaven, clothes impeccable, and Joaquín could almost see the resemblance between his uncle and the mother he'd lost at the age of ten.

Joaquín let Tío Antonio shake his hand and give him a hug, then was lost in the excitement of the baggage being unloaded, and numerous questions thrown at him.

"Ah, but here," Antonio said as he took his niece's arm, ushering her toward the lovely hacienda hidden behind the stucco walls Joaquín had seen earlier. "Come in, all of you. You too, Bain, and we'll see if we can make arrangements," and Bain, always accustomed to being of use, reached up to help one of the servants and the footman with the trunks. "Leave them," Antonio went on. "The servants will bring them in. Now, come, friend, at least stay long enough for a glass of Madeira, por favor," and Bain turned hesitantly from the carriage, following them into the hacienda that was shaded from the lowering sun by a lacey canopy of green from a number of surrounding trees.

It was a little over an hour later when Bain, after having ridden cross-country from the de Léon ranch, reined to a stop and sat his horse gazing off into the valley below him. The sun was beyond the hills already, but light still clung to the top of the ridges even though lamps were being lit in the ranch house.

Leaning forward in the saddle a little, he rested for a

few minutes after the long ride, just admiring the beauty of the land, and remembering how apprehensive he'd been thirteen years ago when they'd all decided to come out here and be a part of it. He never thought he'd ever take to raising cattle and horses the way he had, since he'd detested the plantation life of his in-laws back east. Yet as his brother-in-law Cole Dante often told him, it grows on a man. Especially the untamed beauty of this land, even with the turmoil it was in. Now he was the owner of well over four thousand acres, and someday the Double K, as the ranch was known because of its twin K's back to back, would grow until it was one of the biggest in the area, along with Cole and Heather's Crown D. Most folks didn't know whether Cole used the Crown D as his brand because Dante started with a D, or because, as rumor had it, he was really an English duke. Either way, his place had quickly picked up the name from the brand, which was the letter D with what looked like a crown on top.

Suddenly Bain sighed, straightening in the saddle. If he wanted to reach the ranch house before dark, he'd better not sit around here reminiscing like this, and he dug Amigo in the ribs, reining the sorrel toward a trail that led down the side of the hill toward home.

Brax was the first to see his father coming. He'd been sitting on the rail fence watching the south trail that led down from the hills, and he followed Bain to the back barn.

"The food's cold already," he announced as he watched his father dismount next to Amigo's stall.

Bain nodded. "I figured as much." He began unsaddling Amigo as he watched Brax out of the corner of his eye. "I suppose you're all questions."

Brax began helping. "So what's wrong with that?"

"Nothing."

They worked together for a few minutes, putting the saddle aside, and Braxton began rubbing Amigo down for his father.

"So what's he like?" he finally asked when he couldn't contain his curiosity any longer.

Bain frowned, "Well now, that's a question I don't know as I can rightly answer." He took off his hat, wiping a hand across his brow and smoothing back his hair. "From what I could see the little while I was there, he's a rather proud lad, maybe a bit too proud. Anyway, he doesn't seem to think much of us Texans." His hat went back on.

"I figured as much by the way he shook hands."

Suddenly a sound near the door caught their attention and both men turned, watching Luther, a black slave the Kolters had brought with them from South Carolina years before, come in carrying a strange-looking chair with wheels attached to its legs.

"Well, Luther," Bain said as he caught sight of the chair. "Broke another wheel, did she?"

Luther shook his head. He was every bit as tall as Bain, but not quite as broad through the shoulders, with intense eyes that could look right through a man. He and his wife, Pretty, were devoted to the family, and especially to Blythe, the Kolters' daughter and Braxton's twin.

Luther set down the chair he was carrying, then gazed at it thoughtfully. "I gotta try to find a way to make the wheel, with the brake on it, hold up better," he answered. "Now if she'd just quit losin' her temper at some fella I know, she might not take it out on the chair so much." He looked sideways at Braxton.

"She still mad because I was teasin' her?"

"It ain't teasin' when it hurts, son," Luther said as he knelt down, examining the broken wheel on the chair which looked like it might even have been a rocking chair. "Teasin' makes people laugh, not cry."

Brax flushed. "I thought she would laugh."

"Your sister's not about to laugh at the prospect of endin' up a spinster, and you know it, boy."

"I said I was sorry." Brax looked disgusted. "Sometimes I wish—"

Bain stared at his son. "You wish what?"

"I wish I'd killed the man who crippled her, instead of you."

"The revenge wasn't that sweet, Brax," Bain answered as he watched the fire sparking in his son's gray eyes. Brax was too young to be so intense, but then why shouldn't he hate the man who'd crippled his twin sister? "Come on now," Bain went on as Braxton finished currying Amigo, and threw a blanket over the sleek horse. "You said you wanted to hear about the de Alvarados. I'll tell you on the way up to the house."

They said a quick good-bye to Luther, who was already working on the chair, and by the time they walked into the front hall and Bain hung up his hat, Braxton had already formed a rather negative opinion of the de Alvarados. Yet hoped his father's description of them was exaggerated.

"You mean she's only fourteen?" Blythe complained a few minutes later, while they all sat around the dining-room table discussing the de Alvarados and Bain downed the food the cook had warmed up for him.

"So what's wrong with fourteen?" asked her younger sister, Genée, who'd just celebrated her thirteenth birthday earlier that year. "I suppose it means a person doesn't have any brains."

"It means they should still be seen and not heard," Blythe answered, and watched her sister's gray-green eyes, a mixture of color from both parents, snap irritably.

"So you say," Genée countered, then threw a strand of chestnut hair off her shoulder and looked over at her mother, who was studying the three of them curiously. "Can't you make her stop, Mother?" she asked, pleading with Lizette. "Between her and Brax, you'd think I was a baby."

"Good Lord, I don't know where you children get all the energy to argue all the time," Lizette said shaking her head. "I swear," and she turned to Bain, who was finishing the last of his meal, "maybe they don't have enough to do, dear," she suggested. "With that much energy to devote to disagreeing, I'm sure perhaps, between the two of us, we could come up with something to keep them busy. What do you think?"

"Aw, come on, Ma, we're not really arguing," Brax cut in. "Besides, we're not children."

"Then quit acting like children. If it hadn't been for your teasing, the wheel on Blythe's chair wouldn't be broken."

Brax glanced over at his twin sister, and a feeling of shame made him cringe. "She knows I didn't mean it."

Bythe's smoky gray eyes, such a contrast to her pale hair, bored directly into her brother's. "Yes, I know," she said.

Lizette looked first at one, then the other, and her heart went out to them. They were usually so close in everything. And there wasn't a day went by that Brax didn't still share something from his world with his crippled sister. Yet the frustration of having to live in two different worlds, and watching her brother being able to do all the things she longed to do, often frustrated Blythe to the point of anger. And who better to take it out on than the person closest to her.

"Come on, since I made you mad enough to break your chair, let me be your legs tonight," Brax suggested, and he stood up, starting to pull the chair Blythe was in from the table.

Blythe smiled impishly as she looked up at him. "And drop me? No, thanks."

"Have I ever dropped you?"

"No."

"Then shut up, and we'll go sit outside for a while, until it's time to go bed."

He reached down, picked her up, and headed toward the door with her.

"Watch the hall rug!" Lizette called after them, and Bain watched thoughtfully as his two oldest children left the room.

It was a little cool outside as Braxton set Blythe down on the top front step of the porch that ran the length of the big frame ranch house, then he straightened, looking down at her.

"You want me to get you a shawl?" he asked.

She shook her head. "No, it feels good. The house was too stuffy."

Blythe watched her brother flex his muscles as he sat down beside her, and she envied him those muscles that could carry him to the bunkhouse and back, and run to meet their father when he came home. And she had to admit Brax was good-looking. Even now, he was practically old enough to marry if he wanted. Oh, God, she hoped he wouldn't. Not for a long time anyway. He looked her way, and their eyes caught, the light from the lantern hanging lit on the porch casting shadows across his face.

"I really am sorry, Bly, you know that," he said, apologizing again.

She reached out and look his hand, as she had when they were small children.

"Yes, I know you are," she answered, then dropped his hand and leaned back against the porch rail beside her. "Brax, do you think anybody'll ever love me?" she suddenly asked.

He frowned. "I told you—"

"I didn't ask because of that." She straightened and looked at him for a minute, then gazed out into the night at the stars brightening the sky. "I've thought about it so many times already. I guess that's why what you said earlier hurt so badly. But do you think anyone would? My being crippled like this and all?"

"De Léon does."

"Don't be silly. He's an old man."

"In his thirties?"

"Well, he's old to me."

"But he does like you. Even Grandma Dicia said she thinks he's sweet on you. And you have to admit, he's good-looking."

"Brax, I'm serious," she said, and looked at him wistfully. "I'm talking about love, love. Like Ma and Pa, and Uncle Cole and Aunt Heather, and what Grandma Dicia had with Grandpa Roth."

Braxton's eyes narrowed as he stared at her, the mention of his great-grandfather, who'd been so dear to him, bringing back a lot of memories he wished weren't always so vague. But it was hard to remember things that happened when you were only four, no matter how hard you wanted to.

"I doubt either of us'll ever see that kind of love, Bly," he answered. "Anyway, I don't want to. I want to be my own man, and come and go as I please, and count on no one but myself."

"Then you can't get hurt, right?"

"What do you mean by that?"

"I know you, Brax. I should, we're closer than most. You think I haven't guessed why you shy away from caring too much?"

"I don't know what you're talking about."

Blythe studied her brother's face in the light from the lantern. She knew him so well.

"If you don't love, you won't be hurt if you lose that love, will you? I saw it when we were little and Grandpa Roth died. You've shut almost everyone out ever since then, haven't you?"

"Think you're pretty smart, huh?" Brax stood up and stretched. "But what's wrong with that?" He was staring down at her again. "It hurts bad enough to love you and see you like this. Why love someone else and take the chance of being hurt again?"

Blythe shook her head. "Oh, you ninny," she cried helplessly. "Hurting is part of loving, don't you know that?"

"Not for me it isn't." He felt a pang of fear run through him as he stared at this beautiful young woman who was so much a part of him. "I hate hurting, Bly," and he turned away from her, starting to walk off.

'Where're you going?'

"To see if Luther has your chair fixed yet. "I'll be right back."

Blythe watched him disappear in the darkness, heading across the drive and over to the back barn that was farther back from the house, and her heart went out to him. If only she could follow him, grab him by the shoulders, and shake some sense into him.

Suddenly she turned to the sound of footsteps behind her on the porch.

"Oh, Grandma, you scared me. I didn't hear you."

Loedicia stepped down the first two steps, then sat down beside Blythe and sighed.

"I didn't want to interrupt," she said, embarrassed. "But I couldn't help overhearing. I've been in the servants' quarters checking Corbin's leg. That steer fell on him pretty hard."

"Is it going to be all right?"

"I'm sure it will. He won't be able to ride for a while, but that's probably for the best. Your father's got enough grown men to handle the branding, without having to worry about him and Dexter getting in the way. Besides, Pretty'd rather have the boys here anyway."

Blythe studied her great-grandmother. She was still a pretty woman, even though she'd turned eighty in March. Her hair was almost pure white now, only a few gray streaks left, but the few extra pounds of flesh she'd been carrying for the past ten or fifteen years had smoothed out more than one wrinkle from her face, making her seem far younger than her years. Her violet eyes looked back at Blythe with concern.

"Did you hear Brax and me?" Blythe asked sheepishly.

Loedicia nodded. "Yes, and I guess I can't really blame him. It isn't much fun being hurt, is it?"

"No." Blythe sighed. "But love doesn't always have to hurt, does it, Grandma?"

A faraway look came to Loedicia's eyes, and she drew them away from her great-granddaughter's face and looked up at the Texas sky, remembering a hundred other skies in other places that looked just the same, and she took a deep breath.

"No, it doesn't have to, but it usually does, my dear, one way or another."

"But it's worth it, isn't it?"

Loedicia turned to Blythe again, then reached over and took her hand, squeezing it. "Yes, it's worth it, Blythe, every bit of it, and someday Brax'll understand. Don't worry, someday he'll find someone."

"I hope not for a long time though. I need him, Grandma."

"I know you do, dear, but don't hang on too tight. Remember, you're two people, not one. Besides, you may find someone yourself."

"Out here? Don't count on it—and I don't intend to marry Don Antonio either, no matter how many times he makes eyes at me. He's too old."

"And no one would expect you to."

"Good. Besides, he'd never ask me anyway, and Brax is silly to have even mentioned it."

"Speaking of Antonio, did your father say anything about what happened at the ranch?"

"Only that Joaquín de Alvarado seems to have his nose rather high in the air. Oh, yes, and he's got a fourteen-year-old sister Father says is a spoiled brat."

"Oh dear, and I was hoping . . ."

"What's that?"

"That perhaps having young people around would help Antonio get over the loneliness he's felt since Maria died."

"Good heavens, she's been dead ten years already, Grandma. I barely even remember her. You'd think he'd be used to it by now."

Loedicia stared at Blythe for a minute, then gazed up again at the stars. "One never gets over loneliness, my dear, always remember that. A person learns to live with it and cope with it, but just like losing the use of your legs like you have, it's something you never get over, no matter how hard you pretend you have." Her eyes lowered to the drive, where the vague shadows of Luther and Braxton could be seen. Blythe's special chair Luther'd made for her so she could be pushed around the house being carried between them. "But look, here come Brax and Luther, and I do believe they've got your chair fixed already."

"My lady," Luther said as he set the chair down on the hard dirt patch in front of the steps, his deep resonant voice echoing on the night air. "Your throne awaits."

Blythe looked up into Luther's smiling face, and smiled

back. What would she have ever done without him and Pretty? He'd been her legs for thirteen years now, practically ignoring his own two sons, Corbin and Dexter, to be able to do it, and Blythe was only thankful both boys understood. Blythe knew there'd been no way Luther could have avoided the carriage accident that night, with the rain and all, but there was also no way to argue with a man's guilt. Especially a man like Luther, whose heart was as big as any man's heart could be.

"Well, so who's going to do the honors?" she asked as she gestured with both arms, and Loedicia smiled as Braxton reached out, pulled Blythe gently to her feet, steadying her with his arms about her, then lifted her into his arms and set her back down in the chair.

"And would my lady like a walk before retiring?" he asked as she settled into the strange-looking chair with its funny-looking wheels Luther had confiscated off an old wagon around the ranch yard.

Blythe, affected by his playful mood and the inflection in his voice, lifted her chin haughtily, her pale blond curls bunched onto the shoulders of her dark blue cotton dress, and she gestured toward the yard. "If thou thinkst thou art strong enough to do the deed, fair knight, then push away," she quipped, and laughed heartily as Braxton grabbed the long bar Luther'd nailed to the back of the old rocking chair, tilted the chair back a little, to take the strain off the front wheels, and began shoving Blythe down the path toward the drive. Loedicia knew they'd end up down near the back corral, so Blythe could spend some time with Pegasus, the palomino horse her father'd bought special for her, some four years before, when she'd finally decided she wanted to learn how to ride. She'd named him Pegasus because she said he'd bring wings to her legs, and she was right. She'd become a skilled horsewoman in spite of her handicap, and Loedicia continued to watch them, so young, so full of life.

"She gonna do fine, Miz Dicia," Luther said as he caught the pensive look in Loedicia's eyes. "Don't you worry, Pretty and me, we're gonna see she does."

Loedicia reached out and let Luther pull her to her

feet, then she looked up at this strong black man, who wasn't just a slave, but part of the family, and she sighed. "I know, Luther," she answered softly. "It's just that . . . I guess it's just the foolish worries of an old woman, but with life so unpredictable, especially in these times, I often wonder what's in store for those two. They're not like the rest of us, you know. They're a special breed. . . . Ah well, shall we go in the house? I'm sure Bain's got far more to say about the new arrivals at the de Léon ranch than I could get out of those two," and they both took one last look in the direction of the laughing young couple, then turned, walking up the steps, and disappeared into the house.

Brax caught his breath as he slowed down, then stopped, and he stood panting heavily. They were barely two feet from the corral fence, and he tilted the chair back upright, making sure Blythe wouldn't fall forward.

"Did you have to hit every bump?" she asked, half-laughing, and his smile broadened.

"You've got a pillow on your rear end, haven't you?"

"Oh fine." She reached back, straightening her tailbone into a better position. "I'm glad Pegasus doesn't treat me so rough. Where is he anyway?" and she squinted, lifting her head so she could see over one of the lower fence rails.

"You want to lean up against the rail?" Brax asked.

She nodded, and he helped her from the chair, then propped her up, with her arms resting on the top rail. Pretty had exercised Blythe's legs every day, over the years since her accident, and although her legs had strengthened enough so she could put weight on them, they had never strengthened enough for her to control them so she could walk, and now she leaned an arm out, letting her brother's arm about her waist, with her other arm on the top rail, hold her up, and Pegasus, sensing his mistress was near, sauntered over. She touched his nose affectionately, and cooed to him softly, while Braxton watched.

"We'll go riding tomorrow if you like," Brax said, trying to please her. "I thought maybe we'd go over to the de Léons' and size things up for ourselves. What do you say?"

Blythe sighed. "Does it have to be the de Léons'? I'd rather go visit Uncle Cole and Aunt Heather. It's been ages since I've seen Teffin."

"We'll do that too," he agreed happily. "In fact, we'll see if maybe Don Antonio's nephew wants to go with us. How's that?"

She patted her palomino's nose a bit longer, letting its velvety softness soothe her, then nodded. "All right, we'll go by there first, only I hope Don Antonio isn't at home when we do. Sometimes, the way he looks at me, and the way he's so attentive, makes me embarrassed."

"I told you, he likes you."

"Well, I don't like him. At least not that way, anyway. He's nice and all, but . . . well, even if I did want to fall in love with someone, it'd be someone my own age. Now, help me back to the chair, Brax, will you?" she asked. "My legs are getting tired," and a few minutes later, as he tilted the chair back again and headed toward the house, Blythe leaned over to get one last look at Pegasus as the first faint moonbeams crept down from the hills in the distance, turning his sleek coat as pale as her hair was in its light.

2

The ride to the de Léon ranch the next morning would have been longer, only Braxton and Blythe had taken a shortcut through a dry arroyo, the hilly climb at the end always a challenge for Blythe. Her steed had done well, as had Braxton's mount, Hickory, a pinto Uncle Cole had given him when they'd first come west, years before, and he'd discovered Braxton already knew how to ride.

Now horses and riders moved like one as Brax galloped beside his sister, moving down the long winding drive that led to the walled hacienda. At first when Blythe had started to ride, Luther was always right there beside her. But eventually, as most young people will, she'd rebeled against this practice, so they'd often let her ride out alone, or what she thought was alone, for even though he wasn't right in sight, Luther was always close enough at hand that if she needed him he could reach her, although she was never aware of it. However, when her brother was along, or someone else in the family, the slave knew she was in good hands, so today as they raced side by side, Brax knew Luther was back at the ranch, and Blythe was his responsibility.

"You win," he said, reining up near the wooden gate, and she straightened in the saddle, bristling.

"You weren't supposed to let me win," she shot back.

He looked mortified. "Me, let you? Ha! Tell Father that one. Now come on, let's be a little more dignified, they might have seen us coming," and they straightened their hats as they rode through the gate, and on until they reached the shade from the trees surrounding the house.

Inside the hacienda, Don Antonio was pacing the floor irritably. Now he stopped suddenly, looking over at the young man whose life had been handed to him to guide until he finished growing to manhood.

"So you didn't want to come here. So I didn't want you to come here either, Joaquín," he said testily. "But you are here, and there's no way we can change that now. So while you are here, and until you are old enough to claim your inheritance, I think it would be wise if you at least tried to be nice to those I consider my friends."

"But they are peons, Tío, you saw for yourself. Señor Kolter was going to help the servants. And you heard him last night . . . almost burning his hand on a branding iron? Doesn't he have vaqueros to do the work for him?"

"Sí, he has vaqueros. But you must remember, Joaquín, that the people here haven't been brought up to only ride and strut and act important, as you have. Even young Braxton, Bain's son, is as skilled at working a ranch as any of his father's hands. It's the way they do things."

"I see." Joaquín stood up, straightening the ruffled front of his fancy shirt, and walked to the window of the parlor that overlooked the veranda. Suddenly his eyes narrowed, amused. "Is that why he rides in the daytime with a beautiful señorita?" he asked.

Don Antonio stepped up behind his nephew and frowned as he saw Braxton and Blythe bringing their horses to a halt at the hitchrail out front, and his jaw set stubbornly.

"You will be nice to them, Joaquín, do you understand," he said softly, yet with authority. "They are my friends. And you will speak English to them as much as possible too. They know Spanish, yes, but are more fluent in English, and prefer to use it, as do most Texans."

"As you wish," Joaquín said, and he gave his uncle a frowning look as Don Antonio turned, heading toward the door.

"Come then," Don Antonio urged him. "We can't let them just sit on their horses."

"I thought you had servants to answer the door."

"Sí, I have servants," Antonio answered. "But these two I wish to greet myself. Now come along."

Joaquín hesitated momentarily, then reluctantly followed his uncle to the front hall, where the servants were already opening the door for Braxton.

"Ah, Braxton, hola!" Antonio said, reaching out to shake Braxton's hand.

Joaquín watched the blond young man he'd met in town the day before, hat in hand, pumping Don Antonio's arm vigorously, then he glanced out the door beyond the veranda, to where the woman still sat her horse, hat off, her pale blond hair braided in back, and hanging to her waist, with a few loose curls framing her face.

"You have met my nephew, Joaquín?" Antonio asked.

Braxton nodded. "Sure have. Joaquín?" and he reached his hand out.

"Señor, Braxton, is it not?" Joaquín said in quite good English as he took the younger man's hand. "Sí, we have met." He released Braxton's hand. "But I thought my uncle said you worked on your father's ranch."

"I do, only today's Saturday. All work and no play, so they say." Braxton studied the other young man curiously. "My sister and I were hoping maybe you'd ride with us today," he went on. "After all, if you're going to live around here, you might as well learn the lay of the land."

"What a marvelous idea." Antonio was more than pleased. "I think it'd do you good, Joaquín. Where will you ride?" he asked Braxton.

"Blythe wants to go see Teffin."

"You have time for a cool drink first?"

"Afraid not. At least Blythe said she'd rather not come in this time, if you don't mind."

"Ah, not at all," Antonio said. "But perhaps we can go out and talk to her for a while while Joaquín gets his things."

"Who said I was going?"

Braxton straightened, staring hard at Joaquín. "I won't force you, Joaquín," he said firmly. "I've never forced anyone to be a friend. If you'd rather just sit and twiddle your thumbs all day, that's up to you. Besides, I hadn't thought that you might not know how to ride."

Joaquín's dark green eyes narrowed arrogantly. "You are joking surely, señor."

Brax glanced at Antonio, then back to Joaquín. "No, I didn't think I was. Not everyone knows how to handle a horse, but then, like I said, maybe some other time." Brax turned to leave. "Don Antonio—"

"Wait," Joaquín said quickly, and Braxton stopped, turning back again to face him. "All right, I will go with you, but I have to pick out a horse, and my saddle is in the harness room."

"Hey, good, come on then, I'll help you while your uncle keeps Blythe company. That all right, sir?"

Antonio smiled warmly. "More than all right, my young friend."

They started for the door, and as they walked out it, heading across the veranda to the steps, Don Antonio's eyes rested anxiously on Blythe, although his words were for the two young men.

"You know where the horses are, Brax," he said, gesturing toward the back stables. "Tell García to let Joaquín use the big black I bought from your father last year. I think it will suit his spirit fine," then he greeted Blythe, who was still astride, and he stood talking with her while Braxton and Joaquín walked the length of the veranda, instead of using the front steps, and disappeared around the side of the hacienda toward the long low stables around back.

"You said the señorita on the horse is your sister?" Joaquín asked as he straightened his dark green bolero jacket while they walked down the stone walk at the side of the hacienda.

Brax nodded. "She's my twin."

"Yes, I see where that would be."

"I think your uncle's sweet on her."

"Sweet on her?"

"Yeah, you know, he likes her."

"You mean like a querida—what you call a sweetheart?"

"I knew you'd understand."

"You are really joking with me this time, sí?"

Braxton glanced over at Joaquín. "Why would I joke? He likes her, that's all."

"But he is—"

"He's what?"

"My uncle."

"And she wouldn't have him on a silver platter, I know. But it's fun watching him fawn all over her whenever he gets a chance."

Joaquín stopped, staring at Braxton, confused. "You mean my uncle is courting your sister?"

"Hell, did I say that? You're not listening, friend. I said he likes her, but that's as far as it goes. He's a little old for her, don't you think?"

Joaquín frowned. "Many men take young wives, señor."

"Well . . . yeah, they do."

"Then I think perhaps you are poking fun at my uncle, sí?"

Braxton's eyes narrowed thoughtfully as he stared at Joaquín. "Is that what you think?"

"I am not sure, because you do not seem to be laughing."

"I'm not. I just happened to make a remark about the fact that I think he cares for her. I guess I just think it's odd for such a distinguished man to think there's anything special about my twin sister, that's all."

"But she is a beautiful woman."

"Yeah, I know." Braxton looked down the path toward the stables and the corral. "Only come on, if we're going to get that horse saddled and get out of here, we'd better get a leg on," and he began walking again.

Joaquín watched him for a second, then shrugged and followed, shaking his head.

"So where's your sister?" Braxton asked a few minutes later when they were headed back toward the front of the hacienda, leading a huge black stallion adorned with a fancy silver-trimmed saddle and halter.

"I presume she is pouting in her room," Joaquín answered, then suddenly glanced up ahead to where his uncle and Braxton's sister were waiting for them. "Aha, but I see I am wrong, señor. It looks like Catalina has joined Tío Antonio and your sister."

Braxton caught sight of a head of dark curly hair that blended dramatically with the black silk dress the girl was wearing as she stood near Blythe's palomino, her back to them.

"I've got a sister who'll be fourteen next year," Braxton confided. "Pa said your sister's about the same age. Maybe we should have brought Genée along. I hadn't thought."

"It would have done no good, señor." Joaquín's eyes were steady on his sister. "Catalina can ride a horse like the wind, but I doubt she'd join us."

"Any special reason?"

He glanced over at Braxton, a faint smile tilting the corner of his mouth. "Because she hates Texans."

"And you don't?"

"I do not know them yet, señor."

At least he wasn't illogically stubborn, Braxton thought as they neared the others, then suddenly a frown creased his forehead as Joaquín's young sister turned to greet them, and he was rather startled at the sight of her face. She looked nothing like her brother, whose eyes had a slight slant to them, indicating that perhaps there was Mexican Indian blood in the family line somewhere. Her eyes were large, round, and so dark they looked black, and where her brother's nose broadened somewhat across the bridge, hers was small, quite delicate, and with her ebony hair to make her skin look much lighter than it really was, there was a sensuously animal quality about her, reminding him of a sleek panther he'd seen in a book once.

"Your sister's only fourteen?" Braxton asked as they approached the trio.

Joaquín glanced at him curiously, then chuckled. "Believe me, señor, she may look older, but there is still the heart and head of a child inside her, I assure you. And she has the tongue of a viper to match, so do not be surprised at what she may say."

"Thanks for warning me."

Blythe was leaning forward, stroking her horse's neck, when she caught sight of her brother and Antonio's nephew heading toward them. Thank God, she thought. Another minute with these two, and it'd probably end up spoiling her whole day. She straightened, and her hand tightened on the reins, keeping Pegasus under control.

"It took you long enough," she called out as they approached. "They'll be eating lunch by the time we get there."

"Good." Braxton tried to avoid Joaquín's sister's inquisitive eyes as he swept his hat from his head. "Joaquín, I didn't introduce you earlier. My sister Blythe . . . Blythe, Don Antonio's nephew, Joaquín de Alvarado."

"Señorita." Joaquín was still holding his horse's reins in one hand, but reached up, taking her hand, and to her surprise, he kissed it lightly, then she found herself looking into an intense pair of almond-shaped green eyes beneath a thick head of hair that was a strange mixture of iridescent blue-black, with reddish highlights here and there. He wasn't necessarily handsome, yet there was a strangely rugged quality about him that belied the fancy clothes. "I see you have met my sister," Joaquín said after releasing her hand. "But your brother has not. Señor Kolter, my sister, Catalina Maria de Alvarado. Catalina, Señor Braxton Kolter."

Braxton saw Catalina's chin tilt slightly as her jaw tensed, and instinctively he knew the girl disliked being introduced to him.

"Señor," she said hesitantly.

He put on his best manners, smiling congenially. "Señorita."

Catalina's eyes narrowed as she studied Braxton. She'd seen him yesterday from a distance, but now, up close, he was even more disgusting. His boots were dusty, the clothes he wore faded and near to being threadbare, as were the strange clothes his sister wore. She had to admit, however, with the right attire on, he could possibly be quite dashing. He did have such unusually light blond hair, and his eyes were rather arresting. Such a strange shade of gray, they almost looked lavender. How old did Tío Antonio say he was? But he was a Texan, and that fact overshadowed any of her other feelings. Her eyes sparked insolently as she watched him don the well-worn hat again.

"We'd have invited you along, señorita," Braxton went on as he studied her slight figure, not quite ripe enough to be called that of a woman, but coming very close. "But your brother said you'd no doubt refuse anyway."

"I have refused," she answered. "Your sister already asked, and I told her if I want to ride, I will pick my own time and company."

Antonio's eyes narrowed. "You will go in the house, Catalina," he said. "I will not have my guests insulted like this."

The young girl glared at her uncle, then inhaled arrogantly. "You are as bad as they are, Tío," she countered. "Making me speak English when they are around. Am I in Mexico or the United States?"

"You're in Texas, señorita," Braxton answered, and he reached for his horses' reins, grabbed them, then looked back at her. "We may be part of Mexico, but believe me, we're not Mexicans. Not Santa Anna's Mexicans anyway."

"Thanks be to God," she retorted. "I doubt Santa Anna would want any part of the lot of you."

"Catalina!" Antonio's face was flushed. "You will go immediately to your room!"

The young girl's eyes swept from Braxton, to his sister, then to her brother, before finally coming to rest on her uncle again.

"Do not worry, Tío," she said belligerently. "I would rather stay in my room than associate with traitors to my country," and she whirled around and marched up the front steps of the hacienda, disappearing inside, while Antonio fell all over himself apologizing.

"Por favor, I am so sorry, both of you, forgive her, please. It was bad enough she lost her father, then to have everything around her so strange and new."

"You are too kind to her, Tío Antonio," Joaquín said, interrupting him. "Believe me, there is nothing wrong with my sister that a good hard spanking would not have cured, if it had been applied to her years ago when needed. But I am afraid my father was far too lenient when it came to Catalina."

"Spare the rod and spoil the child, eh?" Braxton asked.

Joaquín glanced at him for a moment, his eyes intense. "That, shall we say, is putting it mildly. Catalina is not just spoiled, señor, but frustratingly obnoxious."

Blythe frowned. "But she's your sister."

"Sí." Joaquín chuckled, amused. "And if I did not love her so much, I would not put up with it. But do not worry, one day she will grow up."

"In the meantime?"

Joaquín's eyes studied Blythe for a moment. "In the meantime, she will no doubt make Tío Antonio's life as miserable as she has made mine, will she not, Uncle?" he said, addressing Antonio.

Antonio stared at Joaquín, his face still flushed. "In the meantime she will learn to be a lady, whether she likes it or not," he answered. "But here, let me apologize for her uncalled-for behavior, and urge you to dismiss it from your thoughts, so you can enjoy the day." He glanced quickly in the direction Catalina had disappeared, then back again to the others. "Don't let this spoil your ride, por favor. And I see you agree with my choice of a horse." He reached out and stroked the neck of the big black stallion Joaquín had saddled. "He complements Blythe's Pegasus beautifully, does he not?"

Braxton was already starting to mount his own horse. "Now Joaquín can see if he rides as well. Ready?" he asked as he settled into the saddle.

Joaquín watched his uncle step away from the big stallion, and was just ready to mount when Catalina called his name from the doorway.

"Un momento," he said, forgetting to speak English, and handed the reins to his uncle. "I will be right back," and he strode purposefully up the steps to the door, where his sister stood on the threshold, his hat in her hand.

"You forgot your hat, Joaquín," she said to him in Spanish, and he inhaled sharply.

"Gracias. But why did you do that, Cat?" he asked. "You could at least try to get along."

"And be a hypocrite like you." Her dark eyes narrowed angrily. "Father would never have allowed this, had he known."

"Father did know, but he also knew blood is thicker than politics, and where a man lives, and what country he calls home, is not as important as whether that man is free to call it home. So unless you want me to rectify the mistakes Father made by letting you have your own way for the past fourteen years, you'd better start acting like a lady, understand?"

"Sí, I understand, but I will not like it."

"No one said you have to like it." His eyes softened as they searched hers. "We are alone now, you and I, my little cougar," he went on. "So just for me, please, you will try?"

"For you I will try, Joaquín, but I can't promise."

He took the hat from her and put it on his head, straightening it to exactly the right angle. "I will tell you all about the Kolters when I return, I promise. Now, adios," and he turned, striding back down the steps, then took the reins from his uncle and mounted. "Shall we, señor, señorita?" he said, looking from Braxton to Blythe, and within minutes they were cantering through the big wooden gate, heading away from the hacienda.

The sky was deep blue, with fragile strands of white stretching across it, the sun directly overhead, as the three riders reined their mounts single file down a sharp incline, then walked them slowly across an open field toward a dusty drive a short distance away. They'd been riding for well over an hour already, and now Joaquín glanced at the young woman riding beside him, her beautiful palomino responding instinctively to every deft movement she made with the reins. He'd noticed way back at the hacienda that, unlike most females, she was riding astride instead of sidesaddle, only, being a gentleman, he'd refrained from mentioning it. Just as he hadn't said anything about the strange clothes she was wearing, which consisted of what looked like a skirt, but was split in the middle, so she could straddle her mount, and he watched her now as they rode along. She could ride, all right. As well as her brother.

"That's the main drive over there," Braxton said, distracting Joaquín from his daydreaming as they neared the long ribbon of road some hundred or so feet ahead of them. "The ranch house is dead ahead about a mile."

"You said this Cole Dante is your uncle?" Joaquín asked.

Brax nodded. "He's Ma's brother. Pa's relatives are still back in South Carolina."

"South Carolina?"

"Yeah, Ma and Pa came out here in twenty-two."

"Then you were not born in Texas?"

"Hell no. That doesn't mean anything, though. Over half the people in Texas weren't born here."

"My uncle was."

Braxton glanced at the sturdy young Mexican at his side. "Yeah, I know," he said. "I just hope you'll remember it. Now come on, if we give the horses their heads, we might get to the house before they finish eating," and he dug his horse in the ribs, hitting the road at a gallop, Joaquín and Blythe neck-and-neck with him. A few minutes later, Braxton was reining Hickory in as they caught sight of some buildings on the horizon.

Joaquín reined up beside him, then all three moved forward again, at a walk this time, and Joaquín tried to make out the lay of the outbuildings. Unlike his uncle's hacienda, there was no wall around the Dantes' ranch, however, most of the buildings were clustered together some distance from one building that looked like it could be the main house. It was two stories high, made of rough-hewn logs, with a veranda across the front. A thin stream of smoke was visible at a chimney toward the back of the place, and as they drew near, he saw a young woman leave the veranda and start walking toward them. Her hair was deep gold, the sun gilding it with amber highlights, and she was holding down the skirt of her pale blue dress so the wind, sweeping across the open prairies, wouldn't expose her petticoat.

A hand shaded Teffin's gold-flecked topaz eyes as she watched her cousins approach the ranch, only they weren't alone today. She studied the rider with them, her eyes narrowing. He was definitely Mexican, and as they drew closer, she realized he was also quite good-looking.

"Who's with them?" Heather Dante asked, and Teffin turned sharply. She hadn't heard her mother come up behind her.

"I never saw him before," she answered.

Heather stood next to her daughter and brushed a loose strand a fiery red hair from her face, to reveal a pair of lovely violet eyes that warmed at the sight of the young people reining to a stop.

Braxton dismounted, flinging his reins over the hitchrail. "Teffin, Aunt Heather." He kissed each lightly on the cheek, then turned his attention to Joaquín, who was also out of the saddle now, and waiting, his eyes on Teffin. She was one of the loveliest young women he'd seen in a long time, and her smile was enchanting as she smiled at him. He stepped forward at Braxton's request and smiled back as Braxton introduced them, and as Joaquín had done when meeting Blythe, he kissed Teffin's hand, as well as her mother's, instead of shaking them, realizing, as he did, that mother and daughter looked nothing alike.

"Señorita, señora. My pleasure."

"You are coming with us, aren't you, Teffin?" Blythe called from the back of her horse, and it was the first Joaquín realized that Blythe was still in the saddle.

"Your sister is in a hurry?" he asked Braxton.

"Not exactly."

"Help her down, will you please, Brax," his aunt said as she put an arm about Teffin, then looked over at her niece. "Even if Teffin does go, Blythe," she informed her, "she'll have to change clothes and saddle a horse. So why don't you all grab a bite to eat while you're waiting."

Blythe looked down at her brother. "Brax?"

"Sounds good to me. Joaquín?"

"Whatever you wish, señor."

Heather smiled, squeezing her daughter's shoulder affectionately. "Good, then I'll see what we can put together," and she released Teffin, then headed toward the house, while Braxton stepped over to Blythe's horse, and Joaquín was surprised to see him reach up, help his sister from the saddle, then start walking toward the veranda, cradling her in his arms.

Teffin grabbed their horses' reins, wound them about the hitchrail, then glanced at Joaquín, who was still standing with his horse's reins in his hand, frowning, as he watched Braxton carry Blythe up the veranda steps and in through the open front door.

"What's the matter?" she asked.

His frown deepened, eyes puzzled. "He carries his sister?" he asked.

Suddenly she understood. "You didn't know Blythe was crippled?"

"Crippled? No, señorita. They said nothing, nor did Tío Antonio. They just rode over to the hacienda . . . I had no idea. . . ."

"That'd be Braxton, all right. I guess sometimes he just forgets. We're all so used to it. But come, Mother's right, you're probably all hungry," and she waited for him to fasten his own horse to the hitchrail, and they followed the others on into the house.

It was late in the afternoon when Blythe, Braxton, and Joaquín finally returned to the de León ranch, after saying good-bye to Teffin back at the Dantes'. Joaquín had turned his horse over to one of his uncle's servants, and now he stood on the steps of the huge hacienda and watched Braxton and Blythe ride back out through the gate, and he thought back over the afternoon, realizing he'd really enjoyed himself.

He hadn't expected to, naturally, and had given it a try only because of his uncle. Now he was sorry the day had ended, and he had to admit the land was every bit as beautiful as his uncle had told him, and so much like some of the mountainous areas down near Montclava.

They'd ridden through dense brush country today, across

dusty plains dotted here and there with scrub trees and bushes, then into more than one water bog, where they had to guide their horses carefully so as not to end up in waist-deep water. Braxton and Blythe both knew the land well, and Joaquín was certain Braxton also knew where every wild steer was from here to what he called the plains and Indian Territory, and Joaquín had been fascinated when Brax had led them to the northwestern reaches of the Dantes' land, where Teffin's father and some of his hands were breaking in some of the wild horses that had been rounded up during the week.

Joaquín had heard rumors about the Comanche's skill with taming horses, and was surprised to learn Teffin's father was adept at it. But then, as Teffin herself told him, her father was part Indian himself, although not Comanche. That too was peculiar, because to look at Teffin Dante, there wasn't any indication she had Indian blood. In fact, her amber hair, with its gold highlights, and lovely topaz eyes had really made an impression on him. He'd thought Braxton's sister was lovely when he'd first laid eyes on her, and yet her loveliness had faded quickly from the moment he'd looked into Teffin's unusual eyes. She was so different. Just something he couldn't explain. And in her green riding habit she told him her parents had given her for her sixteenth birthday last December, and the way she smiled at him, her eyes so warm and friendly, he'd felt as if he'd known her all his life.

Joaquín stood on the steps for a long time watching, until the Kolter twins were completely out of sight, then turned slowly and went into the house, almost bumping into Catalina, who was standing at the foot of the stairs in the entrance hall, waiting for him. Her eyes were hard and unyielding, mouth firmly set, as she stared directly at him.

"I hope you've eaten already," she offered, watching him closely. "Tío Antonio's in a horrible mood, and I doubt he'd appreciate having the servants warm up your food."

"We ate at the Dantes'."

"How nice."

"They're really not all that bad, Cat." He looked down in reproof at his young sister. "Like I said before, since we have no choice but to be here, you could try to be friends."

"With them?" Her dark eyes snapped, bristling. "Don't you remember anything Father told us, Joaquín?" she asked.

"Sí, I remember. But that was when he was alive. Well, he's not alive now, so we have to bend with the wind until it stops blowing, and if that means trying to get along with these tejanos, then that's what we have to do."

"And enjoy it?"

"Why not? What's wrong with that? Just because Father refused to associate with men he considered political enemies—por Dios—men disagree all the time."

"Men?" Her eyes narrowed and she looked at him suspiciously. "What do you mean, men? Who is she, Joaquín?"

"She? She who?"

"You can't fool me." Her eyes gleamed impishly. "You never give in this easily unless—it's not his sister, is it? Por Dios, I hope not."

"It's not anyone's sister," Joaquín retorted. "So don't think you're so smart. Now let's go find out what you did to put Tío Antonio in such a foul mood," and he took her arm to usher her toward the parlor, but she refused to budge. "All right, then tell me here," he said, releasing her arm.

Catalina took a deep breath. "How was I to know he'd get mad?" she mumbled reluctantly.

Joaquín frowned. "Over what?"

"That girl on the horse. All I said was, she sure must not be much of a lady, riding astride like that—how was I to know she rides that way because she's crippled? Nobody said anything—"

"And they shouldn't have to, young lady," Antonio interrupted from the parlor doorway. "You talk of ladies. Ladies treat guests civilly and ladies don't judge others solely by their finances and political leanings. A lady is a lady at all times, regardless of the situation, remember that." Antonio's eyes were blazing as he stepped into the entrance hall, his seething gaze making Catalina's face flush. "But then I guess I can't expect anything different from you, can I? You're your mother's daughter, all right. Rebellious and stubborn." He looked at Joaquín. "And you, are you equally as insensitive too, young man, or did you learn something today?"

"You're being rather hard on her, aren't you, Tío Antonio?" Joaquín said, defending Catalina. "After all, like she said, she had no idea Blythe's legs wouldn't give her strength enough to ride properly."

"Properly? That's just the problem, Joaquín—properly for whom?" He sighed. "I think it's time both of you learned that there's a world outside your own, and people do things differently in that world, whether it's riding, eating, or any number of things."

"Including breaking horses?" Joaquín offered.

Antonio smiled. "Ah, so you did learn something today. Bueno, you can tell your sister all about it while I go tell García which carriage we shall use tomorrow for church."

"We're going to town tomorrow?" Joaquín looked puzzled. "I thought there was a chapel here."

"Sí, there is." Antonio headed for the door. "But for your first Sunday here, I thought it best we attend Mass at the mission to acquaint you with the rest of San Antonio," and he disappeared out onto the veranda and headed for the stables.

Catalina rolled her eyes. "Oh, fine, another venture back to that godforsaken little place. Ah, well, you might as well tell me the worst, dear brother, since you seem to have enjoyed yourself—just what did you learn today?"

"What did I learn, or what are the Dantes and Kolters like?"

She started toward the parlor, letting the skirt of her dress swish crisply as she entered, with Joaquín close at her heels. "The Kolters I saw yesterday, so you can tell me what the Dantes are like," she said as she perched daintily on the sofa. "Tío Antonio said they're related to the Kolters."

Joaquín studied her for a minute, then walked to the front window and stared out, remembering once more his afternoon with the young Texans.

"They're part Indian," he finally said, knowing it would get a rise out of her, and he could hear his sister's quick intake of breath. "But then, so are the Kolters."

"That's impossible. With hair like that?"

"It's on their mother's side." He turned to face her, while Catalina tried to conjure up a picture in her mind of Señora Kolter. She'd only seen the woman from a distance yesterday, but from what little she could see of Señora Kolter's hair below her bonnet, it had looked dark.

"Señora Kolter and Señor Dante are sister and brother," Joaquín went on. "And Señora Dante's got the reddest hair and purplest eyes you've ever seen. Her eyes are just like the old lady's."

"What old lady?"

"The one who was with the Kolters yesterday. Don't you remember?" He hesitated thoughtfully, then continued. "Now, let's see, if I have everything straight, they're all the old woman's grandchildren, one way or another."

Catalina stared at him. "How could that be? If the old woman you said had violet eyes is Señora Kolter's grandmother, and this Señor Dante is Señora Kolter's brother, then how come his wife's the one whose eyes are like the old lady's?"

Joaquín shrugged. "Don't ask me. I'm only repeating what I heard."

Catalina's forehead settled into a frown. "Strange," she murmured.

"You think that's strange. You should see Teffin's father, he can gentle a horse just like the Comanche do."

"Teffin? Who's Teffin?"

Joaquín could feel the warmth beginning to creep into his cheeks, and not wanting his sister to notice, he turned back to look out the window. "I almost forgot about her," he lied, trying to be nonchalant. "She's the reason

Braxton and Blythe rode over to the Dantes'. The four of us went riding."

"Aha!" Catalina's eyes gleamed as she drew her feet up beneath her on the sofa and watched her brother's discomfiture. "And you said— You're a liar, Joaquín de Alvarado!" Her eyes were dancing. "What does she look like?"

Joaquín took a deep breath, his dark green eyes closing as he remembered all too well what Teffin looked like, only there was no way he was going to let Cat know how he really felt inside. She'd teased him enough back home about the señoritas who always made eyes at him. Be damned if he'd put up with it here. Opening his eyes again, he turned back to face her, and straightened, trying to act unconcerned.

"Teffin? Ah, sí." He shrugged. "She looks like any other señorita," he answered. "Amber eyes, light hair."

"As light as her cousins'?"

"Cielos, no, darker. I would say more like the moon at harvesttime perhaps."

"The moon? Harvesttime?" Catalina laughed, and Joaquín felt the warmth creep into his face again. "Joaquín, you're blushing!"

His jaw set stubbornly. "I do not blush, Catalina!"

"Oh, I think it's precious." Her hands flew to her cheeks, her eyes still sparkling. "No wonder you had such a good time today."

"You, young lady, I could kill," he said, reaching for her, but she was too quick.

"Ha! I told you," she chanted, taunting him as she backed away, left the sofa, and moved toward the door. "I told you that if you enjoyed yourself it would be because of a woman!"

"Today had nothing to do with her."

"Then why are you blushing?"

"I am not!"

"Oh no?" She giggled outrageously. "I think you should look in a mirror right now, dear brother, it might surprise you."

Joaquín's eyes narrowed as he glared at her, knowing

she was right and wishing she weren't, because for some reason he couldn't explain, he knew he was blushing, something he never remembered ever doing before. At least not over a woman. He reached out for her again, and once more she giggled, still avoiding his hands as she moved even closer to the door.

"Oh, no you don't," he yelled, and made one quick lunge, almost catching her, his fingertips lightly brushing the smooth material of her silk dress as she ducked away from him, moving into the hall, and made a dash for the stairs.

"I'll thrash you within an inch of your life," he warned, shaking his fist as he stopped behind her at the foot of the stairs.

Catalina, hesitating on the first landing, leaned over the rail and held back another giggle while sticking out her tongue. "So much for you and your Kolters and Dantes," she taunted. "But just remember, dear brother, you were the one who told me no woman would ever make a fool of you, it wasn't my idea!"

Joaquín's fist clenched on the balustrade, knuckles white, as he stared up at her. There were times when he wondered how God could expect a man to love someone just because she was kin, and he took a deep breath, trying to regain the self-control he knew he possessed.

"So, you discovered I like the ladies after all, so who cares, little cougar," he finally yelled, straightening calmly, his hand sliding from the balustrade to smooth back his dark hair, and he tilted his handsome face upward, his chin set firmly. "So taunt all you want, because you and I both know it'll take more than a pair of golden eyes and a pretty smile to catch this hidalgo."

"Hidalgo?" Catalina was still leaning over the rail. "Hidalgo? Since when are you nobility?"

"Since I became the only son of Don Esteban de Alvarado, second son of the third son of Count Ramon de Alvarado of the house of Aragon."

"And you make eyes at an Indian?"

"Hold your tongue, little cougar, or the next time I get

my hands on you, I'll cut it out and feed it to the dogs, understand?"

Catalina's mouth puckered mischievously as she stared down at her big brother, and she could understand why the girls always made a fuss over him. There were few caballeros as handsome as he, but sometimes he just didn't use the brains God gave him. These Texans, oh how she despised them.

"Go ahead, kill me if you will," she answered dramatically, then her voice softened, more serious. "Only please, Joaquín, do not lose your heart to a Texan. I don't know if I could forgive you."

"You? Forgive me?" This time it was his turn to laugh. "You will probably end up marrying one before I do, little sister, so don't be so smug."

"Never!" she shot back, then flicked the hair back from off her shoulder. "I'd rather die first. Now, if you'll excuse me, I'll go to my room. There're some things I'd like to do. And besides, I'm tired of hearing about what a marvelous time you had with those heathens," and without another word she turned, ascending the rest of the stairs, and was lost from view.

Joaquín stood staring after her for some time, then turned and sauntered to the front door, and on outside to stand on the veranda. The sun was gone already, and night shadows had already begun to creep in beneath the trees and bushes, leaving a deep purple haze on the horizon, where a few faint stars were vying to be the first to be seen.

He moved to the top of the steps and gazed out across the long expanse of lawn, and beyond the wall, to the hills, where they had ridden that afternoon, then turned his gaze farther north, in the direction of the Dantes' ranch. Catalina had been partially right, only he'd never let her know that. Teffin's presence had helped him to enjoy the day. From what he'd seen of it today, the Texas landscape alone was enough to warm a man's soul, but seeing Texas with Teffin Dante beside him had been enough to warm his heart as well, and he smiled to himself, not hearing his uncle approach.

"So, you find something amusing, Joaquín?" Antonio asked as he joined him at the top of the steps. He had come up the side steps and now stood beside Joaquín, gazing off in the same direction. "Today you learned a little about Texas, eh?"

"A little."

"So, what you see, you like, is that it?"

Joaquín frowned, wishing he didn't have to be truthful, but Tío Antonio deserved at least that.

"Sí, what I see, I like," he answered after a few moments. "At least so far, with the land that is. As far as the people go, I guess I have yet to make up my mind. After all, one day is not really time enough to get to know anyone, is it?"

Antonio saw the reluctance in his nephew's eyes and knew how hard it was for him to concede even what he'd conceded, and he smiled at him warmly.

"You are growing up, Joaquín," he said proudly. "And I think perhaps someday you will be the man your father wanted you to be, no matter who rules this country," and he put a hand on Joaquín's arm, realizing the young man was so much taller, he'd never get an arm across his shoulders. "So, shall we go in and have a glass of Madeira?" he asked warmly. "Or, if you'd prefer something stronger . . ."

Joaquín turned. "Madeira will do fine," he said, and let his uncle usher him back toward the doorway, where the flickering lights from lanterns were just starting to glow, only although he heard every word Tío Antonio was saying, his mind was still back on the Texas plains with a pair of golden eyes, a smile, and a thousand questions he didn't have any answers to.

3

Teffin was quiet as she set her embroidery down and stood up, stretching her tanned arms as far as they'd go; then she let out a soft sigh.

"Bored again?" Cole asked as he looked up from the letter he was reading, and watched his daughter showing her opinion of ranch life. It was evening, and they'd been sitting in the parlor for some time already.

"Well, there isn't anything to do really, is there?" she answered. "Oh yes, in the daytime I can ride and shoot, that is, if there was anything to shoot at—but what about now?"

"You could help your mother with the dishes."

"And get in Bessie's way? Heaven forbid. You'd think she and Helene owned the place."

"Now don't go off on that tangent again. They've been with us too long, and you know it. Besides, if it hadn't been for Bessie, we probably wouldn't have made it this far, over the years. Your mother needed her then, and she needs her now, only a little help from you wouldn't hurt."

"Oh, Pa." Her small nose wrinkled, the few freckles on it darkening in the lamplight. "You know what I mean—I'm tired of trying to keep myself busy, and at night it seems so much worse. There isn't even anything to read anymore. I swear I've read everything we have half a dozen times already."

Cole held the letter he was reading out to her. "Here, I bet you haven't read this yet."

"I've read it three times since Brax gave it to Mother

this morning. It's from Grandma Rebel, and she said Grandpa Heath and Grandma Darcy are both well. Grandpa Beau hurt his leg when a horse went wild and pinned him against a stone pillar, but he can still walk, and Rachel Grantham, next door, had to quell another uprising that almost turned all of Port Royal into a shambles, and they wish they could all come out again to see us, but they've been too busy with spring planting." She counted on her fingers. "And let's see, the cotton's in, the indigo's in, and they're trying a new strain of rice. Did I miss anything?"

He glanced at the letter for a second, then folded it and stared at her, watching her eyes scan the room, looking for something to do, then, "So, you haven't said," he asked. "What did you think of this young man, this Joaquín de Alvarado?"

Teffin leaned back in her chair again and avoided her father's eyes. "He's handsome enough, I'll say that for him. But a bit conceited, don't you think?"

"I hadn't noticed, but then, I was rather busy when we were introduced. You were with him all afternoon, though. Surely you had a better chance to size him up than I did."

"Oh, Pa, you make it sound terrible. I wasn't sizing him up."

"Oh? I thought all females did a careful study of their prospective beaux."

Teffin's eyes darkened as she looked over at her father. He was a hard man at times, lean and lanky, with dark hair, touched by a hint of ebony, like the feathers of a raven, that gave away his Indian heritage, as did the slight slant of his emerald-green eyes. Only with his tanned face, the lines in it chiseled by the sun and weather, he was still a handsome man at forty. Teffin wondered what he'd looked like when he'd been her age.

"He's not going to be a beau," she answered quickly. "At least I don't think he will. I like him, but—oh, you know, Pa, there's just nothing there."

"Your ma says he's rich."

"He will be when he's twenty-one."

"When's that?"

"A couple of years, I guess. He didn't really say." She squirmed into a better position in the overstuffed chair with its carved wooden arms. "Only I'm still bored, Pa."

"Then why don't you answer your grandmother's letter? Or did you forget the schooling your mother gave you?"

"Don't be ridiculous. It's just that I hate to write."

'And it shows, too. I saw that recipe you gave Blythe the other day. The penmanship was terrible."

"Oh, Pa!"

"I'm serious. You need the practice."

"What does she need practice in?" Heather asked from the doorway.

The parlor was large, with fireplaces at each end, and two doors. One leading to the foyer, the other to the back stairs, dining room, and kitchen, and neither had heard Heather come in from the kitchen. Both father and daughter glanced over to where she stood, just inside the room, but it was Teffin who spoke as she rose from her chair and took a deep breath, letting her mother know how she felt.

"Penmanship," she answered as she started across the room. "So I guess I'll go write a letter and tell everyone back in South Carolina about the exciting life I lead out here," and she brushed past her mother.

"Say hello for us too, dear," Heather added. "And tell them I'll write, first chance I get."

Teffin waved a hand. "Yes, Mother," she said, acknowledging that she'd heard, and they watched her disappear toward the back stairs, her exaggerated gait anything but ladylike, as she went into the dining room.

"I wish there was more for her to do," Heather said, her gaze following her daughter. "But you know the way Bessie is. Even I have to put my foot down at times, or she'd run everything."

"Hey, I thought you liked having Bessie here."

"I do, Cole, honest I do," she answered. "I've grown so fond of her over the years, she's almost like my own mother, but there are still times when she thinks Teffin and I should be pampered like Lizette and I were when we were young."

"And you wouldn't enjoy that?"

Heather saw the amusement in his eyes. "No more than you'd enjoy it if Eli took over breaking the horses. Especially if there was nothing left for you to do around here except sit around twiddling your thumbs all day, or maybe working occasionally on a few pieces of harness, or mending a carriage wheel once in a while, while you tried to look busy."

"I'd hate it." He reached out, took her hand, and drew her to him, pulling her onto his lap. "But then I'm not you."

"Cole!"

"Shush," he admonished, his gaze taking in her face, his warm green eyes dark and compelling. "If Bessie wants to spoil you, let her. That only gives you more time for me."

"And Teffin? You want her spoiled too?"

"Teffin's not spoiled, she's just restless. It's her age. Remember when we were that young?"

Heather brushed a stray hair from her face and tucked it into the knot of red hair twisted at the nape of her neck, then her hand moved to her husband's face, touching it gently, letting her fingers trace his jawline.

"Do I remember?" she asked softly, her violet eyes softening as she gazed into his. "That's just the trouble, dear, I remember only too well. Why do you think I'm worried."

Cole reached up, his hand covering hers, and moved her palm across his lips, kissing the center sensuously, then he brought it to rest on his chest. "Well, you don't have to worry, love," he said, her nearness arousing him, as it always did. "Teffin's high-spirited, I know, but she's got a head on her shoulders too. I think if you just keep her busy enough to keep her out of mischief, everything'll work out." He smiled tenderly. "Besides, there's no place she can get in trouble out here."

"I wouldn't bet on that if I were you, Cole. I have a strange feeling she's going to be no different than the rest of this clan has been over the years. And if I'm right, I think we've got our work cut out for us where Teffin's concerned. Now with this young Mexican showing up—"

"You mean Don Antonio's nephew?"

'Yes, Don Antonio's nephew." Her eyes looked troubled. "You should have seen the way he looked at her."

"I did."

"Then you should know what I mean." Heather's fingers toyed with the collar of the work shirt Cole was wearing, tracing one of the seams she remembered stitching when she made it for him. "Please, Cole, help me with Teffin," she begged. "I almost botched up my own life because I didn't know how to handle the feelings that filled me as I grew up. Help me guide Teffin so she won't have to suffer any of what I went through."

Cole squeezed her hand, his face growing serious as he stared back at his wife, her face softly lined from age and sun, but still the face of the young girl he'd first fallen in love with.

"It's a bargain," he whispered hesitantly. "I'll help you, and you help me, and between the two of us, she'll have to turn out right. How's that?"

"I hope so."

"Now kiss me," and he reached up, pulling her head down until her mouth reached his, and he kissed her passionately, their years together making the kiss all the sweeter for them both.

It was late when Teffin finally set the pen she was using aside on the desk in her bedroom, picked up the last page of the letter she had written, blew on it, drying the ink, shoved the cork back in the ink bottle, added this last page to the rest of her letter, and sighed wearily. She'd managed to struggle through four pages in all, and now she read them over slowly, making sure the spelling was right, and it was legible, which had been a job in itself, and her gaze fell on the remains from three broken pen tips, as well as the crumpled pieces of paper, that proved her father had been right. So her writing wasn't perfect. So what? and she shrugged, quickly deciding to ignore the fact.

Satisfied she hadn't forgotten to include everything and everyone in the letter, she folded it carefully, slipped it into the envelope she'd already addressed, then propped it up against the bottle of ink where it'd be in full view, so she wouldn't forget to give it to the first person heading toward town. This done, she pushed back her chair, stood up, and strolled to one of the windows overlooking the side yard. Resting her hands on the sill, she leaned out. The moon was up, its pale glow reflecting off the roofs of the buildings, deepening the shadows, and making everything seem so unreal. How lonely it looked, and she let her gaze wander to the hills beyond. There were miles and miles of land out there, she thought, with little in between except trees, shrubs, wild animals, and Indians. Yet it was her home.

She was still staring off toward the hills when suddenly a movement out front caught the corner of her eye, and she squinted, leaning out a little farther, and was just barely able to make out the figures of two men on horseback on the drive leading to the bunkhouse out back. That's right, it was Saturday night, and now the rest of the men would start straggling in too, just like always. She pulled her head back in, staring at the open window. The same old thing week after week, year after year. If only . . .

Still weary, in spite of the talk with her father, she turned and gazed about the room she'd known all her life. Grandma Dicia said it reminded her of the bedroom in the log house she'd lived in years before, on the shores of Lake Erie, with its rustic walls and handmade furniture. To Teffin it was bare and uninteresting. But then so was her life.

Boredom—boredom—she thought angrily. At least Brax and Blythe had each other, as well as Genée, to liven things up. But whom did she have? No one. Not even a brother or sister to help the days go by.

A frown creased her forehead. That wasn't true, really. She sat back on the edge of the windowsill and stared across the room thoughtfully. She did have a brother. But where? The frown deepened, and after a few minutes she straightened again, sauntered over, and sat on the edge of the four-poster bed, staring absent-mindedly at a handmade calendar on the far wall. Her brother—it was strange thinking of him.

According to her parents, Case had been kidnapped and sold to Comanche Indians the year before she was born. When he was just a little over a year old, and they'd been searching for him ever since. That's why they'd ended up here in Texas. They'd traced the Comanche this far, when the trail ended.

She lay back on the bed and stared up at the rough-hewn ceiling, wondering. What would he be like today, this brother of hers? Ma said his hair was a beautiful deep auburn color, but then that was when he was small. Would it still be so red, or would it be darker now that he was older? And she said his eyes were like Pa's, dark green, with a slight slant to them. But of course that too could be changed by now. By now he was probably a full-fledged Comanche warrior somewhere, with feathers braided in his hair, and those horrible scars on his chest, like Pa said Comanche warriors had, from having their manhood tested by hanging from some kind of pole.

She shivered at the thought, then sat up and glanced toward the door at the sound of a knock.

"Come in."

"It's me, dear," Bessie said as she pushed the door open and stepped inside. Bessie Taylor and her daughter, Helene, who was now in her early thirties, had been with the Dantes for as long as Teffin could remember, and it was never unusual for Bessie to drop by like this, to see that everyone was settled for the night. Her gray hair was pulled back already, and put in its cap for bed, and the candle lamp she was carrying cast flickering shadows into the folds of the old blue robe she had on. "I thought I saw a light under your door," she said as she shut the door behind her. "Only I thought you were in bed hours ago. The house was so quiet."

Teffin took a deep breath. "I had some things to do."

"Like mooning over that Mexican dandy the twins brought over today?"

"No—like writing a letter."

"Good. You could use the practice." Bessie's gaze wandered to the letter on the desk, and she walked over, letting the light from her lamp mingle with that of the whale-oil lamp on the desk, so she could see better. "Hmm—quite an improvement too," she said, reading the address on the front.

"Did you want something, Bessie?" Teffin asked, irritated by the woman's motherly intrusion, especially tonight when she was already out of sorts.

"Only to tell you Helene finished making the nightgown for you this afternoon. You know, the pattern you helped her draw up the other day. It's in the bottom drawer. I thought you might want it tonight."

Teffin's face flushed, and she felt embarrassed. Bessie's daughter, Helene, was always doing special things for her, and here she was resenting Bessie's prying, when all the woman was doing was trying to be nice.

"I'm sorry, Bessie," she apologized, moving from the bed with a little more enthusiasm, and she went to the dresser and pulled open the bottom drawer. "I guess I've been snapping at just about everybody lately, but I've been so unsettled." She reached in the drawer, took out a neatly folded mound of pale pink silk with lace on it, and unfolded it, holding the nightgown against her as she stood up. "Oh, Bessie, it's so lovely," she cooed, and her hand smoothed it against the rough fabric of the cotton dress she had on. It was lovely. The most lovely nightgown Teffin had ever seen. "Tell Helene I can't thank her enough, will you? She does such beautiful work."

The top of the gown was appliquéd with white silk flowers, trimmed with lace, and just feeling the fragile garment gave Teffin a thrill.

Bessie smiled, watching the young girl's eyes fasten firmly on the nightgown, and she sighed. "When Helene promises, she keeps it. And she did promise. Now, hop into it, and then to bed, young lady, it's late and you don't want to sleep all through Sunday." She started for the door, when Teffin stopped her.

"Bessie?"

"What is it?"

Teffin blushed again, not knowing quite where to start; then, "Bessie, you were with Ma and Pa years ago when my brother disappeared, I know you were. Both you and Helene. But I've never asked you. What do you think really happened to him?"

"Is that what you were thinking about when I came in? Your brother?"

Teffin felt uncomfortable under Bessie's intense gaze, because few people ever mentioned her brother any-more. It was just something no one ever talked about, as if it was wrong to. "Yes, but I don't know why. I guess I was just wondering. Do you think maybe he's out in those hills somewhere with the Comanche? Or maybe they sold him to the Apache or . . . Where do you think he might be, Bessie?"

The crow's-feet at the corners of Bessie Taylor's eyes deepened, and the smile usually gracing her lips faded as she stared at Teffin, wishing she had an answer. It had happened so many years ago, and yet the memory was still just as painful, even for her.

"I don't know, honey, and that's a fact," she answered, a strange faraway look in her eyes. "But wherever he is, I sure hope life's treating him well."

"Me too," Teffin said thoughtfully, and for a few minutes the nightgown was forgotten as both women stared at each other. "Good night, Bessie," Teffin finally said.

Bessie walked back over to the young girl, kissed her, gave her a big hug, then left, closing the door behind her.

The room was quiet for a long time while Teffin stood next to the dresser, then slowly she walked to the bed and began undressing so she could slip into the first really fancy grown-up nightgown she'd ever owned in her life. And a few minutes later, as she lay in her bed with the lamp out, fingering the delicate lace and luxuriating in the feel of the silk next to her young body, while praying someday she'd meet the brother who'd been stolen from her life even before it had started, she drifted off to sleep. However, she didn't dream of Case, not tonight. Instead she dreamt of a tall, handsome young caballero on a black horse with a silver-trimmed saddle, and a smile that had a way of creeping into his fascinating eyes.

It wasn't until two days later when she once more ran into Joaquín. Or did he run into her? She had no way of knowing really. All she knew was she was out riding, heading toward the Kolters' late in the afternoon, when he hailed her from a nearby ridge and came riding over. This time, his sister was with him, and Teffin was surprised. For some reason, the way he'd talked of his sister that first day she'd met him, she'd assumed Catalina de Alvarado wasn't much for spending her time outdoors, but today she certainly was dressed for it in a lovely black riding habit that made Teffin's brown riding skirt and buckskin jacket look anything but fashionable.

"Oh, but I love to ride," Catalina said shortly after they were introduced, her accent much heavier than her brother's. "It is just that you do it so differently here. At home I was always with one of the grooms close by, and my duenna."

Teffin hitched herself more comfortably onto her side-saddle and smoothed her rather worn skirt self-consciously over her leg as they started across a field, heading toward the drive leading to the Kolters' ranch. "Yes, I could see where you'd have a duenna," she answered. "So what happened to her?"

"I am afraid she refused to come to Texas with us. Besides, Tío Antonio says Texans do not have duennas."

"Mexican Texans do. Some, that is."

Catalina glanced over at her brother. "See, Joaquín—it would not have hurt."

Joaquín straightened in the saddle, giving her the same patronizing look she was so used to seeing, then he looked over to Teffin. "You see, my sister is spoiled, Señorita Teffin," he said. "Always wanting what she does not have. Back home, she used to curse the fact that she had to have a duenna. Here, she curses the lack of one."

Teffin looked over at Catalina, and saw the anger in the young girl's eyes, and knew Joaquín's words would probably spoil the day for his sister. However, by the time they reached the Kolters' ranch, Catalina seemed to have weathered the rebuff to the point where she was her old self again, haughty and uncooperative, although Genée, starved for someone her own age to talk to, didn't seem to notice, and after a quick introduction, Genée, her usual friendly self, invited the young Mexican girl to her room so she could show off her collection of fancy buttons. Each one with its own fascinating history, according to Genée.

"Your sister will be disappointed, Señor Braxton," Joaquín said as he helped Braxton catch and saddle Blythe's horse so they could all take a ride before supper. "Catalina will find everything she does boring, and stupidly childish."

Brax had been out on the range all morning, but knowing his sister looked forward to the company, he didn't mind staying in the saddle a few hours longer. He pulled the cinch on Pegasus' saddle tight, folded the stirrup with its leather boot back down again, and glanced over at Joaquín, who was rubbing the palomino's nose, quieting him.

"Oh, I don't doubt that," he answered. "But I think your sister's the one who'll be disappointed, because if I know Genée, she'll not only show Catalina those damn buttons, but drag her out back to her tree house. And I can't imagine your sister climbing trees."

Joaquín's eyes widened. "Your sister climbs trees?"

"Genée's been at it for years, although Ma's tried to discourage her. At least she used to, but it didn't do much good, so instead she let Pa and me put up a tree house for her. That was when she was only about eight or nine. Blythe said she's even got curtains at the windows now, but I haven't been out back to take a look lately."

Joaquín laughed. The thought was incongruous, and a few minutes later as he, Teffin, Brax, and Blythe rode their horses away from the Kolter ranch, heading toward the main road, he looked back just in time to see Genée strolling across the ranch yard toward a huge old tree near the outbuildings, with Catalina close at her heels. Only, as Braxton said, Cat didn't look any too happy.

A smile tilted Joaquín's lips as he watched his sister following Genée, Genée's shining russet hair and bright yellow dress a contrast to his sister's dark beauty and drab mourning clothes, and he was sure Braxton was right. Cat was the one who was in for a big disappointment, because she was so hoping the youngest member of the Kolter family would perhaps be more conservative and femininely genteel than what she had so far learned of the Kolters. Oh well, she was young yet, he thought, she'll learn, and he turned his attention back to his newfound friends, who were in a heated discussion over the rumors about a man named Señor Stephen Austin. It seemed someone had learned he'd been taken prisoner and was being held in Mexico City, and according to Braxton, Blythe, and even Teffin, everyone was really upset over it. However, the political discussion didn't last too long, and soon they forgot all about Señor Austin, and instead were discussing the merits of raising cattle as opposed to horses.

For the next few weeks, Joaquín spent more and more time with Braxton, riding over almost every day during the week, and accompanying his newfound friend out onto the range, where he was quickly learning all about horses, cattle, and surviving in the saddle. Then when the work was done, he, Braxton, Blythe, and Teffin could be seen riding around the countryside or visiting friends in San Antonio, until soon it became quite unusual to see one without the other.

It was the middle of June, and for days now rumors had been growing all over the Texas frontier that relations with the Mexican authorities were really becoming strained. However, at the Kolter ranch, politics was the farthest thing from everyone's mind. Lizette Kolter was turning thirty-six on June 17, and Bain, Braxton, and Blythe were planning a party for her, to celebrate. Although the Kolters' house was large and sprawling, the parlor even dwarfing that of the wealthy de Léon ranch, Bain felt it'd never be big enough to hold all the people who were expected to attend. So he, Brax, and Luther, along with Luther's sons and some of the other men, began cleaning out the main floor of the bank barn, getting hay up into the overhead lofts, and making sure there were no rotted boards in the floor. Luther's son's leg was completely healed now, and he and Dexter were a big help, although they'd rather have been out on the range. However, Dexter, especially, was all muscle, and who better to help with the barrels and boxes to be hefted into the loft along with the hay. Besides, Luther hated to see boys so young out with the cattle, and Corbin had already proved it was dangerous. No, Dex wasn't even twelve yet, and Corbin was a year younger. There'd be plenty of time for roping and branding. So right now they were better off right where they were, and as the floor was cleared, and minor repairs done, Luther thanked God he could work right alongside them.

As the days moved on, the barn took shape, no longer even looking like a barn inside. Lanterns were strung from loft to loft, with ropes and hooks, so people dancing would be able to see, the floor had been swept until every bit of hay and straw had disappeared, and corn-meal had been sprinkled here and there, so the dancers' feet would slide. Tables had been put up near the door for refreshments, and Luther built a sort of stage for the musicians to stand on while they played. The musicians being a trio of neighbors. One with a guitar, one a banjo, and the other with a violin.

To Lizette it was going to be the most beautiful music in the world, though, because it had been so long since she'd been to a real ball. And this would be almost like one. Back in South Carolina there'd been so many balls and soirees, but not out here. An occasional impromptu dance or party over the years was about all they ever had, and she missed the party dresses, fancy food, and excitement. That's why tonight was going to be so special. Her birthday had actually been earlier in the week, on

Wednesday, but no one ever had a party during the middle of the week. So Saturday night was chosen, and now, as she stood in front of the mirror in the bedroom she and Bain shared, staring at herself in the mirror, she wondered if maybe the dress she had on was too flamboyant, especially for her. But then Pretty said it made her look thinner, and Pretty was usually right.

It was a deep green, the color of her eyes, with tucked sleeves and bodice, the skirt so full she had to wear three petticoats beneath it so it wouldn't lie in folds, and she had fixed her hair extra nice, so the emeralds in her ears, and gracing her neck, contrasted with her dark hair. They had been Bain's gift to her, having had his father send them from back east.

A sigh escaped her lips as she squinted, running a finger along a line on her forehead. Gracious, if this kept up, she'd look old before her time. Ah well, that's what worrying could do for a person, and after taking one last look, to make sure she looked her best, she made sure Bain's clothes were laid out for him, then headed for Blythe's bedroom downstairs, responding to a summons only a few minutes before, from Pretty.

Blythe was sitting in her chair next to the side window, looking out, when Lizette came in, and Liz stood quietly for a minute watching her, then spoke.

"Now, what's this I hear about your not wanting to join us?" she asked as she walked toward her daughter.

Blythe's gray eyes were dark, bristling. "I just don't want to be there, that's all," she answered. "I already gave you my love on your birthday, Ma, and like Pa, I wanted you to have a night like this, but you know it'd be foolish for me to try to attend a dance."

"Foolish?" Liz exhaled unhappily. "Now look here, young lady. This is not just a dance. It's a party. There'll be lots of folks who won't dance, so you can't use that as an excuse."

"It's not an excuse."

"Then what is it?"

"Oh, Mother!" Blythe turned away so her mother wouldn't see the tears.

"Blythe, please." Lizette came over and knelt down next to her. She reached out, taking Blythe's hand. "Running away, or hiding, or whatever you want to call it, isn't going to help, you know that. Sooner or later everything has to be faced. And you've never run away before. So why now? Everyone knows you can't walk, so no one'll embarrass you by asking for a dance, and you know everyone understands."

"That's just the trouble, Ma." Blythe's voice broke. "Everybody understands too well. Sometimes I think it'd be better if they just ignored me a little. Instead they wait on me hand and foot, and treat me like an invalid."

"Blythe!"

"Well, it's true. I know I am an invalid, as far as they're concerned, but I'm not really, Ma. Not the way they think. I can do everything except walk. Even ride a horse."

Lizette stared at her daughter. Blythe was seventeen already, and so beautiful, with her pale hair and gray eyes that had just a hint of—what was it, blue? Lavender? They were truly lovely. Most girls her age were either married or at the least spoken for. Yet Blythe was right. She could do everything except walk. Only, unfortunately, walking seemed to be more important to people than anything else. Why, just last week one of the men in town married a blind girl, but where was someone for Blythe? Were legs really that important?

Lizette was still holding Blythe's hand, and she squeezed it affectionately. "Now come on, dear, don't be foolish, please," she coaxed. "Don't spoil the evening for me. Who knows, maybe you'll really enjoy yourself tonight. After all, Teffin and the others'll be there. And Antonio's bringing Joaquín and Catalina."

Blythe sneered. "Great, Genée's going to love that. She still can't stand Joaquín's sister, but then I guess I can't blame her. The girl's absolutely obnoxious."

Lizette eyed her skeptically. "Rather harsh on her, aren't you, dear? After all, it's been a big adjustment for her losing her father like that, without any warning, then having to come here."

Blythe flushed. "I guess you're right, but I just can't help thinking how I could be mean and rude to people too, if I wanted. After all, I've got a reason to be angry with the world. Oh well." She shrugged. "Don't worry, Ma, you can send Pretty in if you want. At least I have a new dress to wear tonight, and I guess I can put up with all of it again, just for you," and she glanced over to her bed, where Pretty had already laid out the lovely red silk dress they'd been working on all week, knowing the soft folds across the shoulders, and bright color, would contrast beautifully with her pale hair, and darken the flecks of silver in her gray eyes. And there was always a slim chance that just for once, somebody'd be there who wouldn't care that she couldn't walk.

Lizette breathed a sigh, kissed her daughter on the cheek, then stood up and left the room, promising to send Pretty right in, then she went back upstairs to check on Braxton and Genée. By the time the guests started to arrive, everyone was dressed for the occasion, in their Sunday best, and waiting just inside the main door of the barn, including Blythe, who looked lovelier than ever, ensconced in the strange wheeled chair Luther had made for her.

The evening had been going so well. There were friends of the Kolters' from as far as Gonzales, and Goliad, who'd end up staying overnight with the Kolters or other ranchers near San Antonio; Juan Seguin, who came with Don Antonio de Léon and his nephew and niece, as well as most of the other officials and shopkeepers from town, along with other ranchers from the area. All in all, the turnout was more than what Bain had expected, especially since so many of the men were off at meetings with Sam Houston and some of the others who were trying to sort out the political mess that seemed to be escalating with every day that went by.

It was late already. The party had been going on for hours, and Braxton stood in the barn near the back, watching the festivities while resting his feet. He'd bought a new pair of boots just for tonight, only they'd been pinching his little toes during every round on the floor, and he was tired of wincing. Now he sighed, straightening, then made his way to the door. Once outside, he strolled down the bank, trying not to look too obvious, melted into the shadows, and made his way around the ground floor toward the back, where the pasture started, then he leaned against the rail fence that kept the milk cows in, and pulled off his right boot.

Damn! It felt good, and he rubbed his little toe, moaning in relief. Realizing the other foot would feel equally as good, he slipped off the boot too, and breathed another sigh. Even with the stockings on, it was such a relief, and he made a mental note to take the boots back to the bootmaker the first thing Monday morning, to see if anything could be done.

He'd been standing, leaning against the fence for some time, when he suddenly realized someone was standing flattened against a tree only a few feet away, and he tensed, trying to squint into the darkness.

"Who's there?" he challenged, but no one answered. His hand moved to his hip, where his gun usually hung in its gunbelt, then he realized he wasn't wearing it tonight. "I asked, who's there?" he called again, this time more forcefully, and a frown creased his forehead as a figure stepped gracefully from the shadows, and he watched Catalina de Alvarado coming toward him, her small figure unmistakable in the dim light from the crescent moon overhead.

She was still dressed in black, and would be until a full year was up, but the dress she had on tonight was made of lace, as was the mantilla, the comb holding her hair beneath the mantilla trimmed with gold, the onyx necklace at her throat, and earrings in her ears, also set in gold, and to Braxton, for some reason, she looked far older than her fourteen years.

His face flushed, embarrassed to be caught with his boots off.

"They're new," he explained when she reached him and he saw her gaze fixed on the boots in his hands.

He'd never remembered seeing her smile before, usually she was full of piss and vinegar, and ready for a fight.

But tonight her mouth tilted teasingly, and her voice, when she spoke, was actually friendly.

"Evidently you need a new bootmaker, Señor Kolter," she said, amused.

"Señor Kolter? That's rather formal, don't you think, ma'am?" he said, surprised. "The name's Braxton."

"Sí, I know, but Tío Antonio says I should treat my elders with respect."

There it was. The sarcasm again. "Joaquín said you're fourteen, that means I'm only three years older," Brax countered with some flippancy. "You call that an elder?"

"You do not?"

"You know better than that." He glanced about, realizing she'd been standing out here alone. "Why'd you come out here anyway?"

She shrugged. "The noise, people—I guess I just prefer it out here. Besides"—her nose wrinkled in distaste—"I have never been to a party in a barn before."

"Too low-class for you, eh?"

"I did not say that."

"But you meant it, right?"

Catalina tried to see Braxton's face more closely, but it was so hard. His hair was silvery in the moonlight without a hat on, but his face was too deeply shadowed.

"You always think the worst of me, do you not?" she asked. "I wonder why."

He stared hard at her, realizing as he had the first time he'd met her that in spite of her youthful insolence, and the bitter sarcasm that proved she was, as her brother stated, haughty and spoiled, she also had a strange effect on him he didn't like. Especially her dark eyes, and the way her mouth moved when she talked. It was a sensual quality that unnerved him, and now here it was again, making his knees feel weird and tying his stomach in knots. He'd have to ignore it, that's all there was to it. Leaning over, he began putting on his boots.

"I guess because I'm not used to having to put up with someone like you," he said, pulling on the last boot. "I've been around my sisters too long."

"Your sisters? You call them ladies? I feel sorry for

you, señor. But then I feel sorry for all Texans, because as soon as my government puts a stop to all this nonsense about freedom and the like—"

"Freedom?" He straightened, looking down at her now, his eyes sparking dangerously. "What do you know of freedom?"

"I know it is a license to kill."

"Who told you that? Your father?"

"My father was a great man, and if he had lived he would not turn against his country as Tío Antonio has."

"Your father was a Federalist, and you don't even know what it means."

"I do too!"

"All right, what does it mean?"

Her chin lifted angrily. "It means that . . . that we are to be free to do as we wish as true Mexican citizens."

"It means that your father believed in states' rights. Something your precious Santa Anna has forgotten exists."

"That's a lie!"

"Is it? Then ask your uncle why your father died, Catalina," he said, hoping to make her understand a little of what was going on. "He sure as hell didn't have a heart attack from overwork. And ask him what happened to all the other Federalists down in Zacatecas who believed just like your father had. Ask him where the hell they are now."

"You are swearing at me again."

"I'm not swearing at you."

"You are too!"

"I'm trying to show you the difference between freedom and tyranny."

"You are trying to justify rebellion!"

"You're impossible."

"And so are you!" Catalina's dark eyes searched his face again. He had turned slightly, and this time the moon was full on it. Besides, he was standing closer to her. His eyes were blazing, jaw rigid, the classic features strong and compelling, as if etched in stone, and a strange, disquieting feeling shot through her, making her inhale sharply. "I hate you, Señor Braxton Kolter," she went on viciously, forcing her voice not to tremble as her knees were doing. "I hate you and your whole family. Do you understand? Now, por favor, if you don't mind, the air here is not as refreshing as I had expected," and turning abruptly, she picked up the edge of her skirt and stalked off, heading back toward the bank that led into the main floor of the barn.

Inside the barn, Joaquín was having the time of his life. In only the few short weeks he'd been here, he'd learned to understand not only the countryside, but the men who were trying to tame it, and although he still exuded an air of nobility in the firm way he walked and the mannerisms taught him from the time he was a child, he'd quickly conformed to the friendly, down-to-earth attitude held by these men who called themselves Texans, and he was enjoying this new freedom he had, to be himself.

He'd been dancing with Teffin most of the evening. A fact that had been noticed by both the Kolters and Dantes, as well as most of the other guests. And Heather, who was more worried than any of the others, and who'd been standing near the tables watching the dancers, frowned when the music stopped and she saw Joaquín bend down to whisper something in Teffin's ear.

"Outside it is so much cooler, Teffin," he said softly.

Teffin looked up at him and smiled, the gold flecks in her topaz eyes shining brighter than he'd ever seen them before in the flickering light from the overhead lanterns.

"We could sneak away, couldn't we?" she agreed.

Joaquín didn't wait for a second invitation. Taking her hand, and tucking her arm in his, he glanced about, then hurriedly began moving with her toward the huge open barn door.

Teffin had been having a marvelous time. Not only had some of the young men from town been overly attentive, but for some reason, Joaquín had let his hair down just enough to make the evening exciting. Usually he was all reserved, never really being himself, as if he were portraying a part in a play. But tonight—even his eyes had a warmth in them she hadn't seen before, and once, while they were dancing, at the way he smiled at her, she'd even felt a strange stirring deep down inside. Now, as they reached the open door, she breathed in deeply, smelling the fresh night air, only to stop abruptly at the sight of Catalina tramping angrily up the sloping bank toward them, mumbling something under her breath neither Teffin nor Joaquín could hear clearly enough to understand.

"Cat?" Joaquín exclaimed, surprised to see her.

Catalina hesitated for a brief second, both feet firmly in place, then dropped her skirts and looked her brother straight in the eyes. "Joaquín, I wish to go home!"

Joaquín's eyes widened in surprise. "Home? But the party, it is still going."

"For you perhaps, not me." She was about to tell him in Spanish, but decided against it. After all, why not let Braxton Kolter's dear cousin know how much she despised them all. "I have had enough of your so-called friend's insulting remarks, and since no one seems to care anyway whether I am present or not, I would much rather be gone."

"Then I guess you will have to leave by yourself, my little cougar," he answered, dashing her demands to pieces. "Because I am not leaving, and I doubt Tío Antonio or Señor Seguin will care to leave either. After all, from what I have heard so far, this is the best—" He glanced down at Teffin. "What do you call it, fiesta? Fandango? Whatever it is, it is the best in years, and I certainly intend to stay to the end."

"Oh—" Catalina's eyes were blazing. "You are as bad as the rest," and she lapsed into Spanish this time, telling him what a terrible brother he was, and what a traitor he was, then she marched off with her head in the air, to find a place where she could sit and sulk.

"Well, I wonder what brought that on," Teffin said as they watched Catalina making her way through the crowd.

Joaquín was frowning slightly, however, he wasn't about to let his sister's passionate dislike of Texans spoil his evening. After all, they weren't all that bad, and once more he took Teffin's arm and they stepped outside.

"Forget her," he said. "She was no doubt talking to Braxton or Genée. You know how your cousins always affect her."

He smiled at her warmly as they strolled down the bank, his elaborately embroidered clothes complementing her fancy blue dress. But when they reached the bottom of the sloping entranceway, he stopped to survey the ranch yard.

"So, where do we go?" he asked, his voice low and vibrantly alive. "Right, toward the road, and perhaps stroll over by the fence, or left toward the bunkhouse and the backyard?"

"Let's go toward the back, where Genée's tree house is. You know, there's even a swing there."

He looked startled. "You've been in her tree house?"

"Why not? I haven't always been grown-up, you know."

Joaquín's eyes softened as he gazed down at her, marveling at how pretty she looked tonight, the paleness of her dress contrasting with the sparkling flecks in her eyes, and as they turned, heading toward the backyard, making their way toward the big old tree, neither of them saw Braxton, who was still standing by the fence, watch them until they melted into the shadows, then he straightened stubbornly and headed toward the house to change his boots so the rest of the evening wouldn't be ruined.

Braxton was almost to the porch when he stopped abruptly, then frowned. Someone was sitting on the steps, only the light from the porch lantern barely outlined the figure. He squinted.

"Grandma? Grandma Dicia?"

Loedicia'd recognized the walk long before Brax got to her. "Your feet really hurt so much you'd leave your mother's grand party?" she asked.

"Only to change them." He dropped down beside her, once more starting to pull off the torturous boots. "But how'd you know?"

"Experience, young man. Experience." She glanced at him curiously. She had seen Catalina leave him, heading back inside the barn. "You and Antonio's niece—another fight?"

"The same one." He sighed. "I swear that girl's not only stupid, but half mule."

"She was born and raised Mexican. What do you expect?"

"I don't know. I guess I just can't understand it when people are so blind."

"She's young yet. The day'll come when she'll open her eyes to what the world's really like."

"Never," he blurted. "Not her. She'll probably die defending Santa Anna's right to all of this."

Loedicia's hand covered his arm and she squeezed it affectionately, her violet eyes deepening with concern. "Just so you don't die proving she's wrong."

His hand covered hers. "Don't worry, Grandma. I'm too ornery to die." He glanced over at her skeptically. "So why aren't you at the party?"

"I've had my fill." She drew her hand from his, and her head tilted back, her gray hair looking even whiter in the moonlight, and her eyes softened. "Let's see, I danced with Antonio and Juan, had a nice long chat with Jim, who, I must say, is still drinking too much, swapped some tall tales about the war with that old trapper from town. You know, the one says he was with George at Valley Forge."

"You mean old Cal Dayton?"

"Is he the one with the front teeth missing?"

"I reckon."

"Then that was him."

"Which war, Grandma?"

"Now you know which war, Brax—or have you forgotten the schooling we struggled through?"

Brax smiled. "Just wanted to see if you remembered. After all, Grandma, that was a long time ago."

"Sixty years?" She sighed. "It's not as long as you think," she answered. "You know, when you're young, fifty, sixty, even seventy years sounds like such a long time away, but after they're gone, you wonder, where did they go so fast?"

Braxton glanced over at his great-grandmother, and a warm feeling filled him as he studied her face. Genée looked like Grandma would have looked when she was younger, except for the coloring, but then so did Ma, and yet Grandma had a warmth and sensitivity about her that neither his sister nor his ma possessed. A kind of aura. Maybe because Grandma Dicia'd lived so long, and knew so much. She'd be eighty-one next March, and yet the only thing old about her was the gray hair and wrinkles. God, how he loved her. How they all loved her.

"And, oh yes," she went on. "I ate too much too. All those sandwiches and cakes."

"You're gonna get fat, Grandma."

"So you'll love me all the less?"

"I'll love you all the more." Braxton reached over with a free hand, cupped her chin, then leaned forward and kiss her tenderly. "But for now, I'm gonna go up and change boots so I can keep on dancing until the musicians go home or there's nobody left to dance with."

His hand dropped, he stood up and started to turn, then suddenly froze at the sound of hoofbeats echoing on the night air, and he squinted, staring off into the darkness toward the drive.

"Someone's coming . . . and fast," he added.

Loedicia straightened, then stood up beside him, stepping down to the ground as a horse and rider emerged out of the darkness.

Brax raised his arm. "Ho! Friend!"

"Brax—that you?" The rider leapt down and ran over, leaving his horse ground-reined in the drive.

Braxton was surprised. "Got here sort of late, didn't you, Gallagher?" he said as the other man stopped at the foot of the steps.

Frank Gallagher was breathing heavily. "I ain't comin' to dance. I come to tell you all what's going on."

Frank Gallagher was shorter than Braxton, with chestnut hair, bushy brows that almost met over a wide nose, and a mouth more like one long thin line, with a jaw so square it gave the impression his head was in a box, and he was three years older than Brax.

"I been ridin' since yesterday morning," he said, still trying to catch his breath as he went on. "There's a whole group gatherin' at San Felipe, and I wouldn't be surprised if, when they're through, they marched right on in to Anahuac."

Braxton's face grew serious, his teasing manner completely gone. "You're sure?"

"Hell no, I ain't sure, Brax. But you know what's been goin' on, and how they been talkin'. Damn! It ain't right they should hold Briscoe and the others, and everyone knows it."

"So what can we do? Houston won't raise a hand yet, you know that. And rumor has it Austin's on his way back."

"To hell with them," Gallagher said. "Houston ain't even a Texan, and Austin's livin' in a dream world. What we're gonna need are men willing to fight." He turned quickly, and started heading toward the barn. "You comin'?" he called back to Braxton, who was still holding onto his new boots and didn't know whether to put them back on or run up and get his others.

By the time Brax was ready to holler his answer, Gallagher was halfway to the barn.

"You're going?" Loedicia asked, her eyes now on her great-grandson.

Braxton stood motionless for a minute, watching Gallagher disappear into the barn, then heard the music stop, and the beehive of shouting that followed.

"Looks like I just might at that, Grandma," he answered. "Guess I'd better go get my other boots," and he turned quickly, bolting into the house in his stocking feet, while Loedicia stood silently, watching him go, then turned her attention toward the barn.

It was coming—coming again into her life, as if the mere struggle to survive each day here wasn't enough. War! War with all the fighting, the blood and chaos. A shiver went through her as she watched a number of young men leave the barn and start heading for their horses, and she wished with all her might that it didn't have to be.

4

The Kolters' ranch yard was full of mounted riders now, the party completely forgotten, as Lizette stood next to Braxton's horse, her hand still on the bridle.

"Talk some sense into him, Bain, will you?" she argued. "What they're planning is foolish."

"But, Ma!" Braxton was in the saddle already, only Lizette had refused to let go.

"She's right, Brax," Bain agreed. "There'll be a time to fight, yes, and when that time comes we'll all be in it. But not now. Not like this."

"Why not like this?" Braxton's gray eyes scanned the rest of the young men who were mounting up.

Most of them were as young as he was, and they too were telling their families good-bye. He reached back, and checked to make sure the bedroll he'd grabbed was secure. "If we wait for Houston, we could be waiting forever. No." His eyes were pleading as he looked first at his mother, then his father. "Please, Pa. I have to go. Make her understand, will you?"

Bain took a deep breath, then rubbed his hand across his chin, the beard he still wore bringing back memories of his own passionate longing for adventure when he was his son's age. Suddenly he nodded, and stepped up, taking Lizette's hand from the horse's bridle.

"No!" Lizette cried.

"It has to be, Liz," he said, his fingers tightening on her hand. "He isn't a boy anymore." He looked up at Brax sitting so straight in the saddle. "You said good-bye to your sisters?" he asked.

Brax nodded. "Yeah, Pa."

"Then go, but be careful son, please, and if all goes well, the next time the rest of us'll be with you."

Brax took a deep breath, relieved. "Maybe there won't have to be a next time, Pa," he said, then glanced beyond his father, to where Joaquín was standing behind Teffin, with his hands on her shoulders. "I suppose I can't talk you into coming with us, can I?" he yelled to his new friend.

Joaquín shook his head. "I am not that much a Texan yet, mi amigo," Joaquín called back. "But I will be waiting. Vaya con Dios."

Braxton threw Joaquín a salute, as Gallagher and the others dug their horses in the ribs, and like a thundering stampede the group of riders, with Braxton riding hard to catch up, disappeared into the night, heading cross-country for San Felipe de Austin, some seventy miles northeast of San Antonio.

For a few minutes not a man, woman, or child moved, the dust from the riders swirling high in the moonlight like a foggy mist, then slowly, as it settled to the ground, a figure moved here, there, and slowly everyone began milling about. Only no one seemed as eager to continue the dance anymore. In fact most of the guests began talking of leaving, and only a few started moving back toward the barn, the rest just talking in a mumbling undertone, the carefree happiness of a few minutes ago completely forgotten.

Joaquín's hands were still on Teffin's shoulders, and he looked down at the top of her head, where it barely came to the middle of his chest, and he began to wonder how she'd accepted his refusal to go with Braxton. Would she think he did it because he was a coward? Or would she understand?

Suddenly his hands dropped, as he felt her start turning, and she looked up at him.

"He shouldn't have gone, Joaquín. Not yet," she said. "Pa says even Houston said it's not time to fight yet."

"Oh? And when will it be?"

"Perhaps never." Her mouth was set in a grim line. "At least I hope not. The thought of fighting scares me."

"Do not worry, Teffin," he said, his gaze lifting from her face to the milling crowd, then back to her face again. "I do not think your so-called Texans would be foolish enough to actually challenge a power like my government. They will no doubt come to their senses long before any shots are fired."

"I sure hope you're right, but I have a terrible feeling this is just the beginning, because you see, I know these people better than you, and they'd challenge the devil himself if they thought he was taking away their right to be free."

"You speak of freedom." He gestured about them. "You come and go as you please, live as you please— work, play, do as you please. Is this not freedom?"

"Certainly, but don't you understand, this is what your Santa Anna would take away from us."

Teffin wasn't as well-schooled as Braxton and her uncle and father in the complexities of the political situation in Texas, but she knew enough to know that the loss of even one aspect of freedom could mean the loss of it all.

"Don't you see, Joaquín," she went on, taking his arm and pulling him away from the others, hoping she could make him understand, "it's not just being able to come and go as we please. It's being able to have a say in how much we're taxed for what we have, being able to defend ourselves if wrongfully accused, living where we want, and traveling where we want, without fear. It's letting us decide what's best for us, and not some men hundreds of miles away, who have no idea what it's even like here in Texas. Why, the Mexican government even tells people what church they're supposed to belong to."

"So, is that so terrible? After all, it is the only church."

"Is it?"

They were stopped now, standing beneath a small oak tree not far from the back porch. Teffin leaned back against it as she gazed up into his face.

"Your government says so, yes, I know, but to make it a requirement for citizenship—belief in God is something a man holds in his heart, not words stamped on paper, Joaquín. Look at Sam Houston, he even took your Spanish names, but it's all a farce. He rarely goes inside a church, from what my father says. And the rest of us. How many of us do you ever see in your church on Sunday mornings?"

He frowned, then nodded. "So this too they will fight over, sí?"

"For all of it, yes, I think they will, and I'm afraid."

He reached up and lifted a small golden curl from the side of her forehead and brushed it back, then his hands slid down the side of her face, the back of his fingers caressing her cheek, and his eyes softened.

"Do not be afraid. For whatever happens Teffin, I will see that no one ever hurts you, ever. I promise this to you."

She reached up, her fingers twining in his, and squeezed his hand, and for the second time tonight a warm flood of feeling swept through her, and she trembled. Perhaps she'd been hasty when she'd told her father Joaquín would never be a beau, but then—it could be like Grandma Dicia told her once. A person can grow on you, and you can grow to love him without even wanting to. Could it be possible? Was Joaquín growing on her? She stared into his dark green eyes, unsure and puzzled. She'd give it time. That's all she needed, time.

"Thank you, Joaquín," she whispered softly. "I only hope that if worse comes to worst, you'll be able to keep your promise."

"Why not," he said softly, and his fingers tightened on hers. "After all, I will be on the winning side."

Teffin frowned. Not because she knew he was going to kiss her, or because she was afraid of her reaction to that kiss, but because she felt like a traitor. No matter how you looked at it, Joaquín was a Mexican, and it would take more than his feelings for her to make a Texan out of him.

His lips touched hers, lightly at first, then as her mouth moved beneath his, accepting their vibrant warmth, his lips became more sensuous, more demanding, and he pulled her hard against him.

Teffin felt so soft and pliable in Joaquín's arms, and for some reason, it seemed so natural for him to feel what he was feeling. It was a fierce longing he'd never felt before toward anyone else.

After a few minutes he drew his head back, straightening a little, and looked down into her eyes again. They were so lovely, even in the shadows, and he knew she'd enjoyed the kiss as much as he had.

"Por favor, forgive me. I should have asked permission," he apologized. "But you looked so lovely—I am forgiven?"

Teffin smiled, her lips still tingling from his kiss. "How could I not forgive a friend?" she answered, and saw him frown.

"Only a friend?" he asked.

She inhaled, her heart telling her to go slowly. "For now." She smoothed the skirt of her dress as she backed away from him, forgetting momentarily about the tree behind her. Bumping into it, she became flustered, and reached up, toying with a strand of her tawny hair before finally getting back her composure. "I think perhaps we should maybe join the others, don't you?" she asked as she gazed toward the barn, where she saw some of the guests starting to leave.

Joaquín was all gallantry. Reaching out, he took her hand, twining her arm in his again. "Sí, perhaps you are right at that," he answered, and they left the concealing shadows and headed back toward the barn.

For the next few days, everyone who had been at the Kolters' party lived in a state of constant strain. Not a word was heard from any of the young men who'd ridden off to join those gathering at San Felipe. However, rumors did circulate that the atmosphere was getting explosive. With Braxton gone now, Joaquín began to spend more and more time at the Dantes', rather than the Kolters'. In fact, it wasn't long before he was riding over every day to join Cole Dante out on the range, where he was quickly making himself indispensable, and he had even become one of the few hands Cole had who could tame a horse Comanche style.

"You'd think he'd been born to it," Cole told Eli late one afternoon when the two old friends were on their way back to the ranch after having spent the day breaking some mares the men had brought in the week before.

Eli glanced over at Cole and frowned. "Gettin' pretty attached to him, ain'tcha?" he called as Cole rode along ahead of him.

Cole took a deep breath and leaned back more comfortably in the saddle. "Reckon maybe I am, I don't know," he answered. "I just wish he weren't such a diehard Mexican."

Eli rubbed a hand across his clean-shaven face, wishing as he always did that they lived in a cooler climate so he could at least grow a short-clipped beard once in a while like Bain Kolter wore. But even a clipped beard itched him like hell in the heat, and he wasn't about to be miserable year-round. So as much as he hated shaving, he'd gone the routine again just this morning.

Eli had been with Cole close to twenty years already, and he glanced at him now, thinking the two of them were as close as any two men could be, even though he was almost a quarter-century older than Cole.

"What'll you do if we get bad news from San Felipe?" he asked, his slate-gray eyes studying Cole curiously as they reined onto a well-worn path, through a grove of cottonwoods. "This could be it, you know."

Cole was staring straight ahead, into the shadows caused by the late-afternoon sun. "If word comes that we go— then I guess we go."

"And Antonio's nephew?"

"Maybe he'll stay here with Mose and keep an eye on the ladies for us, who knows."

"Who says Mose'll stay—besides, what if Joaquín decides to join his countrymen?"

"You think he will?"

"Hell, I don't know." Eli dug his horse a little harder in the ribs, and moved up alongside the big white stallion, sired by the first horse Cole had ever tamed. A horse he'd grown to love, but a horse that had always reminded him of the son he'd lost, because it was to forget Case's abduction, and the tragic knowledge of his and Heather's assumed deaths, that he'd left on that first quest into Comanche territory. That was so long ago. Nevado's sire was dead, and still they had no idea where Case might be. Every trail, every lead had proved false, and now Eli had a feeling he knew why Cole had taken such a liking to Joaquín. "He reminds you of the boy, doesn't he, friend?" he said, finally bringing his suspicions out into the open.

Cole nodded, his tanned face revealing the agony he felt inside. "I reckon that's one way of putting it," he answered. "I guess he's almost what I would have liked Case to be when he grew up. Perhaps a little less of the dandy about him, but—there's just something. Don Antonio should be proud."

"He probably would be, if Joaquín weren't so dead set on takin' the wrong side in all this." He took off his hat, ran a hand through his once-sandy hair, now gray, but sporting a small bald spot in the back, ruffled it to try drying out some of the sweat, then plunked the hat back on his head. "Even at that, though, Joaquín ain't half as bad as that sister of his. Why, she ain't even dry behind the ears yet, and she thinks she's growed up enough to know what's goin' on." He laughed. "I hear tell she thinks Santa Anna's some kind of savior or somethin'."

Cole's hands tightened on the reins. "Just so she doesn't get Antonio and the rest of the Mexicans who are on our side to thinking they might be wrong." His eyes darkened, like the color in a murky pond, anger narrowing them. "Dammit, Eli, we should have gone with Brax, instead of staying back here just waiting. I feel so useless—at least then we'd know what the hell was really going on, instead of walking around wondering. Even Bain regrets not going."

"Don't worry, Cole," Eli assured him, "We should hear somethin' soon. Word's just slow at filterin' back, that's all."

Cole sighed. "I hope you're right." He straightened in

the saddle, and reined Nevado to a halt where the cotton-woods fell away, heralding the top of a ridge, and they could see for miles in the distance.

"You know, I think I like it here in Texas, as well as I liked it near the Arkansas," he said after a few minutes. "Only I sure as hell hope we can find a way to keep things going our way, without a fight."

"And if we have no choice?"

"Then I guess we'll have to, because I've never backed down from a fight yet, and I don't intend to now, nor has Bain either. No, my friend, regardless of how much I hate war, I won't let some Mexican dictator take away what I figure's mine." And he dug his horse in the ribs and headed across the top of the ridge, with Eli close behind on his sorrel, heading onto the trail that led back to the ranch house in the valley below.

The days slowly moved on, and during that time, the only word coming back to San Antonio was that some of General Cos's letters to the troops at Anahuac had been intercepted, and when read, their contents had revealed that Santa Anna, who was brother-in-law to General Cos, was planning to march a division of troops up from Zacatecas, where they had only last month squelched a revolt by slaughtering hundreds of their own country-men. Now their plan was to crush the Texans with the same sort of vengeance they'd used at Zacatecas, and the news hadn't been taken lightly at San Felipe. According to the riders, who were keeping everyone informed, a number of the young men at San Felipe, Braxton in-cluded, had chosen a lawyer from Georgia named William Travis as their leader, and were on their way from Buffalo Bayou, on a sloop called the *Ohio*, with a cannon on board, to launch an attack on the garrison at Anahuac.

"And what a joke that was," Braxton exclaimed some two weeks later as he sat his horse beside Joaquín, telling him about his adventures while they rode out from the Kolters', heading for the open range. "We had one stink-ing cannon, one ball, and barely enough powder to get the damn thing off the ship."

"And yet Capitán Tenorio surrendered?" Joaquín was amazed.

"Hell yes, it scared the pants off him. You see, he didn't know we only had one shot, and we sure weren't about to tell him otherwise. He told Travis he needed a day to decided, only Travis gave him an hour." Braxton laughed as he took off his hat, brushing a couple of flies away from his horse's ears, letting the sun catch his hair and turn it to pale gold before he covered it again. "I wish you could have seen those soldiers pouring out of the place," he went on. "The crowd was yelling for their necks, but Travis knew better. Instead, since there was no place to hold them prisoner, he turned the whole damn bunch out and sent them packing back toward the Rio Grande and General Cos."

"Then you won?"

"Well." Braxton's face flushed slightly. "We did, and we didn't. The men back at San Felipe got scared, and just before I headed for home, they were talking about apologizing for the whole thing. Can you imagine? Here we are, shoving their damn tariffs down their throats and getting away with it, and they're gonna apologize."

Joaquín studied his friend closely. Brax was young yet, with a great deal to learn. "Perhaps this way is better, mi amigo," he said. "If one shot can accomplish what you are after . . ."

"Now who's the dreamer?" Brax glanced over, watching his friend. He'd grown more than just fond of Joaquín. For some reason, the Mexican had grown on him since his arrival last May. Maybe because, in spite of his stubborn loyalty to what he referred to as his country, he was not only a man of honor, but integrity. "By the way," Braxton added, "I hear you've been spending a lot of time with Teffin lately."

Joaquín was riding his uncle's black horse, as he usually did, and he neck-reined the animal to the left, avoiding a low outcropping of rocks, and the expression on his face grew guarded as he looked over at Braxton.

"You disapprove?" he asked.

"Should I?"

"I hope not, because I have a strange feeling she is someone who will be important to my life."

"From what Blythe says, I'd say she's already important to your life."

"Let us just say I am working on it." He frowned. "Your cousin is hard to understand, amigo," he went on as he held his horse back to keep pace with Braxton. "One moment I think she cares, the next, it is as if we are strangers. How is this, por favor? I would like to know what I do wrong."

A grin broadened Braxton's full mouth, and his eyes twinkled. "Now you're learning about women, friend," he said "They're unpredictable, especially in this family. Now come on, let's get a move on, and see if we can find that stallion Pa said he spotted up near the north ridge. If he's got as big a herd of mares with him as Pa said, Uncle Cole's gonna be anxious to know," and he dug his horse in the ribs, challenging Joaquín to keep up as he headed across a flat stretch of ground toward the hills beyond.

They'd been riding for well over two hours already, searching every arroyo and water hole where Brax knew there might be sign of a herd, and now they were well into Indian Territory, and moving more cautiously. There'd been Indian sign a couple of times, but Brax assured Joaquín it was two, maybe three days old, and with the sun high now, their clothes were clinging with sweat.

Joaquín took off the sombrero he'd begun to wear along with the more casual clothes, and wiped his forehead, then squinted as he put it back on, his gaze trying to avoid the undulating waves of heat dancing along the surface of the ground in the distance. They'd been moving across an open stretch of ground for the last half-hour, and he sighed as he spotted a tree-lined slope some distance ahead. Brax had never brought them this far northwest before, and the land was new to him.

"You have been here before, amigo?" Joaquín asked as he saw Braxton's eyes scanning the landscape ahead.

"Yeah, a few times with Pa."

"Then you know where to look?"

Brax nodded. "There's a box canyon about four miles

ahead. The other side of those hills. Could be they're holed up in there."

"And if they are not?"

"Then we keep looking."

Joaquín inhaled, trying to get a fresh breath of air, but there was none. Only the heat, dust, and smell of animal sweat to fill his nostrils.

"There is water?" he asked.

Braxton knew what he meant. The horses were wringing wet, even though they hadn't been riding hard, and he could feel the dry, gritty dust in his own mouth.

"As soon as we reach those trees up ahead," he answered, and Joaquín felt a wave of relief sweep over him.

When Braxton had told him, shortly after his arrival, that summers in Texas were hot, he hadn't thought much of it, since his own home in Montclava had also had hot summers, but in no way had he been prepared for the intense heat permeating the Texas plains. Gone were the rolling slopes of San Antonio and its surrounding trees. The land they were traversing now was barren and dry, with craggy mountains fringing the sky, and rocky arroyos where shade trees were rare, and life consisted of rock lizards and an occasional armadillo. So the line of cottonwoods up ahead was more than inviting.

Joaquín sighed a few minutes later, straightening in the saddle as they reined their horses beneath the sparse shade of the trees, and he followed closely behind Brax, who seemed to know right where he was going.

Minutes later they rode down the opposite side of the hill they'd just ascended, dismounting at the edge of a clear pond fed by a small stream that filtered through a bunch of rocks, before it reached the pond, which emptied at the far end as a trickling brook, then disappeared into a cluster of bushes some hundred or so feet away. Still there was no sign of a herd. Only the hoofprints of a few stray cattle.

Braxton dropped to his knees, pulled his hat off, untied the bandanna from around his neck, and scooped it through the water, bringing it sopping wet to cover his head, face, and neck, then he cupped his hands, lifting handfuls of the cool water to his dry lips while his horse snorted gratefully, siphoning the refreshing liquid into his mouth.

"Well, come on," he urged Joaquín, as Joaquín stood for a minute watching. "Don't worry, it's clear."

"You are certain?"

"Would I be doing this if it weren't?" Brax ran a wet hand through his blond hair, rivulets of water dripping down his face onto his neck, where they settled into his shirt collar. "I know a poisoned hole when I see it. Besides, I've been here enough to know there's not a chance. No alkali and none of that smelly old black stuff within miles."

Joaquín dropped his horse's reins and let the animal move to the water, and while the big black stallion took his fill of the cool sweet liquid, Joaquín joined Braxton, washing away the sweat and dust from this own face, hair, and neck, then he glanced over at his friend as they both stood up.

"So where to now?" Joaquín asked.

Braxton set the hat back on his head, and reached out, grabbing his horse's reins. "To that box canyon I told you about," he answered as he mounted again, and Joaquín followed suit, then suddenly froze, his gaze moving beyond Braxton to a low ridge some distance to the northeast.

"I think we have company, mi amigo," he said softly.

Brax whirled around, then inhaled sharply, his eyes quickly picking up the silhouettes of three warriors against the midmorning sky.

"Comanche," he said, then frowned. "But I don't think they've seen us." He turned back to Joaquín. "Ride out slow toward those trees," and he motioned with his head, back to the trees they'd ridden through only a few minutes before.

"And if they see us?"

"Then we're in trouble."

Joaquín laid the reins across his horse's neck, flexing his heels, and the big stallion turned slowly, heading back the way they'd come, with Braxton and Hickory close behind. Once into the trees again, Brax reined up, then slowly walked Hickory back partway, where he could still see the Indians, and he swore under his breath as he watched them start riding down the trail he knew would bring them to the pond they'd just left.

"We'll have to get out of here, and fast," he stated, then looked about quickly, hoping to find a route where the Comanche wouldn't spot them. After a few seconds he reined his horse into the thickest part of the trees, then yelled back to Joaquín, "Come on!" and he rode off down the trail he'd ridden up only a short time before, with Joaquín close behind. Some hundred feet down the slope, he reined up, then turned his horse to the right, off the trail, and followed the line of trees, keeping beneath their branches as long as he could. A short time later, he sighed in relief as the ground carried him down behind a rock abutment, and he galloped along behind it until pulling Hickory to a halt again when the rocks began to fall away.

"So, are we safe?" Joaquín asked as he drew up beside him.

Braxton's gaze was fixed on the trail behind them. "Not until we've got at least five miles between them and us," and without saying another word, he moved off again, riding down into the old dry riverbed that stretched out ahead of them, knowing it would take them past the Comanche.

It was a little over an hour later, Brax and Joaquín were making their way along the high ridge that ringed the mile-long box canyon Braxton had been heading for, and there, far below in the valley, was the stallion his father had told him about. With him were at least twenty mares. Only this horse wasn't one of the small mustangs they were all used to running into out here on the open plains. He was big, tawny and beautiful, and Brax was certain the sleek horse had to be a throwback to some of the palominos bred in Spain and brought to the Southwest territories by Joaquín's ancestors, because as they watched, their gaze intent on him, as if knowing he was being observed, the animal reared up, threw his head back, then pranced the ground restlessly, letting the sun catch his mane and turn it into a brilliant golden hue. Brax's mother had had a palomino like this once when she'd first come west, and his father had bought one special for Blythe, and now here was another for the catching.

Joaquín smiled. "Cole Dante is fortunate," he said as they watched the animal, Joaquín's dark green eyes transfixed by its beauty. "For such a one, men will pay well."

"If we can find him again, now that we know he exists."

"Why find him again?" Joaquín was studying the horse intently. "You and I can take him."

For a minute Brax wasn't sure he'd heard right, and he drew his eyes from the prancing animal and glanced over at Joaquín.

"What are you getting at?"

"I am getting at nothing. I am telling you I will take the stallion and his mares back to Cole Dante, but for this I will need your help."

Brax leaned forward in the saddle, his gray eyes skeptical. "You'll take him back?"

"Sí, it will not be hard."

"Oh no, just walk right up and slip a halter on him, I suppose."

Joaquín straightened arrogantly. "Your uncle taught me well, mi amigo," he answered. "For what better reason than to bring such as this one back to his rancho?"

Braxton shook his head in disbelief. "But he's wild."

"Sí, that I know. It will make the challenge all the more interesting."

"You're crazy, amigo."

Joaquín laughed, then looked down at the clothes he was wearing. He still had on his calzoneras, but with leather botas laced over them to shield his legs from the heavy brush, and he'd taken the sleeves from one of his fancy jackets to make it cooler, then slipped it on over a full-sleeved shirt that was starting to show wear about the edges.

"Perhaps I am," he answered, as he realized that, at the moment, he felt far removed from the brash young man he'd been only a few months back. But it felt good to relax and get his hands dirty. And how proud he'd be to show Señor Dante what an excellent teacher he had been. "But I still say, I can take him," and he gazed back down to the floor of the canyon. "Only as I say, it will take much doing. So, if you will show me the trail, we will commence, sí?"

Brax inhaled as he stared at his friend. "You're serious aren't you?"

"Why not? To bring such a prize for Señor Dante will be worth it."

Braxton studied Joaquín for a minute, then laughed. "You know, Joaquín, we don't trade our women for horses," he teased.

Joaquín's eyes narrowed shrewdly. "But it would not hurt, sí?"

Brax grinned. "Sí, I guess it wouldn't at that." He turned his mount, reining him toward the trail leading down to the valley floor.

For the next few hours there was no room in Joaquín's thoughts for anything except the stallion he'd made up his mind to capture, and as soon as they reached the floor of the canyon, he set to the task.

First he had to catch him. Taking the lariat from the saddle horn, he hefted it freely in his hands, letting his long tapered fingers get the feel of the rope, then he glanced over at Brax.

"You still think you can ride the mouth of the canyon to keep him in?" he asked.

Braxton nodded. "I know I can, but I could probably get more results if I had something besides my hat to wave."

"Here." Joaquín grabbed the serape he'd had slung at the back of his saddle. "And whatever you do, amigo, do not let him get through. The mares we can round up later, but him—I have a feeling he would run to the sea if he could see the horizon. Here, he will give up quicker. Now, ándale!"

Brax caught the serape, then took off at a gallop, heading for the canyon's narrow entrance, which was only some two to three hundred feet wide, and as he did so, Joaquín eased his own horse forward, only at a slow walk for now, trying to get as close as he could without being detected by the huge animal, which was now at the far end of the mile-long canyon, nibbling on a plush stand of grass.

Easing his mount cautiously, Joaquín closed the space between, moving from bush to bush, and tree to tree, walking his horse leisurely a few feet, then stopping. When he was only a few yards away, however, he suddenly reined up when his horse nickered, and he saw the tawny animal, up ahead, raise his head and sniff the air, ears laid back.

Joaquín had been bent in the saddle, trying to become part of his horse, mingling here and there with the mares, but forgetting that the horse he was on was also a stallion, and now the big black's ears went back hostilely as he stood staring at this wild contemporary. The waiting was over.

With a quick flick of the wrist as he straightened in the saddle, Joaquín's lariat snaked out, coiling into a whirling circle, and he dug his horse in the ribs. The golden stallion, already on guard, tossed his head viciously, then, catching sight of the man on the other horse, took off at a gallop. However, Joaquín was already bearing down on him, the rope singing through the air toward its target, and it met it head-on slipping down over the palomino's sleek neck, with little effort.

Even though Joaquín was ready for the impact, as he slowed his horse and the lariat tightened, the resulting jolt almost jerked him from the saddle. But with a strength surprising even him, he hung on desperately, then quickly gave the animal just enough lead to keep the rope taut, yet let him run, while he rode close behind.

For almost an hour the animal ran, with Joaquín and his mount at his heels, first this way, then retracing his path, heading more than once for the open mouth of the canyon, only to be frightened back by the sight of Braxton, the serape waving as he cut across the trail to turn him. Meanwhile, the mares milled about restlessly, knowing something was happening, but unable to comprehend what to do. Finally, exhausted from the rope cutting off his wind, and the constant moving, the big gold stallion began to slow his efforts, and a short time later Joaquín was facing him from the ground, the lariat wound deftly about his hand as he approached the skittish animal.

Braxton was still near the mouth of the canyon, but seeing that the big stallion had become weary, he'd moved up the side of the hill a short distance, to where he could get a good view, and now he watched fascinated as his Mexican friend, remembering everything Cole had taught him, hobbled the reluctant animal with a piece of the same lariat, put a noose around the stallion's underjaw, then proceeded to talk to the horse in a soothing voice, trying to calm him, while he rubbed the stallion's nose softly and stroked him.

For a long time Brax sat partway up the side of the canyon wall, on his horse, watching, oblivious of everything around him, so it was a complete surprise sometime later when he was suddenly brought back to his surroundings by a hurried command from below, and looked down just in time to see the three Indians he'd thought they'd eluded some four or five miles back on the trail. Every muscle tensed as he watched them urge their horses forward, then bring them to a halt only a few feet inside the box canyon. The three warriors sat for the longest time, looking around, and he hardly dared breathe while they studied the ground, then moved on a little farther, before picking up his and Joaquín's trail again. Luckily they hadn't discovered his tracks leading up the hill as yet and he prayed they wouldn't look up.

He continued to sit motionless and stare at the riders. They were Comanche, all right, and from the look of them, they'd no doubt been separated from a bigger raiding party. Braxton shifted his gaze down to the other end of the canyon. The Indians were heading right toward where Joaquín was engrossed in taming the wild stallion.

Braxton continued to stay quiet until the trio was a good two to three hundred feet into the canyon, then cautiously he turned his horse and headed back down to the canyon floor, and keeping the three Comanche in sight ahead of him, he moved his horse forward, following stealthily, but staying as far back as he could so as not to be detected.

Meanwhile, just ahead of the Comanches, Joaquín, hat off, leather gloves thrown to one side, was working relentlessly on the big stallion, caressing him affectionately and trying to assuage his fears while breathing gently into his nostrils. His warm breath had calmed the palomino considerably, and he was no longer straining against the ropes.

"You see, my magnificent caballo," Joaquín cooed to him in Spanish, "I will not hurt you." His hand stroked the animal's breast as he looked into its eyes. "For you and me it is time to be amigos, sí." His hand moved up to the horse's velvety nose, and he touched it lightly, still talking, unaware that barely ten yards behind him now, three pairs of sloe eyes watched curiously, surprised to see a man they knew was not a Comanche using a technique taught only by their tribe.

Suddenly Joaquín tensed, his hand still on the horse's nose, and he stood motionless for a moment, a weird feeling of apprehension beginning to fill him. Somehow, he knew someone was standing behind him, and he was sure it wasn't Braxton. Perhaps the look in the stallion's eyes as he stared off into space, but whatever it was, he was certain he was no longer alone. Turning his head slightly, he pretended to still be absorbed in the stallion, only his stomach tightened as he caught sight of the three Comanche.

Without hesitating, his words still tender and coaxing, he continued to pretend he'd seen nothing as he leaned against the animal, letting the stallion feel the weight of his body, yet all the while he was keeping the trio just within sight of the corner of his eye. Then he saw something else. Behind the Comanche and a little to their left, he saw Braxton, still astride, rein his horse quickly behind a huge flowering bush, the rifle that had been in the scabbard on his saddle clearly visible in his right hand.

Every muscle in Joaquín's body was alert, waiting, but

for what? Who would move first, Brax or the Indians? He continued to pretend to ignore the intruders, keeping his voice low, the words as calmly subdued as possible, so as not to let on that he knew anyone was there, and as he did, the Indian who'd been between the other two suddenly straightened and urged his mount forward a few feet.

"You! White man!" he shouted in English.

Joaquín hesitated, then straightened, flexing his broad shoulders, and he slowly turned. The Indian's dark sloe eyes were shaded by the frown on his face, but in the sun, his braided hair, with its coup feathers, was flecked with reddish-brown highlights, and although his skin was bronzed, Joaquín would swear he looked like a half-breed.

"You!" the Indian shouted again. "How you do this?" and he gestured toward the stallion.

Joaquín stared at the Indian curiously, determining they were probably about the same age and build, but at the moment the Indian had the advantage. Should he answer in English or Spanish? He'd been talking Spanish to the horse. Straightening arrogantly, his hand reaching back to touch the stallion, more for moral support than anything else, he avoided looking at the tree where he knew Braxton was.

"I was taught by a friend," he answered in English, trying to keep the fear from his voice. He had seen Comanche from afar, but never come face-to-face with one before.

The Indian's eyes narrowed and his head cocked sideways as he studied Joaquín carefully. "You not white man," he said, looking into Joaquín's eyes, which were more sloe than his own. "Who you?"

"Joaquín Luis de Alvarado," Joaquín answered. "And you?"

"Me, He Who Rides." He nudged his white-stockinged horse a little closer. "Who your friend teach you?"

"Señor Cole Dante."

He Who Rides' eyes flickered with recognition, and his hand tightened around the feathered lance he was carrying. "I have heard tell he is enemy of Comanche—you his friend, you die!"

"You know him?"

"I have heard—I do not need to know."

Joaquín's eyes were alert, muscles tense, waiting for even the slightest indication that this Indian or his companions would attack. Still they sat their horses as if they had all the time in the world.

He Who Rides was only some ten feet away now, only Joaquín would have felt better if the Indian wasn't astride. Looking up at him like this was unnerving. He could tell the warrior was as poised for battle as he was. They stared at each other for some time, neither moving, sizing each other up, then suddenly the decision of what to do was taken from him when Brax reined his pinto into the open, his rifle pointing past the other two Indians, directly at the back of He Who Rides.

"Everybody stay put," Brax yelled in English, and loud enough so there'd be no misunderstanding, then he followed it with a jumble of words in a language Joaquín had never heard before.

He Who Rides was still staring at Joaquín, and his eyes narrowed viciously.

"I would not do that if I were you," Joaquín warned as the Indian's fingers began to tighten again on the lance. "My friend is an excellent shot, He Who Rides, and his rifle is aimed directly at your back."

He Who Rides' fingers eased on the decorated lance as Braxton continued in rather stilted Comanche again, then Brax rode forward, as the other two Comanche reined their horses until they were next to He Who Rides, and both Comanche turned their horses so they were facing Braxton.

"You too, fella," Brax ordered, his rifle still aimed at He Who Rides. And slowly, his face hard, unyielding, He Who Rides reined his horse around to face his new intruder. "That's better," Braxton said, relieved he hadn't had to shoot. For one thing, he hated the thought of killing, because for all his brashness, he'd never killed a man up this close before, and he sure as hell didn't want to start with a specimen like this.

The other two Comanche were nothing spectacular, the one to his right even rather puny for a brave, but the Indian who'd confronted Joaquín was broad-shouldered and slim-hipped, with bulging muscles rippling in the late-afternoon sun that reflected off the fancy medallions gracing his bronzed chest. It'd actually be a shame to put a bullet in a man like this.

Braxton rode in closer now, and reached down, taking the lariat from where it hung on his saddle and he threw the rope to Joaquín, who had moved away from the three Indians and was now facing them, while the huge stallion, still hobbled, snorted arrogantly, his ears laid back, eyes wild.

"Here, tie them," Brax ordered curtly. He motioned toward He Who Rides. "Him first."

He Who Rides straightened, tensing, and Braxton's hands tightened on his rifle as he once more addressed the Indian in Comanche, then Braxton looked over at Joaquín.

"When he gets down, watch him," he warned.

Joaquín's gaze was steady on He Who Rides as the Indian swung a leg over and slipped from the saddle after angrily sinking the end of his lance into the ground. It was obvious the Comanche didn't like what was happening, but his respect for the white man's rifle overpowered his natural instinct to fight, so while Braxton continued leveling his rifle on them, Joaquín, using the lariat, tied up all three, both hands and feet.

"And their horses?" Joaquín asked after bending over and checking for the last time to make sure the knots on He Who Rides' wrists were tight enough.

Braxton's rifle was back in its sheath now, and he rode forward, dismounting.

"We could take them along."

"And have the Comanche raid your father's ranch to get them back? That is what they would do, sí?"

"Yeah, that's what they'd do, all right." Braxton glanced about them. "I know—after we get the stallion and mares away from the canyon, we'll tie their horses up near the entrance somewhere."

"You think they will be able to get free?"

Braxton glanced over to where He Who Rides lay on the ground tied hand and foot, and he could physically feel the hatred emanating from the brave's eyes. "It may take a while, but I can just about bet he'll be loose before the sun goes down tonight. So our best bet is to get as far away as we can before dark. Now come on, help me pull him and his friends over to those trees yonder so they don't fry in the sun, then we'll see if that wild stallion's lost enough of his jitters to follow a lead rope," and he let loose of his pinto's reins, walked over, and began dragging He Who Rides into the shade of a nearby tree, while Joaquín helped with his companions.

By the time they'd determined that the animal Joaquín had been trying to tame could be handled cautiously with a rope, then rounded up all the mares in his herd, and were headed away from the box canyon, after tying the Indians' horses in a hard-to-find place some hundred or so yards from the entrance, the sun had already dipped low on the horizon and they both knew night wasn't far off.

"No rest tonight," Brax said as they rode away, making sure the mares were following their stallion, who was being led by Joaquín astride his uncle's big black. "You think you can make it back without any sleep?"

Joaquín laughed, then glanced back toward the canyon where they'd left the frustrated Indians, who'd been calling curses on them all the while they'd been getting things ready to leave.

"To save my skin, I would go without sleep all day tomorrow too, mi amigo," he answered, then his gaze sifted over the tawny stallion he had in tow, its mane and tail fluttering like creamy silk in the late-afternoon breeze. "And for the honor of presenting such a one to your uncle, I would go without sleep beyond that."

Braxton glanced back, following Joaquín's gaze. He was right. With a horse like that, a man could feel like a

THE GATHERING OF THE WINDS 97

king, and he dug Hickory hard in the ribs, hoping Joaquín and the horses could keep up, because he was going to put as many miles between them and the three Comanche before dark as he could.

5

It was early. Too early to be up really, because it was still dark outside, and Bain stretched restlessly, then sat down at the kitchen table, rubbing the sleep from his eyes. He should take time to wash, but wouldn't, and he sighed as Liz set the cup in front of him, poured some reheated coffee into it, then glanced across the room to where Don Antonio was pacing the floor. Antonio de Léon stopped to look out the window for a second, then started pacing again.

"You sure you couldn't use a cup, Tonio?" she asked.

He stopped pacing again, looked over at the steaming cup of coffee in front of Bain, then sighed, shrugging. "All right, so, perhaps I should take time," he answered. "It would do no good to ride out, only to fall asleep in the saddle, would it?"

He came over and sat down opposite Bain, while Lizette brought another cup for him. Pretty had wakened them both only a few minutes before, after opening the door in response to Antonio's frantic pounding.

"You realize we're probably going on a wild-goose chase, don't you, my friend?" Bain said as he shoved a stale biscuit in his mouth, then washed it down with the black coffee. "The boys probably rode too far, and decided it would be better not to travel back after dark."

"Braxton has done this before?" Antonio asked.

Bain shook his head. "No, but then he's never had Joaquín with him before either."

"My point exactly." Antonio tried hurriedly to cool

the coffee in his cup, stirring and blowing on it. "And you admitted they were heading into Indian Territory."

Lizette set the coffeepot back down on the stove, then tightened the sash on her wrapper as she came back to the table.

"He's right, Bain," she said. "They should have been back hours ago."

"I know, I know." He took a deep breath, then reached out and took her hand. "It's just that I guess I hate to think anything could be wrong." He squeezed her hand, then grabbed another biscuit, shoving it in his mouth, and taking his cup with him, he left the table. He had only his pants and a shirt on, and the shirt wasn't even buttoned. "I'll just slip on my boots and grab the rifle and pistols, be right back," and he padded barefoot across the wood floor, disappearing into the dining room.

"Por favor, I am sorry I had to wake you so early, Lizette," Don Antonio apologized as he sipped his coffee. "But I do worry about Joaquín. After all, he was brought up in an entirely different environment than I have given him here. If anything were to happen . . . Besides, Catalina is hard enough to control under normal circumstances. For the clock to strike so early an hour and Joaquín not accounted for—soon the cock will crow too, and it will tell me anything could be wrong."

Lizette reached up, brushing a stray hair back from her face as she stared across the table at Antonio. He was trying not to look too upset, but then she was upset too. Braxton had never been out all night like this, unless he was with Bain or Cole and the men from the ranch. She hadn't even known he hadn't come home until Don Antonio banged on the door. What time was it? Her gaze moved to the clock behind Antonio on the far wall. Four-thirty! If only they hadn't gone to bed so early last night. But she hadn't given it a thought. There were often times he was late getting in, but not this late.

"I'm sure it's probably nothing," she said, trying to assure him. "They're young, adventurous."

"And right there lies the trouble." He gazed over, looking directly into her eyes. "We both know, don't we, how young people have some strange idea they are immortal, only we know they are not. You are as worried as I, are you not?"

"Yes, I guess I am. That's why I wish you and Bain would take some of the men with you."

"Ah, but no, Lizette. It is better we go, just the two of us."

"He's right," Bain said as he hurried back into the room, completely dressed this time, with a gunbelt strapped onto his hip and a rifle in his hand. "So, are you ready?" he asked.

Antonio downed the last bit of coffee in the cup and stood up. He too was wearing a gunbelt, of tooled leather, much fancier than the plain holster Bain's pistol was resting in.

Both men grabbed their hats and headed for the door, with Lizette close behind, a lantern in her hand. They stepped out onto the back porch, and she handed Bain the lantern.

"Be careful," she cautioned as he set his hat on his head. He pulled her to him with his free arm and kissed her.

"Don't worry, Liz, like I said, they probably just went too far and holed up somewhere for the night. We'll find them," and he kissed her again, then both men headed toward the barn, using the lantern to light their way, as the first few patches of daylight began to lighten the sky off to the east.

Lizette turned at a noise behind her. Pretty was standing just inside the door, the flickering light from the lamp in the kitchen illuminating her worried face.

"I thought I told you to go back to bed," Liz said, watching the Negro woman's gaze following the men to the barn.

Pretty shrugged, pulling the sash on her white apron tighter around her middle, then she smoothed the front of it down over the skirt of the plain gray dress she'd slipped into. "Shucks, I couldn't go back to sleep now, even if I wanted to," she answered, her voice filled with concern as she drew her eyes from Bain and Antonio and looked at Liz. "Once that old daylight starts comin' up over them hills, I might's well give up the notion of gettin' any more sleep. Besides, them boys might just come back anytime now, and if they do, they's gonna be hungry. Now come on, why don't you go get some sleep, Miss Lizzie. You's the one looks like you could use it."

Lizette sighed. "I don't think I could go back to sleep either," she said, then turned her gaze back toward the barn, where Antonio sat astride already, waiting for Bain to saddle his horse, and a few minutes later, as the first faint rays of the morning sun began to blend into the gray dawn, turning the sky into gold beyond the hills to the east, Lizette and Pretty stood by the back door of the ranch house and watched Bain and Antonio ride out of the ranch yard, then turn, heading toward the western hills, where night still clung tenaciously to the sky.

"So, where do we start?" Antonio asked as he rode alongside Bain.

Bain looked off to the northwest. "I told him I saw that herd up toward the canyon, so I guess we'd better start there first," and he dug his horse harder in the ribs, and they quickly left the ranch house behind.

For the rest of the morning, as the early light of dawn swept the cobwebs of night from around them, bringing with it the heat of a new summer day, Bain and Antonio rode the trails they felt Braxton and Joaquín would have been most likely to have taken. Only, except for a few stray cattle and an occasional deer, they encountered nothing except the quiet countryside. As the morning wore on, the sun lifting higher and higher above them, Bain was really getting worried. They were well into Indian Territory already, and although Bain had picked up Brax and Joaquín's trail from the day before, there was nothing to show they might have returned.

Suddenly Bain reined Amigo to a halt as they moved up a sloping incline and maneuvered their horses around an outcropping of rocks.

"Listen!" he yelled back to Antonio, and Antonio moved up beside him, bringing his own mount to a halt.

Both men sat rigid, their heads cocked, listening to the

rumble of what sounded like thunder in the distance, yet the sun was still beating down unmercifully.

"Horses?" Antonio asked.

Bain nodded. "Over the hill. Come on."

Both men spurred their horses forward. On reaching the top of the hill, they reined up again, this time staring at the spectacle before them. There, riding like the wind across the flat expanse of land that seemed to stretch out for miles before reaching the ragged purple hills beyond, were Joaquín and Braxton, a pounding herd of horses galloping behind them, following an elegant palomino Joaquín had at the end of a rope. The palomino's tail was raised, the ends flickering skyward, whipping in the wind as he moved, while his golden mane flew high in the air, as if trying to catch the sun. It was a magnificent sight.

"Now, are you through worrying?" Bain said as he looked over at Antonio.

Antonio shook his head. "I do not believe it, señor. It is impossible. They are both too young to accomplish so much."

"I'll let you tell them that," Bain offered, then reined his horse toward the trail, leading down the side of the hill. "Now, come on, let's slow them down a bit before they hit the hills," and he took off down the trail, with Antonio close at his heels.

Braxton was having the time of his life, and so was Joaquín. It wasn't even near noon yet, and they were well over halfway home, without a sign of the Indians they'd left back in the canyon, nor any new ones to add either. They were both tired and sleepy, yet they'd both been sleepy before, with less to show for it.

Brax saw the sloping hills ahead and yelled over to Joaquín, "We'd better slow them down, friend, or they'll stampede right into those trees."

Joaquín nodded, and both riders began to slow their mounts, so by the time they neared the sloping hills a short distance ahead, the whole herd was moving at an ambling trot, then Joaquín suddenly reined his uncle's big black to a stop and shouted over to Braxton.

"There is movement up ahead, near those trees," he

said as the palomino pranced, pawing the ground, disliking the fact he'd been stopped from his headlong run.

Brax had seen it too, and was already reaching for his rifle as he slowed Hickory to a walk.

"Couldn't be Indians," he called over, drawing his weapon from its sheath. "Not warriors anyway. Might be a deer or a stray calf."

"No, see?" Joaquín was pointing to a spot halfway down the hill, to where two men had emerged on the trail, then they were quickly lost again beneath a line of trees that ended at the edge of the flatland they'd been riding across.

"Hope they're friendly," Brax murmured half under his breath. "But just in case . . ." and he cocked his rifle, then let the stock rest on his knee, with the barrel pointed straight up, ready to swing into action if need be, and they started moving again, only slowly now, and cautiously, keeping the restless herd behind them.

Suddenly, as the two approaching riders cleared the trees and began coming toward them across the open plain, Brax let out a whoop.

"Damn! It's Pa!" he yelled, uncocking his rifle and slipping it back into its sheath. "Pa and your uncle," and he took off at a gallop, leaving Joaquín behind with the horses, and he met the two men before they could reach the herd.

"Hey, Pa, look what we got!" he yelled as he neared them. "And there's at least twenty mares in the bargain, unless we lost a few on the way."

He reined in next to his father, dust flying in the hot morning sun, the tiredness suddenly gone from his eyes.

Bain stared at his son's rumpled clothes and dirt-streaked face. "You didn't come home last night, Brax," he said, ignoring Braxton's excitement. "We got worried."

"Oh hell, Pa, we can take care of ourselves." He glanced over at Antonio de Léon. "You should have seen Joaquín," he went on with the same enthusiasm. "You'd swear he was part Comanche, the way he set out taming that stallion."

By now Joaquín was close enough to hear the conversation. "He is a beauty, is he not, Tío Antonio?" he yelled, getting his uncle's attention, and he held the rope up, leading the tawny palomino into full view for them both to see.

Don Antonio's eyes narrowed as he squinted, studying the beast. Joaquín was right, he was a magnificent animal, however, it was going to take more than a few horses to erase the fear that had ridden with both men all morning, and he looked at Joaquín now, his eyes darkening angrily. "Do you not know what we have gone through, young man?" he bellowed, trying not to be too harsh, yet hoping to make him understand. "I thought you were dead somewhere. Your scalp on some warrior's lance."

Joaquín and Braxton exchanged glances, while both men stared hard at them, and the wild horses continued milling about.

"We did see three," Brax said rather sheepishly. "But don't worry, we left them back at the box canyon where we found the horses."

Bain frowned. "Dead?"

"Tied up."

"And you think they're still there?"

"Not hardly . . . but look, Pa, even getting loose, they couldn't follow us in the dark, and we've been riding all night."

"Then I guess you must be tired as well as hungry, right?"

Again both young men exchanged glances, and Bain turned to his companion.

"We're about thirty or so miles from Cole's north camp," he reminded Antonio. "And since most of the horses would end up there anyway, until they're broken what's say we head there now and drop them off before going home?"

Antonio pondered the question thoughtfully.

"I know it means we won't get back to the ranch until late," Bain went on. "But it'd be foolish to try to herd these horses to my place, then only have to drive them north again."

"You are right of course, my friend," Antonio answered after a few more minutes. "It was just that, when we do not return right away . . . I hope Lizette will not send others out looking for us."

"I tell you what," Bain said as he looked out over the herd now, still silently marveling at what these two young men had accomplished. "When we reach Cole's camp, I'll have him send one of the men down to the ranch, then over to your place to let them know all's well. That way, Brax and Joaquín can get some needed food and rest."

Antonio knew Bain was right. Still, is seemed something more should be said. True, they were both all right, but to take such a risk, and worrying everyone so. He looked over at Joaquín. He was sitting straight in the saddle, his eyes gleaming with pride at what they'd accomplished. Ah well, what good would it do to rant and rave? At least he had proved he was growing up. He looked over at Bain.

"Cole and his men won't be expecting us, you know."

Bain grinned. "Who cares? Once he sees that stallion and all these mares, he won't care whether we break up his day or not. That all right with you, son?" he asked.

Brax nodded. "We were heading that way anyway, Pa." He glanced over at Joaquín, whose dark green eyes were still on the stallion he'd captured. "Weren't we, Joaquín?"

Joaquín's eyes shone as he returned Braxton's gaze. "Ah sí, mi amigo, and now I will feel better with four of us to ride herd instead of two. That way, if the Comanche braves we left back there did get loose, it would be four against three this time, instead of three against two," and now it was Bain and Antonio's turn to exchange glances, wondering just how much of a fight the Indians had put up. Ah well, that'd come later. For now, Bain turned back to both young men, and he reined his horse so that Amigo faced the herd.

"Well, that's settled," he offered. "Now, we'd better get going," and he nodded toward the trail they'd just come down. "If we ride hard, we may even make it before the cook puts away the noon dishes," and with that he dug his horse in the ribs, heading back toward the rear of the wild herd, with Antonio at his side, while Braxton, realizing his father and Don Antonio were going to ride tail, reined his horse about, heading the rest of the way across the flat plain, with Joaquín close behind, leading the golden stallion, and they headed for the trail Bain and Antonio had just left.

It had taken the four riders longer than they thought to reach the northernmost reaches of the Dantes' land, where Cole had put up a couple shacks and some corrals where he and the men could break the horses they caught before taking them to the main corrals at the ranch house where buyers could see them. Some they sold locally, others were driven east to Nacogdoches and the Sabine, where they were sold to speculators from back east. Any place a market could be found, Cole usually found it, and it was what he liked doing.

Now he stood dumbfounded, the lariat with the golden stallion attached to the other end resting in his hand, as he stared at Don Antonio's nephew, Joaquín.

"You really mean you want me to have him?" he said, his dark green eyes studying the young man curiously. "You go to all that trouble, then turn him over to me?"

Joaquín straightened proudly. "If you had not taught me, he would not be here, sí?"

Cole glanced over at Bain. True, Bain had sent the two of them to find the stallion, but to bring him back like this, with his whole brood of mares . . . He'd never dreamed . . .

"I know you mean well, Joaquín, but I can't take him," Cole finally said, and held the rope out for Joaquín to take. "You should know that. You caught him fair and square. You risked your life to bring him in, and he belongs to you."

"But I brought him for you!"

Cole saw the disappointment in Joaquín's eyes. "Why?" he asked.

Joaquín could feel the flush starting to heat his face.

"Do I have to have a reason, other than that I want you to have him, as my friend?" he asked.

Now it was Cole's turn to blush, and he ran a hand through his dark hair. "Well now," he said, his gaze moving from Joaquín, to the stallion, and back again to Joaquín, "I'd be honored to accept him from you, Joaquín," he said. "Except for one thing."

"Oh?" Joaquín frowned.

"That horse you're riding belongs to Antonio there, doesn't he?" he asked.

Joaquín nodded. "Sí."

"And I happen to know you didn't bring any horses with you when you came north, did you?"

"No, Señor Dante."

"Then don't you think it'd be a mite selfish of me, being able to pick and choose any damn horse I want, the way I can, if I accepted such a fine specimen as this from you, and left you with nothing to ride?"

"I . . ." Joaquín was at a loss.

"I'll tell you what, Joaquín," Cole went on, watching the young man's face intently. "I'd be honored as all hell to have a stallion like that—who wouldn't?—but to be truthful, I'd feel like a bastard taking him, and knowing by all rights he should be yours. So I'll tell you what I'm going to do. I'm accepting him, Joaquín, and I'm proud as the devil to do so, but now that he's mine, I'm turning right around and presenting him back to you, as a token of my friendship, and I don't want to hear any more arguing on the subject, understand? Since he's mine, I'll do with him however I want. And this is what I want," and he held the lead rope out again for Joaquín to take.

Joaquín stared in frustration. What could he do now?

"So go ahead, take the horse, Joaquín," Antonio urged warmly. "You do not want to hurt Señor Dante's feelings, do you?"

"But that is not what I planned," he began to argue.

"To hell with what you planned," Brax cut in. "If Uncle Cole says the horse is yours, then take him, friend. Believe me, it isn't every day he gives away a prize like that."

Joaquín hesitated momentarily, then slowly reached out and took the lead rope from Cole. "I will do this," he said, his voice deep with emotion. "I will accept the horse back as a gift from a friend, but I pledge that someday I will bring you a gift you will not give back, even in friendship," and he ran his hand down the palomino's head to his soft velvety nose, then led the horse away, with Braxton beside him.

Bain stared at his brother-in-law curiously for a few minutes, but it was Antonio who spoke.

"Thank you, Cole," Antonio said, his gaze following his nephew as Joaquín and Braxton headed for one of the corrals. "I thank you for helping my nephew learn what it is to be a man. A real man."

"Don't thank me," Cole answered, his eyes also on the two young men. "Thank Brax, there. He may be headstrong at times, and think the world revolves around Texas, but he's the one making a man out of Joaquín."

"But you are fond of the boy, sí?" Antonio asked.

"You mean Joaquín? Sí, I'm fond of him, Tonio," Cole answered, his sloe eyes a bit misty. "He reminds me of what the son I lost might look like today, only instead of sombreros and calzoneras, he's probably wearing feathers and war paint."

"Which reminds me," Bain cut in. "Brax was saying they ran into a trio of Comanche up by the box canyon, and one of them I think you might find interesting."

Cole's eyes shifted from where Brax and Joaquín were to Bain. "Oh?"

"You ever hear of an Indian called He Who Rides?" asked Bain.

"He Who Rides?"

"Brax said that's what he called himself. Evidently while they were being tied up, Brax caught some of what they said here and there, and seems this particular brave hasn't been in the territory too long. I guess there's some drifters came down from up Santa Fe way, and he's with them."

"So what's different about him?"

"Well, Brax said his hair's more red than black, for

one thing, especially with the sun on it, and he'd swear the Indian's eyes were either green or hazel."

Antonio saw the look of anguish in Cole's eyes. "Perhaps this time it will be the one," he said.

Cole took a deep breath. "You're sure Brax said his eyes looked green?"

Bain nodded toward Braxton. "Ask him."

Cole reached out, grabbed Bain's arm, and squeezed it hard. "You damn bet I will," he said, then hurried off without another word, heading toward where Brax and Joaquín were talking to some of the men now, and showing off the palomino.

For the next half-hour Cole made Braxton and Joaquín go back over the whole affair in the canyon, drinking in every part of description they gave him, and later that evening, back at the ranch, he sat in his bedroom on the edge of the bed, one boot in his hand, his thoughts miles away.

"You're not sorry you let Joaquín keep the horse, are you?" Heather asked from the vanity, where she sat brushing her hair.

Cole shook his head, coming back to the present. "No . . . no, that's not what I was thinking of," he answered. "It was something else. Only I don't know whether to let you get your hopes up or not."

"I don't understand." She was in her nightgown already, and set the brush down, turning to face him, the dim light from the lamp on the vanity in front of her casting very little light across the room. She stood up, walking toward him, to see his face better. "Cole?"

He'd been holding one of his boots and staring off into space. Now he set it aside and pulled off the other, then started taking off his pants.

"I didn't tell you earlier, because I wasn't sure I was going to do anything about it, but now I think I have to," he said, and while she stood quietly, watching him finish undressing, he told Heather about the young Indian Brax and Joaquín had encountered on their recent escapade.

"Do you really think . . ." she asked as he slid beneath the covers.

He was on one elbow, staring at her. "Brax said his hair had too much red in it for him to be pure Comanche. And he looked close to the right age."

"Oh, Cole, if only . . ."

She walked over, blew out the lamp, then hurried back to the bed and crawled in beside him, her head resting on his arm as she cuddled close.

"I'm going to send Eli out," Cole said as he held her against him in the darkness. "If anyone can learn something, he can."

"But that's dangerous, isn't it?"

"Not for him. At least not as dangerous as it would be for me. Some of them still consider him a friend. After all, I'm the one they blame for taking their mustangs. He just works for me, that's all."

"But do you really think they'll tell him anything?"

"Even if they don't, he can find out indirectly from some of the old trappers out there he knows. Anyway, it's worth a try, love. If this Comanche they call He Who Rides is really Case, I've got to know."

"In a way I hope he isn't," she mused absentmindedly. "Because if he is, I doubt he could ever be our son again. Not now. Not after being with the Indians so long."

"That's something we'll have to face when the time comes." His lips brushed her forehead. "Now, let's close our eyes and pray that this time the trail won't lead to a dead end," and he kissed her full on the mouth, then pulled the thin sheet up over them to keep the flies off in the morning, because of the open window, and he sighed hoping the breeze, ruffling the leaves on the trees just outside the window of the log house, would last all night, because if felt so good in the summer heat.

The next few weeks moved along slowly for Cole and Heather, and even Teffin became restless. They'd told her about He Who Rides even before Eli'd gone, mostly because they knew Braxton and Joaquín would no doubt tell her anyway, and even she had begun to hope, as did Bessie and everyone else at the ranch, when they too were told what happened. Why, Mose Wheatley, a free black who'd been with the Dantes as long as Bessie, and who usually spent his time working the horses for Cole, even took over Eli's job with the men, while he too anxiously waited for the old trapper's return, since he'd been more than just fond of Case's nurse Tildie, who'd been traded to the Comanche with the boy. And it still hurt Mose terribly, wondering over the years what might have happened to her, and if she were even still alive, because he'd always felt their kidnapping had been his fault, since he was the one who'd been left in charge that long-ago fateful day. Tildie had been in her mid-teens then, such a loving girl, never complaining, always happy and smiling, and just the thought there was a chance she might still be out there somewhere made him eager.

So everyone at the Dantes', as well as at the Kolters', waited impatiently for Eli's return, while the rest of the summer, waiting for neither time nor man, moved steadily on, its days filled with what most summer days on the Texas frontier were filled with, work.

But night was the hardest time, because there was time to think, and brood, and wonder. And it was on just such a night, more than six weeks after he'd left, that Eli, tired yet glad to get back, slid off his horse and walked the last few steps up the walk toward the back porch of the Dante's ranch house.

It was a Saturday night, and late. At first he'd planned to spend one more night out under the stars, but the closer he'd ridden toward home, the better the thought of sleeping in a bed had sounded. Only now, glancing around and realizing everyone was probably asleep already, he was skeptical about letting them know he was back, because if he woke Cole up, the others would no doubt wake up too, and he still wouldn't get any sleep in a bed tonight. He stood on the back porch now, staring at the closed door for a few minutes, debating whether to just wait until morning or not, when the door slowly opened and the decision was made for him.

Bessie's daughter, Helene, hadn't been expecting anyone to be standing on the porch this time of night, and she hadn't heard Eli ride up the drive. Half-asleep yet, she'd been heading for the outhouse, and now she stood stock-still, staring at his vague form out on the porch, barely visible in the darkness.

He sensed her terror and blurted, "Shh, it's me!"

"Eli?" She'd been about to scream, and sighed now, relieved. "You scared me half to death," she said, stepping back so he could enter the kitchen, and he walked in, then turned, waiting. "You want me to wake Cole now?" she asked as she went to the table and lit the lamp.

Eli watched her closely as she set the glass chimney down over the candle flame. Helene was in her thirties now, and sort of pretty in a quiet way. Her dark brown hair was tied back with a bright red ribbon that clashed with the pink wrapper she was wearing, but he could see the edge of the skirt, of the red nightdress she had on beneath the wrapper. She finished making sure the light would stay lit, then turned toward him, her big brown eyes studying him thoughtfully.

"I hope you have good news," she said as she started toward the dining room to go upstairs. "Because I'd hate to be waking them up for nothing."

"You wake them and I'll let them decide that, young 'un," he said, treating her as he always did, as if she were still the same quiet, unassuming child they'd rescued from the steamboat mishap so many years ago. Only she was no longer, a child. Still quiet and unassuming, Helene was almost like a part of the house, helping her mother, sewing for the family, and keeping to herself.

"Unnatural, that's what it is," Eli'd often told Bessie when they'd discussed the fact that Helene had discouraged the attentions of every man who'd ever tried to court her. Bessie'd only shrugged, blaming it on the fact that Helene had been through so much over the years, it was only natural she'd shy away from really caring for any one particular person. However, Eli had his own suspicions about whom she cared for, especially whenever he saw her wearing the Indian-bead necklace Cole had given her when she was a girl. Only he'd always kept his suspicions to himself. Now he watched her glide from the room like a phantom, the flickering light from the lamp seeming to follow her for a second or two until she was gone from sight.

By the next afternoon everyone knew Eli'd come home, including the Kolters and de Léons, and late in the day Joaquín and Teffin rode side by side heading for a quiet, secluded place on the Dantes' four-thousand-some acres where the three cousins and Joaquín often spent their Sunday afternoons. Only, Brax and Blythe couldn't come today. The Kolters had ridden into town instead, and Teffin slowed her horse as she and Joaquín neared the running water cascading from the rocks above into the clear pool of water that was surrounded by trees and wildflowers. Although summer was almost over, the weather was still hot, the day one of those lazy ones better spent just lying around in the shade.

Joaquín, wearing better clothes than the old sombrero and workclothes he'd been wearing during the week, reined his horse to a stop, dismounted, then helped Teffin down. Her feet touched the ground, and she tucked the white shirtwaist into her blue riding skirt while he tethered their horses to a tree a short distance from the water. He was riding the palomino now, and patted the stallion's nose affectionately before joining Teffin at the edge of the pond.

"I think you're falling in love with that horse," she said as she took off her hat, letting the sun turn her dark gold hair into a shining mass of yellow, the natural curls clinging to the perspiration on her forehead where the hat had been resting.

He smiled, his eyes all too revealing. "I think I have fallen in love with more than my horse," he answered, his voice low and husky, the tremor in it making her tense.

He started to walk closer.

"Please, Joaquín, don't spoil it. Please?" she begged. "I told you before, I'm not ready to love anyone yet. I don't even know what love is."

"But you do care, sí?"

She flushed. "Yes, I care, you know I care. I like you, and there are times when you're not around that I do miss you—but I don't know if it's love or friendship really—and I have to be sure."

"Then I will be patient until you realize it is love." He reached out, took her hand, then led her to an old log they always sat on, and the two of them sat down. "So, now, you said you would tell me what Eli discovered on his journey to the Comanche, did you not?"

She smiled. "That's better, only it wasn't too much really. However, he did learn that He Who Rides got his name because he rode into one of the Indian camps on the back of a horse, and without benefit of escort of any kind, and they had a hard time getting him off the horse. At first they couldn't figure out why he fought them so, because he was only a few years old at the time. It wasn't until he tried to walk that they realized he'd broken his leg at some time or other, and it wasn't healed as yet." She reached down, picked up a pebble, and tossed it into the pond, watching the circles flare out from it, her golden eyes gazing intently at the water until it was still again. "From what Eli says, his leg never did heal the way it should, and he still has a slight limp from it."

"Then he has no parents?"

"No. None that anyone knows of."

"So he could be your brother, right?"

"Pa thinks he is."

"Your mother?"

"She's afraid he is."

He frowned. "How do you mean, afraid?"

She turned to look at him. Joaquín had become precious to her in so many ways. She could talk to him about almost anything, and he'd listen. If only her heart wasn't so unsure.

"Ma's afraid that if he really is Case, he won't ever acknowledge the fact, and if he is and he does, she's afraid the Comanche's influence on him will make it impossible for him to ever become a part of our world again."

"She may be right."

"I know." Her eyelids lowered before his steady gaze, and she sighed. "For years I've often wondered where my brother was, Joaquín," she said softly. "Now that there's a chance we might have found him—"

"Only how can your father be sure?"

"He can't really, I guess, unless we could find Tildie too."

"Ah, sí, the slave girl you said was with him."

"So I'll probably never know," she mused unhappily. "Nor will Father, because Eli knew Tildie, and he said the Comache told him He Who Rides was alone when he rode into their camp."

"There were no scars your brother had, no marks from birth, to say who he is?"

"None. Only his description. Ma said he had dark red hair, almost black, and green eyes slanted just like Pa's."

Joaquín reached out and took her hand. "I wish I could help in some way," he offered.

She squeezed his hand. "You have helped," she answered. "Just by being here," and she smiled again.

Joaquín loved to watch Teffin smile, because when Teffin smiled, her whole face lit up, eyes sparkling as if someone had thrown gold dust into them. A warm sensation swept through him, and he stood up, pulling her to her feet, and he smiled back, his arms closing around her to hold her close.

Again as she had a few times before, Teffin didn't fight him—in fact, unlike a few moments before, she welcomed his arms. It was comforting just to be held like this. She didn't want to hear words of love, not now, not just yet, but it felt so good to let someone else share the hurts and doubts so they didn't seem so huge anymore. She drew her head back for a moment and stared up at him. Joaquín was so tall compared to her. The top of her head barely reached his chin, and she sighed, leaning close again, resting her head on his chest, the velvet of the blue suit he had on soft and warm against her cheek.

"Thank you for being here, Joaquín," she murmured. "You have no idea how it helps."

"I think I do," he whispered back, and was just about to reach down and tilt her face up toward his, to let her know what was in his heart, when the sound of hoofbeats echoed through the grove of trees, and a few seconds later, a rider broke into the open, the pinto he was on prancing to a stop next to where Teffin and Joaquín's horses were tethered. Braxton dismounted, breathing heavily. He stopped briefly, and stared at them, then flushed.

"Sorry, didn't mean to interrupt anything," he said, then walked over to where they were standing, as Joaquín's arms fell from around Teffin. "But I knew you two would be out here."

Teffin frowned. "What is it? What happened?"

"Don't worry, nobody's hurt or anything," he explained quickly. "But while we were all in town today, a fella came riding in and said Austin's out of that Mexican jail and back in San Felipe. Landed at Velasco on the first of the month. Only that ain't all. Word is there's over a thousand Mexican troops just south of the Rio Grande, waiting for orders to move."

"And Austin?" she asked, wondering if the time he'd spent in the Mexico City jail had changed him any.

"He's finally decided to fight, and all hell's broke loose. Pa's packing now to head for San Felipe, and I guess your father's going with him."

"What about Case?"

"Hell, Tef, there's not even any proof the Indian is Case, you know that. Besides, this is more important now. He Who Rides'll have to wait."

Joaquín had listened quietly to Braxton's words. Now he spoke. "You are going too, mi amigo?" he asked.

"Not just yet. Pa said I gotta stick around and see to the ranch. At least for now." He looked again at Teffin. "He let me ride as far as your place with him, though, and your pa said he wants to see you before he leaves, and they're anxious to get away before dark."

"They're leaving that soon?"

"Have to."

Teffin looked from her cousin to Joaquín. "We'd better hurry then," she said, and within minutes the trio were reining their horses through the trees, away from the quiet and peace of their tranquil pond, and out into the sunny afternoon, into the outer world of chaos Teffin knew it would soon become.

Bain and Cole had been gone for weeks already, and word was quickly filtering in from every source that men were gathering from all over, in response to the call to arms. It seemed Stephen Austin had been guest of honor at a dinner just a few days after his return from the prison in Mexico City, and during the dinner, he had not only denounced Santa Anna as a tyrant and butcher, but given his sanction to the war cries his contemporaries had been voicing for so long. And now, word had also come through that Sam Houston had been made head of the army of men who were organizing.

"Oh, how I wish I could be there," Brax said one afternoon while he and Joaquín were on their way to the de Léon ranch after a hard day on the range. "It doesn't seem right I should have to stay here and take care of the ranch. Hell, Ma knows what to do. So does Luther."

"Are you really that eager to fight, mi amigo?" Joaquín asked.

Braxton straightened in the saddle, flexing the muscles in his shoulders that had broadened some over the summer, and he sighed.

"Sorry, Joaquín," he apologized, flushing a bit. "I know you still consider Mexico your country, but I can't help feeling like I do." Brax was leading a string of five horses behind him, and he turned in the saddle now, making sure they were still all right. "I only wish you'd forget that silly notion of yours that Mexico's claim in this country can be salvaged, because I'll bet my life, when it's all over, there won't be any Mexican Texans."

"Sí, you are betting your life, mi amigo," Joaquín answered, then shook his head. "I only wish there was an easier way to settle this."

They were nearing the big wooden gate that kept intruders from reaching the de Léon hacienda, and suddenly Brax reined up.

"Hey, look," he said, nodding ahead to the adobe walls. "The gate's closed."

Joaquín frowned. Don Antonio never had the gates

closed during the day, only at night, and a weird feeling swept through Brax as he saw Joaquín raise his arm and call, hailing someone to open the gate for them. Then, as they eased their mounts to a walk and Brax made certain the string of horses he had were still all intact, he and Joaquín rode into the yard, the gates closing quickly behind them.

"What is it? What has happened?" Joaquín asked seconds later as Don Antonio hurried across the veranda and down the steps, his face somber.

Antonio stopped abruptly. He was pale, his dark eyes worried. "It has come to this," he said anxiously, his voice breaking. "Santa Anna has declared the government in San Antonio no longer in charge, and the town has been taken over by a Mexican colonel who's already sent a detachment of troops to Gonzales and ordered them to turn over the cannon they have there."

Brax slid from the saddle, but still held the rope on the horses he'd been bringing over to Don Antonio, and his eyes darkened as he realized what the older man was saying. He'd been to Gonzales the year before, when he and his father had driven some cattle there to a ranch just outside of town, and he looked at Don Antonio in disbelief.

"You mean that old brass relic they've had sitting around to keep the Indians scared off?" he asked.

"Sí," Antonio answered angrily. "And so ridiculous is it that I would laugh if it were not so tragic. But I cannot laugh, my young friend," he went on. "For they've also taken Juan's authority from him, and they are doing what they will to those in town they think are siding with the rebels. San Antonio is in chaos, and most are fleeing north, trying to escape what they fear is to come."

Joaquín had also dismounted, and he'd been watching his uncle closely. "I do not understand," he said, joining the conversation. "There have always been troops in San Antonio, at least from what I could see when we were in town. So why now, all of a sudden, are you acting as if it's a sacrilege, Tío Antonio?"

Antonio glanced at Joaquín, wishing the young man could have embraced the Texas cause as he had.

"Because the troops there now are a sacrilege, Joaquín," he said bitterly. "They are not just Mexican troops, but puppets manipulated by General Martín Perfecto de Cós, Santa Anna's brother-in-law. The man who bloodied Zacatecas. No, they are not just Mexican troops, my dear nephew, they are bloodthirsty criminals who would have their own way, no matter who suffers for it."

"I think you exaggerate, Tío," Joaquín said, his gaze intent on his uncle's face. "To you, anyone opposing your idea would no doubt be a bloodthirsty criminal. And as for the people running away, I see you did not run."

"Because I have nowhere to run to. Besides, by staying here, perhaps I can help in some way, who knows?"

Joaquín took a deep breath. "You really expect me to believe my government would persecute innocent people?" he asked. "I'm sorry for you, Tío Antonio, and you too, Braxton, but I cannot in all fairness agree with your rebellion and your accusations."

"No one says you have to, Joaquín," Antonio assured him. "But someday you will understand what we do, and why."

"You say they've sent troops out to Gonzales?" Brax asked.

Antonio nodded. "Sí, a few days ago. By now the townfolk there could all be dead.

"I doubt that." Braxton's eyes lit up. "Pa wouldn't let me go with him, but I can sure as hell go and find out what's happening at Gonzales." He handed the string of horses to Antonio. "Oh, here, I almost forgot. These are the ones you picked out the other day. They're all broken and shod. You can pay Ma for them later."

He turned, mounting into the saddle as Catalina came bounding down the steps, her eyes on her brother as she purposely ignored Braxton.

"Oh, I am so glad you are back today, Joaquín," she said. "Did Tío Antonio tell you? Thank God! It looks like we will soon be able to act like true citizens of Mexico again, instead of being forced to conform to these heathenish Texas ways."

Antonio's eyes narrowed as he turned to his niece, and

his jaw clenched viciously. "If you really knew what you were talking about, young lady, I would turn you over my knee," he yelled angrily. "But since your stupidity comes from being ill-informed, and not from a sadistic mind, I will excuse it." He called one of the servants to take the string of horses back to the stables, while Catalina stared at him, her dark eyes flashing angrily, then he reached out to shake Braxton's hand. "Godspeed, my young friend," he said, his voice more subdued. "But will you not go home first, to tell your mother where you go?"

Brax shook his head. "There's no time. It's over seventy miles to Gonzales. I'll let Joaquín ride over to tell Ma."

"No, I shall tell your mother myself," Antonio said. "Only be careful, Braxton—there are soldiers everywhere —and hurry back."

Brax reached down; he was carrying a knife and pistol in his gunbelt with a rifle in the scabbard of his saddle. A must out on the range.

"Don't worry, I shouldn't be gone long. One day, two—three at the most," he said. "And tell Ma not to worry, I can take care of myself."

"You are sure this is what you must do?" Joaquín asked, wishing with all his heart his friend would change his mind.

"Sí, it's what I have to do," he answered. "I have friends in Gonzales, Joaquín, and they don't deserve this."

"You will take some food with you?" Antonio asked.

Braxton shook his head. "Not hungry really. I guess I'm too excited," and he turned his horse to go, then glanced back. "Adios, amigos, and don't forget. Tell Ma you got the horses, and I'll be back as soon as I can," and he rode toward the gate, then reined up waiting for it to be opened.

"You mean he is really going to that town, that Gonzales to try to help fight the army?" Catalina asked incredulously.

Joaquín frowned. "Unfortunately, my dear sister, I'm

afraid he is," he answered, and saw her eyes darken as she drew her gaze from Braxton to rest on him.

"Then there is only one thing you can do to make all of this right," she said, her jaw clenching deliberately. "You must go join the army, Joaquín, it is what Father would have wanted."

"You are out of your mind, young lady," Antonio stormed. "Joaquín will do no such thing. I forbid it!" But they were words he never should have spoken, because no sooner did Braxton ride out of the gates of the de Léon rancho than Catalina's suggestion, along with Antonio's heated words, began to weigh on Joaquín's mind, turning his next few days into an endless battle of conscience versus duty. And a few days later, he too rode through the gates of the de Léon rancho, heading for San Antonio, not to join Braxton, but hoping to join the Mexican Army as a scout.

6

Braxton had been riding hard all night, and now the warm morning breeze was full on his face, holding back the sleep from his eyes. He'd been lucky so far. After skirting San Antonio so he wouldn't be spotted by any Mexican soldiers, he'd kept off the main roads just enough so he could still keep his direction, yet wouldn't run into anyone. Now, as he topped a ridge and reined Hickory up, staring off into the distance toward where he knew the town of Gonzales to be, he was more certain than ever that he was too late. At least for any fighting.

There was the brass cannon big as life, sitting across the river in a wagon bed, with a crude sign on it reading "Come and take it!" and the wagon was resting on the ferry they used to cross the river. From what he could see now, however, everything was as quiet as it had been the last time he'd been here. Giving Hickory a nudge with his heels, he moved forward again, more slowly this time, gazing about for any telltale signs of battle.

Maybe Don Antonio had been wrong. Maybe it had all been rumors. Hickory picked his footing down the side of the hill, then Brax kept him moving forward until suddenly, just a few hundred yards from the ford of the Guadalupe River where he'd planned to cross, he saw the first signs of battle. There, on this side of the riverbank, were boot tracks, horse tracks, wagon tracks, a few discarded long rifles, and a number of other items such as a plume from a soldier's hat, a piece of a shako with the mud and dirt ground into it, as well as an occasional canteen or abandoned piece of uniform with blood smeared on it, and a number of handmade pikes.

Brax stopped Hickory and studied the scene for some time, leaning far over in the saddle, trying to read the sign. Suddenly he smiled. Antonio said they'd sent the cavalry out. A mistake, to be sure, because any fool knew most Texans live on their horses, and from what Brax could tell, he'd say it looked like the soldiers had been the ones who'd retreated.

He was still staring at the ground, and was just about to rein Hickory into the ford, when a voice called from across the river.

"Ho! Friend or foe there?"

Brax looked up, and waved his hat. "Reckon I'm a friend," he drawled. "That is, if you're a Texan!"

"Then put on your hat and come across."

Brax set the hat back on his head and reined Hickory the rest of the way into the water, glad it wasn't any more than a couple of feet deep here. But he still couldn't see the face of the man who'd called, because the sun was at the man's back. He rode up onto the opposite bank.

"You're too late for the fight," the man said when Brax reached him and reined Hickory to a stop. "We killed one Mex, but the rest of them got away. The name's Ferris," he went on, reaching his hand up. "Charles Ferris, but most folks just call me Champ."

Brax took the man's hand. "Braxton Kolter here. Glad to meet you, Champ."

The handshake was hard, firm, both men's hands callused, and now Brax could see the other man's face. He was older, that was for sure, with a scar on his right cheek, and blue eyes that crinkled in the corners, as if they found the world amusing.

"I'm surprised you didn't run into a few stragglers on the way," Champ said while Brax dismounted. "They lit outta here yesterday morning like the devil was on their tail."

Brax reached out affectionately and stroked Hickory's head as he gazed off toward the town, which was still some distance to the north. "Didn't use the roads," he offered. "I came cross-country."

Champ nodded. "Smart lad."

They started walking together toward town, with Brax leading his horse, and Brax realized, after walking only partway there, he apparently wasn't the only newcomer, for men were lounging all over at the side of the road leading to Gonzales. Talking, drinking, and bragging about who did what in their encounter the day before with the soldiers.

"Reckon I'm not the only visitor, eh?" he said as he recognized a couple of friends from San Antonio. Then he stopped, sizing up a group of men who were in the middle of a heated discussion. "What's that all about?" he asked.

Champ squinted in the early-morning light as he glanced toward an old shack where Braxton had been looking. He frowned. "That's Moore, Burleson, and Somerville going over what happened yesterday with some of the men," he explained. "Colonel Moore's the one who led the attack against the soldiers yesterday. Everybody else wanted to wait until they came across the river, but he wouldn't have no part of it. So we took the cannon across on the ferry, and caught 'em with their pants down. Sure was a pretty sight too."

Brax took a deep breath and kept on walking, "Where you from, Champ, Gonzales?" he asked.

"Hell no, I got a place between here and San Felipe. Happened to be headin' toward Goliad, when I got here and discovered what was goin' on." He glanced over at Braxton. "You got kin in Gonzales or somethin', kid?"

Brax didn't like being call kid, but he overlooked it. "Nope, but Pa's up with Houston or Austin someplace, along with my uncle, and I just thought maybe I could give a hand."

"Good lad. But looks like there won't be no need. You plannin' to stick around?"

"It all depends." Braxton continued walking slowly and taking in everything he saw.

By the time they reached the center of the small town

of Gonzales, he'd come to the conclusion that the sparse inhabitants of the place had been reinforced by a large number of outsiders, and according to Champ, there'd been well over a hundred men who'd routed the dragoon of Mexican soldiers the day before. Trappers, farmers, shopkeepers, you name it, they were there, with everything from old Kentucky rifles to confiscated tomahawks. Some even had homemade pikes, and Champ said more than one farmer carried nothing more than a pitchfork into battle. "Anything that'd get the job done," he said proudly.

Brax stood in the center of town now. It was a far cry from what it had been the last time he'd been here. Men seemed to be all over the place. Some were even propped against trees or whatever they could find, to sleep away the effects of last night's celebrating of their victory.

He let out a soft sigh as he stood quietly for a few minutes and stared down the main street, then his eyes narrowed thoughtfully. For some weird reason, he suddenly began to wonder just what the hell he was doing here. And he hadn't even taken time to ride out and tell Ma. So why? It didn't make sense. Was it because he'd wanted to be a part of it? Was it because he was tired of listening to the news secondhand, and here he'd have a chance to help make that news? This was something close enough to home to make him feel needed, and wanted, so it wasn't as if he was completely out of touch. And yet now, as he stared at the men milling around, men who, like him, had no call to be in Gonzales, except they heard there was going to be a fight, he realized they hadn't even needed him, and he still felt like an outsider.

Straightening, he turned at the sound of Champ's voice beside him. "What's that?" Brax asked, bringing his thoughts back to where he was, and why.

"I said, if you're hungry, there's a cantina over yonder. Some of the town women took it over, and they been dishin' out food for the past few days, startin' around sunup. Reckon they knowed a man can't fight on an empty stomach."

Brax's hand delved into his pocket, and he fingered a

few pesos, wishing he'd taken time to ride back to the house to tell Ma himself, 'cause she'd probably have made him bring money with him. "I haven't got much on me," he offered, disappointed. "How much does it cost?"

"Anythin' you can give. They ain't particular. If you don't have nothin', then you don't pay nothin'. Reckon they're glad just to have us all here. Come on," and he started walking toward a low stucco building where men were already lining up outside the door.

Brax was restless. The morning had been dragging for him. Three times he'd made up his mind to go home, then changed it abruptly. Once when he'd been talking to a couple of men from San Antonio who'd been with them earlier at Anahuac, then again when he'd heard one of the ladies of the town thanking a group of men for coming, and expressing how much more secure she was because they were all there, and again when rumors began to filter back that the dragoons were heading back toward Gonzales again. The rumor had proved false, and he'd just about made up his mind to leave again, figuring they didn't really need him, when he suddenly found himself listening to an old friend of his father's named Ben Milam, who was talking about heading for Goliad, where everyone knew General Cós had left a detachment of men to guard the supplies he was going to need, and keep a road open for him to San Antonio. Now, while Brax listened to this new idea, all thoughts of heading back home began to vanish again, and by nightfall that day, after gauging the rest of the sentiment in the town, and realizing there really was a reason for him to be here, Brax settled down with Ben Milam and a bunch of other men to get a good night's sleep before heading out in the morning toward Goliad, about a hundred miles or so to the south. He was going to fight dammit. This time there'd be no late arrival, and not just listening to the news. He'd be a part of it, and as he tried to get comfortable on the ground, using his saddle for a pillow, he hoped Ma wasn't going to be too mad at him. After all, it wasn't right he should stay home and let Pa and Uncle Cole do it all. He'd go just this once, and he closed his eyes with a prayer on his lips, hoping the fluttering feelings in his stomach were due to excitement rather than fear.

The next morning, however, the fluttering was still there, and although Brax tried desperately to deny it, the fluttering stayed with him all the way to Goliad, and he was rather glad the ride there was a slow one, since they had to keep off the main roads in order to make the attack a surprise one. Champ had come along too, and Brax was glad. It wasn't that he was a coward. Hell, he'd fought Indians right alongside his pa, hadn't he? And he'd carried a gun since he was old enough to sight down the barrel. It was the way they were going to attack that was making him apprehensive. Like with that Indian attack back at the box canyon. To shoot an Indian flying on horseback or sneaking among the bushes was a lot easier than shoving a knife in his gut or watching his eyes when you pulled the trigger.

But Ben said they were going in after dark, one at a time and damn, he never done anything like that before. Would it be any different than gutting a deer or butchering a steer? He glanced over at Champ, riding beside him that first day, and wondered what the hell he was doing here, and yet, that first night when they'd bedded down, he'd known all too well what he was doing here. He was fighting for Texas, that's what. Just like Pa and Uncle Cole had fought for the United States back in the war, and they hadn't been much older than he was.

It had been like that all the way to Goliad. One minute, he was glad he was here, the next, he wasn't quite so sure. So by the night of October 9, as he crouched in the shadows at the edge of town, after leaving Hickory with some of the men a good quarter-mile back, and waited for the signal to move in, his insides felt like they were twisting into little pieces. He checked the knife in the sheath at his gunbelt, then made sure his pistol was ready, with the rifle slung over his shoulder, since it too might be needed. And it was dark. Hell, it was so dark he could hardly see the buildings just ahead of him, yet knew they were there. The waiting was agony. First he'd sweat, then chill, and finally, after what seemed like hours, the waiting was over, and all hell broke loose.

Brax saw the flash of the sentry's rifle at the same time everyone else did, and with that flash went all the anger, frustration, and fear he'd been harboring for days. Without hesitating, yet keeping his head down, he began to move forward with the rest of the men.

They'd been keeping well hidden ever since moving in shortly after dark, and now Braxton's muscles, stiff from the cramped quarters they'd been forced to hide in, hurt slightly as he moved stealthily along, keeping the others in sight, yet staying tense and alert for the slightest movement of the enemy. He could hear shots, and suddenly, glancing off toward an alleyway between two houses, his heart skipped a beat as he recognized the vague outline of a soldier. He started to call to Champ, then realized the man was no longer there. Somewhere in the last few seconds they'd been separated. Well, this is it, he shouted silently to himself, and turned back toward the alley. There wasn't even time to think. His trigger tightened on the pistol, the shot vibrating in the night air, and as if mesmerized, he watched the soldier's eyes widen in disbelief. Then, before he even had time to ponder what was happening, the soldier he'd just shot was quickly shoved aside from behind, and another took his place. Coming at Brax furiously, the soldier's cry of anger and frustration cut into Brax like the wail of a puma protecting her young, and instinctively the empty pistol flew to Braxton's left hand, while his right came up with the knife from his sheath. And as he'd done to more than one animal in his years on the range, as the soldier lunged toward him, Brax drove the knife deep, twisting and gouging as it hit bone and tissue, then he yanked it back out and straightened, breathing heavily in the darkness as a voice close behind hollered, "Here, this way, we've gotta reach the chapel before they regroup." Brax turned, wiped the blade on his pant leg, and without looking back, followed Champ and the rest of them toward the old church the soldiers had been using as their headquarters.

To Brax it seemed like the fighting had gone on forever, but according to what Champ told him later, it had taken no time at all before they were battering down the door to the Mexicans' headquarters and counting the loot from their night's raid. Which consisted of some three hundred stands of arms, a few artillery pieces, and close to ten thousand dollars, as well as stores and provisions Ben Milam knew General Cós would be counting on.

All in all, the night had been a successful one, and it wasn't until morning, when Brax stood with some of his comrades guarding the twenty-five soldiers who'd surrendered with their colonel, that he really had time to stop and think about the night's events. He shuddered now as he watched the sun begin to fill the horizon, heralding a new day, while he purposely avoided the faces of the soldiers he was guarding. Hardening his heart to the remembrance of the sight of their comrades' faces as they'd contorted in pain when his knife had ripped their bodies to shreds, he had a hard time keeping from throwing up. It was one thing to gut an animal, but another to a gut a man.

His jaw clenched hard, his gray eyes steadily watching the hills in the distance, knowing the soldiers last night were only the first. If Texas was to win her freedom, there was no way to avoid repeating that fight over and over, and he sighed now, wishing he had gone home when he had the chance, yet knowing why he hadn't.

It was close to noon when Joaquín, astride the golden palomino he'd named Compadre, rode into San Antonio, past the soldiers who were lounging about, and reined up in front of the same government building where he'd alighted from the family carriage that first day he'd arrived in San Antonio some months back. Only, his heart was much heavier now. He'd known for some time, there'd been all sorts of trouble in Texas, but had never really let it concern him, especially since his arrival. He'd been enjoying himself too much, and ignoring all the signs, but now they could no longer be ignored. He was Mexican, as his father had been, and his mother, and unlike his uncle, he couldn't turn his back on his country. Especially without reason.

They said Santa Anna was a dictator, a tyrant, a greedy man who wanted nothing more than to rule Mexico with an iron fist. Well, who were they? Texans, that's who. Naturally they'd decry Santa Anna—they wanted Texas for themselves. Catalina was right. Shots had been fired, according to the news filtering back to them, and he could no longer ignore the fact that he'd have to take sides. Now, as he slid from the saddle and addressed the soldier guarding the door to General Cós's headquarters, he did so with mixed emotions.

"Por favor," he began in his native tongue, "I would wish to see the general in charge—is that possible?"

The soldier looked him over curiously.

"Not hardly," he answered. "He's at home eating."

"Ah, sí, then I will find him," he said, remembering Tío Antonio had said the general had taken over one of the homes in town, and he turned, grabbing Compadre's reins, and led the horse from the plaza, then stopped in front of a lovely home that had once belonged to a family who had fled when the soldiers came. A few minutes later he was ushered into a dining hall that could easily seat a few dozen men. General Cós was busily eating.

"I hope this is important," the general said as he set down his napkin and stared at Joaquín.

Joaquín inhaled sharply, yet stood his ground. "I would like to enlist," he said firmly, and saw the general's eyes sharpen.

"So, why do you tell me? Recruiting soldiers is something I gave up doing years ago, young man. I have officers to handle that. Why do you bother me?"

"Because I do not want to be just a soldier."

"Oh?" The general's dark eyes narrowed shrewdly. "And what rank do you wish to hold? Perhaps you would like my job, is that it?"

"I wish to be a scout." Joaquín's eyes were filled with pride. "I have been in Texas long enough that I know my way about, at least as far as the Comanche territory. And

I would be much more valuable to you in that respect than as a regular soldier."

"I see." General Cós was fingering a glass of wine near the edge of his plate. "In other words, you would turn on your countrymen?"

"They are not my countrymen. I have become friends with many who call themselves Texans, sí, but Mexico is my country, not Texas. I was born and raised in Montclava."

"And your name?"

"Joaquín Luís de Alvarado."

"You live here in San Antonio?"

"Not here, no. My uncle, Antonio de Léon, has a rancho some miles west of town."

"Ah, sí." The general hesitated as he studied Joaquín. "I have heard of your uncle. And he has sanctioned your joining the army?"

"Tío Antonio? Madre de Dios, no. He has said I am too young."

"And how old are you?"

"Old enough to know that I must do this."

"Your age?"

"I was nineteen in August mi general."

Martin Cós stared at the young man before him. It was obvious he was not only well-educated, but intelligent too. An asset to any man's army. Still, with Antonio de Léon as his uncle . . . Word from his informers had linked de Léon's name with that of Juan Seguin, who had already shown himself as a traitor the day they'd marched in. And speculation about de Léon was also running high. He began to wonder if perhaps the young man he was watching so closely had been sent here to spy on them. Well, there was only one way to find out if he was truly on their side.

"You say you know the rancheros in the area?" he asked, his fingers still toying with the wineglass.

"Sí."

"Then perhaps you would know where we could buy some horses." He caught a glimmer of hope in the young man's eyes. "We lost a few on our way, and could use about ten head."

"Only ten?"

"Sí, that would do for now." Martin Cós leaned closer as he flicked the end of his dark mustache. "You know, then, where we could find them?"

"I know a ranch where they are sold, sí, mi general."

"Bueno." The general took a sip of his wine. "Then if you will take some of my men there with you, and buy ten of their best stock, I will consider your loyalty, and let you serve as a scout. Is that agreed?"

Joaquín was pleased, although he wasn't sure how the Dantes were going to take to him showing up with a bunch of soldiers. Teffin should understand, though. After all, she'd understood when he'd told her he was leaving. At least she said she did. Now suddenly he wondered if maybe she was just trying to be nice. Well, he couldn't think of that now. All he could think of now was, he was going to get a chance to defend his country. He straightened proudly.

"Agreed, mi general," he answered, and within half an hour he was riding back out of San Antonio, heading for the Dantes' ranch, with a number of soldiers accompanying him.

Heather was tired. She and Mose Wheatley had been working the horses all day. Exercising them and rubbing them down. Their only relief was the break they'd taken at lunchtime, and now they were back out at the far end of the corrals again, riding, riding, and riding.

Shortly after Cole and Bain had ridden off, the hired hands had started to leave too. All that were left now were Mose and Eli and another hand who hadn't been with them long enough to think Texas was worth fighting for. He was probably in his mid-fifties, wore a scar on his right cheek, went by the name Shem with no last name, but knew how to break a horse. Not the way Cole did, however. He did it the white man's way, with spurs and perseverance. He and Eli were still up at the north camp this afternoon, and Heather, who'd been exercising a roan with a blaze on its forehead, helping to get the mare more used to the saddle, suddenly reined her to a stop as she spotted a dust cloud in the distance.

Right away her hand went to her hair. She was a mess. She'd been wearing Cole's pants ever since he'd left, since she'd taken over so much of his work, and she rested a hand on her leg as she watched a number of riders emerging from the dust cloud.

"Mose!" she called, turning back to where Mose was rubbing down another mare.

Mose lifted his head, the hat he wore covering his bald head, making the muttonchops at the sides of his cheeks look even bushier. His dark face glistened with sweat, only he didn't answer, just gazed off to where Heather Dante was staring, and he left the mare, moving to stand over beside her.

"Who you reckon it is, Miz Heather?" he asked.

She frowned. "One looks like Joaquín."

"That traitor?"

"Shhh—we don't know that. Leastways, we have no right to accuse. After all, he was brought up Mexican."

"Humph!" Mose made no bones about how he felt. Actually, the only reason he hadn't taken off himself was that he'd promised. But that didn't mean he was on Joaquín's side. No sirree! "Looks like he's got soldiers with him, Miz Heather," he said. "Want I should get the gun?"

"No—don't. Just stay here, Mose and I'll ride out to meet them. You can open the gate for me."

Mose didn't like it. "I'll open the gate, but I go too, ma'am," he offered. "On no account am I gonna let you talk to those men without me bein' there."

So after opening the gate for her, then closing it behind him, Mose vaulted into the saddle of his own horse that was tied just outside the corral. Both he and Heather rode down the lane past the barn and bunkhouse, and within minutes were confronting Joaquín and the soldiers near the hitching post in the front yard.

"Well, Joaquín, I see you kept the promise you made

to Teffin," Heather said as she greeted him, still in the saddle.

Joaquín's face was grim. "I am not a soldier yet, Señora Dante," he answered. "But if my mission today is successful, then I will become a scout for the Mexican Army."

Mose frowned, shifting his stocky frame in the saddle as he studied the young man. "So, what's your mission?" he asked.

Lieutenant Rodriguez, still in the saddle himself, sneered as he looked at Mose, then he addressed Heather. "You let your slaves speak for you, señora?"

Heather's violet eyes darkened. She didn't like the man's looks. His eyes were shifty and hard, his mouth a thin line that gave the impression he was continually sneering.

"He's not a slave," she said. "He's a freeman, and yes, I let him speak for me, And I too ask, what is your mission, Joaquín?"

"We have come to buy horses."

Heather's eyes narrowed as she reached up, lifted the floppy old hat she was wearing, and tucked a stray strand of red hair back where it belonged, then set the hat back on her head. "I see, and you expect to buy them from me, right?"

He smiled hesitantly. "Sí."

"Then I'm afraid your mission will not be accomplished, Joaquín," she said as she relaxed more in the saddle. "With Cole not here, I'm not selling."

"But . . . I do not understand. Just a week ago you sold a string to a gentleman from up north of town."

"They were promised."

"And the ones to my uncle?"

"They too were promised."

Joaquín stared at her, frowning as he began to understand, but it was Lieutenant Rodriguez who spoke.

"Do you not see, Señor de Alvarado," Rodriguez offered. "The señora is trying to tell you she refuses to sell horses to the Mexican Army. Am I not right, señora?" and he looked directly at Heather.

"That's one way of putting it."

"You realize we could just take them?"

"No!" Joaquín's eyes hardened. "We will not use force. We came to buy horses, not steal them. If they are not for sale, then that is the end of it."

"You mean you are just going to ride away and leave all of those horses here?" the lieutenant said, gesturing toward the corrals in back, where some twenty to thirty horses were milling about, and he began talking in Spanish. "There are just two of them against all of us, you fool, and I do not intend to go back without horses."

"Speaking Spanish won't help your situation either, Lieutenant," Heather countered in English. "You see, we happen to speak it quite fluently, it's just that we prefer English."

Heather saw the lieutenant's eyes tighten, and knew by the look in them he was furious.

"Besides," she went on, "there are not just the two of us. There are others in the house, as well as men working in the barn." The last was a bluff, and she knew Joaquín knew it, yet hoped he wouldn't give her away. "So you see, all I have to do is let out one yell, and I'm afraid you and your men would be the ones who were outnumbered, not us."

Lieutenant Rodriguez studied her thoughtfully for a few moments. The señora was a lovely woman. Obviously older than he, but tanned as she was from working out-of-doors, there was a sensual quality about her. He finally drew his eyes from her and glanced over at Joaquín.

"She is telling the truth?"

Joaquín too was watching Heather, and knew she'd been lying. But he also knew, for some reason, he couldn't let the lieutenant know. Maybe because he didn't like the way the lieutenant was looking at Heather, but it wasn't just because of the horses.

"Sí, she no doubt tells the truth," he answered. Then asked Heather, "Is Teffin home?"

Heather took a deep breath, relieved he hadn't given her away. "She rode over to see Blythe," she answered, truthfully this time, and Joaquín nodded.

"Gracias." His hands tightened on his horse's reins as

the big palomino moved restlessly. "Only, por favor, would you do me a favor, Señora Dante?" he asked.

"What's that?"

"Do not let her ride alone anymore, señora. Por favor, I would not want harm to come to her, and things are not as they used to be, comprende?"

Heather glanced over to the lieutenant, then her gaze sifted over the men with him. They were a cruel-looking bunch, and she knew Joaquín realized it too.

"Don't worry, she knows the hills," she answered. "But I'll try to keep her here as much as I can."

"Bueno." He turned to the lieutenant. "Shall we head back to town now, Lieutenant?" he asked, maneuvering Compadre so the horse was between Lieutenant Rodriguez and Heather.

Rodriguez' jaw clenched angrily, but he wasn't about to let this young hidalgo know he didn't like returning empty-handed, so he reached up, tipped his shako, and smiled cynically as he began reining his horse around toward the road.

"I am sorry we could not come to terms, señora," he said, his voice low, menacing. "But perhaps another time. Adios," and he called to his men, ordering them to ride out.

"I am sorry, Señora Dante," Joaquín apologized, hoping Heather wasn't too upset with him. "But I had no idea you would not be willing to sell your stock."

"To the Mexican Army? Surely you of all people should understand, Joaquín," she said. "Cole's out there somewhere getting ready to fight them, and you expected me to give them the help they need to destroy him? Hardly." Her hands tightened on the reins of the horse she was riding, and she leaned over, patting the animal's head. "I'd rather die than let them have even one horse, knowing it could possibly mean Cole's life."

"I am sorry . . . por favor . . ."

"Yes, I know you're sorry," she went on, realizing he was flustered and upset too. "But that won't make you change your mind either, will it? As you've told us so often, Joaquín, you're Mexican, not Texan. So go play

Santa Anna's games with him, but don't be surprised if Teffin isn't sitting around waiting for you if and when this is all over."

She was right and he knew it. Teffin had told him as much the night before he left, but he had no choice. Catalina was right, they were both right. They had been told only what the Texans had wanted them to hear. Hadn't he lived in Mexico? Grown up there? Texas was a part of Mexico, and that's the way it should stay. Joaquín straightened in the saddle, his green eyes darkening hostilely.

"So, we have chosen sides, señora. I was hoping it would not have to be, but I must go the way I know to be right. I only wish you could understand."

"Oh, I understand, Joaquín. Believe me, I do understand. But I only pray someday you'll realize you made the wrong choice."

"So, we shall see, shall we not?"

Rodriguez was near the end of the drive already, and he turned in the saddle and yelled, "You coming de Alvarado?"

"Sí!" Joaquín called to him, then turned for one last good-bye. "Tell Teffin I will be back," he said deliberately. "Adios," and he rode off, joining the soldiers at the edge of the drive, while Heather and Mose sat quietly in their saddles, watching.

"What the Sam Hill were they doin' here?" Bessie called to them as she stepped out onto the front porch. "I was gonna come out, but I never did feel any too easy around them soldiers."

"Don't worry Bessie," Heather called to her as she reined her horse around to head back toward the corrals. "They just wanted to buy some horses, only I wasn't selling."

"Good!" she answered. "The boys got enough trouble from them fancy soldiers without furnishin' horseflesh for 'em to ride on," and she turned and went back into the house.

Mose was still staring after the soldiers, his dark eyes,

beneath his hat, troubled. After a few minutes he reined his mount about and moved over beside Heather.

"You don't suppose we're gonna have any trouble outta them soldiers, do you, Miz Heather?" he asked thoughtfully as they rode back up the drive. "If so, I could maybe ride north and have Eli and Shem come down to the house and help us here for a few days. What do you think?"

Heather too was wary. "I wonder . . ." she mused as she turned her gaze back to the road, watching them disappear in a cloud of dust. "That's a good idea, Mose, maybe you'd better," she finally said. "Only, be careful, the Comanche have been moving in a lot closer, now that they realize the men are gone, and I'd hate for anything to happen."

"Don't worry, ma'am." He straightened, flexing the muscles across his broad shoulders, his eyes twinkling, amused. "I been around these dang horses so much since I joined up with Mista Cole that I ride 'em as good as them Comanche do. They spot me and they're gonna have to do some skittin' if they even wanna keep me in sight. I'll be back with Eli and Shem before dark," and he dug his horse in the ribs, taking off at a gallop, heading back beyond the corrals where the horses were kept, and to the hills beyond, until he was lost from sight.

Heather continued heading back toward the corrals, knowing there were still horses to feed and curry, and yet she was apprehensive. The horse was at a slow walk as she pondered what to do, then finally, making up her mind, as she neared the back of the house, she rode up to the back porch, dismounted, and took the steps two at a time.

Helene glanced up from the table where she was shelling corn for the chickens, surprised to see Heather back in the house.

"Did your mother tell you what's been going on?" Heather asked Helene, and the younger woman nodded.

"Said they were after some horses."

"Only they didn't get them." Heather moved to the

sink, grabbed the dipper sitting in the wooden bucket on the counter, and took a long drink. "But I'm worried," she went on after wiping her mouth on the sleeve of Cole's old workshirt she was wearing. "I hadn't thought when I let Teffin ride over to see Blythe . . . I think I'd feel better if maybe you'd ride over and see she gets back all right. Will you do that, Helene?"

Helene frowned. "You think they'll make trouble?"

"I don't know, I'm not sure. Only Tef doesn't even have a rifle with her, and I hadn't thought these hills might be crawling with vermin walking on two legs instead of four."

Helene set the bowl aside and stood up, wiping off the corn dust from her hands on the apron. "You want me to leave right away?" she asked.

"I'd appreciate it. I'd go myself, but if those soldiers happened to come back, I wouldn't want you and Bessie to be here alone. And please, Helene, be careful," she warned her. "Stick to the trails we usually use, instead of the road, I think it'll be safer. And take the extra rifle by the fireplace in the parlor. I know you know how to use it."

"You think all that's necessary?" Bessie asked from the doorway, and Heather turned toward her, taking her hat off and wiping her brow.

"I hope it won't be, Bessie," she said, her voice firm yet hesitant. "But I can't take the chance. I lost a son because I didn't think it could happen to me. I'm not going to lose a daughter for the same reason." She put her hat back on, and looked back over at Helene, realizing she wasn't as used to riding as everyone else, yet it wasn't as if she'd never ridden at all. "I'll saddle a horse for you," she offered. "And meet you out by the barn," and she turned toward the sink, took another drink from the dipper, then went back outside, heading for the harness room to get a saddle.

It was close to dark by the time Joaquín and the soldiers he'd escorted to the Dantes' returned to San

Antonio without the horses, and now Joaquín stood in front of General Cós, trying to explain.

"I do not confiscate horses from friends," he said stubbornly. "There are other rancheros around, and I am certain that in a day or so you will be able to buy any number of horses from one of them."

"So you just left them there, is that it?" He snapped his fingers. "Just like that, you decide what is best for the army of Santa Anna, right?"

Joaquín flushed. "That is not it at all, mi general," Joaquín answered. "The Texans always say Santa Anna is greedy, that he is a dictator, that he takes what he wants regardless of who gets hurt, and I call them liars. Now you would have me believe it is the truth?"

Martín Cós hesitated as he stared hard at Joaquín de Alvarado, not knowing quite what to make of this young man. Then a shrewd idea crept into his thoughts. De Alvarado was certainly loyal to Santa Anna, but he was also a young man of integrity, and he had breeding. He would be an asset to Santa Anna as a scout, but only as long as he held Santa Anna in great esteem, as long as he thought Santa Anna to be the savior of Texas, as some called him already. To disillusion him now would be the worst thing he could do. Besides, he had learned the boy's uncle was influential in the area. It would be well to humor him.

"No, it is not the truth, Señor de Alvarado," Martín Cós answered. "Santa Anna wants only peace from these rebels. I did not mean 'confiscate' the way it sounded. I just thought perhaps you could have done more to persuade them to accept the money for the horses. After all, they are needed for the army."

"As I said, there was no way to force the issue without using violence, and I would not do that to a friend."

"So . . . then I guess we will have to search further, my young friend, won't we?" he said. "As you say, we do not want to cause harm to any of the good people of Texas. But in the meantime, I will write a letter of introduction for you to take to General Santa Anna, advising him to take you on as a scout, and I would ask that you also carry a report to him for me that he must have. I can trust you with it, can't I, señor?"

"Sí, sí, I will guard it with my life, mi general."

"Bueno, then you are excused, and I will call you when it is time for you to leave." General Cós stood up and put an arm around Joaquín's shoulder as if he were a good friend. "For now, though, señor, find yourself a meal and some rest, for you will no doubt be riding most of the night."

"Gracias, mi general," Joaquín answered, and started to leave.

"And, oh yes," General Cós added as Joaquín reached the door, "send Lieutenant Rodriguez in, will you, Señor de Alvarado, I would have a word with him too."

Joaquín left, having no reason to mistrust General Cós. Yet, later that evening, as lights began to flicker from the windows of the houses in the town of San Antonio, and the cool breezes of the October night settled down on the countryside around it, while Joaquín Luis de Alvarado reined his palomino, Compadre, past the stucco buildings in the town square, through the plaza, and out onto the Camino Real, heading south toward the Rio Grande and Santa Anna, back in San Antonio, Lieutenant Rodriguez and the men who'd been with him that very afternoon also slipped out of town. Under the cover of darkness this time, they headed once more for the Dantes' ranch to the northwest, with orders from General Cós not to return without the horses they'd been told to bring back earlier in the day. No matter what the cost.

7

It had been dark for hours, and yet Heather couldn't sleep. Maybe she'd been wrong. After all, she had no other suspicions to go on, except for the way the lieutenant had looked at her. And besides, surely Joaquín would never agree to such a thing. He had been upset when he'd ridden out, yes, but to come back and steal the horses . . . ? Yet, if General Cós ordered it . . . After all, Joaquín had cast his lot with their enemies. How far would he go?

She tried to get more comfortable in the hay, scratching her arm where the dried grasses made it itch. She and Shem were in the haymow of the barn, where they had a good view of the two corrals in back, while Mose huddled against the watering trough inside the corral, and Eli lay sprawled on the back roof of the chicken coop, about fifty feet from the corral. And even though the house was dark, she knew Bessie was at the kitchen window with Helene, while Teffin sat at her bedroom window with a rifle, watching the drive. She glanced over to where Shem lay, his head resting on his arm, eyes shifting from the road out front to the corral and the hills beyond.

Shem was older than Mose, close to Eli's age, with a thick head of curly gray hair, short wiry beard, and a thin sharp nose with a bump right in the middle, and sharp, deep-set eyes that never missed a thing going on around him. He'd been with them close to six months already, and had proved his worth more than once against the Comanche.

142

His head raised, she saw him tense, and her heart leapt into her throat.

"What is it? Did you see something?"

He was motionless for a second, then she saw him relax. "Weren't nothin' ma'am. Just a couple deer prowlin' around them trees t' other side of the corral a ways."

Heather sighed, relieved, then once more tried to find a comfortable spot so she could maybe get a little sleep. It had to be late already, close to midnight, with the moon high as it hung a sharp crescent in the sky, and it was tilted slightly, as if it just got through spilling out all the stars that were scattered around it. She shivered. There was a coolness in the air, and as Heather snuggled into the straw and closed her eyes, she pulled Cole's old jacket closer around her for warmth.

God, how she missed Cole. It wasn't just that she'd had to take over with the horses. Actually, she had to admit she was enjoying that part of it. It was the lonely nights with no one to hold her and make love to her. His love was what she missed the most. And they'd heard so little from the men. Only one letter so far, and it had been so vague. Not even a hint as to what was happening.

She had just started to doze when suddenly Shem poked her with his foot.

"Miz Dante, ma'am, you awake?"

She jerked to a start and sat up. "What is it? Are they here?"

"I think so, look!" and he pointed toward the road, where a number of horsemen were coming. They were about two hundred feet from the drive, and moving slowly now, and Heather, who had crawled up next to Shem, glanced over toward the house, to the window where she knew Teffin was, hoping Teffin wouldn't take any shots before they were ready.

But Teffin hadn't seen the riders yet, as she stared out the window, because there was a tree next to the house, and it was obstructing her view. Instead, she glanced toward the barn, where her mother and Shem were, and anger filled her. Ma was wrong. She just had to be, and this was all going to be for nothing, she just knew it, she kept telling herself. Maybe Joaquín hadn't accepted their loyalty as Texans, and maybe he was stubborn and pigheaded when it came to Santa Anna and Mexico. But there was no way Teffin would believe he'd do such a horrible thing, and just take the horses. Not Joaquín, and especially not to the Dantes'.

Suddenly she tensed, alert. The window was open, and she knelt on the floor, peering out over the sill as she heard the sounds of leather and harness. Someone was coming up the drive. She swore softly under her breath—something Teffin rarely did—because it was a soldier, all right. She could see moonlight reflecting off the brass ornaments on his hat and uniform, as well as the rifle he carried, and now more soldiers were coming behind him. She could hear all too clearly the rhythmic creaking of their saddles.

Her hands were sweaty, and she rubbed them dry on her pant legs, anger replacing the doubt she'd felt only moments before. She was wearing a pair of her father's pants, held up with a piece of rope, and had on one of her shirtwaists, with her hair pulled back and fastened with a ribbon. At first her mother had told her she was to go to bed and let them handle it, but after a good hour of pleading and convincing, Ma had realized that if what she suspected was right, and someone did show up, Teffin would probably help anyway, even though she'd been told not to. So instead, Heather had given her a rifle too, but with orders not to shoot unless she was forced to.

Now Teffin's eyes widened as she kept her head at the window, peeking out gingerly, and watched the soldiers riding quietly in, no doubt figuring everyone was asleep. She glanced toward the barn, where she knew Ma and Shem were waiting, knowing they'd no doubt seen them too, then to where Mose was in the corral. The chickenhouse, with Eli on the roof, was out of sight at the back of the house, so there was no way she could see if he was still there.

Her mouth was dry, stomach fluttering wildly, as the soldiers continued walking their horses past the house, and on back toward the corrals, then suddenly, when they were only some twenty feet from the gate of the first corral, Teffin saw Mose stand up, leaning against the fence inside the corral, so it was harder for them to see him.

"Hola, señores! That's far enough!" he shouted, surprising them.

As the soldiers reined their horses to a halt, Teffin counted them in the moonlight. There were six.

Lieutenant Rodriguez squinted into the darkness, recognizing the voice he heard as that of the stocky slave that had been with Señora Dante earlier in the day. That meant she'd probably been bluffing, and he was no doubt the only hand on the place, he thought. Bueno. A movement near the watering trough in the corral caught his eye, and with a sharp command to his men to hit the ground, he leveled his pistol and fired.

Men and horses scattered, and Mose, surprised the soldiers hadn't backed off, ducked down behind the trough and slid across the ground under the bottom rail of the fence until he was out of the corral and behind a bush not far from the carriage shed. While he'd been scurrying to better cover, though, Eli had cut loose with a shot from the chickenhouse, Shem and Heather from the barn, and Mose could hear the soldiers cursing, yelling, and trying to figure out where all the shots were coming from as they scurried for cover in the dark.

There was some horse-drawn machinery near the front of the barn, along with some cordwood, and Rodriguez crouched behind the wood, breathing heavily as he loaded his pistol again. He'd already determined there'd been shots from above, in the barn behind him, as well as some from what looked like a chicken coop the other side of the drive. And since he knew the man in the corral had been the slave who was with Señora Dante this afternoon, he figured he'd underestimated her, and she hadn't been lying, when she said there were others around.

With his pistol loaded again, he glanced about, trying to see where his men were. One was right at his elbow, but he couldn't see the rest.

"Where are all the men?" he asked hurriedly, keeping

his voice low. The private behind him inhaled sharply, his eyes scanning the ranch yard.

"I do not know, Lieutenant. The last I saw, they were on foot, and running toward the house."

Lieutenant Rodriguez' gaze shifted to the ranch house, and he was certain he saw Corporal Martinez climb over the rail of the back porch and flatten himself against the log house. That could mean the house was empty, he thought, but the thought was premature, as he saw what looked like movement at one of the upstairs windows that overlooked the drive. He pulled off a shot toward the window, and heard the bullet splat into something. The movement was gone.

"Damn, they're shooting at Teffin!" Heather exclaimed, and leaning as far out of the hayloft as she could, she drew bead on where she'd seen the flash from Rodriguez' gun, and pulled the trigger.

Once more a volley of shots rang out.

"It will do you no good to fight, Señora!" Rodriguez called out from behind the stack of firewood. "You know you are outnumbered."

"Oh, am I?" Heather whispered to Shem, and instead of giving up, she'd reloaded and sent another shot the lieutenant's way.

Rodriguez swore as the bullet missed his head by inches. He searched the yard with his eyes. Their horses were still in the drive, ground-reined as they'd been trained, only they were out in the open, where there was no chance for his men to get to them without being seen. He knew, however, that Martinez was only a few feet from the back door.

"Martinez!" he called out.

"Sí, Lieutenant?"

"See who is in the house!"

Heather's heart sank. "Stay out of the house!" she yelled down to them. "They have nothing to do with this."

"Martinez?" Rodriguez yelled again.

"Sí, Lieutenant."

Heather held her breath as the ranch yard grew silent,

then suddenly a shot rang out from the house, followed by a couple of screams, what sounded like wood being splintered, and a few seconds later Martinez' voice echoed across the yard.

"Just two women, Lieutenant," he yelled, then caught his breath. "Only they promised they would give no more trouble."

"Bessie?" Heather yelled.

"Don't worry, I'm all right, Miss Heather," Bessie called from the darkness. "You just don't give 'em those horses like you said. Me and Helene's all right, don't worry."

Then they hadn't gone upstairs and found Teffin, Heather told herself quickly. Thank God. Only what did she do now? She couldn't let them have the horses. Not like this, not after all they'd gone through, and yet she couldn't let anything happen to Helene and Bessie.

"The horses, señora?" Rodriguez called to her.

Heather's jaw clenched angrily. "Over my dead body," she yelled back.

"That can be arranged too!" he answered, and was quickly ducking behind the woodpile again as shots came now from all around him. Eli, still on the roof of the chicken coop, tried to aim where he thought the man was, and Mose, close, but still unable to see Rodriguez, shot at one of the soldiers he'd spotted near the back porch.

"We can kill the two in the house," Rodriguez called out when the shots ended.

Heather was reloading again. "You'd never leave this place alive."

The hair on the nape of Rodriguez' neck prickled. She was probably right. Still, there had to be a way. Suddenly he turned to the soldier behind him.

"You think you can get into the barn without being hit?" he asked.

Private Salazar glanced behind him to the huge log barn. There was a window a few feet behind them.

"Sí," he answered quickly.

"Bueno, then get inside and fire it," he ordered.

Salazar stared at him for a minute, then smiled. "Ah, sí, Lieutenant," he answered. "And then should I pick them off as they drop from the loft?"

"No, fool, I will take care of them in my own way, but just make sure it gets hot for them, comprende?"

Salazar nodded, then rose to his feet, and crouching, headed toward the open window of the barn, slipping in unnoticed.

It had been quiet for too long, and Heather didn't like it. There'd been no movement anywhere, not even in the house. The last shot that had been fired was when Eli had left the chicken-coop roof and run in a zigzag toward a huge oak tree closer to the house. Rodriguez and some of his men had peppered the darkness, but Eli's hearty war whoop had let her know he was still all right. That had been at least five, maybe ten minutes ago.

She shifted in the hay, trying to see if Rodriguez had moved or not, when suddenly she froze. Her nose twitched, and she straightened, suddenly forgetting everything but the air around her. She took a deep breath.

"Oh, my God, Shem, fire!" she gasped.

Without waiting to confirm her words with his own nose, Shem scurried from the mound of hay he'd been stretched out on and leapt to his feet, running to the edge of the loft, where he stood staring down at the floor of the barn, which was quickly being consumed by flames.

Heather was beside him in seconds.

"My God, what do we do?!" she cried.

Shem reached out, holding her back. "We don't panic," he answered, then took her hand, leading her toward the ladder. "But we can't stay here."

"That devil, I'll kill him!" she muttered viciously when they reached the ladder.

Shem made sure the flames were still confined to the hay near the stalls before letting her get on the ladder, and they started to climb down.

Meanwhile, inside the house, Teffin was more scared than she'd ever been before in her life as she crept through the dark dining room, trying to remember where everything was, so she wouldn't make noise. All she had to do was knock something over to ruin the surprise she was planning for them, and her hand gripped the rifle she was carrying even tighter, pressing it even closer to her body, so she wouldn't accidentally hit something with it in the dark.

She'd taken off her boots and put on the moccasins she used for slippers, and now she hesitated at the door to the kitchen, remembering there was a board there that usually squeaked loud enough to wake the dead. Taking a deep breath, she lifted her foot high, stretched as far as she could, and moved into the kitchen, sighing with relief when there was no accompanying squeak to give her away.

It was lighter here in the kitchen with the back door open, and now she could see Bessie and Helene out on the porch, only she knew there was a soldier standing with them. Let's see, she told herself confidently, all she had to do was to step through the door with her rifle aimed at the soldier, and then she'd have the upper hand. But what then? Well, she wouldn't worry about that now. First she had to get the drop on him, and carefully, so as not to let him know she was around, she began to creep through the open kitchen door, her knees trembling, mouth set in determination. Suddenly her hair stood on end, and she gasped, startled, as she heard someone yell, "Fire!"

Without thinking, Teffin closed the few feet to the door quickly, the rifle and soldiers momentarily forgotten as her gaze rested on the barn which was beginning to glow orange-red inside, with thick smoke starting to pour out the windows and doors.

"Ma!" she screamed hysterically, and the soldier who was holding the pistol on Bessie and Helene whirled around just in time to catch her as she ran out onto the porch.

"Hey, where are you going?" he blurted.

Teffin began to squirm, fear for her mother driving caution from her. "Let me go! Ma!" she shrieked, then suddenly quit fighting him, and froze, staring incredulously toward the barn, where she could see her mother and Shem's figures silhouetted in the open doorway to the haymow.

"Oh, my God, they'll be killed," Bessie gasped as she grabbed Helene's arm. "We gotta do something."

Martinez' fingers were digging into Teffin's arm, but he was still holding a gun on Bessie. "You will stay where you are," he warned, but he hadn't counted on Bessie's stubbornness. With one quick movement she whirled around, and at that same instant Teffin too went into action. After a quick kick to the shins by Teffin, Bessie's arm flew out, knocking the gun from Martinez' hand, and before he even realized what was happening, all three women were off the porch and running toward the burning barn, surprised to run into both Mose and Eli, who were now paying no attention to the soldiers, while they hollered orders up to Heather and Shem in the hayloft, and prayed they'd get out without being hurt.

Heather's eyes were smarting, and her lungs hurt from the thick smoke, yet she knew this was the only way out. They'd been halfway down the ladder when the straw and hay had ignited directly below them, shooting flames straight up at them, and they'd been forced to retreat to the hayloft. Now she was close to panicking.

"Swing the rope in farther, I'll catch it," she yelled to Shem, who had used a pitchfork somebody'd left in the haymow to reach out and grab the rope from the block and tackle that was used to hoist straw and hay into the barn. He swung the rope in, then nodded as she caught it.

"You first," he said.

She wasn't about to argue, as she glanced behind them to where fire was already creeping into the loft, while below them Eli and Mose, with Teffin, Bessie and Helene watching, were holding on to the other end of the rope.

Eli cupped a hand to his mouth and yelled to them, oblivious of the soldiers, who'd all left their hiding places now and were regrouping, pistols at the ready, as they too stood fascinated, watching the couple in the barn trying to flee the fire.

The whole barn was a glowing inferno now, with flames leaping from the roof, turning the night sky bright orange, and Heather knew there wasn't a moment to lose. Wrapping the rope around her leg, and hanging on as hard as she could, she let Shem shove her out, her weight full on the block and tackle, and as quickly as they could, Mose and Eli lowered her to the ground. Once safe, her only concern now was for Shem, and by the time they hauled him down too, then moved back away from the heat, the whole barn was lighting up the sky for miles around.

Heather's face was smudged from the smoke as Teffin hugged her, and now, as Heather realized there was nothing more for them to do except watch it burn, she also became aware of the soldiers standing behind them, their guns trained on them, and knew there was no way they were going to keep the horses now. Her only relief was there hadn't been any animals in the barn, except for a few cats, who'd no doubt been able to get out on their own.

"So now, see," Lieutenant Rodriguez said as they all stood near the back porch, watching the roof of the barn fall in, "you would have no place to keep the horses, even if you didn't want to give them to me, now would you?"

Heather whirled around, her arms still around Teffin. "Get out of here, you bastard!!" she yelled, the rancid smell of the smoke burning her eyes. "And don't you dare touch those horses, or I'll kill you!"

Rodriguez laughed. "You! Come, señora," he said, his laughter drowned by the crackling flames. "I will take what I want, and you will do nothing, comprende?"

"Don't be so sure there, Lieutenant," Eli cut in, sizing the man up, and figuring he had his eyes on more than the horses. "Just because I look like an old man don't mean I am one," he went on. "I got a pistol pointing right at you from under this here hat of mine, and if you so much as step forward, I'll blast you to kingdom come. Now, you comprende?"

Rodriguez stared at Eli, then straightened irritably. He should have kept a closer eye on the men instead of the women, and his gaze moved to the hat the old man was holding in his left hand, then he glanced toward the other two men. The one, who'd been in the barn with Señora Dante was still standing next to the old man, but the black must have slipped away in the commotion.

Rodriguez swore softly to himself as the black's voice confirmed what he'd been afraid of. "And I'll back him up," Mose yelled from somewhere near the corral.

Rodriguez stood motionless for a long time, then took a deep breath. "I will take the horses," he finally said.

"Not tonight you won't," Eli answered. "Because if either you or any of your men take even one step toward them corrals, you'll be the one who'll get the first bullet."

Rodriguez bit his lip. To go back empty-handed again? Anger surged inside him. And he wanted the woman too. Well, he couldn't have everything, but he would have the horses. "Then I'm afraid you'll have to shoot," he said, calling Eli's bluff. "Because I intend to get them and ride out, whether you like it or not."

Eli stared at him hard, "Then take them and get!" he said.

Heather started to protest, but Eli refused to listen.

Rodriguez called back over his shoulder. "Mount up, men."

Martinez started to interrupt.

"I said mount!" he screamed at his corporal in Spanish, and this time Martinez clamped his mouth shut and hurried over, helping the rest of the men with their horses, while Salazar grabbed the lieutenant's horse and brought it over to him.

Neither man said a word as they both mounted, then Rodriguez turned in the saddle, his gaze resting on the pistol Eli no longer had hidden under his hat.

"You are wise, señor," he said to Eli, while his eyes snapped dangerously. "For if you had shot me, the whole lot of you would be dead now, and you know it."

"And you are wise too, señor," Eli offered fiercely. "For if you were to take anything other than the horses, you too would be dead. Do I make myself clear?"

"Perfectly," Lieutenant Rodriguez answered, and glanced for a moment toward Heather and the young woman she'd been protecting. Mother and daughter, he thought furiously, and they could have been his. He turned back, looking once more at the old man, then quickly turned to his men. "¡Ándale!" he called as he dug his horse in the ribs and headed for the gates to the corral, and a few minutes later he and his men drove every mare and stallion from the corral and out into the moonlit road, heading back toward town, while Heather, Teffin, and the others watched disheartened, as the huge barn continued to burn the rest of the way to the ground.

It was one of those lovely mornings Bain had always looked forward to when he was home. The air was brisk, with just a hint of warmth to it, with the sky starting to turn as blue as the chicory growing alongside the dusty road they'd been trudging down the past few days, and although he was stiff and sore from sleeping on the hard ground, he felt better than he had for weeks. Last night he'd slept with Amigo's reins tied to a tree branch directly overhead, and now he stretched, glancing over next to him at Cole, who was lying back with his head resting on his arms, his eyes wide open, staring up at the early-morning sky.

"How long you been awake?" Bain asked as he sat up, shaking the cobwebs out, and rubbing his chin, realizing his beard needed more than just a trim.

Cole's gaze shifted from the clouds overhead to his brother-in-law. "Saw the first lick of dawn," he answered.

"So how come we aren't on the road already?" Bain looked around. Usually they were on their way long before this, so by the time the sun came up, they'd have left at least two or three miles behind.

"Don't ask me," Cole said lazily. "I just take orders, I don't make them."

"Oh, oh, here comes old windbag now," Bain said as a

buckskin-clad figure emerged out of the waning darkness a short way down the road. The man was yelling and kicking at the long line of stirring men who lay beside the road and overflowed into the nearby fields.

When he got to Bain and Cole, he waved, acknowledging they were awake already, then continued on to the next group of men.

"Maybe Austin overslept," Bain said as he stood up, followed slowly by Cole. "You know, he looked really tired last night when he rode by checking the line."

Cole stretched, then sighed. "You thought so too?"

"Hell, he looked like he was asleep on his horse."

"He was. Why do you think we stopped early last night?" Cole stared off at the rest of the men, stretching and getting to their feet. What a conglomeration.

Somewhere between four and five hundred men had answered the call to arms the men at San Felipe had sent out. Some from as far away as Georgia, Louisiana, and a half-dozen other states back east, as well as Mexicans who'd fled north across the Rio Grande from Santa Anna, and a number who'd been born in Texas yet felt betrayed by their government. Cole and Bain had ridden down from San Felipe and joined this group about two days before they'd left Gonzales on October 13. It seemed like ages ago, yet they'd been marching only about two weeks.

The men had started calling themselves the Volunteer Army of Texas weeks ago—only from the looks of them, they were anything but an army. Equipped with everything from guns, knives, and broadswords to tomahawks and hatchets, they were riding mules, mustangs, Indian ponies, and even fancy horses like the ones Bain and Cole rode. Then there were the men on foot. Men who'd either lost their mounts, were too poor to own horses, or had left them for their families to use. They trudged wearily along the dusty road with only the clothes on their backs, a weapon or two, and a bedroll made up from old quilts, blankets, anything they could get their hands on. But wherever they came from, whether in buckskins or fancy clothes, each, in his own way, seemed to have a score to settle or a grievance to be made right, according to him. Whether personally, against the Mexican government and Santa Anna, or just what the man stood for. Whatever, each man here had his reasons.

Cole rubbed the stubble on his face, hoping maybe this morning, since they were getting a late start, he could get a decent shave. And there was a creek, only some fifty feet or so from the road, making the prospect even more appealing. It had been years since he'd had so much brush on his chin, and he disliked it. For one thing, it always reminded him of the years he'd been on the run from the law, and all the heartache of losing Case. Besides, when he'd reached Texas and ridden with some of his Comanche friends, in order to pass for an Indian he'd had to be clean-shaven, and he'd gotten so used to it that even this much of a beard bothered him.

He reached over and untied Nevado from where he was tethered, on a different branch from Bain's horse, Amigo, and he began leading the big white stallion off toward the trickling brook.

Bain glanced over at him, "Where you headed?"

"Think I'll grab a quick shave while Nevado breaks his thirst. Care to come?"

"Hell, why not." Bain untied Amigo and began leading him. He caught up with Cole. "You think anything's really going to come of this, Cole?" he asked as they picked their footing through the overgrown field they had to traverse before reaching the stream.

Cole glanced back at the rest of the men. They were stretched out as far down the road as the eye could see. Gathered in groups here and there, with makeshift campfires, trying to get decent food in their stomachs before the day's long march started, and keeping their spirits up by bragging about what they were going to do to Santa Anna and his brother-in-law, General Cós, when they chased them out of Texas.

"Reckon it will," he drawled. "That is, if more men don't decide to go home like they been doing."

"At least they come back after getting the chores done."

"Yeah? So what happens if Cós and his men decide to meet us halfway? Hell, Bain, it's going to take every man we've got to get through this. We can't just sit around waiting for men to take off and go home whenever they get a hankering to. You think I wouldn't like to see Heather and Teffin? I'd give my right arm to go home right now, too, but you know damn well that's not how wars are won."

"Don't you think you're being rather hard on them, though?"

Cole had been made a captain his first night after arriving at Gonzales, and he looked over at Bain as they reached the stream, then he took his razor and a piece of soap from Nevado's saddlebags and handed Bain a small broken piece of mirror.

"Hold this, will you?" he asked, then knelt down while the horse drank, and he started lathering his face, using the cold water from the stream while he talked, his voice sounding peculiar, lips moving into various awkward positions as he tried to see into the piece of mirror Bain was holding for him. "All depends on what you mean by hard," he answered. "They made me a captain in this damn army, Bain, and by God, if they're going to have an army, they should act like one. Now, if that means they'll have to do extra duty for lighting out without asking, then that's their problem." He had started shaving, nicked himself, then tried to wipe off the blood. "Hell's fire, when I was in the army, a man was a deserter if he left the ranks without permission. This army should be no different."

"But we're not fighting the same kind of war, Cole."

"Aren't we?" He finished shaving and took the mirror from Bain, then wiped his razor off and put everything back in his saddlebags. "All wars are the same, Bain. They're fought to be won," he went on. "And you can't win them without discipline of some kind. Hell, I don't care if some of the men feel they gotta go home for a spell, Bain. After all, we haven't really fired any shots yet. All I ask is that the men assigned to me come up and ask first, so I don't wake up some morning and discover I'm sitting on Cós's doorstep all by myself."

Bain knew Cole was right, yet he'd felt sorry for two of

the men who'd decided to come back the day after they'd left Gonzales, and they'd ended up spending an hour at attention with their rifles while the rest of the men relaxed.

"Hell, they'll fall asleep better tonight," Cole had remarked, but Bain couldn't help his feelings, even though he had to admit that fewer men from Cole's outfit took off than from any of the others.

So far, Bain and Cole had managed to stay together, and both were glad. Although they'd never been extremely close at the time Bain married into the family, that fact had changed since the Kolters' arrival in Texas. Now they were as close as brothers.

They grabbed their horses' reins after slapping some of the cold water on their faces and arms in an attempt to wash up some, then headed back toward the road, leaving a number of other men back at the stream doing the same thing.

The rest of the morning moved along as usual, although no mention was made as to why they'd started the day so late. By the time the sun was climbing high into the sky, they were well on their way again.

It was late afternoon, and the men were already tired. They'd been moving steadily all day, not even stopping to eat, but grabbing their food on the run. Dried jerky, hard bread, and whatever else they could lay their hands on, and now they had slowed considerably. In fact, as Cole turned in the saddle, he frowned, watching the line of men behind him. It looked like someone was trying to make his way through them on horseback. His frown deepened.

"Who you suppose that is?" he asked as Bain too turned in the saddle.

"Whoever it is, the men look excited."

Bain and Cole kept their horses moving slowly, yet still kept glancing back, and suddenly Cole's mouth twisted into a lazy grin and he pulled the brim of his hat down somewhat farther against the afternoon sun.

"It's Houston," he exclaimed as they recognized the horseman. "Wonder what he's doing here."

Bain too wondered, since they all knew Houston was

supposed to be back in San Felipe attending the consultation that was supposed to take place on November 1. But
then this whole thing was so much organized confusion, it
was hard to tell just what was going on half the time.
Even Jim had made the remark that he wished Austin
would make up his mind what rank he wanted him to be.

"Half the time he calls me Colonel Bowie, and the
other half Major," he'd said while they'd sat around the
campfire talking the other night.

Jim had ridden into camp some days back, bringing a
half-dozen Louisiana volunteers with him, only he hadn't
stayed long. He and a Georgian named Fannin had struck
up a quick friendship, then lit out with close to a hundred
men to scout the roads up ahead around San Antonio.
Cole and Bain had both wanted to join them, but Jim
insisted they were better needed in the ranks. Now,
however, no one seemed to know where Jim was, or
Fannin either, for that matter. Just like everything else
that was so unorthodox about this whole war, word had
got back that Bowie and Fannin got to arguing, split their
men up, and went their separate ways. So it was no
wonder now that Houston should be riding along the
road toward San Antonio instead of attending the meetings back in San Felipe, where he was supposed to be.

Bain glanced over at Cole. Cole had known Houston
from his days in the army, during the war. Both had been
with Jackson at Horseshoe Bend, against the Creeks, and
more than once since Houston's name had begun to be
bandied about in political circles, Bain had heard Cole
tell the story of how he'd pulled an arrow out of Houston's thigh back during the fighting. Cole had been a
young inexperienced lieutenant then, and Houston had
had to threaten him to get him to do it. Actually, Cole
had done such a sloppy job he swore Houston'd probably
never admit they'd known each other, even though they'd
fought a number of times after that. But Cole had been
surprised a couple of years back when he'd run into
Houston on a trip to Nacogdoches with a herd to sell,
and the "General," as they all called him most of the

time, not only remembered him, but remembered the incident too.

"Hell's fire, who wouldn't remember a man who did to me what you did?" Houston had remarked. "Besides, for a second there I thought you were one of them Creeks, got hold of a uniform somehow, and was infiltrating," he'd added. "Only I knew you wouldn't be an Indian, the way you pulled out that arrow. I dang near bled to death."

Now Bain watched Houston's eyes light up as he saw Cole. There was only two years' difference in the men's ages. However, although Cole was the younger, he looked more like ten years younger than just two. Drink, trouble, and the life of a sporadic wanderer had taken their toll on Sam Houston. He straightened in the saddle, tilting the hat back on his head, as he rode up to them.

"Thought you were supposed to be in San Felipe, Sam," Cole said as they shook hands.

Houston swore. He was a big man, and took advantage of it, his size often intimidating even his friends.

"Was," he answered. "Only we don't have enough delegates for a quorum." He glanced ahead down the road, toward San Antonio. "Where's Austin?" he asked.

Bain nodded. "You're almost there, General. You got about half a mile to go."

"Good." Sam glanced at Cole, Cole's sloe eyes reminding him so much of the past, then he studied Bain. "You two should have stayed back in San Felipe with me," he added.

Cole shook his head. "I sell horses, Sam."

"And I help him."

"That's just the trouble." Houston looked away, and sighed as he gazed off toward where the line of men was still making its way along the dusty road. "The men who'd do the most good for politics, and really give them their due, always seem to know better'n to get mixed up in them, don't they? Ah well . . . at least I tried." He shrugged, then nodded. "Adios," and he set his horse at a comfortable trot, so he could catch up with Austin, his long legs sticking out on each side of the little Spanish stallion he was riding.

Cole watched him go with mixed feelings. Sam Houston was a fighter, he knew that, but he was ambitious too, and Cole wondered just what the man was expecting to get out of all this. He turned to Bain as they continued riding along with the others.

"You know you should go back with him, don't you Bain?" he said. "After all, ever since all this started, they've been begging you to be a delegate."

Bain gave Cole a disgusted look. "Hell, Cole, you know how I feel about politics. I never was any good at keeping my feelings to myself and buttering people up. That's why I never followed after Stuart when he went to Congress." He smiled. "Besides, one politician in the family's enough," and he nudged Amigo to go a little faster, to keep up with the rest of the men on horseback, who were also moving a little faster now, Houston's arrival giving them a new burst of energy and enthusiasm.

That evening the long column of men made camp earlier than usual again, and the next day, much to Cole and Bain's surprise, the whole day was spent with Houston and Austin arguing over whether to release the delegates to attend the consultation back in San Felipe, or not.

Finally, after a number of speeches and a great deal of haggling, it was put to the men for a vote, and it was decided that all the delegates who weren't staff officers would go back with Sam, leaving only three staff officers, Wharton, Travis, and Austin, behind. Austin didn't like it, but there was nothing he could do, since the men voted on it. So he gave the delegates their leave, and watched Sam ride out of camp with them, hoping they hadn't made a mistake, because that evening as the men settled down to wait for morning and another day's long march, there was an undercurrent of restlessness among the volunteers that hadn't been there before.

The next morning, as usual, Cole, Bain, and the rest of the men were roused early, campfires were put out, and they were on the road toward San Antonio de Bexar long before sunup. Only, as they headed down the rutted road, some even barefoot, having worn out their shoes days ago, no one had any suspicion that up ahead, closer to town, Bowie and the men he'd taken with him to scout around were being attacked by well over a hundred Mexican lancers on the open plains at La Concepción.

Braxton sighed as he shifted in the saddle. They'd been riding hard for what seemed like an eternity already, and now, as he rode into the shallow stream, then began moving up the low incline into the grove of trees stretching up ahead onto the hill, he glanced at the men around him.

They'd left Goliad a few days before, following Ben Milam, with the promise that they'd catch up to Austin and the rest of the men somewhere along the road to San Antonio, but so far, all they'd caught up with were a few disgruntled Mexican soldiers who'd been sent out to scout the road to Goliad, and a supply wagon with food confiscated from some of the farmers in the area.

The scouts they'd disposed of quickly, but the soldiers guarding the supply wagon were a different matter. However, by the time they left the road that led from Goliad and headed cross-country to pick up the road from Gonzales, they not only had full stomachs, but a good supply of staples, and the hunger that had gnawed at Braxton's belly ever since leaving home had been appeased.

Now, however, as they neared the crest of a small hill, Braxton's stomach might as well have been empty again, the way it felt. Only minutes before, while they were splashing their way through the stream, they'd heard the telltale crack of rifles from up ahead, and now, as Brax reined up beside the others, squinting hard to see through the morning fog, the rifle shots were joined by cannon fire, and he tensed. There was fighting up ahead somewhere, that was for sure.

"Wait here!" Ben yelled, and Brax held Hickory in check, along with the others, while their leader moved forward far enough to clear the trees.

After a few seconds, he motioned for the rest of them,

and Brax was one of the first to move. In seconds he was beside Ben, staring in awe at the scene before him.

The sun wasn't up as yet, and fog still clung to the ground, swirling up in patches here and there and obstructing part of their view. Yet they were able to see that a number of Texans, looking more like ghostly apparitions than men, were in the process of holding back what looked like the whole Mexican Army. Even the cannon fire didn't seem to be slowing the Texans down as they charged, like specters, out of the morning fog.

Ben glanced at his men, knowing the odds were against them, yet knowing they couldn't just sit there and watch.

"Who's with me?" he asked hurriedly, and there was a chorus of shouts.

Brax looked at the men around him. He'd known, before they answered, what they were going to say, and before he really had time to contemplate whether he agreed or not, he and Hickory were moving forward into the fray.

Half an hour later, breathing heavily, Brax dropped to the ground behind an old overturned wagon and stared back to where the men he'd been running with were turning the cannon around so they could use it against the soldiers they'd taken it from, and he sighed. For a minute there, he hadn't been sure he'd make it, especially when a rifle shot grazed his arm, and he glanced down now, then reached over, tracing the jagged fabric where it'd torn a hole in his left sleeve. The skin was just barely broken, only he couldn't figure out why it was bleeding so much.

Grabbing a handkerchief from his pocket, he wiped it off, and kept at it till it stopped bleeding, then shoved the handkerchief back in his pocket. Lifting the hat from his head, he wiped his brow, then reloaded both pistol and rifle just in case. This done, he leaned his head back against the wagon bed, trying to get a second wind, yet hoping he wouldn't need it, while all around him the cries of battle went on.

"Well, I'll be damned. What the hell are you doing

here, boy?" a voice suddenly bellowed from in front of him, and Brax jerked upright, his eyes flying open.

There, crouching on one knee, disheveled, dirty, and panting heavily, was Jim Bowie.

Brax flushed, sitting up straighter, and lifted his hat from the ground, his eyes glued to Jim's face.

"I reckon I'm doing the same thing you are, Mr. Bowie," he answered. "Shootin' at Mexican soldiers."

Jim scowled, wiping a hand across his mouth where blood trickled from a cut. "Hell, you are. Bain know you're here?"

"Nope."

"Thought as much." He drew his eyes from Braxton's face, then eased up a bit, peeking over the top of the wagon bed. The fog was beginning to lift now, and he was glad. It'd make things easier. He brought his attention back to Braxton.

"How'd you get here?" he asked.

"We were at Goliad."

"You with Milam?"

Brax nodded, and Jim thought for a moment as he glanced back, watching the men with the cannon.

"Suppose you can do me a favor, boy?" he asked, looking back again to Brax. Jim saw Braxton's gray eyes harden, and knew Brax probably resented being called boy, but at the moment he didn't much care. "Don't worry. I won't tell you to go home," he assured him. "I'll leave that to your pa."

"Then what?"

"I need someone to go get Austin for me, that's what. Can you do it?"

"Why not?"

"Where's your mount?"

Brax figured Hickory was within earshot, and he put two fingers in his mouth and blew. Seconds later he saw the pinto heading across the field at a trot, and blew again.

"Right there," he answered, his eyes on the animal.

Jim caught sight of him too, and nodded. "Good."

Hickory reached them quickly, and Brax got to his

feet, but stayed crouched, reaching for the reins. "And be careful, boy," Jim cautioned. "He should be a couple miles back by now. Tell him to get here fast."

"Right." Brax eased up a bit, and slipped the rifle into its scabbard, then jammed his hat down hard on his head. "Wish me luck," he yelled as he shoved the pistol into his gunbelt, and he leapt into the saddle with one fluid motion, and as Jim turned back toward the wagon, resting his own pistol on the top of it, to cover him, Braxton dug Hickory in the ribs, dashed madly across the field, with shots echoing after him, and out onto the road toward Gonzales, leaving a puff of dust behind to mingle with the disappearing fog.

Brax had been riding for quite some time, and he was still riding hard. He'd gotten away clean, and now he was pushing Hickory to the limit, and the pinto was responding for all he was worth. The fog that had cooled the ground earlier had already been replaced by a blazing sun that was gradually filling the horizon, with the sky above it deepening to a hazy blue, erasing any possibility of rain. Braxton was glad. It was going to be a good day, he just knew it, although there was a nip in the air that hadn't been there yesterday, and he was glad he'd picked up a heavier jacket back in Goliad, since he'd left home in his shirtsleeves.

Home! The thought was provoking, and as he galloped down the road, he couldn't help but wonder what Ma thought. She was probably still mad, and he didn't much blame her. The least he could've done was take time to say good-bye. But then if he had, she'd have probably talked him out of it. Then where would he be? Back home, that's where, while everyone else did the fighting for him. And he couldn't do that. Not this time. Although as he raced along the road now, the slight nick on his arm burning as the air hit it, he knew there were moments back in Goliad when he'd wished he had stayed home.

Suddenly his thoughts went to Joaquín, and he swore softly under his breath. He was leaning low in the saddle now, trying to make time, and he reached out, patting

Hickory's neck. Joaquín was an enigma. They'd tried so hard to make him see how things were, but it was as if he were blind. Well, even though Joaquín's sympathies were with Santa Anna now, maybe when this was all over he'd feel differently. At least he hadn't gone off and joined the Mexican Army as his sister had wanted him to do. Anyway, that was something.

Catalina! Just the thought of her was irritating, and he shook his head vigorously trying to erase the image of her dark eyes and smug smile, when he spotted some men up ahead on the road. Reining up briefly, he made sure they weren't Mexican soldiers, then gave Hickory his head again, until he reached them. He pulled the horse to a halt.

"Where's Austin?" he asked breathlessly, and all of the men pointed in unison to a rider who was quickly bearing down on them.

"What is it! What's happened?" Austin asked as he pulled back on the reins. He spotted Braxton. "What is it, boy?"

Brax was so sick and tired of being called boy, and son. Hell, he was almost eighteen, wasn't he? Only now wasn't the time to argue the point, and especially with someone like Austin. He swallowed his pride again, his only sign of annoyance the way his gray eyes darkened.

"It's Mr. Bowie," he blurted, trying to keep Hickory calmed down. "He said to come on the double, they've been attacked."

Austin frowned. "How far ahead?"

"Two, maybe three miles."

Austin was still weary, the long march having taken its toll, but he inhaled sharply, then turned to his men, starting to give orders, and within minutes the men who were on horseback were quickly disappearing from sight down the road, with the foot soldiers in hot pursuit.

Brax watched them for a few minutes, and was just about ready to join them when he realized how heavily Hickory was still breathing. So instead, he reined the pinto over under a tree a few feet from the road, where they could both catch a second wind, and he started watching everyone streaming by. They were both panting now, horse and rider, and Brax reached out, stroking the gelding's neck affectionately.

Suddenly, as he watched the road, trying to take it all in, and marveling how so many men could be all in one place at the same time, he squinted, took off his hat, rubbed the sweat from his forehead before it had time to get into his eyes, then shaded them from the early-morning sun as he caught sight of a huge white stallion making its way through the throng of excited men, with a reddish-brown horse beside it.

"Pa?" he gasped in astonishment, his voice barely audible, and he swallowed hard, frowning as the rider on the sorrel turned his way and Brax could see his face clearly. "My God, it *is* Pa," he mumbled half to himself, and he sat there, just staring in disbelief, while out on the road Bain and Cole were trying to keep the men in some sort of order.

Word had filtered back down the line that Bowie was in trouble, and although Cole, with Bain's help, was managing well, he sure wished to hell these men had been more disciplined. He shouted for them to move faster, then happened to glance over at Bain, who suddenly wasn't moving at all. Instead, Bain was sitting his horse right in the middle of everything, and he was staring off to the side of the road, where the figure of a lone rider was visible beneath a tree.

The sun wasn't very high yet, but with most of the tree's leaves already fallen for the winter, it shone strongly highlighting the rider's pale blond hair. Cole saw Bain watch closely as the rider put the hat he was holding back on his head, to keep the shards of sun filtering down through the partially bare branches from getting in his eyes, and Cole frowned.

Bain continued to stare, squinting thoughtfully. He wasn't sure, but something about the way that man sat in his saddle . . . and the horse was a pinto. He reined Amigo a little closer, then suddenly knew he was right, and he continued to stare incredulously while the men hurried past him.

"What is it, Bain?" Cole asked, wondering why he'd stopped instead of starting to hurry down the road with the rest of the men.

"It's Brax, I'm sure of it!" Bain called back to him, and he spurred his horse anxiously, maneuvering him sideways through the throng of men until he reached the edge of the road.

Bain pulled Amigo to a stop some ten feet from the rider, and both father and son sat astride, staring at each other.

"Hi, Pa," Brax finally said, loud enough for Bain to hear, and his eyes shifted sheepishly.

Bain didn't know what to say. He was mad, frustrated, and shocked all at the same time. Brax was supposed to be out at the Double K.

"What the hell are you doing here?" he finally shouted as he rode in even closer.

Brax flushed self-consciously. "Not here, Pa, please. Later, okay?" he pleaded, frowning as he glanced around, hoping none of the men on the road had heard.

Bain opened his mouth to say something else, when he was suddenly joined by Cole, who had also realized that the lone rider was Braxton. Cole's sloe eyes were already taking in the fact that Braxton's clothes looked like he hadn't been home for weeks, and there was what looked like partially dried blood on the sleeve where his jacket was ripped.

"Braxton's right, Bain," Cole said, his big white stallion prancing impatiently. "So he's here, so let's talk it over later. Right now we've got to keep these men moving. Now, come on!" and he started turning Nevado.

Braxton had been watching his father's face, and for a minute he wasn't quite sure what Bain was going to do. Then he sighed, relieved as Bain's gray eyes bristled, and he said, "Your uncle's right, we'll talk about it later," and he too began turning his horse back to the road.

"But you'd better have one hell of a good explanation about all this, young man," he shouted over his shoulder as he finished turning the animal and began following

Cole, who was already filtering back among the hurrying men.

Braxton stared after him in awe.

"Well, come on, son!" Bain urged, trying to be heard above all the noise as the tide of men began sweeping him along. "Are you coming or not?" and Braxton was totally surprised.

"Hey, yeah, Pa . . . yeah!" he yelled back, giving his horse a kick in the ribs, and he too joined the hurrying men heading down the road toward San Antonio, glad he had a reprieve from what he knew was going to be a hell of a good tongue-lashing, from his pa. At least for a little while anyway.

8

By the time Austin and the reinforcements reached Bowie, there wasn't a live Mexican soldier in sight, and the men were all in a heated argument with Jim as to whether they should press right on into town or not. Since only one of their men had been killed, and very few wounded, they'd somehow come up with the ridiculous conclusion that either they were invincible or the Mexican soldiers didn't know how to fight, and they were determined to follow them right on into General Cós's headquarters and take over.

However, Bowie was against it, as was Austin when he arrived. So now, instead, with Austin in command, they began to grumble and complain as they set up camp, each group of men seeing to its own needs.

It was still morning, and Braxton dropped the firewood he'd gathered on top of the pile where Uncle Cole had told him to put it, then turned to head back across the field to see if he could find more, when he stopped suddenly, watching his father approach. Oh, oh, he thought. Well, he knew it was coming.

"Hi, Pa," he said when his father reached him, and Bain studied his son curiously.

"I think it's time we had that talk, Brax, don't you?" he said.

Brax could see his father was still irritated, and he shuffled his feet nervously, then hooked a thumb in his gunbelt. "I reckon."

Bain exhaled expectantly. "So?"

"So what do you want me to say?"

169

"Well, you could start by telling me why you left your mother and sisters out at the ranch alone."

"Hell, Pa, they're not alone."

"Oh, I see. I suppose you expect Luther to defend them if anything happens."

"Well, he does know how to shoot."

"So do Grandma Dicia and your mother, but that doesn't mean they can defend themselves against Comanche." He was furious. "I left you there, Brax, and I did it for a reason. Why couldn't you just do what you were told for a change?"

"Because I thought I could help. I wanted to be a part of it. Cós was already in San Antonio, I had to do something."

"So you decided to fight."

"And I did a hell of a good job of it too, Pa." Braxton's strong face was flushed, eyes glistening. "Ask Ben and the others, they'll tell you."

"They already did, but that's not what I'm mad about. I know you can fight, Brax, I've fought beside you dozens of times, remember? Why do you think I haven't had to worry as much about the ranch since I've been gone? I never dreamed—"

"But it was so close, Pa."

"So are the Comanche." Bain's eyes were troubled. "And what about the soldiers? What if they decided not to stay in town?"

"Hell, Pa, they wouldn't bother going all the way out to the Double K."

"We've got horses, haven't we? And cattle! An army has to be fed, and they don't care where the food comes from." He looked over at his son, his face hard, unyielding. "How long you been gone?"

"Two, maybe three weeks. I lost count."

"Well, you're going back, and now."

"Aw, Pa!"

"No, not 'Aw, Pa!' You'll go, and that's that."

"How? The place's crawling with soldiers."

"It was crawling with them when you left too, and you got through all right."

"Jesus Christ."

"And don't swear. You know your ma doesn't like it." He studied Brax for a minute, watching his son's face flush with resentment, and knew what Brax must be feeling. He'd fought like a man, killed like a man, and now was being treated like a child. Bain had to make him understand. "Look, son," he said, hoping Brax wouldn't let his words go in one ear and out the other, "I need you at the ranch, that's all there is to it."

"I know, Pa, I know . . ."

"Then go, dammit. And if anything's happened to your mother and sisters while you've been gone . . . well, we'll take that up when I get home. Do I make myself clear?"

Brax took a deep breath, feeling miserable inside, because he knew Pa was right, and he didn't even have an excuse for leaving, except he was tired of getting all the news secondhand. Just once he'd wanted to be a part of it. How shallow a reason it was now when he thought back over the past few weeks, and the danger he'd not only put himself in, but his family too.

"All right, I'll go, Pa," he answered, tears glistening in his eyes as he admitted to himself he'd been fighting those very guilt feelings ever since he'd left. Ignoring the tears, he glanced at the men around him. "Just as soon as I get the fire built that I promised Uncle Cole," he finished.

"No, you'll go now, Brax," Bain insisted. "I'll fix the fire. If you leave now, and ride hard, you'll be home before dark, even working a wide circle around town. Now, where's your horse?"

"Around someplace." Brax stuck two fingers in his mouth and blew, his usual way of letting Hickory know he was needed, and the frisky pinto came trotting casually across the campground from where he'd been vying for a patch of good eating, with a number of other mounts. "Do me a favor, will you, Pa!" Brax asked as he watched Hickory approach. "Don't tell the others you sent me home, okay? Just tell them I had to leave."

Bain stared at his son, realizing why Brax had asked him. "If that's what you want," he said.

Brax reached out, grabbing Hickory's reins.

"It is," he answered, then climbed into the saddle. "Oh, and one other thing, Pa."

"What's that?"

"You can tell Uncle Cole, if you want. And, Pa!"

"Yeah."

"I love you, Pa, take care," and before Bain could stop him long enough to tell him the same, Brax dug Hickory in the ribs and rode out of camp, heading northwest, hoping to circle the town of San Antonio de Bexar and get home without getting caught, and hoping his father hadn't seen the tears in his eyes.

Braxton was worried. He'd been riding for most of the day, and it was still daylight, but he'd had to circle farther northwest than he'd planned, in order to avoid running into soldiers. Then he'd had to ride south, into Comanche territory, so he was approaching the ranch from the west, where there were no roads, only trails through the hills. The Double K and Crown D both bordered Indian Territory, and he moved cautiously now, realizing the shadows here and there were starting to deepen, the sun dipping lower on the horizon with every moment, yet he knew the ranch was still some distance ahead.

Circling the quiet glade where he, Blythe, Joaquín, and Teffin had spent many a Sunday afternoon, he crossed the small brook that flowed into the lazy pond inside it, and moved onto the trail he knew led to the Double K, then reined up, his eyes straining as he studied the ground. It hadn't rained for a number of days, and the ground was extremely dry, making the dirt path look like powder, and he tensed as he saw the unmistakable outline of unshod horses in the dust.

Leaving Hickory's back, he hit the ground, then stopped, quickly reading the sign. Too many horses to count, only they'd all been heading east, none west. Anxiously now, he leapt into the saddle again and gave Hickory his head, eating up the trail as fast as he could, until finally he pulled the gelding up short, at the top of the hill, where the trail led down to the back corral. Pa usually had a bunch of steers in the corral to be herded to market, but since Pa's been gone, there were only the few stragglers he and Joaquín had rounded up before he'd left. Again he felt guilty. With him home, he and Joaquín could maybe have taken a few north to San Felipe or one of the other towns, and suddenly he realized the enormity of what he'd done. Not only had he left Ma and his sisters unprotected, but with him gone there was no way they could get any money if they needed it, and he began to wonder what they'd been living on.

Suddenly he started to urge Hickory forward. He pulled the animal up again, this time maneuvering him behind a clump of scrub bushes that were still holding tenaciously to their leaves, and he peered over the top of the browned leaves, staring down the hill in the direction of the ranch, where a slight movement caught his eye. It was near the carriage house, opposite the corral, and at the back of the big log ranch house, and he held his breath as he watched a figure move stealthily, heading toward the tree that held Genée's tree house.

Only, as quickly as the figure moved, a shot rang out from the house, and he saw the Indian go down. Straining his eyes, the setting sun behind him helping, Brax managed to pick out the rest of them. Hidden behind whatever was available, which included the bunkhouse, barn, chicken coops, outhouse, and corral fences, were about a dozen Comanche, their horses grazing idly halfway down the slope.

They couldn't have attacked more than an hour ago, because the sign he'd seen had been fresh, and he wondered. How long could Ma and the others hold them off?

Cursing softly to himself, he watched another Indian try to move in closer, only to be driven back with the others. However, he knew, as the sun dipped even further in the sky, that once it got dark, things wouldn't be quite so easy. All the Comanche had to do was wait, then move in under cover of night. He couldn't let that happen. Reining Hickory about, he moved cautiously, so as not to be seen, until he'd disappeared from their view down the other side of the hill, then, giving Hickory his head once more, he headed toward the Crown D, where he knew he could get help.

Half an hour later he was riding across the open plain from the southwest toward the Crown D, his gaze glued to the remains of the huge barn that had once stood in the ranch yard, unable to believe his eyes. He was so dumbfounded by what he was seeing, he hadn't even noticed Heather, who had spotted him riding across the field, and reined up to watch, then started riding out to meet him. She'd been working her horses as usual, and by the time he saw her, she was halfway across the field already.

"My God, Brax!" she exclaimed as she reached him, and now suddenly all questions about the burned-out barn were lost to him as he confronted her.

"You gotta come, Aunt Heather," he begged. "And where's Eli and Mose?"

"What is it? What's happened?"

"It's Ma. They're pinned down by Comanche, and we gotta get back there before dark."

Heather's mouth went dry as she pulled the hat off her head of thick auburn hair and lifted the hat high, waving it to get attention while she called back to the corrals, "Eli, Mose, Shem . . . get your rifles, tell Bessie we're going, and come on, the Comanche are raiding the Kolters'!" She turned to Braxton. "Teffin went over last night to spend a few days," she said, her violet eyes darkening to a deep purplish-blue, and Brax knew what she was trying to tell him. Come hell or high water, they had to make it.

A few minutes later, riding hard, and hoping to beat the first shadows of evening to the Double K, Braxton, his Aunt Heather, wearing her husband's old clothes and riding beside him, flanked by the three hands from the Crown D, reined away from the sight of the burned-out barn and headed off into the hills to the south, and the trail that led back home.

Meanwhile, back at the Double K, Lizette closed one eye, squinting as she peered through the slit in the shuttered window, trying to determine where the Comanche were hiding. There had been at least twenty when she'd first spotted them riding down the hills out back, and now she was certain they'd been able to whittle them down to about a dozen. It hadn't been easy, though, and now she was really scared. It'd be dark in less than an hour, and once darkness settled over everything, there'd be no way they could see the bastards creeping in.

At least now they could catch movement, and with each side of the house covered, there was a chance. But after dark . . . ? She straightened, set her rifle down, and moved carefully away from the window, then hurried through the big house, making sure everyone was still in place.

She'd been at the window in the guestroom upstairs, at the back of the house, so she was facing all the outbuildings. Grandma Dicia and Genée were in Braxton's room in front, across the hall from her, while Pretty and her elder boy, Dexter, stayed in the parlor downstairs to watch that side of the house. Luther was in Dexter and Corbin's room so he could watch the drive, as well as the outbuildings, from downstairs, with Corbin at the window in the dining room downstairs, where he could back up his father if need be. Even Blythe was in her bedroom, adjacent to the front hall downstairs, with a rifle eased out the shuttered window, while Genée's old wet nurse, Dodee, who usually was so scared she shook uncontrollably when anything like this happened, was upstairs in Genée's room with Teffin, where they had a good view of the side yard.

Satisfied everyone was still in place, Lizette returned to the guestroom, and once more took up her vigil. Time was moving so slowly, and she knew the Comanche were just biding their time, waiting for the sun to go down, yet there was nothing more she could do.

She slipped the rifle barrel through the hole in the shutter again, then squinted, peering out. It was so quiet out there, and to make matters worse, the sun was disappearing below the horizon, and she was staring right into a red sky that was blinding, while the shadows, left behind, deepened.

A noise from behind made her turn, and she sighed as Genée stuck her head in the darkening room.

"Grandma said not to light any candles, Ma," she said quickly. "She said even a slit in the window can be seen in the dark."

Lizette nodded. "Tell her not to worry, and remind her we've been through this before."

"Yeah, but Pa was here then."

"I know that too. Look, just go back with Grandma will you, Genée," she said wearily. "I've got enough problems without worrying about you two."

She watched Genée shake her head and leave, then Lizette bent forward again, brushing the dark hair from her eyes as she once more peered through the crack in the heavy wooden shutters, her green eyes intense.

Suddenly she tensed, and bit her lip. Something moved down near the corral where the horses were, only it wasn't a horse. One of the Indians, crouching low, was trying to reach the gate. The corral was off to the left of the cornfield, and she leveled her rifle, getting a bead on him.

The explosion nearly split her eardrums, but she only clenched her mouth all the harder against it, then looked out the slit again. Nothing was moving. Not even the strange bump on the ground only a few feet from the corral gate, and she was so glad Bain had taught her how to shoot. It gave her a strange feeling, though, as she stared outside, realizing the Indian she'd shot at was lying out there dead. Even like this, it was hard to get used to the fact that you'd actually killed someone.

Straightening abruptly, she turned at another sound behind her. This time it was Teffin, and she hurried in unceremoniously, dropped to the floor beside Lizette, and reached up, pushing the shutter open a bit. "Aunt Liz, look!" she cried, pointing off toward the hills behind the Indians, and Lizette's head joined Teffin's so she could get a better view. As she did, she caught sight of riders on the hill. They were still some distance away, and with the setting sun behind them, it was hard to see.

"More Indians, you think?"

Teffin shook her head. "I don't think so, Aunt Liz. I'd swear one of those horses is a pinto, look!" and as they watched expectantly, crouched behind the upstairs bedroom window, the riders dipped down below the horizon, where they were no longer silhouetted in the setting sun, and Lizette and Teffin watched Braxton, Heather, Eli, Mose, and Shem come riding down the back hill to catch the Comanche in a cross fire.

He Who Rides saw the pinto at the same time his companions did, only, unlike them, he didn't want them to leave.

"I have a score to settle," he told the brave beside him.

The other Indian shook his head. "It is no time to settle scores," he argued as the riders coming toward them started shooting. "And it is no time to take the horses either. Now come, before they start shooting from the house too," and he grabbed He Who Rides' arm, pulling him with him, and they headed for their horses, where the other braves were already mounting.

It was still light enough out, and Heather, who'd learned from Cole to shoot from the saddle, let out a holler as she rode side by side with the men down the hill toward the back corrals. Two of the Indians were trying to reach their horses, and she was just as determined that they wouldn't. Her finger tightened on the trigger.

"Damn!" she yelled seconds later as the Indian she'd aimed at leapt onto his mount, and she reined up for a second, pushing the old hat she was wearing back a little further on her head, figuring it'd help her see better so she could reload. Only there wasn't time. With a quick jerk of his horse's reins, the Indian whirled his horse about, and for a second Heather held her breath as she looked him dead in the face. Only he wasn't looking at her. He was astride his mount, the animal prancing the ground skittishly, but the Indian was staring at Braxton, his expression filled with hate.

Heather sucked her breath in, frozen in the saddle. It was He Who Rides, it had to be, she thought. The setting sun had turned him to red-gold, and it was impossible to see his face clearly, but she knew it for certain a few seconds later as Braxton too caught sight of him. Only, instead of shooting, both young men just stared hard at each other for what seemed like an eternity, the hundred or so feet separating them vibrating with emotion, then He Who Rides whirled his horse to the right and headed past the cornfields and off to the north, following close behind his companions, until they were out of sight.

Braxton let loose with another shot, just for good measure, that was joined by a lone shot from the house, then all grew quiet.

Heather still hadn't moved, and Brax rode Hickory forward, reining up beside her.

"That was him, wasn't it Brax?" she asked.

He nodded. "Yeah, that's why I didn't shoot him."

"I thought as much." Heather's gaze was on the spot in the distance where the Indians had disappeared, and she shuddered. "Maybe you should have," she said, her voice breaking. "After all, Brax, even if he is Case, he's too set in his ways now to ever be our son again. He'll never be anything but a savage."

Eli had ridden up beside Brax, and he saw the sadness in her eyes. "Don't count on it, Miss Heather," he said, trying to be reassuring. "Remember, he didn't kill Braxton either. Now come on, let's get down to the house," and as they rode down the back drive, past the corrals, and the tree that housed Genée's tree house, then stopped, dismounting by the back porch, Heather thought over what Eli had just said.

He was right, she thought. Eli was right. He Who Rides hadn't killed Braxton. They'd looked each other straight in the eyes, close enough to know there was no mistake, and yet He Who Rides hadn't fired either.

Only, Heather had no way of knowing, as she turned and started up the back steps to enter the kitchen of the big log house, that at that very moment He Who Rides, while putting distance between himself and the Double K

Ranch, was also cursing his luck because he'd run out of ammunition for the white man's weapon he'd been using, hadn't brought his bow, arrows, or lance, and hadn't had a chance to use his knife or tomahawk. Next time, he told himself silently. Next time, son of the devil, I will not make that mistake, and he whipped his horse harder, promising himself that someday, when that next time came, the white man with the golden hair would die.

Lizette had never been so glad to see anyone before in her life as she opened the kitchen door and saw Heather standing on the threshold. After hugging her enthusiastically, and greeting Eli, Mose, and Shem, she turned her attention to Braxton, who had been lingering a little longer than necessary at the top of the porch steps, since he knew the danger was past. He walked hesitantly forward now, and stood in the doorway, the light from the candle lamp Pretty had just lit falling across his face, and she didn't know what to say.

She wanted to shout at him and ask him what he thought he was doing by leaving them the way he had. Yet, she was so glad to know he was all right, and thankful he'd arrived when he did, that she stared at him now with mixed feelings.

"Hi, Ma," Brax said from where he stood in the doorway, and as her eyes caught his, for a brief second he wasn't sure whether he should have come home or not.

Suddenly he saw her deep green eyes soften, the tiny crow's-feet in the corners crinkle just enough to let him know it was going to be all right, and she flung her arms about him, holding him close.

"Oh, Brax!" she cried, tears filling her eyes. I've been so afraid . . ." She choked back a sob, drawing her head back so she could see his face again. "I should thrash you, young man," she said, her voice trembling with emotion. "Where've you been?"

Brax held her from him, looking deep into her eyes. "I saw Pa, Ma," he answered.

"You saw Bain?"

"He's back just the other side of Bexar with Uncle Cole, Mr. Bowie, and practically the whole Texas Army."

Luther, who'd been standing next to his wife, stepped forward. "You mean they're plannin' to march on the town?"

Brax shook his head. "Don't think so," he answered, and while Pretty lit a fire in the cook stove and started making supper for them, since it was already getting late, Brax greeted everyone else enthusiastically. He was the center of attention now, and after giving Blythe an extra kiss and hug, they moved to the parlor, lighting the lamps on the way and opening the shutters, and while they waited for supper, Brax gave them an accounting of everything he'd been through since leaving home some weeks ago.

It was late now. Eli, Mose, Shem, and Heather had already headed back toward Uncle Cole's, taking Teffin with them, although she would rather have stayed, now with Brax home. But Heather felt it was better she stayed closer to home, especially after what Brax had told them about the army being so close. She knew anything could happen, so Teffin hadn't argued. Before leaving, however, Eli and Shem had taken the bodies of the Indians who'd been killed up to the top of the hill and left them—in the hopes that their companions would return for them—and promised to come over and bury them the next day if they hadn't.

Now Brax sat on the floor in the parlor in front of the fireplace, watching the glowing embers burning lazily. He'd often thought of this moment back in Goliad, and on the cross-country ride with Ben and the others, but never dreamed he'd be experiencing it so soon. In a way he felt cheated, wishing Pa had let him stay, and yet he was needed here too. Today had proven that.

Pulling his legs up and hugging them to him, he cringed at the thought of what might have happened if he hadn't arrived, and he drew his gaze from the burning wood and turned to look about the familiar room, with its chinked log walls. Everybody else was already in bed, exhausted after the long siege by the Indians. Only Brax couldn't sleep. Aunt Heather had told him about Joaquín and about the barn and the soldiers when they'd been on their way over from the Crown D, and it had been haunting him ever since. Now, as he sat quietly watching the fire, he thought back over that conversation, and he began to wonder: What was Joaquín doing now? Where was he? And more important, why had he done such a stupid thing?

According to Aunt Heather, the last time she'd seen Antonio de Léon he'd told her Joaquín had been sent south to scout for Santa Anna. Brax was having a hard time believing it. They'd been such good friends. How could he have turned on them like this? It didn't make sense. But then nothing about any of this seemed to make sense anymore. According to Uncle Cole, Austin and Houston were fighting over who'd lead what, and half the men back in San Felipe weren't even sure they wanted anyone to lead anything. All anyone seemed to know, or care about, was that they all hated Santa Anna and the government he controlled. And yet Joaquín had elected to join them. Damn him!

Brax had changed his clothes, and was wearing a clean blue shirt Blythe had made for him, and a pair of buckskin pants. His fingers ran lovingly across the stitching on the shirt sleeve, as he thought of all the work his sister had put into it. At the thought of his sister, he remembered Joaquín's sister, and he inhaled deeply, wishing he could forget Catalina even existed. He was so absorbed in blaming her, for perhaps talking Joaquín into doing what he'd done, that he didn't hear Grandma Dicia step into the room until she spoke. She had a shawl around her shoulders, covering the flannel wrapper that was over her nightgown.

"Brax?" she asked as she walked over. He turned, reaching up his hand.

"You can't sleep either?" he asked.

She took his hand, squeezing it as she lowered herself into the armchair beside him. Most women wore nightcaps, but Loedicia had always hated them, and now, as Brax studied her, he watched the firelight turn her gray hair a lovely golden red, while softening the deep wrinkles in her aged face and making her violet eyes look brown.

She smiled down at him. "You were thinking of your friend, weren't you?" she said.

He frowned. "How'd you know?"

"I've seen the look before." She was still holding his hand, and released it, then pulled the delicately embroidered shawl tighter about her. It was chilly tonight, and the fire felt good. "Besides, I know you, young man. Friendships mean a great deal to you, don't they?"

"Do they? I thought so once. Now I'm not so sure." He inhaled deeply, then turned back toward the fire. "I thought I knew Joaquín, Grandma," he went on. "I know we hadn't known each other very long, but there was something there . . . he was like the brother I never had. Was I that far wrong?"

"Were you?"

He turned to face her. "What do you mean?"

"Think, Brax," she urged, her voice low, hushed. "Think back to the way he acted. You say you thought you knew him. How did you know him? What was he like?"

Brax sighed, frowning. "Gosh, Grandma . . . he was . . . he was like me, I guess."

"Honest, kindhearted, and loyal, right?" she offered.

He flushed. "Well, yeah . . . I guess you could say that."

"Then why does it surprise you that he did what he did?"

"What do you mean?"

Loedicia's eyes searched her great-grandson's face. "Joaquín was born in Mexico. Is it any wonder he'd give his loyalty to Santa Anna?"

"But the man's a bloodthirsty tyrant!"

"You know that, and I know that, but you see, Joaquín hasn't learned it yet."

"And when he finds out?"

"If and when he does, he'll no doubt realize his mistake."

"How can you be sure?"

She drew her gaze from his face and stared at the fire for a few minutes, then looked back at him again.

"Did you know that at one time, when I first met your Grandpa Roth, he was a captain in the British Army?" she asked.

Braxton eyed her skeptically. "But . . . that couldn't be," he retorted defensively. "He was a member of the Philadelphia Light Horse Troops, then joined Marion in South Carolina. He used to tell me about his adventures all the time . . . and Ma said . . ."

"I know." Loedicia smiled warmly. "But he was a British soldier before that, and a loyal one too, until he suddenly realized what the rest of us were fighting for."

"And you think maybe Joaquín . . . ?"

"I think perhaps you shouldn't hate him too much, Brax. After all, the qualities you saw in him before are still there. And can you imagine how hard it must be for him now, feeling deep down inside he's doing the right thing, and yet knowing all the while that what he's doing could ultimately hurt all the people he cares for so much. And especially Teffin. I think we all know how he feels about her. It takes a special kind of person to have that kind of loyalty."

Brax stared at her for a few minutes, watching her eyes. Grandma was so smart, and had seen so much of the world.

He smiled. "Thanks, Grandma," he said, and sighed. "I think maybe now I can sleep, how about you?"

She smiled back. "I can try." She took a deep breath. "At least I don't have to worry about you tonight," she answered. "Just your father and uncle," and as she stood up, he followed her to her feet. "So tell me," she went on as they headed for the stairs. "Are you going to stay home now, or are you going to break your mother's heart again?"

"Aw, Grandma . . ."

"Don't worry, Brax, I guess she expected it, in a way. But please, dear, if you do decide to go again, tell her, will you? It hasn't been much fun living with her these past weeks. Bad enough your father was gone, but when you left . . ."

"I promise, Grandma," he said as he let her hold his arm while he escorted her up the stairs. "If I do decide that I have to leave, she'll be the first to know."

"Good." She crinkled her nose and winked at him. "That's my boy," and her hand tightened on his arm as they reached the top of the stairs.

For the next few weeks life at the Double K was in a strange turmoil. From all outward appearances, things seemed normal, yet underneath it all, the unrest was maddening. It was dangerous to travel the roads or go into town because of the soldiers, and yet life had to go on.

Word of the clash between Bowie's men and the soldiers had reached all the surrounding territory, and everyone was waiting to see what would happen next. Nothing did. Instead of attacking, the Texans dug in. Some near the old mill in the bend in the river just north of the ruins of the old mission fort folks had begun calling the Alamo because of the cottonwoods there. While others camped to the east, near the powder house, and still others literally trenched themselves along the San Antonio riverbank, where they'd set up a battery placement for the cannon brought to Austin by a volunteer group of soldiers from New Orleans. Men were coming from all over now, and the Mexicans, with General Cós still in command, had settled into what they considered two advantage points. One in town, the other inside the old fort that the Texans, unfortunately, seemed to have surrounded.

The weather turned cold, and still nothing happened. Now and then Antonio de Léon would stop by the ranch with news of a skirmish here or there, and so far Cós's men seemed to have the upper hand. But then one day shortly after the first of December, Antonio rode into the ranch yard of the Double K with the startling news that Austin had left the army in charge of someone else, the men got tired of waiting, and following Ben Milam, who'd been urging them to follow him, had attacked and even now were fighting in the streets.

Don Antonio and Juan Seguin, because of the positions they'd held with the Mexican government at one time, and because they were also of Mexican blood, had been successfully using every opportunity they had to learn what they could, using a false friendship with Cós and his soldiers to further the Texans' cause. Only now, unfortunately, Juan had been found out, and Antonio was the only one left to gauge the enemy's strength. Although the Dantes and Kolters both knew what he was doing, Catalina was ignorant of it, and often reveled in the knowledge that her uncle had finally come to his senses and was helping the Mexicans. Now her only hope was that he'd realize that the sooner he quit associating with the Dantes and Kolters, the better it would be for all of them.

Fortunately the Double K and Crown D ranches, as well as many of the other homesteads in the area, were far enough from town that they were hardly aware any fighting was going on. However, in their hearts they knew, all of them. And although Lizette refused to let Brax out of her sight, she prayed every night that they wouldn't get hurt.

It was Tuesday afternoon, the second Tuesday in December, and the weather was cold, as it had been for a number of days now. Blythe watched her mother throw another log on the fire, then she stared back down at her knitting. She'd taken an old shawl of Grandma's apart because they hadn't been able to buy any new yarn, and she was making a scarf and hat for Genée for Christmas. She stared at the silvery blue yarn on the needles. War! War! That's all they ever talked about anymore. This whole stupid war! But then it wasn't really stupid, she knew that. It was just that she missed Pa, and worried about him something fierce, as did everyone else.

Dexter and Corbin had tried to slip into town unnoticed, figuring nobody'd bother a couple of slaves minding their own business, but it was useless, and too dangerous to even go past the marketplace, so they'd turned around and come back. But they had learned that Ben Milam had been killed, a fact that had bothered Braxton more than he let on. But since that day, no one had even ventured near San Antonio, and Don Antonio hadn't come over either, so they had no idea at all how things were going.

Blythe knitted a few stitches, then glanced over at her mother again, where she stood in front of the parlor window staring off toward the road. It seemed like she was standing there more and more every day now, and Blythe prayed hard it'd soon be over.

Suddenly she heard her mother gasp, and she settled the knitting in her lap as Lizette let out a yell.

"Oh, God!"

"What is it, Ma? Who's there?" she cried anxiously, but Lizette couldn't even speak.

Her eyes, glued to the road out front, were watching two riders coming up the long drive toward the house. One was riding a huge white stallion, the other a sorrel, only the one on the sorrel was bent over, huddled against the cold gray day, and she didn't know if he was doing it to keep warm or because he was hurt.

"It's your father," she said simply, then half-ran to the front door, throwing it open wide, and just stood waiting, afraid to move. "Cole! Bain!" she cried frantically from the doorway, then began to run toward them, and as Cole slid from the saddle, she reached Bain's horse. Before Cole even had time to warn her, Bain fell into their arms, and they had to struggle to keep him from hitting the ground.

Within minutes the front yard was crowded with Pretty, Dodee, and Genée, while Blythe sat on the porch in her chair with the wheels on it, waiting.

"You run up and get the covers back, Dodee," Lizette ordered as she and Cole worked at getting Bain into the house. "And, Pretty, get some water boiling. Genée, go find some bandages. Now hurry, your father's hurt."

All three disappeared quickly, and only Blythe was left to watch them half-drag her father into the house. As they carried him up the steps to her parents' room over the parlor, all she could do was sit at the foot of the steps with tears rimming her sad gray eyes, and pray.

Dodee pulled the covers back a little farther on the four-poster bed, then watched as Miss Lizzie laid Mr. Bain on the bed, and she trembled.

"You want I should do something else?" she asked unsteadily.

Lizette was unfastening Bain's shirt, and she glanced back at the girl. "No, that's fine. Just go make sure Pretty doesn't need you to help her," she said. Lizette looked over to the other side of the bed, where Cole stood waiting, and she realized he too had been limping. "You should have let us know. We'd have brought a carriage," she admonished.

He shook his head. "Not near town you wouldn't." He straightened, looking about the room, the split-log walls with their mudded cracks reminding him of his own home. "There's nothing safe near town right now, Liz. You should know that." He sighed wearily. "The fighting's been door-to-door for two days now, and it's getting worse."

Lizette fumbled under Bain's shirt. He was still only half-conscious, and she looked up from his face, glancing toward the door, where Grandma Dicia had appeared.

Loedicia had been taking a nap when she'd heard the commotion, and she still wasn't fully awake. She stared at Cole curiously.

"I'm not dreaming, am I?" she asked.

Cole sighed. "No, you're not dreaming, Grandma," he answered. "But Bain's been hurt. There's shot in his shoulder, more in his thigh, and a bayonet wound in his arm."

"Well, here then, move aside so I can help," she insisted as she came the rest of the way into the room, and with deft hands, gnarled from age, yet skilled in what she was doing, Loedicia helped Lizette strip her husband's feverish body and clean the wounds, then she turned to Cole, who also had a nasty cut on his leg, where a lance had barely missed the tendons.

By the time Brax rode in from the range, with Dexter

and Corbin in tow, along with some ten steers they'd rounded up, Bain was sleeping comfortably in bed, Cole's wound had been cleaned and dressed, and Cole was getting ready to ride the last few miles home.

"I'd better go with you," Brax suggested as they stepped out onto the front porch, but Cole shook his head.

"Hell no, there's no reason for that," he said. "I'm not hurt that bad. Besides, even if I fell asleep in the saddle, Nevado'd get me home all right. One look at the barn from a distance, and he'd head on in without me having to even use the reins." Suddenly he froze, looking from one to the other, seeing the strange looks on everyone's faces, and his own face paled. "What is it? What's wrong?" he asked.

Brax turned on his mother. "You mean you haven't told him?"

"Told me what?" Cole was livid. "What the hell's going on anyway? What's the matter with all of you? You said Heather'd be glad I was home, so why the long faces?"

"It isn't Heather, it's . . . well, it's the barn," Lizette answered hesitantly. She'd forgotten about it until now, since it was nothing new to them, and without trying to be too hard on Joaquín for bringing the soldiers in the first place, she told Cole all about the loss of the horses and the burning of the barn. As she did, she saw his eyes darken ominously.

"So, the young Mexican chose sides, did he?" Cole's hands clenched on the brim of the hat he was holding. "Well, I guess we all knew it was coming, didn't we?" he went on. "I only hope he doesn't think that when this is all over he can just wander back into our lives and we'll accept him again. Because I'll tell you, Brax"—and he turned to his nephew, his green eyes cold and distant—"if he ever does come back, I don't want him to ever set foot on my place again, do you understand?"

Brax hadn't remembered ever seeing his uncle so angry before, and he nodded reluctantly. "Yeah, Uncle Cole, I understand," he said.

"Good." Cole set the hat on his head, pulling it down harder against the light drizzle that was beginning to fall outside, then he looked at the others. "I'll be over in a day or two, to see how Bain's doing," he said quickly. Then, already having said his good-byes to everyone before Braxton's arrival, he stalked off the porch, mounted Nevado, and headed across the side yard to the field and the trail that led toward home.

Heather was in the lean-to Eli and Mose had built at the side of the carriage house, where they could keep the horses, until something could be done about building another barn. They had cleaned up much of the mess, stacking it all in a huge pile in the field behind the barn, but she hated to even look at the spot anymore. She and Teffin had been working the new batch of horses Shem and Eli had brought in. Shem had broke them to the saddle, and it was her job to do the rest, between everything else she had to do. Ah well, it was better than just wandering around trying to look busy, and she remembered her conversation with Cole last spring.

In a way, his going off to fight had been good for Teffin, and Heather glanced over to where Teffin was rubbing down the mare she'd been teaching to cut out cattle, like she'd watched her father do so many times. She'd told Heather it hadn't really been that hard to learn. It was just a matter of remembering. If Cole hadn't gone, Teffin would probably still be walking around all day hunting for something to do. Now, however, she was kept so busy she didn't even have time to ponder over her feelings for Joaquín anymore.

And that was another thing Heather was pleased about. Since the night of the fire, Teffin hadn't even spoken Joaquín's name. And if he were guilty of planning the raid Lieutenant Rodriquez' men had made, it was best Teffin lost interest in him now, before her heart was broken entirely.

Heather finished rubbing down the roan she'd been getting ready so Eli could take him north, in hopes of selling him at San Felipe, along with the one Teffin had been working, as well as the three others out in the corral. She sighed. It wasn't just selling the horses that made her glad Eli was going north. The main reason was, she'd talked him into coming back by way of San Antonio, in the hopes he might run into Cole and Bain somewhere. After all, that's where they'd been when Brax had left them. There was fighting, sure, but Eli could handle himself.

Weary and tired, she set the curry comb aside, threw a blanket over the horse's back, and walked to the open end of the lean-to. She was just ready to call back to Teffin, asking her if she was through, when she caught a movement at the edge of the woods the other side of the field, behind what was left of the barn. Her first instinct was that it was Brax on an errand for Lizette, because the rider had emerged from the trail they used to reach the Double K. But as the rider drew closer, the big white stallion looking dirty gray in the falling rain, she let out a squeal, started running, then stood in the misty rain, her curly hair straggled about her face and neck, oblivious of how she looked as she waited for him to reach her.

Cole's gaze was on Heather from the moment he saw her dart from the lean-to, and he urged Nevado faster, galloping now, while trying to ignore the burned-out ruins of the barn. He was keeping his eyes and thoughts on the woman only, knowing that in her arms was the comfort he needed, the reason for his existence. When he was barely ten feet from her, he pulled back on the reins, slid quickly from the saddle, and limped anxiously toward her, then stopped.

"Heather!"

"Cole!"

It was a time of enchantment for both, a time of renewal, a time of forgetting the lonely months behind them, and as Teffin watched from inside the lean-to, having heard her mother's excited cry, Heather was lost in Cole's arms, and tears ran down Teffin's cheeks. Pa was all right. He was home, and he was all right. Thank God!

Three days later, as the rain let up and the sun came out again, trying to warm the earth, Antonio de Léon made a surprise visit to the Crown D Ranch to inform the

Dantes, before heading for the Double K next, that General Cós's army had surrendered, not only the Alamo fortress, but the town, and plans were being made to send him and all his men back south, across the Rio del Norte, with the promise that they never again raise arms against the Texans.

The town, the territory itself, was now in the hands of the free Texans. And as Teffin stood in the parlor listening to Don Antonio's news, and heard her mother exclaim that it was going to be a good Christmas after all, she wondered plaintively where Joaquín was and what he was doing. Then later, at the Kolters' Double K, as Braxton listened to the news, he too wondered the same thing.

That night, in San Antonio de Bexar, in spite of the dead and wounded, and in spite of all that had gone before, there was dancing in the streets.

9

It was April 19 already, and well on its way into the year of 1836. So much had happened since Joaquín had ridden away from his uncle's hacienda just outside of San Antonio those long months ago. So much he wished he could change, yet he knew he couldn't. How cruel life was, to teach a man honesty and loyalty as a youth, then try to deny it existed once he grew to manhood. He'd been so foolish, and his uncle so right.

He had stood on the hill overlooking the small village near the river and watched the soldiers burn and kill, and tried to excuse them by telling himself the people who were dying had aided the enemy. But it hadn't worked.

He'd stood in Santa Anna's tent weeks later, as they neared San Antonio, and watched the man he'd once practically revered order the deaths of innocent women and children, claiming they'd given food to the Texans, and he hadn't said a word. Tears rimmed his eyes now as he sat his horse, remembering. He'd been a coward. He knew that now. Even later, when he did speak up, he'd let them talk him into believing they were right.

He glanced at the darkening sky overhead, feeling the tears roll down his cheeks. As if that wasn't enough, he'd stood inside the wall of the Alamo only a few short weeks ago and watched Santa Anna's soldiers drag the bodies of the Texans who'd defended it into a pile, then was forced to smell the roasting flesh, as the odor permeated everything, when the bodies were burned. God! How it stank. His one consolation had been that the only body he'd recognized had been that of Mr. Bowie, Bain

Kolter's friend. That had been bad enough, though. He'd been so ashamed, he hadn't even let his uncle or anyone else know he was even near San Antonio.

Perhaps that's what had finally brought him to his senses. Or was it watching Santa Anna afterward strutting about like a peacock with that young woman he'd talked into marrying him? A farce of a marriage that meant nothing. Or maybe it was listening to the soldiers who'd been in Goliad laughing over the slaughter of unarmed men who'd been promised their freedom.

Unable to pinpoint the exact moment he'd decided he'd been helping the wrong side, Joaquín wiped the tears of anger from his eyes and straightened in the saddle. Well, he had a job to do, if he was going to prove his worth to the Texas Army, and he couldn't get it done sitting here. Nudging his palomino in the ribs, he rode down the hill, picking up the trail along the river, then crossed a bridge before heading into the swampy area. It was close to sundown, and he was keeping to the growing shadows as much as he could, so as not to be seen. He remembered crossing here before. That meant the town of Harrisburg wasn't too far ahead. At least what was left of it.

He'd accompanied Santa Anna's troops on their drive north from San Antonio, as far as the outskirts of a place called Morgan's Point, or more recently, New Washington. But that was as far as he'd gone. Instead, while Santa Anna was enjoying himself at a local plantation with one of the female slaves, Joaquín had talked a stableboy out of a change of clothes and now the scout's uniform he'd worn was gone, and he was dressed in a pair of old black pants that were tucked into his boots, and a dark brown shirt, the sleeves so long, he had to roll them up. And he was without a hat.

The missing hat he didn't mind too much, because the early-evening breeze felt good on his head. But he missed not having a jacket of some kind, with pockets to put things in. He still had his rifle and pistol, though. He had backtracked Santa Anna's trail, knowing Houston had to be somewhere around. Now, if only he could sneak up on their camp and identify himself before getting shot. He began to wonder apprehensively, as he rode along: Did they have a password? What if they shot first, then decided to find out who he was? His stomach was tied in knots, and he was just about ready to change his mind and light out for home and Catalina and Tío Antonio instead, when the sound of men talking filled the air, and he tensed, cocking his head, trying to distinguish what they were saying, but could only make out a word here and there. What he did hear, though, was in English, and he knew he'd found Houston. Now what to do?

The question was answered for him when a rustling in the bushes to his right made him whirl around and he caught sight of an old Kentucky rifle pointed right at his chest.

"Going somewhere?" the voice belonging to the man holding the rifle asked.

"I am looking for Señor Houston," Joaquín," answered truthfully, and although his insides felt like jelly, his voice was strong and firm.

"Señor?" The man stepped out of the shadows, but still kept Joaquín in his sights. He was bearded, buckskins dirty, eyes hidden beneath the low brim of a sweaty old hat. "You're a Mexican then, right?"

"I am a Mexican, sí, señor," Joaquín answered, head held high. "But so are others who fight Santa Anna. Am I not right?"

"Oho, so you fight the devil, do you, lad? Well, we'll just find out about that, won't we? Now, off the horse," he ordered. "And move straight ahead."

Joaquín studied the man for a minute, then dismounted, and leading Compadre, he started walking in the direction where he'd heard the men talking. Within minutes he'd begun to pass more men, who almost looked like twins to the man holding the gun on him. Most of them were bearded, unwashed, and wore their hair to their shoulders, where it was often matted, less often tied back with a leather thong, and their clothes were muddy and torn.

This was Houston's army? he thought as he let his gaze

move from one to the other, and suddenly he stopped, but the man behind him poked him with the rifle.

"Over there," the bearded Texan ordered, and a few minutes later, while the shadows of light continued to deepen, Joaquín found himself standing next to a huge bear of a man who was checking the cinch on his horse's saddle.

"Got something for you, General," the bearded man said.

Sam Houston studied the young man before him, then straightened. Sam was tired. They'd just finished crossing the bayou on an old raft that nearly drowned the lot of them, and although he was glad they'd all made it, the incident hadn't tempered his mood any.

"Now, I know you're not one of my men," he said, noting Joaquín's smooth cheeks and clean clothes. "So who are you?"

"My name's Joaquín Luís de Alvarado, señor," Joaquín answered. "I am the nephew of Don Antonio de Léon, a good friend of Señor Juan Seguin."

"You know Juan?"

"Sí."

Houston glanced at the man who was holding the rifle on Joaquín. "Go find Seguin for me," he said, then looked back at Joaquín. "So, why are you here?"

"Because I think I can help. You are General Houston, sí?"

Sam nodded. "So, how can you help?"

Now was where Joaquín knew he could get into trouble, but there was no other way. "I have been a scout for General Santa Anna," he said, his voice hushed, hoping only Señor Houston would hear. "I know what his plans are, and I wish you to have them."

"You do?"

"Sí, señor. I have watched much wrong being done by the man I thought to be the savior of my country," he confessed sadly. "I had not believed what I thought were lies about him. But I have learned they were not lies. That the man who calls himself Santa Anna, El Presidente, is everything they say he is, and more. So I have come to offer to you what I know. That Santa Anna is at what you call New Washington, with close to eight hundred men, and that General Cós has been ordered to meet him at a place called Lynchburg, with at least five hundred more, and that in two days' time Santa Anna plans to move against you from this place called Lynchburg."

Houston's eyebrows raised. "Well, you're quite informed, aren't you, lad?" He studied Joaquín curiously. "but how do you know all this when it's obvious you're not old enough to be one of his trusted generals?"

"I was one of his trusted scouts."

"I see." Sam stroked his horse's neck affectionately. "You say Santa Anna is at New Washington?"

"Sí."

"Then he didn't follow Burnet and the others?"

"Only as far as Morgan's Point, what you call New Washington."

Houston was apprehensive. The last he'd heard, Santa Anna was chasing Burnet and the rest of the government officials who'd fled Harrisburg, and everyone was predicting he'd follow them all the way to the coast, and Galveston. If this young Mexican was telling the truth, that meant Santa Anna wasn't even twenty miles ahead of them.

Sam was still questioning Joaquín cautiously when Juan Seguin emerged out of the group of men and stopped a few feet away, staring at Joaquín. He was dressed much like the rest of Houston's army, his only claim to his Mexican heritage the serape slung over his shoulders and the sombrero on his head.

It wasn't quite dark yet, and Joaquín could tell by the shocked look on Juan's face that he hadn't expected to be standing face-to-face with his old friend's nephew. At least not here, in Houston's camp.

"Ah, just the man I want to see," Houston said as he caught the surprised look on Juan's face. "You know Señor de Alvarado?" he asked.

"Sí." Juan's eyes narrowed shrewdly. "I know Joaquín. Only what is he doing here?"

"He claims to have changed sides."

"Well, well," Juan exclaimed. "So the proud young peacock finally discovered what this is all about, eh?" He studied Joaquín for a moment longer, then strolled closer, looking into his eyes and noting the flush that tinted Joaquín's face at the word "peacock." "His uncle said it would happen, but I did not believe him. I guess he knew Joaquín better than the rest of us."

"Then you think he is telling the truth?"

"It all depends. What has he told you?"

Joaquín spoke up. "I told him that Santa Anna is at what you call New Washington, waiting for reinforcements he sent for, and he plans to attack in two days' time, when they arrive."

"At Lynchburg," Houston added.

Juan rubbed his chin thoughtfully. "It could be true. After all, those papers Deaf Smith and his men confiscated said that reinforcements were on the way."

"I know." Sam pondered the situation.

They'd just had the hell knocked out of them crossing the bayou, and he knew the men were muddy and tired. Yet, if they kept going, and marched all night, getting along on as little sleep as possible, they could get to Lynchburg ahead of Santa Anna, and be waiting for his soldiers when they came in, which was much better than letting Santa Anna wait for him and his men. He looked steadily at Juan.

"Do you think maybe the men can keep right on moving, Juan?" he asked.

Juan shrugged. "Who knows. Men have done the impossible before, many times, señor."

Sam wasn't sure.

"Santa Anna thinks you are beaten already, Señor Houston," Joaquín offered, trying to help him make a decision. "I was hoping my information could help prove him wrong."

Sam looked at Juan again after listening to Joaquín. "You think I should trust him, friend?" he asked. "I'd hate to get the men halfway there and suddenly find myself surrounded by Santa Anna's soldiers."

Juan was closer to Joaquín now, where he could see his

eyes more clearly, and after a few questions to satisfy his own doubts, he nodded.

"Sí, you can trust him, General," he said, "And to prove it, I will be with him every step of the way. In fact, I will see that he accompanies our scouts on the road ahead, just to make sure."

Sam sighed. "Good, then take him into the ranks and introduce him around. And, oh yes, tell the men to gather around, I'll have some words with them."

"What is he planning to do?" Joaquín asked a few minutes later as he walked away from Houston, leading his horse behind him, while following Juan.

"I have a feeling we will not be sleeping much tonight," Juan answered. "And if what you say is true, I have a feeling we will also be breathing down Santa Anna's neck before long."

Suddenly Juan reached out, stopping Joaquín as a lone figure stepped out into the open only a few feet ahead of them. Joaquín looked over at Juan curiously, then felt a shiver run down his spine as Cole Dante snarled, "What the hell are you doing here?"

Cole's eyes were bristling dangerously as Joaquín turned toward him, startled.

Joaquín stood motionless, staring at the man he'd once considered a friend. Cole's hair too was long now, like the others', his buckskins muddy, chin no longer clean-shaven, and Joaquín knew by the tone of Cole's voice that the friendship was all but over, as far as Cole was concerned.

"Señor Dante . . . ?" How could he explain? How could he make him understand? "I do not know . . . I am no longer with them, señor," he blurted hastily. "Do you not see? Por favor . . . we can be friends again, yes, sí . . . ?"

"Friends?" Cole's fists clenched savagely as he stepped closer. "You call yourself a friend? You bastard! I should kill you for what you did to me and my family."

He started to lunge at Joaquín, but Juan stepped in between, a hand on Cole's chest to hold him back. Joaquín could understand Cole's being angry because they'd been on opposite sides, but . . . what was he talking about? He had no idea . . .

"I don't understand," he protested. "I did nothing . . . Teffin! Teffin is all right?"

"Teffin? What do you care about Teffin, or any of the rest of my family, for that matter? And I trusted you!"

"But what did I do?"

"Do? You burned down my barn, stole my horses, and almost killed my family, that's what you did! And you have the nerve to ask, 'What did I do?' " Cole's jaw clenched fiercely as he stared into Joaquín's dark green eyes, looking for remorse. Instead he saw shock and pain.

"Kill them?" Joaquín shook his head. "Madre de Dios, Señor Dante, I did not try to kill them," Joaquín said. "I swear it. I have not seen them since the day I took some soldiers to your place to buy some horses and Señora Dante refused."

"Oh, she refused, all right, and then you brought those bastards back after dark and took them, didn't you?"

Cole was breathing heavily, anger at Joaquín upsetting him more than he'd been upset since the night he'd fought Heather's first husband and killed him for beating her. He wanted to tear into Joaquín with the same abandon.

"Listen to him, Cole!" Juan urged as he held Cole back, knowing that if he didn't calm Cole down soon, they'd need more than one man to keep him from killing Joaquín. "Listen to Joaquín," he begged Cole frantically. "He said he didn't try to kill them."

"He brought the soldiers out there, didn't he? How do I know he wasn't in on the whole thing? Just because he didn't show his face . . ."

Joaquín shook his head, and there were tears at the corner of his eyes. "I would not do such a thing, mi amigo," he pleaded, his voice breaking. "As God is my witness. When Señora Dante refused to sell the horses, I made the soldiers leave. If they returned, it was without me, señor, for that very night, when I returned to San

Antonio, I left town, heading south, and I have not been near the Crown D since."

Cole didn't know whether to believe him or not. And yet Heather had assured him there'd been no sign of Joaquín that night. Still, he had brought the soldiers there in the first place. How could Cole not believe that Joaquín too was at fault?

"What's he doing here, Juan?" Cole asked again, the timbre in his voice deep, ominous.

Juan relaxed momentarily, still keeping a hand on Cole's shirtfront. "Seems he has changed sides, mi amigo. And has told Houston where he can find Santa Anna."

"You're sure it's the truth?"

"Must be. It goes right along with what Deaf Smith learned off that courier he waylaid."

"Hmmmmm . . ." Cole still wasn't convinced.

"I have been a fool, Señor Dante," Joaquín began slowly. It was hard to admit you'd made a mistake, especially one so grave, but Joaquín knew he had no other choice. "All of you were right, and I was wrong, señor," he went on. "General Santa Anna is even worse than you imagined. I only hope the information I brought your General Houston will help right any wrongs I may have done. But believe me, I would never do what you accuse me of doing. Not to a friend, regardless of whether we believe the same or not. I never dreamed the soldiers would return . . . I should have suspected. Will you forgive me for taking them there in the first place, and for not believing all of you right from the start?"

Cole straightened, and Juan dropped his hand from Cole's chest. Was Joaquín telling the truth or not? Cole wanted to believe him, and yet . . . Bain was back at the Double K, still nursing his wounds because of Santa Anna's soldiers, the Crown D had no barn because of them, and the Indians were making life miserable for both ranches, with most of the men gone except Braxton, Luther, Eli, Shem, and Mose. And even his own leg hadn't healed properly yet, leaving him with a limp. All because of Santa Anna. Yet Joaquín expected to just change sides, and everything would be all right again. Could he? Or had too much happened?

Cole stared hard at the young man he'd once befriended. If he were telling the truth . . . He took a deep breath. "You swear by all that's holy?" he asked.

"I swear," Joaquín answered. "If I had only known . . . I would never have left San Antonio. In fact, if I had known then what I know now, I would have gone to Gonzales with Braxton when he left, instead of volunteering my services to General Cós. But I did not know. I had to see with my own eyes."

Cole still wasn't certain. War could do strange things to people. Yet Joaquín had always been a young man of integrity.

"Por favor, Señor Dante, forgive me for being a fool!"

Cole rubbed his beard thoughtfully, then glanced at Juan. "Houston believed him?" he asked.

"Like I said, everything he says coincides with those dispatches. Only the dispatches didn't tell us right where Santa Anna is. So Joaquín's information, if right, can mean the difference between victory and defeat."

"It's that important?"

"To Houston, sí. And I think I know why. He just asked me if I thought the men could keep moving. Have you thought what would happen, Cole, if, when Santa Anna and his army got to Lynchburg, we were there waiting for them?"

Cole's eyes narrowed shrewdly, and he looked at Joaquín. "Is that really what you want, Joaquín?"

Joaquín straightened proudly. "I want General Santa Anna dead," he answered. "If that means marching to this Lynchburg with your General Houston, then I will be the one to take the first step." His face was open, his expression all too revealing, and Cole could see tears in his eyes. "Por favor, Señor Dante, I ask you again . . . have pity on a fool."

Cole stared hard at Joaquín. How could he refuse such a humble plea? His eyes softened, and he inhaled sharply. "You're not a fool, Joaquín," he said, and tried to smile a bit. "A dreamer perhaps, and rather gullible at times.

But a fool? Never. I'm just glad you came to your senses, that's all," and he stuck out his hand.

"Then you believe me?"

"I believe you."

Joaquín needed no more invitation, and he reached out, grabbing Cole's hand, shaking it vigorously. "Gracias, señor," he said, his voice breaking on the words. "You will not regret it. You will see."

"I'd better not," Cole said, his lips twisting into an affectionate half-smile amidst the beard he'd been swearing to shave off every morning. "Or I'll slap the hell out of you. Now, where the devil'd you get those clothes?" he began, and as they walked away, Cole criticizing the clothes Joaquín was wearing, while promising to find him a hat and a jacket the first chance they had, and applauding Joaquín on the good care he was taking of his palomino, Juan sighed with relief, glad he hadn't had to coldcock Cole, and pleased that his friend's nephew was finally showing his true worth.

It couldn't have been more than a half-hour later, after a rousing speech from General Houston that brought forth the resounding cheers of "Remember Goliad" and "Remember the Alamo," when the undaunted army of Texans, following their commander and struggling to pull two cannon they'd brought along with them, began to move away from the banks of the bayou and out onto the road Joaquín had just traversed. However, after crossing Vince's Bridge, instead of following the road southeast as Santa Anna's army of men had done, they veered off the main road and headed northeast, following the bayou toward Lynchburg, Lynch's Ferry, and the San Jacinto River.

It was early afternoon. Houston's army of men had marched all night and managed to reach Lynchburg early in the morning, as dawn was creeping up on the ferry from the east. And now, after a breakfast of dough cakes made with flour confiscated from some of the ferryboats that had been loaded by Mexican sympathizers for Santa Anna's army, and beefsteaks from some cattle Juan, Cole, Joaquín, and a number of other scouts had rustled, brought in, and slaughtered, the men, their bellies full, had regrouped back from the ferry a ways, along the bayou, with most of the men entrenched in the woods near the water. The cannon they'd affectionately begun calling the Twin Sisters were out in the middle of the knee-high grass on the plain before them.

They had seen smoke curling into the air from the direction of Morgan's Point, just south, beyond Peggy Lake earlier, and when the scouts Houston sent to keep an eye on Santa Anna finally returned to camp, telling him about a skirmish they'd had on the road with some Mexican scouts, Houston knew Santa Anna was on his way, and everything Joaquín had told him had been true.

Now Joaquín leaned against a tree, the jacket he was wearing, taken from one of the Mexican sympathizers at the ferry, pulled around him to ward off a chill. He wasn't cold. Far from it. Not cold the way most folks thought of cold. It was the thought of what lay ahead that forced the goose bumps to rise, and lifted the hair at the nape of his neck, while twisting his stomach in knots.

Some of the men had started eating again, but just the thought of it now had no appeal. He stared up at the sky beyond the trees, and the river. By all portents, it was going to be another miserable day. The sky was still gray, with the smell of rain in the air, and the temperature had dropped considerably the past few hours. A prayer came to his lips as he watched the rest of the men, seemingly unconcerned, as they went about their business.

Suddenly someone shouted, an alarm was given, and Joaquín stood up, hugging the tree he'd been sitting against, the rifle from his scabbard in his hands. He'd kept Compadre beside him while he'd rested, and the big palomino nudged his shoulder affectionately.

"Get back, amigo," Joaquín urged, grabbing the animal's reins, and he held him back while continuing to watch.

"They're coming, all right," Cole said from beside him, and Joaquín looked back over his shoulder. He hadn't heard Cole come up. "Looks like Santa Anna wants to find out just what he's up against," Cole went on. "Houston sent Colonel Neil and some men out to the cannon."

"Then we shall fight?" Joaquín asked.

"Now hold on there," Cole cautioned him. "Right now we're just going to do some picking back and forth. Get a bead on the soldiers, boy, but watch!"

Although Joaquín's rifle was aimed at the Mexicans, his gaze was glued to the Twin Sisters, and he watched the men getting them ready for action, while what looked like a whole dragoon of soldiers was forming across the grassy plains. Suddenly both Joaquín and Cole turned at the sound of a horse behind them, and were surprised to see Houston riding up through the line of men, urging them to shout as loud as they could when the cannon roared, to make the enemy think there were more men here than there were.

As Houston moved quickly, riding in and out among the trees, an occasional shot from the Mexican Army's twelve-pounder would crash into the trees above him, breaking off a limb or two, but otherwise doing little damage. Joaquín frowned, then turned back toward the clearing.

Finally it was the Sisters' turn to bark, and as Houston neared the far end of the line of men, Joaquín and Cole both cheered their lungs out as the Sisters roared. First one, than a few minutes later, the other, and Joaquín saw an explosion in the enemy's ranks, a couple of mules hit the ground, and one of the officers looked like he'd been hit.

"Santa Anna will not like that," Joaquín offered as he tried to catch his breath from all the shouting, yet keep a bead on them with his rifle.

"I don't doubt it," Cole answered. "Let's just hope the next one's as accurate. Look!" As Cole nodded, Joaquín saw that Santa Anna had evidently decided to send a charge of men to take the cannon, as a group of infantry soldiers broke away from the others, moving head-on toward it.

The Sisters spoke again, spewing scrap metal into the advancing soldiers, felling some, and forcing others to retreat, and once more a chorus of cheers rang through the woods, almost deafening Joaquín's ears, as shots also rang out along the line of men. Even he took a shot at one of the soldiers, his jaw clenching angrily when he saw the soldier he was aiming at go down.

By the time the skirmish was over a short while later, Colonel Joe Neill had been wounded in a freak accident when a ball of shot ricocheted off some metal on Houston's bridle and hit Neill in the hip, and Houston had been forced to give his aide, Hockley, command of the cannon, but the soldiers had been held at bay, and their twelve-pounders had been hit.

Most of the Texans were in high spirits now. Their stomachs were still full from the unusual breakfast Juan and the rest of the scouts had supplied, and their first encounter with the enemy had been successful. And one of the men, Colonel Sydney Sherman, who'd brought a group of volunteers with him from Natchitoches, was insisting that he and his men should be given permission to follow through and capture the enemy's cannon. Houston refused. In the first place, the cannon had been hit, making it's usefulness to Santa Anna ineffective, and second, there was too much chance in getting that close to the line.

Instead, Houston ordered him to take his cavalry, and only reconnoiter, not going past the timber line.

"That's like letting a roadrunner loose in a snake pit and expecting him to just watch," Cole told Joaquín as they all watched Sherman and his men head out of camp. Cole's words were prophetic moments after the horsemen disappeared, when shots were heard and Houston rode from camp cursing, only to meet Sherman on his way back.

One man had been killed, two wounded, and several horses were gone, and it wasn't a surprise to anyone when Houston stripped Sherman of his command, refusing to listen to any pleas that he hadn't purposely started the fracas, and gave the command to a young man named Lamar, who'd proved his worth by rescuing one of the wounded men.

"Well, Houston just made himself another enemy," Cole mused as he and Joaquín watched the goings-on. "But I doubt it could have been avoided."

"I thought Señor Houston wanted to fight," Joaquín questioned, frowning.

"Oh, he does." Cole's gaze rested on Houston, who was standing some fifty feet away. "But not unless, and until, he says so."

"I see." Joaquín watched Houston for a minute, then looked around at the men. "Then I have a feeling we will not fight any more today, mi amigo," he said relaxing some. "For it looks like Señor Houston has lost all interest in the enemy at the moment."

Cole agreed, as he too watched Houston talking to the wounded men and making his way through the camp, urging everyone to get some rest, since there was no way of knowing just what the rest of the day would bring.

Joaquín and Cole, as well as Juan Seguin and the others, took Houston at his word. And as quiet settled over what undoubtedly was the Mexican Army's line of battle forming to the south, just north of Peggy Lake, as they saw barricades of saddles, baggage, and whatever else the Mexicans could find to use as a breastworks for their cannon build up, they let the guards on duty take over, and fell asleep, curling up exhausted on the wet ground beneath the trees. And as a slow rain began to fall, the rest of the men dug in too. That evening, when Houston also retired to a well-drained spot away from the river, his head resting on his saddle for a few precious hours of sleep, no signal taps were heard as the rain began to let up some, and he dozed off, joining his men.

The next morning, as the drum beat reveille, bringing everyone to life again, Joaquín and Cole stirred, and Cole poked Juan.

"Come on, old friend, they're calling us," he said.

Juan stirred wearily, muttering something, and started to turn over.

"No you don't!" Cole admonished. "If we fight, you fight too, amigo."

Juan rolled onto his back and opened his eyes. "It has stopped raining?" he asked.

Cole laughed. "Hell, it stopped last night before Houston closed his eyes."

"I would not know," Juan answered, rubbing the sleep from his eyes, and he sat up, glancing over at Joaquín. "So, do you think we will fight today?"

Joaquín shrugged. "As Señor Dante says, that, señor, is up to your General Houston."

"You know what I think?" Juan said, lowering his voice so only his two companions would hear. "I think Señor Houston will fight today, and do you know when?"

Cole eyed him skeptically. "When?"

Juan smiled. "Do you remember yesterday morning, Joaquín, when General Houston came over and asked you whether Santa Anna takes a siesta or not?"

"Sí."

"You said he did, right?"

"Sí."

"Then think, mi amigo. What better moment to catch Santa Anna unprepared than with his pants down."

Joaquín and Cole both stared at their friend in surprise.

"It is perfect, do you not see?" Juan went on, his voice barely a whisper. "Santa Anna forgets that Texans don't take siestas." He lifted a finger conspiratorially. "Mark my words. Sam Houston is not a man to ask idle questions of anyone. I will bet you we will fight before the day is over," and Juan was right, although for a while Joaquín and Cole thought perhaps he'd guessed wrongly.

All morning long an undercurrent of tension seemed to permeate the camp. Some of the men had become ill, due to exposure and any number of other reasons, and those who weren't ill were restless. Again breakfast consisted of dough cakes and beef. Although the sun was finally trying to dry out the land, and a brisk warm breeze began blowing, it didn't seem to help anyone's spirits as the morning dragged on.

Then suddenly a new fear began to grip the camp as someone spotted a column of soldiers marching up the road from Vince's Bridge.

"Reinforcements?" Cole asked as he and Joaquín stood with Juan watching.

"Sí," Joaquín answered.

Only Houston, knowing the morale of his men could be shattered if they knew Santa Anna's reinforcements had arrived, told them instead that the men they were watching were some of the same soldiers they had seen the day before, and that Santa Anna wanted to try to make them think they were reinforcements to dishearten them.

"But he's wrong," Joaquín tried to tell Cole a few minutes after Houston had disappeared along the line of men. "I know General Cós's soldiers when I see them."

"Then don't tell anyone else you know, boy, because if you do, you'll have Houston to contend with, understand? He says they're not Cós's troops, then they're not his troops, comprende?"

Joaquín frowned. "Not really," he answered. "But I guess your Señor Houston knows what he's doing."

The rest of the morning continued to drag on, and Joaquín was as restless and jittery as the rest of the men. He felt his chin. He was going to need a shave, but how? He'd left all his gear when he'd left Santa Anna. Ah well, he'd never had a beard before. There was always a first time. He looked over at Cole. They were sitting on tree roots, letting their lunch digest, while watching their horses munch grass near the riverbank.

"How do you think I would look with a beard?" he asked, surprising Cole.

Cole cocked his head this way, then that, studying Joaquín's face and noting the black stubble, already visible.

"Like the rest of us, I reckon," he answered. "If you can get it clipped, the ladies will think you're an Adonis, but if you end up with a bush like this"—and he ran a hand into the beard on his chin—"they won't come near you, even for the time of day."

Joaquín sighed. "Does Teffin like men with beards?"

"Teffin?" Cole's eyes crinkled in the corners. "I was wondering when you'd be bringing her up."

"Well, does she?"

"I never asked her." Cole studied Joaquín closely. How glad he was that Joaquín realized he'd been fighting for the wrong side. "You really like Teffin, don't you?" he said after a few minutes.

Joaquín felt the heat creeping into his face, and knew he was blushing. "Is it wrong to like a woman?"

Cole took a deep breath. "Never," he answered. "You know, men tease each other about them, and try to pretend love and romance are women's ideas, but believe me, there isn't one man here, I'd say, who hasn't kissed at least one female in his lifetime and enjoyed it. So no, my friend, there's nothing wrong with liking a woman, or even loving her. But just make sure when you find that woman that you never stop letting her know how you feel. I almost lost Teffin's mother twice, Joaquín," he went on. "And believe me, if we manage to get through all this, I hope I never have to leave her again."

"That is how I feel for Teffin, Señor Dante," Joaquín said, and Cole could tell it took courage for him to admit it. "And if we make it through, I would ask you if I may have your permission to court her."

Again Cole was surprised. "If we come through this, and it's all right with my daughter, you'll be welcome at the house anytime, Joaquín," he answered, and saw relief in the young man's eyes. "In fact, you can come over and help us build the barn back up, how's that?"

"Oh, sí," Joaquín answered. "I would be glad to, señor. I only wish I hadn't been foolish in the first place, and perhaps you would not have to build it again."

"And maybe they'd have found our place anyway, even without you. So let's put that behind us, all right?" He gazed around, noticing the men seemed to be forming small groups up further among the trees, away from the riverbank. "Come on, I think maybe we'd better go up now and find out what's going on."

They were halfway back to their spot beneath the trees where they'd spent most of the morning when they realized Houston had ordered an assembly and roll call. Tethering their horses on low-lying branches, Joaquín and Cole joined Juan and the rest of the men standing at attention. When roll call was over, those who were unable to stand to be counted were kept out of the ranks, and the rest finally given their orders. The first order was food. It was three in the afternoon already, and Joaquín would have been pleased with the order, except he couldn't figure how Cole and the others could eat at a time like this. It was evident Juan had been right, and reinforcements or not, they were going to do the impossible.

Buffalo Bayou was at their backs, the San Jacinto River on their left, and the Mexicans dead ahead, across the plains, the only way out being down the road toward Vince's Bridge, close to eight miles away.

Joaquín ate what little he could, then glanced over at Cole.

"Got your rifle ready?" Cole asked.

"Cleaned it this morning again."

"Nervous?"

Joaquín took a deep breath. "Should I be?"

"Hell yes, my insides are screaming."

"Then sí, I guess mine are too," he answered. "You think this is finally it?"

Cole nodded. "Just like Juan said. It's siesta time, right, Joaquín?"

"Sí, but I was right too. Cós's men have arrived, señor."

Cole nodded. "I know, but remember, don't tell anyone else."

"I won't."

"Good."

Cole finished his food. "Sure you don't want another bite?" he asked.

Joaquín shook his head. "My stomach couldn't take it, señor."

Cole tucked the last piece of dough cake in his mouth, chewing it until he could swallow, then stood up, flexing his muscles. He'd lost weight since they'd been on the march, but the muscles in his calves were still firm from all the riding, although there were times he'd walk just for the exercise.

Joaquín stood too, and was straightening his shirttail, tucking it into his pants, when Juan hurried up.

"Get your horses and follow me," he said quickly.

Cole and Joaquín untied Nevado and Compadre and led the horses away, following after Juan, who was making his way along the line of men, working his way away from the river toward the opposite end of the woods, gathering a procession of men and horses behind him as he went. Finally he stopped in front of Colonel Lamar, the man Houston had given Sherman's command to, and a short while later, as men began to form all down the line, infantry, regulars, and the like, Cole, Joaquín, and Juan found themselves mounted on their horses and staring out from among the stand of trees across the top of the knee-high grass of the plains toward where Santa Anna's men were camped, waiting for a signal to move forward.

Joaquín was nervous, his eyes squinting in the afternoon sun. Well, this was it, he thought. If he had to go, he'd rather go this way, with friends on each side, and he looked first to his right, to where Cole sat ramrod straight in the saddle, rifle butt resting on his knee, then to the left, where Juan sat, his dark eyes straight ahead, rifle also pointed upward.

Joaquín drew his eyes from the two men, made sure his own rifle was ready, finger on the trigger, and winced, fighting the reins for a few seconds as Compadre became skittish.

"Whoa, boy, whoa," he soothed, then leaned forward, whispered softly in the horse's ear, "Soon it will be over, mi amigo. Then we shall go home."

He straightened again as Lamar came riding along the line checking, making sure everything was in order, and still they sat. The waiting was horrendous. Sweat ran down Joaquín's neck, making his shirt stick to his back, and still they waited. He hadn't been able to find a hat, and the sun made him squint as he sat listening, trying to hear what was going on further up the line. It was impossible to see through because of the leaves on the trees and all the underbrush. There was nothing he could do except wait, and waiting was nerve-racking.

His hands grew clammy, mouth dry, as again Lamar rode past, giving a few words of encouragement here and there and trying to keep the more restless from breaking ranks.

Finally, after what seemed like an interminable time, Lamar eased his horse to a stop at the front of the line of men and waited. This was it, thought Joaquín, and he swallowed hard, jaw set in determination.

Joaquín guessed it must have been close to four o'clock when Lamar gave the signal, and each man, nudging his horse in the ribs, slowly began to move forward. The sun was hot, breeze still blowing off the river, and Joaquín felt it catch a wavy strand of his hair, flicking it onto his forehead, yet he ignored it.

Somewhere in the distance he could hear a drumroll, and the incongruous strains of a song he'd often heard played at the dances and fandangos back in San Antonio. The drum was loud, fife shrill, as the strains of "Come to the Bower I Have Shaded for You" mingled with the creak of saddles and thud of horses' hooves as they moved along. It was an eerie tune, as if Houston were mocking Santa Anna with his invitation. Joaquín's knuckles on his left hand were white as he held the reins.

They rode down a shallow ravine, dusty and dry in spite of the rain the day before, and yet no man broke ranks. Joaquín had no idea whether the cavalry were the only ones moving, or if the infantry was also on the march, because his gaze was shifting alternately from Lamar, to the route his horse was taking, and back to Lamar again, glimpsing only occasionally what lay ahead.

They had just passed the ravine, some sixty men on horseback, moving stealthily through the tall grass now, when suddenly Joaquín felt a chill run down his spine as a sentry somewhere yelled.

"Sentinela, alerta! Sentinela, alerta!"

They'd been seen, and as quickly as the Mexican's shout filled the air, the Mexican infantry and artillery started firing, only their aim was too high, the cannon-balls crashing into the trees behind Joaquín, while the musket balls fell short.

As the enemy cannon continued to fire, Joaquín heard the answering fire from their own cannon, and from the yelling, he knew the enemy was scattering. Still the horses kept moving forward, rifles at attention, and Joaquín could hear no other rifles except those of the enemy.

When? he thought, as a cannonball zoomed overhead. When would Lamar give the signal? But there was still no answer, only the constant drumming and incessant music. Lamar had given strict orders that no one was to shoot until he ordered it, and Joaquín was certain he was going to die before General Houston had Lamar signal his men.

Suddenly Joaquín's palomino broke stride, as did some of the other horses, when a rider tore across the field from the direction of the road to Vince's Bridge, and Joaquín fought to get Compadre quieted down as he heard Deaf Smith yelling that Vince's Bridge was down. His startling announcement was followed closely by a couple of stray shots from somewhere, then seconds later Houston's voice was heard above the clatter of horses, men, and cannon, warning the men not to shoot, to hold their fire and stay low. Still the line of cavalry kept slowly moving forward.

Finally, when Joaquín was certain they'd end up riding right through Santa Anna's tents without having fired a shot, he heard the first volley from the infantry, then seconds later watched Lamar raise his arm. With rifles exploding all around him, and flanked by Cole on his white stallion and Juan on his sorrel, Joaquín spurred his palomino forward amid the frenzied shouts of "Remember Goliad!" and "Remember the Alamo!" The charge was on.

10

It hadn't rained for at least two days, and the ground had dried out enough so that dust was settling on Catalina's black skirt as she and Tío Antonio rode along in the small buggy. She wished now he'd used the big carriage and had a driver, at least then she wouldn't have to put up with the powdery dirt. Tío Antonio was even walking the horse, but it didn't help much. April was almost over, and she was glad she wouldn't have to wear black much longer. It'd be a year this coming Saturday, April 30, since her father had died, and the mourning would be over. At least as far as outward appearances were concerned. Actually she'd always mourn his passing.

Glancing over at her uncle, she straightened the bonnet on her head, disgusted that she'd been forced to wear it, and sighed. She hated bonnets, and would rather wear her mantilla, but naturally mantillas couldn't keep the sun off in an open buggy. Her eyes snapped irritably.

She hadn't even wanted to come along, but Tío Antonio had insisted it was time she saw what the soldiers had done to their beautiful town. Santa Anna had taken most of the soldiers with him on his drive north, but there was no way anyone could deny they had been there. The once-lovely homes that had belonged to many of Antonio's friends had been used to house some of the soldiers, and they'd taken little care to keep them nice. Food and supplies had been confiscated from shopkeepers with little thought to payment if money wasn't available, and the memory of Santa Anna's storming of the old mission at the edge of town was still uppermost in everyone's mind.

Because of this, tension was at a peak. Even those who had welcomed the Mexican general's arrival at first had sighed with relief when he'd moved on, and when General Cós and the rest left to reinforce Santa Anna's troops, leaving only a small garrison behind, the sighs of relief were even more pronounced.

Then two days ago, word had filtered back to them that Houston's troops had defeated Santa Anna up near the San Jacinto River, and the Mexican troops were already heading south again for the Rio Grande. At first Don Antonio hadn't believed it, but just yesterday he and Braxton had ridden in close enough to town and saw the first Mexican soldiers coming down from the north, and they watched from the rolling hills on the outskirts of town as the soldiers passed through, one regiment after another. Tired, weary, and belligerent because they weren't returning as victors.

Now, with most of the soldiers already aware of Santa Anna's defeat, Don Antonio had decided it was time Catalina quit defending them so highly. He'd told her that perhaps if she saw the reactions of the other townfolk to their presence, it'd help persuade her. So here they were on their way home now from a dull and boring journey she didn't even care to be on.

Even though the rumored battle had ended the fighting some five days ago, on the twenty-first, soldiers were still pouring down the roads toward the river some were claiming was now the new borderline between Mexico and what most folks were already calling the Republic of Texas, even though no definite orders on the matter had come from anyone. However, Don Antonio had been assured by the soldiers he'd talked to that the rumors of the battle were true, and pretending to still be neutral about the matter in hopes of learning anything that might help, he had ridden from the town as peacefully as he'd arrived.

"So, now are you convinced the war is over?" he asked Catalina as they rode along under the late-afternoon sun.

She looked at him in disgust. "Perhaps your Texans think it is over, but I will bet those soldiers we saw did not think so." She smiled smugly. "That officer I was talking to just before we left said he imagines they will reorganize again once across the river. After all, he said there are hundreds of soldiers who never even reached Texas Territory."

"I see. And that is what you would want? You learned nothing from the Alamo or any of the rest of it?"

"I learned that your Texans are stubborn, sí," she answered. "I learned they would rather die than admit they were wrong."

"Catalina! Catalina! What am I going to do with you?" His hands tightened on the reins as he maneuvered the buggy around some ruts in the road that were so deep they were still tacky from the previous rains. "How old are you now, Catalina?" he asked.

Her chin tilted proudly. "You know I was fifteen on the twenty-eighth of March."

"That's right, you are fifteen. And do you not think at the tender age of fifteen that perhaps you are not quite qualified to know the difference between good government and bad?"

"Ha!" Her dark eyes blazed furiously. "You call what is going on now a government?" she asked. "Tío Antonio, there wasn't one person back in town who seemed to even know where the men who are supposed to control your Texas government are. And you call it a government?"

"You are impossible, young lady, and you know it," he answered bitterly. "Since you hadn't been in town for so long, I was hoping perhaps a visit might help you to change your mind, but you and your brother are like two peas in a pod. I only hope he was not one of those lying on the battlefield up near Lynchburg. For if he was, I'm afraid there'll be no living with you."

"If he died, then he died for his country, Tío," she answered, but there were tears in her eyes. "Mexico will always be our country, no matter what!"

Don Antonio exhaled disgustedly. He'd never known anyone quite so stubborn, and with a flick of the reins he set the buggy at a faster pace, hoping the bumps they were bouncing over would purge some of the sassiness out of her; while a short distance ahead, in the hills to the north, two lone riders, tired and weary, yet pleased at being so close to home, were making their way down a long, rather steep hill.

Cole turned to Joaquín beside him and frowned. "You're not still worried about our leaving, are you?" he asked.

Joaquín thought for a minute as he reined Compadre around a small tree, then moved closer to Cole. "No, Señor Dante. At first I thought perhaps we should wait until the whole matter of Santa Anna was settled. But as you say, they are probably still arguing over what to do with him."

"And getting nowhere," Cole assured him. "Hell, the men were never really any kind of regular army anyway, at least you weren't, and I figure my job was over. Let the politicians do the rest. Besides, I've got a barn to build, and I can't do it if I'm sitting up north wet-nursing Santa Anna and his men." Cole grinned. "One thing I discovered about the Texas volunteers when I first joined, Joaquín, is there's no such thing as desertion. They just call it going home," and he urged Nevado a bit faster toward the bottom of the hill as he spotted a swirl of dust in the distance along where he knew the road was. "Come on, let's go see if it's somebody we know," and now both men spurred their horses a little faster. Reaching the foot of the hill, they started across the plain, traversed by the rutted road, keeping their horses at a steady pace.

Neither rider looked anything like he had barely a few days back. Before leaving the battlefield up north, Cole and Joaquín had plundered some fairly decent clothes from the enemy officers' well-filled trunks, they had shaved, Joaquín leaving a mustache, both had trimmed their hair, and they looked half-decent for a change, their white breeches and matching silk shirts a contrast to the fancy black vests and boots they had on. Even Cole's old worn hat had been relinquished, and both men wore sombreros they'd found along the way, so they were a strange sight as they rode along with the afternoon sun so bright one had to lift a hand to shade the eyes in order to see.

"What's this!" Antonio exclaimed as he began to slow the buggy, his thoughts no longer on his niece as he watched the two riders approaching from the hills to the north, and he reached for the rifle he always carried with him.

"Tío!"

"Calm down, Catalina," he cautioned her as the horse began to falter, slowing considerably. "It need not be anything to worry about."

"But who?" One hand was up against the rim of her bonnet, shading her eyes. "Who would be riding way out here?"

"It could be Brax, or someone from the Crown D."

"Or it could be Indians too!" she cried breathlessly.

The buggy was barely moving now, and suddenly Antonio took a deep breath, pulling it to a stop.

"Well, I'll be damned," he blurted as he recognized the riders, and a frown creased his forehead. "What are they doing here, and together?"

Joaquín and Cole had recognized the driver of the buggy about the same time he'd recognized them, and Joaquín glanced over at Cole, realizing he too knew who it was.

"How do I tell Tío Antonio what happened?" he asked as they drew closer.

"You mean about changing sides?"

"Sí."

"I wouldn't worry about him if I were you. It'll be that sister of yours who'll need an explanation, and I doubt anything you say will have any effect, unless she's done a lot of changing herself since you've been gone."

They were approaching the buggy at a loping canter now, and Cole raised a hand in greeting. "Don Antonio!"

Both men reined to a halt only a few feet from the buggy, while its two occupants continued to stare at them dumbfounded.

"Well, you could say something," Joaquín said, his face flushing self-consciously. "We are not ghosts, you know."

Antonio's eyes were on Joaquín, as were Catalina's, and still the silence was all too heavy.

"I am sorry, Joaquín," Antonio finally said, hoping to make his nephew feel better. "But someone has to lose in a war. I am just glad you were not hurt." Suddenly he frowned. "But tell me, how is it you are here? We heard that all of Santa Anna's men are prisoners, along with the general."

"Because I was not with Santa Anna," Joaquín answered, and saw the wary look in his sister's eyes. "You see, I fought beside Señor Dante and Juan Seguin, with General Houston's cavalry."

"You what?" Catalina shouted, suddenly coming to life.

Joaquín rode closer to the buggy. So close he could have touched her if he'd leaned over, and he gazed down into her face. "You heard the first time, Catalina," he answered. "In fact, I was the one who told Señor Houston where Santa Anna was, that he hadn't continued on to Galveston, but was hoping to attack the Texans near Lynchburg."

"You? But why?"

"Because I discovered what kind of a man he is, that's why."

"You mean you discovered what they wanted you to believe," she cried. "Don't you understand that?" She shook her head. "I was proud of you, fighting for our country, Joaquín, a true patriot, and now you . . . I am ashamed to call you my brother!"

"Then don't," he snapped back. "Only remember, Catalina, one day you'll grow up and find out things are not just simply black and white, and that loyalty is not blind, but must be deserved."

Catalina took a deep breath, her eyes dark and hateful, as she looked away from her brother to where Cole sat his horse, watching.

"I suppose you are proud of yourself, are you not, Señor Dante?" she said, her voice unsteady. "But I will warn you, as I have told Tío Antonio and anyone else who cares to listen. You Texans may claim your freedom now, but as far as I am concerned this land will always be a part of Mexico, as I am a part of Mexico, and no one will ever convince me otherwise."

"So, are you going to welcome me home regardless?" Joaquín asked, trying to ignore her hostility as best he could. "Or will you be stubborn and pretend you no longer have a brother because he doesn't agree with everything you do?"

Catalina's lips pursed, and she wanted so much to vent her anger on him, to pound her fists against his chest and punish him for betraying their country, yet as she stared into his face, the familiar green eyes boring into hers, she knew she could never hate Joaquín. He was too much a part of her, and tears filled her eyes.

"Yes, I will welcome you home," she answered, her voice breaking. "And I am glad you are not hurt, but there is one thing I will not do."

"Oh?"

"I will not congratulate you!"

"Well, I will," Antonio said boisterously. "And I am proud of you, Joaquín." He stood up as best he could, and reached across to shake hands with Joaquín, who leaned over, grasping his uncle's hand firmly.

"Gracias, Tío Antonio," Joaquín answered, then released his hand and looked back at Cole, while Antonio sat back down. "Well, it appears I am home, señor," Joaquín said as he leaned back lazily in the saddle. "But if you wish me to go the rest of the way with you . . . ?"

Cole shook his head. "No need," he said. "I could use some time alone to think." His hands tightened on Nevado's reins, and the big white stallion tossed his head impatiently. "But remember, you promised me an extra hand with a hammer, amigo, right?"

Joaquín grinned. "Sí, and remember what else we talked of . . . I will hold you to your promise also, señor."

Ah yes, Teffin, Cole thought as he remembered their conversation that day by the bayou. "As I said before," he assured the young Mexican, "you are welcome anytime, Joaquín. Now I'll be on my way. Antonio, Señorita

de Alvarado . . . and I shall see you soon, amigo, right?"
and he turned, waving, and rode ahead of them, spurring
his horse into a gallop, knowing he was nearing the fork
in the road that led northward, on the last leg home.

It had been warm all day. Teffin and Helene had been
doing some quilting, and had brought the quilting frame
outside under the trees since it was so stuffy in the house.

"It's cool here," Teffin said as she worked on the
stitches, crossing a patch of calico that had been part of a
dress she'd once had. "I feel sorry for Mother out in the
hot sun with Eli and Shem."

Helene glanced over at Cole's daughter, realizing as
she had these past few months that Teffin was really
growing into a lovely young woman. Strange, though,
how she didn't seem to resemble either of her parents.
Her eyes were an unusual topaz color. Cole's were green,
Heather's violet. And even her hair was the color of pale
honey, with golden highlights to it. So different from
Heather's fiery locks and Cole's dark ones. But then
Helene was glad Teffin didn't look like her mother, otherwise she probably wouldn't have grown to love the girl
as if she were her own daughter. And she was glad Teffin
didn't look like Cole either. It was bad enough seeing
him every day and knowing he belonged to someone
else. If his daughter had looked like him, she'd never be
able to be around her so much without being reminded,
and hurting even more.

"Your mother seems to enjoy riding out with the men,"
she said as she watched Teffin busily working the tiny
stitches. "You'd think now, with some of the men drifting back, she'd stay at the house."

"I think she does it to keep her mind off Pa."

"Perhaps."

They worked quietly for a few minutes longer, the only
sound their breathing, the occasional call of a bird nearby,
and Bessie's voice floating out the window as she sang
while she worked inside the house.

Helene drew her eyes from the quilt and looked up at
the horizon. The sun was getting low in the sky. That

meant Heather and the men would be coming in from the range soon. Sometimes she wished Heather wouldn't come back, that she'd be hurt out there, but then she wasn't supposed to think that way, was she? You weren't supposed to hate anyone. Isn't that what her mother always said? But how did you tell your heart not to hate when it was denied fulfillment? How many years she'd loved Cole, and she reached up self-consciously, fingering the unusual beads he'd given her those long years ago for her thirteenth birthday. She'd been wearing them ever since he'd left for the fighting, promising herself not to take them off until he came home.

Slowly her gaze wandered from the horizon in the west, back over to the burned-out barn, then on to the road out front. Suddenly she hesitated, staring at a swirl of dust off in the distance, and she tensed, since few people ever rode this far from town.

"There's a rider coming," she said.

Teffin looked up, then squinted, trying to see if it was more than one, then frowned as a lone figure was revealed against the cloud of dust he was stirring up.

"Whoever it is, he's coming fast," Teffin answered, and stuck her needle into the material. Standing up quickly, she was just ready to run for the house when she saw the rider was astride a big white horse. "Pa!" she cried, and started jumping up and down.

Right away Helene knew she was right. "Oh, my God!"

"Pa! It is Pa," Teffin continued yelling. "And Ma's not even home!" Teffin didn't even wait for Helene, but took off at a run toward the road, holding up her skirt all the say.

Cole was at least a quarter-mile away yet when he caught sight of Teffin, and his heart skipped a beat. Already Nevado was at full gallop, and he wasn't sure he could get anything more out of the stallion, still he tried. When he was almost there, he reined up, then leapt from the saddle and met Teffin with outstretched arms.

"Oh, Pa!" she sighed as her arms went around his neck and she held him close. "I was hoping. Oh how I was hoping you'd get home soon."

Teffin felt so soft and supple in his arms, and after holding her close for a few minutes, Cole drew back, grabbed her face in his hands, kissed her on both cheeks, then stared down at her, marveling at how pretty she looked in her calico dress.

"Don't you look lovely!" he exclaimed, his warm green eyes boring into hers, then he looked surprised. "But you've changed, grown up more."

Teffin flushed. "Don't be silly, you haven't been gone that long."

"It seems like years instead of months." His hands dropped from her face to the shoulders of her pink calico dress, and he gazed off behind her toward the house. "Your mother?" he asked.

"Mom's out on the range."

Suddenly he smiled. "I don't think so," he said, and she saw his gaze shift from the house to the trail way back beyond the corrals, to where some riders were just starting to work their way down to the back corrals.

Heather, Eli, Shem, and some of the men who'd been slowly drifting back the past few days were tired from the heat and dust, and Heather, who was in the lead, was trying to figure out where she was going to get money to buy herself a new pair of boots, since hers had gone through on the bottom this afternoon. She gazed off beyond the house toward the road out front, her thoughts miles away, then suddenly reined up as she realized someone was standing in the road talking to Teffin, and he was standing beside a white horse.

Pulling her hat down some to shade the late-afternoon sun in order to see better, she suddenly inhaled, then let out a cry that brought her companions up short, and while they watched curiously, she spurred her horse forward into a gallop and took off down the lane between the corrals, heading past the house.

Helene's heart sank as she heard Heather cry out, and she watched Heather riding frantically, trying to reach Cole. Helene's mouth pursed bitterly. She'd been so hoping, but now, with Heather home, Cole would hardly say two words to her, as always. She just knew it. It was as if she didn't even exist when Heather was around. It was only when Helene happened to catch Cole alone that he seemed to forget who she was and treated her differently. Of course he'd never told her he cared, but he had to, otherwise why did he always remember her birthday? And the beads. She fingered them again, and her eyes grew misty as she watched Heather reach Cole and Teffin.

Cole was as anxious as Heather was, and he reached out, grabbing her horse's bridle as Heather pulled back on the reins, then he caught her in his arms as she left the animal's back, his booted feet churning up the dust as he twirled and looked down into her face. As he tightened his hold on her, Heather's hat fell back, resting behind her head, and Cole drank in her crimson hair, tanned face, and weary smile.

"Oh, God, how I've missed you," he murmured.

There were tears in her eyes. "Me too." They both laughed. "I mean I missed you too," she explained. "And I was afraid you wouldn't come home."

"Oh, love!" Cole's mouth came down on hers, warm and caressing, and for a few moments they were both oblivious of Teffin standing only a few feet away, or the others who were watching from the house. When the kiss finally ended, Cole drew his head back, then glanced over at Teffin, her face slightly flushed. "I've got good news for you too, young lady," he said, then his hand came up, touching Heather's face lovingly, and he gazed down into her eyes again. "Only first, I want your mother to know that I hope with all my heart I'll never have to leave her again," and he kissed her once more, a light kiss this time that seemed to seal his words on her heart, then they grabbed their horses' reins, and holding hands, with Teffin leading the way, while she walked backward so she wouldn't have to take her eyes off her parents, they all traversed the last few hundred feet to the house.

Teffin had been full of questions all the way, and by the time they reached the others, Cole had already told her about Joaquín's change of heart and the part he'd played in the victory they'd won over Santa Anna. That evening, after a joyous welcome home from everyone else at the Crown D, for the first time in months Cole fell asleep with his head on a soft pillow and Heather in his arms, and the next morning woke up to a new day, with no more bloodshed staring him in the face. For Cole Dante and the rest of his family, the war was over, and slowly now, as each new day dawned, life on the Texas frontier began to take on a semblance of what it had been before the war came along to change it.

Bain's wounds, which had kept him home from the fighting at San Jacinto, had finally healed, leaving him with a bad leg, necessitating the use of a cane. However, he could still ride a horse, and spent hours in the saddle, reluctantly leaving the roping and branding to Braxton and the younger men. But he was still boss, and under his guidance the Double K once more began to prosper, as did the Crown D now that Cole was home and in charge.

Spring had always been roundup time, and now, this year was no different, although it started later than usual. And after a few weeks they even started building the barn at the Crown D back up again. It was slow, tedious work at first, however, because the logs had to be cut farther north, where there was timber available, and hauled all the way to the ranch. And there were no lumber mills in this part of Texas either yet, so once again, instead of using finished wood, as they'd have done if building back east, the barn went up using split logs, as Cole had done the first time. While everyone was trying as hard as possible to get life back to normal again, Don Antonio, after frequent visits to San Antonio, San Felipe, and Washington on the Brazos, kept them informed on the formation of the new government of what was now being officially called the new Republic of Texas.

However, out here, in the rolling hills where the threat of Comanche raids was far more important to everyone than what Houston and Austin were doing, and where life was controlled by weather and work rather than meetings and legislation, all anyone cared about was that they were free to live the lives they'd always wanted to live, without being forced to bow to a government that wanted to enslave them or run them out. So little attention was paid to politics anymore, except that everyone would be there when it was time to vote.

It was the second week in June already. The first section of split logs for the new barn had finally been set in place, and they were waiting for the hands to bring a new load down from up north. Joaquín had begun spending a great deal of time at the Crown D shortly after his arrival home, and now Teffin sat on the front steps of the house, remembering last Saturday when he'd come over and helped put the logs in place. He'd stayed for supper that evening, and afterward they'd taken a walk back beyond the corrals and bunkhouse to where the trail led partway up the hill, and they'd sat for a long time on an old log, until it was almost dark, watching everything going on down here at the house.

Teffin liked talking to Joaquín. It seemed as if they had so much in common. They both loved horses, and much to Teffin's surprise, Joaquín even knew how to read English, as well as Spanish. Something a great many Texans couldn't even do. One thing both Ma and Aunt Liz were always emphatic about was schooling, and Teffin imagined Grandma Dicia was really at the back of it all. There were two things in Teffin's family that were always expected. One was to be educated, and the other was that neither the men nor the women ever chewed or rubbed snuff. That too they always credited to Grandma Dicia, who'd always considered the habit a nasty one, and had instilled the same sentiments in her children and grandchildren. And although Don Antonio had begun smoking cigarettes some years back, neither Joaquín nor Catalina had ever taken up the practice. Many Mexican children did smoke, though, and Teffin was glad Joaquín didn't.

The only thing bothering her about her friendship with Joaquín now, however, was that she was afraid he was growing too serious, and she just wasn't all that sure of her feelings toward him.

It was early afternoon, she was sitting now on the front steps, leaning back against the post that held up the roof over the veranda, staring off down the road, trying to analyze those feelings, when she frowned, a speck of swirling dust in the distance letting her know there was a rider on the road. The rider was some distance away yet, but it was unusual to see anyone on the road this time of day. At least anyone who had any business being there. It was only a few hours after lunch and all the men, including Joaquín and her father, were still out on the range.

Straightening, with one hand over her eyes in the hopes she could see better, she fixed her eyes on the rider, watching intently as he approached, and as he drew nearer, she could see he was riding a black mare with a white blaze on her forehead. The rider's clothes were those of a cowhand, although they were also black, including his hat and shirt, and he rode easily in the saddle, as if it were a part of him. When he was only a couple hundred feet from the house, Teffin figured he must have seen her too, because she saw him suddenly shift into a different position and flick the reins, the horse breaking into an easy canter as they rode between the wooden posts on each side of the drive, then he reined up at the end of the front walk as Teffin stood up and took a few steps toward him.

The rider took off his hat, and Teffin could see his face now, the sun on it full. He looked to be perhaps twenty or so, with blue-green eyes, dark wavy hair, and the most incredible pair of dimples she'd ever seen on a man, yet the bronzed skin and small scar on his left cheek, as well as the intense look in those blue-green eyes, let her know the smile he was bestowing on her was a rarity.

"How do, ma'am," he drawled, and for a second Teffin didn't know what to say. There was something about him. The eyes, the way he smiled. And his voice was so low and vibrant, it almost made her shiver. Yet he wasn't really handsome. Not in a pretty way anyway. "You live here, I presume?" he asked.

She nodded.

"Your pa home?"

"No . . . no, he's not here, but Ma is," she added quickly, finally finding her voice.

He glanced back toward the corrals and bunkhouse, then over to what would someday be the finished barn, then back to Teffin again.

"Where is your pa?" he asked.

She hesitated for a second. "What do you want him for?"

"Well, I reckon that's my business, don't you?"

"Maybe." She stared at him, then flushed as she felt his eyes sift over her from head to toe, then they seemed to soften as they caught hers, and held.

"Look, sorry if I came on a bit strong there, but the name's Kaelen, and I'm lookin' for a job. They told me in town your pa could use some help."

Teffin was surprised. Kaelen—the name fit him for some reason. She was glad he wasn't Will or James or some other common name. This time she smiled back, only it was a provocative smile she couldn't quite seem to control, and her eyes twinkled.

"Whyn't you say so in the first place," she said. "He's out on the range, won't be back until just before dark. Only I wouldn't bother him out there if I were you. Leastways I doubt you'd find him, since I imagine you don't know your way around. I could show you, though, if you want."

He studied her thoughtfully for a second. "No need," he answered, relaxing some in the saddle. "I guess I can wait until he rides in. That is if you and your family don't mind. Besides, I could use a cold drink."

Teffin was just ready to ask him in the house when Mose, who'd been repairing a latch on the gate to one of the corrals out back, joined her. He'd seen the stranger ride up.

"Miss Teffin, there somethin' I can help you with?" he asked.

Teffin blushed, knowing it was Mose's way of watching over her. "This is Kaelen, Mose," she said, introducing the black man to Kaelen, and as Kaelen stretched out his hand, his leg swung over the saddle, and he slid to the ground.

"Mose," he confirmed, and his hand gripped the other's firmly. "Glad to meet you, Mose."

Mose's eyes narrowed slightly as he felt the firm handshake, yet there was something about the young man . . . he couldn't quite put his finger on it but . . . he almost looked familiar, especially around the eyes, and he was so tall.

"He's lookin' for a job," Teffin explained as Mose released Kaelen's hand.

Mose took in the young man's scuffed boots and well-worn clothes. "You been ridin' far?" he asked.

"Too far. Figured I'd light a spell."

"Well, I'll tell you," Mose said as he glanced at Kaelen's hands, "I could use a hand out back till the boys gets back, if you'd care to help me, and you can ask the boss when he rides in."

Kaelen looked pleased. "Sounds right nice to me," he answered. "If the young lady thinks her pa won't mind."

"Mose always handles the men when Pa isn't around," she said. "If he says it's all right, then it's all right."

Mose winked at Teffin, the bushy side whiskers at his jawline bunching up as his mouth widened in a grin. "You'd better go tell Bessie there'll be one more for supper down at the bunkhouse tonight, Tef," he said. "And tell your ma I finished fixing that bridle for her half an hour ago if she still wants to go ridin'."

Kaelen studied the young woman this black man had called Teffin, and a sadness filled him. She was so lovely, her eyes such an unusual color, and for a brief moment he wished he hadn't decided to come to the Crown D. Then, as he drew his eyes from her face and looked over to the house, the outbuildings, and the land surrounding it, before looking back at her again, he knew he'd had no other choice.

"You name's Teffin?" he asked.

"Yes, Teffin Dante," she answered. "And you're Kaelen what?"

"Just Kaelen," he answered, then turned to Mose.

"Now, where's that work you said you had?" he asked. "Even if your boss doesn't hire me, at least it should be enough for a free meal."

"You'll tell Bessie?" Mose asked.

Teffin nodded, then watched the man named Kaelen grab his horse's reins and follow Mose, walking off toward the back corral, his long, lean frame moving easily.

"Who's that?" Heather asked a few minutes later when Teffin reached the porch again and her mother came out.

"Says his name's Kaelen. He's looking for a job."

"He know how to break horses?"

"I didn't ask. Neither'd Mose, but he's going to help Mose until Pa comes home, and see what he says."

Heather frowned. "You know your father could use another hand, Teffin," she said. "A lot of the men haven't come back yet, and I'm wondering if they ever will."

"I know." Teffin smiled impishly. "Besides, he's good-looking, Ma. Did you notice? And he's got the biggest dimples."

"And he's no doubt a drifter too, so don't get your hopes up. He'll probably never stay in the same place long enough to break in a bed." She put an arm about her daughter's shoulder. "Did Mose say whether he had my bridle fixed yet?"

"Oh, yes, he finished it half an hour ago."

"Good, then I'll ride out to meet your pa when it's time."

"May I go too?" she asked. "It's so boring around here again now, with Pa home. I wish you could talk him into letting me help work the horses again. I really liked it."

"I know you did. So did I, but he says the mistress of the Crown D isn't going to end up looking like a cow-hand, and I guess maybe he's right. The calluses on my hands are nearly gone now, and I must admit they were rather ugly."

"But, oh, Ma, wasn't it fun watching the horses cut out a calf or work the end of a rope, knowing you were the one who taught them. It's so much more fun than just shelling peas and sewing."

"But far more dangerous. Your pa's right, Tef, but you can ride out with me if you want to. I'll be leaving at the usual time."

Teffin nodded, then left her mother on the porch, while she went into the kitchen to tell Bessie there'd be one more for dinner down at the bunkhouse.

All the hired hands ate at the bunkhouse, but Bessie cooked their food. At least for now. Cole had promised her that as soon as he could, he'd put a stove up in the bunkhouse and hire a cook just for the men, since he was planning to hire more hands than he'd had before. He said he figured Bessie was doing enough already just with what she had to do at the house, and now, with the war over he was planning to see about opening new markets for his horses, meaning he'd have to have more men.

So later that afternoon, after Teffin and Heather rode out to meet him, telling him about the young man who'd shown up that afternoon, Cole had readily hired Kaelen, even though Joaquín had been skeptical since Kaelen wasn't willing to tell anyone his last name. But then, as Cole told himself later, Joaquín had no doubt noticed the enthusiastic way Teffin was talking about the young man, and Joaquín's suggestion that Cole might be better off not hiring the stranger could be prejudiced by more than a suspicion that Kaelen was running from something. Besides, he'd told Joaquín, half the people in Texas were running from something or someone.

So the next morning, when Joaquín rode over to the Crown D to ride out with Cole and his men, the new hand rode along with them, and as Teffin watched from the house, sitting upstairs in the empty guestroom where she knew she'd have a good view and not be noticed, all she could remember was the unusual light in the new hand's eyes, and the warm smile he'd given her when they'd first met.

The summer seemed to be going too fast for Teffin. Here it was well past the Fourth of July already, and even though they didn't celebrate it here in Texas, Grandma always made sure they never forgot it.

Kaelen had been at the Crown D for over a month already, and during that time Teffin had managed to be alone with him so few times it had begun to be a game with her. Always it seemed like someone else would be there. In the evening and on weekends it was Joaquín, the rest of the time it was Mose, Shem, Eli, or one of the other hands. However, she often found herself alone with Joaquín, a fact that wasn't helping at all because she knew now after meeting Kaelen that Joaquín was only a dear, lovable friend, and would always stay only a dear, lovable friend. But Kaelen . . .

Every time she ran into him, her heart danced outrageously and her stomach felt like it was full of butterflies. At first she tried to ignore the things she was feeling, telling herself it was just because they lived so far from civilization and she rarely met anyone new. But after three other men showed up and were hired, as well as someone who had worked for Cole before, and not one of them made any kind of impression on her, she began to admit the truth. She was falling madly in love for the first time in her life.

Only she never said a word to anyone, not even Blythe. And she was sure Kaelen was beginning to feel the same way about her too. He had to be. Because every time they met, whether they were alone or anyone was around, she could feel his eyes on her, the depth of emotion she saw in them almost frightening in its intensity. Yet the few times they had been alone, he'd said nothing. No indication whatsoever that he cared. But a woman knows. A woman always knew. Mother had been right when she told her she'd know when the right man came along, and she'd known it for sure last night.

Last night she'd said good-bye to Joaquín, then instead of coming right in, she had walked over by where the new barn was going up, not knowing Kaelen was inside looking the place over. It was dark out already, and the moon was up, Joaquín having left rather late. Something he was prone to do a lot lately. And Joaquín had even kissed her good-bye. A kiss he'd seemed to enjoy, but a kiss that had left her feeling empty inside.

At first when she'd run into Kaelen in the barn, he'd acted quite impersonal, but after a few minutes he'd asked if Joaquín was her steady beau.

"He thinks he is," she'd told him, and she'd sworn he had frowned, but there was no way she could prove it. They'd talked a little while longer, about a lot of different things, then started to leave the place, heading for the house, when she had tripped on a chunk of wood someone had left in the way, and Kaelen had caught her, breaking her fall. At first she'd tried to brush his arms away, but as he held her close, looking down into her eyes, for a minute she'd been so sure he'd been going to kiss her, and she quit struggling. But instead, after staring at her for the longest time with the moon falling on her face, all he'd done was take a deep breath, close his eyes for a brief moment, as if fighting a battle within himself, then tell her to go on into the house.

Teffin hadn't wanted to let go of him. She hadn't wanted to leave, but when he'd opened his eyes again, looking into hers, his expression had suddenly been so cold and unfeeling it was frightening. All the warmth that had been there only moments before had disappeared, and as she thought back over it now, on her way to the corral to get her horse, she was still as puzzled as she had been last night.

When she reached the corral, it took Mose only a few minutes to catch her mare and saddle her, and as Teffin sat astride in the special skirt she'd made so she wouldn't have to wear her father's old pants, since she didn't like riding sidesaddle anymore, and maneuvered the roan off toward the back of the barn to the trail leading to the Double K, she sighed. Maybe she'd only been imagining what had happened last night, making more out of it than it was, and yet . . . Letting the hat fall from her head so the wind would blow through her hair, she lifted her head thoughtfully and set Jubilee at an easy trot. She was going to have to think this over, and there was no better way to work the kinks out of your mind than a long hard ride.

She had told Ma she was going to go see Blythe, but had never intended to go near the Double K. Instead, a good half-mile onto the trail that led there, she reined her little mare, Jubilee, onto another trail heading southwest toward the pond in the quiet glade where she and her cousins often spent Sunday afternoons. It was quite a distance from even the Double K, but she was sure it'd be all right. After all, she'd been there alone before a number of times.

It was so quiet and peaceful in the glade this afternoon when she finally rode in, and she dismounted slowly, then tied Jubilee to a nearby tree, leaving the reins low enough so the mare could nibble. She needed this time to think, some time to herself, and there just wasn't any at the house. She was wearing the white shirtwaist she usually wore with her dark blue suit, and she tucked it in at the waist of the buckskin skirt she had on. What a grand idea it had been to make the skirt, she thought as she glanced down at it. She and Ma had each made one, and they were so comfortable, they'd decided they were going to make more. After all, Blythe wore them all the time, and no one complained. Checking the buttons on the front of her shirtwaist, she made sure they were all still fastened, then sighed.

The afternoon was warm, and she fanned the top of the shirtwaist, letting the cool air in as she sat down on the log where she and Joaquín spent so much of their time, and she started to go over the past few weeks. She couldn't have been sitting there more than fifteen minutes when suddenly she heard the unmistakable beat of horses' hooves against the earth, and voices carried to her from somewhere close by.

Quickly, without taking time to gauge where the voices were coming from, or how close they might be, she jumped up, ran to Jubilee, untied her, and led the mare hurriedly off toward the far end of the small glade to where a thick covering of vines made a natural screen beneath the trees, and she slipped behind them with the horse, just in time, her hand covering Jubilee's nose to keep her from nickering.

Standing motionless, her eyes squinting to see through a small break between the thick leaves of the wild-grape vines, Teffin held her breath, watching as between ten and fifteen Comanche rode into view. Her heart was pounding so loud she was certain they'd hear it, yet they were so intent on what they were talking about, they didn't seem to even care to look to see if anyone was around. If only she knew Comanche like her father and Brax, she'd be able to tell what they were saying. Whatever was going on, they were certainly excited.

Her eyes moved to the man who seemed to be their leader, and suddenly her heart sank. It was He Who Rides. It had to be. The description was too accurate, and besides, she'd gotten a good look at him that long-ago day last year when he and some warriors had attacked the Double K. Her gaze moved from his face, and now she felt a chill run down her spine. There were fresh scalps on his coup belt, blood still red on them. It was then she saw the fancy rug one of the braves was using on his horse instead of a blanket. She'd seen that same rug only two weeks ago when she and Ma were in San Antonio. One of the ranchers' wives a little further to the south had bought it to use in the parlor. Teffin's gaze wandered back to the scalps, and tears welled up in her eyes. One was salt-and-pepper gray, she was sure of it. She bit her lips to hold back the tears. The Sherwoods had been middle-aged, and Bain had warned them to find a place closer to town when they'd first moved here two years ago, because there were just the two of them. But they wouldn't listen.

For a long time she watched, then sighed, relieved when it looked like they were finally going to leave. Only instead of heading back toward Indian Territory, as she figured they would, evidently all keyed-up over one successful raid, they left, using the same trail she'd come in on, and she felt her heart skip a beat. That meant they were heading for the Crown D, and the only ones there besides Ma, Bessie, and Helene were Mose and two of the hands. Not enough to hold off that many Indians for very long. She stood for a minute pondering, then quickly climbed onto Jubilee and reined her out of the woodland glade into the afternoon sun, heading northwest. She'd circle around the Comanche and ride fast toward where her father had one of the line camps, hoping to find him and let him know the Comanche were heading toward the house and had already raided the Sherwoods'.

Teffin had been riding hard, and her mouth was dry, sweat running into her eyes. She patted her horse's neck affectionately. Poor Jubilee was tired too, only Teffin couldn't stop, not now. Suddenly she reined up at the sight of the two riders about half a mile ahead, just disappearing into an arroyo. Whipping Jubilee even faster, she threw all caution to the wind. By their silhouettes she was sure the men worked for her father, and she was proved right a few minutes later when Jubilee, grinding loose gravel, skidded to a stop in the sandy bed of the arroyo, and she yelled to Kaelen and Eli, who were riding up ahead.

Both men whirled their horses about, and seeing who it was, dug them in the sides, hurrying back to meet her.

"Thank God!" she cried when they were within earshot, then explained breathlessly when they reached her. "Eli, the Comanche are headed for the house, you gotta tell Pa. Where is he? He might be able to get there in time if he rides hard."

Eli turned to Kaelen. "He should still be near the river with the men. I'll head out there, you stay with Teffin," and before the younger man could even try to protest, Eli was heading down the dry arroyo and up the side to the northeast, toward where Cole and the men had been chasing a herd they'd seen earlier.

Kaelen watched him go, then looked at Teffin. "So now what do we do?" he asked.

"I imagine we head toward the line camp, since Pa'll probably head through there on his way to the house."

"Let's go then," he said, and breathing heavily, still winded from the long run, Teffin spurred Jubilee around, and they headed back up the side of the arroyo the way she had come.

"Where were you and Eli heading?" she yelled over as they galloped side by side, hoping to meet up with the rest of the men Eli'd gone after.

Kaelen glanced over at her. "We were following the tracks of a stallion that had separated from the others. Evidently he fought over the mares with another stallion and left the herd. The stallion we'd been following was hurt pretty bad."

"Oh! Well, I'm just glad you were there. I hope Eli finds Pa!"

"I'm sure he will. Now come on, let's quit talking and ride!" and with that he lay low on his horse's neck, and she followed suit, both of them giving their horses their heads.

At least five miles were behind them now as Teffin slowed her horse some and straightened in the saddle to maneuver Jubilee down the side of another steep hill. At first as she plunged over the side, the mare's footing was sure and steady, then suddenly Teffin felt Jubilee stumble, her leg slipping into a hole, and before Teffin even had time to get ready for it, her body left the saddle, and the next thing she knew she was flying through the air toward a pile of brush some ten feet away, right in the middle of the hill.

Her first instinct was to scream, but there wasn't even time, and hitting the ground, her head was snapped so hard she cringed, almost passing out. Shocks tore through her clear to her toes, then once the initial impact was over, she took a deep breath and opened her eyes. She'd shut them just before landing, and now, with her body still trembling from the fall, she glanced back up to see if Jubilee was all right, and sighed when she saw the horse, only frightened by the near-fall, go crashing the rest of the way down the hill riderless.

Exhaling angrily, she was just ready to yell a few nasty words to ease her humiliation, when suddenly her ears caught the sound of the rattlers, and she froze. Only it was too late. Horrified, every nerve in her body screaming, she watched transfixed as the snake, moving like lightning, sank his fangs deep into her thigh and right through the buckskin riding skirt she had on.

11

Kaelen had been halfway up the hill again when he heard her scream, and realizing the scream was one of fear, not pain, his gun was in his hand already as she slid from the saddle, climbing the last few yards on foot. By the time he reached her, Teffin had managed to find an old piece of a broken branch, and although tears were already flooding down her cheeks, she had a death grip on the stick, and was wielding it like a club, in case the rattler decided to strike again.

One shot was all Kaelen needed. Although the shot missed, it landed close enough to scare the snake off.

"Where'd he get you?" Kaelen asked as he watched the snake slither away, then holstered his gun and knelt down beside her.

Teffin was fighting back tears. "On the leg," and she pointed to a small spot, not quite on the outside of her right thigh, where two small damp holes were visible. The underbrush was scratching her, and she started to move.

"No, stay still," Kaelen cautioned. "The more you move, the faster it travels. In fact, I've got to stop it from going too far if I can."

Reaching up, he grabbed the bandanna from around his neck, ripped the leg of her skirt open, using a knife from the sheath on his gunbelt, then put the bandanna around her thigh, pulling it tight and tying it.

"Now I'm going to have to get you to the bottom of the hill as fast as I can," he said. "Then I've got to take care of that bite," and he reached out, not even waiting for an answer from her, picked her up in his arms, keeping her legs low, and carried her the rest of the way down the hill, slipping and sliding most of the way.

On reaching the bottom, he ran quickly to the shade of a small cottonwood nearby and set her down.

"Where are the horses?" she asked as she looked around, realizing they weren't in sight.

Kaelen glanced around, then quickly stood up, puzzled himself over the fact that neither horse was around. Then, as his gaze rested on the far end of the ravine they were in, he cursed softly as he saw the two saddled horses disappearing around a bend with the stray stallion he and Eli had been searching for.

"Looks like they decided to leave home," he said, then forgot them again as he knelt down and once more took out his knife. His gaze moved from her leg to her eyes. "You know what I have to do now, don't you?" he asked.

Teffin shuddered. "Oh, God!"

"Do you want to bite on something?"

"No." She ground her teeth, clenching them tightly, and shut her eyes, both hands doubled into fists. "Go ahead," she said, and felt him begin cutting away the rest of the skirt fabric, leaving her whole thigh bare.

It was a nasty bite, and Kaelen tensed, knowing there was no time to waste. The rattler had been an old one, and the fangs had gone deep. He looked at Teffin's face, her eyes closed, anticipating the pain, and he knew she had no idea how bad it was really going to be.

"Scream if you want, Tef," he said, his voice breaking, and she opened her eyes, looking into his, her own filled with fear.

"It's going to be that bad?"

He nodded. "I've got to cut deep."

She inhaled stubbornly, then exhaled, tensing. "All right, I'm ready," she said again, but he knew she wasn't, not really. Especially when he began the first cut, and her body went rigid, the pain bringing an agonized shriek to her lips.

One more quick cut, and he sheathed the knife, then

turned her partway on her side, so her thigh was easier to reach, and he set to work. While she lay there sobbing, her face pressed against the ground, he bent over, his mouth against the cuts, and began sucking out the blood as fast as he could, spitting it aside in the dirt. After keeping the rhythm up for a good fifteen minutes or so, making sure he'd gotten out all the poison it was possible to get, he sat back on his heels and finally looked at her face. The first he'd looked at her since the first cut.

"Is it over?" she asked as she stared back up at him. Her face was streaked with tears and dirt, and she looked so helpless.

He nodded. "I think so. How do you feel?"

"Terrible."

"Sick or what?"

"I feel like I'm going to throw up."

"Then go ahead."

She turned from him, leaning on her elbow, and lost part of her lunch. Wiping her hand across her mouth, she looked back at him. Kaelen was staring at her leg, no doubt wondering what to do next.

"Now what?" she asked.

"Now I've got to clean it somehow. If I had my horse, I'd have some water. The canteens are tied to the saddle."

"There's a spring a short way from here," she said, then flushed. "But I don't think I can walk."

"That's no problem. Where is it?"

"The horses were headed there."

He looked back down to the end of the ravine.

"It's just around the bend. I've been there a number of times with Pa."

"Then I guess that's where we go."

"You can't carry me all that way."

"Who says I can't?" He checked her leg, loosening the tourniquet a bit and noting that it was beginning to swell more, then put his arms beneath her and picked her up. "You're light as a feather," he said. "I just wish I had something to cover your leg with, though, because of the dust and dirt."

"You have a handkerchief?"

"Blew my nose on it earlier."

"Oh . . . what about my shirtwaist?"

He stared at her curiously. "Your shirtwaist?"

"I'm wearing a chemise. It wouldn't be as if I were naked."

"But . . ."

"You'll need bandages too, won't you? At least until the horses come back and we can get home."

He set her back down and helped her remove her shirtwaist, his fingers barely touching her skin as he helped peel it from her, then he wound the shirtwaist around her leg so it covered the bite, hoping no dirt would get in, and he picked her up again.

The sun was sinking lower in the sky as he made his way along the rocky floor of the gully, keeping an eye out for Indians, while all too aware of Teffin in his arms. He'd tried to avoid her ever since that first day, and yet it had been pratically impossible. The feelings she'd stirred in him were the kind a man couldn't easily ignore, and he'd fought them until he was so frustrated he wanted to scream. This wasn't supposed to happen. It was wrong, insane, and with each step he promised himself he was going to come down to earth, accept the reality of it as it was, and purge the feelings he had for her once and for all.

Yet, here he was, holding her close, watching her golden hair catching the deep shadows of the setting sun, and feeling her soft flesh against his callused hands, while her eyes studied him intimately, sending shivers clear through him.

Teffin was frightened. Not of Kaelen. She'd never be frightened of Kaelen, but she'd seen men die of snake-bite before, and it wasn't a pretty sight. All she could think was, what if he hadn't gotten enough poison out? It didn't take a lot, and she felt so sick to her stomach. Any other time, being in Kaelen's arms would be paradise, but now all she was aware of was she had to hang on to him, her life depended on it, and she began to wonder if Eli had found her father, and what might be going on back at the house. God! She hoped they were all right.

Her arms tightened about Kaelen's neck, and her head went down onto his shoulder. "I feel horrible," she murmured helplessly.

He stopped. "You going to throw up again?"

"I don't think so . . . I just feel so dizzy and sick."

He started walking again. "We're almost to the bend."

A few minutes later, he carried her around the bend where the horses had disappeared earlier, and there was the spring, bubbling out of some rocks a short way up the side of the ravine to his right. It was seeping over the stones and dirt, onto the ground below, where it formed a shallow pool, then was quickly soaked up in the sandy soil of the arroyo. There wasn't a horse in sight. Evidently they'd quenched their thirst and moved on.

"Damn!" he muttered under his breath.

He could use Sheba about now, or even Teffin's Jubilee. Well, no use wishing. He had to do with what he did have, and he climbed up the side of the gully, still carrying her, until he reached the base of the spring, then he set her down and removed the shirtwaist from the wound.

Standing back up, he gazed about. There was nothing he could use to catch water in. Teffin watched him through dim eyes. Her thigh was painfully swollen, and she felt so weak. Kaelen looked puzzled, and she tried to talk to him, only she was disoriented, and her tongue wouldn't move the way she wanted it to.

He saw her lips move, and knelt down, only there was no way he could understand what she was trying to say. Already the poison he'd been unable to suck out of the wound was having its effect on her, and he didn't like it. He had to find some way to get water to it. Even a small amount, only it had to be clean. If his hat weren't so sweaty, he could use that. And hers was just as bad. Well, he had to do something.

Moving closer to the spring, he cupped his hands in the cold water to see how much they'd hold, then washed them as best he could before finally filling them again and carrying the cold, clear water to her leg, letting it cleanse the wound. Over and over again he made the trip back and forth from the spring to her leg, with the cold water, until he was sure he'd cleaned it enough, then, paying little attention to the fact that her shirtwaist was one of her best, he ripped both the sleeves off, tied them together, and wrapped the wound again, still keeping his bandanna tied firmly in place, but not too tightly on her leg, just above the wound.

The sun was almost over the horizon already, and now he was starting to get worried. Without the horses, there was no way he could get her back to the house, and yet he hated the thought of spending the night out here in the open with her. For one thing, he knew she was going to be delirious most of the night, and she'd no doubt chill, and he didn't even have his jacket to wrap around her. On top of that, he was afraid he might not have gotten out enough poison. All he didn't need was for her to die, and an ache filled him at the thought.

He didn't want Teffin to die. She couldn't, and he knelt beside her, picked her up, and started walking again. Somewhere there had to be shelter of some kind where he could take care of her and keep her safe until morning, if it came to that.

He had walked a good two miles already, praying Eli or someone would come along, hoping he wouldn't encounter any more rattlers, and keeping his eyes peeled in case Sheba or Jubilee showed up. No such luck.

Night shadows were creeping into what had once been shade now, and the last few streaks of daylight were flirting with the stars to the east as he stumbled along in the heat, knowing the night would be sultry with no breeze stirring. He was still following the ravine, and was just about ready to give up on finding any kind of shelter, when he saw the dark outline between the boulders some twenty feet up the side of the gully.

By the time he reached the cave, he was tired, hungry, and so glad to be able to sit down, he just sat, not even bothering to put Teffin down first. She was on his lap, and he leaned his head back against the side of the cave, her head resting on his shoulder, with her warm breath on his neck. He shivered. What was he to do now? What if she died?

"Oh, God! Please, don't let her die," he prayed aloud, and held her close, his heart filled with the love he had for her. The love he knew could never be.

His eyes were closed, and he opened them, straightened, then looked around. It was getting darker by the minute, and soon the cave would be pitch black. Knowing he couldn't just sit here, he finally laid her on the floor and stood up, his blue-green eyes searching the place for something, anything he could use to build a fire or hold water. There was nothing. Well, dammit, he'd find something.

Mad at himself, and the whole situation, he moved to the cave entrance, stepped outside, and began gathering up anything he could find. Just forty-five minutes later, he was once more sitting near the entrance, before a small fire this time, a stick in the coals, roasting bulbs of some desert lilies he'd dug up, while silently thanking Eli for showing him how tasty they were. At least they'd fill his stomach and keep him going so he could take care of her. He only wished he could get Teffin to eat them, but she was in a daze yet, the effects from the poison still with her.

As soon as he had eaten the bulbs, Kaelen set his hat aside, then gathered Teffin into his arms again to wait. The fire was going out, but he wouldn't need it now. Teffin was flushed, her skin clammy, and he wished there was more he could do for her, but this he could do. And holding her close, his arms around her, he made sure she was comfortable, preparing to spend the night with her in his arms, even though it was hot and humid, and he knew the sweat would be dripping off him by morning.

He knew Teffin was chilling, yet he was glad the fire went out because the heat would have been worse for her, driving the poison all the faster through her body. His lips brushed her hair, and he sighed. This would be as close as he'd ever come to her again, and he knew it. The one and only time he could hold her, and as she mumbled something, then moved closer in his arms, he closed his eyes and tried to close his heart against his feelings too, only it wasn't that easy.

The night had gone slowly, and now Kaelen stirred, then realized where he was, and what was happening. He opened his eyes, and much to his surprise, Teffin was awake, staring at him.

"Hello," she whispered weakly.

He frowned. It was barely light outside, the sun just starting to fill the sky with pink and gold, and he was surprised to see her so lucid.

"How do you feel?" he asked. She tried to smile, only it was an effort, and her face was still streaked by the dirt from her tears the day before. "I don't really know, except that I'm comfortable," she answered hesitantly. "Did you hold me all night?"

"I guess I did."

"Thank you."

"My pleasure."

"Am I going to be all right now?"

"I imagine. But you still didn't say. How do you feel?"

She frowned, and looked directly into his eyes. "Do you really want to know?" she asked. "Or are you just being polite?"

"I don't understand."

Mustering up all the strength she could, but still weak from her bout with the poison, Teffin reached up, touched the scar on his cheek, then let her fingers trail down across his lips. She felt him stiffen.

"I'm feeling fine, and I thank you," she murmured, and before he could warn her not to, her lips moved to his, touching them lightly at first, then, unable to pull away, she moaned incoherently, melting against him, and she kissed him long and hard.

At first Kaelen tried to fight it, then knew he was lost as the kiss swept through him like a whirlwind, settling deep in his loins, and even though he fought against it, he could feel his own lips responding to hers, and his arms drew her even closer, and he kissed her back.

Teffin knew by Kaelen's response he'd been wanting to kiss her for a long time, but she'd never dreamed it would be like this, and in spite of her weakness from the poison, she felt the kiss clear to her toes. Oh, how she loved him. The kiss was ending, and she opened her eyes, expecting to see the love in his eyes she just knew would be there. Instead, she cringed, and her face went pale. He was staring at her as if he hated her, his lips still quivering, the scar on his cheek livid, his eyes filled with fury.

"Why did you do that?" he asked, his voice breaking, its harshness grating in her ears.

She pushed herself back some in his arms, so she was looking directly at him. "Because you wanted me to," she answered. "Didn't you?"

"Because I . . . ? Oh, God! This is impossible."

"Impossible? What do you mean, impossible? You've been . . . well, I thought you cared."

"That's just the trouble. I do," he said, his voice bitter as he shook his head. "But it can never be, Teffin, don't you see? No, you wouldn't . . . how could you? Damn! I shouldn't have come here!"

"Why did you?"

"Because I had to."

"What do you mean, you had to?"

"I can't tell you. Not yet anyway."

"Oh, I see. You come into my life, make me fall in love with you—"

"Don't say that."

"Why? What's wrong with it? Why can't I fall in love with you?"

"Because you can't!"

"Why?"

She was still partway in his arms, and he wished he didn't have to let go, yet it was time she knew the truth before matters got any worse. His eyes softened, and sadness filled them.

"Because I'm your brother," he answered, and his voice trembled with emotion.

Teffin stared at him dumbfounded. "You're what?"

"You heard me, I'm your brother. Well, your half-brother anyway."

"What are you talking about?"

"I'm talking about us," he said, trying to make her

understand. "I'm talking about you and me, and why we can't be in love—I'm your half-brother, Teffin. Don't you understand? Cole Dante's my father too."

Teffin's head began to move back and forth slowly, falteringly, as she continued staring at him, yet she couldn't force herself to move from his arms.

"It's not true," she finally said, her voice unsteady. "It can't be. You're making it up . . . it's not true. I only have one brother, Case, and he was sold to the Comanche. I don't have a half-brother."

"Yes, you do. Now listen to me, Teffin. My name's Kaelen Baldridge, you have to accept it. Ask your father about Lily Baldridge, he'll tell you."

Her eyes were on his again, and she wanted them to show her he was lying, but they never faltered.

"Years ago, when your mother and brother were kidnapped, and your father thought your mother was dead, he almost married my mother," Kaelen went on, trying to explain. "Unfortunately, they didn't wait for the ceremony, and I'm the result. When your mother showed up again alive, my mother and her brother, Zeke, went to New Orleans, where I was born. My mother never married, Teffin. In fact, she died shortly after I was born, and Uncle Zeke raised me. We've traveled around a lot, but he always told me if anything ever happened to him, I was to find my real father, Colton Dante. I believe at one time they called him Duke, am I right? That's why the Crown D?"

Teffin couldn't believe it. This wasn't happening. Not to her. It couldn't be. "You're sure?" she murmured as her heart began crumbling into little pieces.

"Positive."

There were huge tears in her eyes. "But why? Why didn't you say something right away?" she pleaded. "Then maybe I wouldn't have . . . maybe we could have . . . Oh, God! Kaelen, why?"

Kaelen's heart felt like it was strung out on a hide rack to dry, and it hurt. "Don't you think I would have if I'd known this would happen?"

"But you knew right from the start. I could feel it whenever you looked at me. If only you'd said something."

"Would it have made any difference? Does it make any now?"

She choked back a sob as she realized what he meant. Would it have made a difference? The feelings were still there now, even though she knew the truth. The warmth inside at the sound of his voice, the sweet sensations that crept through her when their eyes met. It was still there. Even if she had known he was her brother right from the start, would any of it have been different?

She was a little unsteady, but finally pried herself from his arms, only she still couldn't stand up. "What do I do now? How do I go on, Kaelen?" she asked, her eyes searching his.

"I could ask myself the same thing, Tef." He looked as unhappy as she felt. "Do you think I've enjoyed the past few weeks? Feeling myself drawn to you, and yet knowing it was wrong? Do you think I liked it? It's been hell!" He shook his head. "If I could change it, I would, but I can't."

She shook her head, tears glistening in her eyes. "It isn't fair! It just isn't fair!"

"When was life ever fair?"

She swallowed hard, then glanced off, outside, to where the sun was already beginning to fill the shadows and reheat the earth that had never completely cooled down during the night, and she wanted to lash out at the agony inside her. Her brother! It just didn't seem real, and yet . . .

"When are you going to tell Pa?"

"I don't know." Kaelen sighed. "I wanted to tell him that first day, but couldn't. Then the longer I waited, the harder it was . . ." He ran a hand through his dark hair, and she stared at his face, noticing, as she had so many times already, that even when he wasn't smiling, it was easy to tell where his dimples were. "I guess I was hoping I could get him to know me, and maybe like me first, and it'd be easier," he said. "And then there's your ma."

"Ma?"

"I don't like the idea of hurting her, and I know it will." He flushed, his jaw tightening. "Look what it's done to you."

"Mother's not in love with you."

"Teffin!"

"Well, it's true. My God, Kaelen. Do you know how I feel? Can you even imagine what it's like? I'm in love with my brother! My own damn brother!"

He winced at the look on her face. If only he could hold her and make it right, but all he could do was just sit there and watch the hell she was going through, while he died inside too.

"I'm sorry," he blurted, for lack of something better to say. "If I could undo it, I would, but it's too late for both of us."

Her eyes caught his, and she stared at him hard. He was telling her . . . Oh, what a mess they were in. She wiped her eyes with the back of her hand, smearing even more dirt on her face, and he'd have laughed at how ridiculous she looked if he hadn't been so torn inside.

"So now we know how we feel," he went on, trying to weather the storm of emotions they'd been drowning in. "So now we end it."

"Is it really that easy?"

"I didn't say it'd be easy, but it has to be done."

"I know . . . I know." She brushed a stray hair back from her face, her eyes misty with tears, then took a deep breath. "So, like I asked, when will you tell Pa?"

"I don't know. I should tell him when I get back, I suppose."

"No, not yet, please. Don't tell him so soon. Give me a few days. If you tell him now, they're liable to guess the truth about us, and I wouldn't want that."

"Why should they do that?"

"Because when you first came, I told Ma . . . well . . ." This time it was her turn to blush, and she could feel the heat in her face. "I told her I thought you were good-looking."

"What did she say?"

"She told me to forget it, that you were just a drifter,

and probably wouldn't even stay long enough to break in your bed at the bunkhouse."

"I wish she'd been right."

"Me too."

Kaelen studied her face. Was she beautiful only to him, or did others see her in the same light? he wondered. Well, no sense torturing himself by what he wished could be. She was his sister, and that was reality.

"All right, I'll wait a week, how's that? Enough time?"

"I think so."

"Teffin, I mean it, I'm sorry."

"I know." She sat up straighter, trying to use strength she didn't really have, and he realized that physically she still wasn't strong.

"Let me check your leg," he suggested, reminding her of why they were there together, and she watched him get up, moving to her right side, where he knelt down and untied the makeshift bandage. He had removed the tourniquet during the night.

Although she was no longer feverish or delirious, he knew they could still have problems when he saw her leg still swollen.

"Hungry?" he asked.

"Not really."

"Well, you'll eat anyway," he said. "I'll be right back," and he walked away, outside, into the morning sun, leaving her by herself.

At first she thought he'd be back in just a couple of minutes, but it wasn't until some twenty minutes later that he finally came into the cave again, his arms loaded with firewood, pockets bulging with more desert-lily bulbs, and a grin on his face.

"Guess what I found?" he said as he began laying the wood down where he'd had the fire the night before, setting the sticks so he could light them with a few pieces of dried grass to catch the sparks from the flint he carried in his pocket.

"I can't imagine," she answered.

"Our horses." He leaned down, blew on the grass until it took hold, then pushed it back beneath the twigs and sticks. "I guess they got tired of following that stallion and began wandering on their own. I tied them up at the bottom of the ravine."

"Then we can go home."

He looked over at her, his eyes looking straight into hers, and an ache settled in his breastbone. "Yeah, we can go home," he answered, then reached in his pocket and pulled out the flower bulbs. "But first we have something to eat. It's going to be a long ride back."

Half an hour later, with her stomach battling the intrusion of the wild-lily bulbs, Teffin let Kaelen carry her from the cave, down the side of the ravine to where the horses were, then let him put her up on Jubilee. It was surprising how weak she still was, even though she'd been bitten the day before. Her leg was swollen, though, and she knew as long as there was still some poison in her system, she'd feel the effects.

"Can you ride?" he asked as he handed her the reins.

She nodded. "I think so."

"Good." He walked to his own horse and mounted, then rode over beside her. "Ready?"

His eyes were fixed on her face, and for a moment he thought she was going to burst into tears again as she had once while they were eating, but instead, she bit her lip, holding them back.

"May I ask you something first?" she said, her voice tremulous.

"What's that?"

"If I weren't your sister, Kaelen, if I were just anybody, instead of who I am, would you love me?"

Kaelen took a deep breath, his eyes boring into hers. She had put her hat on, and it wasn't as easy to see her face, but that didn't matter. He knew it by heart. The curve of her lips, the way her eyes crinkled when she frowned. Would he love her? What a foolish thing to ask, yet she had asked it, and she deserved an answer.

"Forever," he answered simply, then pulled his hat down a little more to shade his own face from the sun, so he wouldn't have to see the anguished look on hers. "Now come on, let's move," and without saying another word, he dug Sheba in the ribs, and Teffin followed him on Jubilee, heading back toward the trails leading home, hoping they wouldn't run into any Indians on the way.

Some mile or so ahead in the gravelly arroyo, Cole and Eli were riding slowly following the faint trail Kaelen's boots had left the night before. With the ground so dry, there were times the tracks were so hard to see, Eli had to dismount, yet others when they were deep where the ground was softer, without so much rock and gravel.

"He has to be carrying her, Cole," Eli said as the clear outline of where Kaelen had walked ran ahead of them down the middle of the ravine.

"Where are the horses?"

"Run off? Maybe they ran into those bastards we drove off yesterday. Them redskins were in a mean mood when they rode away from the Crown D."

"If they'd run into He Who Rides, neither Kaelen nor Teffin'd be walking," Cole offered.

Eli frowned. Cole was right. "Then what happened? There wasn't a thing where we picked up their trail."

"Who knows." Cole shrugged, his sloe eyes squinting in the morning sun, and he pulled the hat down farther on his forehead to see better. "At least we know they're on foot, at least Kaelen is, and we know they stopped at the spring. Anything else, I won't guess at, only that we find them in one piece."

He and Eli had left the ranch house to search for Teffin and Kaelen shortly before sunup, having decided it'd be foolish to attempt going during the night. They had reached the ranch the day before, shortly after the Indians had attacked, and it hadn't taken He Who Rides long to realize he was outnumbered, so he and his braves took off back to the hills with the plunder they had left from their raid on the Sherwoods'. But since it was so late in the day by the time the whole encounter was over, instead of riding back out to continue hunting the horses they'd been after, Cole and the rest of the men gave up for the day and just stayed at the house, waiting for Kaelen and Teffin to show up. Only they hadn't.

When they all realized something was wrong, it was

way too dark to start searching, so they'd waited until morning, then left early enough so they'd be well on their way by the time the sun was up.

Cole rode along now, keeping his thoughts to himself. He liked Kaelen. The young man had proved his worth more times than he'd expected out on the range, and whenever Cole needed a volunteer for a job, Kaelen was always there. Even Eli had picked Kaelen when he needed help with something, and Eli had remarked to him more than once that even though Kaelen had evidently had a rough life, he didn't seem to be afraid of hard work. Nor was Kaelen afraid of any of the other hands either. But he was always so solemn and quiet, and he kept to himself so much, the men began to speculate that maybe the law wasn't too far behind him.

However, Cole didn't think so, and he was sure Kaelen was younger than he led them to believe. Although he looked at least twenty, Cole was sure he was closer to eighteen, only Kaelen never mentioned his age. No matter, though. At the moment Cole was positive, no matter how old the young man was, or why he'd shown up at the Crown D looking for a job, if anyone could take care of Teffin, and keep her safe, it was Kaelen.

They were at least a mile or two past the spring when Eli reined up and pointed ahead, and there, riding toward them, right down the middle of the gully, were Teffin and Kaelen, on Jubilee and Sheba.

Cole and Eli spurred both their horses at the same time, while up ahead, Kaelen pulled back on the reins, grabbed his hat, and started waving it, then spurred his own horse into a loping canter as he called to Teffin.

"Come on . . . am I glad to see you two!" he yelled as he drew close enough to be heard.

"Are you all right?" Cole asked when he reached them, then he caught sight of Teffin's bare arms and chemise, saw her torn riding skirt with the shirtwaist still bandaged around her thigh, and he frowned. "What happened?"

Teffin's hands were so tight on Jubilee's reins her knuckles were white. "A rattler," she answered hurriedly, so Pa wouldn't get the wrong idea. "If it hadn't been for Kaelen . . ." She glanced over at Kaelen, remembering all too vividly that Pa was Kaelen's pa too, and now suddenly she could see the resemblance.

Cole was off his horse already, and was untying the makeshift bandage on Teffin's leg. He lifted it gingerly. The wound was clean, but it was still red and swollen. Retying the bandage, he looked up at her.

"You're not dizzy, are you?"

She shook her head. "Not now, but I was awfully sick last night."

Cole patted her hand, then went back to his horse and mounted up. He looked over at Kaelen. "How can I thank you, Kaelen?" he said, as Nevado pawed and pranced impatiently.

Kaelen straightened in the saddle, studying the man he knew was his father, and wishing he hadn't promised Teffin to wait a week. Kaelen's face was solemn, his blue-green eyes hard, unyielding. "Don't worry, I'll find a way someday," he said, surprising Cole. "But for now, let's just say I'm glad I knew what to do, and let it go at that."

Cole reached out his hand. "We can shake on it anyway, can't we?" he said. "Because I do thank you for what you've done."

"If you want," Kaelen shook hands with Cole, purposely avoiding Teffin's haunted look, and both Teffin and Kaelen were glad the conversation was mostly about the Indian raid for the rest of the ride home.

Teffin ended up spending the next two days in bed. It wasn't too bad, really, because it gave her time to think, and by the time the weekend rolled around, she had made a decision she knew was the only one she could make, under the circumstances.

Grandma Dicia and Blythe had ridden over in a buggy one day to visit her, and Joaquín had dropped in both evenings while she was confined, and it was Joaquín's visits that were uppermost in her mind now as the weekend drew near.

It was early Saturday morning. The weather was hot,

and although her leg was still bandaged, the swelling was gone. Ma said it'd leave a scar. She hoped not. But then it didn't really matter, did it? She hadn't seen Kaelen since they'd come back that day, at least not up close. A couple of times she'd watched him from the house, working out back near the corrals, and she'd spied him from the guestroom upstairs when he'd ridden out with the other men yesterday morning.

She was up in her room now, and glanced into the mirror on her dresser, fixing her hair. It was almost getting too long again. She loved it when it hung to her shoulders and was long enough to tie back in a queue, but it was halfway to her waist already, and was so hard to manage. Well, a simple ribbon around it would have to do. It was close to eight o'clock already, and Joaquín had said he'd be over by then to help with the barn.

She was wearing a new dress today, one Helene had made for her, and it was the prettiest shade of blue, with just a touch of matching lace inserted in the puff sleeves and around the heart-shaped neckline. Actually, it was the first new dress she'd had on in over a year. Since the night of Aunt Liz's birthday party when Joaquín had kissed her that first time. They hadn't had any party for Aunt Liz this year, or anyone else either, and she'd been disappointed because she'd often daydreamed about what it would be like to dance with Kaelen. Now, though, she was glad they hadn't, and an ache settled inside her as she thought back over what Kaelen had told her.

She'd made him promise to wait a week before telling Pa, and that left only three days now for her to do what she had to do. If only she hadn't told Ma how good-looking she'd thought Kaelen was that day he'd arrived. And if only she hadn't tried to flirt with him so much. Well, at least she hadn't confided in anyone about her feelings for him. That was one thing in her favor. And now, if Joaquín would just help her out by being as attentive as he usually was, by the time Kaelen did tell Pa the truth, no one would suspect she cared for him in the slightest.

Satisfied she looked fine, Teffin left her room, went to

her parents' room, found a small bottle of perfume on their dresser, one Pa had given Ma for Christmas a few years back, and figuring today was as special as you could get, but knowing Ma'd say no if she asked her, put a dab behind each ear, then trailed the stopper down to the base of her throat. After putting it back, she left the room, went downstairs, grabbed a piece of fresh-baked bread from the kitchen, after arguing with Bessie and Ma that it was enough breakfast, and was outside sitting on the front steps when Joaquín rode in, dismounted, and joined her, as she had figured he would.

His eyes were smiling, their green depths admiring how pretty she looked in blue, as he sat next to her on the step.

"Señor Dante is not at the barn yet?" he asked.

"He's still eating breakfast."

"Bueno. Then I will have time to ask you."

She eyed him curiously. Joaquín was was always full of surprises. "Ask me what?"

"To go to church with me in town tomorrow."

"Church?"

"Sí, church. You are Catholic, are you not?"

"Well . . ." She looked at him rather sheepishly. "We're supposed to be. At least we joined the church when we had to, but except for when we're required to, we never bothered to go much, and now, since Mexico no longer gives the orders . . ."

"You mean you would just quit going?"

"That doesn't mean we don't believe in God," she explained. "It just means we have our own way of worshiping Him, that's all."

He looked concerned as he studied her face. "But I have to get married in the church," he said, frowning. "It is expected of me."

"What does that have to do with me?"

"You do not know?"

She was staring at him intently, knowing full well what he meant, yet leading him on coyly. "I'm not sure . . . what do you mean, Joaquín?"

He reached out, took her hand, and smiled, his tanned

face was such a contrast against the white shirt he was wearing. It had been a good shirt once, with ruffles down the front, and full sleeves, but after being worn a number of times while Joaquín was working with Cole, it was no longer fit to wear with the fancy suits he rarely wore anymore.

"But you didn't say. Will you go with me tomorrow?"

"How can I? Your house is closer to town than ours. By the time you came for me, we'd have to leave at dawn to get there on time."

"You could stay at our place. Tío Antonio would love having you."

"And Catalina?"

"She would no doubt ignore you. But it would be fun. You could ride over with me when we're through on the barn, stay the night, well-chaperoned naturally, we could attend Mass in the morning at the church, with Tío Antonio and Catalina, then have a picnic lunch on the way over here later in the afternoon."

"Have it all thought out, haven't you?"

He smiled. "I was going to ask you today while we were at lunch. I am glad I can ask you now. It will give you more time to say yes."

"And if I don't?"

"I will be heartsick." He stood up slowly, his gaze moving from her face to the barn, where the men were beginning to gather, then he looked back down to where she still sat on the step. "I will give you until noon to decide," he said hurriedly. "Only please." His smile broadened. "Do not say no," and with that he began reaching for Compadre's reins.

The horse had been standing ground-reined, nibbling on a tuft of grass while they talked, and Joaquín started leading him away.

"I guess your father is ready," he said hastily. "I will claim my answer at the noon hour," and he continued walking toward the barn as if he'd just arrived, turning Compadre over to Mose, who'd put him in the pasture at the back of the barn with some of the other horses and the few cows they had, instead of in the corrals with the horses that weren't broken as yet.

Teffin stood up slowly and walked to the side of the house, watching as her father joined the men. Kaelen was there too, and even though she didn't want it to, her heart constricted agonizingly at the sight of him. She inhaled deeply. Well, there was only one way she was ever going to be able to put Kaelen out of her heart, and that was to put him out of her life, and the only way she could do that was by making a new life for herself somewhere else, and if that meant getting married, well, she'd rather marry Joaquín than anyone else. At least she liked Joaquín, which was more than she could say for any of the other young men around San Antonio. Now, the question was, would he ask her, and she turned quickly, went back to the porch, into the house, and on to the kitchen to ask Ma if it was all right for her to spend the night at the de Léons', well-chaperoned of course.

12

After an engrossing weekend for Teffin, spent at the de Léon ranch, attending church with them, and having a romantic picnic with Joaquín in a small wooded glade on the de Léon property, Teffin and Joaquín returned to the Crown D Sunday evening and informed everyone they were betrothed, with the wedding date being set for a year from this coming August, on the nineteenth. Five days after Joaquín's twenty-first birthday.

"That way I will have my inheritance," he informed them proudly.

In a way, everyone had been expecting it, the way Joaquín had been paying court to Teffin since his return from the fighting, but still it was rather a surprise because Teffin, although letting him monopolize most of her time, had never seemed very enthusiastic about their friendship. At least not the way most girls in love were. She never mooned around and acted lovesick. But then, Teffin wasn't like most girls her age, and kept a great many feelings to herself, rarely confiding in anyone. So her family accepted the announcement without reservations.

Teffin would have liked the wedding to be this coming August, so she could get away from the Crown D as soon as possible, but de Alvarado family tradition more than social convention won out, and they'd have to wait at least a year. A prospect Teffin wasn't looking forward to with much relish, because she knew once Kaelen revealed his true identity, Pa would never let him leave the Crown D. Especially since there was so little hope of ever finding Case. Even if He Who Rides did prove to be

260

her long-lost brother, it was unlikely he'd ever return to them, so it was inevitable that Kaelen would take the place of the son Cole had been mourning for so many years.

It was late Tuesday evening. Joaquín had ridden over that afternoon as usual, after making sure everything was going well at his uncle's ranch, a job Antonio had relinquished to him after his return from San Jacinto, and a job Antonio had assured him it would do him well to learn, so he could be master of his own rancho someday. And after eating supper with the Dantes, he and Teffin had spent some quiet time together, making plans, before he'd ridden off toward home again.

Now Teffin, with mixed feelings, watched him disappear into the night. She liked Joaquín. So much so that she felt guilty for what she was doing. Yet, it was the only way. First of all, now that everyone knew she was going to marry Joaquín, no one would suspect how she really felt about Kaelen, and after she was married to Joaquín . . . well, she could put Kaelen out of her life once and for all, except for an occasional visit home.

She was still standing in the dark at the edge of the drive near the front walk, where she'd been standing when Joaquín kissed her good-bye, and she took a deep breath, then turned to go into the house. It was a hot night, extremely hot, and instead of going in, she hesitated. At this point, the thought of being upstairs, sweltering in her room, wasn't any too pleasant, so, turning slowly, she began to stroll back along the drive, past what would someday be the new barn, then across the back lawn to the outhouse, where she took advantage of the fact that it was empty. After coming back out again, she continued her sauntering, until she finally ended up at the back corral where the horses were trained.

It was really dark out, and even a little spooky without the moon up yet, and with a light breeze rustling the leaves on a tree near the edge of the drive, it was rather frightening. However, not wanting to go back as yet, but not wanting to stray too far from the house either, she wandered over to the tree, leaned back against its trunk for a few minutes, then slid to the ground and wrapped her arms about her knees, folding the soft material of her green dress about her legs. Leaning forward, she moved her arms up across her knees, then rested her head on them as she gazed back toward the house.

It was well past ten already, and only a dim light shone from the kitchen window. Bessie, usually the last one into bed, often went in about nine-thirty or so, and evidently she'd left a light on for Teffin.

Teffin sighed, then suddenly straightened as a noise caught her attention, and she glanced over across the drive toward the bunkhouse, just in time to see the door open and one of the men come out. Whoever it was stood quietly for a few minutes just outside the door, and from the faint pinpoint of light she could see, she realized he must be smoking one of those cigarittos, like Don Antonio smoked. Most of the hands just chewed, or used snuff. But she'd seen Kaelen smoking occasionally, and she began to wonder.

Her question was answered when the lone figure suddenly straightened, and she knew by the fluid movement of his hard-toned muscles and catlike walk that she'd guessed right. It was Kaelen. Had to be.

Although Kaelen had yet to see his twentieth birthday, he was at least an inch taller than Cole, only his body was still lean, the muscles sinewy, giving the appearance of someone who'd been in the saddle more than on the ground. Which she imagined was probably true.

He strolled across the drive to the corral, and she stood up, then saw him lean against the top rail, staring off into the night at nothing in particular. Her first thought was to go back to the house, and she even started to head that way, then turned back one more time and stopped, watching him again for what she promised herself would be only a second, when he suddenly whirled around, perhaps sensing she was there. No matter the reason, it was too late now to keep going toward the house, and her insides tightened anxiously as she saw him toss the cigaritto down, crush it into the ground, then start toward her.

Kaelen had thought he was alone. He'd been the only one awake in the hot, sweaty bunkhouse, and he just had to get a breath of air. Even Eli was snoring up a storm when he'd slipped out. Ordinarily he'd have been sleeping already too, after a rough day with the horses, but tonight wasn't just any night. Not only because of the heat and humidity, but because tomorrow he planned to tell Cole Dante who he really was. He'd given Teffin her week, and now he knew why she'd wanted it, and as he walked toward her now, wondering what she was doing so far from the house this late, he began to think perhaps his first instinct the day he'd arrived, to just run and forget the whole damn mess, would have been the wisest thing to do. But then if he had, he'd never have gotten to know her, would he? He straightened firmly as he approached.

He'd spotted her the minute he'd turned, and although it was dark, there was no way he could mistake who it was. He'd watched her too much not to know every line, every curve. They were seared into his memory like a bad dream, and were just as frightening to his emotional stability. At first, in her pale green dress, she was only a vague apparition against the grass and trees, but as he drew nearer, he could almost see her face.

"Teffin?" he asked, just to be certain his eyes weren't deceiving him.

"I thought that was you."

He frowned. "What are you doing so far from the house?"

"The same thing you're doing, I guess."

"Hardly."

Now that he was closer, she realized his head wasn't the only thing bare. He wasn't wearing a shirt either. All he had on were pants, boots, and some sort of chain around his neck that hung down into the rippling muscles of his bronzed chest.

"Then what are you doing?" she asked.

"Trying to find the right words to tell your father who I really am."

"It shouldn't be that hard, should it? You just tell him."

"Just like that, huh? What if he calls me a liar?"

"He won't."

"How do you know?"

"Because I know Pa. Oh, he'll probably deny it at first, because he won't want to admit to anything that'd hurt Ma, but in the long run, he'll face the truth."

"Like you did?"

"What do you mean?"

"Teffin, you don't have to marry Joaquín, you know. There'll be someone else who'll come along someday."

"No there won't."

"Yes there will."

"Not for me, never, Kaelen. I know that just as sure as I know you're standing here. You see, I'm being honest with myself. I have to be. I know how I feel about you will never change, only there's nothing I can do about it, but I also know I have a life to live. So for me, Joaquín's the only answer, don't you see? I do like him, so I'll fill my life with him, and ignore you, if I can. That way maybe I'll survive."

He reached out to touch her cheek lightly, a gesture meant to console, but one he shouldn't have made, because instead of merely caressing her cheek, his hand cupped her face, and he stared at her hard, stepping even closer. He wanted to hold her, caress her, smother her face with kisses, yet the folly of committing such a sin made him stop.

He hadn't wanted to love her like this. He'd wanted to love her as a sister, and God in heaven, why couldn't he? Why did it have to tear his guts out every time he looked at her? What the hell was God doing to him, anyway? Her eyes were colorless in the dark, but the expression on her face was all too revealing.

"I'm sorry, Tef," he murmured. "I'd leave now if I thought it'd do any good, but it wouldn't." His hand moved from her head, down the side of her face to her shoulder, then dropped down and stopped at her waist, his strong fingers gently kneading the flesh beneath her thin dress.

"Where would you go?" she asked, her eyes intent on his face. "No, you belong here, Kaelen, as much as I do. All I hope is that the time goes fast, and the pain'll soon ease. For now . . ."

They stared silently at each other for a few struggling moments, then, "But why does it have to be Joaquín?" he finally asked, his blue-green eyes steady, unflinching. "Why can't you wait awhile?"

She wanted so badly to throw herself against him and scream at God for what He'd done to them; instead she tried to smile.

"Because he cares," she answered. "It's as good a reason as any. And I'll try to help you all I can with Ma and Pa too, I promise," she went on. "After all, I always wanted a brother." Suddenly tears sprang to her eyes.

"Don't," he whispered. "Not like this." He took her hand, squeezing it, and lifted it to his lips, kissing her fingertips tenderly. "Don't cry for us, Teffin. I can't love you the way I'd like to, no, but there's no law says I can't love you at all. Every man has a right to love his sister, doesn't he?"

"I guess . . ."

"And remember another thing too, Tef," he went on. "If that Mexican ever hurts you in any way, you come to me, understand?" His eyes darkened, the emotion in them so intense it was frightening. "I'll kill him before I'll let him hurt you, ever."

The tears were still glistening in her eyes. "He won't," she assured him. "Like I said, he loves me."

Kaelen tried to smile. "Lucky man." He glanced back toward the house, and saw the dim light still on in the kitchen. "Come on, I'll walk you back," he offered.

She shook her head. "I'd best go alone." Her eyes were still on his face. "You'll tell Pa tomorrow then, for sure?" she asked.

He nodded. "For sure."

"Then good luck." She twisted gently from his grasp, all too aware of her fingers running across his bare chest in the attempt, and not wanting him to see the new tears in her eyes, she began to hurry away.

"Good night, Tef," he called after her.

She turned as she walked, slowing down a little, and waved hesitantly. " 'Night, Kaelen," and she turned back toward the house, again, trying not to appear to be running away, but that's exactly what she was doing, trying to run away from her heart.

Kaelen watched her disappear into the house, his own feelings in a state of upheaval, then he turned and strolled back to the bunkhouse, knowing all he had left to him now was another restless night while he waited for morning.

The weather the next afternoon was still dry, the sun unbearably hot, when Kaelen rode into camp beside Eli, then dismounted, tethered Sheba with the rest of the hands' horses, and strolled over to where the men were gathering everything up, ready to call it a day.

"Where's Dante?" he asked Shem, who had just left the corral where the wild mustangs were.

Shem glanced about, then pointed off to where Cole was examining the hoof of one of the mares his men had brought in that afternoon. Kaelen straightened, and reached up, taking off his hat. Well, he'd promised himself as well as Teffin he'd tell Dante today, so he'd best get to it. Holding his hat in his hand, he hurried over to where Cole was.

"Excuse me, Mr. Dante . . ."

Cole glanced up, then went back to examining the mare's split hoof. "What can I do for you, Kaelen?"

Kaelen's hat was in both hands now, and his face was flushed, the scar on his cheek outlined in red. "I'd like to talk to you, sir, if I may," he said.

"Go ahead, talk."

Kaelen glanced around. There was no way he could talk here. "If you don't mind, sir," he began, "it's something rather personal."

Cole dropped the horse's hoof and straightened. "Oh?"

"I was hoping maybe you'd let the others leave, and we could follow a bit later. If that's all right with you, sir."

Cole's eyes sifted over Kaelen. The young man looked way too nervous. "You in some kind of trouble?"

"No, sir."

"The law's not after you?"

"No, sir."

"Then what the hell's the fuss about?"

"Please, sir." Kaelen had straightened too when Cole stood up, and the flush on his face deepened as he realized he was about an inch taller than this man who was supposed to be his father. "It's important, Mr. Dante. Not just to me, but to you too. Please, sir?"

"Me?"

"Yes, sir."

"Now how on earth could what's bothering you be important to me?"

"Believe me, sir," Kaelen took a deep breath, his blue-green eyes studying his father's face. "It's not only important to you, but it's something I don't think you'd want me to just blurt out in front of everybody. At least not till you've had a chance to chew on it for a while, sir."

Now Cole was really confused. He liked Kaelen, even though he did seem to be a loner, and all legs. Yet, everyone was tired and anxious to get back to the ranch, including himself. Today had been harder and rougher than usual. Oh, well, what the devil.

"All right, Kaelen." Cole glanced around and saw that most of the men were already hitting the saddle. "I'll tell Eli we'll be along later. But this'd better be worth it," and he walked off, heading toward Eli and the men.

Kaelen watched the last of the riders disappear down the trail, then waited, trying to pick the right words as Cole headed toward him. A mockingbird sang somewhere in a nearby tree, and Sheba pawed the ground, anxious to join the other riders, seeming to know instinctively that when the sun sank low on the horizon, it was time to head for home. Kaelen felt the sweat clinging to his dark hair even with his hat off. He was nervous as all hell.

"All right, Kaelen," Cole said when he reached him. "What's it all about?"

Kaelen sighed. "I don't know just where to start," he answered, and glanced around. "Can we sit down, sir?"

They walked a few feet to a bench where the men usually sat to eat lunch. It was near one of the corrals that was empty now, the horses having been taken back to the ranch with the men. Sometimes Cole left them here until they were partially broken, with a few men guarding them, an old shack serving as the men's shelter. But with the Indians still raiding, he'd begun to do most of the breaking back at the ranch, and had even enlarged the corrals there.

He and Kaelen sat down, and Cole glanced over at the young man again. "I'm waiting," he said.

Kaelen wished he could die. Bad enough he was a bastard, but now he had to let the world know too. Either that, or be a loner the rest of his life. He looked over at Cole Dante, the man's sloe eyes steady and strong. No, he didn't want that. He didn't want to spend the rest of his life drifting. He wanted Dante to know. After a brief pause, he plunged in, sink or swim.

"Does the name Baldridge mean anything to you, sir?" he asked.

Cole tensed. "Baldridge?" He eyed Kaelen suspiciously, because the name brought back memories he'd near forgotten. "If it does?" he countered.

Kaelen was nervous. "My name's Kaelen Baldridge, sir," he blurted. "Uncle Zeke said that when he was gone, I should look you up."

"Your Uncle Zeke?"

"I'm not doing this right at all, am I, sir?" Kaelen apologized hurriedly, and could have bitten his tongue. "You see, my mother was Lily Baldridge, sir. I mean, Mr. Dante. You did know Lily Baldridge, right?"

"Yes, I knew her." Cole's voice was barely a whisper, and he was staring hard at Kaelen now, as Kaelen's face turned red.

"Well, according to her, you're my father, sir," Kaelen said, his voice breaking.

Cole opened his mouth to say something, but nothing came out, and his eyes were filled with disbelief. His son? Kaelen his son?

"You . . . she told you this?" he asked, his thoughts suddenly flashing back to the early spring of 1818, when Lily came back into his life, and he thought Heather was dead.

"She didn't come right out and tell me, no, sir," Kaelen answered. "Leastways not that I can remember, because I was only three when she died. But Uncle Zeke always said . . . and she gave this to him to give to me, and he said when, and if, I ever looked you up, I should show it to you," and he reached inside his shirt, pulling out the chain Teffin had noticed there the night before. There was a small round silver snuffbox at the end of the chain, and he opened it, taking out a piece of paper, unfolding it carefully. "Here," he said, handing it to Cole. "You're to read this."

Cole reached out and reluctantly took the paper from him, his eyes still on Kaelen's face. The young man's features were unsmiling, his jaw tense, eyes alert for Cole's slightest reaction. Holding the paper where he could see well, Cole drew his eyes from the young man's face to the paper, and noticed it was quite old, and yellowed with age, the creases ready to give where it had been folded, but the words had been written in nice dark ink, and were still legible.

"My dear son, Kaelen," it began, and as Cole kept on reading silently to himself, the words tore at his heart.

I am not much with words [it went on], but because I know there are only a few days left for me to be with you, I must write this so you will understand. When you were conceived, your father and I thought his wife and son were both dead. We would have married, had she not returned, and when I left, your father did not know you were already growing inside me. This knowledge came to me some weeks later. I have never loved anyone else but your father, Kaelen. I never could, and when you are full-growed,

I would like you to forgive me if what I have done has hurt you, but I loved your father very much. I always called him Duke, because it was the name I first knew him by, but his real name is Colton Dante. Folks call him Cole. I think you will grow up to be much like him, and I am glad. I only wish I could see you full-growed. I would be so proud. Your father was last known to have land northwest of the Arkansas River, near Fort Smith. Perhaps someday, if you can forgive us both for bringing you into this world without the proper words having been said by a preacher, you will find it in your heart to look for him. Meanwhile, always remember that I love you, and I wish I could be with you always.

> Your loving mother,
> Lily Baldridge

Written by hand this sixteenth day of January, in the year of Our Lord, 1822.

There were tears in Cole's eyes as he read the last few words and the signature, and he stared at the letter for a few minutes, then took a deep breath.

"Why didn't you show me this the day you arrived?" he asked as he looked up from the letter.

"I was going to at first . . . but then, I guess I just didn't know how to go about it. I used to rehearse what I was going to say, and how I was going to say it, but it just never sounded right. Then when the time came, I just couldn't seem to do it. And then the longer I waited, the harder it got. I finally decided it was either tell you or leave, and I sure as hell don't want to leave."

Cole suddenly felt so old as he studied Kaelen for some minutes, then frowned. "No wonder there was something familiar about you," he said. "You look a lot like your ma, but your eyes are a different color. Hers were brown, if I remember right."

"That's what Uncle Zeke said."

"You never really knew your ma then, did you?"

"She died right after I turned three, and I only have a few vague memories of her. Me and Uncle Zeke were together after that, just the two of us, up until about a year ago, when we tried to outrun some Indians up north near what they call the Platte River, and he didn't make it. I been loning it ever since."

"I see." Cole was still in a mild state of shock. A son! He had another son! Suddenly his stomach tightened, and a shiver ran through him. My God! What was Heather going to say? Good Lord! His gaze fastened on the scar in Kaelen's cheek, the young man's tanned face, nice-looking in a rugged way, attesting to the fact that there was no denying he was Lily's son. And with the letter . . .

Cole was still holding it. Folding it, he handed it back to Kaelen, who slipped it back into the little silver snuffbox.

"So, what do I do now?" Kaelen asked as he clicked the little box shut.

Cole's eyes were intense. "What do you want to do?"

"It all depends."

"On what?"

"You, sir." Kaelen wasn't about to crawl, yet he had to be truthful. "If you believe what Ma wrote, and you're willing to accept me, I'd like to be your son, sir."

Tears welled up in Cole's eyes. "You'd like to be my son? Looks more like you are my son. There's no 'like to be' about it."

"Well . . ." Kaelen's face turned every shade of red. "I know I am, sir, I realize that, but I also know there's no law says you have to claim me either, sir. If you were just to tell me to leave, well, I guess I wouldn't have any other course but to go, would I?"

"You think I'd do that?"

Kaelen inhaled sharply. "You'd have every right, sir."

"I see. Then you're leaving it up to me, is that it?"

"I guess you might say that."

"You're damn well right you might say that." Cole stood up and thrust a hand in his pocket, took a couple of steps, then whirled back around to face Kaelen. "Did you ever wonder what I was going to tell my family?"

Kaelen shrugged. "Not really."

"I didn't think so." Cole rubbed his chin thoughtfully. "Damn! What am I going to do? What am I going to say? How do I explain you?"

"I'm sorry, sir. I guess I shouldn't have come, should I?"

"Don't say that. Just sit there for a minute and shut up." Cole continued to stare at Kaelen for a few seconds, sizing him up.

He had to admit Kaelen was a young man a father'd be proud of, but it wasn't going to be easy explaining him. Not at all. To Heather or anyone else. What to do? He scowled, his gaze moving off to the corrals and the shack, remembering these past few weeks, and how Kaelen, in spite of the fact that he kept to himself so much, had fit in with the ranch work. He also remembered the way Kaelen had taken care of Teffin the other day when she'd been snake-bitten. Then suddenly he almost laughed at himself. What was he arguing with himself about? He knew damn well he wasn't going to turn Kaelen away.

He drew his gaze from the work area and looked back over to where Kaelen still sat on the bench, his fingers nervously curling the brim of his hat. "How old are you, Kaelen?"

Kaelen stood up. "I'll be eighteen in December, sir."

"You look older, and you're taller than I am."

"I reckon. But then Uncle Zeke was tall too."

"I know, I remember." Cole rubbed a hand over his eyes, took off his hat, and ran a hand through his dark hair, realizing Kaelen's hair had that same blue-black sheen, and he smiled, the hat covering his head again. "All right, boy," he finally said, and Kaelen's heart felt strangely full. "I don't know what's going to happen when we get back to the ranch, or just how I'm going to explain this whole damn thing without getting myself in a peck of trouble I don't really need right now, but there's no way I'll refuse to accept what's mine." He walked over and looked into Kaelen's blue-green eyes. They were misty, he was sure of it. "Do we shake on it, son, or are you game for a fatherly hug?"

Kaelen's face turned crimson, but before he had time to say either way, Cole's arms were around him, and there was no longer any need for the anger and indecision that had been so much a part of Kaelen's life for so long, and he smiled, the dimples in his cheeks filling with silent tears. The first he'd cried since Uncle Zeke died.

Cole released him, backing away. "So you were right," he said, watching the expression on Kaelen's face, and realizing the tense, wary look had left the young man's eyes, to be replaced by a relaxed look of acceptance. Only he saw tears too, though he never mentioned them. "So I did have to chew it over. So now, let's head back to the ranch, and you can tell me all about you, and Zeke, and the years we've missed," and his arm was about Kaelen's shoulder as they headed for their horses.

On the ride back to the ranch, however, Cole made Kaelen promise not to say anything to anyone about their conversation until he'd had a chance to talk to Heather alone first, and now, later that evening, Cole stood in the library that was also his business office and faced Heather, whose face was white and drawn.

Telling her about Kaelen had been one of the hardest things he'd ever had to do, but there was no way he could keep something like this from her. He stared at her now, wishing he could read her mind.

"Well?" he finally asked when the silence became overpowering.

Her violet eyes were withdrawn, cold. "Well what?"

"What do you mean, 'Well what?' I just told you Kaelen was my son."

"I know."

"So do something, dammit! Yell at me, scream . . . call me names, but don't just stand there staring at me."

"I don't know what to do," she answered helplessly. "What does a woman do when her husband tells her he's fathered a son without her?"

"You make it sound like I was unfaithful. I thought you were dead. But it's the truth, and it has to be dealt with."

"Why? Why does it have to be dealt with?" Tears sprang to her eyes. "Why doesn't he just ride out and pretend he never came?"

"Is that what you want? What you really want?"

"He's lived without you this long, hasn't he? Why does he need you now?"

"Because he's alone, love. Can't you understand that? I can't pretend he doesn't exist."

"Well, I can!"

"No you can't. You can want it, but you can no more ignore it than I can.'

"Oh yes I can." She shook her head, her voice catching on a sob. "Why did he have to come? Why did it have to happen? I don't want it, Cole," she pleaded. "You already have a son!"

"Do I? Do I really?" Cole's eyes were dark and stormy, like the sea. "Where's my son, Heather?" he asked bitterly. "Where's the man you say is my son? Out raiding our neighbors? Out in the hills somewhere with feathers in his hair and scalps on his coup belt? Oh, God, love," and he reached out, taking her hand in his. "I've got a chance to have a real son again, just like you have your daughter. Would you deny me my own flesh and blood?"

She bit her lip, tears filling her eyes, as the hurt coursed through her. His flesh, but not hers. Lily had given him what Carl Palmer and the Comanche had taken from him, and she hadn't been a part of it, and it hurt. True, he'd thought she was dead, but it didn't lessen the pain any. She pulled her hands free and walked to the window, staring out into the night, then closed her eyes, the past suddenly all too vivid in her thoughts.

There had always been that chance, just like there had been with her. Even now there were times when she looked at Teffin . . . It had been so long ago, though, and the past could be so real at times. Yet . . . she could accept the fact that Cole had turned to someone else when he thought she was dead—after all, she was guilty of doing the same thing, and she had known he was alive. But it was another thing to have to look at the results of that union every day, and be reminded. Cole had done it, but could she?

"I don't honestly know if I can do it, Cole," she finally said, and turned again to face him. "I hate her for giving you another son. Something I couldn't seem to do, and I don't know if I can look at him every day and not hate him too."

Cole moved toward her, his hands reaching out to rest on her shoulders. "Will you try, love?" he asked, his gaze steady on her face.

She reached up, her fingertips touching the frost at his temples. She loved him so much.

"All right, I'll try," she murmured. "But it'll take time getting used to."

Cole sighed. "I knew you'd understand, love," he whispered. "You always do," and as he pulled her into his arms, kissing her, Heather suddenly remembered the conversation she'd had with Teffin the day Kaelen arrived, and she thanked God nothing had come of it, and Teffin was to become Señora de Alvarado, and she kissed her husband back with a fierceness that revealed the strength they were all going to need to see this thing through.

A few minutes later, when Teffin was summoned to the library and told about Kaelen, she tried hard to act both surprised and shocked. But her best performance of all was when she met Kaelen as her brother for the first time in front of her parents. She knew it would only be natural for the two of them to be self-conscious under the circumstances, and she was just as pleased as Kaelen was that their nervousness and obvious discomfiture were construed as the result of the news that had just been thrust upon them, rather than the fact that Teffin knew already and they were both dying inside because of it.

For everyone else at the Crown D, the news of Kaelen's parentage and his moving from the bunkhouse into what had once been one of the guestrooms in the main house was accepted with mixed feelings. Eli and Mose smiled knowingly, and chorused that they'd always thought there was something familiar about the lad. Helene was non-committal, which didn't surprise anyone, and Bessie just shook her head, wondering what was going to come of it, while the hired hands, although beginning to treat Kaelen with a little more respect now, said very little, except to tease him occasionally about his new status.

The strangest reaction of all came from Joaquín. Not only did he seem relieved to learn of it, but Kaelen's new position in the Dante household ignited what looked like a friendship between the two that hadn't existed before, and Cole made the remark to Heather he was sure it was because Joaquín no longer considered Kaelen competition for Teffin's affections, and was more secure in his relationship with her.

It certainly wasn't because Joaquín had felt Kaelen was beneath him socially before, because, far removed from the way Joaquín had been when he'd first arrived in San Antonio, there was now none of the aristocratic snobbery that had once been part of his life.

As for the Kolters and the rest of the Dantes' neighbors, to them it was a combination of shock and disbelief. Yet, once the truth was accepted, life once more rolled along as it had before, and it wasn't long before Braxton even began including Kaelen in the excursions he often took to town, and who knew where else, since Joaquín deserted him more often than not, to be with Teffin.

The days rolled on, summer drew to a close, and even though conditions at the Dante ranch were often strained, Teffin was surviving. How? She had no idea how, because there was no way to escape Kaelen completely, although she tried every chance she had. And as the days wore on, she wished more and more that he'd never come into their lives because of the pain.

However, with Heather, just the opposite seemed to be happening. The more she tried to hate Kaelen for taking the place of the son she'd lost, the more she realized it was a fruitless task. How did you hate a young man who treated you like a queen? Like the mother he'd lost when he was so young? And even though he was still much of a loner, quiet and even mysterious in some ways, revealing little of the years behind him, Heather had to admit to herself she was beginning to think more and more of him as a son.

Summer waned into fall. Elections were held in Texas in September, with Sam Houston becoming president of

the new republic, and Mirabeau Lamar, who'd led Joaquín
and Cole on the charge at San Jacinto, as his vice-president,
while at the Crown D, the new barn was finally up, the
ranch was prospering again, and by Christmas it would
have seemed like there'd never been a war, if it weren't
for the constant threat of more trouble from the Mexican
soldiers camped just across the Rio Grande, as well as
the Indians, who were less a threat, but more a reality.

Even Houston's new government was unable to make
peace with the tribes, and every time a ranch was raided,
and stock driven off, more and more the victims talked of
He Who Rides, and more and more Cole wished he
knew whether the fierce Indian was his other son, or just
another white captive who had turned Comanche.

As usual, after the Christmas holidays, time went by
quickly. New settlers began moving in, and before anyone realized it, spring was gone, the war's end was already well over a year behind them, and it was early
summer 1837. Houston, as most people felt, was doing a
good job as president of what had now been officially
recognized by the United States as the Republic of Texas;
some members of what were no longer the Texas Volunteers, but the Texas Army, were still arguing whether to
raid across the big river into Mexico or not; and the new
republic was agonizing in its birth throes, with money
worries as well as foreign affairs, but at the Crown D,
summer had brought Teffin enough problems of her own.

Far removed from politics, she found herself caught up
in preparations for her coming wedding, which was now
only a little over two months away. Although Teffin had
finally managed to convince herself she was doing the
right thing, the past few months had been torture for her.
No matter how much she and Kaelen tried to act like any
normal brother and sister, there were times when the
undercurrent of tension between them almost became too
much for either to bear. A look, a few words said, and
Teffin always knew why Kaelen would ride off by himself
somewhere and be gone for hours. It was the same reason she'd hibernate in her room writing letters she didn't

really want to write to her grandparents back in South Carolina.

So although she was apprehensive at first over the wedding plans, she knew deep inside it was the only solution. Just a little over two months, she kept telling herself, and she'd get away from it all.

She stood now before the dresser in her room, making sure the dress she had on would be all right to wear today, because she wanted to look extra nice. It was a little fancier than her other dresses, with pink lace trimming the darker rose-colored cotton, and she was wearing a straw bonnet, since she had none to match the dress.

She stared at herself in the mirror, wondering what it would be like to wear some of the ball gowns her mother had told her she'd often worn, and for a brief moment Teffin wished she'd been brought up back east, instead of here, where the closest thing to balls were fandangos, barn dances, and husking bees.

Ah well, there was nothing she could change now, except her last name. But then, maybe being Señora de Alvarado would open up new worlds for her. Who knew?

Today Joaquín had foregone his usual participation in the workings out on the range, as had Cole. Joaquín had become as skilled as Cole at training horses, and with his uncle's permission had spent more time at the Crown D than at home. But today they had all made plans to ride into San Antonio, Cole to take care of some business regarding his horses, Heather because she just wanted to get away, and Joaquín and Teffin to meet Joaquín's old nurse, Matilda, who had come all the way from Monterrey, Mexico, for their wedding.

Joaquín had told Teffin that Matilda had been with him for as long as he could remember. And although she was a slave, his love for her was more like that for a dear friend. She'd nursed him through sickness, encouraged him when he'd failed at something, and when his mother died, Matilda had taken her place in his heart. However, when his father died, because Matilda was a slave, the lawyer said she had to be sold with the rest of the de

Alvarado possessions, and she had been bought by a family who had taken her to Monterrey.

Joaquín had been heartsick, but there was nothing he could do at the time. Now, however, with his twenty-first birthday only weeks away, Tío Antonio, who had begun a search for the woman some months back, had made arrangements for her to be bought from the people in Monterrey and brought to San Antonio as a wedding gift for Joaquín, and word had arrived at the hacienda by messenger the day before that she was in town waiting for someone to come for her. Since Cole had been planning a trip to town already when word arrived from Joaquín, Cole sent a message back inviting Joaquín to join them, and they'd be glad to pick him up, then drop him and his old nurse off afterward. Joaquín had accepted, and now, as Teffin glanced out the window at the sound of the carriage they were going to use as her father maneuvered it to the front walk, she took one last look in the mirror to make sure she looked all right, then grabbed her white parasol and headed for the stairs.

After picking up Joaquín at the hacienda, the rest of the ride to town went so quickly that for a few minutes Teffin forgot what Joaquín was supposed to mean to her. Perhaps because Ma and Pa were along, she didn't know. But they laughed together at nonsensical things, sang a few songs Joaquín said were making the rounds of the taverns and cantinas lately, according to Braxton, talked about the weather, politics, and the price of the wild mustangs Cole was breaking, which was now up to four dollars a head. A fact he was pleased about. And it was more like they were one big family.

When they finally reached town, riding past the marketplace toward the plaza and the inn where Matilda was supposed to be staying, it took a few minutes for Teffin to remember why she and Joaquín were there, and how close the wedding was. But as soon as Joaquín helped her from the carriage, they said good-bye to her parents, promising to meet them back here in front of the inn when their errands were done, and they started inside, there was no mistaking what lay ahead.

"Now remember," Joaquín said as they headed down the upstairs hall toward the room where the innkeeper said Matilda was, "I haven't seen her for over two years, and she may not have been told where she was coming, and why. The men Tío Antonio sent after her were told not to tell her anything. That it was to be a big surprise."

Teffin smiled at the anxious look on Joaquín's face. He had grown a mustache since coming back from the war, and it made him look so much older, and actually more handsome.

"Don't worry, I'll let her see you first, so the surprise will be all the better," she answered.

He squeezed her hand, then stopped in front of one of the doors, knocked, and it was Teffin, who was surprised a few seconds later when it opened. She had expected to see an ancient old lady, almost as old as Grandma Dicia, with gray hair, a wrinkled face, and a few extra pounds.

Instead, the door was opened by a strikingly proud black woman in her mid-thirties, with dark penetrating eyes shining from an equally dark face, her thickly matted hair pulled back on all sides and twisted into a bun at the nape of her neck, and she was wearing a black dress that seemed to emphasize her solemn looks, only her hair was so kinky that occasionally a wisp of it would escape the bun and fall here and there, softening her austere features somewhat. The only jewelry she was wearing was huge gold earrings.

Teffin's first impression of her was one of dismay, for Matilda looked so cool and aloof, and Teffin had wanted to like her. Then suddenly, the moment the woman's eyes fell on Joaquín, her whole foreboding countenance just seemed to fall away, and in spite of the stern look they had first encountered, Teffin found herself looking at a warm, glowing smile that literally lit up the woman's face. And when Joaquín finally quit hugging his old nurse and introduced her, saying, "And this is my betrothed, Teffin," it was no surprise to Teffin to find herself being swept into the woman's arms too, as Joaquín had been, and cooed over like a mother hen.

"I always knew my boy would marry well someday,

Miss Teffin," Matilda said a short time later while they stood in front of the inn with Matilda's luggage piled beside them and waited for Cole and Heather to bring the carriage. She spoke English with a decided Spanish accent, generously flavored with a hint of the drawl most southern slaves used, and she went on, "When those Mexican fellas came and bought me, and we started up here, I had a feelin' deep inside where I was really headin', cause I knew, if there was any way at all for my boy to be near me, he'd see to it. You see, I got faith." She glanced over at Joaquín, her eyes warm with love, then she looked at Teffin and smiled that warm smile again. "Besides," she said, lifting her head haughtily, the pride visible once more in her bearing, "we been together too long to go our separate ways, and I knew he knew it."

Teffin smiled back. "How long have you been with Joaquín, Matilda?" she asked.

The black woman's eyes grew distant, as if she were seeing something long past. "Since he was a babe," she answered as she came back to the present. "And that's a long time ago, Miss Teffin." She straightened her bonnet, pulling the brim forward a bit more against the sun. "But Joaquín didn't say, señorita—he said your name is Teffin, but Teffin what? I did not catch the last name."

"It's Dante," Teffin answered hurriedly. "Teffin Dante, and here come my parents now," and she lifted her hand, waving at her father, who had just driven the carriage around the corner of the street, coming from the direction of the plaza.

Matilda had frozen at the sound of the name, and now she stared transfixed as Cole and Heather made their way toward them, only no one, not even Cole and Heather, caught the panic-stricken look on her face.

Instead, Cole was pleased. He'd made a good contract to sell some horses, Heather had managed to get the material and ribbons she'd been after, and things were looking up. He flicked the reins, pulled the carriage to the edge of the boardwalk, then wound the reins so they wouldn't drag, and jumped down.

"Told you I wouldn't be long," he said as he took a deep breath and looked at his daughter and Joaquín.

Then his gaze shifted to the black woman, still standing beside Joaquín. Suddenly he frowned, unable to quite grasp why, but she looked familiar.

"Oh, my God in heaven!" Matilda moaned, her head shaking from side to side as she stared at Cole. "Por Dios," and with those words she began to slip to the ground in a dead faint, only Joaquín caught her as soon as her knees began to buckle, while everyone else sprang to life.

Lifting her limp body into his arms, Joaquín entered the inn again, followed closely by Cole, Heather, and Teffin, and the innkeeper let them take Matilda to his quarters in the back, where Joaquín stretched her out on his bed. Heather, who had hurriedly climbed from the buggy to follow them, began loosening the neckline of Matilda's dress, to help her breathe easier, then felt Matilda's forehead. The black woman's eyes were still closed, but her breathing was deep and even.

Heather straightened. "I'm sure she'll be all right. I imagine the long trip might have been too much for her." She glanced down at Matilda again. "Look, she's opening her eyes."

They all stared down at the black woman on the bed, only it was Matilda who spoke, her voice barely audible at first, the strange accent she had distorting her words some.

"You all don't know who I am, do you?" she asked, her eyes moving from Heather to Cole, then back to Heather again, and suddenly, as she talked, the hair on the back of Heather's neck began to prickle, and she felt the gooseflesh rise on her arms.

"I'm Tildie, ma'am," Matilda went on, her voice breaking, and there were huge tears in her eyes. "Oh, my God, Miss Heather." Her voice suddenly grew stronger. "I'm Tildie!"

Heather hadn't moved, nor had Cole. Both were just staring at Tildie as if in a stupor, afraid to believe, yet listening to every word.

Joaquín looked at the Dantes, then back to Matilda, and then to the Dantes again, his expression puzzled and confused. "Caramba! What is going on?" he asked. "I do not understand."

Matilda reached out, her eyes searching Joaquín's face, and her fingers groped for his hand. He was standing at her left, with Teffin beside him, the Dantes on the other side of the bed.

"It is for you, my niño. Do you not understand?" Matilda said, squeezing his hand. "It is them! Your real parents. There is no longer any need for the lies."

Joaquín's eyes darkened, and his hand tightened on hers until his knuckles were white. "What lies?" he asked, his face still puzzled. "Matilda, what is this?"

Tildie closed her eyes, then opened them again, and they were glistening with tears as she continued to stare at Cole and Heather a few minutes longer, then she looked back at Joaquín again. "Your name is not Joaquín Luís de Alvarado, my niño," she answered, half-whispering, her voice strained. "Señor de Alvarado bought you from the Comanche Indians to take the place of the real Joaquín de Alvarado, who had died only a few weeks before. It would have been the real Joaquín who would have been twenty-one on August 14 this year, not you. You will not be twenty-one until November. You see, your real name is Case Dante, and you are the son of Heather and Cole Dante."

13

Teffin lay on her bed, staring at the ceiling, her eyes still red from crying, her insides still hurting savagely. Her whole world had suddenly fallen apart again, in just one day. There was no more Joaquín, no more wedding, no more way to escape the torment she'd been going through this past year. Her whole world was one great big mess, and she wanted to scream.

Yet, as badly as Teffin felt for herself, she felt even worse for Joaquín, rather Case, as they now called him. It had been three days since the black woman Tildie had revealed his true identity, and no one had seen him since. He'd returned to Don Antonio's hacienda just long enough to tell him and Catalina what had happened, packed a bedroll, mounted Compadre, and ridden away without so much as a backward glance, and Teffin knew he had to be hurting inside.

The black woman had explained how, after being traded to the Comanche those long ago years, they'd ridden for days, running into a small caravan of Mexicans hauling goods inland from the coast. Don Estéban de Alvarado and his wife had been journeying toward their new home in Montclava with the merchants, and when they saw Case, he'd reminded them so much of the son they'd lost at sea only a few weeks before that they'd bought him, including Tildie in the bargain. However, Tildie couldn't speak Comanche or Spanish at the time, and when she tried to tell them her name, they thought she was saying "Matilda" instead of "Me Tildie", and the name stuck. Not knowing how to read or write, with no way of ever finding her way back home again, and threatened with being sold to someone else if they did try to leave, or if she told anyone, even Joaquín, the truth about their son, Tildie had accepted her fate, and became Matilda, letting Case become Joaquín Luís de Alvarado.

Teffin closed her eyes, her thoughts running back over the past few months, and she shivered at the thought of what might have happened had the black woman not shown up. She'd have been married to her brother. The very sin she was trying to run away from. The whole thing was hopeless, and she opened her eyes again, her fingertips lightly touching her lips as she remembered all the passionate kisses she had shared with Joaquín.

It was all so impossible. She couldn't have Kaelen, and couldn't have Joaquín. Her lips pursed angrily. She had to start thinking of him as Case, if that was at all possible. Sighing disgustedly, she sat up, then looked over toward the door as she heard the knob turn.

"Who is it?"

"It's me." Heather stepped inside, and Teffin looked away.

"I won't come down anymore," she said. "I just can't, not yet."

Heather walked to the bed and stood near it, looking down at Teffin. "Case is back," she offered.

Teffin glanced up. "Is he all right?"

"Yes, your father's talking to him."

"Is he going to stay?"

"I don't know." She studied her daughter curiously. "It'll be hard for him if he does. He loved you, Teffin."

"I know." Teffin felt the heat on her face, and knew her face was probably crimson. "But don't worry, Ma, he can stay here, because I'm the one who's going."

"You? What are you talking about?"

Teffin stood up, walked to the window, and stared out, a lump sticking in her throat as she caught a glimpse of Kaelen working on a broken fencepost out front.

"I know now what I'm going to do, and in a way, I guess it's what I'm supposed to do." She turned to her mother, her eyes hard, unfeeling. "I'm going to become a nun, Mother," she announced carefully.

Heather's eyes widened. "You're what?"

"You heard me."

"You can't be serious."

"I'm quite serious. There's a convent up near St. Louis. I remember one of the priests in town mentioning it one time. It's the Sisters of St. Joseph. I've written them a letter. It's there on the desk," and she nodded toward the small desk on the other side of her room. "I'm sure they'll accept me."

"This is ridiculous, Teffin," Heather exclaimed. "You're not even a good Catholic."

"That's not my fault."

"Oh, Lord, here we go."

"Well, it isn't. I can't help it if the only church is way in town, and you and Pa hardly ever go."

"Teffin, we accepted the Catholic faith only as a prerequisite for living here, and you know it. I never told you you had to be Catholic."

"Well, I am. I was christened one, wasn't I?"

"That's beside the point."

Teffin wasn't about to be persuaded to give up her decision. What did she care anyway? Didn't everybody always say, as long as you believed in God, it didn't matter what church you went to? So why the big fuss? Walking over, she picked up the letter that was already addressed, and stared down at the envelope.

"There's nothing you can say that'll change my mind, and that's all there is to it, Ma," she said. "I only hope I get an answer right away."

She didn't, though. It was three months before she had her answer, packed her clothes, and was ready to ride away from the Crown D, and during that time, everybody, including Blythe and Grandma Dicia, tried to talk her out of it.

"You know you won't be happy, dear," Grandma Dicia had said while visiting one Sunday afternoon. "You were baptized Catholic, yes, but you know in your heart you weren't brought up one."

"I was going to be married in the church."

"I know." Grandma patted her hands. "But marriage to a man, even as a Catholic, is far different from being married to the church. And that's what being a nun is, dear, marriage to the church."

Even Joaquín—Case—had tried to dissuade her.

"It will not help to run away, and you know it," he said the first evening he was home. "I discovered that the hard way." He was still wearing the mustache he had worn as Joaquín, and she had a hard time thinking of him as anyone else, although she could understand now why she had liked him so much as a friend. Brothers were supposed to be friends.

"But I have to go," she answered truthfully. "It's not just what happened to us, Joaquín . . . I mean, Case . . . it's just everything."

"But to give your life to the church . . ."

"You said it was the only church."

"Sí, I said that, and it is for me . . . rather it was. I do not even know myself now if I still believe what it tells me."

"You don't mean that."

"But I do. You see, I had a lot of thinking to do when I rode away from here the day Matilda told me about myself. First of all, I had to come to some sort of, what you say, understanding about my feelings for you. It is not easy to stop loving someone, Teffin."

She nodded. "I know."

He reached out and took her hand, looking deep into her eyes. "I will always care, you know that," he said, trying not to lose the perspective it had taken him so many days to find. "And as long as I live, I will have a special place in my heart for you. But I also know you will never be mine to love as a wife, and I do not like this, but I will accept it, just like I had to accept the fact that I am not the true son of Don Estéban de Alvarado. You have only to accept me as a brother, Teffin, but I must change my whole life, and come to terms with these new things, and at the same time give you up, but I do not run away."

"I'm not running away. It's what I want."

"It will be a mistake."

"It won't be the first I've ever made."

"But it will be the most foolish."

"I guess I'll be a fool then, because I intend to go."

It was the same argument she gave Kaelen when he tried to talk her into changing her mind. Her decision was made, and nothing was going to deter her.

Unfortunately it rained the day Teffin finally had everything in order and left the Crown D. It had taken the whole summer for all the paperwork back and forth from St. Louis, but now the day had come. Heather and Cole were going with her and Helene in the closed carriage as far as Galveston, then she and Helene would go the rest of the way alone, sailing to New Orleans, and on up the Mississippi by steamboat.

At first Teffin rebelled against even having Helene along, but when her father insisted it was either Helene or her mother, she opted for Helene, because she knew if her mother came along, she'd try to argue her out of doing what she was doing for the whole trip.

It rained all the way to San Felipe, but the next day the sun came out and the last part of the trip to the coast was more enjoyable. There had been little laughter in Teffin's life lately. How could there be, when she was forced to live under the same roof with both Case and Kaelen. The situation was impossible, and the farther from the Crown D they rode, the more impossible she realized it had become, so that the long, tedious journey was like a tonic to her. By the time she and Helene stood on the deck of the ship taking them to New Orleans and the Mississippi River, and watched the harbor at Galveston receding in the distance while they waved good-bye to her parents, she'd made up her mind that no matter what, she was going to try to be the best nun the Sisters of St. Joseph ever had.

However, resolutions are easier made than kept, and it wasn't long before Teffin began to realize Case was right. In fact, after an exciting steamboat ride up to St. Louis, her introduction to convent life left much to be desired.

In the first place, all during the long riverboat ride she'd fought back and forth with her feelings, knowing she had to get away, and knowing it was not only for her sake, but Kaelen's too. Only the closer they came to St. Louis, the more she began to question just what she was getting herself into. The only problem was, she was just stubborn enough not to want to admit it.

And when they finally arrived at the convent and the mother superior paraded out the clothes she was to wear, showing her the drab cell-like room that was to be hers as a neophyte, and told her the strict rules she'd have to abide by, the only thing that kept her from going back home was the pain that still filled her breast at the memory of Kaelen, and she became more determined than ever to stay, even though Helene gave her one last chance to change her mind.

The steamboat ride had really been a new adventure for Helene as well as Teffin, and Helene had been hoping that after seeing some of the young men on the boat, and just generally associating with the other people, as well as realizing there was life beyond the Crown D, Teffin would end up going back home with her. However, she hadn't counted on Teffin's stubborn pride, nor had she any idea what Teffin was really running from. Perhaps if she had, she would have used different tactics to talk her out of staying, but every mention of returning home was met by an obstinate "Never!" from Teffin. So, after making sure she was settled in, Helene said her good-byes and headed back to the waterfront for the long journey home alone, while Teffin tried to assimilate herself into convent life.

At first Teffin didn't mind too much, adhering to the rigid rules, although having her beautiful golden hair cut almost to her scalp brought tears to her eyes. However, obstinacy and a determination that she was doing the right thing made her gulp back the tears and try to accept the life she'd decided on. Besides, she thought as the hair fell from her head, she had six months in which to make her final decision. And later that first night, as she lay on her cot after evening prayers, she vowed she'd make it, even though her pillow was wet with tears.

Almost five months later, Teffin was still at the convent, all right, but oh, those last few months had gone terribly slowly. The monotonous prayers in the morning and evenings bored her to death, the work was dull and uninspiring, and the rules absolutely ridiculous. In the first place, Teffin had always felt she could talk better to God in her own words, instead of with a lot of prayers someone else made up. And she'd always talked to God whenever she felt like it too, which always seemed to be when she was either thanking Him for something, or asking for His help. But to repeat the same old words seemed to have no connection to God for her at all. It was just something to say and do because the mother superior said so. And unlike the mother superior told her it would, somehow she knew it never did a thing for her soul.

Nor did the sewing, or floor scrubbing, or even the books they read make her feel any closer to God. Many a night she lay on her cot remembering back to the ranch, and felt she'd been closer to God there, when she'd worked with the horses for Pa, than she felt now, or even when she was kneeling down before the altar on Sundays.

Grandma had always told them God didn't need buildings, or fancy words, or all the traditions men heaped up before Him. He was just there all the time for you to love, and that meant loving His Son, and accepting Him too. You didn't need a lot of folderol. It was as simple as that.

Now, this afternoon, as Teffin knelt in the garden at the convent, staring down at the row of young peas she'd been weeding, Grandma Dicia's words came back to her so loud and clear it was like a bell ringing in her head, and she just had to listen.

She sat back on her heels, ignoring the dirt covering the front of her clothes, and glanced over at the wall surrounding the place to keep the world out, and she thought back over everything that had happened since she'd arrived. They'd cut her hair. Why? She lifted her hand, letting a finger slide beneath her habit. It was longer again, starting to grow out. But for the life of her, she couldn't understand why they'd cut it in the first place. What did having short, stubby hair have to do with loving God?

She'd always thought sisters became sisters to devote their lives to God, but did they really? Is that what God wanted them to do? Shut themselves off from everyone and everything? She drew her gaze from the wall and glanced across the garden to where two of the other novices were working. Sister Anne and Sister Therese. Of all the girls in the convent, she'd become closer to them than any of the others, and yet, she didn't really know them all that well. She did know, though, that they were here, not so much because they loved God, but because if they had stayed in the outside world they'd have had to make decisions and live their own lives. It was more a matter of survival. And all the others. So many were running away, just like her, and what better place to run to? Here they did what they were told, had clothes on their backs and food in their mouths. When they weren't fasting.

That was another thing. If Mother Philomena thought she was going to make Teffin stop breaking the rules by making her fast in repentance for her sins, she was sadly mistaken. All it ever did was cause her to eat double helpings at the next meal. After all, Teffin told herself time after time, didn't the Bible say it wasn't what went into a man's mouth that defiled him, but what came out, because what came out came from the heart? Then what good did making her go without food do?

It wasn't just that, though. It was everything. And she didn't like have having to be called Sister Felicita either. So who cared whether any of the saints were named Teffin or not!

She leaned over again, going back to her weeding, and pulled up a big fat weed, then stared down at it, not really seeing it at all. All she could see was years of pulling weeds, with her hands dirty, nails broken and cracked, and her knees sore. Then there'd be hours of sewing, and maybe even teaching other people's children, if she decided to teach. And those long hours of monotonous prayers ahead of her. Suddenly she squeezed the weed until her fingers hurt.

"No! I won't. I can't," she finally mumbled to herself, then sighed. "But if I don't, what else is there?"

Leaning back on her heels again, she watched the other two sisters once more, then bit her lip as she pondered her alternatives. There was only one other place she could go where life might hold some chance of being normal for her again. Only, knowing mother superior, there was no way she'd give Teffin her permission, because on the day she and Helene arrived, although Mother Philomena had made sure Teffin understood that if at any time she was dissatisfied, she could leave, she had also made sure they knew if Teffin quit, her parents would have to be notified, and Teffin would have to wait for someone to come take her home. A place where Teffin didn't want to go.

No, if she went, it would have to be on her own, without anyone's permission. It was the only way she could avoid ending up back in Texas. And more and more every day now, she knew she couldn't keep on pretending. She had to leave. She just didn't belong. Each time she said the Hail Marys and tried to say a rosary, she felt like a traitor to Jesus. After all, the Bible said Jesus was the only way to get to heaven, not through His mother, the saints, or any of the rest of it. No wonder Ma and Pa never went to church, she thought as she pondered her feelings. They'd probably have made lousy Catholics too.

The weed dropped from her hand, and she stood up, brushing the dirt from her habit in response to the ringing of a bell inside the church. Well, if she was going to go, she was going to have to figure out a way to go, and she'd have to do it all by herself too, because she knew Sister Anne and Sister Therese, who had already started to leave the garden would never keep a secret like that from anyone, let alone Mother Philomena.

That afternoon, as prayers began in the chapel in the

convent of the Sisters of St. Joseph, one novice, mouthing the Our Fathers and Hail Marys without really paying attention to what she was saying, had her thoughts on anything but her devotion to God. Instead, as the memorized prayers fell softly from Teffin's lips, her mind was running back and forth over how she was going to accomplish the decision she'd made only a few hours earlier, so that it would cause the least stir and be the most successful. Later that evening, by the time vespers were completed, the whole plan had been settled on, its execution only a few days away. That is, if all went well and she was able to get her hands on the clothes she'd arrived in that had been put away for safekeeping, just in case.

The next day, shortly after morning prayers, Teffin stood in the mother superior's office and faced the older woman, whose eyes were studying her as if she'd just encountered the devil himself, instead of a young woman of nineteen who had simply decided convent life wasn't for her.

"You're absolutely positive?" Mother Philomena asked as she eyed Teffin, her dark eyes accusing.

Teffin was tired of explaining. "If I was any more positive . . . I . . . I just don't want to be here. I've told you why, and that should be enough, shouldn't it?"

Mother Philomena's fingers drummed on the desktop in front of her, and she took a deep breath, sighing unhappily. "I was so hoping we could do something with you, Sister Felicita," she said, her voice harsh, unyielding. "But it seems you've done nothing but break the rules and try to do things your own way since the day you arrived. So maybe it's for the best, who knows. But you will have to stay here until your parents or someone responsible comes for you. You do understand that, don't you?"

"I know I have to go home, if that's what you mean, but since I no longer wish to remain, isn't it possible for me to have some of my own clothes back to wear until I leave? After all, they are mine."

"You don't seem to understand, my dear. I can't give you your clothes back. At least not until the day you leave. You see, if you were to wear your street clothes, you would set a bad example for the other girls. No, sister, you may not have your clothes back yet. I'll write to your parents first and we'll make arrangements, but until the day you set foot out of the Sisters of St. Joseph, you'll remain in your habit. Do you understand?"

Teffin took a deep breath, her topaz eyes sparking dangerously. She hadn't expected this. "Then you refuse me?"

"I refuse to let you wear your street clothes, yes. As for leaving us, perhaps it's better you do go," she went on. "Because we don't want some one here who lacks a true calling. Now, if you don't mind, I do have duties to perform this morning," and she walked out from behind the desk and opened the door for Teffin to leave.

Teffin didn't move, though, and she stood for a minute staring at Mother Philomena.

"Well," the older woman said. "What is it now?"

Teffin had been holding her breath, and she exhaled. "I guess . . . well, I was thinking . . . maybe . . . I think I've changed my mind. I think maybe I'll give it a little more time, Mother Philomena," she finally said, surprising the mother superior. "After all, I have been here not quite five months. Maybe I'm being a little too hasty."

"Then you're going to stay?"

Teffin tried to hide the hostility gnawing her insides. "Yes, I've decided to stay, at least until the full six months is up."

"Well, fine, then I won't have to write your parents. But for now, sister, we do have things to do, and you've wasted enough of my time," and again she waited for Teffin to leave.

This time Teffin obliged her. But that evening as Teffin sat in her room staring out the window, she knew that leaving the Sisters of St. Joseph was going to be a harder task than she'd expected, because she needed those street clothes, and they were safely locked away in a storeroom behind Mother Philomena's office.

Two nights later, while the empty halls of the convent echoed with the melodious chanting from the chapel during vespers, a lone figure made its way along the deserted hallway outside the mother superior's office, then hesitated for a minute before opening the door and slipping inside. Half an hour later Teffin sat in the dingy cell she called her room and checked to make sure she had everything from home, including the handbag she'd brought with her. She'd managed to pilfer the key for the storage room from Mother Philomena's office, but now her problem was that the handbag was empty, and there was no way she was going to get out of St. Louis without money. It was the only part of the plan she hadn't come up with a solution for as yet.

She had feigned a stomachache so she wouldn't have to go to vespers tonight, and now she leaned back against the pillow on her bed and sat for a long time pondering. Where on earth was she going to get enough money to leave? Then her gaze fell on the Bible on the stand next to her cot. It was new. Had been given to her by Uncle Bain and Aunt Liz when she'd left home, only she wasn't going to need it now, and it was a fancy, expensive one. Besides, it was a Catholic Bible, she told herself, and she had a feeling that when she left here, it'd be a long time before she ever saw the inside of a Catholic church again.

Reaching over, she picked the Bible up, fingering it carefully. It should be worth something. Maybe even enough to get her all the way to South Carolina and her grandparents, because that's where she'd decided to go. It was the only place left to her where she wouldn't have to ever see Kaelen again.

Determined now to make her own way, later that evening, while everyone else slept, Teffin, her street clothes tucked beneath her arm, slipped quietly from the room, crept through the corridors on tiptoe until she reached the back door, then moved stealthily outside. After shutting the door quietly behind her, she climbed up the small apple tree at the end of the garden, to reach the top of the wall surrounding the convent, then slid down over the other side, melting into the darkness, where she hoped to find a place to change her clothes.

The next morning, as the sun began to filter into the sky, diminishing the stars and bringing the city of St.

Louis to life again, Teffin stood in front of an old store, its windows full of all forms of bric-a-brac, and waited for it to open, hoping no one from the convent was looking for her as yet. She'd left her novice habit rolled up in a ball and stuffed into an old rubbish barrel in the alley near where she'd changed clothes, and although her hair was still shorter than any other woman's on the street, at least she didn't feel out of place in her deep russet dress and matching bonnet.

She had spent the night huddled in that alley, and now she stood for some time, the Bible tucked under her arm, waiting for the shop to open, and every time someone went by, she'd hold her breath. Finally, after what seemed like ages, an elderly man arrived, opened the door, and stepped inside, with Teffin following close behind. A few minutes later, she left the shop behind, heading for the docks this time, with enough money to at least get her as far as New Orleans, she hoped, and maybe farther. The Bible had been a good one, with gold lettering on the cover, and fancy pictures inside.

"Just the kind they like out at the convent," the old man had said as he handed her the money.

Now, as Teffin walked away, nearing the river, where she'd planned to buy passage on the next steamboat heading out, she couldn't help smiling at the thought that indirectly, if one of the sisters from the convent bought the Bible she'd sold to the old man, Mother Philomena would be helping her run away.

Teffin's ticket, when she bought it, was for New Orleans, as she had wanted. Only it had taken almost all her money. What she'd do for more to buy passage the rest of the way to Port Royal, she'd worry about when the time came. For right now though, all she wanted was to find something to eat, because she hadn't eaten since the night before, and as soon as the *Southern Star* pulled away from the docks, she made her way toward the galley to see what she could find.

Her long journey up to St. Louis with Helene had already introduced her to life on the river, so it was nothing new to her this time, and even though she hadn't been able to afford a big cabin like before, she had had enough money for a small one that reminded her of her room back at the convent, because there was just barely enough space for a bed and dresser. However, it sufficed. Only now, the second day out of St. Louis, she began to have another problem. There was one man on board who was really staring at her all the time, and it made her rather edgy, since she was traveling alone.

Most of the day he was with a younger man, and both were in buckskins, so she assumed they were trappers who'd come down out of the mountains to the west. But there were times when the older man was all by himself, and more than once she'd caught him staring at her intently.

Finally, toward evening on the third day, while she stood on the upper deck watching the sun turning the sky to a golden red before dipping down below the trees, she sensed a movement close by, and turned to find herself staring right at the older man, who was slowly bearing down on her from the other end of the promenade.

Her first instinct was to run, but he was rather a handsome man, in a dashing way. His dusty blond hair was edged with gray, and his dark brown eyes were so intense they made her shiver, the crow's-feet in their corners driven even deeper by the dark tan on his face. And he walked so forcefully and solidly like a man who was sure just who he was and where he was going.

"Excuse me, miss," he began when he finally reached her, and she saw that the broad-brimmed hat he carried was new compared to his buckskins. "I know I'm a stranger, miss, but . . . I must talk to you, if you'll permit me."

Teffin straightened nervously, her gold-flecked eyes studying him warily. "Go ahead," she answered, after looking around to make sure they weren't alone on deck.

"Thank you." Then he hesitated for a second, as if unsure how to begin. "I know you'll probably think I'm just saying this to try to strike up a conversation, my dear," he said, his voice not as confident as his walk had been. "But believe me, I mean it as a compliment, really

I do, although you'll probably think it's a strange one. But you see, you're the very image of my younger sister when she was about your age." His eyes shifted to take in her hairline. "Your hair, the color of your eyes." His hand disappeared into the inside pocket of his buckskin jacket, as he once more looked at her face. "Here, look at this," and he held out a small enameled miniature for her to take.

Teffin reached out, then gazed down at the delicate portrait in her hand, and a frown creased her forehead, gooseflesh making her skin begin to crawl, for the young woman in the picture, whose portrait had been so painstakingly painted, could very well have been herself. It was uncanny.

"She's your sister?" she asked as she studied it.

"Her name's Frances. Frances Harley, only when she was your age she was Frances Brooks."

Teffin's frown deepened as she stared at the picture of the young woman who looked like her.

"Now you know why I was staring, Miss, ah . . ."

"Dante," Teffin answered, her thoughts still wandering. "My names Dante. Teffin Dante."

Suddenly she looked up, realizing the man hadn't moved. He was standing motionless, as if he'd seen a ghost.

"Is something wrong?" she asked.

"May I ask how old you are?" he asked, his voice husky with emotion. "Please, it's important."

Teffin wasn't exactly comfortable with the way her conversation with this stranger was going. Yet he didn't seem to be the sort of man she should be afraid of. Actually, he was much older than she, and seemed more the type a girl would ask to help her if she needed it, and she relaxed just a little, but still held the picture, keeping herself at a distance.

"I'll be twenty in December. Why?" she answered, and for a second she was sure she caught a hint of tears in his eyes.

"Is your mother's name Heather, Teffin?" he asked, surprising her, and this time she knew his voice had a definite break in it. "And does she have beautiful violet eyes?"

Teffin's head drew back, and she stared at him suspiciously. "You know my mother?" she asked. This was crazy.

"If her name's Heather Dante and she has violet eyes, and she's married to a gentleman named Cole Dante, then yes, I know your mother," he said, his voice still strained. "And I believe I know you too."

"I don't understand."

"I think I do now," he said, then looked about, spotting a bench a few feet away on the deck. "Please," he said, gesturing toward it. "Will you sit down, Miss Dante, and I'll try to give you the only explanation I know of that could be the reason you look so much like my sister. And by the way, Miss Dante, my name is Brooks. Ian Brooks, if that helps."

At the moment, however, nothing was helping, and Teffin studied him for a minute, then moved to the bench and sat down. Ian Brooks came over and sat beside her, only he still hadn't bothered to take the enameled miniature from her.

"Have you ever heard my name, Miss Dante?" he asked, his eyes searching her face.

"No, should I have?"

"I wasn't sure. But you do know that years ago, your mother was once kidnapped and thought dead, right?"

"You know about that?"

"Yes, I know about it, In fact, I was with your mother before she reached Cole Dante again," he answered. "I helped her to survive in the wilderness, and brought her back to Fort Smith."

Teffin stared at him in disbelief, flabbergasted by this new turn of events, then suddenly she glanced down at the enameled portrait she was still holding, and a weird sensation began to sweep through her.

"Your mother returned to Fort Smith in May of 1818, Miss Dante," Ian Brooks continued. "And you were born in December. That's only eight months, my dear. A woman's confinement is usually nine . . . and you look exactly like Frances did when she was your age."

Suddenly Teffin knew what he was trying to tell her, and the strange uneasiness she'd been feeling ever since first seeing the picture began to grow stronger.

"Are you trying to tell me my mother and you . . . that . . . that I'm your daughter?" she gasped, and saw the man's eyes darken with concern.

"It's the only explanation there is." His voice was barely a whisper so anyone standing nearby wouldn't hear. "Don't you see? You certainly don't look like Cole Dante, now do you?"

Teffin's gaze moved from the picture to his face, and she looked directly into his eyes. He was trying to tell her he was her father?

"You and my mother?" She shook her head. "No, not Ma, she'd never do anything like that. No . . . I don't believe you," she cried.

"Then maybe you can tell me why you look exactly like my sister?"

"That isn't fair!"

"Isn't it? Miss Dante, Teffin, I know both your parents. I knew them years ago, and I have a strange feeling they've known all along who your real father is. They'd have to, and believe me, there could be no other explanation."

"But you and Ma . . . she let you . . . ?" Her face grew crimson, and she just couldn't say the words.

"I loved your mother, Teffin, I still do," he said, trying to make her understand. "And just for a while she let me love her. If that was wrong, then I'm sorry, but it did happen. Your father knew it, and yet he forgave her. But the facts are still undeniable. You're my daughter, Teffin Dante, mine and Heather's, not hers and Cole's, and there's no way any of us can deny it. Especially not now that I've seen you."

Teffin had been watching Ian Brooks's face closely, while tears gathered in her eyes. Not Pa's daughter? Oh, God! She was Teffin! Teffin Dante! Then suddenly a wild exhilaration began to catch at her, and her eyes widened.

It was incredible! She wasn't his daughter! Pa wasn't her father! And if this man was right—this man who called himself Ian Brooks—if he was right, and she wasn't Pa's daughter, then she wasn't Kaelen's sister either, was she? Oh, my God! She wasn't Kaelen's sister!

"Do you know what this means?" she asked, suddenly looking happy instead of sad, as he'd expected, and Ian was puzzled at the change. "No, you don't know, how could you," she went on, the tears now streaming down her cheeks. "It's the answer to all my prayers. Oh, thank you, Mr. Brooks, thank you, thank you, thank you," she cried. "Because you see, if Pa's not my pa, then I'm not really Kaelen's sister, and oh, Mr. Brooks, if what you say is true, you've just made me about the happiest person on the face of the earth."

For the next half-hour, while the sun went down and the stars began to fill the sky and the steamboat plied its way downriver, Teffin and Ian Brooks sat on the promenade deck breathing in the tangy night air of April, and talked. They talked about the years before Teffin was born, and the weeks and months Ian and Heather had shared together. How Heather lost a baby she was expecting, then broke her leg, and how Ian took care of her. And they also talked about the years after Teffin's birth. The years Ian had missed. Teffin even told him about Kaelen and Case, and how she'd been running away.

"But now, don't you see, if you're right, Mr. Brooks," she said as she sat looking at this man, who no longer seemed so much a stranger to her, "If you are really my father, then Kaelen isn't my brother, and I have every right to love him after all, don't I?"

Ian Brooks stared at her thoughtfully, his heart in his eyes. If only he'd known. But what good would that have done? It still wouldn't have changed his life. He'd told Heather he was a wanderer, and here he was, still wandering. Actually, he had his aide, Lieutenant Warren Russell, were heading now for the Texas frontier to map out some of the area for the United States Army, an assignment that definitely wasn't in the best interests of the Republic of Texas, and therefore had to be done without its knowledge. An assignment he wasn't free to tell anyone about. Not even this newly found daughter of his.

But to find her after all these years—and she had to be his daughter. She looked so much like Fran it was frightening. Even the unusual topaz color of her eyes that had a way of catching golden highlights when the light caught them just right. How many times he'd seen Fran's eyes do the very same thing.

He smiled. "Where do the Dante's call home now?" he asked, trying not to let anxiety at discovering who she was scare her. "I knew they'd left the Arkansas River territory, but have no idea where they went from there."

"We live in Texas now," she answered, her fingers absentmindedly caressing the face of the miniature while she stared at him. She was still in a mild state of shock over what he'd revealed to her, and her insides were all a jumble. "Pa and Uncle Bain have ranches about thirty miles or so west of San Antonio."

"That's Indian Territory, isn't it?"

"Comanche, yes, sir. But we've managed to survive."

"You're going home now?"

"Not exactly. At least I wasn't," she answered, and looked down at the picture she was still caressing. "But now . . ." She looked over at him again.

"Now it all depends on whether I go home with you or not, is that it?"

"Oh . . . would you?" she asked. "If I went home and told Ma what you just told me, they'd say I was touched in the head or something, but if they heard it from you, and saw this picture . . ."

Again Ian smiled, and this time Teffin knew she saw tears in his eyes as she handed him back the miniature, and he nodded. "I can't think of anything that could stop me," he answered, and he gazed down at the picture of his sister, then tucked it back into the inside pocket on his buckskins again, and for the rest of the evening Teffin couldn't believe what was happening. More than once, she actually pinched herself to make sure she wasn't dreaming.

Later that same evening, as Teffin sat in the sparse cabin she'd been assigned to, and glanced out the only window, directly above her bed, she stared up at the stars above and talked to God, the only way she knew how to talk to Him, from the heart.

"Thank you, God," she whispered softly as she wiped a stray hair away, where it was curling into her ear, then listened to the paddle wheel of the steamboat slapping the water as it rolled on through the night. "Thank you for listening to my prayers. Grandma was right, you know. I can see that now. I don't need all the rest of it. All I need is You. I prayed so hard that somehow I'd find a way to be with Kaelen, and now I know why You had me be so stubborn in my decision to go to St. Louis, even though we both knew I wouldn't be happy there. And You were the one who helped me to get the key to Mother Philomena's storeroom so easily that night so I could get my clothes, because You knew he'd be on this boat, didn't You? Oh, thank you, God, I'll never forget as long as I live, and I'll never ever doubt what You can do, ever again."

She took a deep breath, her heart fairly bursting inside at the thought that she was really going home. And with her father too. A sigh escaped her lips as she slid down on the bed and cuddled the small hard pillow beneath her head, in the hopes of maybe finally being able to fall asleep.

"And thank You for helping me find my real father," she murmured, and with that her eyes shut, a smile graced her lips, and she began to relax, while down the corridor, in another cabin, Ian Brooks sat on the edge of his bed explaining to Lieutenant Russell just why a young woman named Teffin Dante was going to be traveling with them all the way to the Texas frontier.

"It's a perfect cover, don't you see?" he said as he watched Warren putting an edge on the knife he always carried in his sheath. "And a legitimate reason for us to be out there too. What more could we want?"

"And if they become suspicious?" Warren tested the knife by shaving a few hairs from the back of his hand. "Remember, Major, if any of those Texans get so much as a hint of what we're doing, there'll be the devil to pay."

"You don't think Houston knows what's going on back east?" Ian asked, then shook his head. "Hell, Warren, why do you think he ended up in Texas in the first place? You know damn well this was probably planned all along. Dammit, I'll bet you that within less than ten years Houston and his Texans will be begging to come into the Union. And when that happens, we won't have to trust their maps and surveys, either, we'll have our own, and we'll be one jump ahead of them when we're really needed. You can take it for what it's worth, but I'll bet the White House had its eye on Texas long before Jackson even sent Houston down there. So what we're doing it just getting things ready. Now, with Teffin joining us, and giving us a reason for being out there, it'll only make our job easier."

"And she's really your daughter?"

"She's really my daughter." Ian stretched out on the hard bed, his hands behind his head, and watched Warren put away his knife, then cup his hand over the candle lamp in the wall sconce to blow it out. "And tomorrow I'll introduce you," Ian said, then sighed as the cabin was plunged into darkness. "Good night, Lieutenant."

"Major . . ." And a few minutes later, all that could be heard was the splash of the paddle wheel as the sound floated in through open window above their heads, and the deep breathing of Lieutenant Warren Russell, who was already asleep. For Major Ian Brooks, however, it was going to be a long night, and he knew it, as his thoughts began to wander back into the past, to the woman he'd given his heart to so long ago, and to the night his daughter was conceived. A night that had haunted him often over the years, but a night he never wanted to forget.

The next morning, Lieutenant Warren Russell was introduced to Teffin Dante as her newly found father's friend and traveling companion, and Ian Brooks explained to her that he'd already told Warren the circumstances of their meeting, and the obvious conclusions they'd come to, and Warren agreed to follow along with them to the Crown D.

For Teffin this whole new change of events was almost overwhelming, and she was having a hard time keeping everything in the right perspective. She was ecstatic over the fact that there was no longer anything to keep her and Kaelen apart, and yet her heart ached for Pa. Was he going to understand that she wasn't going to toss him aside as if he'd never existed? He'd still be her pa as far as she was concerned. Maybe he wasn't her real pa, like Mr. Brooks said, but he was the only pa she'd ever known. So it wasn't as if he wouldn't still be her pa. But he was going to be hurt, and so was Ma.

If only there was a way to accept what was happening without letting it touch their lives. But there wasn't, and as the *Southern Star* continued traversing the muddy waters of the Mississippi River, making its way closer and closer to New Orleans with every day that passed, Teffin prayed God would somehow ease the blow she knew was coming for her parents.

In the meantime, Ian Brooks was busily playing the doting father to the daughter he hadn't known existed. It was Ian Brooks who watched over her like a hawk, making sure none of the other passengers annoyed her or caused her any problems, and Ian Brooks who had left the boat with her one afternoon only a few days before revealing his part in her life and helped her pick up two new dresses and a small brocade bag to keep them in, since she'd left the convent with only the clothes on her back. And it was Ian Brooks who paid for her passage on the sailing ship that took them from New Orleans to Galveston, and Ian Brooks who, as they left Galveston, let her ride behind him on the horse he'd brought with him all the way from St. Louis. And it was Ian Brooks, with Warren Russell's help, who watched over her and helped her on the long journey home through the wild Texas countryside. And during all that time together,

Teffin began to understand a little more about the father she had never known, and what she learned, she liked.

Now, weeks later, her russet suit rumpled and dirty, her nose still peeling from too much sun all at once, but with her heart singing inside, Teffin sat astride Ian's horse and held tight to the buckskin-clad man sitting in front of her, then glanced over to Warren riding beside them, and tears filled her eyes. She was almost home. Only a half-mile more down the road, and life was going to be good again. She just knew it, and her arms tightened on Ian's waist.

"We're almost there," she said, her voice tremulous, expectant.

Ian's head turned, and he glanced down over his shoulder, seeing only the top of her head. "You'll be all right?"

"Yes, I'll be all right," she answered, although her stomach was full of butterflies. "Now let's hurry, so we can just get it over with," and with that, Ian nudged his horse into a loping canter, for he too was anxious. Not just to claim the daughter he'd found after all these years, but to see once more the woman he'd always loved, the woman who'd given his daughter birth.

14

It was midafternoon. Heather stood on the veranda, leaning on the broom she'd been using to sweep the porch, and she stared off toward the front gate, watching as two horses continued moving toward the house. She had spotted them turning off the main road a couple of minutes before, and was trying to figure out who it might be. A hand shaded her eyes, only it didn't help. All she could make out was that the lead horse carried two riders, and one looked like a woman, her bonnet barely visible behind the man's buckskin-clad shoulder, her kid shoes sticking out behind his moccasined feet.

It wasn't until the rider on the first horse reined up at the end of the front walk, slid down, then reached back up to help his companion down, that Heather gasped, recognizing Teffin. Teffin's face was dirty, her once-beautiful traveling suit a wrinkled mess, but her eyes were shining with enthusiasm as she started up the walk and met her mother halfway.

Heather had leaned the broom against the porch railing and quickly descended the steps, and now she quickened her pace at the sight of Teffin.

"Good heavens! What are you doing here, and like this?" she asked as she grabbed her daughter's shoulders and stared at her.

Teffin grinned sheepishly. "Is that any way to say hello, Ma?"

Heather bit back a sharp retort as her violet eyes took in her daughter's unkempt appearance. She seemed to look all right physically.

"I guess it's not," she answered, and pulled Teffin into her arms, closing her eyes to absorb the feel of her young body more lovingly, then she opened them again and once more confronted Teffin. "Now, how and why?" she asked, her eyes on Teffin's face.

"Not yet, Ma, please," Teffin begged, and glanced back behind her to where Ian stood, holding his horse's reins, while Warren sat, still mounted, as if he wasn't sure whether they'd be welcome or not. "There's someone I want you to meet, Ma," she went on. "He brought me safely all the way from St. Louis. Come on," and she grabbed her mother's hand, pulling Heather with her toward the two riders who were waiting.

Most of the front walk was in the sun, but the big oak out front shaded the end of it, as well as part of the drive, and Heather's eyes settled on the first rider, who was standing next to his horse. When she'd started toward him, he'd turned for a second, his back to her, rearranging something on his saddle, but now, as she drew closer, he turned back to face her, and she stopped abruptly, pulling her hand from Teffin's grasp.

Her knees suddenly felt like jelly. It was him . . . yet it couldn't be! She swallowed hard, unaware that the late-afternoon breeze had lifted some of her dark red curls and gently plastered them against her cheek, or that she was still in the sun, and it had caught the rest of her hair, turning it to fire. All she could do was stare at the buckskin-clad figure of a man she'd thought never to see again. A man she'd thought of so often over the years, whenever she'd looked at her daughter.

"Ian?" she gasped, her feet glued to the stone walk, and a hand flew to her breast to keep her heart from leaping right out.

He looked so well. There were a few more lines in his face, yes, but they only made him look more rugged, and instinctively she knew that, true to his word, he'd never settle down in one place. The buckskins attested to that.

Ian's hand tightened on his horse's reins as he stared at what, to him, was the most beautiful woman in the world. And she hadn't changed, not really. Oh, the wrinkles were a bit deeper around her eyes perhaps, and her figure had filled out and matured some, but the years had been kind to her.

"Hello, Heather." His voice broke on the name. "It's been a long time."

Teffin stood motionless for a few seconds, just watching the two of them, then, eager to take an edge off the shock she knew her mother must be feeling, she took Heather's hand again and continued pulling her toward the end of the walk.

"He said he knew you and Pa," Teffin said, her face flushed, only Heather was still staring at Ian. "He's told me a lot of things, Ma," she went on, hoping her mother was listening. "A lot of things I think I should have been told a long time ago."

Heather inhaled sharply, Teffin's voice finally breaking through to her, and color floated into her face, which had previously been pale from shock.

"I don't understand," she finally said, looking at Teffin first, then Ian, then over to the other rider, who was still mounted. "What's going on?" Her eyes rested on Teffin. "Why aren't you in St. Louis?" She looked directly at Ian. "And why are you here?"

"I think I'd better let Teffin explain that," he answered. "But maybe this'll help," and he reached into his buckskins, taking the small enameled picture of his sister out, and he handed it to Heather.

Heather straightened, trying to keep her composure as she took the small portrait from him. Then she looked down at it, and her jaw tightened. "Who is she?"

Ian was watching her closely. "My sister."

From the look on Heather's face, he knew there'd be little explaining to do as to why he was here.

Teffin could never in all her days have imagined the impact her arrival at the Crown D with Ian and Warren was going to have on everyone's lives. If she had, perhaps she wouldn't have arrived so unexpectedly. But then, no one had prepared her for Ian Brooks either.

By the time Cole and the men rode in from the range, Heather had managed to weather the shock enough to at least act rational, but after seeing Cole's reaction to Ian's presence, Teffin suddenly knew things weren't going to be as easily settled as she'd thought, and she wished she'd had the foresight to make Ian promise not to say a word to either Ma or Pa about her feelings for Kaelen until after she'd had a chance to talk to Kaelen first herself.

Luckily, though, Kaelen and Eli weren't with the men late that afternoon when they rode in. Seems they'd left to hunt a cougar that had been raiding the back corral and killed one of the horses. She was glad, because this way, she didn't have to contend with Pa and Kaelen at the same time. As it was, Pa wasn't taking it any too well, and Teffin sat in the library now, cringing, while she watched the anger smoldering in his sloe eyes as he confronted Ian.

"You had no right to tell her!" he yelled, his face livid.

"Why? Because you're afraid to face the truth?" Ian was just as mad. "You should have told her years ago."

"Told her what? I had no proof. Besides, she was my daughter, and that's all there was to it."

"Just like that? No suspicions? No doubts? You never gave it a thought?" Ian laughed bitterly. "Come on, Cole, I know you. You're smarter than that."

Heather was standing behind the chair Teffin was sitting in, and Cole glanced over at his wife, his face troubled, the pain in his eyes all too revealing. How right Ian was. How many times over the years he'd looked at Teffin and wondered. Suspicions? They'd always been there, yes, but no one had ever put proof to what, until now, had only been conjecture. Now there was no more guessing, no more reason to wonder. Cole shuddered. The miniature Ian had so generously shared with them had shattered forever the illusion that maybe she really was his daughter after all, and had just been born early.

Cole's dark green eyes moved from his wife's face, their gaze settling on Teffin, and he knew regardless of who had fathered her, and in spite of Ian's insistence, in Cole's heart Teffin would always be his daughter, not Ian's.

"Yes, there were suspicions," he finally said, his voice harsh, unyielding. "But they didn't mean a thing, Ian, not a damn thing. Not to me. I've loved her, raised her, and by God, you had no right to tell her any of this."

"I see. In other words, you were willing to just let her go all through life believing she was your daughter regardless of how it might hurt her, is that it?"

"What are you talking about?" Cole's eyes darkened. "How could being my daughter hurt her?"

"That's right, she said you didn't know." Ian looked over at Teffin. "I think you'd better tell them, my dear," he said, the concern in his face all too apparent.

Teffin felt the heat in her face, and knew it was turning crimson. She hadn't wanted to tell them. Not just yet, but then . . . maybe Ian was right, and they should know before she confronted Kaelen.

"Well?" Cole urged as they all stared at her.

"I don't know how to tell you."

Heather's frown deepened. "What is it, Tef?"

Teffin swallowed hard, then looked up into her mother's face. "Do you remember, Ma, the day Helene and I sailed out of Galveston, when you asked me how I thought running away from St. Louis was going to solve anything? Well, I gave you an answer then. Do you remember?"

Heather thought for a minute. "You said it may not solve anything, but at least it won't make matters worse."

"And I was serious, Ma. You see, I couldn't stay here any longer. Not the way things were. It was either leave or die of heartbreak, because I couldn't go on living under the same roof with the man I loved and keep my sanity."

Heather's heart went out to her. "Oh, God! I had no idea you loved Case that much."

"Case? Lord, no, Ma. I don't love Case. I never did. The only reason I was going to marry him was that I couldn't marry Kaelen."

"Kaelen?" Cole was dumbfounded. "You and Kaelen?"

"Ridiculous, isn't it?" Teffin's eyes glistened with tears. "We both knew what was happening, but knowing doesn't always save the situation, and for us it was hopeless. But now . . ."

"Now Teffin doesn't have to hurt anymore, Cole," Ian offered. "Don't you see? Because she doesn't have a half-brother named Kaelen anymore, only a half-brother named Case."

Cole stared at Teffin, his thoughts running back over the night Teffin and Kaelen had spent together when she was snake-bitten, and he remembered how, after Kaelen moved into the house, the way the two always seemed to be either trying to avoid each other or snapping at each other irritably. And he also remembered some of the looks he'd seen pass between them. Yes, it had been there all along, but he'd been too blind to see it. For the first time in his life he felt defeated.

"You really love him?" he asked.

She nodded. "Very much."

Heather turned to Cole, and they exchanged glances, then he stepped over and knelt down in front of Teffin. "You know I love you, don't you, Tef?" he asked.

She nodded. "Yeah, Pa, and I love you too."

"Then will you forgive me?"

"There's nothing to forgive. Not really," she reminded him. "You had no way of knowing for sure. I can't blame you for that."

"If I had been certain . . ." He took her hand and looked into her face, so like the portrait on the enameled miniature Ian carried with him. "Will you tell Kaelen when he gets back, or shall we?"

Teffin felt her heart lighten at his words, and she squeezed his hand, then leaned forward, her arms circling his neck, and she hugged him.

"I'll tell him, Pa. Just as soon as he gets back. Don't worry, I'll tell him," and there were tears in her eyes as she looked up at Ma and her real father, who was watching Ma too, his own eyes misty.

Although everything had been settled in the library that evening, things were still tense at the Crown D. In the first place, Teffin had begged Pa to let Ian and his friend, Warren Russell, stay for a while. At least until after Teffin had broken the news to Kaelen and things had been decided one way or another there. And Kaelen and Eli still hadn't returned by bedtime that night, so Ian and Warren were put up in one of the guestrooms.

It was close to two in the morning when Teffin, still sitting on the back porch where she'd sneaked to after everyone else had gone to bed, saw the two riders making their way down the back lane toward the house. She'd almost fallen asleep twice in the chair already, but now every nerve in her body was wide-awake as she watched the horses and riders stop at the bunkhouse, where one of them got off and went inside, while the other continued on toward the barn, leading the other's horse after him.

It wasn't hard for her to recognize Kaelen's long, lanky stride when he reached the barn and left the saddle, leading the horses inside. That graceful, easy way he had of moving. She pulled the sash on her pink wrap tighter, made sure the slippers were all the way on her feet, and lifted herself from the chair, gliding silently down the porch steps to make her way slowly through the darkness.

Inside the barn, Kaelen was tired. Tired, sweaty, and disgusted. They'd tracked the damn cat halfway across Comanche territory, almost running into an Indian village in the process. And for what? The bastard had gotten clean away, losing himself in a mountain of rocks and boulders just the other side of Painted Creek. Well, maybe they could pick up his trail again tomorrow, only maybe this time it wouldn't take them so long to get back to the ranch.

He was hungry too. The rabbit Eli'd shot had been a scrawny one, and it had been digested hours ago. Sighing wearily, he led Eli's horse to its stall, unfastened the cinch, removed the saddle, then hefted it onto the side rail, followed closely by the saddle blanket. This done, he took off the reins and bit, tied him in, then turned his attention to Sheba.

The mare looked as tired as Kaelen felt as Kaelen took off the saddle. Suddenly he froze at the sound of a noise behind him, near the door. He'd lit the lantern that hung between the stalls when he'd first come into the barn, and now he whirled around, squinting, trying to adjust to the dim light, so he could see into the shadows.

"Who's there?"

Teffin stepped forward, and heard Kaelen's sharp intake of breath.

"My God! What are you doing here?"

She smiled, and he frowned, then tensed even more as she walked toward him. Her golden hair was shorter than it had been when she'd left, and it was framing her face like a halo, with her eyes warm and intense, the lantern deepening their topaz color to a rich bronze.

She looked so pretty in pink, it nearly took his breath away, the nightclothes she wore barely hiding her firm, lithe body from him.

"I . . . I don't understand . . ." he began, but was unable to finish.

Her smile faded as she continued walking toward him, the skirt of her nightclothes skimming the straw on the floor, then she stopped abruptly and looked up at him. He was so tall.

"I have a surprise for you," she said.

He was still holding Sheba's saddle, and tossed it aside onto a nearby sawhorse, then faced her, finally finding his voice again.

"You mean your being here isn't the surprise?"

"That's only part of it."

There was something about the look on her face . . . she looked so . . . how could he put it? So contented, so pleased with herself, and there was no longer the pain in her eyes as there had been those long months before she'd left for St. Louis. How many times he'd run from that look because he couldn't bear to see it anymore. But now . . .

"Do you remember when I asked you if you'd love me if I weren't your sister, and you said you'd love me forever?" she asked.

His mouth tightened. "I remember."

"Then love me, Kaelen. Love me forever," she murmured happily. "Because I'm not your sister. I found out I'm not Cole Dante's daughter. I never was."

Kaelen's eyes narrowed skeptically as he continued to stare at her, the love in her eyes making her whole face light up. Yet, what she'd just said was impossible, wasn't it? He shook his head.

"That can't be."

"But it is."

She reached up, her hand touching the front of his shirt. He was sweaty, and smelled like horses, but she didn't care. All she cared about was that she loved him, and as they stood there in the barn, with Sheba nickering occasionally for attention because Kaelen had forgotten to finish taking care of her for the night, and while the flickering light from the whale-oil lanterns cast dancing shadows around them, Teffin stood in the circle of Kaelen's arms and told him all about Ian Brooks and the confirmation that had come from Ma and Pa.

"So you see," she said, finally finishing her story, "there's no blood tie between us and there's no reason anymore why you can't love me forever, if you still want to."

"If I still want to?" He was estatic, and cupped her face in his hands, drinking in the love he saw mirrored in her eyes. "Oh, God . . . you're sure there's no mistake?" He just couldn't believe it was true. Things like this just didn't happen to people, and especially to him.

She sighed. "There's no mistake. The whole thing's true, Kaelen. In fact, I've already told them how I feel about you."

"And they weren't upset?"

"A little shocked, but they accepted it."

"Thank God!" He gazed into her eyes with a tenderness that made her tremble, and his head began to descend slowly, as if she were fragile and might break. Then lightly, as if touched by the wind instead of flesh, his mouth caressed hers in a kiss of longing so remarkably passionate, it ripped right through her like a whirlwind, and fought its way to every nerve in her body, making her tingle all over.

Her eyes were still open, as were his, and it was unnerving to watch his expression while his lips played on hers, lightly, sensuously, then he drew his head back, the flickering light playing in the waves of his dark hair, and he closed his eyes, sighing.

"How long I've been wanting to do that," he murmured, then once more looked down at her. This time his hands dropped from her face to her shoulders, and he drew her closer into his arms. "How many times I've dreamed of what it would be like to hold you like this, and be able to love you. I want to marry you, Tef," he went on huskily. "I want to marry you, and have babies with you, and grow old together, and . . ."

Suddenly he stopped talking, and his eyes hardened, the scar on his face more prominent than she'd ever seen it before. "You will marry me, won't you?"

Now it was Teffin's turn to kiss him. "Yes, oh yes," she whispered, and reaching up, she pulled his head down, their lips met, and in the quiet of the barn, with only the dim light from the lantern to see by, Teffin poured out her soul to him in that kiss.

Then, after taking care of Sheba, they blew out the lantern and left the barn arm in arm, making plans for all their tomorrows on the way back to the house.

The wedding of Teffin and Kaelen was set for the second week in May, which was not quite two weeks away, and during that time Ian and Warren, using the excuse that they wanted to be around for the wedding, stayed in the area, riding about the countryside together, supposedly trapping and hunting, while secretly doing the work they'd been sent to do. Much of their time was spent in the open range, but occasionally they'd stop by the ranch or spend some time in San Antonio. But mostly, they rode the frontier.

As Ian had told Warren, coming here with Teffin had been a godsend, giving them time to come and go as they pleased, so that by the time the day of the wedding rolled around, they were well over halfway through mapping out the area.

Since the emergence of Texas as a republic, and with religious restrictions no longer applying, a number of Protestant ministers began moving into the territory. And much to the astonishment of the village priest, Don Antonio de Léon had offered to let Teffin and Kaelen be married at the chapel on his rancho, with a Protestant minister officiating, since Teffin had requested a Protestant ceremony. Then there'd be a reception afterward in the ballroom at the hacienda. He felt it was the least he could do for a young lady whom he had at one time hoped would be his niece. Besides, she was the sister of the young man he still loved as a nephew, even though his name was no longer Joaquín. Not wanting to hurt her father's old friend, Don Antonio, and realizing that, under the circumstances, it would be the wisest thing to let him have his way, Teffin and Kaelen made arrangements with him, and the wedding day arrived with all its splendor.

The nuptials were officiated at in the early afternoon, with festivities expected to go on into late evening, and everyone from ranch hands to San Antonio city officials was invited. Even the Kolters' ranch was deserted today, with everyone at the wedding, and the weather was warm and balmy, as if trying to do something special for the bride and groom, who looked doubly handsome in their wedding finery. It was one of the few times any of them had seen Kaelen in anything except work clothes, and Teffin couldn't get over how marvelous he looked, while Heather sat with tears in her eyes and mixed feelings in her heart.

It was late afternoon, the ceremony had been over with for hours, and Blythe sat on a bench in the courtyard at the de Léon ranch, where she could see in through the doors to the ballroom where the couples were dancing, while her toes tapped a staccato rhythm in time to the music. If only she could get up on her feet and whirl about like everyone else was doing. Her pale blond head bobbed and moved with the rhythm as well, and she could feel the beat vibrating clear through her as the tempo of the guitars began to pick up.

Clasping her hands in front of her on the lap of her dark green organdy dress, she tried to still the urge to just fling herself off the bench and try to be one of the crowd. It was so hard not to care. And she did care. Just

yesterday she'd tried to stand alone again, and failed
miserably. Her hands opened, and she smoothed the
skirt of her dress, letting her fingers glide over the fancy
embroidery work she'd done on the skirt. It was three
tiers, each with with its own design of silky white roses,
blue violets, and pale green leaves. She'd made the dress
especially for today, with Pretty's help.

Even Genée had a new dress for the occasion, she
thought, and watched her young sister dance past the
doorway with one of the young men from town. Genée
was sixteen already, and really growing into quite a young
lady, and there were so many times Blythe envied her the
strength in her legs.

Blythe looked away, then flushed as once more she
caught herself looking directly into the eyes of a man
who had been pointed out earlier to her as Ian Brooks's
friend. This was the umpteenth time since the ceremony
she'd caught him standing around staring at her. She had
seen him from a distance over the past few days, since
Teffin's return. Once from inside a closed coach, when
she and Grandma Dicia had ridden into town. Another
time from the kitchen of the Crown D when she was
visiting Teffin, and he and Teffin's real father were riding
out of the ranch yard with Uncle Cole and his hired
hands. Then, one day she saw him from her bedroom
window at the Double K, when he and Ian Brooks rode
over to talk to her pa about something. At the moment,
however, he was standing next to Case, and both were
enjoying the drinks in their hands.

Warren took another sip of ale, then licked his lips as
he studied the girl in the courtyard who was sitting all by
herself while everyone around seemed to be ignoring her.
She'd been looking right at him only a second ago, and
he wondered why she'd blushed, as if embarrassed. He'd
seen her earlier in the chapel, sitting with the Kolters,
and had managed to single her out again a number of
times since the ceremony. Only he had no idea who she
was. Now, here she was, like a breath of fresh air in this
land of cactus, mesquite, heat, and stucco. Funny he'd
never seen her before today, but then most of the past

few days he'd been out in the wilds. In fact, that's where he and Ian had been spending all of their time lately.

He turned to Case. "Who's the pretty lady?" he asked, motioning with his head toward the bench where Blythe sat.

"My cousin."

"I thought I'd met all your family."

"You met Brax?"

"Yeah."

"His sister."

Warren took in her pale hair and even features. "I should have guessed." He took a long swig of ale and licked his lips again, straightening. "How about an introduction?"

Case frowned as he took his eyes from Blythe and looked more closely at Warren. Warren was a handsome devil, almost too good-looking, and there was an air of the Don Juan about him. Case had noticed it earlier one day when he'd ridden into San Antonio with the man for some supplies, and he'd also sensed it earlier in the evening shortly after the dancing started, when he'd been flirting with some of the ladies. He wasn't sure he wanted to introduce him to Blythe.

"Well?" Warren asked, his fingers caressing the mug of ale.

Case took a drink of his own ale, then shrugged thoughtfully. What the hell. Maybe it'd perk Blythe up some if someone besides Don Antonio paid her some attention.

"After you, Señor Russell," he said, reverting easily to his Mexican upbringing as he gestured toward Blythe, and he followed Warren through the crowd of merrymakers to where Blythe sat alone.

The courtyard was at the back of Don Antonio's hacienda, with the ballroom to the right, and a small fountain bubbled up in the center of the courtyard, trickling into a small lily pond. Blythe was near the pond, where light from above, where the courtyard was open to the sky, could filter down. With the afternoon sun playing in her pale hair, she had no idea how lovely it made her look.

Warren hesitated a few feet from her and let Case

overtake him, then he straightened his tie. He was wearing a black jacket tonight, small string tie, and white shirt, an outfit he'd had tucked away in his saddlebags. But he still had on the buckskins and the old boots he wore in snake country that he'd managed to polish up so they'd look half-decent.

He licked a finger surreptitiously and reached up, slicking back a lock of coffee-colored hair, then smiled as he stepped up behind Case.

The introductions were the easiest part for Blythe. It was when Case excused himself and walked away right afterward that left her disconcerted.

Warren sat on the bench beside her and glanced over, ignoring the people around them who were talking and laughing and making such a buzz of commotion it had even been hard to catch her name.

"Case said you're Braxton's sister," he finally said.

"We're twins."

He grinned. "I should have known."

"We look that much alike?" Her mouth tilted in an impish smile. "Don't let Brax hear you say that."

"I meant the hair," he corrected. "Let's face it, there aren't many people walking around with hair the color of you and your brother's. Especially around here." His eyes caught hers, and he smiled. "And such lovely gray eyes. Are you sure you're real?"

Blythe laughed softly. "Too real," she answered, and smiled back.

She liked his smile. It was rich and open. As if it was meant just for her.

"Would you care to dance?" he asked.

Her smile faded. "I thought you said you knew my brother."

"I do. But what does that have to do with your dancing?"

"He didn't tell you?"

"Tell me what?"

She could feel the heat on her face, wishing she didn't have to say it. "I can't dance," she said softly, then before he could misunderstand, she went on, "You see,

I'm crippled. That's why I haven't moved from this bench for what seems like hours now."

Warren felt his heart sink inside him. Such beauty, such unadulterated loveliness to be imprisoned in a useless body. He glanced down at her kid shoes, the toes just visible at the hem of her dress.

"You can't move your legs at all?" he asked.

"Oh, I can move them," she said, and shuffled her feet a little, although it was an effort. "I just can't stand on them." She tried to smile. "Sometimes it's a blessing though, really," she went on. "I don't have to help with the housework, so I can spend more time with Pegasus."

"Pegasus?"

"My horse."

"You ride?"

"Certainly I ride. He's a beautiful palomino. I let him be my legs."

"And the rest of the time?"

"I have Luther and Pretty. And Brax, when he's not off chasing the girls or out on the range. He and Luther made me a special chair I use at home. Only it's too bulky to put in a buggy. so I'm out of luck when I leave the house."

"And you've been sitting here for hours?"

"It seems like it."

Warren stared at her for a few minutes, then made a quick decision. "Then I'd say you deserve a change of scenery." He set his mug of ale aside on the bench, stood up, then reached down and held his hands out to her.

"What . . . what are you doing?"

"Hush!" he answered. "Just take my hands."

"But I can't stand up."

"Then I'll help you." He reached down, put his hands at her waist, and lifted her to her feet. "Now put your arms around my neck, hurry," he said while he continued to hold her steady.

Blythe hesitated for a minute, then, as his hands loosened at her waist, and his arms replaced them, holding her tightly against him, her arms went around his neck.

He was looking down into her face and she felt a twinge of expectation run through her, making her breathless.

"Do you know what you're doing?" she asked.

"Exactly." He winked. "Now, are you comfortable?"

"Comfortable?"

"Yes . . . do you feel like you're going to fall or anything?"

"No. But I don't understand."

"And you don't have to." He started to walk away from the bench, holding her upright in his arms, and he felt her arms tighten frantically around his neck.

He was heading directly for the ballroom, where the music had slowed to a lazy waltz, and Blythe felt a lump in her throat.

"Oh, please . . ." she begged, but he ignored her protest.

"I bet you've never danced in your life, have you, Blythe?" he said as he moved steadily through the crowd, carrying her. "I bet you have no idea what it's like to glide around a dance floor, and let the music carry you along, do you?"

She was staring up at him, her eyes filled with tears. Only they were tears of anger. He was going to make a fool of her. She just knew it.

"Let me go," she whispered. "Please, Mr. Russell, let me go."

"It's Warren, Blythe," he corrected her as he stepped inside the ballroom. "And I'm not going to let you go. Not until I've had a dance with the most beautiful woman I've ever seen," and with those words his arms tightened, even tighter, about her waist, and he moved onto the dance floor, swaying rhythmically to the music, her useless legs not even touching the floor.

Blythe knew her face had to be crimson. Especially when Braxton danced by, a startled look on his face. Within minutes the whole room was abuzz as other heads also turned to watch. But for the first time in a long time, Blythe didn't care that people were staring. In fact, she didn't seem to even notice their presence anymore as she was caught up in the music and the feel of

Warren's body molding itself to hers. She was in heaven, if only for a little while. The dance seemed to go on and on, then when it finally ended, Warren stood for some time looking at her, his blue eyes warm with desire, God, she was beautiful, and he had a feeling he could have her all to himself too.

He smiled. "Hungry?" he asked.

She took a deep breath. "To be able to dance, even like this . . . thank you."

"My pleasure." With one quick movement he swung her up into his arms, cradling her against him. "And now for a bit of fresh air," and he began making his way toward the French doors along the side wall, then stepped into the garden outside.

There were few people in the garden, and most of them went back in when the music started up again, more lively than before.

Warren finally found a bench where he could put Blythe down. It was in a very quiet spot in the garden, far back near some of Don Antonio's flowering cacti, where they were screened from the ballroom by a barricade of creamy pink yucca blooms. However, there was a small shade tree next to the bench too, where the afternoon heat couldn't reach as well. He sat her down gently.

"So, now, was that so bad?" he asked as he stood looking down at her.

They were both in the shade, and the shadows made his eyes appear to be even a deeper blue in his tanned face. There was a big wave in his hair just above his forehead, and the rest of his hair curled slightly behind his ears, then rested just above his collar. His eyebrows were thick and a little bushier than most perhaps, but they arched perfectly, defying the square line of his jaw. It was the first time she'd taken a few minutes to really scrutinize him, and she liked what she saw. However, she had no idea how old he might be, but suspected he was close to thirty.

He'd asked if the dance had been bad. At first she'd been scared half to death, but the minute he'd started swaying to the music, the fear had left her, to be replaced by a hunger to know what it was like. A hunger that still wasn't satisfied because she felt as though she could have let him carry her through dance after dance all day, and on into the night.

"It was marvelous," she answered. "Almost like riding Pegasus. When I'm on him it's as if I'm whole again. As if the whole world's mine for the taking."

"It is," he said, then put a foot up on the bench beside her and bent down, leaning an elbow on his knee as he studied her face.

Braxton had said he was twenty, that meant she was also twenty, and he'd bet almost anything she'd been paid little court, if any at all, over the years. If so he wouldn't have found her sitting alone in the courtyard.

"What are you doing tomorrow?" he asked.

She laughed. "Recuperating from today. Why?"

"I thought maybe you might go riding with me."

She stopped laughing, and stared at him, the color rising in her face again. "You really mean that?"

"I always like to take pretty girls riding on Sunday afternoons."

Blythe thought back over the dance this man had just introduced her to. No one, not even Brax, had ever thought to do something like that for her, and as she studied Warren, responding to his charming smile and the deep tremor in his voice, she realized that except for Don Antonio, he was the first man ever to ask her to go riding. And except for Don Antonio, he'd no doubt be the last.

"All right," she said, accepting his invitation. "Only if you don't mind, I'd rather meet you on the trail away from the ranch so my family won't know."

"Any special reason why?"

Her cheeks were pink again. "Because I have a brother who likes to tease me, and doting parents who hover over me as if I'll break." She pushed a lock of pale blond hair back over her shoulder and tilted her head provocatively. "Just for once I'd like to do something on my own without having to listen to a lot of comments and lectures about it later, all right?"

"In other words, they try to run your life."

"That's one way of putting it, I guess. But, you know, when you have to depend on other people the way I've had to depend on them, sometimes it can be suffocating."

He smiled. "I know what you mean. Something like being in the army."

"You were in the army?"

"Maybe I'll tell you about it someday. But for now, I want to learn all about you. What you like, what you don't like, and why you named your horse Pegasus," and for the rest of the day, on into the evening, Blythe was overwhelmed by Warren's attention, because he never left her side except to perhaps bring her some food or an occasional drink.

However, Don Antonio, watching from a distance, had strange misgivings when he realized as the evening wore on that the young frontiersman who had ridden into Texas with Teffin's father was making a decided impression on Blythe, because for some reason, he didn't like the man. It was nothing Warren said or did, only the way he said it and did it. Something Don Antonio couldn't quite put his finger on, and he expressed his opinion late in the evening, shortly before the reception was over, while he stood talking to Grandma Dicia.

"I hope you will watch over her, Loedicia," he said as he watched Warren present Blythe with a glass of punch. "She is not used to the flattery and attention most men are so quick to ply women with. And it is usually so far from sincere."

Loedicia, too, was watching Blythe. Had been watching her all evening, and for the first time in years she could see laughter in Blythe's eyes, and it was obvious to anyone who took time to notice, that Blythe was having a good time.

Loedicia drew her gaze from her great-granddaughter and looked over at Don Antonio. The poor man wasn't taking any of this well. Not at all. For the past few months, since Blythe's twentieth birthday, he'd really begun to court her in earnest. At least it was obvious to everyone at the Double K that that was what he was doing. It had all started with the Sunday afternoon he'd run into her when she was riding, then it had escalated to his coming by the ranch quite often, supposedly to see Bain, but ending up spending most of the evening with Blythe. He'd even asked her to go riding with him occasionally. His actions had been rather subtle, but no one had been fooled much by them.

Loedicia studied him for a minute, this kind, gentle man. He was hurting inside, and it showed.

"Don't worry, Antonio," she said, her strong voice belying her eighty-three years. "It's just that she's young, and having a gentleman like Warren Russell pay her court is a novelty. By the time she returns home, the novelty'll no doubt be worn off. Meanwhile, I'm glad she's enjoying herself for a change."

"Ah, sí," he answered, not wanting Loedicia to think he would be cruel and deny her a little happiness. "I just do not want her hurt, that is all, Loedicia. She is too lovely a flower to be crushed in full bloom."

"And you're in love with her, are you not, Antonio?"

Don Antonio's cheeks darkened to a deep pink as he avoided Loedicia's violet eyes and gazed off to where Blythe and Warren were talking animatedly.

"You are too perceptive, gracious lady," he answered. "Only, por favor, you will tell no one, sí?"

"I'll tell no one," she said, and smiled knowingly as she looked back to where Blythe was enjoying herself, laughing and carrying on with Warren Russell.

That evening, the first ones to ride away from the de Léon rancho were the new Mr. and Mrs. Kaelen Baldridge, driving a small buggy with their trunks tied to the back, and heading for some land at the southeastern corner of the Crown D where Kaelen, Case, and Cole had put up a crude log cabin for them during the days preceding the wedding. Land Cole and Heather gave to them for a wedding present. Teffin was ecstatic, Kaelen was all smiles for a change, and Blythe's heart was happy as she watched them ride away.

After the bride and groom were gone, however, the rest of the guests lingered on, and it was late when they too finally began to dispose, carriages moving one at a time through the big swinging gates. Mingling in among the carriages were a number of men on horseback, including Ian Brooks and Warren Russell.

Warren had said good-bye to Blythe a few minutes earlier, and now, as he sat his horse, watching the moon shroud the carriage she was riding in as it disappeared through the big wooden gates ahead of them and on into the night, he smiled, hoping she wouldn't forget to meet him tomorrow afternoon as planned.

His smile faded quickly, however, as Ian rode up next to him. They'd been staying out in the brush lately because of their work, and were heading back for camp tonight.

"I've been looking for you," Ian said as he maneuvered his horse around a buckboard with a family in it, then let it become lost in the darkness behind him as Warren tried to keep up with him.

"Don't worry, I'm not lost," Warren said.

Ian frowned. "I didn't say you were." Warren's face was shadowed beneath the broad-brimmed hat he was wearing, and Ian wished he'd cornered him while it was still light so he could see his face. "I want you to leave her alone, Warren," he warned the younger man.

Warren tensed. "Who the hell you talking about?"

"The crippled girl, that's who, and you know it." Ian's sable eyes were blazing. "I'm not blind, Lieutenant, I saw what you did on that dance floor, and you spent the whole rest of the day with her too." His jaw tightened angrily. "I won't have it, Warren. Not again."

"Hell, Major, you're making mountains out of molehills." Warren tried to look relaxed. "I just saw to it the lady had a nice evening, that's all."

"Well, make sure that's all it is, one evening." Ian was hot and testy as they rode along under the warm, starry night. "I don't want the young lady hurt, understand?"

"Don't worry, Major, we've got too much work to do yet for me to spend my time dallying about with the locals. I'll probably never even see her again," and as they rode off toward their camp somewhere in the hills,

Ian had no idea that Warren had no intention of leaving Blythe alone, and was already quietly fantasizing about his rendezvous the next day with her.

The next afternoon rolled around quicker than Blythe thought it would, although the morning had seemed to drag by. But now, here she was astride Pegasus, wearing her buckskin skirt, riding boots, and one of her best shirtwaists, and she'd worn the new tan felt hat Brax had given her for her birthday back in February. She hadn't worn it much, preferring her old beat-up straw, but today was an occasion, and she wanted to look her best.

Maneuvering Pegasus around a bend in the trail that led from the Double K toward the Crown D, she was surprised to see Warren already waiting for her. The afternoon was a hot one, and when she first caught sight of him, he was off his horse, resting beneath a small pin oak, while his horse grazed on some grass nearby. His hat was pulled down over his face to keep off the flies, and his legs were stretched out, arms crossed over his chest.

At the sound of her approach, he sat up, startled, then leapt to his feet, hat in his hand, and she presumed maybe he'd fallen asleep. After all, everyone had left the de Léons' rather late last night. Even she hadn't heard the roosters this morning, and as she rode closer, she wondered how Kaelen and Teffin had fared on their first night alone together. Well, it was an experience she'd probably never have, she thought. At that moment, however, she reached Warren and he smiled at her, that gorgeous smile of his making his eyes come alive, then he leapt to the saddle, facing her, and suddenly she wasn't sure of her last thoughts. Maybe there was hope for her yet.

"Well, hello," he said, reining his horse closer to her, his gaze taking in her clean-scrubbed look, for he had noticed the night before how Blythe wore nothing to enhance her looks whatsoever, and he was sure she probably never even bothered to pinch her lips or cheeks as most women did. Instead, her skin, lightly bronzed from the hours she spent riding under the open sky, had its own highlights, with a natural blush to her cheeks, making her gray eyes look even lighter, flecks from blue and green to violet running rampant through them. And this, contrasted with the fair hair, bleached almost white from the sun, made her look more like a portrait an artist might create to describe Helen of Troy or one of the other beautiful women in history, rather than a flesh-and-blood woman.

Warren couldn't take his eyes from her as she smiled. "You're late," he said.

"You're early," she replied, refusing to accept his accusation. "At least if you go by the clocks at the Double K." She pulled Pegasus to a stop and the palomino tossed his head smartly.

"Then forgive me." He pretended to act penitent. "So, are you ready for a long ride?"

"Where to?"

"There's a marvelous place I discovered just the other day. It's about an hour's ride from here. Now, if that's too far . . ."

She looked at him skeptically. "In which direction?"

He nodded toward town. "Northwest. Don't worry, I wouldn't take you anywhere near the Comanche. I don't want to take a chance on losing you."

Besides, he thought to himself as they urged their horses forward, heading down the path toward the main road, Ian's scouting in that area today and I sure as hell don't want to run into him either, and he smiled over at Blythe, neither rider aware that some hundred or so yards away, hidden completely by the brush and trees covering the countryside, Luther sat his faithful steed, as he always did when Blythe was alone on Pegasus. And as the riders moved forward, he too moved with them. Not close enough to be noticed, but just close enough to be there if needed.

That first day with Warren was one Blythe was sure she'd never forget. Somehow he'd found a lovely canyon, with a river flowing through, and trees galore, with wildflowers running all the way up the riverbank. Delicate columbine, monkshood, wild poppies. Some were already in bloom, others budded, ready to burst forth. Unlike so much of the dry land around San Antonio, it was cool here, the grass thick, like sitting on goose down when he lifted her from her horse and set her down in it to rest.

As isolated as the glade was back near the Double K where she and her brother and cousins had spent so many delicious hours just basking in the summer's warmth and enjoying themselves, it was even nicer here. Probably because of the company, she assumed. She glanced over at Warren, stretched out in the grass beside her, leaning on an elbow while he dissected a blade of grass and stared at her.

"I'm sorry I'm so boring," she said, her face coloring slightly.

His mouth tilted into a half-smile. "Don't be silly. You're not boring." His eyes darkened, the blue in them so intense it made her shiver. "How could anyone as lovely as you be boring?"

"But I don't know anything about the world, or all the places you've probably been. I've never been farther than San Antonio. And I've only seen that from the back of a horse or the seat of a buggy or wagon."

"They never take you to town?"

"Oh yes, I've been there a lot of times, but there's no way I can go into the stores or anything. I did visit Mr. Bowie's house a few times when I was younger, though Pa used to carry me in. That was before his family all died. Afterward he wasn't around as much, though."

"Bowie died at the Alamo, didn't he?"

"Along with some of Pa's other friends, yes." She looked off across the river, her thoughts wandering. "You know, I've never seen the Alamo," she said after a few minutes. "It's the other side of the river, and Pa says there's nothing really to see except a crumbling old building."

He studied her face for a few minutes, letting her last few words sink in, then he got a brilliant idea.

"Would you like to see the mission?" he asked.

"You mean you'd take me?"

"I'll take you anywhere you want to go, lovely lady,"

he whispered huskily, and moved closer to her, so she had to look up into his face. "When would you like to go?"

"Next Sunday?"

He shook his head. "Tomorrow," he murmured. "I don't think I could wait until Sunday," and before Blythe had a chance to even try to protest, his lips found hers and he pressed his mouth hard against them, while his hand went to her shoulder and he eased her back in the grass.

Blythe lay beneath Warren, staring up at him now that the kiss was ending, and her face was flushed, her insides quivering as she realized he had awakened feelings in her she'd told herself long ago were feelings she was supposed to ignore. Cripples weren't supposed to need loving like normal people, she'd made herself believe. At least that's what most people thought. Her legs were dead, so the rest of her was supposed to be dead too, wasn't that it? But it wasn't. Oh, Lord, it wasn't, and right now her body was more alive than it had been before, and it was frightening.

"What's wrong, Blythe?" Warren asked.

Her hand moved to his shoulder, and she held him back as she continued to stare up at him.

"I . . . I don't know," she answered truthfully. "You see, I've never been kissed like that before."

"What a waste." His hand moved to her face, where his fingers gently plucked a stray hair from her cheek, and he tucked it down beside her ear. "Hasn't anyone ever told you how lovely you are?" he asked.

"No."

"Then you're in for a treat, Blythe Kolter," he went on, his voice vibrant with emotion. "Because I intend to tell you as often as you'll let me," and again he bent down, his lips sipping at her mouth lovingly, while his hand cupped her face, holding her so she couldn't turn away.

Blythe wanted to scream, cry out. One part of her told her to go easy, be careful. The rest of her body told her to let go and feel for the first time in her life, and the battle between the two was slowly being lost by her common sense. Her eyes were closed, while sweet sensations ran through her from the tips of her toes to the top of her ears, even running down her spine into the small of her back, then leaping like liquid fire into her loins. She didn't want him to stop. She never wanted him to stop, but suddenly he did, and she looked up into his eyes, her breasts tingling for his touch. Her body on fire.

"Warren!"

He kissed her again hungrily. "I know," he murmured, then sighed, his mouth close to hers yet, "I feel it too, Blythe. I've felt it from the moment we met."

"Is that why you danced with me?"

"And why I asked you to come riding with me." He leaned back on his elbow again, letting his head rest on his hand as he looked down at her. "I don't care about your legs," he went on. "A man doesn't fall in love with legs, and I do think I'm falling in love with you, Blythe Kolter."

"You don't even know me."

"Don't I?" He ran the back of his free hand down the side of her face, and saw her shiver. "I know I couldn't take my eyes off you yesterday at the wedding," he went on. "And I can't stop looking at you now. There's something about you, Blythe, something I just can't put into words. It's a feeling here, deep down inside," and he touched his hand to his chest. "Like I said, I think I'm falling in love with you, Blythe Kolter," and with that he leaned over once more, his lips on hers again, and for the first time in her life Blythe knew she was falling in love too, while some distance away, at the top of a small hill, Luther sat stoically on his horse, cursing himself for having to spy on Blythe like this, yet frowning, because he wasn't certain he liked what he was seeing.

15

The afternoon after Teffin's wedding was the start of a new existence for Blythe. Only, one she decided to keep from the family as long as she could. In the first place, she knew Warren wasn't exactly the prize catch of the year. Especially for a girl in her circumstances, although he'd confided in her that he wasn't just a wanderer, but had special reasons for being here, only he wasn't free to divulge them. At least not yet. That was why he'd been so willing to go along with her deception, he'd confessed while they were riding one afternoon. Because until his work was done, it was better no one learned the true reason why he and Ian Brooks were there.

To Blythe, whose life had been filled with endless days of boredom, the idea that Warren was on some sort of secret mission was as intriguing as the fact that she'd fallen in love with him, and she wasn't about to let anyone else in on it, not yet. She had no idea that one other person did know about her and Warren, and Luther, his loyalty to her never wavering, had all he could do to keep from letting the others know.

How many nights he'd fought with his conscience over what he knew. Yet, something kept holding him back. Maybe because for the first time since that horrible night on the road back in Port Royal when the carriage crashed, he saw true happiness in Blythe's eyes. For so many years he'd had to face the empty look in them, knowing there was every possibility love, the kind of love he and Pretty had, would never be there for his babe, as he called Blythe. But now things had suddenly changed, and he didn't want to be the one to spoil her life for her again. So every day when she rode out of the ranch yard at the Double K to meet Warren, Luther kept up his vigil. And every afternoon when she returned, he prayed he was doing the right thing by his silence.

Blythe, however, had no idea of Luther's dilemma, because she had never ever suspected over the years that Luther had been following her. And because of his covert actions Luther had become more adept than the Comanche at hiding in the brush, so that even Warren, a man accustomed to the wilderness, was unaware of his presence.

And now, as Warren and Blythe rode along one afternoon on a high ridge overlooking the vast countryside, with its hidden canyons and rolling hills, where they'd spent so much time over the past few weeks, neither was aware that Luther had been eying the sky for the last half-hour, watching the same rain clouds gathering that they were watching.

"We're going to get wet," Blythe said as a low rumble roared off in the distance, then echoed across the hills. "We shouldn't have come so far."

Warren frowned, then glanced about. He'd been so engrossed in telling her all about what it was like back east in New York, he hadn't kept his eyes on the sky, and if he didn't think of something, and quick, they wouldn't just get wet, they'd be drenched.

They'd ridden south today, and as he gazed off into the distance, he happened to remember a place he'd seen when he'd been mapping the area a short time back.

"I have an idea, come on," he said, and kicked his horse hurriedly in the ribs making sure she was following.

Descending the ridge after only some ten minutes of riding, he quickened his pace, and his eyes searched the sky, watching the storm clouds get lower and lower as they continued to roll in. They probably wouldn't make it, but even if they didn't, it'd be better than weathering the whole storm in the open.

By the time they topped the small knoll, then dipped down into the lush valley and Blythe caught her first sight of the tumble down shell of the partially burned cabin, the rain had already begun to blow into her face, and her shirtwaist was sticking to her.

Warren reined up next to the porch of the old cabin and quickly dismounted.

"Come on," he said, holding his arms out to her. "Before it gets worse."

Blythe practically fell into his arms, and being slippery, he held her even tighter as he carried her up the steps and onto what was left of the porch. The roof was hanging, ready to fall, and there was no door as he stepped over the threshold, but there was enough roof once inside to keep the rain off. Whoever had built the cabin had built it well, and he assumed the evidence of charring and broken furniture, as well as bullet holes in the door, meant it had taken more than the natural elements to make it look like this.

"The Sherwoods," Blythe said as he carried her to an old mattress on the floor near the fireplace, and he looked at her curiously as he sat her down.

"Sherwoods?"

"It must be their place." She wiped the rain from her eyes and took off her hat, shaking the water from it. "The Indians raided them some years back." She glanced toward the fireplace, to where a broken figurine lay in the dust and rubble. "I remember when the Sherwoods spent Christmas at our place once, and Grandma Dicia gave them that figurine for a present," she went on. "They used to stop by occasionally, and Mrs. Sherwood had always admired it. It was something my great-grandma brought with her years ago from South Carolina." She set her hat down and reached out her hand. "Would you hand it to me, please, Warren?"

His own hat was off, and he flicked the water from it, threw it beside hers, then walked over, picked up the pieces of figurine, and brought them to her.

"Pretty, isn't it?" she said when she'd pieced it together.

He'd been watching her closely. "Not half as pretty as the lady holding it."

She smiled, used to his flattery now. "You're incorrigible."

"I'm in love with you."

"So you've been saying."

He knelt beside her on the mattress and reached out, touching her shirtwaist.

"You're soaked to the skin."

"I know."

"Better take it off."

The figurine was forgotten as she stared at him. "I can't do that."

"You'll catch cold if you don't."

The rain was battering now against the cabin's weakened walls, seeping in here and there where the mud that was chinked between the logs had loosened, and it blew in fiercely through the windows where the shutters hung, half-off. And it was colder now with the rain. She shivered. Only it wasn't just the rain making her shiver, and she knew it.

"Come on," he coaxed, and began tugging at her shirtwaist where it was tucked into her skirt. Her hands covered his, stopping him.

"Warren?"

"I won't hurt you," he whispered, his blue eyes gazing deeply into hers. "I could never hurt you, Blythe."

She stared back at him for a minute, then her hands slowly eased on his, letting him pull the shirtwaist from her skirt and unbutton it.

Blythe trembled again as he slid the shirtwaist down over her shoulders, leaving only the chemise plastered against her skin, and she knew her nipples had hardened against the wet clothes. Something she'd been hoping wouldn't happen.

Her arms slipped from the sleeves of her shirtwaist, and he tossed it aside on the remains of an old chair to dry, then concentrated his full attention once more on Blythe. His hand moved to her face and he cupped her chin, looking at her sensuously, knowing that she too was aroused. He moved his hand down, caressing her neck, and watched her already rigid breasts peak even harder.

God! He wanted to touch her, hold them, bury his face in them, but would she let him? Moving his hand deftly, he pushed the strap of her camisole aside and bent down his lips gliding over where the strap had been.

"I love you so much, Blythe," he whispered as his lips lingered near her ear, and she threw her head up, letting his lips cover her bare flesh and work their way farther and farther down her throat, until they reached her breastbone. His hands eased her back on the mattress, he pulled the ribbons on her chemise, and it fell open.

Blythe started to cry out, only he buried his face in her soft flesh, quickly breaking down all the barriers she'd put between her and her feelings over the years.

She was alive! Oh, God! She was alive. And she was feeling and what she felt had nothing to do with her legs. It had to do with her heart, and things down deep inside her. Things no one had ever told her about, thinking she'd never know them. But she did know them. Oh, Lord, she did. And when Warren lifted his head, his tongue leaving her flesh, and looked down into her face, he knew she was as ready as he was.

"It'll be good. You'll see, my love," he whispered, and gently reached down to unfasten her riding skirt.

One part of Blythe wanted to protest, the other didn't care. He was going to make love to her and she knew it. He was going to do to her what her father did to her mother, what Ian Brooks had done to Aunt Heather, what men had been doing to women for centuries, and what she thought she'd never know. If she stopped him now, there might never be another chance for her. Just once to know what it was like, to experience, to understand; oh, dear God, she had to know. For the first time in her life she had to know what it was to be a woman, to be loved. And instead of stopping him, she tried to help. Only Warren didn't need any help.

Her eyes were closed, yet she knew he was looking at her as his hands pulled the skirt from her body. Still she lay quiet, holding her breath. Then she felt the drawers follow her skirt.

"You're beautiful," he murmured, and she was. The most beautiful creature he'd ever seen, and for the first time in years he suddenly wished he'd turned and run from her when he'd first seen her. But then, if he had, he wouldn't be here drinking in the long length of her young body, so ripe for the taking, would he? and he stripped hurriedly, then stretched out beside her, and she opened her eyes.

"Don't be frightened," he reassured her, and his hand moved to her flat stomach, then moved up slowly to caress her breast. "Love is worth waiting for, darling, and worth giving in to, and I'm going to love you with every fiber of my being, Blythe Kolter," and slowly, deliberately, his mouth came down on hers once more, and Blythe forgot she was crippled. That her legs couldn't respond. And even later, when, after kneading her eager flesh gently, he drew her hips up and plunged deep inside her, Blythe knew she didn't need her legs to be a woman. Not anymore, for she felt every thrust, every joy, every sweet sensation flooding her body. No, she didn't need her legs, not ever. Not as long as she had her heart.

As she lay in Warren's arms afterward, knowing that for her, life would never be the same again, outside the cabin the rain was streaming down Luther's face and soaking him clear to the skin while he watched and waited for the storm to let up and the two people he'd been following to come out of the abandoned cabin.

The rain had lasted a little over an hour, and now the sun was out, its heat beginning to penetrate Luther's waterlogged clothes, making steam rise from them as he still sat hidden in the bushes, watching Blythe and Warren riding away from what was left of the Sherwoods' place. He frowned, his thoughts far removed from the miserable condition he was in. All he could think of was the look on Blythe's face as that Russell fella carried her from the cabin and put her on her horse, and the way she'd made sure all her clothes were straightened before riding off. It was the natural gesture of a woman who had something to hide.

All the rest of the way back to the ranch, that scene kept haunting Luther, until finally, after giving Blythe time to ride in and give her mother a trumped-up story about finding an overhanging cliff where she didn't get too wet, he entered the barn on the lower side where she wouldn't see him, put his horse away, and went looking for Grandma Dicia. The one person in the world he felt would know what he should do.

Loedicia was on the front porch.

"Miz Chapman, can we talk?" he asked.

He was in dry clothes now, having changed when he reached home.

Loedicia squinted a bit. The rain had cooled the air some, but the sun was still just as bright, and being low on the horizon, it didn't help the eyes much.

"You followed her again today?" she asked.

Luther glanced about to make sure Blythe was nowhere around, since the window to her room faced the porch.

"That's what I wants to talk about, Miz Chapman," he said.

"Getting tired of spying, are you?"

"I ain't spyin', Miz Chapman, you know that. I'm only protectin' her. There's all kinds of rattlesnakes there, and some of them got legs. That's what I want to talk to you about."

"Two-legged rattlesnakes?"

"Yes, ma'am."

"Maybe you should tell her ma."

"First I'd like to tell you. If that's all right."

Loedicia sighed. Luther was always coming to her first with his troubles. She'd tried years before to convince him she wasn't boss at the Double K just because she was the oldest person around, but he didn't seem to care.

"All right," she answered. "Then tell it. What has Blythe been up to that has you so worried?"

For the next few minutes, while Loedicia and Luther took a leisurely stroll from the house, making their way toward the vegetable garden in back, the black slave told Blythe's great-grandmother all about Blythe's recent excursions with Ian Brooks's young friend Warren Russell. Even making sure Loedicia understood that their meetings were far from platonic, and ending with his fears of what might have transpired today.

"You're not sure, though?" Loedicia asked as they stood next to the garden and she stared up into Luther's worried face.

"No, ma'am. I only gots my feelin's. But I know people, and I know my babe. I saw her just a few minutes ago, and there was somethin' about her . . . somethin' happened in the cabin today, Miz Chapman. I'm sure of it."

"Then maybe you'd better talk to her ma this time, Luther," Loedicia said, and watched a few minutes later as Luther headed toward the house again.

Lizette stood in the doorway of Blythe's bedroom and stared thoughtfully at her daughter. Blythe was in her special chair, sitting in front of the mirror, just staring at herself. Something Lizette had never caught her doing before. Now, when she thought about it, Blythe had been doing a lot of things the past few weeks she'd never done before, like wearing her best hat just to go riding, and the bottle of perfume they'd given her last Christmas was almost gone already. Something very unusual for Blythe, since she said she was only going to use it for special occasions. After all, it had come all the way from back east. Lizette wondered. Could Luther be right? Well, only one way to find out.

Blythe turned as her mother stepped into the room. She was surprised to see Ma this time of day because she was usually in the kitchen with Pretty and Dodee getting supper ready.

"Something wrong, Ma?" she asked.

Lizette paused and stopped a few feet from Blythe, her eyes on the girl's face. Luther was right. There was something different about her, but what?

"You tell me," Lizette said.

Blythe frowned. "I don't understand."

Lizette reached behind her, shut the door that led into the front hall, then walked over and shut the other door, leading to the hall outside the kitchen.

"Now maybe we can talk," she said, although she wasn't really sure how to start. Well, might as well plunge right in. "I want to know what's going on between you and Warren Russell."

Blythe was startled, and her face showed it. How did Ma know?

"I don't know what you're talking about." She tried to act innocent.

"I'm talking about you and Warren Russell. I know you've gone off riding with him almost every day the past few weeks. And I know you were with him today. What happened in the Sherwoods' old cabin today, Blythe?"

"You've been spying on me!"

"No I haven't."

"Then someone else did it for you."

"It wasn't spying."

"No? Then what do you call it?"

"Remember, you're crippled, dear. You can't just go riding around the countryside by yourself like other folks do."

"So you had me tailed? Oh, Ma!"

"Only in case you needed help. Not to spy."

"Is there a difference?" Blythe thought of all the kisses she and Warren had shared, and the intimate moments they'd had together, and her blood boiled at the thought that someone had been watching. "Who was it?" she asked.

Lizette shook her head, her bright green eyes evasive. "It doesn't matter who it was."

"It matters to me!" Her hands clenched on the arms of her chair, the knuckles white. "How could you do this, Ma? How could you subject me to such a thing?"

"Well, if you'd let Warren meet you here at the house, like you should have, nobody would have followed you. It was only when you went out alone that I wanted someone nearby. After all, dear, you know very well we don't live in the safest territory in the world."

"So that justifies what you've done?"

"No, it doesn't justify it, any more than your answer has justified what you've done." Lizette's eyes narrowed as she stared at her daughter. "I asked you, Blythe, what happened in that cabin today?"

"What makes you think something happened?"

"Instinct maybe . . . I don't know, but I do know you seemed so different when you came home today." She hesitated. This wasn't going well. Not at all. "Look, dear," she began, trying to ease the situation some. "I'm not asking so I can condemn you. I only want to help you, because I don't want anything to hurt you."

"Hurt me?" Blythe stared hard at her mother. "How can love hurt me, Ma? Warren loves me, and I love him. So how will that hurt me?"

"Oh, Blythe." Lizette wanted to grab her daughter, shake her, and try to make her understand. "Because he can't marry you. He has no way to provide for you. He and Ian are wanderers, drifters. How can he take care of you?"

"I don't want to be taken care of, I want to live. I'm tired of being protected and fussed over. Let me be a part of the world, Ma," she pleaded. "Let me know what it's like to laugh and cry and love, and if I make mistakes, then let me make them just like you did. It's a part of being alive." Tears sprang to her eyes. "Please, Ma, don't chain me to this chair, and this house. I'd rather die because I took a chance on living than die because I wore myself out wheeling this monstrosity about," and she looked down at the chair Luther and Brax had made for her. "If Warren can give me that, then I don't care what I have to go through."

"Has he asked you to marry him?"

"No, not yet. But he will, I know. It's just that he can't right now. Not until . . ." Her voice faded.

"Until what?"

"I'm sorry, Ma. I can't tell you. It's . . . well, he's on some sort of special assignment or something. He and Ian Brooks both, only he said he can't tell me about it. Or anyone else, but I think it has something to do with the army."

"Why do you think that?"

"It's no proof, really, but one day when we were riding, I noticed a paper sticking up out of his shirt pocket, and it had 'U.S. Army' printed on it, and the brand on his horse is U.S. Army too."

"Ian told your pa they bought them at an army post a few years back."

"Maybe they did. I don't know. All I know is I love him, Ma. The only reason I didn't tell you was that I wanted to do something on my own for a change. Just once I wanted to be me instead of relying on somebody else. But what happened in that cabin today, Ma, is my business, and only mine. It's between me and Warren and nobody else, not even you have a right to interfere."

"In other words, he made love to you."

"I didn't say that."

"Then why are you blushing?" Lizette bit her lip, anger and frustration at knowing what her daughter was going through fighting with the love she had for her. "Oh, Blythe, I was hoping you wouldn't make the same mistakes I did, and it has nothing to do with your legs, believe me. I was hoping someday a nice young man would come along, and he'd see past your chair—"

"He has, Ma, he has." Blythe's eyes were shining. "You'll see. Why, I bet he'll ask me to marry him any day now."

"I hope you're right, dear," Lizette replied anxiously, "I sure hope you're right."

However, at that very moment, not ten miles away, Warren was riding into the camp where he and Ian had been staying the past few days. Ian was there already, stirring up the fire to roast a couple of rabbits, and the coffee was perking already. It smelled good.

Warren slid from the saddle, ground-reined his horse in a nearby patch of grass, then strolled over, stretching to get the kinks out.

" 'Bout time you rode in," Ian said as he fanned the flames a little harder with his hat to catch the rest of the wood. "Got caught in a storm, I see."

Warren's buckskins were still damp in places, even though the sun had been out for the past couple hours he'd been riding.

"Where'd you hit the rain?" Ian asked casually.

Warren shrugged. "Here and there."

"Where's here and there?"

"What is this, Major, an inquisition?"

"Might call it that," Ian straightened as the fire took hold. "I asked you, Lieutenant, where'd you get into rain?"

Warren studied Ian Brooks for a minute. The major's eyes were hard, unyielding. "Southwest of here, near that river I was mapping the other day. Why?"

"You're a liar, Lieutenant."

Warren's eyes narrowed, the blue in them darkening ominously. "Where do you get off calling me a liar?"

"Because that's what you are. There wasn't a drop of rain west of here. Not all day. Now, are you going to tell me where you were?"

"I told you where I was."

"The hell you were. You been messin' around with that girl, haven't you?"

"So what if I have? I've been doing my work too, haven't I?"

"Damn you!" Ian was incensed. "That girl is Cole Dante's niece, you fool. She's not some little tart you can kiss off when we ride out of here."

Warren's jaw tightened stubbornly. "I know exactly what that girl is," he said, his voice low, controlled. "She's the loveliest thing this side of the Mississippi."

"Lovely enough to leave your wife for? Or have you forgotten what's waiting for you back in New York?"

"Have I ever forgotten before?"

"Every time you look at a pretty face, you forget. At least for a while." Ian was at his wits' end. "Goddamm it, Warren, you know very well you're not about to give up Amy, the kids, and all that money. When this job's over, you'll go back home for a while just like you always do, until you get itchy feet again."

"So who the hell is it hurting?"

"It's hurting that girl, that's who."

"Oh, Christ, Ian, I'm only helping her live a little. The kid's been smothered all her life with family breathing down her neck all the time. Now she's learning to live a little, that's all. So what's the harm in it?"

"So I want you to break it off, now, before it gets out of hand. Besides"—Ian began to sharpen a stick to use on the spit he was making for over the fire—"we'll be leaving in another week, heading farther north, deeper into Comanche territory, and I doubt we'll be heading back this way."

Warren glanced over at his superior officer. They'd been together off and on for a lot of years now, and he liked Ian. Even if the old man, as he often thought of him, was a bit stodgy. But then Ian didn't seem to need a woman the way most men did. At least not anymore, and Warren thought of Heather Dante. It seems the major had sown his own wild oats at one time.

Ah well, Ian was right about one thing, though. Warren wasn't about to give up Amy, the boys, and a few million dollars for a girl who couldn't even walk, even if she was a beauty. But he wasn't going to give up a good thing, either. Not until he had to. Only, what Ian didn't know wouldn't hurt him. Warren'd just have to be more careful from now on, that's all.

"All right," he agreed, knowing he'd never keep his word. "I'll break it off tomorrow. Only I won't enjoy doing it, Major. Not a damn bit," and he reached down, picking up one of the rabbits Ian had shot, handing it to him to put on the stick to turn over the spit.

Some time later, after they'd finished eating, Ian eased himself from the ground where he'd been sitting and strolled over to the horses. They rarely even unsaddled them before dark, just in case they'd have to light out in a hurry, and he reached out, checking his horse's cinch, then ran a hand down the side of its neck.

"Think I'll go for a little ride," he said, glancing off toward the hills to the east. "Haven't visited with the daughter in a while, and won't get to after we leave." He patted the horse's nose. "Don't mind, do you?" he asked.

Warren shrugged. "Hey, don't let me stop you. It's been a long day," and as Ian mounted and rode off, Warren settled down next to what was left of the campfire, his head resting on his bedroll, and let his thoughts wander back over the afternoon he'd spent with Blythe, and hoped tomorrow would bring more of the same.

Ian didn't like having to lie like that to Warren, yet felt justified because he knew damn well Warren had lied to him. He could tell by the look in Warren's eyes that the man hadn't the slightest notion of breaking it off with Kolter's daughter. Just like the last time, he thought. Well, it wasn't going to happen again, he'd see to that, and as soon as he was far enough away from the camp, he changed directions, and instead of heading northeast, headed southeast toward the Double K, knowing he probably wouldn't get there till after dark.

Shimmering lights flickered from inside the ranch house as Ian made his way down the back trail past the corral, cornfield, and the carriage house with the bunkhouse built at the back. He glanced over toward the chicken coop and garden, then smiled to himself as he saw the tree where Kolter said his youngest daughter had had him build a treehouse years before. It must be nice to watch kids grow up, he thought, then remembered the years he'd missed with his own daughter. Wiping a tear from his eye as he reached the hitchrail out back, he dismounted, then stood for a minute scrutinizing the back porch. Someone was sitting on the steps, only all he could see was the silhouette in the light from the kitchen.

" 'Evenin'," he said as he strolled over.

Braxton stood up, turning slightly so he was recognizable. " 'Evenin'. Somethin' we can do for you, Mr. Brooks? It is Ian Brooks, right?"

"You have good eyesight, son. And a good memory too." He hadn't seen Kolter's son more'n three, four times at the most since he'd been here.

"Yes, sir."

"Your pa home?"

"Pa? Yeah, come on in."

It was over an hour later when Ian, his supposedly friendly visit over, rode away from the Kolter ranch, heading back toward the camp he shared with Warren Russell, while back inside the big log house at the Double K, Blythe sat in her special chair, just staring out her bedroom window into the night, not really seeing it at all. How could she, for the tears in her eyes?

She hadn't wanted to believe Mr. Brooks, and it had been such a temptation to yell at him and call him a liar, but with Pa sitting right there, she hadn't dared. All she could do was sit there heartsick and listen. Even now she didn't want to believe him. Yet he had no reason to lie.

Warren was married, he'd said. Had been married for eight years to a woman who came from a wealthy New York family. A woman named Amy, who was the mother of his two sons, four and six. Ian Brooks had told them Warren's wedding had been the social event of New York's summer season back in 1830, since both Warren and his wife had come from such prominent families. Only, along with his bride, Warren had also acquired the fortune Amy's millionaire father had left her, and he'd never have to work another day in his life.

However, according to Mr. Brooks, Warren had always had itchy feet, and could never stay in any one place too long. So he'd bought himself a commission in the army for a while. That's when Ian had run into him. That didn't last, though, and now he just liked taking off to explore some, whenever he got the notion. Only in spite of his shortcomings, Ian assured them all that Warren was a smart man, and an asset to have around, especially out on the frontier and up in the western hills. He never had mentioned a thing about the secret mission Warren told her they were supposed to be on. But then, if Warren wasn't telling her he was already married, he was probably lying about that too.

Blythe reached up and wiped away the tears with her bare hands. She felt so empty inside. Empty and angry and betrayed. She loved him! Oh, God, how she loved him! And just today . . . remembering how she'd surrendered herself to him, and the way his body had taken hers, she buried her face in her hands, trying to bury her shame. Only it was impossible, and again the tears came.

She wanted to run outside and hide somewhere in the night, anywhere, so she wouldn't have to face the world again. But there was nowhere to go even if she could run.

Her hands slowly lowered from her face, and she gulped back the sobs as she heard footsteps, and realized some-one had come into the room. Wiping her eyes again quickly, she turned.

"Has he gone?" she asked her mother.

Lizette nodded. "Your pa said he'd walk outside with him."

"He came just to tell me, didn't he, Ma?" she said.

"I think so. I'm not sure. Maybe he stopped by to see your pa about buying some fresh beef to dry, like he said, and it just happened to come out in the conversa-tion. Who knows."

"You believe that?"

"I'm sure your pa does."

Lizette hadn't told Bain about Blythe's meetings with Warren. It was just one of those things you didn't tell your husband. Not until you had to, because if you did, who knows what he might do. So she was glad that if Ian had discovered what was going on and decided to come over to let Blythe learn firsthand about the man she thought she loved, he'd had the sense to do it the way he had, and just dropped the information as if it were part of his normal conversation.

It had been a cruel way for Blythe to learn the truth about Warren, but the only way Ian knew to do it with-out giving away Blythe's secret to her family. And know-ing Warren the way Ian knew him, he knew Blythe's family would be very unaware of what was going on.

Now Lizette stood just inside Blythe's bedroom where she'd stood earlier in the day and again studied her daughter. Gone was the light that had shone from Blythe's eyes earlier in the afternoon, and the warmth that had softened her mouth. Her eyes were already red from crying, and her cheeks were blotched. Lizette watched her lift her head and close her eyes against the pain, the flickering light from the lamp at her bedside casting shad-ows over her face.

"I'm sorry, Bly," Lizette said, her voice breaking. For

she felt every tear Blythe had shed. "I wish I could have softened the blow some for you."

"Softened it? Oh, come now, Ma, didn't I just tell you this afternoon to let me make my own mistakes? Well, I really made a first-rate one this time, didn't I? Dumb, stupid Blythe couldn't see past her nose. Fell for the first man who looked at her twice." Her fists clenched on the arms of her chair, and she stared back out the window. "I could kill him!"

"I know how you feel."

"Do you? Do you really, Ma? How could you possibly know how I feel? You've got Pa to love you. You've always had Pa to love you. You never had to worry about a pair of useless legs nobody wants to have anything to do with." Her eyes narrowed, cold, unfeeling. "You know, I always told Brax he was a fool for being afraid to love. Well, maybe he has the right idea after all. Maybe it's better to close your heart and try not to feel. Where did love get me?" She pushed a stray hair out of her face. "I should have stopped fooling myself a long time ago, Ma," she went on. "No handsome hero's going to come riding into my life and rescue me from this chair. I know it now." She sniffed back a deep sob that hurt. "Yeah, Brax has the right idea. Well, two can play Mr. Warren Russell's little game, if that's what he wants."

"What are you talking about?"

"Don't worry, Ma, I'll handle my own mistakes." Blythe's face was unreadable. There were tears there, yes, but there was anger too, and Lizette was at a loss. "Now, will you push me to the bed, Ma," Blythe went on, her voice unsteady. "I think I'll try to get some sleep," and Lizette watched her daughter cautiously for a second, then grabbed the handle at the back of the chair and pushed Blythe across the room to her bed.

The next day was sunny, and at first when Blythe said she was going for a ride that afternoon, Liz looked at her hesitantly.

"Don't worry, I'm not going to meet Warren," Blythe said as Luther helped her into the saddle. "And don't try to have anyone follow me either, Ma, because if you do

I'll only lose them." She took the reins in her hands. "I just want to be alone," and she rode away from the front walk, heading down the road at a fast gallop, then, once out of sight, veered off the road and across the open range toward the valley where Warren had taken her that first day, unaware that Luther, making sure she hadn't spotted him, and being true to what he'd been doing ever since she'd learned how to ride, was quietly following her trail.

Blythe was furious as she rode on, reining Pegasus toward the edge of an incline, then leaned back so she wouldn't slide forward in the saddle. She hadn't wanted to lie to Ma, but it was the only way. No one was going to talk her out of this. No one.

She'd cried herself to sleep last night. Ashamed, angry, and brokenhearted. But with the light of dawn, all that was left were the tears and anger. Warren had made a fool of her. He'd taken advantage of her loneliness and had played her for a fool.

The bastard! The dirty filthy bastard! Well, he wasn't going to get away with it that easily. If she suffered, he was going to suffer too, if even only for a little while. Her gaze moved to the gun she always carried in the scabbard of her saddle. Pa had taught her, Brax, and Genée how to shoot as soon as they were big enough to sight down a rifle barrel, and by God she was going to make him sweat for what he'd done to her. She reached out, fingering the rope slung over her saddle horn. The rope Ma hadn't noticed she'd been holding when Luther lifted her into the saddle. A rope just for you, Warren Russell, she whispered softly to herself, and she nudged Pegasus even harder in the ribs. She sure as shootin' didn't want to be late. Not today.

Warren was restless. He'd been working all morning in the hot sun, and had decided to take a swim in the river while waiting for Blythe. At first he'd thought to finish before she got there, but the more he thought of it, the more he decided maybe he ought to take his time and still be in the water when she arrived. After all, it wasn't really all that deep here, not even up to his shoulders, and if he worked things right, he just might be able to talk her into joining him. Only it seemed like he'd been in the water for ages already, and still no sign of her. Hoping she wouldn't be too much longer, he laid his head back in the cool water for a few seconds, letting it soothe the back of his neck, while he tried to imagine what it'd be like to hold her against him and let the water caress their bodies while he kissed her. Hell, just because her legs wouldn't work . . . he could carry her to the water. His eyes closed and a smile played at the corners of his mouth.

Unbeknownst to Warren, Blythe had already arrived, and was sitting quietly on Pegasus only a few hundred feet from the water, watching him. And the longer she watched, the madder she got, until finally she reached over, slipped the gun from its sheath, rested it on her knee, then nudged Pegasus to move forward.

Her gun was one of those new revolving-breech rifles Pa had brought back with him from a trip he'd taken back east last year. He'd given her and Braxton each one for their birthday, and she'd become quite adept at using it, a fact she was rather proud of. She readied it now as she rode into the open where Warren could see her. Watching him straighten, then spot her, she started forward, and rode closer, letting him come toward her in the water. This was better yet, she thought, and waited until the water was waist-deep on him, then called out.

"That's far enough, Warren!"

Warren stopped, slipping slightly on a rock, and he frowned as he looked across the water to where she sat her horse; then he saw the rifle aimed right at him.

"What the hell . . ."

Blythe knew he'd seen the gun, and she held it steady, aimed right at his chest. "Stay right there," she went on. "Unless you want a hole clean through you."

Warren tried to laugh. "Come on, Blythe, what the devil are you doing? Put that thing down."

"Why?"

"Because you'll get hurt, that's why. A joke's a joke."

"I'm not laughing, Warren, and I won't get hurt either.

I told you before that I can shoot as well as my brother, remember?"

The current was pushing gently at Warren's bare legs as he stood in the river, and he felt a chill run through him at the sound of her voice. She was right. She wasn't laughing. He straightened, combing the wet hair back from his face with his fingers.

"So, why are you aiming at me?"

"Because I found out something about you last night, Warren," she answered. "I found out you're a dirty rotten skunk!"

Warren's eyes narrowed as he continued to stare at her, and she went on.

"I found out you've got a wife, kids, and a couple million dollars you don't intend to part with, and all that sweet talk yesterday was just that. Nothing but talk."

"Now look, honey," he began, and started to take a step. She pulled the trigger and a bullet whizzed by his ear.

"God damn, what the hell are you doing?" he yelled, but the bullet had stopped him.

"I told you to stay put!"

"Look, this isn't funny anymore, Blythe." Beads of perspiration rolled down his face in spite of the cool water. "Now, put that thing down."

"Not on your life." Blythe's gray eyes never wavered. "You took something from me, Warren Russell," she reminded him. "Something you had no right to, and by God, you're going to pay for it."

Warren swallowed hard. Good Lord, she was going to kill him!

"Hey, look now," he began, trying to talk some sense into her. "It's not worth hanging for, is it?"

"It is to me." Blythe nudged Pegasus forward, moving closer to the edge of the water. "But then who's going to hang me?" she asked. "After all, nobody even knows we've been seeing each other, do they? So who's to say some Indian didn't put a bullet in you?" She sneered. "Don't worry, I won't hang."

"Come on, be reasonable, Blythe," he pleaded. "So I made love to you. You enjoyed it, didn't you?"

Yes, she'd enjoyed it when it was happening, but whether she liked it or not had nothing to do with it. He'd stolen too much from her. It wasn't just yesterday. It was all the past few weeks that should never have been. Tears filled her eyes, only he couldn't see them.

"So did you," she yelled back. "That's just the point. You made a fool of me, Warren Russell."

"I made a woman of you, Blythe Kolter!"

"Damn you!" She let loose with another shot that drew blood this time, and he reached up, massaging his injured ear.

"Hey!"

"What's wrong, Warren? You don't like the sight of blood? Or just your own?"

"You're crazy."

"Crazy? No, I'm not crazy, just mad." She hadn't really meant to actually hit him. She'd just planned to make him sweat. But this was better yet. Now, if she could really turn his knees to jelly . . . She aimed again, just above his left shoulder. This ought to do it. "You're a son of a bitch, Warren Russell," she hollered at him. "And you're going to pay for what you did to me!"

Her finger began to squeeze on the trigger. Only just at that moment, someone shouted from behind, distracting her, making her lose her target, and as the shot rang out and she stared out across the water in disbelief, she saw Warren grab at his left shoulder, where blood was already beginning to seep between his fingers.

"My God!" Ian cried as he rode in close, leapt from the saddle, and stared at her. "What are you trying to do, kill him?"

Blythe's eyes were like saucers as she looked down at Ian, then they both glanced out over the water.

Warren was making his way toward them, blood covering his left shoulder and chest, his face pale as he tried to stay on his feet until he got out of the water. He went down on his knees for a second, and Ian started to head for the water to help him, then stopped abruptly, and he and Blythe both turned back quickly toward the woods behind them as Luther, horse and all, came crashing through the underbrush and into the open river glade, his own rifle cocked, ready to defend Blythe.

Luther'd been watching from the ridge to the south, and had started forward the minute he'd seen the gun in Blythe's hand. Only it had taken him a while to ride down from the ridge.

"Go get him," he yelled to Ian, who nodded, then turned again and made his way to the water, wading in and grabbing Warren so he wouldn't stumble anymore.

Luther slid from the saddle, rifle still cocked as he strolled over, watching Ian help Warren from the water, then he tensed as he saw Warren's wound was worse than he'd thought.

"Oh, my God, Luther. I didn't mean to kill him, just scare him and make him sweat a little," Blythe cried as she watched Ian half-dragging Warren's naked body from the riverbank.

When he reached solid ground, Ian eased Warren out of the water, laid him in the grass, then headed for his saddlebags to get something so he could stop the bleeding.

"He gonna make it?" Luther asked.

Ian glanced over at the black slave, whose gun was still cocked, as if he wouldn't hesitate to use it.

"Probably, but no thanks to her." Ian looked over at Blythe for a second, then concentrated on opening the saddlebags.

Luther and Blythe both watched Ian take some things from the bags, then head back to where Warren lay in the grass, but before starting to work on his shoulder, Ian grabbed Warren's shirt from where his pile of clothes lay and tossed it over him for modesty's sake. Then he began to wipe and probe with his fingers.

"The bullet's still in him, and it's deep," he finally said as he stood up and looked back at the blond young woman who was still on her horse, and the slave who evidently felt it his duty to play bodyguard to her. "He'll need a doctor."

"No," Luther said, and his voice left no room for

controversy. "There'll be no doctor, not from town," he went on. "You gets him on his horse, Mr. Brooks, and you takes him back to your camp, and you takes that bullet out yourself."

"Hey, look," Ian said, his face grim. "I don't give a damn about that gun you're pointin' at me, but I do care about Warren, and I think you care about this little lady here too. And believe me, if Warren dies, she's in real trouble, and you know it. Now, you want to take that chance?"

Luther stared hard at Ian for a few seconds, then decided, "All right, you takes him to town," he agreed. "But on one condition. You tells the doctor he was in a skirmish with some Injuns, understand? Because if you tell him the babe here done shot him, I'm gonna tell the whole world she did it 'cause he raped her, and we'll see who hangs. You get my meanin'?"

Ian didn't like it, but what could he do? They had to get the bullet out. Actually, he could do it himself if he had to, but not here. There'd be too much chance for infection.

"You win," he finally said. "Only she just better hope he doesn't die," and he pointed to Blythe, then went over, picked up Warren's clothes, and began to put them on him. "And you," Ian said as he stared down into Warren's pain-racked face. "I hope to hell this teaches you a lesson, goddammit."

Warren was breathless from the pain, his voice unsteady. "Hell, she didn't have to shoot me!"

"You're lucky she didn't kill you. Now come on." He shoved the last boot on Warren's foot, then came around behind him and began lifting him from the ground. "Well, you could give me a hand, you know," he said, looking over at Luther.

Luther stood for a minute sizing up the situation, then relaxed, uncocked his rifle, put it back in its scabbard, and looked up at Blythe.

"Don't you worry, babe, there ain't nobody's gonna get you in no kinda trouble over this, I'll see to that. 'Cause even if he do die, and they learn you done it, my story's gonna be the same, and folks is gonna say you just did what you had to do."

By this time there were tears in Blythe's eyes as she watched the expression on Warren's face when Ian tried to move him. She nodded, gulping back tears, the anger and frustration replaced by fear of what she'd done.

"Don't worry, Luther, just help him," she said, and while Blythe watched, trying to ignore the tears trickling down her cheeks now, the two men managed to get Warren onto his horse, put the reins in his hand, then mount themselves, and the foursome rode away from the riverbank, Luther and Blythe heading southwest toward the Double K while Ian and Warren rode off toward San Antonio, with Ian riding close enough to Warren to try to keep him from falling out of the saddle.

16

Blythe looked sullen as she rode along beside Luther. They were halfway home already but she'd still talked very little to him about the shooting. In the first place, it wasn't just Warren who she felt had betrayed her. She'd never dreamed Luther was the one who'd been following her all these years. If she'd been smarter, she'd have figured it out, though. Who else but Luther would want to be bothered with her?

She glanced over at him furtively. "You know I'm mad at you too, don't you?" she said.

"Yep." His mouth pursed as he pulled his hat a little farther on his forehead to protect his eyes better from the afternoon sun. "Figured you'd be," he went on. "That's why I made sure you didn't see me."

"Then why didn't you just stay home?"

"If I had, you'd be in a nice peck of trouble right about now, wouldn't you babe?"

Blythe sighed. He was right, really. And it wasn't just today. Actually she'd been lucky over the years, riding all over creation the way she did with so many Indians around. And it just took one wrong thing to turn your life upside down, like today. And if he hadn't been there . . .

"It's just that I thought I was so grown-up, Luther."

"You is, babe, you is." Luther moved a little closer to her, and his eyes warmed at the sight of her fragile face, all suntanned, her eyes pleading. "Grown-up don't mean what goes on on the outside, babe," he went on. "Grown-up is what you is on the inside. And believe me, you's growed. If not, you'd have shot that fella back there clean through the heart the first time. No, babe, grown-up don't have nothin' to do with me followin' you all these years. Grown-up is how you accepts things that comes along. And you's mighty growed-up, babe."

Blythe smiled. Good old Luther. He always could make her feel better when life looked the bleakest.

"I wonder what Pa's going to say," she said after they'd ridden a short while longer.

Luther rolled that one around in his head for a minute, then straightened in the saddle. "Well now, he don't really have to say nothin' does he?"

"You mean we don't tell him?"

"He didn't know you was seein' the skunk, did he?"

"No."

"Then why tell him it's over?"

"But it isn't over, Luther. What if Warren dies?"

"Like I told Mr. Brooks back there. Either way, his friend'll come out on the wrong end of the stick if he don't tell people the right story. 'Cause there ain't no-body would blame a lady for defendin' herself from the likes of that Warren fella."

"I hope you're right."

"Don't worry, I am."

"What about Ma?"

"That's different. But you let me handle your ma, understand?"

Blythe blinked back the tears that had been trying to reach the surface for the past mile or so. It wasn't easy to have your heart twisted and wrung out like an old piece of laundry, without feeling it inside. Even though she hated Warren now for what he'd done to her, it was hard to just brush aside the tender moments they'd shared as if they'd never been.

That evening, back at the ranch, Blythe lay in bed staring across her room toward the far wall where a picture hung over the fireplace. It was a painting Don Antonio's wife had given to Blythe when Blythe was just a child. The woman had painted it only the year before she died, and it was of Blythe when she was about seven years old. Her hair was falling about her shoulders, and she was standing in a field of flowers. Blythe remembered how she had always thought how marvelous it was the way Maria de Léon could paint, and especially from memory, because Blythe had never even sat for the portrait.

Well, Blythe wasn't that innocent little girl anymore. She was a woman, and she'd almost killed a man today. The thought was frightening, because she hadn't been defending herself as she'd done so many times when they'd been attacked by Indians. No, she hadn't shot in self-defense. She'd shot in anger. And even though she knew she'd only been trying to scare Warren, just knowing how close she'd come to ending his life was frightening.

She closed her eyes, then opened them again as she heard the doorknob click and her mother came in.

"Feeling better?" Liz asked.

Blythe sighed. "I knew by the look on your face at dinner that Luther told you, didn't he?"

"He told me." Lizette's green eyes took in Blythe's discomfiture. She knew her daughter was still hurting.

"Are you going to tell Pa?"

"And have him kill Warren for sure? No, dear. Ordinarily, I don't keep things from your father, but there are times when to tell him would be worse than not telling. And this is one of those times."

"I'm sorry, Ma." The tears Blythe had been fighting ever since the shooting suddenly burst forth, flooding down her cheeks. "I didn't mean to do anything wrong, I just wanted someone to care."

Lizette sat on the bed beside Blythe, pulled her daughter into her arms, and held her close.

"I know," she whispered softly, just letting Blythe cry herself out. "It's not much fun seeing your cousin get married, and your sister start having boys court her, and know it's something you can't have. So you grab at whatever you can. I know all too well how you feel."

"But, Ma—!"

"Hush, Blythe, there are things about me . . . you have no idea, but believe me when I say I know exactly what you're going through."

Blythe wiped her eyes, drew herself back, and stared at her mother, wanting to believe her. Yet Ma had always had Pa, hadn't she? A frown creased her forehead as Ma took her hands and squeezed them, then smiled.

"Don't worry, dear," Liz said as she looked into Blythe's red-rimmed eyes. "You're young yet. Love will find you, and when it does, it won't be with the likes of a man like Warren Russell either. I know right now it hurts, but it won't be forever. Now try to get some sleep, and don't worry about Warren, he'll live. He just got what he deserved, that's all," and she helped Blythe to get down further into the covers, then blew out the light for her and left the room.

Blythe lay in the dark for a long time with tears in her eyes before finally dropping off to sleep.

The next few days went without incident, although rumors did filter back from town that Ian and Warren had had a skirmish with some Indians, and Warren had been wounded. Other than that, nothing more was said about the incident, and Blythe was relieved, although she had quit going riding every day as she had been doing the past few weeks, and went out only occasionally for a short ride.

It was on one of those short rides, on a Sunday afternoon, two weeks after the shooting incident, with Braxton riding along beside her this time, that Blythe ran into Don Antonio de Léon. Today was the first she'd ridden with her brother for weeks, and it felt good again to be together as they made their way down along the lower end of the Double K range. Suddenly Brax reined up and pointed off to a hill a short distance away.

"Well, look who we bumped into," he said.

Blythe glanced over, to see Don Antonio and Case moving down the hill single file, and as she too reined her horse to a stop, Braxton called to them.

Both men waved, and Braxton grinned. "I think Case spends more time with de Léon than he does with his pa."

As they watched them, Blythe was inclined to agree. Even though Case lived at the Crown D and had accepted his role as Cole and Heather's Dante's son, his life as Joaquín de Alvarado was still so much a part of him that it was hard to let go, and even though Don Antonio was only a family friend, Case still treated him more like a real uncle.

"Hola," Don Antonio greeted them as he and Case reined up a short time later. "What a pleasant surprise."

Blythe glanced over while the men were all greeting each other, then tried to smile as Don Antonio sidled his horse closer to Pegasus.

"Well, Blythe, buenos días, my dear," he said, and as she looked into his eyes, Blythe somehow knew Don Antonio wasn't just passing the time of day. "Why is it I haven't seen you out riding lately?" he asked.

She tried not to, but blushed horribly. "I guess we just didn't happen to be in the same place at the same time, that's all."

His eyes studied her curiously. It seemed as if she always blushed when he spoke to her. Could it be she knew how he felt? She had grown into such a beautiful woman, and he loved her so much.

"Perhaps then you will finish your ride with me today," he said, glancing over for a second to where Case and Braxton were talking. "I believe I just heard your brother invite Case to join him in town. And if I know Case as well as I think I do, if there are females involved in the day's activities, he will not only say yes, but beg to go." He looked back over to Blythe. "That means I would be able to ride back to the ranch with you, if you will let me."

Blythe had been watching Don Antonio the whole while he'd been talking, and as she looked into his face now, a strange warm feeling flooded her. Strange how, since she'd grown up a little more herself, he didn't seem quite as old as he used to. The other day Pa had mentioned Don Antonio had just turned thirty-six. That wasn't so old really. Actually, today he looked almost ten years younger. His dark eyes were alive, expectant, and the hint of a smile at the corners of his mouth made her feel more relaxed.

She too glanced over at Braxton just as he and Case both looked their way.

"I have a feeling you're right," she said, then called over to her brother, "I suppose you're going to desert me again."

Brax laughed. "Oh, come on, Bly." He reined Hickory over next to her mount. "I don't get to town all week, and I had to stay home last night. You wouldn't begrudge either of us a little fun would you?" He looked over at Don Antonio. "You wouldn't mind riding back with her, would you, sir?" he asked.

"I would love to ride back with her," Antonio answered, then looked at Blythe again. "But she has not said yet whether she is willing to let me."

Brax looked at his sister. "Bly?"

"Naturally I don't mind." She looked first at Case, then at her brother. "Only you two had better not get into any more trouble like last time, or Pa and Uncle Cole'll be skinning you alive for sure."

Brax grinned. "Hell, that wasn't any trouble," he said. "Besides, we didn't start it. It was that Yankee and his loud mouth." He pulled on the reins, quieting his pinto. The horse was restless and anxious to get moving. "So, do you care?"

"No, go ahead," she said, and Case winked at her, his way of thanking her, and both of them hollered, waving good-bye as they dug their mounts in the ribs and took off at a gallop.

"What is this trouble? Is there something I missed?" Antonio asked while they watched the two of them getting smaller in the distance.

Blythe's gaze was on her brother, who was quickly becoming a speck against the horizon. "Nothing real serious," she said. "It's just that they got into a fight at the cantina about two weeks ago, and Pa and Uncle Cole had to pay for the damage to the chairs and tables. That's why Brax has been so short of money lately. Pa's been taking it out of his wages."

"Then at least Brax will learn, will he not?"

Blythe smiled. "If he ever grows up."

Don Antonio knew well what she meant. "You must remember, my dear, boys never really grow up," he said. "They may grow somewhat wiser and the years may creep up on them, but in their hearts they are always part little boy." He straightened in the saddle, then glanced about. "So, would you like to ride a bit more before we head back to the Double K, or would you prefer to just head for home?"

Blythe looked over at him again. What a striking figure he made in his fancy Mexican clothes, the brilliant shades of blue enhancing his swarthy good looks. His horse's saddle was trimmed with silver, and even the hat he wore was edged with the precious metal, as were the filigree buttons that bordered the legs of his calzoneras, while tooled leather boots were shoved neatly into his elegantly fashioned leather stirrups. She forgot so many times just how wealthy the man was. No doubt because he was so nice. Most men with his land and money were snobs.

She smiled at him, and he smiled back.

"You have decided?" he said.

She nodded. "I think I'd like to ride a bit longer, if you don't mind."

His eyes lit up. "I would feel sad if you didn't." He looked about again. "So, which way?"

She reined Pegasus about in the direction of the trail she and Braxton had been riding, and in minutes they were disappearing down it, and Blythe was laughing and talking with Don Antonio as if the last few weeks with Warren had never even happened.

However, at night, back at the Double K, it wasn't always so easy to forget, although it seemed with every day that passed there were fewer and fewer days ending with tears on her pillow at night. And with each new day that dawned, Blythe began to see even more and more of Don Antonio.

He rode over in the evenings and sometimes during the day, coaxing her to go riding with him, and they'd end up being gone all afternoon. Even on Sundays he began showing up with a carriage and driver, and talked her into riding into town with him, to just get her out of the house and into new and different surroundings.

One Sunday afternoon he even had her over to dinner, much to the chagrin of his niece. The years had done nothing to temper Catalina's attitude toward the Texans, whom she still considered foreigners who had taken over her country, but in spite of Catalina's curt reception and contentious manner, Blythe had to admit she had a good time.

Catalina was all of seventeen already, and Blythe tried to understand how she had felt at seventeen. So she ignored Antonio's niece as much as she could, concentrating only on Antonio, who was not only attentive, but trying so hard to please her, there was no way she couldn't enjoy herself. After that afternoon, it seemed as though she began to see even more of him, and then finally, one day while they were out riding, he reined his horse to a halt and called her to join him.

Blythe nudged Pegasus forward, then was surprised when Antonio left the saddle and held his arms up, reaching for her.

"Come," he said, his voice exceptionally vibrant, the lilt in it more animated than it had ever seemed before. "I wish to show you something."

She stared down at him, suddenly wary.

"Por favor, please, I will not hurt you. I would never hurt you, mi querida," he said.

Only Blythe remembered Warren telling her the same thing, and she still hesitated.

"You are frightened of me?" Antonio suddenly asked, surprised.

Blythe shook her head, and finally held out her arms to him, and he lifted her from the saddle, then cradled her against him while he carried her to the edge of a high cliff where she could see for miles in all directions. Far off, like a tiny dot in the distance, was the de León hacienda, its walls easily defined in the huge panorama.

Antonio was standing at the edge of the cliff, his feet set firmly, and now he looked from the scene before them, right into her eyes. She stared back at him.

"It is all yours, mi querida," he whispered softly as he held her close. "The land, the hacienda, and I would give you the moon and stars if I could, if you will but say yes to me." His face was like an open book as he looked at her, and Blythe wanted to cry. "Por favor, I am asking you, Blythe Kolter, I know I am older than you, but the age does not matter. Not for the love I have for you. I would ask you, will you marry me, mi querida? Will you be my wife? I have wanted to ask you for so long now."

Blythe had expected to be surprised if any man asked her to marry him after what had happened with Warren, but coming from Tonio, as she'd begun calling him lately, it was no surprise at all. She stared at him for a long time, feeling the strength in the arms that held her, and seeing the love in the eyes looking into hers. It was a look she had never seen in Warren's eyes, and a look that wrenched at her heart, because although she really liked Don Antonio, she knew deep in her heart it was more the love of a friend she felt, and she didn't know what to do.

"I have shocked you, sí?" Antonio said.

Her arms tightened around his neck and she tried to make him understand. "No, you didn't shock me," she answered. "It just that . . . you say you love me, Tonio, but I don't think I know what love is."

"Then I will teach you."

"And if I never learn?"

"Then I will have the love for both of us."

"That's not fair."

"To you? Or me?"

"To you."

"Oh, but you are wrong, querida." His voice was deep with emotion. "To say no to me would not be fair, for it would cut my heart as surely as it would if you were to use a knife. No, my dearest one. I have loved you for so long, and all I would ask is to make you happy."

There were tears in Blythe's eyes. What should she do? If only she could hate him, it would be so easy to say no, but she didn't. In fact she really did like him. There were times when she even began to wonder if, since she didn't really know what love was all about, she might even be starting to fall in love with him, but marriage? Marriage required so much. She would have said yes to Warren the first time he kissed her, if he had asked, and yet he had done nothing to prove his love for her as Tonio had been doing.

She breathed deeply, knowing her face was still flushed. "Do I have to answer today?" she asked.

He looked disappointed, but only for a moment, then smiled. "Ah, but no, mi querida," he said as his arms tightened to hold her more firmly. "For such a decision I should not have expected an answer today, I will wait for my decision until you are ready, because I want you to be sure." He looked out again across the plains to where his hacienda sat basking in the summer sun, the pride on his face too apparent. "But I want you to remember, mi querida, what I have will be yours too, and gladly," and this time when he faced her again, for the first time since he'd come courting, he leaned forward, his mouth covering hers, and kissed her slowly, yet passionately. Something he'd been wanting to do for a very long time.

That night Blythe had so much to think of, and after Pretty helped her to bed, she lay for a long time with her head resting on her open palms as she stared at the ceiling. It wasn't just leaving home, and the security of this room, that bothered her. Although she knew she'd miss it. But what would she do when he tried to take his marriage rights?

She knew what it had been like with Warren, but she had thought she loved Warren. Closing her eyes, she tried to imagine what kind of lover Tonio would be, only it was so hard. Would she be scared, would she even want it? Oh, God! If only she knew what to expect. And Catalina! She could just imagine how the girl would feel, having an aunt only a few years older than herself, and a gringa to boot. If nothing else, Blythe would love to marry him just to spite Catalina. Only marriages weren't decided on in order to spite someone. No. If she decided to marry Tonio, it would be for other reasons, not spite.

Opening her eyes again, she raised up on her elbows

and stared toward the fireplace where the picture of her hung. It was too dark to actually see, but that didn't matter because she'd looked at it so often over the years she knew it by heart.

If she were like the little girl in that picture, with two strong legs to stand on, she wouldn't even be contemplating an answer to Tonio's question. But she wasn't like her. That little girl had the use of her legs, a liberty the artist had taken true, but there was the difference. She had told Ma no hero was going to swoop down out of the hills and rescue her from her chair. Well, maybe she was wrong. Maybe she was just looking for him to ride in from the wrong direction. After all, what would be so wrong in her becoming Don Antonio's wife, Doña Blythe de Léon. A little strange perhaps, but not altogether unthinkable.

She sank back onto her pillow again and continued staring at the ceiling. Well, whatever decision she finally made was going to be frightening. Because either way, if she said no and stayed here, there was every possibility she'd spend the rest of her life at the Double K. Yet, if she said yes, she'd be moving into a new world she'd never been a part of before.

Determined that her decision, when she made it, would positively be the right one, Blythe finally closed her eyes again and tried to get a little sleep.

The wedding of Don Antonio de Léon and Blythe Kolter was set for September 28, the last Saturday in September. It was only about a month and a half away now, and Blythe had been so busy with the preparations since her decision to say yes that she had paid little attention to other things going on around her. That's why she hadn't even noticed when the time for her menses had come and gone without them showing up. They had been due the first week in July, and here it was the second week in August when Liz, suddenly realizing there's been no rags to wash out for Blythe for some time now, stopped scrubbing her own and went looking for her daughter.

As usual, Blythe was on the front porch working on her wedding dress, embroidering the flowers around the flounces that would billow out on on the skirt. Liz stopped and watched her for a second, then joined her.

"Look, I'm almost through Ma," Blythe said, and held up the material she'd been working on.

"That's pretty, dear."

Blythe frowned. "Well, you could be more enthusiastic about it."

"I am, believe me," Lizette said. "But there's something we have to talk about, and I don't know where or how to start."

"You're not going to try to talk me out of marrying Tonio again, are you?" Blythe asked. "Because really, Ma, I have a feeling that for the first time in a long time, I'm doing the right thing."

"No, I'm not going to try to talk you out of it," she answered. "Only I think before this whole thing goes any further, you'd better tell him that you're pregnant, don't you?"

Blythe froze, staring at her mother, her face slowly draining of color. "Pregnant?" she gasped, then suddenly let her thoughts carry her back to that day with Warren, and the realization she'd been so wrapped up in everything that had been happening and the the past few weeks . . . my God! Ma had to be right, and she set the billowy material aside, embroidery and all, and stared at her stomach, remembering abruptly how hard it had been to fasten her chemise the other morning, and thinking she'd put on a few pounds. She hadn't felt well at breakfast the past few days either.

"How long has it been, Blythe?" Lizette asked.

Blythe shook her head in disbelief. She was so stupid. "Oh, Ma . . . not since way back in June sometime, I think."

"Warren?"

Blythe nodded, unable to talk because of the lump in her throat.

"That's what I was afraid of. And Antonio hasn't touched you, has he?"

She shook her head.

"Oh, my dear." Lizette leaned forward, squeezed Blythe's hands, then reached up, brushing a stray hair back from Blythe's forehead. "He has to know, dear, you do understand, don't you?"

There were tears in Blythe's eyes. "Oh, Ma, how do I tell him? What do I say?"

"I wish I knew. But he has to be told."

"I know, I know," she said tearfully, and the next afternoon, after spending a restless night trying to think of what to do, when Antonio came over to take her riding, Blythe made up her mind that one way or another she'd tell him today, before the afternoon was over.

As usual lately, she and Antonio would ride to the glade where she and Braxton, with their cousins, had spent so much time when they were younger, and he'd carry her from her horse to the log they used for a bench. It wasn't far from the water, and they'd sit there for a long time talking, he'd kiss her a few times, tell her how much he loved her, then they'd head back to the ranch again.

They were sitting there now, and Antonio glanced over at Blythe. Something had been bothering her all day, he was sure of it. She was too quiet. Her laughter didn't ring true, and more than once he'd caught her staring off into space with tears in her eyes.

"What's wrong, querida?" he finally asked after studying her curiously for a few minutes.

Blythe took a deep breath. "I have something to tell you, and I know it's going to hurt you, and I don't know how to start."

Antonio held his breath. "You are not changing your mind, are you?"

"No, but I think you will," she answered, and before he could tell her she was wrong, she not only told him she was quite sure she was pregnant, but confessed her whole sordid affair with Warren. Including her attempt to make him pay, and the results of her anger.

By the time she finished, she was sobbing, wishing she could die, or at least just go hide somewhere, anywhere

where she wouldn't have to see the look on Tonio's face. Still, he had listened quietly, commenting very little. Now he stared at her for a long time, then finally reached out, touching the side of her face gently as he gazed at her.

"Do you love him?" he asked, his voice breaking.

"No, I don't think so. I thought I did then, but now I'm sure it wasn't love. It was just that I needed someone to care."

He seemed to take in what she said while he stared at her; then, "Do you still want to marry me, Blythe?" he asked.

"I'm so ashamed . . ."

"I didn't ask if you were ashamed." He wiped the tears from her face with his long fingers, then held her face in both his hands. "We all do things we are ashamed of, mi querida," he said as he looked at her. "Even I. You think I am a saint? I am far removed from sainthood, mi amor. Many times I did to women what he did to you, and I did not love them. It was for pleasure, and pleasure alone, so who am I to condemn you for what you have done? All I ask is, do you still want to marry me?"

"And the baby?"

He hesitated a moment, and she held her breath.

"Since this . . . this Warren Russell and Señor Brooks are no longer in the area, I assume he does not know of it, am I right?"

"Yes."

"Then if it is a girl, you shall name her, and if a boy, then I will take that privilege."

Blythe couldn't believe it. "You would accept the child as your own?"

"Rather than lose you, sí, mi querida."

"Oh, Tonio!" Tears glistened in Blythe's eyes, and he kissed her softly, then held her for a long time. Afterward they talked for the rest of the afternoon, while Antonio continued to reassure her he loved her, and Blythe knew again this was right.

So the wedding plans didn't change, and Blythe saw a new side of the man she was to marry. A side of him she had never dreamed possible, as he not only made his hacienda ready for her, but had his servants construct a new chair for her, with carved handles, larger wheels, so she could reach down and move herself, and plush cushions to make her more comfortable.

However, three weeks before the wedding Blythe woke up one morning with a bloodstained bed and cramps so bad she was doubled up in pain, and even though Lizette called Pretty to Blythe's room to help, before the sun went down that evening neither Blythe nor Antonio had to worry anymore about what to name the baby she'd been carrying. Or what to name any child in the future either. Because not only did Blythe lose the baby, but due to the injury to her years before, her body had never fully developed as it should inside, and her disfigured womb was also ripped from her, being expelled in one mass along with the baby.

Pretty had all she could do to keep Blythe from losing her life as well, since she bled profusely, but with Pretty's skill, and loving care, everything was soon under control again. Although Blythe went through a horrible ordeal for the next few days.

However, by the time the day of the wedding arrived, she was looking forward even more now to being married, because although she had had mixed feelings about losing the child, and felt sad because she'd never experience the joy of having a baby of her own now, she also felt relieved that she was no longer coming to Antonio carrying her shame.

Finally, on September 28, with family and friends in attendance, Blythe sat in her chair at the chapel at the de Léon rancho, dressed in the frothy white dress with its billowing skirts and fancy embroidery, a delicate tiara gracing her pale hair, and exchanged vows with Antonio before the village priest, becoming Doña Blythe de Léon. And although the ceremony was a quiet one, the festivities afterward were anything but quiet as the guests ate, drank, and danced until way after dark.

It was very late. The guests were gone and the festivities over. Blythe sat upstairs in bed in the master bedroom where Antonio had carried her after everyone was gone, and she watched the door, waiting for his return. He'd said he'd be back up shortly, and that had been almost an hour ago. Naturally she felt he was making sure she had enough time to prepare. She didn't have her chair upstairs here yet, but Antonio had assigned a servant named Rosita to take care of her, and although the woman was efficient and polite, it wasn't like having Pretty, and Blythe had felt so awkward being helped into her nightgown, then into bed.

Pretty had been like family to Blythe, and had been all Blythe had known since she was a baby. As she sat now, looking about the strangely alien room with its Spanish atmosphere, the extent of her new husband's wealth apparent in the expensive furnishings, she knew it was all going to take more getting used to than what she had first thought. The Double K was a well-run ranch, and considered one of the bigger ones in the area, but its split-log house and plain furnishings were nothing compared with the elegance Don Antonio had in his home. Now she was part of it.

She glanced toward the huge double doors, called French doors, that opened onto the portico at the front of the house. It was dark outside, the light from the lone candle lamp on the dresser trying unsuccessfully to reach out into the darkness. However, the breeze from outside was far more aggressive than the dim light, and Blythe breathed in deeply, smelling the fresh scent of the fragrant flowers that twined in the trellis just below on the veranda.

She was wearing a pale blue nightdress Pretty had helped her to make, and was propped up against the goose-down pillows on the huge mahogany bed. Her hands smoothed the thin cotton sheet covering her legs. Even the border of the sheet was embroidered with fantastically brilliant flowers that matched the borders on the pillowcases. Hands trembling slightly, she ran her fingers across the stitching, feeling the silken flowers beneath them.

If only she wasn't so nervous, and she remembered the disgusted look Catalina had given her just before Tonio

started up the stairs with her. Catalina had been on her
way to her own room after having had another argument
with Braxton just before he'd left, and Blythe assumed
the look had been in retaliation for her being Brax's
sister. Whatever the look was for, she hoped with all her
might that Catalina wouldn't carry her vendetta against
the hated gringos, as she referred to most Texans, into
her relationship with Blythe, or it was going to make life
as the hacienda miserable for everyone.

Suddenly Blythe turned at the sound of footsteps in
the hall, and a moment later Antonio entered the room.
He stood just inside the door, staring at Blythe for the
longest time, and the longer he stared, the more self-
conscious she became.

"Ah, mi querida, por favor, forgive me," he said as he
closed the door behind him and finally walked to the
chair the other side of the bed and began taking off his
chaqueta. "I did not mean to stare so. But if you only
knew how lovely you look." Again he saw Blythe blush,
and it warmed his heart.

She had made a mistake, yes, he thought as he watched
her, continuing to undress as he talked about some of the
people who'd come to the nuptials, but now it would only
be easier for him because he knew for certain he would
never hurt her. He had hurt his first wife that first time,
although he hadn't wanted to, and it had almost ruined
him because of it. So, in a small way, he thanked Warren
Russell, while still condemning him in his heart.

He was down to his pants now, his chest bare, and he
hesitated a moment, glancing over at her. She'd been
staring at him while he took off his shirt, but now her
eyes were diverted, and she was looking down at the
fancy sheets. He tossed his shirt aside and sat on the bed,
watching her closely.

"I embarrass you, mi querida?" he asked.

Her eyelids lifted and she gazed up at him. "Silly, isn't
it?" she said, her voice strained. "You'd think I'd know
what to expect."

His gaze softened as he looked into her eyes. "You are
still innocent, mi amor," he went on, and reached out,

taking her hand in his. "And I love you all the more for it."

He drew her hand up, kissing the back of it softly, then opened it, pressing his lips to her palm, and Blythe sighed, realizing she liked it.

Her gaze lowered to Tonio's chest, and she watched the muscles rippling beneath the mass of dark hair that covered it, and suddenly she felt her heart begin to pound. Warren had been muscular, yes, but his body had been long and sinewy, every muscle hard like iron. Antonio was so different. He was shorter than most men, yes, but what people had always accepted as extra poundage was really a stocky build which proved to be sturdy and muscular without an ounce of fat on it. Blythe suddenly felt drawn to him.

Gingerly she reached out and touched his chest, then saw his eyes become languid, and he trembled. Pleased at the feel of him she rested her palm against him, then ran her fingers to his shoulder before pulling her hand away again.

"Ah, but no, do not stop, mi querida," he whispered as he gazed deep into her eyes. "Touch me, love me all you wish, and let me know you want me as much as I want you," and to prove what his heart was feeling, he leaned closer, his mouth covering hers, and kissed her hungrily for the first time since he'd known her, knowing this time his want of her would be fulfilled. This time he could love her as he'd always yearned to love her, and when the kiss was over, he slipped from the rest of his clothes, climbed in beside her, and when Blythe felt his hands molding and caressing her, then let those same hands arouse her and hold her so she too could feel, while he made love to her, his soft words reassuring her that she was all he had ever wanted, she knew that this time it was right. And the only reason there were tears in her eyes when she lay in his arms afterward, letting him hold her, was that she knew that although she cared, she could never love him the way he loved her.

17

Even though Blythe's life quieted down some after her marriage to Don Antonio, life for the rest of her family remained as hectic as ever, as Grandma Dicia often made it a point to tell Blythe whenever she came calling.

First of all, Teffin informed everyone she was expecting, Case and Braxton rode off and joined the Texas Rangers, and Helene, who had been with the Dantes for years, had run off with one of the ranch hands and no one seemed to know where she was. It was just as well, though, Loedicia confided to Blythe, since the woman had caused some trouble between Heather and Cole back when all the mess over Kaelen and Teffin had been going on.

"Thank God it didn't amount to anything, though," Loedicia told Blythe one afternoon when they were having tea. "But you know, being in love with your uncle the way she's been all these years, it's probably better this way."

Blythe had been shocked. She'd had no idea. But then Helene had been such a strange, quiet woman. Now that Blythe thought back over the many times she'd visited at the Crown D, she knew Grandma Dicia was right. The only thing that bothered her now was how Helene could have gone on living there all those years under those circumstances.

As the days and months rolled along, Blythe finally began to feel like she was a part of Tonio's home, even though she didn't actually run it, as most women would.

It wasn't that Antonio didn't trust it to her care, but

loving her so much, he didn't want her to tax herself with things he considered unnecessary. So her days were spent just doing whatever she wanted, and it was with a great deal of surprise one afternoon that he discovered her sitting in her chair in the small studio downstairs off the library, an easel in front or her, sketching the cacti in the garden outside near the ballroom.

"I didn't know you could draw, querida," he said as he studied the strong bold lines on the paper.

Blythe studied what she had done. "I didn't either," she answered, and turned to him. "I was almost afraid to try when I found them. They were Maria's, weren't they?"

"Sí." He looked around at the small studio, which was much as it had been years ago when his first wife was alive. "But it is yours now, if you would like it."

Blythe didn't know what to say. She had seldom mentioned Tonio's dead wife, not knowing what his feelings were, but now . . .

For the rest of the summer her days were spent with the easel in front of her, and at Christmas he presented her with her own paints, and for a while it seemed to take the place of the family she could never have. And although she'd never experienced the same depth of blissful yearning with Tonio she had known that day with Warren in the old burned-out cabin, she felt sure that maybe she was finally beginning to fall in love with him, because she could feel herself starting to care.

It was Antonio who became restless as time went on. Every day he'd watch Blythe struggle from bed, either with his help or with the help of Rosita. And every day he'd watch her legs move, but never enough to really be of help. And when he made love to her, he reveled in her response, stronger than he'd ever imagined it could be, and he began to wonder. Finally one day, some two years after their marriage, after returning from a trip he had taken to Mexico City on business, a trip she couldn't accompany him on because of her condition, he informed her he had a surprise for her that would be arriving within the next few weeks. However, he wouldn't tell her what it was.

Used to surprises from him by now, Blythe just kissed him and promised she'd be patient, then went back to her painting, expecting a new necklace or perhaps some silk for a new dress.

It was early morning, a little over a week after Antonio had told her about the surprise. Blythe had finished the painting she'd been working on the day before, so when her brother showed up and asked her to ride into town with him, she jumped at the chance. After all, she hadn't seen Braxton for months. He'd informed her that he and Case had been patrolling in Comanche territory lately instead of along the Rio Grande, and she was glad he'd taken the time to stop by.

"I shouldn't really," he said as they headed toward San Antonio. "But I had to run an errand in town anyway. Figured what they wouldn't know wouldn't hurt them. Besides, a fella has to make sure his twin sister's being treated right, doesn't he?"

Blythe glanced over as they rode along. Just like Brax, she thought. Even the Rangers weren't going to tame him.

It was a lovely day the sun hot, with a cool breeze blowing down from the north, and when they arrived in town it seemed as though everyone else had thought of the same thing, as they rode past the crowded market toward the plaza.

San Antonio had grown a great deal since the end of the war, and although the inhabitants were still mostly Mexican, more and more each day settlers were arriving from the United States. Some were building up the town, others looking for land, and most of the settlers out on the frontier lived in one-room cabins yet, with crude fencing and outbuildings, the way the Kolters and Dantes had when they'd first arrived. Now, here were more to add to them, Blythe thought as she and Brax rode past a train of six wagons, furniture piled high on them, and the effects of an already long journey apparent in their shabby condition. She began to wonder where they were planning to settle, or perhaps were they just passing through? She watched them curiously as they made their way through the dusty streets.

Brax had promised her that all he had to do was pick up something in town, then ride back to the Crown D to meet Case before heading out on patrol again. So a short time later, after dodging a number of oxcarts, loose chickens, and some people on foot, they reined up in front of one of the older buildings. Brax dismounted, tying his horse to the hitchrail, then strolled inside, leaving Blythe waiting on Pegasus.

Relaxing in the saddle, Blythe nodded to a gentleman passing by whom she knew to be a business acquaintance of Tonio's, then she reached down, patting Pegasus' neck as the stallion moved restlessly, evidently frightened by the noisy arrival of a freight wagon that had just entered the plaza from the south, from the direction of the Camino Real.

The mules pulling the wagon were loud, the harness and wheels even louder, and the driver was trying to drown them all out, while beside him on the seat sat a tall stoic gentleman, hat on, chaqueta slung over one arm in hopes of being cooler. As the wagon neared the spot where Blythe was waiting, the man's gaze suddenly settled directly on Blythe, and she felt a tingling sensation begin to run through her from her ears clear down to her toes.

The stranger's eyes were dark, his skin as swarthy as Tonio's, but there was something about his face, about those eyes, and Blythe couldn't tear her own gaze away as the driver pulled the wagon to a halt right in front of her.

"This here's San Antonio, fella," the driver said to the man on the seat beside him. At the moment, however, his passenger seemed to be completely engrossed in the young woman astride the horse only a few feet away.

She was beautiful, he thought as he continued to stare. The loveliest creature he'd ever seen, and a strange feeling shot through him.

"I said this here's San Antonio!" the driver repeated, louder this time. Finally the man drew his gaze from the young woman and looked at the driver.

"Ah, sí. Muchas gracias," he said, then reached behind the driver, grabbing a bag. "You will take down my trunk too, sí?" he asked.

The driver nodded, then twisted the reins around a bar at the front of the wagon and climbed down. His passenger also climbed down, but on the other side, where he set the bag he was carrying down, and walked to the back of the wagon to help the driver, who was already unfastening some rope from about a large trunk.

Good Lord, he's tall, Blythe thought as she continued to watch the wagon's passenger. She'd swear he had to be at least an inch or so taller than Kaelen, and Kaelen was taller than both Pa and Uncle Cole.

She watched the tall, dark stranger toss his chaqueta over the side of the wagon, then join the driver, lifting the trunk to the ground. Once free of the trunk, he reached up, took off his wide-brimmed black hat, grabbed a handkerchief from the pocket of the chaqueta where it lay, and wiped his brow, and Blythe marveled at the dark curls that clung to the sweat on his forehead. She had never seen a man before who exuded so much masculinity and yet seemed quite unaware of it as he put the hat back on his head and grabbed his chaqueta while watching the driver return to his seat. Once on the seat, the driver untied the reins, and with the same exuberant fervor in which he entered town, he yelled to his mules again, not only startling them but also causing a near-panic with Pegasus.

When the mules charged toward him, Pegasus reared back, threw his head high, then bolted right for the stranger, who jumped quickly to one side and made a grab for him, catching Pegasus' bridle, only to be dragged for at least ten feet before Blythe finally managed to convince the palomino he wasn't riderless.

"I'm sorry," she yelled down at the stranger as she held the reins tightly to keep Pegasus from bolting again. "I'm awfully sorry!"

The stranger was spitting dust from between his teeth as he let lose of Pegasus's bridle now that the animal seemed to be under control again. He began brushing more dust from his clothes.

"Madre de Dios! Why do you not learn to ride the beast first before you get on his back!" he snapped as he ran a hand over his hair to get the dirt out. "You could have killed me, and yourself too."

"I do know how to ride."

He eyed her skeptically, then reached down, picked his hat up from the road, and flailed it against his leg to clean it off.

"If that is what you call riding, señorita, then I feel sorry for the horse." His eyes were bristling irritably. "And I suggest from now on you try walking, it is safer. Now—" he set the hat back on his head and flipped the dust from his chaqueta as he talked, then shrugged into it—"do you suppose perhaps you would be able to direct me to the alcalde's office, or would you call him constable? Sheriff? Whatever, do you think perhaps you could hold that mount of yours in check long enough to point it out to me?"

Blythe's face was crimson. Of all the nerve. Her eyes narrowed, and she stared at him. "Why should I?"

"Because I just saved your life."

"Saved my life? I was born on a horse, señor."

"Then I suggest you tell the horse that, señorita, because I do not think he knows." He straightened arrogantly. "Now, where is your law enforcement?"

A self-satisfied sneer tilted the corners of Blythe's mouth. "If you weren't so busy criticizing my riding, señor," she said, enjoying the moment tremendously, "you might have noticed that you're standing right in front of it."

The stranger's eyes darkened, and this time it was his turn to blush as he turned and read the sign over the door of the building. Then he looked back at Blythe.

"So we are even, are we not, señorita?"

Blythe's jaw tightened hard as she stared at him, her gray eyes intense. "Even? Far from it, señor." Pegasus pawed the ground again. "We will only be even when and if you apologize!"

"Apologize? You are saying this was my fault? Never, señorita," he said, and turned, pulling the tails of his chaqueta firmly, as he marched toward the door of the building where Braxton had disappeared.

Just as he reached for the knob, the door opened and Brax came out.

"You are the law?" the stranger asked.

Brax hefted a thumb up, motioning behind him. "Inside, señor." Then he watched as the Mexican entered, closing the door behind him after first taking one last glance back to where Blythe sat on Pegasus.

"Well, wonder who he is," Brax said as he mounted Hickory.

"Who knows." Blythe glanced toward the door where the tall dark stranger had disappeared. "But whoever he is, he could use a lesson in manners." She drew her gaze from the building and looked over at her brother. "Ready?" she asked.

"Ready," he replied, and they turned their mounts around, then moved across the plaza, once more dodging a congestion of carts and carriages and people, unaware that the newly arrived stranger had left the building again and was now standing in the road next to his luggage staring after them, his dark eyes narrowing curiously.

Blythe glanced over at her brother as they rode out of town, following the road that wound along beside the river.

"Do you have to go back right away?" she finally asked.

He smiled, the two-day growth of beard he was sporting the same pale color as his hair, making his tanned face all the darker. "You trying to tell me you'd like to look at something like this across from you at the dinner table tonight?"

"You could shave first."

He reached up, rubbing the stubble on his chin. Damn! It was a long time since he'd sat at a decent table. They'd been eating anything they could, anywhere they could find it lately, including rattlesnake and lizard. Still . . .

"What do I do about Case? He's expecting me to show up at the Crown D."

"I'll have Tonio send someone over to tell him you'll be late."

"He probably would like that." Brax gazed off down the road, then took his hat off, wiped his brow with his hand, flicking the sweat off his fingers, put the hat back on, and glanced over at her again. "You win," he said. "I just hope your cook has something good on the menu for tonight," and he grinned, straightening in the saddle as they both urged their mounts a bit faster.

Antonio was quite pleased to have Braxton join them for dinner that evening in spite of the fact that, even with his face clean-shaven, Braxton didn't exactly present the usual appearance of a dinner guest. But Antonio liked Brax. Always had, so he overlooked the soiled buckskins, dirty boots, and gunbelt Brax wore even when eating. It was Catalina, however, who was upset by his presence.

Being her usual self, she did everything she could to aggravate him. However, tonight, for some reason Brax refused to take the bait. In the first place, he didn't want to hurt his sister by starting an argument in her home, and besides that, he'd been away so long that in spite of her sharp tongue and insulting behavior, he discovered he was glad to see Catalina again. Realizing reluctantly that her dark eyes and flashing smile still had a way of bothering him, although he'd never admit to her, or anyone else for that matter, that they had the slightest effect on him.

It was early yet, but dinner was over, and they were just ready to leave the table, when one of the servants came in. Don Antonio excused himself, asking Braxton if he'd mind wheeling Blythe into the parlor, since a caller had arrived and was in the library waiting for him. So Braxton, Blythe, and Catalina went directly to the parlor, where Catalina, infuriated by Braxton's apparent refusal to argue with her, tried to think of as many ways as she could to get a rise out of him. Again to no avail. All he did was smile and agree with her. And it was during one of her tirades, on how the Rangers were nothing more than a vicious bunch of cutthroats and outlaws, that her uncle returned and Blythe's face paled as she got her first glimpse of her husband's caller. He was the tall dark stranger she and Brax had met earlier that day back in San Antonio.

"Ah, you see, I am glad now that you have stayed, Braxton," Antonio said as he entered the room. "For I want you also to meet our new guest." He walked over to stand near his wife's chair. "Mi querida, Catalina, and Braxton, I wish you all to meet Dr. Mario de Córdoba, from Mexico City. The doctor and I met during my last visit to Monterrey, where he was visiting a colleague."

Braxton was quick to shake hands, Catalina curtsied, but Blythe just stared.

Never in her wildest dreams would she have thought the man knew Antonio.

"And this is my wife, Blythe, Doctor," he introduced her, after introducing the other two.

Blythe nodded, realizing that the doctor's face was as flushed as her own.

"I'm afraid we have met earlier in town, Tonio," she said, hoping to ease some of her embarrassment.

Dr. de Córdoba's expression was remorseful to say the least, and although he tried not to show it, at the moment he wished he could crawl into a hole somewhere and never have to come out.

"Sí, that we did," he offered, his eyes boring into hers. "And I believe I owe the señora an apology. Am I not right, señora?"

A smile played about the corners of Blythe's mouth as she remembered earlier in town when he'd said he'd never apologize to her. Her eyes twinkled knowingly.

"Apologize? How nice of you, señor—or should I say 'doctor'? But the whole thing was my fault, I'm sure." She turned her head, looking over at Antonio. "You see, dear, Pegasus decided to get a bit frisky, and I'm afraid he almost ran the good doctor down, and it seems the doctor thought I would be better off walking than handling . . . what was it you called my palomino, a beast? Anyway, I'm sure neither your doctor nor I am any the worse because of the incident."

Antonio reached down, took her hand, and smiled. "Then we will talk no more of it," he said. "But you are wrong, mi querida. Dr. de Córdoba is *your* doctor, not mine. I have told him of your accident, and he thinks perhaps he can help you."

Blythe's hand froze in her husband's grasp, and a cold chill ran through her.

"No . . . oh, please, no, he can't," she said, her voice strained as she stared at the man standing before them. "There were all sorts of doctors when I was small back east, before we came here . . . there's nothing he can do."

"Por favor, please. Will you let me try, señora," Mario said as he studied this beautiful young woman. "There are so many new methods now. We have learned so much."

"And if you fail?"

"Then I will at least have tried."

Blythe continued to stare at him for a few minutes, then looked at Braxton. If only . . . But to get her hopes up and then fail . . . "What do you think?" she asked her brother.

Braxton watched her closely, almost able to read what she was thinking. "I think your husband loves you very much even though you can't walk, Bly," he answered. "But I also think, for your sake, that you should at least give it a try."

Actually the decision as to whether she would let the doctor try to cure her or not had nothing to do with whether her husband loved her as she was, or whether she'd be too disappointed at a failure. What neither Braxton nor Antonio realized was that her hesitation at saying yes right away was brought about mostly from her feelings for this tall handsome stranger who had come into her life.

He was the first man since Warren Russell who had evoked such feelings in her by just a look from his dark, penetrating eyes, and she was afraid if she said yes, those feelings would erupt into emotions she'd never be able to handle. She was attracted to this man in ways she had no right to be, but how could she explain a thing like that to Tonio? And how could she even explain it to herself? But ever since this afternoon and their altercation in town, Blythe had been unable to forget the man. Now, if she agreed to let him try to see if he could make her walk again . . . She was in a quandary, and it wasn't until after a great deal of soul-searching on her part, and pleading from her husband, that she finally gave in.

So that night Dr. de Córdoba took up residency in the guestroom at the de Léon hacienda.

"And you'll do everything he says?" Braxton asked as he was leaving.

Blythe nodded. "And probably a few things he doesn't say too."

They were in the foyer, just the two of them, and they both laughed, then Brax bent down, kissing her on the cheek.

"So where to now?" she asked.

He straightened, then reached down and took her hand. The days were long now and the sun was still riding low on the horizon.

"To get Case, then who knows where," he said, and kissed her again. "Just so I make it before dark," and she understood.

Brax never wanted her to worry. They were still close in spite of the miles separating them.

"Take care." She squeezed his hand, then released it.

"You too," and he walked out the door, literally bumping into Catalina, who was outside on her way in. "Well, good-bye to you too," he said as he placed his hat on his head and smiled.

Catalina's eyes blazed furiously, and she looked ready to tear him apart. "Good riddance, you mean," she said through clenched teeth. "And I hope you fall from your horse and break your neck, Braxton Kolter," and she turned to flounce away into the house, only Braxton was too quick for her.

In one deft motion he grabbed her arm, turned her back to face him, pulled her against him so she couldn't wrench free, and kissed her full on the mouth. The longest kiss Blythe had ever seen a man bestow on a woman.

When the kiss was finally over, he drew his head back, looked Catalina dead in the eye, said, "Adios, my little cougar," as Case had often referred to her when they were younger, then bounded down the front steps two at a time, leapt to the back of his horse in one powerful motion, and rode out of the gate, never looking back.

Blythe was as flabbergasted at her brother's actions as Catalina, and she watched now as the young woman stood on the veranda staring after the horse and rider that were disappearing in the distance. Then, before Catalina could discover she'd seen the strange encounter that had gone on between these two people who supposedly hated each other, Blythe reached down and grabbed the wheels on her chair, pushing herself off toward the parlor, where Tonio had said he'd meet her after showing the doctor to his room.

The next few weeks at the hacienda were a real trial for Blythe as she spent almost every waking moment with the doctor, who not only examined her legs, but wrote down the particulars of the carriage accident she'd been in, as well as going over every symptom she had ever had, from the day it occurred until now. He even went over her personal history, and although Blythe told him of her miscarriage and the results, she let him think it had happened after her marriage to Antonio.

Sometimes the doctor put weights on her legs and had her try to move them, and one day he even took her for a ride to a nearby river and took her into the water with only her chemise and drawers on, so he could watch her legs float, to determine just how much mobility she might have. There seemed to be nothing he wouldn't try if he thought it might help, but nothing did. That's why, early one afternoon a little over a month after the doctor's arrival, Blythe found herself lying facedown on a table the doctor had had the servants bring to the master bedroom. She was wearing her chemise and drawers, but there was a sheet over her back, and another covering her buttocks, while the doctor's hands worked their way down her spine to the small of her back.

Mario was becoming frustrated. He wanted to help her so badly, but each time, he ran into a blank wall. There was some life in her muscles, yes, but not enough, and for some reason they refused to get any stronger. All he could think of was that the nerves had been crushed too, but then, if that were so, why any feeling at all? Because she could feel. He'd known that the first day he'd examined her and watched the gooseflesh rise on her legs at the touch of his hands.

He stared at her head for a moment. She was resting it on her arms, and her eyes were shut. He wondered. Was she asleep? He didn't think so, and as his hand moved across her spine, his fingers deftly identifying the vertebrae and trying to piece together the puzzle of bone and tissue that refused to work as it should, he saw her tremble, and knew she was awake.

His hands kneaded her back slowly as he searched for something, anything, out of place. So many times these things could be so well-hidden. Especially an injury from so long ago.

Suddenly he tensed as he realized his fingers weren't just searching, they were enjoying the feel of her beneath his hands. A sensation quite alien to him because he'd always been able to disassociate himself from his patients. However, now, for the first time, all the ploys he'd ever used before to accomplish it didn't seem to be working. His hands stopped momentarily, and he stood motionless.

"What is it?" she asked, sensing something was wrong.

He inhaled sharply, his hands beginning to move again, and opened his mouth to answer, when there was a knock on the door. Leaving the table hurriedly, he walked over, opened it, and thrust his head out.

"Por favor," Rosita began, her face flushed. "But the señora's madre, she is here to see her, and insists that she see her now, señor. She is waiting in the parlor, and por Dios, she is upset."

Blythe had heard, and she raised her head, calling to him, "Tell her I'll be right there," she said, and watched him repeat the answer; then he shut the door and turned back to Blythe.

"I will go down and send someone up to help you," he offered, but she stopped him.

"And who will carry me down, pray tell?"

He stared at her for a moment. "You want me to?"

"Why not you?" She pushed her chemise down and pulled her drawers up beneath the sheets, then sat up, letting her legs dangle over the side of the table. "Just hand me my dress, I'll only be a minute. Besides, it'd be silly to send someone else up when you're already here."

He walked to the chair where her blue silk dress lay, picked it up and handed it to her, then waited for her to slip it over her head so he could fasten it up the back.

"Before you go downstairs, there is something I must tell you, Blythe," he said, and she finished putting her arms in the dress, then stared at him. "You do not mind giving me a few minutes before we go?"

She shook her head. "No, go ahead."

"Bueno." He paused then walked around the table and began fastening the buttons at the back of her dress.

"First of all, I am not here purely by accident," he began, his fingers working slowly, to give him time. "You see, many years ago I had a brother. His name was Emilio Sancho de Córdoba, and they called him Sancho the Bloody. I believe you have probably heard of him."

He saw her shoulders tense, yet went on. "My brother was a pirate, sí, and although I loved him, I knew the life he led was wrong, and I also knew that because of him a young girl lost the use of her legs in a carriage accident on a rainy road one night in South Carolina a long time ago, and I have been trying to make up for that night ever since. I was fifteen at the time, Blythe Kolter de Léon, and you were that little girl, and since then I have helped many others to walk again. But now the one person I wish to walk more than anyone else in the whole world, I seem to be able to do nothing for." His fingers clenched about the last button, then he let go. "I would say your mother is upset because she has discovered my presence in this house, and I wanted you to hear the truth from me first, rather than her."

He walked around from behind her and stood staring down into her warm gray eyes that now held a hint of . . . What was it? Disbelief? Sadness? If only he could read her thoughts. He had been here only a little over a month, but already Mario knew he had fallen in love with this exquisite creature.

"Do you understand what I'm trying to tell you?" he asked.

She nodded, unable to speak as she looked up at him. Mario de Córdoba! The name had meant nothing to her, but Sancho the Bloody? Tears welled up in her eyes.

"You knew I was here?"

"Sí . . . although not until I met Don Antonio. At first, when your father killed my brother, I shouted that I was going to avenge his death. They were the ravings of a boy who had not grown up as yet, I'm afraid. Then later, when I realized the extent of suffering my brother had caused to so many people, I decided the best way to make amends for what he had done was to try to stop some of the world's suffering. So I began to study medicine. Sometime back I happened to run into an old classmate of mine who is at present living in Monterrey, and as men will, we began to discuss friends, when your husband's name came up. But it wasn't until months later, when I visited my friend at his home in Monterrey, that I learned who you were, and I had hoped perhaps I could repair the damage my brother had done."

"Does my husband know?"

"How could I tell him it was my brother who did this to you?"

"But you knew he'd find out."

"By then I was hoping to be able to tell him you would walk again."

"And can I?"

"I don't think so."

"Then what will you tell him?"

"The truth. What else can I do?"

Blythe studied his face as he stood looking down at

her. So many times these past weeks she had wished she weren't married to Antonio. She had felt it that first day in town, when she and Mario de Córdoba had clashed over her horsemanship, and again here at the house the first time he'd walked into the parlor. She had hoped never to have those feelings again, and yet here they were, and she wanted to hate this man who was causing them. Yet knew she couldn't.

"Then I guess you'd better take me downstairs, hadn't you?" she said.

"Perhaps I should."

He bent down, picking her up, and cradled her in his arms.

"We forgot your shoes," he reminded her, glancing down at her feet.

She smiled, her arms tightening about his neck. "So who needs shoes when they can't walk?"

He hesitated a moment, the feel of her in his arms affecting him as it always did, and prayed his feelings didn't show on his face, then headed for the door.

It had been almost two months since anyone from the Double K had stopped by to visit at the hacienda, but that wasn't unusual. Everyone was so busy lately, and the ranches were so far apart. Besides, with Brax and Case gone, and Teffin married, it just seemed like everyone had his or her own life to live. Lizette stood in the parlor now, fidgeting nervously with the fan in her hand while she waited for Blythe to come downstairs. Liz was wearing one of her best dresses, a green silk, and had left her straw bonnet with the flowers on it in the foyer with the maid. She reached up, fluffing the ruffle at her throat, then checked it make sure she hadn't forgotten to put on her emerald earrings.

Let's see, she thought, how many years ago was it? Almost twenty, and if Luther hadn't gone to town for supplies this morning, it could have been days yet before she learned he was here. Mario de Córdoba! Just the name had a way of unnerving her. Still, what if she was wrong? The name de Córdoba wasn't all that unusual. What if it was the wrong Mario de Córdoba? She was just about to try to convince herself that she was being ridiculous and overly concerned after all these years, when she heard voices in the hall, turned toward the door, and stared in disbelief as Mario carried Blythe into the room and stood just inside the threshold, holding her in his arms.

It was Sancho, yet it wasn't Sancho, this tall dark Spaniard. The family resemblance was striking, only Mario's hair was much curlier than his brother's had been, and the cruelness that had dwelt in his brother's eyes was missing in Mario's. But he was just as big and swarthy, his good looks masked by a ruggedness that his brother had also had. A roughness that could be charming as well as fierce.

"Hi, Ma," Blythe said when she realized her mother was staring awkwardly at the man who was holding her, then she looked at Mario. "My chair's over near the fireplace."

Mario, who had been staring as curiously at Lizette as she'd been staring at him, drew his gaze from Blythe's mother and walked over, setting his patient in her special chair, then he called one of the servants, who was in the hall, to get something for her mistress to put on her feet, before finally facing Blythe's mother again.

"Señora Kolter," he acknowledged, surprised at how kind the years had been to Bain Kolter's wife. She was still carrying extra pounds, as she had years before, but in spite of them, she was still a lovely woman. "I suppose I should have let you know right away that I was the doctor who was treating Blythe, should I not?"

"You think that would have helped?" Lizette had felt a sense of urgency in her visit today. Bain was out on the range with the men, and she'd had Luther bring her over in the buggy. She had to see Mario before Bain did, although she really didn't know why. Unless it was because of all the memories she knew seeing him would bring up.

"I am not my brother, señora," he said as he straightened, standing next to Blythe's chair.

"But you look like him, except for the scar and the beard."

Mario reached up to his right temple, to where his brother had had a deep scar, then rubbed a hand across his smooth-shaven face.

"And what is inside is different too," he said. He had to make her understand. "My brother was hurting inside, and he took his anger out on the world around him. I have had no reason to seek revenge on anyone."

"Not even Bain?"

"Not even your husband."

"Then why are you here?"

"To help your daughter walk again. I am a doctor and surgeon now, señora, and if there is any possible way at all for her to walk, I hoped to find it."

"And Antonio knows who you are?"

"He knows who I am, sí, but not that my brother was the man responsible for crippling his wife."

"And when he finds out?"

"He won't care," Blythe cut in, and Lizette's eyes wavered as she glanced at her daughter, then back to Mario. "All he wants is for me to walk again," Blythe went on, hoping she was right. "It won't matter at all to Tonio."

"What will not matter to me?" Antonio asked from the doorway, and all three turned.

Blythe knew Antonio had ridden to town earlier, but had no idea he'd be returning so soon. Usually his business in town took all day.

"Well, what is it?" he asked again as he looked from one to the other while they stared at him. Then his gaze stopped on Blythe's mother, whose presence was unusual this time of day. Most of the time she'd come to visit in the evening with Bain.

"It's about your doctor here," Lizette answered, and saw Don Antonio frown. "You see, Antonio, the man who's responsible for Blythe being crippled was named Emilio Sancho de Córdoba, and he had a younger brother named Mario, who just happens to be your good doctor here."

Blythe saw the color drain from Antonio's face, and an anger like she had never seen before filled his eyes.

"You do not mean this!" He glanced over to where Mario still stood next to Blythe. "You? It was your brother?"

Mario's jaw clenched stubbornly. "Sí, my brother, not me!"

"But you knew?"

"Sí, I knew. Why do you think I came here?"

"To seek vengeance for your brothers' death, no doubt, why else?" Don Antonio's eyes darkened. "Bain Kolter told me years ago how he ran Sancho through with his sword. Why would you not want to kill the man who killed your brother?"

"Because I am not like my brother, that's why!"

"Please, Antonio," Blythe began, but he cut her off.

"No, mi querida, no, please! Do not plead for him, I will hear none of it. He came here under false pretenses—"

"But, Tonio—"

"Enough!" Antonio was furious. "To think I let the brother of the man who did this to you live under the same roof with us. Madre de Dios! Doctor or no doctor, he has no right to be here. I will not have it for any reason, do you understand?" and for the first time since their marriage, Blythe found herself on the receiving end of the anger she had occasionally seen her husband display when he felt wronged. "He will pack up and go now, do you hear me? He will go at once, and never come back again, ever!"

Blythe was at a loss. Her husband was being unreasonable. He wasn't even giving Mario a chance. Fury blazed in her own eyes as she stared at Antonio, then suddenly she turned toward the door and shouted, "Rosita!"

Surprisingly, Rosita was on her way into the parlor with a pair of soft doeskin moccasins for Blythe's feet.

"Forget them!" Blythe said as she reached down and began wheeling herself from the room. "I want you to help me," and she looked back at her husband, who was still so livid with rage he hadn't the slightest idea what his treatment of her was doing to her emotions. "As for you, Tonio, go ahead," she said. "Be stubborn, don't listen to me. But just remember, I'm the one who was crippled, not you," and she continued toward the door, letting Rosita push her the rest of the way out into the hall.

Once in the hall, she looked back over her shoulder at Rosita, who by this time was cowering at the fury in Blythe's eyes, something she'd rarely seen in the years the de Léon's had been married.

"Put those moccasins on my feet, then take me to the stables," Blythe ordered her.

"But—"

"I said the stables, Rosita!"

"Sí señora." Rosita frowned, hoping Don Antonio wouldn't blame her for what her mistress was having her do, then she pushed Blythe through the courtyard, out the back way, and down to the stables, where Blythe ordered one of the grooms to saddle Pegasus. And with the groom helping her into the saddle, within minutes she was riding out the gates of the hacienda without even a hat on her head, hoping to ride out her anger over Tonio's treatment of her.

Back in the parlor, Antonio's anger was already starting to subside as Mario continued trying to make him understand why he was there, and his reason for being so secretive about his past.

At first Antonio did nothing but shake his head. But then slowly, as Mario pleaded his cause, and the words began to penetrate the resentment inside him, Antonio suddenly realized how foolish he was being. You didn't judge a man by what his brother was. And Mario was right. Antonio would never have let Mario come if he had known. Before long, even Lizette began to understand, so that by the time Blythe and Pegasus were leaving the gates of the hacienda far behind them, Antonio had already changed his mind and was actually asking Mario to forgive him and stay. Mario accepted.

"So now I presume I had better go tell Blythe everything is all right again," Antonio said, excusing himself. "I will be back shortly."

Lizette glanced over at Mario de Córdoba, who was now standing near the French doors. "I'm glad we were wrong about you, Mario," she said after Antonio had left the room.

His smile was rather forced. "De nada," he answered. "I am used to being, how you would say, misunderstood. It took me many years to climb out of the shadow of my brother's name."

"And your sister. Where is she now?"

This time Mario's smile was genuine. "Ah, Elena," he mused, and she'd swear a chuckle escaped his lips. "Eric and Elena are married and still living in Havana and running the business Tío Emilio left to them, while trying to keep track of their seven niños, who, unfortunately, are as scheming and devious as their mother."

"You're joking."

"But no, Señora Kolter. They had one right after another, and would have eight now, if the first one had not died at birth."

Lizette thought back to those long-ago days on board ship with Sancho's sister, and the way she had tried to make Lizette believe those terrible things about Bain. And the consequences of all the other things Elena had done. Now the thought of Elena chasing after a brood of children pleased her. A strange revenge, true, but Lizette had raised three children of her own and could just imagine what having seven would be like.

She was just ready to ask Mario if Eric seemed happy, when Don Antonio rushed into the room.

"She is not here." He looked worried. "Blythe is gone!"

Lizette frowned. "What do you mean, gone? Where could she go?"

"She made Rosita take her to the stables, then rode out on Pegasus. But why?"

"Why?" Mario stared at Don Antonio. The man actually had no idea what he'd done. "When was the last time you yelled at her?" he asked.

Don Antonio looked surprised. "Do not be ridiculous, Mario." He'd been calling the doctor Mario for some time now. "I did not yell at her. I simply told her you were not going to be staying, that's all."

"And the way you said it?"

"Cielos santos! Do not tell me she is upset over that. I was not mad at her. I was angry with you."

"But she does not know that." Mario was rather surprised that Antonio would be so blind to Blythe's feelings. But then in the little over a month he'd been at the hacienda, he'd begun to realize that Antonio's love for his young wife was a rather strange love. Seldom did Blythe cross him, or have any reason to. It was as if he always made sure life around her ran smoothly, and in doing so, Blythe had little chance to learn to adjust to disappointments, either in their relationship or in her environment. "Perhaps you should ride after her, Don Antonio," Mario suggested.

Antonio looked pensive for a moment, then glanced to the clock on the mantel. "I would like very much to, but I'm afraid I'm expecting a gentleman from town who is due here at any moment, and I must talk to him, and today." He hesitated a moment, then looked at Lizette. "What shall I do?"

Lizette remembered the furious look on Blythe's face, and she wasn't at all sure what her daughter might do under the circumstances. Besides, she didn't like the thought of Blythe being out there alone, any more than Don Antonio did.

"Perhaps Mario could go after her," she said, and saw Antonio's eyes light up.

"Ah, sí, that would be the thing, and he can explain to her that all is well again." He looked over at the doctor. "Mario?"

A few minutes later, while Antonio stood on the veranda saying good-bye to Lizette Kolter, then watched his mother-in-law being helped into her buggy by Luther, he glanced up and out, toward the front gate, just in time to see Mario de Córdoba disappearing through it on horseback. Mario would bring her back, Antonio thought to himself as he watched the doctor ride away. Mario would bring her back, and all would be well again. He was sure of it.

18

Blythe knew the mistake she'd made after riding only the first mile, yet wasn't about to turn back. She should have taken time to change clothes and put on a hat and boots before leaving. But if she'd done that, she might have lost her temper even more, and really said things she shouldn't. So this was probably for the best.

The top of her head was burning from the heat of the sun, and her armpits were wet with sweat as she spotted a grove of cottonwoods and rode toward it. It would be cooler under the trees but a lot of good it'd do her. She couldn't get off her horse and sit and enjoy the shade, and for the first time in a long time, she cursed Mario's brother for what he'd done to her.

Mario! She pulled Pegasus to a halt beneath one of the trees, and just sat quietly in the saddle, remembering the look on his face earlier when he'd told her about his brother. She hadn't cared, not really, because she knew he was no more like Sancho than she was like Genée. He was Mario, and a warmth flowed through her at the very thought of his name. Irritated by the all-too-familiar feelings she was experiencing, she reined Pegasus away from the tree again and moved on.

She'd been riding for well over an hour already, and suddenly realized this was the first time she'd ever really been riding alone. Before she'd always thought she was alone, but Luther had always been following. Since her marriage she'd never ridden without Antonio, or Braxton or Case if either happened to come along. And a few times Catalina had joined her, but never had she left the hacienda by herself until today, and she didn't even have her rifle either.

Suddenly the thought was exciting, and a little frightening too, and as she reached down, lifted her dress to unfasten her petticoat so she could drape it over her head, she remembered she hadn't taken time to put it back on. That meant she had no way to keep the sun off her head. Ah well, maybe she could keep in the shade as much as possible.

Her temper had simmered down a bit, but she was still smoldering over Tonio's treatment of her. Never, since they'd been married, had he ever talked to her like that. But then she'd never interfered like that with him either.

Still bristling from the encounter, she happened to turn slightly, glancing behind her as she rode. Suddenly she froze, and pulled Pegasus to a halt. Raising a hand to shade her eyes, she frowned, then recognized the rider's long torso above the horse, and the black broad-brimmed hat he wore, with the sides slightly tilted, that gave away his identity.

Her hands were crossed and resting on the horn of her saddle while she waited for him.

"Where are your bags?" she asked when Mario reached her.

"I won't be needing them."

"You mean he changed his mind?"

"I changed it for him."

"How?"

"Like I said I would do. I told him the truth."

"I'm surprised he believed you."

"He had no reason not to."

She eyed him curiously. "You came to take me back?"

"Do you want to go back?"

"No. Not yet, anyway. I'm still mad."

"You are upset, Blythe de Léon. Only dogs go mad."

"Well, when you're treated like a dog . . ." She straightened in the saddle. "He had no right to talk to me like that."

Mario studied her for a moment. "I think you are spoiled, señora," he said, then smiled as he dismounted.

"But come," and he walked over, holding his arms up to help her from the saddle. "I think you should rest a bit. You have been in the saddle for well over an hour."

Blythe stared down at him, then glanced about. "There's no place to sit."

He looked about. They were on a flat plain with no trees, no hills, and no place to sit except the rough ground. Not even any soft grass. "You are right." He returned to his horse and climbed back into the saddle. "So we shall find one."

Half an hour later, with their horses tethered to a nearby bush, Mario was carrying Blythe toward a plush stretch of grass beneath the trees where they'd be out of the sun. It was secluded here. A spot that looked like no horse had ever set foot on it, and yet Blythe knew they were still on de Léon land.

He went down on one knee, and suddenly her arms tightened about his neck.

"Please, don't put me down yet," she begged.

He frowned. "Why?"

"I don't know why. Should I know why?"

He took a deep breath, but continued to put her on the ground, leaning her back against a large boulder that shielded them from the open range beyond the trees.

"I think you are still angry with your husband."

"No, it's not just that. You know it isn't."

"Blythe . . ."

"I know, I'm a married woman, and besides, I'm crippled, right?"

"You are a married woman, sí, but as for your ability to walk . . . of that I do not give a damn."

"Then please, Mario, help me."

"Help you? Cielo di mi vida, I too need help where you are concerned. My hands try to alienate themselves from feeling when I touch you . . . it is impossible. My heart tries to tell me it is wrong when I look at you and feel what I feel inside. And I go to bed at night, lying there thinking of you with him, and I wish I had never come."

"Then I wouldn't have known you."

"And would that not be better for both of us?"

"Would it?" She was gazing into his dark eyes, and for the first time in her life Blythe realized the mistake she had made by marrying Tonio.

You couldn't teach someone to love you, not the way she loved this man who was staring back at her. You could teach a person to care, and to love as a friend, but love like she felt at this moment could never be taught. It was something that just happened between two people, and she knew Mario felt it too.

Reaching up slowly, she touched his face, then let her fingers move to his lips, and they trembled beneath her touch.

"I know it's wrong," she whispered, her voice filled with emotion. "But I have to know for certain. Will you kiss me, Mario?"

Mario's breathing was heavy, his body trying to fight what his heart wanted so badly, and he reached up, took her hand from his lips, then leaned forward until his mouth brushed hers, gently at first, as if tasting to see how sweet it would be. Then suddenly she melted against him, and he found himself lost in the wonder of her as the kiss lengthened and deepened.

Suddenly there was no turning back, no end to what they were both feeling, even though Mario ended the kiss.

"It isn't fair," she murmured against his lips.

"I know."

"What shall I do?"

"I wish I knew."

"Make love to me, Mario." Blythe was no longer the innocent girl she had been with Warren Russell, and this was so much more. "I need you."

"And I want you. I've been falling in love with you ever since that first day when you almost ran me down. I knew it then, but didn't want to believe it."

"Why?"

"Because I have no room in my life for love."

"And yet you love me?"

"Sí . . . sí. I love you so much it hurts when I am near you."

"Then stop the hurting for both of us, please, Mario . . . please make love to me!"

Mario reached out, holding her face in his hands. "How can you be sure, mi querida? It has been only a little over a month. Maybe it is just that you are angry with him . . . maybe you are still upset."

"No," she answered, and her eyes filled with longing. "It's as if I've always known you."

"And I you," and with this confession, Mario drew her close in his arms, then moved her to where she lay prone in the grass. And with the late-afternoon sun trying hard to peek at them through the leaves, Mario made love to her for what he told himself would be the first and only time, and it felt so good, so right, even though they both knew it was wrong.

Blythe was still on her back in the grass with Mario over her, his bare legs warm against her, the fire still filling her very soul, while his lips brushed her neck, then pressed against her ear.

"I have found heaven in your arms, Blythe," he whispered, and kissed her neck again.

Her hands moved up his chest and she marveled at how firm and muscular he was, and at how naturally she had responded to him. There was none of the pretending, none of the feelings of inadequacy she'd felt so often with Tonio. And yet . . .

"Oh, Mario, what do we do now?" she asked.

He raised up, looking down into her face. "What do you want to do?"

"I don't want to hurt Tonio."

"If he learns of this, he will not only be hurt, but he will kill me, and with good reason."

"I know." Her arms tightened about him, her hands moving slowly against his bare flesh, then she pushed him away so she could look up into his face. Her hand left his torso, and she reached up, touching his cheek, running her hand down along his jawline, the feel of him intoxicating to her senses. She'd grown to love him so much, and yet she couldn't hurt Tonio. He deserved better. "It's no good, is it, Mario?" she finally said.

He shook his head. "Not for us."

"So what do we do now?"

His dark eyes searched hers. "I think we should talk," he said, and kissed her softly, then moved from over her, stood up, put his clothes back on, and helped her with her clothes. Then he helped her sit up again against the rock and sat down close facing her so they could talk.

"Now, you asked what we are to do," he said, and he reached out, taking her hand, holding it gently in his. "I have been thinking ever since you asked it. There is nothing we can do." He saw the hurt in her eyes. "You said yourself you cannot hurt him."

"But I love you."

"And I you. I think we have both known it for some time, have we not?" He leaned forward and kissed her again, tenderly, then straightened back up. "But what we feel has no right to be, we know that too, and what happened today must never happen again, and we both know that too."

"But how can we . . . ?"

"We have to." He squeezed her hand hard. "If he even so much as suspected . . . I don't want this, mi querida, I wish with all my heart I could just sweep you into my arms and keep you there always with me, but life is not always so generous with us."

"Why?" she asked, tears springing to her eyes. "Why can't life ever be simple?"

"Who knows." His voice was deep with emotion. "All I know is that somehow we will have to live with this, and yet not let him ever suspect."

"How can I hide how I feel?"

"How? The way you pretend with him even now. You think I have not the eyes to see?" He remembered back over the past weeks since his arrival. "You have not the love for him, yet he thinks you do. Is this not pretending?"

"But pretending to love is easy. Pretending not to love is hard, because it hurts inside."

"I know." He sighed. "But it can be no other way. You are married in the church, and we both must ask forgiveness for what we have done, and pray God may give us the strength to never let it happen again. For your sake, as well as mine, it can be no other way, mi amor."

Blythe heard his words, and knew he was right. Yet to lose him was like losing a part of herself.

"I don't want to lose you."

"Never will you lose me," he answered, and reached up, touching her face, remembering what it was like to pretend she was his, if only for a little while. "No matter what happens, whether you walk again or not, I have made a decision." She looked puzzled, and he went on. "I'll still be your doctor, mi querida, I would not want it otherwise, but I have decided to open an office in town where I will be able to help others as well. That way, no matter what, I will still be able to be near you and know that all goes well with you."

"When did you decide this?"

"Weeks ago, when I knew I had fallen in love with you."

"Oh, God, Mario. Hold me close for just a moment, please!"

How could he deny her? and he reached out, pulling her into his arms, and held her for a long time.

Finally he released her, holding her at arm's length to look into her face, where the tears still glistened on her cheeks.

"I will always love you, mi querida. I want you to know that." He looked into her eyes. "No matter what, no matter the years that go by, you will always be with me in my heart. But I cannot kill the spirit of Don Antonio by even thinking to take from him what is his. Can you understand that? As much as I love you, I could not do this."

She nodded, more tears joining the ones already cascading down her cheeks. "I know," she answered, her voice unsteady, the hurt inside unbearable. "And I won't ask you to. I'll try to be content just knowing. But, oh, it will hurt," and she gulped back a sob. "Oh, how it will hurt."

"One kiss," he whispered, his own heart aching, the tears glistening in his own eyes. "Just one last kiss, mi querida, and then we will love only with our hearts," and this time when he took her in his arms, they clung to each other as if they were both drowning, knowing this kiss would have to last them for a lifetime.

By the time Blythe and Mario returned to the hacienda, Antonio's meeting with the gentleman from town was over and it was close to dinnertime, but since Blythe was exceptionally tired, she'd begged off joining the men, and after a much-needed bath, she had Rosita bring her food to the bedroom upstairs that she shared with Antonio.

After eating the light meal of fried beans and chicken wrapped in a tortilla, with tea to wash it down, Blythe barely sipped at the champurrado Rosita had brought her, its thick creamy chocolate extremely rich following the spicy sauce she'd had on the beans and chicken. Really, she hadn't really felt like eating at all, but knew if she didn't Tonio'd start wondering why, and she didn't want to do a lot of explaining. So she had forced the food down, and was now trying to do the same with the chocolate.

Only forcing the thick chocolate down was far different, and she had only about half of it gone when Antonio came in.

"Well, so have you rested sufficiently?" he asked as he walked over, took off his chaqueta, then removed the small string tie at his throat and unbuttoned his shirt collar. "I have been a bit worried. Mario said you rode far today."

"I guess I didn't realize." She set the cup down on the tray that straddled her lap.

"And that is my fault," he said, walking over to the bed. His dark eyes studied her face, and as she stared back at him, she suddenly realized his hairline was starting to recede a little. "I should never have spoken to you as I did," he went on, apologizing to her. "It was entirely uncalled-for on my part. Can you forgive me?"

Tears rushed to her eyes. She should be asking him to forgive her for what she had done today. Her mouth opened, but nothing came out.

He saw the tears. "Ah, but no, mi querida, do not cry,

please. I will never hurt you again in any way. I promise. Not even if you deserved it, would I hurt you," and he smiled affectionately. "Now, por favor, mi amor, wipe the tears, so I may talk with you without the weeping," and he handed her a handkerchief from his pocket.

Blythe blew her nose, then wiped her eyes, glad he thought the tears were because her feelings had been hurt.

Antonio was sitting on the edge of the bed now, and he studied the room for a few minutes, then his gaze came back to his wife's face.

"Mario has decided to leave," he said, and Blythe hoped the anguish didn't show in her face. "Oh, no, not Texas," he continued. "But, as he says, there are others he can help, and to stay here as he has been doing . . . he says he feels, how can I say . . he is right, mi querida. It is selfish of me to keep him here at the house. He will still be your doctor, but he said the last time he rode into town he was looking for a small villa that would be perfect for his needs. So I have told him, if you say yes, I will not hold him to the promise to stay here. Do you agree?"

Blythe wanted to shout to him that she hated the idea. That she would go with Mario too, if only Tonio would let her go. But to do so would be madness. Instead she nodded.

"If that's what he wants," she answered. "After all, who am I to have to my own private doctor?" and she forced her voice to conform to the words, her reward being a broad smile from her husband, who then leaned over and kissed her gently.

"I knew you would agree," he said as he drew his lips from hers. "Now, finish the champurrado and we will see who will win the game of chess we started yesterday, before I try to make up to you for the misery I caused you this afternoon," and he walked toward a small table at the other end of the room where a chess game was set up, while Bythe stared at the thick chocolate before her, knowing that Tonio meant to make love to her before they went to sleep, and she wondered how she would get through it, after this afternoon.

The next morning, Blythe slept later than usual, so that Antonio and Mario were both gone by the time she showed up at the breakfast table. Antonio to a business meeting in Goliad from which he wouldn't return for at least two days, and Mario to make arrangements to move into the house in town as soon as he could. Only Catalina was around, and as usual she was staying as far away from Blythe as possible. Probably up in her room reading, or perhaps in the sewing room.

Blythe picked at more of her food than she ate, then afterward had Rosita push her onto the veranda out front, where she could catch a bit of breeze while she tried to sketch the scene for a new painting she'd decided to try. Only there was little breeze stirring today.

Finally, restless and out of sorts, bored with the picture she just couldn't seem to get interested in, she called loudly for Rosita, had Rosita call one of the male servants to carry her upstairs, where she changed clothes, then was carried back downstairs, where she ordered Rosita to take her to the stables.

"Oh no, you cannot go riding alone again, señora," Rosita argued. "The señor Don Antonio say if we let you go alone again, he will see we live to regret it."

"Don't be ridiculous. He's never punished any of you."

"But there could be a first time. No, señora. The riding clothes you may wear, but the horse will not be saddled unless there is someone to ride with you."

"I'll ride with her."

Blythe hadn't heard Mario come in, and the sound of his voice made her heart skip a beat. She looked over at him while Rosita shrugged.

"Sí, señor," Rosita said, and glanced quickly at her mistress, knowing the battle was lost, then she headed for the stables to tell the groom to saddle Pegasus and put the saddle back on the doctor's horse, while Dr. de Córdoba brought her mistress from the house.

"When will you be moving out?" Blythe asked as he

pushed her chair across the courtyard toward the back door.

"Tomorrow. That's why I'm going to ride with you today."

She looked back at him, her eyes questioning, and his voice dropped so low only she could hear it.

"No, mi querida, that's not why . . . I just want to be with you alone for a while, that's all. But no, we don't dare, not again."

She breathed deeply, disappointed, yet knowing he was right, and within a few minutes they were riding out the front gate and beyond the walled hacienda, heading for the Double K. It had been a long time since Blythe had been home. Even for just a visit.

Blythe and Mario had been at the Double K close to half an hour already. Having ridden in shortly after lunch, Pretty had rounded up something for them to eat, and now, their stomachs full, they sat on the front porch of the split-log house visiting with Lizette, Genée, and Grandma Dicia, who was sitting on the bottom of the steps fanning herself with the ornate little fan she always seemed to have either in the pocket of her dress or hanging from her wrist.

Loedicia wasn't necessarily listening to the conversation behind her, however. Instead her thoughts were on the story Lizette had told Bain when she'd returned from seeing Antonio and Blythe the day before, and also on the doctor, who'd ridden over with Blythe today. Mario de Córdoba had to be at least in his mid-thirties, and Lizette had said that he looked a great deal like his brother. Now Loedicia understood why Bain had been so quick to believe the worst of his wife those long years ago. For Mario de Córdoba was not only a handsome man, but there was a special charm about him.

Loedicia breathed in the cooler air from the fan, and glanced back up to where Blythe sat in the old chair Luther had resurrected for her to sit in. Loedicia watched her great-grandaughter's face. Blythe's eyes were on the doctor, and Loedicia felt a pang of hurt run through her.

The look in Blythe's eyes . . . she'd seen it earlier when Blythe and the doctor had first arrived, and now Loedicia's heart went out to Blythe, because Loedicia felt sure Blythe was in love with the man.

Loedicia sighed, turning away from the visitors again, and let her thoughts wander, as they often did nowadays.

She glanced down at her hands, the fingers slightly deformed from arthritis. Who would have thought it? She'd always thought she'd grow old the way she'd grown up, in perfect health. If anyone had told her she'd live to be in her eighties, and have aches and pains like everyone else, she'd have laughed. Only it wasn't so funny now, and she let the fan rest in her lap for a minute while she relaxed her wrist and stared out toward the road.

Suddenly she straightened, straining her eyes, then turned, interrupting the conversation behind her.

"Genée, come here, child," she said, and pointed off toward the road as Genée came over and sat beside her. "That is someone coming, isn't it?" she asked.

Genée brushed a mass of russet hair back from her face and gazed off in the direction Grandma Dicia had pointed, to where a small cloud of dust hung low over the horizon.

"You're right, Grandma."

Now suddenly the conversation behind Loedicia quickly began to die out as everyone else caught the movement, and all eyes became centered on the road out front, where two riders were slowly materializing on the horizon.

"It's Brax." Genée was getting excited. "It is, I know it is. I'd know old Hickory anywhere."

"But who's with him?"

"It isn't Case, Grandma. I know that too, 'cause that's not Compadre, it's a roan."

Loedicia's eyes were glued to the man on the roan. There was something familiar about the breadth of the shoulders, and the way he sat a saddle. Yet she had no idea who it might be. She shifted her gaze to the other rider. Genée was right. It was Braxton. It had been months since they'd seen him, although Blythe said he'd been to see her the day Mario de Córdoba had arrived.

The riders were still some distance away, and Loedicia looked back to Braxton's companion. What a contrast. Brax was still wearing the same dirty old buckskins, rumpled hat, and worn boots he'd had on the day he'd ridden out and joined the Rangers. However, the other rider was not only wearing a suit, but a natty suit of slate-blue cloth, with what looked like a dark blue velvet rolled collar, and the coat was buttoned neatly at the waist, without a wrinkle. Around his neck was a high silk stock of creamy satin, with layers of satin cascading down the front of his shirt, and as they rode close, Loedicia caught the sparkle of what looked like a gem amid the satin, while the man's nankeen trousers, although smudged here and there, fit him to perfection, and were worn over Wellington boots. They were clothes seldom seen this far west, and Loedicia frowned as she saw the wearer reach up, take off his beaver hat, wipe the sweat from his brow with a handerkerchief from his coat pocket,then tuck it back, his gloved hands depositing the hat back on his head at a jaunty angle, while he worked on the horse's reins, trying to keep the frisky animal under control.

Genée was standing now, and Loedicia stood up beside her. She had caught a glimpse of golden hair on Braxton's companion, and now as the two riders maneuvered their horses through the open gate out front and started up the drive, drawing closer, Loedicia's heart gave a little flutter as she caught a good look at the dandy riding with Brax.

He was the image of his father and grandfather, except for the sloe eyes, and she knew right away who it was.

Seth Locksley's stomach was fluttering wildly as he rode beside his cousin, wishing Braxton had let him stop someplace to buy some different clothes. He'd felt conspicious all the way from Austin. Why wouldn't he, among men like Braxton and the rest of these Texans? Most of them had never even seen coat and pants that matched, let alone the latest fashions from abroad. At least not the men he'd met so far. But then he'd met so few. Even in Austin, the lack of fashionably dressed men was acute, and he marveled as he thought back to his short stay there.

He'd never been in a log house before, nor had he had the slightest idea, before coming to Texas, that men could live in such austere surroundings. Yet the enthusiasm the men he'd met had for their capital, carved out of the wilderness and still nothing more than mud streets and a bunch of log cabins, was amazing.

He glanced over to Braxton and smiled. What luck running into his cousin's son. But then maybe it wasn't just luck. Seth had been wanting to come to see his grandmother and the rest of the family ever since leaving the ship at Galveston, but at the time he'd had no idea it'd be so hard to do. In the first place, the Texans had no coach service. Even if they had, most of the roads were used more for farm carts and horses. The few private carriages that traversed them more often than not fought ruts all the way. That was when they were passable. And unlike England, or even the eastern cities of the Americas, there was no way he could just ask anyone where the Double K property holdings were. It seemed everyone had heard of San Antonio, but knowing the Kolters was another matter altogether.

He'd planned to just make his way south from Austin, and inquire about the Kolters when he finally arrived in San Antonio, but now, having run into Braxton just the day before he'd planned to leave, had saved all that. His cousin's son not only seemed to know the whole of Texas by heart, but had proved to be a damn good traveling companion, and Seth was really looking forward now to seeing the rest of the family.

He drew his gaze from Braxton and looked off toward the big log house, then slowed his mount some as he realized there were a number of people lounging about the front steps of the place, which was one of the biggest he'd seen so far.

"Hey, looky there," Brax said as he glanced over at his mother's British cousin. "Looks like we got here right at teatime."

Seth frowned. He'd been hoping maybe no one would

be around when they arrived. At least not until he could find something to wear that didn't make him feel so out of place, because more and more, as he rode through this raw land, he'd begun to like it. He was sure it was starting to grow on him.

"Who all's there?" he asked in his clipped British accent.

Brax straightened to see a bit better as they jogged along. "Ma," he said, spotting his mother, who was sitting beside Blythe. "And hey, my sister's there too, the one who's married, and I think that fella beside her's a doctor, if I remember right. Met him a while back when I stopped at her place." He reached up, pulling his hat forward a little to help shade his eyes. "That's Grandma near the steps with Genée."

"The one who was born at our place?"

"That's right."

Seth had been only a little over two years old when Lizette Kolter had stayed at Locksley Hall in England and given birth to her daughter Genée, but he'd heard the story more than once from his mother. He looked everyone over as carefully as he could while Braxton talked, but when his gaze caught up with the young woman he knew had to be Genée, he suddenly froze, his face grew hot, and he felt a strange warmth begin to tingle just beneath his breastbone. Dammit all, he thought as he looked directly at her, I'm blushing. I'm sure of it. My face is probably red as a beet. And as he continued to stare at her, he was more sure of it than ever as he realized she was staring right back at him with the biggest pair of greenish eyes he'd ever seen. They looked like they were on the verge of turning gray like the eyes of a cat, and her russet hair was sprinkled with iridescent highlights of blue-black that attested to the Indian blood he knew flowed through her veins, as it did through his. She was a young version of the elderly woman who was standing beside her, and who was also staring at Seth, but from a pair of violet eyes that had dimmed some with age.

Seth smiled at the look on his grandmother's face,

knowing his arrival was a complete shock to her, and following Braxton's lead, he reined his horse to a halt, slid from the saddle, and wound the reins about the hitchrail at the end of the walk, while Grandma Dicia and the others just stayed where they were and stared.

"Well, what kind of greeting is this?" Brax called to them as he stood next to his horse, staring at the whole lot of them. Then he glanced over at his companion. "I think you've scared 'em out of a week's growth, Seth," he said. "Like you said, we should have found you some decent clothes. Come on," and he grabbed Seth's arm, and the two of them started up the walk.

Loedicia was watching the two young men closely. It wasn't that she didn't want to run and throw her arms about them both, it was just that their arrival had been so unexpected, and sometimes it was hard for an old lady's legs to manage the feat. That didn't mean her heart wasn't pounding expectantly, though. It had been so many years since she'd seen Seth, and yet she knew it was him, as did Lizette. The family resemblance was too obvious.

However, standing beside Loedicia, Genée had no idea who this strangely dressed young man was. In fact, she'd never seen anyone dressed quite like this before, and she was having a hard time trying to keep herself from laughing out loud.

It wasn't until Seth and Braxton were almost to them that Loedicia's legs finally began to do what she wanted them to, and she stepped forward.

"Seth?"

"Grandma Dicia?".

"Oh, Seth!" Loedicia raised her arms, and he walked right into them, burying her against him, while Braxton greeted the rest of the family and shook hands with the doctor, who had left Blythe's side just long enough to reach Brax's hand.

Seth's arms eased from around Loedicia as Mario sat back down beside Blythe, and with a grandmother's pride, Loedicia stood back, gazing up at this young giant who brought so many memories back to her of another tall blond giant of a man she'd given so much love to years ago.

"If someone had told me, I never would have believed it," she said, shaking her head.

"I came over as a diplomatic courier," he explained. "There are a number of us who've been sent over to try to negotiate a working relationship with your new republic."

Brax laughed. "In other words, his father didn't know what to do with him, so he got him an appointment to a good government job, figuring it'd keep him out of trouble for a while."

"Instead, they sent me to your remarkable shores." Seth gazed about at all the outbuildings, surprised to see such a big place this far west. Most of the places they'd ridden past so far were one- and two-bedroom cabins with a few domestic animals wandering about. But this . . . "I say, you've really built a gem of a place out here, haven't you?" he said as he looked back at everyone.

Brax grinned. "You can thank Ma and Pa for that."

Seth glanced at the woman he assumed had to be Braxton's mother. "Cousin Lizette?"

"Hello, Seth." Lizette had been watching her uncle's son, realizing that his eyes reminded her of his mother's. Seth's mother, Lady Ann, who was half Delaware Indian, had eyes like that, dark, sloe, and shining. "How long will you be here?" she asked.

He shrugged. "I may never go home."

"He likes it here." Braxton was pleased. "And these," he said, introducing them, "are my two sisters, Blythe and Genée."

Seth nodded toward Blythe, whom he remembered was crippled. "Señora de Léon, am I right?" he asked.

"Cousin Seth."

"Then this has to be Genée," and he looked down at the young woman standing only a few feet behind his grandmother now. From up close she was even prettier, and looked younger than what he knew her to be. For she had to be all of eighteen. "Genée."

Genée was having a horrible time trying to keep from

laughing at her mother's first cousin. He was every bit as tall as Brax, only with his hair swept back on the sides the way it was, with the curly hair in front of his ears growing down the side of his jaw almost to his chin, he gave the impression of being rather effeminate. A condition his rugged looks and muscular build, all too apparent beneath the fancy clothes, gave a lie to. Now, why on earth anyone so obviously masculine was willing to give everyone the opposite impression, was beyond her. But then maybe that's how all the Britishers dressed. Who knew? She curtsied. "Cousin Seth."

Brax introduced him to the doctor, then looked at his mother. "We're hungry and tired," Brax said as he walked over and put an arm around Lizette's shoulder. "You don't suppose maybe Pretty might have something she could scrape up for us to eat, do you?"

Lizette looked at him dubiously. "I think you'd better go wash up first," she said, the pungent aroma of horse, sweat, and dirty buckskins assaulting her nostrils. She looked over at her newly arrived cousin. "You did hear the description of a Texas Ranger, didn't you, Seth?" she said. "He rides like a Mexican, tracks like a Comanche, shoots like a Kentuckian, and fights like the devil. Only I swear he smells like the hogs."

"That's only because I don't have room to carry a trunkful of clothes and a tub on the back of my horse," Brax said, defending himself. "Besides, I don't smell like a hog. A horse maybe, but not a hog."

Everyone laughed, and within minutes Seth too was enjoying himself, although there were times, as there had been since he'd first set foot in Texas, when he had a hard time following what they were all saying. The Mexican doctor with Brax's sister was bad enough with his heavy Spanish accent, but the rest of them . . . Although supposedly speaking English, they sure had a strange way of doing it. He had no idea that Blythe and Genée were thinking the same thing about him. Especially Genée.

She had never come in contact with anyone quite like Seth Locksley before, and it was fascinating to her as they all followed the two men into the house and visited with them while Pretty gave them some food.

It was late afternoon by the time they were all talked out and Blythe decided it was time for them to leave. So Mario put her on her horse, they bid good-bye to everyone, then rode out of the ranch yard, heading back toward the hacienda.

"I like your cousin," Mario said as they waved good-bye on their way through the front gates.

Blythe smiled. "But he talks so funny. Besides, he's Ma's first cousin, not mine."

"Then he would be perhaps your second cousin, sí?"

"Once or twice removed, I suppose." She dug Pegasus a little harder, enjoying the feel of the afternoon breeze on her cheeks as she lifted her chin.

She'd been as surprised as everyone else to see Seth in Texas. Although he was only twenty, his father, Teak, actually the Earl of Locksley, was their mother's uncle, and their grandmother Rebel Dante's brother, and they rarely heard from him. Not that the earl was all that snobbish, being British nobility and all, but mail between the new Republic of Texas and England, or anywhere else for that matter, wasn't all that reliable.

Blythe tensed, then glanced over to where Mario was riding beside her, his gaze steady ahead on the terrain they were crossing, and she wondered what he was thinking.

"I'm glad you're not leaving until tomorrow," she said. "In fact, I wish you didn't have to leave at all."

"I know." He frowned, looking over at her. "But I must, you know that." He moved his horse even closer to her. "I am not a saint, mi querida. And to be in the same house with you every day, under the same roof . . . it was hard enough before. Now it would be sheer torture."

"For me too."

"Then I know you understand."

She sighed. "Well, at least we have today," she said, and pushed the hat back off her pale hair, letting the balmy breeze cool the perspiration that was making it curl about her forehead. "I'll have the servants fix your

favorite meal tonight." Her eyes began to dance as she
looked over at him. "Then we'll sit on the veranda until
the moon comes up." She hesitated, but only for a moment, then tears came to her eyes. "God, I'm going to
miss you."

"And I you, but we have no choice. Now"—he tried
to stop her tears—"we will race to the cutoff, and I will
win, sí?"

She sniffed, grabbing the reins tighter. "Not on your
life!" she cried, hoping to mask her pain, and with a
quiet dig in Pegasus's sides, she sent the palomino flying
off toward the trail that led home, with Mario galloping
beside her neck and neck.

Later that evening, as Blythe, Mario, and Catalina sat
at the dinner table eating the meal Blythe had ordered
cooked especially for the doctor, Blythe wished with all
her heart they didn't have to share it with Catalina. Not
just because she wanted to be alone with Mario, but
because she'd realized some weeks back that Catalina
was also taking more than just a passing interest in Mario.

Although Mario had never given Catalina the least bit
of encouragement, and had conducted himself with the
utmost propriety with his host's niece, something he
couldn't say about his host's wife, Blythe could understand how Catalina could become smitten with him. He
was not only charming and friendly, but there was just a
touch of aloofness about him that could be considered
intriguing. This, coupled with his ruggedly handsome features, could be devastating to any young woman. However, it wasn't much fun having to sit here through another
meal and watch Catalina trying every way she could to
make Mario pay court to her.

Even later, out on the veranda, Blythe continued to
have her evening ruined, as Catalina not only kept right
on flirting outrageously with Mario, but as was her usual
demeanor, tried to hurt Blythe every way she could by
subtly making little cutting remarks about Blythe's family
and Texans in general. Something she never got away
with when her uncle was around. And tonight she seemed

to be making up for that fact, even though Mario more than once stopped her, just as Antonio often had to.

By the time the moon came up and the stars came out, Blythe was almost in tears, although she never showed it. It wasn't really because of what Catalina said or did, however. It was just the fact that the young woman was there. She was used to Catalina's sarcastic remarks and moods by now, but she had so much wanted to spend some time alone with Mario, just the two of them. Only it never happened. Right up until the clock in the foyer chimed eleven, Catalina sat right with them. And she stayed right with them until, some twenty minutes later, Rosita came out to find out when Blythe was going up, since she was the one who would have to help her into bed. And once more, she had on other such occasions when she felt obligated for another's welfare because of her crippled legs, Blythe cursed Mario's brother for what he'd done to her. However, not wanting to keep Rosita up too late, and realizing Catalina wasn't about to leave them alone, Blythe looked over at Mario, the light from inside the house too dim to really see his face, yet she could see his hair and jawline easily.

"I suppose I'd better go up," she said. "It's rather late."

"I'll carry you."

He lifted himself from the chair.

Blythe could sense Catalina's animosity.

"You are coming back down?" Catalina asked.

He shook his head. "Like your aunt says, the hour is late." He walked over behind Blythe, and turned her fancy chair toward the door so he could push it inside to the bottom of the stairs. "And in case I miss you in the morning when I leave, remember, I am only moving to town so we shall meet again, Catalina. Buenas noches," and he turned back, concentrating on getting Blythe's wheeled chair through the front door, while Catalina stared after him, her dark eyes mirroring both anger and frustration.

A few minutes later, while Mario was carrying Blythe up the stairs, he looked into her eyes and frowned.

"You are crying?" he asked, his voice barely a whisper so Rosita, who was following them, wouldn't hear.

"I wanted it to be just us," she murmured. "It's the last night we have, and she monopolized it."

"I knew you were there."

"But it wasn't the same."

They reached the top of the stairs, and he waited for Rosita to open the door to the master bedroom so he could take her inside. Seconds later, as he lowered her onto the bed, while Rosita went to the dresser to take out her nightclothes, Blythe's head came close enough to his so her lips brushed his cheek lightly. Mario felt his knees tremble.

"I'd better leave," he said, his voice husky, unsteady, as he tried to sound casual in front of Rosita. "I'll no doubt see you in the morning before I go. But in case I don't, adios, Doña Blythe," and he started toward the door opening it, then looked back for a moment, very aware that Blythe was having a hard time holding back her tears. Wishing he could do something about it, yet knowing he couldn't, he stepped into the hall and closed the door behind him, then turned to face Catalina, while inside the room Blythe, whose eyes had been following him, saw the encounter seconds before the door closed, and she cringed.

It was well over an hour later, and Blythe lay alone in the big bed she usually shared with Tonio, gazing about the dark room, trying hard to keep her mind from imagining all sorts of things as she'd been doing ever since Rosita had left her. Ever since watching Catalina meet Mario in the hall, she'd been in a quandary. What if Catalina had followed him to his room and seduced him? After all, as Mario told her, he wasn't a saint. No man was. But that was a stupid thing to even think. In the first place, Mario wouldn't do something like that, and besides, as much as she knew Catalina hated her, Blythe had to admit she didn't think Catalina would do such a thing either. But then she had never thought she herself was capable of doing the things she'd been doing, had she? Oh, God! If only . . .

Suddenly she tensed at the sound of a click, as if her bedroom doorknob was being turned. Lifting her head cautiously, she stared toward it. The room was lit only by the moonlight coming in from the French doors to the portico, and the windows, but she could vaguely see the door open, and a figure move stealthily into the room.

At first she'd thought perhaps Antonio had come back from Goliad, but as her eyes adjusted, defining the tall figure in the semidarkness, she knew instinctively who it was.

The door closed silently behind Mario, and Blythe heard the familiar slip of the lock Tonio always bolted to keep everyone out when he was alone with his wife, then Mario walked quietly to the other side of the bed, slipped off his robe, and climbed in beside her. She watched expectantly, her body aching for want of him, her eyes grasping the full impact of what they were seeing as they blurred with tears.

"You were too sad," he whispered as he leaned on one elbow, looking down at her, and he reached out, touching her face, sensing the tears that were still there. "Never could I leave you like that. And when your lips touched my cheek . . . ah, mi querida, this will be my good-bye to you. One night to last us forever in our hearts," and with those words his mouth covered hers, and he made love to her until early morning, when he finally slipped reluctantly back to his own room, knowing even though he would see her again, and never be far from her, it was the last time he would ever hold her in his arms.

19

Almost a year had gone by since Mario had moved out of the de Léon hacienda and Seth Locksley had arrived in Texas, and during that time both men had decided this was where they belonged. Mario's medical practice in San Antonio helped keep his thoughts off the hidden yearnings of his heart, and there had been no more illicit trysts with Blythe, only his contact with her as a doctor and friend of her husband. But Seth, being younger and less experienced than the good doctor, was having a horrible time where his heart was concerned. In more ways than one.

His final decision to stay in Texas, rather than return to England with the rest of his diplomatic party, had been met with skepticism, disbelief, and downright anger. None of them could understand how the son of an earl, with all the advantages English society held for him, could possibly give it all up for a country where no one was immune from Indian attacks, the politicians were still fighting among themselves, and the treasury was on the verge of bankruptcy. Even his close association with the new Texas government didn't sound any too promising as far as they were concerned.

However, Seth didn't care what they thought. His older brother, Quinn, was going to inherit the title anyway, so what did it matter where he was or what he did? So he might as well do what he wanted. After getting his first glimpse of the Texas countryside on his journey to San Antonio with his cousin Braxton, he needed little more persuasion to realize that being a part of this land was what he wanted. And after getting a good look at Genée the day he rode into the ranch yard at the Double K, he knew that somehow she was going to be all wrapped up in whatever that future was, even though she didn't seem to take him too seriously at the time. When he had finally had to leave the Double K again, some weeks later, heading back toward the capital, he had still been just as frustrated over her inability to see him as anything other than her mother's British cousin as he had been when he'd first arrived. However, he'd felt the time would come when she'd discover he was more than just a cousin.

That had been almost a year ago, and now, as Seth rode along, following the wagon in front of him, he glanced over at the men he was with. José Navarro was one of the commissioners, asked personally by President Lamar, who had succeeded Houston as president of the new republic, to accompany a contingent of some twenty or so freight wagons from Austin to Sante Fe in hopes of opening up trade with Santa Fe, and in the process try to get the support for Texas from the citizens of what was now referred to as New Mexico, and Seth had been appointed to him as an aide. Only from what Seth had heard by way of his cousins, and some of the new friends he'd made, the mission they were on wasn't exactly a wise one.

Now, as he gazed about at the columns of soldiers, most on foot, having lost their horses along the way when the Indians raided, he had a feeling his friends had been right because things weren't really going any too well. Not only had they run low on provisions, and been forced to stay alive by killing Indian dogs that had gone wild, when they couldn't find other game, but the man leading them, General Hugh McLeod, had been forced to split the train in two when they couldn't get the wagons up over Cap rock. Seth, and the men he was with, had stayed with the wagons, even though it meant dodging Indians most of the way. Then, farther on, the general had split their factions again, sending some of the other commissioners to San Miguel, where they were to recruit Mexicans sympathetic to their cause.

Seth straightened wearily in the saddle as he looked around him at the men that were left. When they'd left Austin back in June, there'd been somewhere near three hundred of them. Soldiers, civilian traders, and the men Seth was with. Now he was lucky to be looking at even half that many. Hardly any wagons were left, most having been caught in prairie fires that had also taken the lives of a number of soldiers, while the rest of them had been picked off by the marauding Indians. And they'd even lost the cannon they'd been so proud of.

Actually, they'd gotten lost after only the first few days out, and Seth had been wishing they'd had his cousin Brax along instead of McLeod. The general might think he knew Texas, but not the way the Kolters, or even the Dantes knew it.

However, wishing wasn't going to help. At the moment, all he could do was keep his eyes on the wagon ahead and try to keep the dirt out of his eyes. McLeod had told them the day before that they were close to the border, and Seth smiled cynically to himself as he took off his battered hat and ran a hand through his blond hair, wiping the sweat from his brow in the process.

How anyone, let alone a soldier on horseback, could know when he was near to the borderline the Mexicans felt shouldn't even exist, was beyond him. Even the land looked the same. Dry, dusty, and unfriendly, and he began to wonder why Texas even wanted it. Ah well, who was he to question President Lamar?

He rode along at a slow pace, the creaking of the wagon ahead and the constant jangling of harness on the mules pulling it keeping in rhythm with his horse's gait, and he wondered if they were going to have to go without food again tonight. Suddenly there was a shout from up front, and Seth reined up, glancing over at the man beside him.

"Wonder what bloody trouble we're in now," he said.

The man shrugged. "Quién sabe?"

José Navarro never had cared much for this Britisher the president had stuck him with. It wasn't really anything the young man did, because actually he seemed to have an uncanny way of surviving, even when the odds were against him. Twice already, once during a prairie fire, and later when one of the wagons had been swamped at a river crossing, everyone was so sure he'd been done in. Yet he'd come riding right through the smoke and fire without even a scratch on him, leading the mules that had been hitched to the wagon. Then he'd showed up in camp half a day after being swept downstream while trying to help with the crossing. The men were beginning to think he had a charmed life, although Navarro doubted it. Navarro figured it was just dumb stupid luck, and he drew his gaze from Seth, looking off toward the lead wagon to see if he could see what was going on.

A few minutes later, Seth watched skeptically as one of the soldiers came running toward them. "What's wrong?" Navarro hollered.

"Everything!" Lieutenant Snyder slowed down, panting heavily, and stopped next to Navarro. "The general says as how you'd all best come up front. There's a whole passel of Mexicans out to meet us, and he don't think they're a welcoming committee."

Navarro frowned. "How many are there?"

"Hell, I don't know. Looks like the whole damn town of San Miguel."

Seth didn't like it, especially after the warnings he hadn't heeded, but he reined his horse around the wagon they'd been following and staying next to Navarro, cantered along the line of wagons that was stopped now.

When they were some fifteen to twenty yards from the lead wagon, Seth reined his horse to a halt and stared in fascination at the huge crowd of Mexicans. Some on foot, others on horses, but all armed, with everything from machetes to rifles. While in front of them, astride a fancily decorated mule, was one of the fattest men he'd ever seen. With him was a man named Lewis, who had been with one of their group that had headed toward San Miguel earlier, and they were talking to General McLeod. Even a few Indians were among the Mexicans.

Seth scowled. "Wonder who the fat chap is?"

Navarro had reined up and was staring too. "It looks

like we are about to find out, señor," and Seth watched
closely as the general turned reluctantly to his men, shouted
some orders, then spurred his horse around and rode
wearily back toward where Seth, Navarro, and some of
the others waited.

General Hugh McLeod reined up in front of José
Navarro. "Well, gentlemen, here's what we have," he
said as he slumped in the saddle, knowing he looked
unimpressive with his uniform so dirty it was hardly
recognizable. "The pompous gentleman on the horse is
using Lewis as an interpreter. Although I doubt he really
needs one. Anyway, he says he's the governor. Now that
should mean something to you, right?"

"It means they knew jolly well we were coming. How?"
Seth asked.

"Cuernos! Locksley, they no doubt have scouts on
every hill from here back to the Pecos River." Navarro
maneuvered his horse so he could get a better look at the
Mexican. "What does Governor Armijo want?"

"Says they've already captured the other two groups
we sent on ahead, and he wants us to surrender too. Said
if we do, he'll send us back home. If we don't, they'll kill
the lot of us right here."

Seth sneered. "And you believe him?"

Navarro looked thoughtful. "He might be telling the
truth. Hmmm . . . and it'd be better than trying to fight."
He looked around at the sorry-looking survivors they had
left. "Let's face it, we're in no condition to even try to
defend ourselves."

Navarro's gaze moved through the crowd of Mexicans.
They were primed, ready for a fight, and it looked like
they'd enjoy it. Armijo had known they were coming, all
right, and he wouldn't doubt that the guide who'd gotten
them lost right after they'd left Austin was working for
Armijo.

General McLeod watched José Navarro's perusal of
the Mexicans. "So, what is it?" he said. "Do we give up
or go down fighting?"

Seth's jaws set stubbornly. "Any way to stall him?"

"What would that gain?" General McLeod wasn't sure

he liked this young upstart the president had sent along with Navarro and the others. Maybe he knew how to talk his way around Englishmen, but what made him think he knew anything about Texans, or Mexicans either for that matter. "Governor Armijo could have had the soldiers ambush us miles back if they'd wanted us dead," he argued. "I say we go in quietly, gentlemen." He looked at the men, including Seth, and one at a time they all nodded agreement.

All but Seth. "I'll go along with you because I have no choice," Seth said as he once more let his gaze drift to the fat man on the mule in front of the others. "But make sure you understand one thing, gentlemen, I think you're making a bloody mistake."

"What would you have us do?"

"Turn around and try to make a break for the hills. I'd rather die on my feet and free than in a prison."

No matter what Seth said, however, the general was determined, and a few minutes later, as Seth watched all the Texans stacking their rifles in one of the wagons, he suddenly had the strangest foreboding. And as he sat his horse, fingers caressing the gun in the gunbelt at his own waist, wishing he didn't have to give it up, he prayed they'd all get out of this mess alive, while wishing he'd taken his cousin's advice and not come along at all.

The sun was beating down relentlessly, white sand stretching out as far as the eye could see, and Seth kept his hand over his blistered face, wishing he had a hat. He had no idea how many days ago—maybe it was weeks—they'd left San Miguel. Time seemed to be standing still, and it was the same thing day after day, hour after hour. He thought back to the day they'd surrendered their weapons.

As soon as the men were devoid of their guns and knives, the Mexicans had moved in, put them under guard, tied them together with rope, and then marched them into San Miguel, where they'd been stripped of their clothes and given nothing but a blanket apiece for covering. Then they'd been thrown into prison with the others who'd already been captured, where they discovered two of the commissioners had been shot a few days before, without even having a chance to negotiate their own freedom, let alone peace. It seemed the governor was a friend of Santa Anna's, and since Santa Anna had once more risen to power in Mexico, none of them had had a prayer right from the start.

Now, after being given just enough castoff clothing to cover them, and being tied together like animals, they were being herded toward Mexico City, so their captors said, only Seth knew few were ever going to make it there. Many were already dead, their bodies left scattered back along the trail for scavengers to feed on. Thank God, he was still going, though, and Seth took his eyes from the man staggering ahead of him, and glanced down at his bare feet. Already the blisters had turned to calluses and they were almost as tough as leather. It was the first time in his life he'd ever been glad his mother was half American Indian, because he was certain it was the Indian blood in his veins that was keeping him alive.

Their captors, besides feeding them barely enough to survive on, seemed to care little whether they lived or not, and often pushed them beyond their physical endurance, and Seth had watched man after man fall dead in the heat, from either starvation or exhaustion. He'd also watched the soldiers shoot them for no other reason than that they couldn't move. Then they'd cut off their ears before throwing the corpses into the brush alongside the trail, the dried ears being proof when they reached Mexico City that the prisoners were dead and accounted for rather than escaped.

It was a sickening sight, and Seth licked his parched lips, trying to find moisture that wasn't there, then looked up ahead, realizing they were coming to the end of the miles of sand they'd been trudging through the past few days. With the sun dipping lower on the horizon, he'd hoped and prayed they'd stop soon so he could get Salezar off his back. Usually the men were tied about three feet apart with rope, only occasionally Captain Salezar, who was in charge of the prisoners, would leave a few men untied so he could torture and torment them along the way. Today Seth had been one of them.

Seth took a deep breath, wondering, as he had since leaving San Miguel, if he was ever going to see Genée again. Even though he knew she didn't care for him the same way he cared for her, he still had hopes. After all, she was almost twenty and hadn't married any of the local men in the area as yet. At least according to what Brax said the last time he'd seen him. Besides, thinking of her kept his mind off the pain.

Squaring his shoulders and trying as hard as he could to keep going, and think of everything except what was happening to him, Seth finally sighed some hours later, and dropped onto a soft patch of grass, then gazed behind him where night shadows were just starting to filter into the white sands they'd left behind. They were finally stopping for the night.

Captain Salezar walked over and threw a canteen of water at him. "One swallow, señor," he said.

Seth picked the canteen up slowly in his sunburned hands and raised it to his lips, opening his mouth as wide as he could to make the swallow worth while. Suddenly the tip of a bayonet was sticking into his neck just below his jawbone.

"I say one swallow, bastardo!" Salezar reached out, grabbing the flask from him, and threw it to the next man in line.

Seth wiped his mouth, his sloe eyes studying the captain insolently. The man knew little English. Just enough to make Seth understand what he wanted, and Seth knew even less Spanish, although it was easy to decipher some of the words, like "bastardo." Now, he was sure he knew what that meant.

He watched Salezar move down the line of men, then Seth turned away, taking in everything around them. The soldiers were already building fires for the night to keep away predators, and he watched them intently. There were well over a hundred mounted soldiers to guard fewer than a hundred men, because that's what they were down to now, and from what Navarro said the day they'd started out, Mexico City was still nearly a thousand miles away. At this rate they'll all be dead by that time.

His gaze rested on one of the Mexican supply wagons where the soldiers who did the cooking were busy slapping together some corn cakes for the men. Sometimes Seth and the others would receive only a pint of cornmeal for their day's ration, and at other times only an ear of corn per man. However, once in a while they'd run into a small village, and the people would feel sorry for them and give them food. Salezar never stopped the villagers. Maybe because he wanted to keep the prisoners alive so he could torture them just a little more. Then there were evenings when they'd eat the soldiers' leftovers, which often consisted of the corn cakes Seth knew were called tortillas, filled with mushy boiled beans that had been cooked days before and were usually wormy. Always the food was cooked for the soldiers first, and by the time Salezar decided to let the prisoners have some, it was moldly and fetid.

Seth's stomach gave a lurch at the thought of having to eat his food with his eyes shut again tonight, so he wouldn't see the bugs wiggling in it. He quickly turned away, looking off toward the hills to the east. At least it was keeping him alive. Suddenly a thought struck him, and he drew his eyes from the rolling horizon and took inventory of all the soldiers.

For the past few nights, when they'd been tied, the soldiers hadn't been as attentive to what they were doing. No doubt weary themselves. In fact, all any of the prisoners had to do was sit there with crossed wrists, waiting for the ropes. Maybe this was finally going to be his chance.

He stared at the soldiers for some time, then turned his attention to the other men who'd been captured with him. Most of them were in as bad shape as he was, if not worse. But there was something he had that they didn't. His youth. At twenty-one, he was one of the youngest to have come along on the expedition, and with his inborn will to survive he was ready to try anything to accomplish it. Anything within reason, that is. Some of the others had tried to get away already, only to be shot. They hadn't picked the right time. His father had always said: When you're in trouble, use your head. God gave it to you to think with. Hell, he was thinking now, and he was sure his idea would work. Besides, he'd rather die alone in the hills than in the hands of the Mexicans, and have his ears sent on to Mexico City as if they were trophies of some sort.

The sun was setting earlier every evening, and he guessed by now, since daylight seemed to be gone so quickly, that before long it'd be midwinter. If he was going to make any kind of break, he'd have to do it soon, or not at all. And he knew he had to try.

Glancing at the sky, he watched the low-lying gray clouds off in the distance. He had spotted them earlier, and it was a sight he'd seldom seen so far on their long trek south. His eyes studied them anxiously. Without any breeze blowing they might not even reach the encampment until morning. However, just in case they did, he looked over the terrain to the east, picking the best route he could take, then as darkness began to obliterate everything around him, except the cooks' fire, he found and picked up a small stone, partially flat and about an inch in diameter, then he sat back and waited.

The clouds that had rolled slowly over the camp a few hours after dark had begun to drop a slow, steady rain on the prisoners and soldiers, and now it was falling heavily as Seth sat up a bit straighter and wiped it from his eyes, looking around him. In spite of the rain, or because of its cooling effects, he wasn't sure, the men all seemed to be sleeping soundly tonight, including some of the soldiers who were supposed to be standing guard. Wrapped in oiled slickers they'd confiscated from some of the Texans' wagons, the soldiers were propped up against wagon wheels and trees, their rifles under the slickers to keep them dry, while their companions, who were also supposed to be on guard duty, milled about the soggy fires that had sputtered out hours before, hoping for the rain to let up.

Seth smiled to himself as he lay on the ground and pulled his hands up close to his chest, twisting the ropes that were holding his wrists, so the small stone would fall out from between his wrists, where he'd had it furtively hidden, when they'd come along to tie them. It had been just enough extra so that once it was dislodged, the ropes were loose.

If it had been hot, the water in Seth's eyes would have been sweat instead of rain, as he worked the ropes now, slipping his hands back and forth to loosen them even more, then suddenly they slipped away, and he slid a hand out, followed seconds later by the other hand.

He had hardly dared move at all, with the other prisoners so close, and it made the task harder. Now, however, he was free, only he was going to have to watch even closer. If even one man was awake and made any noise at all to cause the soldiers to look over, all could be lost. He hated having to leave the others like this, but knew trying to take someone else along with him would be folly. As it was, he wasn't even certain he could keep himself alive for long, or even get clear of the camp. His only hope was that the rain would not only cover his departure but also obliterate his trail.

Certain he wouldn't be noticed as the rain began to fall a little harder now, Seth took one last quick look to make sure the men beside him hadn't been disturbed, then glanced over again to where the soldiers were standing around cursing the weather, then he began to slide along the ground a few inches at a time until he was far enough so he could roll under a bush, where he lay for a few minutes holding his breath. Then, satisfied he hadn't been observed, he got stealthily to his feet, and in a crouched position, ran along a line of what Braxton had called yucca plants before climbing up and over a sandy hill, where he'd noticed earlier there'd been no trail for anyone to follow, with the rain washing his footprints out of the sand, and he disappeared into the dark, rainy night.

It was early morning, and Seth lay in the shelter of one of the huge caverns, looking out at the rising sun. He'd been free for over a week already, and still couldn't figure out how he was still alive. Maybe it was because the rotten food the Mexicans had fed him on the long trek from San Miguel had accustomed him to being able to swallow just about anything, and made it possible for him to live off some of the most disgusting vermin he'd ever set eyes on. That, and the wild plants along the way.

Leaning back against the wall of the huge cave he was in, he sighed, gazing all around. He'd never seen anything quite like this place. It was nothing but caves and more caves, and he'd almost gotten lost in them yesterday afternoon when he'd first stumbled on them. They had afforded him shelter for the night, though, and that's what he'd needed most. He wondered what the soldiers thought when they had no ears to take back to Mexico City for their missing prisoner. He imagined Salezar would find some way to get a set of ears, though, even if it meant cutting them off a dead Mexican somewhere along the way. One thing was certain, Salezar had left San Miguel with a certain number of prisoners, and since all were to be accounted for when they reached Mexico City, Salezar'd have to think of something.

After satisfying his hunger with a handful of some kind of mushrooms he hoped wouldn't kill him, and the remains of a lizard he'd caught the evening before, Seth reluctantly left the cave he'd spent the night in and headed east again, his eyes bloodshot, the scabs on his face from the blisters that were healing where the sun had burned him while he was a prisoner beginning to flake some beneath the headpiece he'd made from the long tails of the flimsy shirt he'd been wearing. He was certain it looked ridiculous, but since he doubted he'd run into anyone who'd see it anyway, he moved on, not only watching for the Indians he knew he'd have to avoid but also looking for anything edible along the way.

The days moved on, one into another. Seth had been moving cross-country for well over two weeks now since leaving the huge caverns. His clothes hung on him worse than before, but he was still alive, and so far he'd managed to stay free. He'd come close to capture once, when he'd gotten downwind from an Indian village, and the scent of cooking had almost lured him too close. But he'd made up his mind that no matter how hungry he got, there was no way he was going to give up what had been so precious to attain. So he'd moved on, saying a prayer over the raw fish he'd eaten that night, caught in a small stream he'd waded through shortly before dark set in.

Now he was moving through a sandy arroyo, trying to find a place where he could scale the other side and wouldn't have to work too hard at it. The lack of good food had really taken a toll on his muscles, and his tall broad frame seemed to be weakening more and more with each day. If he were more skilled at surviving on his own, he probably would have been in better condition. As it was, there were many nights he tossed and turned on the ground with stomach cramps, so sick he felt like he'd die, after eating something he'd been certain wouldn't hurt him. By now, though, he had just about figured what would make him sick and what wouldn't, only the what-wouldn'ts were getting scarcer every day. At least that's how it seemed.

A trickle of sweat rolled down into his eye, and he reached up, taking off his makeshift headdress, then wiped the sweat back into his hair. He'd washed it in a shallow creek the day before. Actually it hadn't really been deep enough for a bath, but he'd sat in the water, then lain down in it, letting the water wash over him, even getting his clothes wet and he had felt better for a while. The days weren't quite as hot now as they had been when he'd escaped, and he'd been glad that his clothes had dried by the time the sun went down, because it cooled off at night.

Setting the headdress back in place, he was just ready to make sure of his bearings and start off again, when he froze, his eyes firmly glued to a hill just to the southeast, where a line of some thirty or forty horsemen was moving along, just far enough away that all he could do was distinguish horse from man.

His first instinct was to run, because he was right out in the open, but knowing they'd spot him for sure if he did, instead he dropped hurriedly to the ground, moved as close to a small scraggly bush as he could, and held his breath.

The line of horses continued moving slowly, and as Seth watched, the blood suddenly began to course wildly through his veins, and he felt as if he'd explode as he recognized what looked like a band of Texans, rifles primed and ready for anything.

After pondering for a few minutes, trying to figure out how to get their attention without having them shoot first and ask questions later, he suddenly decided on the best procedure. Getting to his feet, he reached up, pulled off the makeshift headdress so they could see the color of his hair, and began shouting, "Remember the Alamo! Remember the Alamo!" over and over again. It was the only thing he could think of that would show them he was a friend. Finally he stopped, and stood quietly, the headdress still clenched in his sunburned hands, waiting to see what they'd do.

Up on the ridge overlooking the deep gully, Jack Hays glanced back at his men, signaling for them to halt, and they all drew rein, each man staring at the strange apparition some hundred or so yards below them. The man had been shouting and yelling. Now he stood stock-still, just staring. Could be a trap, Hays thought as he squinted, the battered hat on his head shading his eyes from the afternoon sun.

"What do you think?" he asked the Ranger next to him, and Brax Kolter took a deep breath.

"Want me to find out?"

Hays nodded. "Go ahead."

"I will go also," Case said as he rode in closer to his cousin. Jack looked from one to the other. "All right, the two of you then," he said. "But don't take any chances. He Who Rides knows we're after him, and he'd do anything to catch us in an ambush."

Brax and Case both nodded, then reined their horses aside, breaking away from the rest of the men until they found a place that wasn't too steep, and leaning back in the saddle, they rode their horses deftly down the hill, sliding partway until they reached the floor of the dried-up old riverbed.

Both men had been riding with Hays for months now, tracking the Comanche, who were once more raiding west of San Antonio now that they'd found new chiefs to replace the ones killed at the Council House meeting in San Antonio the year before. Now, after the successful raid they'd staged down through the Guadalupe Valley, having been defeated near Plum Creek on their return, they had regrouped, and word had filtered east that they were gearing for another raid. Captain Hays was going to see to it that this time the advantage would be his, and the new chiefs would learn their place. He Who Rides was but one of those new young chiefs, and if Hays could catch them all together, he'd put a stop to the raids before they started. So they'd been out searching.

Brax and Case were two of the best assets Hays had in his troop, with Kolter practically growing up out here on the frontier, and Brax had taught Case everything he knew. Together the two men were like an army in themselves, even though they were younger than most of his men, more his own age. Hays watched both of them anxiously, his gaze often shifting to the surrounding hills as they rode in slowly.

"Well, I'll be damned!" Brax exclaimed as he reined Hickory in close enough to get a good look at the towheaded man in the baggy white Mexican pantaloons and shirt, who was standing motionless now, just staring at them.

Seth couldn't believe his eyes either, and he blinked them quickly, then shook his head, starting to laugh, a dry throaty laugh that made him cough.

"Seth?" Brax asked. Except for the hair, eyes, and height of the man, this dirty disheveled figure, covered with blisters and sores from the sun and weather, looked nothing like the man he'd said good-bye to back in Austin in the spring. "It is you, right?" he asked again.

Seth shook his head, his shoulders drooping wearily as he just stood there staring, then he watched Brax slide from the saddle and hurry to him.

"What the hell are you doing here?" Brax asked as he caught him around the shoulders, then helped him toward a rock a few feet away, so Seth could sit down.

Case too was off his horse now, and both men stood looking at Seth, waiting for an answer.

"I'm trying to get back to civilization, gentlemen," Seth said calmly in his clipped British accent, just as if he were passing the time of day. Then he proceeded to give them a shortened version of everything that had happened the past few months, both to him and to the others. "You were right, Brax," he said as he finished the hurried narration. "It was a stupid thing to try to do. But Lamar sounded so sure it'd work."

"So much for Lamar." Brax looked over at Case. "I'm glad Houston's back in control again."

Seth stared at him curiously. "Houston?"

"We have had an election while you were gone, cousin," Case explained quickly. "And when Señor Houston hears of this, we will no doubt have an explosion too." He stared down at Seth's bare feet.

"He'll ride with me," Brax said, knowing what Case had in mind. "I'll see if Hays'll let me take him back to the Double K. Let's get him on my horse."

A few minutes later, trying to hide the tears in his eyes, Seth sat behind Brax, holding him around the middle as tight as he could, while Hickory picked his footing back up the hill, with Case following close behind on his palamino, Compadre.

It took only a few minutes to let Captain Hays in on who Seth was and what he was doing there, and for a minute Hays was almost ready to forget the Indians and try to stop Salezar instead. However, caution and experience had taught him that decisions made in anger were usually the ones most regretted. So instead, he instructed Brax to see to it that his cousin got back to San Antonio, while he told Case to go on to Austin to let the president know what had happened to the Santa Fe Pioneers, as the men who had been with Seth had called themselves.

It was a decision Hays knew was the right one as he watched the two Rangers plying Seth with water and dried biscuits before setting off on their trip, while he and the rest of his troop headed northwest again toward where Seth had mentioned passing by a big encampment of Indians. Maybe he'd finally gotten lucky, Hays thought, glad Kolter and Dante's cousin had told them about the Indians. Maybe this time he'd locate the Comanche camp, and a grim smile crossed his lips as he reined his horse on down into the arroyo, with his men close behind.

Seth watched the rest of the Rangers disappearing in the distance as he swallowed a mouthful of dry biscuit, washing it down with water, then he looked at Braxton and Case.

"I was never so glad to see anyone in my life, gentlemen," he said, smiling his sun-baked face showing a myriad of wrinkles. "Only, what are you all doing so far west?"

"Trying to locate that Indian I was telling you about before," Brax answered as he took the canteen from Seth and put it into his saddlebag. "We've had rumors that he and the rest of the new young chiefs are getting ready for another big strike. Only if we can get to them first, we can probably put a stop to it. That's why Hays was eager for the information you gave him. Now, you ready to go?"

Was he ready to go? Seth wiped wet biscuit from the corner of his mouth and stood up, stretching to his full height. He was somewhat relaxed for the first time in days, even though he knew the ride back wouldn't be easy. "The sooner you gents get me out of here, the better," he said as he put the makeshift headdress back on his head for want of a hat. "I'm as ready as you are," and with that they all mounted up. For the first part of the journey back home, Case rode along with Braxton and Seth as far as the Devil's Sinkhole, then remembering his orders from Hays, he veered off, traveling the rest of the way to Austin by himself, while they rode farther south, heading toward San Antonio and the Double K.

Seth felt as if he'd been asleep forever as he opened his eyes and stared up at the ceiling. Yet he knew he couldn't have slept long because it was still daylight outside. It had been early in the afternoon when he and Brax had ridden into the ranch yard, and Cousin Liz had ordered Pretty to help Brax put Seth right to bed for some much-needed rest, while she and Dodee, the slave girl who'd been Genée's wet nurse when she was a baby, made him some chicken soup. The soup being Lizette's remedy for everything from croup to consumption.

Exhausted from the long days of riding, and after the horrible days alone in the wild after his escape, Seth had dropped off to sleep quickly, and was stirring now for the first time. It had been good to sleep without fear, and he thought back over the nights he had lain out in the open, wondering whether he'd ever open his eyes again.

Suddenly a noise at the door caught his attention, and he turned his head as Pretty walked in carrying a bowl of soup, followed by Braxton and Genée.

Seth's sloe eyes stayed on Genée longer than normal before settling back on Brax. "I say, don't tell me you're still here?" he said.

Brax, who was still wearing the same buckskins he'd had on when they rode in, strolled over to the other side of the bed where the back window of the room looked out over the chicken coop and cornfields.

"Came to say good-bye," he said as he lifted the edge of the curtain and looked off toward the hills, then he turned back to Seth. His cousin looked better already. "Now that I know you'll make it, I've still got a job to do. If Hays hasn't done it already." He ran a hand through his pale blond hair, which was curling past his ears, his gray eyes steady on Seth. "Pretty here'll take real good care of you. And if I know Genée, she'll spoil the hell out of you. So take care."

Seth reached up, hand outstretched. "Thanks, Brax."

Brax shook his cousin's hand, then straightened. "Remember, Pretty, go easy on the soup, all he's had is biscuits, jerky, and some beans and coffee. His stomach isn't used to good victuals yet."

Pretty smiled as she set the soup on the stand beside the bed. "You tellin' me how to do my job?"

"Nope."

"Then git, and see to it you come back alive, understand?"

Brax's mouth curved into an impish smile. "See, she really loves me," he said, then he glanced at Genée, who'd been standing at the foot of the bed staring curiously at Seth. "And as for you, little sister, treat your cousin right this time, and stop acting like he's some sort of freak that happened to fall out of the sky one day. He's more man than you've seen in a long time. And especially more than that no-account lawyer Ma says has been coming out to see you lately."

"He's not a no-account," she said, blushing over his statement. "Just because he wears glasses."

"Hell, I don't care if he wears glasses." Braxton's eyes darkened viciously. "But when he isn't in saloons, he spends his time trying to find ways to prove the land around here doesn't belong to who it belongs to. And I don't like anybody who thinks they're gonna ride in here and start tellin' people who've been here for years that they don't own what they own."

Genée straightened stubbornly. "He isn't doing any such thing."

"Oh no? Then why has Don Antonio been spending so much time in the judge's office in San Antonio lately? Hell, he was born on the land he owns, and now your friend's trying to say it's not his."

"You just don't understand."

"Braxton's right, honey," Pretty said as she began getting her patient ready for his soup by propping the pillows up while he sat up. "Next thing you know, he'll be tellin' your ma and pa they don't belong here either."

"Oh, you two, I hate you!" Genée wasn't about to stand around and be humiliated, and in front of Seth too. "I'll come see you later," she said, looking directly at her cousin, then glanced over at her brother. "After he's gone," and she turned abruptly, marching out, slamming the door behind her.

Pretty handed the bowl of soup to Seth, realizing that except for the fact that he'd been so tired before, he was strong enough to feed himself, then she looked over at Braxton.

"You ought to be ashamed, Brax," she said, a frown creasing her dark forehead. "Even my boys don't fight as you and your sister do. And you's usually the one who goads her on too."

"Hell, Pretty, Genée's just too picky, that's all. You ever heard her definition of her future husband?"

Seth, who'd already started eating the soup, stopped for a minute, listening eagerly.

"According to her, he's going to look like one of those Greek gods Ma has pictures of in those books we used to read. With muscles bulgin' all over him, and a face pretty enough to be a girl's. Only he has to be strong enough to protect her from other men, and still be genteel and have some book learning. Christ Almighty, she'll be an old maid before she finds anything like that out here."

Pretty stared at Braxton for a minute, then slowly smiled as she turned her attention to the Kolters' cousin, who was once more sipping quite gentlemanly at the soup. "Well, now, I didn't know that's what the girl had in mind," she said rather smartly. "But if that's what she says she wants . . . stranger things have been known to happen, you know."

Brax laughed. "You're as bad as she is. You're all dreamers, the whole lot of you." He hitched up his gunbelt, then took one last look toward the window, where night shadows would soon start filtering in among the trees. "Well, I'd better be off. Have to say good-bye to Ma and Luther yet, then I think I'll ride out to the range where Pa and the men are branding before heading northwest." He looked down at his cousin in the bed again. "Don't worry. You'll be on your feet in no time. Some new skin, and about fifty or sixty pounds, and you'll look good as new."

Seth's mouth was still sore from his parched, cracked lips, and the hot soup burned it a little, but it tasted so good. "Thanks again, Brax," he said as Braxton started for the door. "I owe you a favor sometime."

A few minutes later, Pretty stood by the window in the

bedroom with Seth and stared out, watching Braxton ride up the back trail past the cornfield and on toward the hills.

"I wonder if he'll make it back this time," she said, and Seth hesitated for a moment, watching this black woman who had raised Braxton from a baby, and he too wondered if he'd ever see his cousin again.

The next few days were like heaven to Seth. Eating when he was hungry, resting when he was tired. But most of all he had Genée to talk to, and for the life of him he couldn't figure out why she and Braxton argued so much, because she was so easy to get along with. Well, most of the time anyway. They'd take long walks in the afternoon, sit on the porch in the evenings, and after the first week, they started riding a short way from the ranch.

It wasn't until the afternoon he invaded her tree house that he learned the extent of Genée Kolter's temper. They'd been getting along quite well until then, with only a few minor disagreements. And he wouldn't have even been in the tree house if it hadn't been for Luther. The women were in the house, Pretty and Luther's sons, Dexter and Corbin, were in the barn, and Luther had asked Seth to help him fix the fence in the chicken yard. Right near the old tree where the tree house was, where some animal had been trying to get to the few chickens they had.

They were almost finished, when Luther suddenly straightened, his gaze resting on a spot beyond Seth's shoulder. Then his voice dropped a volume as he whispered, "Don't look now, son, but there's four Injuns riding just t'other side of the corn patch, and comin' down the hill. I wants for you to grab my rifle there, and scoot up into Miss Genée's tree house, and keep a bead on 'em while I go warn the boys in the barn and the ladies in the house. Then I'll find out what they wants."

Seth felt the hair on the nape of his neck stand on end, but without hesitating, he grabbed the black slave's rifle and did as he was told, keeping as close to the ground as he could until he reached the tree. Once there, he flattened himself against it, glad that the ladder to get into it was on the side away from the Indians' view. Scurrying up as fast as he could, he tried to get his big frame comfortable inside, then peered out the small slit of a window just in time to see the four riders clear the cornfield, ride past the tree he was in, and rein up near the house just as Luther and Lizette came out onto the back porch and walked down the steps to the drive.

Seth couldn't hear what was being said, but he could see the rifles being pointed furtively at the Indians from a couple of windows of the house, as well as two from the barn. And with him in the tree house, the Indians wouldn't have a chance.

He was motionless as he watched, his hand on the trigger, the rifle all ready, then finally he sighed and relaxed as the Indians talked a little longer, Lizette brought some food for them from the house, and they started riding out again, toward the front gate, and on toward town this time.

"It was Kiowas!" he heard Luther call to the boys in the barn. Seth leaned back for a minute against the walls of the makeshift fort to relax. Then he saw the pictures. Strange he hadn't paid any attention to them when he'd first climbed up into the place. But ringing the walls of the sturdy tree house Bain Kolter had built for his younger daughter were some four or five hand-drawn sketches of what looked like the pictures from a book on Greek and Roman mythology, as well as one picture that looked like it was a composite of all of the men in the others. Only the man in the composite picture was wearing clothes more like those of a Texan. Seth was still staring at the pictures curiously a few minutes later when Genée, having been told by Luther where Seth was, popped her head in, followed hurriedly by the rest of her.

"You have no right!" she began, her face livid. "You have no right . . . what are you doing up here anyway?"

"Hey, you saw the Indians . . ."

"But you didn't have to come here." Even though Genée didn't really use the tree house to play in anymore, it had become a quiet place where she could come sometimes just to be alone. She stared at Seth, her eyes filled with anger. "I suppose now you'll laugh and make fun of me."

He frowned, "Why?"

"Because of them," and she gestured toward the pictures.

"Not at all. In fact, I was going to ask you who drew them."

"Hah! You want to make fun of them too, I suppose!"

"I do not." He straightened some, and took a better look at the pictures. At first he thought they were torn from a book, but they were on coarse paper that looked like it had been taken from a ledger, and he knew they'd been hand-drawn. "You did them, didn't you?" he said.

She looked at him skeptically. "And if I did?"

"Why, they're jolly good. Quite better than many I've seen in museums."

"You've been to museums?"

"In London, certainly. And I'd say you have quite a flair for the arts."

"You're not just saying that so I won't be mad?"

"Believe me, Genée, I'd never do anything to purposely make you angry, even though you do look absolutely fascinating when you're up to a good fight. But I mean it. You have a real talent."

Genée still wasn't sure. "I probably should tear them down," she said as she reached for one of them. "After all, I'm not a little girl anymore."

He grabbed her hand before she could tear the picture from the wall. "No," he said. "Don't. You don't have to be a child to like good art. Leave them."

"But it's so silly."

His dark eyes were on her now, and he felt a warmth rush through him as he realized for the first time how long her lashes were, and how delicately they framed her gray-green eyes that suddenly looked more green than gray.

"Nothing is ever silly if you enjoy it," he said, his voice husky with emotion. "I like your drawings."

"Now I know you're making fun of me!"

"Don't be ridiculous."

"Oh, so now I'm ridiculous."

"I didn't say that." He was still holding her hand, but she wrenched it free, and sat for a minute staring at him.

Genée had gotten to know Seth much better during his stay this time at the Double K, and even though they'd gotten along quite well so far, there was something about him . . . for some reason, whenever he was around she felt restless. It wasn't really anything he did, or even said. It was the way he looked at her. As if she were a little girl he had to patronize. Well, she wasn't a little girl, she was a woman. At least that's what she kept telling herself. And he had no right to delve into her personal things like this either. None at all! All he'd have to do was tell everyone about the pictures, and she'd never live it down.

"I want you out of here," she said, her eyes sparking dangerously. "And I want you out now, and don't you ever speak to me again, Seth Locksley," and with that, she reached up, tore every one of the pictures down, then crawled from the tree house, vowing silently that no one would ever get another chance to make fun of her over them, ever again, while Seth watched her curiously, trying to figure out why she was so cussed mad, when he hadn't really done anything wrong.

Her anger didn't stop in the tree house either. At the dinner table that evening, she threw dagger eyes at him, even bringing a comment from Bain about the good mood she was in. His comment, however, only proved to bring on an equally disturbing look for him. Then later, when everyone else gathered in the parlor, instead of joining them, she quickly excused herself, preferring the back porch instead.

Even Loedicia was in a quandary over her great-granddaughter's mood this evening, and Genée wasn't surprised to look up from the bottom step, where she was making marks in the dirt with a long stick, to see Grandma Dicia come out the door.

"I thought I'd find you here," Loedicia said as she stood at the top of the stairs, then descended a few steps, where she stood looking down at Genée. "Now, what's this all about, young lady?"

"What do you mean, what's it all about?"

Loedicia was used to people trying to avoid her questions. "Don't pretend you don't know." Her eyes studied Genée's intently. "Not only have you been treating Seth like he's a stranger all evening, but you've been acting like the rest of us didn't exist either. Why?"

"Oh, Grandma!"

"That won't suffice either, and you know it. Now, what has he done that's so terrible? I thought you were getting along fine."

Genée flushed, and looked up at Grandma Dicia. "We were," she said, then bit her lip.

"So what happened?"

"He went in my tree house!"

"Oh, good Lord, child. What's so terrible about that? You never go in it anymore anyway. I'm surprised your father hasn't torn it down by now."

"But I do go in it, Grandma. Sometimes I just like to go up there and sit and read, or draw pictures."

"Then what's so terrible about Seth going in it?"

"You wouldn't understand."

"Try me."

"I can't!"

"She's upset because I saw some pictures she drew," Seth said from the top of the steps, and both of them turned, neither having heard him.

"See? See what I mean?" Genée yelled, and stood up, her eyes condemning him. "I hate you, Seth Locksley," and she ran off, heading right for the tree house. Even though she was in a dress, she climbed up as fast as she could, although night shadows were already starting to creep in among the trees.

Seth watched her disappear inside, then looked at his grandmother as he came down the steps. "She thinks I was making fun of her," he said. "But she's too sensitive. Actually she's a lovely artist, and all I did was tell her so."

Loedicia had seen the warm look in Seth's eyes when

he'd gazed off toward the tree house, and inwardly she smiled to herself. How easy it was to read her grandson's feelings. "Why don't you go tell her again," she said. "Maybe this time she'll listen."

"And get my head bitten off? She said I'm never to go up there again."

"Oh, pooh! What can she do to you? You're bigger than she is. Go on, tell her, only tell her how you really feel about her too, it just might help."

He frowned. "What do you mean, how I really feel?"

"I'm not blind, Seth." She brushed a white curl back away from her age-wrinkled face. "I know when I see a young man in love. So if you intend to do anything about it, do it now, because I have a feeling that lawyer friend of hers is going to be popping the question to her any day now, and I'd hate for her to say yes to the wrong man."

"But she doesn't love me."

"Who said so?"

"I say, Grandma." He shrugged. "You don't treat someone you love the way she's been treating me. Especially today."

"You do when you don't want to admit that you love him." Loedicia was sure she was telling the truth. "She's in love with you, I'd bet my life on it." She gave him a little shove. "Now go on, Seth, go to her. If you don't, I'm afraid you'll regret it."

Seth wasn't sure, yet . . . Grandma Dicia usually knew what she was talking about. He straightened, squaring his shoulders, then took a deep breath. I'll do it, he said silently to himself, then, "You better be right, Grandma," he said as he looked at Loedicia, "or I'm really going to be in trouble," and he stalked off toward the tree house, following after Genée, while Loedicia watched, a prayer on her lips and hope in her heart.

Genée couldn't believe it. She hadn't even been up here five minutes, and already Seth was sticking his head through the door in the floor. She drew her legs up, her back against the wall, and wrapped the skirt of her calico dress about her legs.

"What do you want?" she asked. "I thought I told you to stay out of here."

"You mean you really meant it?"

Her greenish eyes narrowed, and her mouth pursed angrily. "Every word."

"No you didn't."

"Get out of here, Seth Locksley!"

He was already pulling himself up into the cramped quarters that couldn't have been much bigger than five feet square and five feet high. Once inside, he tried to stretch out as best as he could.

Genée watched furtively as he settled down across from her. "I told you to leave."

"Why?"

"You know why."

He smiled, and she realized some of the blisters he'd had on his face from the sunburn were going to scar. Especially on his forehead.

"What did you do with the pictures?" he asked.

"What do you care?"

"As I said, they're good."

She tilted her head up stubbornly. "If you're through with your compliments, I'd like to be alone."

This time he chuckled outrageously. "You're really precious. You know that, don't you?"

She was fuming. "And you're terrible." She pulled her legs up tighter, then reached up, knocking the hair back behind her shoulder, her eyes smoldering. "Now, will you please let me be?"

"No." He shook his head, his voice lowering as his eyes bored into hers. "I will not let you be, Genée Kolter." He straightened as best he could, and moved over closer to her, knowing there was no way she could get away. "And I will not go either. By Jove, you're going to listen to me whether you want to or not. I love you, Genée," he said, his voice breaking. "I've loved you ever since that first day I rode into your ranch yard and set eyes on you. And if you don't tell me you love me too, I'm going to hound you to death until you'll have to love me, or else. Do I make myself clear?"

Genée's eyes were like saucers as she stared at him. "Well," she exclaimed, her voice unsteady. "Well, I never!"

"Neither did I." He flushed over his own boldness. "I wasn't planning to do it like this. Honest I wasn't," he said, suddenly embarrassed over what he'd done. "I was going to catch you out in the moonlight, with your hair all silvery and soft, and your eyes glistening like diamonds. And I was going to be gentle, and romantic, and . . . oh hell, I've made a bloody mess of the whole thing, haven't I?"

Genée started to laugh, then cry, then shook her head. "I just don't believe it."

"Now who's being laughed at?"

Genée shook her head harder, suddenly realizing why she'd felt so uneasy whenever Seth was around, and why he'd always irritated her so. It had nothing to do with hating him. On the contrary, she'd been fighting just the opposite feelings. She started to laugh again, the small tree house ringing with the sound.

"See, see," he said. Now it was his turn to look hurt. "I knew I'd make a fool of myself."

"Oh no." She found her voice quickly, and reached out, touching his face where the scars from his horrid ordeal were faintly visible. "I'm not laughing at you, Seth. Never. I could never laugh at you. I'm laughing at me, not you," she went on. "Because you see, I love you too. I guess I always have, only I didn't want to admit it because you weren't anything like the man of my dreams."

"You mean the one Brax described?"

She nodded, then looked at him sheepishly. "At least I didn't think you were at first. Yet the more I get to know you, the more I realize now that the only difference between you and the man I drew in those pictures is that he's on paper and you're here."

Seth stared at her hard, wondering if he was really awake or if he was dreaming. "I don't intend to stay here, you know," he said as he took her hand from his face and held it tightly while he watched her eyes closely. "Just as soon as I'm really on my feet again, I'm going back to Austin. There's a lot to do yet to make this country what it could be, and I want to be a part of it. You can understand that, can't you?"

"Oh yes."

"And you'd be willing to leave here and follow me to Austin?" he asked.

"Are you asking me to marry you, Seth Locksley?"

He squeezed her hand nervously. "I think I am."

"Then yes, oh yes, Seth," she cried. "I think I'd follow you back to England if that's where you wanted to go," and before Seth had a chance to even realize he had absolutely nothing to offer her, not even the clothes on his back, he found himself holding her in his arms in the cramped tree house, his lips on hers, returning a kiss he'd only hoped someday would be for him, but was now his wholeheartedly.

20

Seth's wedding to Genée was set for April 1842, and the only thing that marred it was Mexican troops who, on the sixth of March, streamed across the Rio Grande, capturing the towns of Goliad, Victoria, Refugio, and San Antonio. For a while no one seemed to know what was going to happen. Then, as quickly as they had materialized, the soldiers retreated, before the militia could even get organized, and headed back across the border, as if they had just been testing the Texans. So the festive wedding in the parlor at the Double K went on as planned, and Lizette watched the last of her children leave home, heading north with her new husband.

With Genée gone now, living in Austin, and with Braxton God knew where, Lizette began visiting Blythe more and more as the days went on. That's why she and Grandma Dicia happened to be at Blythe's place late one afternoon early in mid-September when Rosita came rushing into the parlor, her face pale, eyes wide with fright, both hands pressing her cheeks, and carrying on in Spanish so fast Blythe couldn't understand a word she was saying.

"Good heavens, Rosita, will you slow down," Blythe said, and glanced at her mother and Grandma Dicia.

Rosita stopped, then burst into tears. "Oh, señora," she cried. "It's Manuel!" Her voice caught on a sob. "He says there has been trouble . . . there are many soldiers . . . they are all prisoners, and that Señor Don Antonio's been hurt!"

Blythe's heart constricted as she stared at Rosita, unable for a moment to grasp the enormity of what the woman was saying, then slowly Blythe straightened, her eyes intense.

Manuel was her husband's driver when Tonio used the carriage, and today Tonio had ridden to town in the carriage, where he had an appointment in court, regarding the ridiculous claims against his ownership of the land. "Where is he?" she asked, her voice breathless.

Lizette and Loedicia were both on their feet now, and Lizette moved over to Blythe. "Let me go see, dear. You stay here."

"But she says he's hurt!"

"Not badly perhaps." Lizette turned to Loedicia. "You stay with her while I find out what's going on."

Loedicia nodded, and she and Blythe both watched Lizette leave the parlor, following Rosita. Only Lizette wasn't gone long. When she came back in the room, her face was pale.

"I'm . . . I'm sorry, Blythe," she said as she stared at her daughter, wishing there was some way she could ease the blow. "He's out in the carriage. They let Manuel bring him home, but it's not good." She walked over and knelt down in front of Blythe, taking her daughter's hands in her own.

"They?" Blythe asked.

"The Mexican soldiers. They've crossed the river and taken San Antonio again. Only this time they've not only taken over the town, but tried to take over the people too. Manuel says it's a mess. Antonio was waiting for his say in court when they burst in and took them all prisoners. Only he wouldn't accept it. There was a struggle . . . I think you'd better send someone for Mario."

It was late. The sun had gone down hours ago, and Blythe sat on the lounge chair upstairs on the portico that adjoined the master bedroom, gazing up at the stars above her, tears rimming her eyes. Tonio had been so good to her, too good, and she didn't deserve it. He had married her in spite of her past, and given of himself so freely, and it wasn't fair that he should be the one to go.

She closed her eyes, remembering his last words, spoken only moments ago, and she wanted to scream. He knew! Dammit, somehow he knew Mario was in love with her. Had he known she returned that love? She remembered the look in her husband's eyes just before he took his last breath, when he made Mario promise to take care of her, and she frowned. No, she was sure Tonio had no idea how she felt about the man who was trying so hard to save his life. If only Mario had. But the bullet had lodged too deep, and done too much damage. Damn the Mexicans! She bit her lip and turned at a footfall behind her.

Only she and Mario were left upstairs now, the others having gone downstairs right after Mario had pulled the spread up over Tonio's head.

"I did all I could, you know that," Mario said as he stepped out of the room onto the upstairs balcony. He started to roll down his sleeves.

Blythe nodded. "I know." She turned abruptly, looking up into his face. "I did love him, Mario. I did," she said, her voice breaking. "Not the way I should, I know, but I did love him."

He finished buttoning his cuffs, walked over, pulled up a wicker chair, set it in front of her, then deposited his tall frame into it, so he was on her level.

"No one says you didn't love him, mi querida. You know that." He was trying to soothe her. "You could not live with a man like Antonio as long as you have without feeling something for him."

"Oh, Mario!" She leaned forward, and so did he, his arms closing around her.

"Go ahead, cry," he urged as he held her close. "Get it out of your system. But remember, what happened to him has nothing to do with your feelings for him. It has to do with General Woll's soldiers and their ridiculous raid. I don't want you feeling guilty."

She sniffed, then pushed him away and reached up wiping her eyes. "What do I do now?" she asked.

He shrugged. "What do you want to do? You'll probably own all of this now, you know. At least I assume he left it to you. Although he might have left part to Catalina too."

"No . . . at least from what he always said, it should be mine."

"That means you're a rich widow." He squeezed her hands. "I didn't mean that like it sounded."

"I know."

"But you are a widow now, Blythe."

"I know that too."

"And I still love you, you know that."

"Tonio knew it too, didn't he?"

"Sí."

"How long?"

"He confronted me with his suspicions shortly after I moved out, and how could I deny it, when everything I did when you were around gave me away? But he never knew about us, mi querida. Believe me. He thought the feelings were solely one-sided. If he had ever known, or even suspected, we loved each other, he would never have let me live. We both know that. He felt, as long as my love wasn't returned, he had nothing to worry about, and you played your part well, mi querida."

"Maybe it hasn't been all playacting after all, Mario," she said as she glanced back into the bedroom, where the bedspread covered her husband's body. "Because I have the strangest, empty feeling inside, knowing he's gone."

Somehow Mario understood. He'd seen death often, and learned much about life, and because he loved Blythe so deeply, he understood. That's why, although he wanted so badly to kiss her, make love to her, and show her that now there was nothing to stop them from being together, all he did was hold her hand and try to console her.

A day and a half later, as cool breezes rolled down from the nearby hills, Mario stood with Blythe and her family at the funeral service in the de Léon family graveyard behind the chapel and watched Don Antonio's body as it was lowered into the ground with prayers being said over it. Then, once the funeral was over, he quickly rode away from the hacienda, heading toward the Salado Creek, about seven miles northeast of San Antonio, where word had gotten back to him that the Rangers had set up camp and were hoping to ambush the Mexican troops. If so, they were going to need a doctor.

During the next few days, while Blythe wheeled herself from one room to another at the hacienda, trying not to feel guilty over her husband's death, Mario moved from one place to another along the lines of fighting, trying to take care of Mexican and Texan alike. Paying little heed to which side the man he was treating had been fighting on, only that he was a wounded man in need of help.

Finally, nine days after their unexpected invasion of San Antonio, the Mexican soldiers who were left when the Texans got through with them at Salado Creek once more straggled back down across the Rio Grande, but not until first sending the rest of the men who were in the courtroom that day with Don Antonio on to Mexico City ahead of them. There the men from San Antonio were thrown into prison with the surviving members of the ill-fated Santa Fe expedition Seth had been on, and all over Texas everyone was up in arms. So much so that by November a troop of Rangers led by Ben McCulloch had joined with a force of Texas volunteers under General Alexander Somerwell, and they were all heading south, not only to see what damage they could do, but hoping to free the prisoners the Mexicans had taken with them.

Unfortunately, this expedition failed as miserably as the expedition to Santa Fe had, because refusing to heed the advice of Ben McCulloch and General Somerwell, who shortly after starting the journey realized they were getting in over their heads and started to retreat, some of the men elected themselves a new leader and continued on toward Mexico with some three hundred men, only to run into more trouble than they could handle. By the time New Years' Eve of 1843 rolled around, they themselves had been captured, and were all being marched on to Mexico City as prisoners too, barely escaping immediate execution at a place called Meir.

For a while the Kolters and Dantes were worried that Braxton and Case were among the men who'd been taken prisoner, since rumor had them riding with Ben

McCulloch. However, one day some six months later, they rode into San Antonio, to report to the Ranger office as usual. Then afterward Brax, accompanied by Case, went to visit Blythe, only to discover that Tonio was dead and that Catalina, having turned twenty-one a month after her uncle's death, had received her inheritance and left for Monterrey. Her departure hastened by the fact that she'd learned of Blythe's feelings for Mario, and their plans to marry when the year of mourning was up.

Happy for his sister, but disappointed that Catalina had never been able to understand what being free of Mexico meant to Texans, Brax rode on to the Double K to spend a few days with his parents, while Case headed in the direction of the Crown D, not only mourning the death of the man who had been so much like a father to him but also hoping perhaps this time, when he saw Teffin, the old hurts wouldn't be there anymore.

Although he'd put his feelings into order years before, it was still hard for Case to watch her and Kaelen so obviously happy together, without feeling something inside. So after only a few days of Bessie's cooking, his mother's pampering, and bouncing Teffin's little three-year-old daughter Loedicia on his knee, when his sister came to visit, Case woke up early one morning, put his old clothes back on, kissed everyone good-bye, and rode out on the trail that led to the Double K, hoping that Brax was ready to leave too, because he knew only time and distance were going to heal old hurts. Not only because of Teffin, but because Don Antonio was no longer there either, and there were tears in his eyes as he turned one last time, taking a look at the house, then pulled his hat down firmly on his head, dug Compadre in the ribs, and disappeared down the trail, knowing his parents were still standing in the ranch yard watching him.

Three years had gone by since Brax and Case had ridden away from home again without looking back. Three years of fighting Indians, outlaws, and the weather. Three years of lonely nights, interrupted only occasionally by some equally lonely woman in a town they might happen to come across, and as they rode along now, the cooler weather of late winter causing them to turn the collars of their buckskins up, Case pulled his gaze from its scrutiny of the horizon and glanced over at Brax, wondering why his cousin had so suddenly decided they should head home.

Their captain had been glad to give them leave, but even if he hadn't, Brax would no doubt have left anyway. That's the way he was. Case reached up, smoothing the mustache he still wore, while he watched Braxton. Brax was now twenty-eight, not quite two years younger than he was, and Case wondered if Brax felt as old, because at the moment, as they rode along the plains of northern Texas, past a herd of grazing buffalo and headed south, Case felt ancient.

They hadn't had a decent meal for ages now, and his right shoulder where he'd taken a bullet the year before still bothered him when the weather grew cool. So it'd be good to get home for a while. He rubbed his shoulder for a second, then once more scanned the endless horizon. Texas was now a state, a fact that often made him feel strange. He had started life as an American, and it looked like he was destined to stay one, his years in Mexico as Joaquín seeming like a dream. Only it wasn't, and more than once the reality of those years had made him hurt inside.

"Why so quiet?" Brax asked as he glanced over at Case, realizing his cousin had hardly said two words during the last two miles.

Case maneuvered Compadre around a salt bush, moving closer to Brax as he did.

"I was just wondering what everyone was going to say when they see us," he answered. "After all, it has been a long time since we have been home, cousin. The years go so fast."

"Too fast. I feel like an old man already."

"You too?"

Suddenly Case frowned as he pulled back on Compadre's reins. Brax instinctively followed suit.

"What is it? What did you see?"

"Over there." Even though his hat was on, Case shaded his eyes more as he continued watching the hillside where he was pointing, some quarter-mile away, where there'd been movement only moments before. "Indians, you suppose?"

Brax was squinting too. Suddenly his eyes picked up the same movement. "It isn't Comanche, that's for sure. Come on," and he started moving forward again, slowly this time with his eyes on the hill, and Case alongside.

"Hell, it's a woman," Brax exclaimed as they drew closer.

Case frowned. Brax was right. It was a woman. An Indian woman, and she hadn't spotted them as yet. She was too busy trying to cut down a small sapling on the side of the hill. Both riders halted their horses again, watching her.

"What the devil is she up to?" Case said as he watched her swinging her tomahawk at a small oak a short way up the hill.

Brax straightened in the saddle. "Let's find out," and he nudged Hickory forward, his gaze moving from the woman to the landscape surrounding her, then back to the woman again.

They were about a hundred feet from her now, and suddenly both reined up as a man's voice rang out loud and clear.

"That's far enough, m'sieurs!"

Case looked over at Brax, his hands tight on the reins. "Who says so?" he yelled back.

"I do!"

They could see two horses and a pack mule now near the foot of the hill, but still couldn't see who was talking. Although whoever it was evidently could see them. The woman had stopped and turned now, facing them, and Case was surprised to see that she was younger than he'd first thought, quite pretty, and except for the clothes and the way she wore her hair, didn't look one bit like an Indian.

"Where do you suppose he is?" he asked Brax in a half-whisper.

Brax nodded toward a large rock a few feet from the horses. Then Case saw it too. The barrel of a rifle was pointed right at them.

"Indian or white man?" Brax called out.

"Who wants to know?"

"Rangers."

"Aha! Then ride in closer, m'sieurs."

Case looked over at Brax, and they slowly reined their horses forward, stopping a few feet from the rock as the man behind it stuck his head up, and they both stared in awe.

The man looked ancient, but had a full head of pure white hair and showed a complete set of front teeth as he grinned.

The grin faded, and he screwed up his wrinkled face, his hard brown eyes studying them. "Your names, m'sieurs?" he asked.

"Braxton Kolter."

"Case Dante."

"Dante?"

"Sí. Dante. My father owns a spread near San Antonio. And you?"

The old gent's eyes narrowed. "Gervaise, DeMosse Gervaise, m'sieurs," he answered, his voice cracking with age, though it still held the same deep resonance it had when he was younger, and showed a decidedly French accent. "And that, m'sieurs, is my daughter, Moonflower."

They both looked at the young woman, who was walking toward her father now, the tomahawk still in her hand.

"Come here, Moonflower," DeMosse said, gesturing toward her, and she quickened her steps.

"My papa is sick," Moonflower said as she knelt down by the old man. "And his leg is now broken."

"My horse got spooked." DeMosse coughed a little, and it was obvious he was trying not to cough at all. "The lungs, m'sieurs," he explained.

Brax and Case exchanged quick glances, then both dismounted.

"You're a trapper?" Brax asked.

"Oui. That is, I was a trapper until age let me know I was losing more pelts than I brought home."

Case had been watching the man closely. "Just how old are you, señor?" he asked.

The old trapper's eyes crinkled mischievously. "How old would you say?"

"I have no idea."

"As close to a hundred as I want to get, m'sieurs," he answered, and coughed again. "And no doubt as close as God will let me get too, if this keeps up."

"I was hoping to reach one of your doctors to look at him," Moonflower said as she handed her father a handkerchief, then gave him back his hat from where he had set it aside, so it wouldn't show up over the rock he'd been hiding behind. "He has been like this for many moons now, and it only gets worse."

Brax looked over toward the pack mule, then back to Moonflower. "Where are you coming from?"

"Just north of the canyon," her father answered for her as he shoved the handkerchief into the pocket of his buckskin jacket. "I been trapping all over Indian Territory for some forty to fifty years now. Ever since the big river got civilized."

"You mean the Mississippi?"

"Oui, m'sieur." He tried to move into a better position, and flinched with the pain, his hands moving to the makeshift splint his daughter had evidently put on his leg. Now Braxton saw the stump of another tree she'd cut down and used for the splint.

"I was going to make a travois to haul him on until the leg healed enough," she said as she stood up, her eyes settling on the half-cut sapling.

"Then allow us," Case offered.

So while the old man kept watch for hostiles, Brax and Case set to work, and with Moonflower's help soon had a travois ready to haul her father on.

While they worked, and with some prodding from Brax

and Case, they learned that Moonflower was the daughter of the old man's third wife. He had outlived all of them, however, and although he'd left children, grandchildren, and great-grandchildren back with the Cherokee, he'd wanted his youngest daughter, Moonflower, to be brought up as a white woman, since she looked more French than Indian.

"She is the only one of my children who does not look Indian," he said proudly while they were fastening him on the travois. "Can you imagine, m'sieurs. A man of seventy-six fathering such a beautiful little thing like that."

Once more Brax and Case exchanged glances, while Moonflower blushed, embarrassed by her father's statement.

"Cuernos!!" Case exclaimed as he made sure the old man was secure on the travois, while trying to figure out Moonflower's approximate age. He added quickly in his head. "That means you are almost a hundred, señor?"

"Like I tell you, m'sieurs," DeMosse Gervaise said, his weathered face lined with age, yet still showing the traces of the strength it once had. "Three more years, if God lets me," and he coughed again, this time a long hard cough that drew blood.

While helping Moonflower, Brax and Case had also promised to see to it that she and her father reached the nearest settlement, although she wasn't any too happy about the arrangement, consenting to let them help only because her father was in the condition he was in. Actually, she hated all Texans, so she informed them in her stilted English that was seasoned occasionally with some French, as was her father's.

"I was but twelve when your Texans drove us from our lands to the east, near the Neches River," she said while they were mounting up to start their long trek southward. "I saw my brothers and uncles die for no other reason than that they were Indian, and the only reason I am bringing my father to the white man's world is that it is his last wish," and she dug her horse in the ribs with her moccasined feet, leading her father's horse and the travois down the hillside, while Brax and Case stared after her for a moment, then joined her, urging their horses past her and into the lead.

They'd been traveling for two days already, and were camped tonight on the banks of a small stream miles yet from any kind of settlement, let alone a town. Case was sitting by their small fire sipping on a second cup of coffee when he began to realize that DeMosse was staring at him. In fact, now that he thought back, the old man had been staring at him hard all the evening before too.

Suddenly DeMosse gestured, and Case moved over, sitting down on the grass beside him.

"You want something?" he asked.

The old man looked thoughtful. "I wish to ask a question, m'sieur," he said.

"Go ahead."

"I have been running your name over in my mind. Dante . . . Dante." He hesitated momentarily, then went on. "I knew a Dante once. Or should I say I met a Dante once, many, many years ago. It is so long I must think hard."

Case let him gather his thoughts together, then listened curiously as the man went on.

"Ninety-three . . . no, ninety-five, it was in ninety-five, I am sure, when we were at Fort Locke and he was there with him."

"Him?"

"The man who took from me the only woman I ever truly loved." He took a deep breath and coughed, then continued. "You see, we had escaped from Thayandanega, a feat in itself, and I had hoped to make her mine. But he was waiting for her when we reached the fort, and this Indian, I have been trying to think of his name . . . Beau, oui, that was it, Beau Dante, part Indian, part French, he was with Chapman."

Case was no longer sipping his coffee. Instead he was staring hard at DeMosse Gervaise. "My grandfather's name is Beau Dante," he said, his voice hesitant.

DeMosse frowned. "But no, it could not be."

"He is part Indian also," Case explained quickly. "His father was a chief of the Tuscarora."

"But you are Spanish."

"It is a long story, señor," and Case told him of how he was kidnapped, and the results, as he knew them, and of being brought up as Joaquín de Alvarado.

"So," DeMosse said. "It is a smaller world than we think, is it not?" and he glanced over to where Braxton was making sure his Colt repeater was clean and loaded. It was a gun that had fascinated Captain Hays when he'd first seen it. So much so that he'd sent one of his men back east to get more, and now all the Rangers had them. "I have heard you call him your cousin," DeMosse said, his eyes still studying Braxton.

"Sí. My father and his mother are brother and sister. In fact, you said the man who took the woman from you was named Chapman? That was my mother's maiden name, and is my great-grandmother's last name."

Case saw DeMosse Gervaise's eyes take on a strange look of disbelief, and for a minute the old man looked as if he were in a daze. "She is still alive?" he asked, his voice hushed.

"Sí."

"Is her first name Loedicia?"

"Sí."

"I do not believe it . . . it is too much." He shook his head slowly, then said. "Where is she?"

"At the Double K. She lives with Braxton's parents."

The old man closed his eyes, his head bent back, and Case watched him closely. DeMosse Gervaise, this trapper who'd seemed to come right out of nowhere, had just told him he'd once been in love with Grandma Dicia. It didn't seem possible, but as they continued talking, and Brax came over and joined in the conversation, not only did they realize that what the old man said was true, but the rest of the evening was spent listening to the story of how DeMosse Gervaise had once been a French spy. How he'd met Grandma Dicia, and their remarkable journey cross-country together shortly after her first husband, Quinn Locke had died.

By the time they settled down to sleep that night, Brax and Case taking turns at guard duty, since they were in Comanche territory, DeMosse had changed plans, and instead of having the two Rangers take him and his daughter to the nearest settlement, it was decided, much against Moonflower's better judgment, that they would accompany the two Rangers all the way to San Antonio, so DeMosse could see Loedicia again. A dream he claimed to have cherished for years, and a dream he'd always prayed would come true, even though he'd been sure it never would.

They had been traveling for a little over two weeks already, and were about fifty miles or so from the Double K. The going had been rough with the travois, but so far they'd managed to avoid the Comanche, although many times Brax and Case had caught signs, proving they were still around.

Even though Hays and his troop of Rangers had done a great deal over the years to rid the frontier of any threat from them, too many of them had managed to elude him and his men, and were still a threat to anyone who dared cross their path. The Comanche had seen what happened to the Cherokee and Creek, and vowed it would never happen to them, and lately they'd been making good their vow. Especially He Who Rides, who seemed to have a special vengeance declared against the white man.

As they rode along now, Case was glad they hadn't run into him, and hoped that's all they'd see the rest of the way in, was signs, because the young Comanche warrior seemed to get special satisfaction over bedeviling them, as he had often done over the past few years when their paths had crossed. No doubt he was remembering their first meeting in that box canyon.

Case was riding rear guard, bringing the pack mule, and he glanced ahead to where Moonflower rode, leading her father's horse with the travois on it. When they'd first run into Moonflower and her father, she'd had her hair, the deep amber color of burnt honey, in one long braid down her back, with a beaded headband around her forehead, and she'd been wearing a buckskin dress, leggings, and a fur-trimmed coat against the winter chill. Now, she still wore the coat, but beneath it she had on a dress of bright blue silk her father said they'd brought with them from up in the hills. It had been part of the loot left over from a raid one of DeMosse's sons and some of the other braves had made against the white men some years before. It wasn't exactly the latest fashion, naturally, and was rumpled from having been washed and not ironed. Nonetheless, it made a striking difference in Moonflower's appearance.

Last night when she'd first put it on, Case had noticed right away how much lighter her eyes looked. In fact he'd noticed her eyes from that very first day they'd met. Unlike most Indians', her eyes were pale brown, only they also had flecks of amber and gold running through them, and for the first time since Case's tragic love for Teffin had been denied him, he suddenly found himself looking at a woman as something more than just a means to appease the loneliness inside him. And as he rode along now, watching her hair, still in its braid, but without the headband, trailing down in back of the funny little straw hat her father had insisted she also wear with the dress, he wished things were different between them.

Moonflower looked nothing like a Cherokee, true, but her heart was certainly Cherokee. All during the trip so far, she'd not only been cool and aloof toward both Brax and Case, but made sure they knew she was only here because of her father. Case thought perhaps she had left behind a young buck she was in love with, but according to the old man, she'd never looked twice at any of them.

She had proved to be a good cook, though, and Case wished now they hadn't run out of cornmeal flour last night because the corn cakes she knew how to make would go well with the young deer he'd shot that morning and slung across the back of the pack mule.

For the rest of the afternoon, as he rode along, Case's thoughts kept wandering back to Moonflower, and that evening when they finally made camp, he made up his mind that whether she liked it or not, he was going to try to break down the barriers she'd set up between them.

Case was stirring up the fire. He and Brax had skinned the deer earlier and butchered it, cutting venison steaks for Moonflower to cook over the fire for them, and now they were roasting the rest of the meat to take with them. It was skewered over the fire on a spit, and Brax, Case, and Moonflower were taking turns rotating it.

Case made sure the coals were good and hot, gave the spits a good turn, then glanced around, looking for Moonflower. She had a way of disappearing every evening after they ate, and it bothered him. Not that he worried about what she was doing, but just because she was part Indian, she thought there was nothing for her to fear.

He saw a movement in the trees down near the stream they were camped by, and took a step toward it. It was Moonflower, all right, she'd been swimming again, no doubt somewhere upstream. He frowned as he watched her fastening up the back of her dress, her wet braid hanging over her right shoulder.

"'You do not listen too well, do you señorita?" he said when he reached her.

Her expression quickly told him she could care less. "I am not a, what you say, señorita," she replied, catching the hook at the back of her dress and fastening it, then flipping the long golden braid back over her shoulder. "Besides, I do not like being dirty, so I will bathe if I wish."

"It's worth losing your scalp for?"

"Who said I would lose my scalp? I am sister to the Comanche. So why would I fear them?"

"Because they are not Cherokee, that's why."

"You are an old woman." She started to brush past him, but he caught her arm.

"Do I look like an old woman?" His dark green eyes bored into hers, the late sun filtering through his black hair, highlighting it here and there with streaks of mahogany.

No, he didn't look like a woman, anything but. Only she wasn't about to let him know that.

"For the last two weeks we've been riding, and all you do is look at us with hate in your eyes," he said after staring at her for a few minutes. "What is it? What have I done to you that you should hate me so?"

Moonflower's chin tilted skyward. "You are a Ranger, that is enough."

"Oh, I see. Then it isn't really me you object to, but what I do."

"Oui. As far as you are concerned as a man, to you I have no feelings at all, but as a Ranger, I hate you."

"Why, because I protect women and children from being terrorized by the Comanche?"

"Because you kill my people."

"The Comanche are your people?" His eyes narrowed. "I see you've met few Comanche, Señorita. The Comanche is brother to no one except Comanche." He frowned. "You mean your father hasn't told you this?"

"My father has lived with the Indians many years."

"But not the Comanche."

He watched a stray hair fall onto her forehead, and she brushed it aside. "Look, m'sieur," she said, her voice bristling. "I am doing as my father asks, oui, but I do not have to like it. As for you and your friend, I do not have to like you either."

Case's eyes moved to hers, and as they met, he saw a flush creep into her cheeks. "Aha, but you do like me, do you not?"

"Like you? I despise you."

"Is that why you keep glancing back as we ride? Because you hate me so?"

"I do not."

"Oh, but you do." The corners of his mouth tilted, amused. "And last night while we were eating, I saw you watching me again."

"You have been mistaken, m'sieur."

"Have I now?" Shadows were already creeping into the trees around them, and Case knew Brax was at the other side of the camp talking to DeMosse. He reached out, his arm circling her waist, and pulled her against him.

"Am I also mistaken when I tell you you are lovely when your eyes shine like that?"

"Let me go!"

"I will when I am ready."

"Now!"

Instead his mouth covered hers, and he kissed her long and hard, literally taking her breath away as his lips moved against hers hungrily.

"Now," he finally whispered, seconds later, as he eased his hold on her.

For a minute she just stood staring at him, and he could see she was as shaken from the kiss as he was, because it had been a kiss filled with all the longing he'd been carrying in his heart for her the past few days.

"You . . ." She cleared her throat, bringing her voice back down to its normal volume instead of the ridiculous squawk that was issuing from it. "Why?" she asked, her lips trembling. "Why did you do that?"

Case still held her against him, and he didn't really know what to say except that he'd wanted to. However, you didn't tell a stubborn, bullheaded woman like Moonflower that you kissed her just because you wanted to.

Moonflower was still staring up at him, waiting for an answer, only her heart was pounding so hard she was sure it was going to stop altogether, and her knees still felt strangely weak. He'd had no right to do this to her. None, she thought angrily.

Her eyes were on his, and suddenly a warm sensation flowed through her as she remembered the feelings the kiss had dredged up from deep inside her. Feelings she knew existed because she'd felt inklings of them the first time she'd set eyes on Case. Only they were feelings that she didn't want to admit, even to herself, were capable of coming fully to life.

"Well?" she asked, hoping to still her heart, her voice still unsteady as she prodded him for an answer. "Why?"

Case hesitated as he studied her face, sensing her discomfiture. "Do I have to have a reason?" he asked.

"You kiss me, but do not know why?" Her eyes darkened furiously, and he suddenly realized there were faint freckles scattered across her small nose. How precious she looked. Especially when she was mad. "Then I tell you, M'sieur Case Dante, you do not ever do it again, understand?"

His eyes looked deeply into hers. "Just what are you afraid of?"

"Nothing!" She pushed him away, her face flushing deeper than he had known it to do before, as she stared back at him, then her jaw tightened angrily. "Just keep your hands off me," and she turned abruptly, moving hurriedly across the camp toward where her father sat talking to Braxton, while Case stood watching her go.

Later that evening, after the last of the venison was packed away so they could get an early-morning start, Moonflower sat near the fire and glanced over to a large boulder some hundred or so feet from camp, where Case sat on first watch, and she thought back over what had happened earlier.

Her hand went to her mouth, touching her lips lightly where his lips had been, and she remembered the wild tingling feeling that had coursed through them at the time. Only it didn't make sense. Any of it. She hated him. Just like she hated all Texans. At least that's what she'd been telling herself ever since first laying eyes on him.

So he was nice-looking. So what did that matter? Many men were nice-looking. Hadn't the man who'd killed her mother been nice-looking, but that didn't make him a nice person. She was right to keep herself away from Case Dante. After all, look what he was doing now, sitting up there on his rock, just hoping a Comanche would come along so he could shoot him. Didn't he know that all Indians wanted was peace? Hadn't her father proved that by living peaceably with them all these years? And the Comanche was no different from the Cherokee. How could he be?

Oui, she thought, disregarding any good feelings for these two Rangers who were helping her and her father, by still clinging to the hatred she'd been nurturing since she was a young girl. They are no different from any of the other bloodthirsty Texans, and she grabbed her blanket, curled up by the fire, and tried to sleep, hoping she could forget the unexpected consequences of Case's kiss.

However, instead of forgetting about it, her dreams were filled with it, and with Case, and by the time she opened her eyes on a new day, she was no longer just angry with him over it, but furious, and refused to even talk to him all morning unless she was forced to.

Even when they stopped for lunch, she kept her distance. That evening, after forcing herself to join in the preparation of the food, yet still keeping her distance from him as much as possible, she just couldn't stay around any longer and be reminded. So she wandered off by herself to pout, while trying to come to grips with what she was feeling inside, because she just couldn't seem to get that ridiculous kiss out of her mind.

She'd been strolling along for some minutes now, her moccasined feet automatically avoiding everything that might crack, and every fallen leaf that could be heard crunching underfoot.

Winter would soon be over, and although winters were never as fiercely cold here farther south, as her father said they were back east, or even up in the northern mountains where her tribe had camped, they were still cool enough at times to put a light frost on the waters and cause some of the trees to lose their leaves.

It had been warm enough tonight, though, and she had left her fur-trimmed coat back in camp. Now, however, with the sun almost gone, she shivered.

Suddenly she froze at a slight sound, and stood motionless, listening. A bird sang from up ahead a few feet, then flew across her path, disappearing into the jumble of tangled brush. Still she didn't move. It was so quiet she could hear herself breathing. Yet for some strange reason the hair on the nape of her neck prickled, and she held her breath.

Sensing instinctively that someone was behind her, she turned her head slowly, expecting it to be Case again, coming to torment her, then gasped as she stared into the hard bronzed face of a Comanche warrior who was flanked by two more warriors as fiercely painted as he was.

For a second neither the Comanche nor Moonflower said a thing, but just stood quietly staring at each other. Then, sighing with relief because it wasn't Case, and certain she had nothing to fear, Moonflower relaxed, lifting her hands to signal she was a friend.

The Indian in the middle, the one with the fierce scowl, let a smile curve his lips, then laughed and said something to the men with him in what Moonflower supposed was Comanche. The warriors with him grinned too, then the Indian in the middle, who was obviously their leader, grew serious as he walked toward her, limping slightly, and stopped so close she could see the color of his eyes. They were green like Case's, but held no warmth or understanding as his did.

"Where you learn sign language?" He Who Rides asked in stilted English this time.

Moonflower stood her ground unafraid. After all, hadn't all the tribes met up at Bent's Fort only a few years back to prove they should all be one in each other's councils?

"From my mother and my brothers," she answered in her own clumsy English, her father's French influence still noticeable.

He Who Rides stared hard at her, taking in her golden hair, topaz eyes, and the freckles Case had also seen beneath her suntan.

"Do not mock me!" he said, his voice harsh, unyielding. "Now, where did you learn to speak with your hands? From the Ranger you are squaw to?"

"I told you!" Moonflower felt her stomach tighten, and suddenly fear began to grip her as she watched this tall warrior shake his head.

"You lie! You are a white woman. Squaw of the dark one who has stolen Comanche's secrets, and for that you will suffer," and before Moonflower even had a chance to try to make a break for it or let out a scream, he'd grabbed her arms, pulling her to him, one arm holding her like a vise, the other covering her mouth, while he whistled softly. Another Indian who'd been hiding a short distance away in the brush emerged with four horses.

Moonflower wished she could yell, but the Indian's hand clamped even tighter, and all she could do was kick and flail, her moccasined feet and feminine strength no match against his hardened muscles. With one deft motion her captor reached down, ripped part of the ruffle from the skirt of her dress, and tied it over her mouth as a gag, then tied her wrists the same way, and hurriedly deposited her on his horse, before hefting himself up behind her. And with one last look back in the direction of the camp, where he knew the Rangers and the old man were, He Who Rides dug his stallion hard in the ribs and rode ahead, toward the other side of the small clearing they were in, pleased that he'd captured the white woman right out from under the noses of the Rangers, and smiling smugly he rode into the trees just beyond the clearing, then disappeared into the growing darkness with his companions close behind.

21

The fire was simmering down to a warm glow as Case drew his eyes from it and let his gaze wander to where Moonflower had vanished in among the trees barely a half-hour before. He'd wanted to stop her, and had even started to, then changed his mind as he remembered the hateful looks she's been giving him all day.

Now, however, he frowned. It was getting a little too dark, and she wasn't back yet. Usually when she did wander off, she always came back before shadows began to creep in among the trees. It was a precaution not only he and Brax but also her father had always insisted on.

Worried, he stood up, stretching, then glanced over at DeMosse. "I think I will see where Moonflower is," he said. "She does not usually stay on her walks so long."

DeMosse's eyes twinkled as he took in the anxious look in the younger man's face. For all Case's nonchalance, the Frenchman was certain Case felt more than just concern for the girl's welfare.

"Good," DeMosse said, trying to get into a better position, the splint on his leg as uncomfortable as all hell. "I have been worried myself, m'sieur," and seconds later he sighed, content in the knowledge that from what he had learned of the two men so far, both Brax and Case were men of integrity. Moonflower could do far worse than to let this young man care for her.

Case had watched the direction Moonflower took, and now, as he moved along through the trees, he had to agree the land was inviting. Birds sang, a rabbit scurried, trying to reach its burrow before dark, and the scent of trees and earth was strong, without the smell from the smoldering campfire to spoil it.

Suddenly he stopped. He was in a small clearing, at least three, maybe four hundred feet from camp, and still no sign of her. He stood quietly for a long time listening, but all he could hear were the birds and the occasional rustle of some small animal nearby.

He was just about to call her name when his gaze moved from beyond the clearing to where the trees were thick, some having lost their leaves, others still stubbornly keeping theirs, and he caught sight of the ground just ahead of him, where the grass had been trampled. Hurrying forward, he knelt down and picked up a small thread of material. It was bright blue silk, barely a few strands, yet at the sight of it his heart constricted in terror.

Still holding the small bit of silk, he stood up, and this time studied the ground behind him and in front of him, then swore softly to himself as he headed back toward camp.

Brax and the old man were having a laugh over one of the old man's stories when they heard Case shout.

Brax stood up, frowning. "What the hell's the matter?" he yelled.

"They have Moonflower," Case called back as he cleared the woods and hurried to the campfire, then began gathering up his things from where he'd been sitting earlier.

It was Brax's turn to pull first guard duty, so Case had spread his bedroll out near the fire. He rolled it up.

"You're not going after her?" Brax asked.

"I'm not?"

"Hey, look, it's getting dark out. How far do you think you'll get once the light's gone altogether?"

"Further than I will if I stay here."

DeMosse was staring at both of them, his eyes troubled. "But why would the Comanche take her, m'sieurs? She is a Cherokee. All she has to do is tell them."

Case was checking to make sure his gun was loaded. He was wearing one identical to the five-shot repeater

Brax wore, one he'd sent all the way back east for last year. He dropped it into his holster.

"Your daughter may be Cherokee, Señor Gervaise," he said as he looked around to make sure he hadn't forgotten anything. "And she may act Cherokee, and she may talk Cherokee, and even know sign language, but as far as the Comanche are concerned, they will take one look at her and say, 'white woman.' And I don't think I have to tell you what they do to white women."

DeMosse's jaw tightened, his mouth working nervously, and he looked at Braxton.

"If my leg were not broken, I could follow them, m'sieurs, even in the dark," he said. "But as it is . . ." He looked down at the splints, then back up to Braxton's face. "Please . . . m'sieur."

"You're right," Brax said, realizing what the old man was getting at. "But first we'll have to find the makings," and he began searching the landscape with his eyes.

Case too knew what the old man meant, and within a few minutes he'd managed to locate a small scrub pine tree not far from camp, and while darkness began to obscure everything around them, he and Brax set to work, using the pine tar and some clothes from the bundles on the back of the pack mule, ripping them to smear with the tar, to make torches to take with them.

"You're sure you'll be all right here alone?" Braxton asked DeMosse when they were finally ready to leave.

DeMosse nodded as he patted the rifle beside him. "I will be fine, m'sieurs. All I ask is that you bring her back," and a few minutes later there were tears in his eyes as he watched the two Rangers move out of camp, leading their horses, heading for the clearing where they could pick up the tracks of the Indians' unshod horses, and he sighed, looking at the food they'd left for him. It was close at hand, as was the wood for the fire, only he hoped they'd be back before he had to use it.

Braxton and Case had been moving steadily through the darkness, and it wasn't until they came up over the top of a small ridge and gazed down into the valley below that they realized they'd been traveling faster than they'd expected to. But it had rained some a few days before, and the ground was still damp, leaving an easy trail to follow, even though they knew the Comanche were trying to cover it.

Now, up ahead and below them, about a mile in the distance, they could see the flickering light from a campfire. They were sure now that not only had the Comanche stopped, but were so confident they weren't being followed that they'd even made camp for the night.

Both men doused their torches quickly, then climbed into their saddles, the first time since leaving camp, while up ahead Moonflower sat a few feet from a cottonwood tree and watched the Indian who had captured her drop down to the ground next to her in front of the fire.

"Tell me, white squaw," he said as he looked over at her. "You say you are Cherokee. Then how you know white man's tongue?"

"You know it too," she answered.

He Who Rides' hand snaked out like a whip, hitting Moonflower's jaw, and she grimaced from the pain.

He had removed the gag from her mouth when they'd eaten, and she was sure he felt safe enough now that he wouldn't have to bother putting it back on again. But he had tied her hands and feet with leather thongs now, and was carrying the pieces of her dress tied to his coup belt, where a number of dried scalps hung.

Moonflower spit blood from her mouth and tried to sit up straighter, having been knocked sideways from the blow, and she suddenly thought back guiltily to the way her brothers had treated many of their captives over the years. Was it any wonder the white man feared them.

She had already told him her father was a French trapper, and he'd called her a liar. And her statement about her mother having been killed by the Texans when they drove the Cherokee from their homes when she was a little girl also brought the same accusation.

She stared at the Comanche now, realizing Case had been right. While the Cherokee was trying to learn to live alongside the white man now, the Comanche still wanted no part of him. And this Comanche who had stolen her away was convinced she was a white woman, leaving no possible way for her to talk him into believing otherwise.

He Who Rides knew the white woman was staring at him, and his expression grew insolent.

"You like what you see?" he asked.

She shuddered. "I spit on you," she retorted, and proceeded to wallow a wad of spit in her mouth, aiming it for his face. Her aim was far from true, however, as the spit hit the ground, and He Who Rides laughed.

"If you were really Indian squaw, you would not miss."

She glared at him, only he went on.

"But since you are not Indian . . ." He looked over at his comrades, said something in Comanche she couldn't understand, and all four laughed.

Moonflower felt the heat flood her face.

"Do not worry, white woman," He Who Rides said as his gaze dropped to the low neckline on her bright silk dress. "I know what to do, even with white woman."

Moonflower's eyes narrowed as she stared at this Indian who told her his name meant He Who Rides in the white man's tongue. If her hands and feet had not been tied, she'd have followed the spit with a good swift kick, but even at that, the moccasins she wore probably would do little damage.

He Who Rides saw the anger in the white woman's eyes, and his own eyes darkened dangerously. Why was it that white women always seemed to have such an effect on him? Why was he always aroused so much easier by the sight of a pale face and light hair, so different from the maidens back in the village? Was it because he too had once been a white man?

He remembered nothing of the life he had led before joining the Comanche. Yet how often his Indian mother had spoken of the day he rode in to join them, with his leg mangled beyond the medicine man's repair.

Was that why he was now feeling these strange uncontrollable yearnings for this white woman? He moved closer to her, and reached out, touching the long braid that hung over her right shoulder to just above her bosom. Sometimes his own hair had the sun in it too, unlike the dark shiny hair of his Comanche brothers.

Moonflower continued to stare at this strange Indian, who, she knew by the color of his eyes and hair, was not truly an Indian, only raised as one. Yet he was far more Indian than she. Her eyes watched the look on his face, while his fingers fondled her hair, then she stiffened as his hand dropped from her amber braid, to cover her breast, and as his fingers cupped it, she heard the Comanche's quick intake of breath.

She tensed, waiting expectantly, wondering what was going to happen next. She didn't have long to wait. With one deft motion his fingers caught the top of the dress, and she closed her eyes, listening to it rip, the cool night air hitting her bare breasts.

Never having worn a white woman's dress before, Moonflower hadn't known to put a chemise on underneath, and the only reason she knew to wear a petticoat was that her father had told her. The petticoat did little to help her now, however, as He Who Rides shoved her back down to the ground, then leaned over her, looking down into her face.

Moonflower's eyes were open now, and with her wrists tied in front of her, she laid them across her chest, trying to hide herself from his eyes. With one quick motion he grabbed the rawhide thongs that held her wrists tight and lifted her arms above her head, pinning them to the ground, his hand so large and sinewy it covered both her wrists.

A scream started to well up inside Moonflower, but she held it in check, remembering that Indian maidens didn't scream and carry on like white women. She would show him. But in spite of the courage she tried to talk herself into having, she was terrified. Many times over the years she had seen white women her brothers had brought back to camp after a raid. Many were out of their minds completely, others did nothing except whimper and cower, their bodies bloody and bruised. As a child she had often wondered why. Then, as she grew up, she had learned why, and yet she had never tried to stop them. Why? Because she felt the women deserved it by being born white? No woman deserved this, and she clenched her teeth as she stared up at He Who Rides, who was already lowering his head to her breasts, his teeth gnashing expectantly, while his free hand began searching beneath her skirt.

Suddenly a shot rang out, and He Who Rides' face contorted with pain as he flinched, and Moonflower realized he was hit. In quick succession two more shots were heard, but by now He Who Rides was on the ground beside her, the fire at his back, her body his shield.

She knew he had been hit, but had no idea where, because it was hard to see with the flickering firelight behind him.

The other Indians were shouting and grunting orders to each other. At least two of them were. The third one was lying facedown in the grass to the right of the fire, and wasn't moving at all. Moonflower hoped he was dead.

Only she had no idea who might be shooting. He Who Rides had covered his trail, so he thought, once they'd left the camp behind, so she knew it couldn't be Kolter and Dante. At least she didn't think it could be.

However, at that very moment Case was less than thirty feet from her, his body pressed hard against the ground. He and Brax had left their horses a few hundred feet back and come in on foot. They'd been planning to try to lure the Comanche away from the fire one at a time, but when Case saw what was happening to Moonflower, he reacted quickly. Now he saw Moonflower react just as quickly.

Realizing He Who Rides was using her as a shield, but also realizing he no longer had her pinned to the ground, Moonflower pushed with her feet, turning sideways in the grass, and began to roll away from the fire and the Comanche as quickly as she could.

He Who Rides shouted something, but it was lost to Moonflower in her flurry to get as far from him as she could. Grabbing for her, he missed by inches, and furious now, he raised up slightly, blood beginning to seep onto the left sleeve of his buckskin shirt as he tried to scramble forward to stop her. But Moonflower was agile in spite of being trussed up, and within minutes she had rolled to the dark shadows beyond the firelight, leaving the Comanche behind.

Small sticks, stones, and gravel had scraped her skin where the dress had been ripped from her, but Moonflower didn't even care. All she wanted now was for whoever was shooting to be a friend rather than foe.

Suddenly she felt the rough bark of a tree against her arm, and knew she'd rolled as far as she could. Looking back toward the fire, she froze and lay motionless, watching transfixed as she saw He Who Rides, crouched and still coming after her.

Another shot rang out, and He Who Rides dropped to the ground again. The shot was followed by two more, and one of the other Indians grabbed his head, spun around, and fell in a heap.

There were only two left, including He Who Rides. But who was doing the shooting? It was impossible to tell exactly where the shots were coming from, but it sounded like one of the snipers wasn't far from where Moonflower lay, the other off to her right a few yards, so that the Comanche were in a sort of cross fire.

He Who Rides lifted his head one more time, to show he wasn't hurt, and now Moonflower saw in the flickering firelight the silhouette of a knife in his hand. The blood on the sleeve of his shirt was evidently from a superficial wound, because it seemed to have no effect on his prowess whatsoever as he dove for safety behind a half-rotted log at the edge of the small clearing they were in.

For a moment the whole place was silent, not a bird, not a cricket, nothing interrupting the darkness, and she held her breath. Then, as if torn reluctantly from his lips, He Who Rides broke the silence.

"So, He Who Steals Horses from the Comanche, you have found me," he shouted to Case. "But it will do you no good. The white man cannot see in the dark like the Comanche, and his rifle, once having spoken, is slow before it speaks again, while my blade is swift and silent. So tonight you will die!"

Case took a bead on the log where He Who Rides was hiding, then changed his mind. He wanted to make every shot count, and since he couldn't see the Comanche warrior, to shoot now would accomplish nothing. Case's gaze moved to the general direction where he'd seen Moonflower roll along the ground. She was at least fifteen feet from the log where He Who Rides was hiding. He could vaguely see the dark outline of her body where she lay against a tree.

He Who Rides' only surviving companion had disappeared at the other side of the camp beyond the fire, so Case figured he'd let Brax take care of him. Case's main objective now was to get to Moonflower before He Who Rides.

Quickly sizing up the situation, he kept as low to the ground as he could, and moved from the cover he was hiding behind. He knew He Who Rides would probably catch his movements, even in the dark, but he also knew He Who Rides had undoubtedly left the rifle he usually used back by the campfire, or he'd have fired it long ago. And that went for the Indian's bow and quiver of arrows too. Case knew that all the Comanche had with him behind the log was his knife, and He Who Rides wasn't about to throw that. If the Indian used the knife, it'd be up close, hand to hand, and Case felt secure in that knowledge as he made his way as silently as he could through the darkness, moving from tree to bush, edging closer and closer to Moonflower.

He Who Rides stuck his head up once more above the log and looked like he was ready to come after Case, forcing Case to fire another shot. Then, as soon as the shot splattered into the log, He Who Rides started to leave the log again. Once more Case pulled the trigger. This time He Who Rides dove back to the cover of the log, cursing softly to himself, while Case hesitated for a second, his eyes on the log, hoping the Comanche wouldn't come at him again, because if he did and Case missed in the darkness, he'd have no time to reload his revolver, and he had only one bullet left in the chamber now.

Instinctively realizing the second bullet coming so fast after the first had shocked the Comanche warrior, Case moved forward again, more swiftly this time, toward the tree where Moonflower lay.

Moonflower could hear the soft rustling, and knew it had to be either Braxton or Case, because the Rangers had shown her the magic guns they had that could shoot five times without stopping to reload, and the last two shots fired at He Who Rides had been fired too quickly not to have come from one of their guns.

Her heart was pounding wildly. Then she heard his voice, barely a whisper. It was Case, and he had managed to reach her.

Case holstered his gun and drew his knife from its sheath as he hugged the ground near Moonflower.

"Shhh . . . hold your hands up, I will cut them free," he said.

Tears were in her eyes as she held her hands over her head to where she knew he was, then felt his hand holding her wrists while his knife cut the leather. As soon as her hands were free, Moonflower began to sit up to untie her feet.

"No," Case cautioned, sensing what she was going to do. "Keep down. The other Comanche is not in sight. He could have reached his rifle or bow. Stay flat, I will go around the tree to cut them."

She did as he said, relaxing back against the ground again, and once more heard the faint rustling, and a few twigs snap, as Case made his way around the tree so he could reach her ankles.

Just as he got to the other side of the tree, he hesitated, a spark of fear bristling the hairs on his neck, as he heard a garbled scream off to his right, where he knew Brax was. However, seconds later he relaxed again as the last of He Who Rides' companions came staggering out of the darkness and fell sprawling on the ground, just missing the fire. That meant He Who Rides was alone. A fact that at any other time would have brought taunts from Case, only right now his first concern was Moonflower.

Keeping as close to the ground as he could, Case reached out, grabbed her ankles, and started slicing away at the leather rope that held them. Just as the last one fell away and Moonflower realized she was free, she looked off toward the log where He Who Rides was hiding, only he wasn't behind it anymore. Incensed by the death of his last comrade, He Who Rides had taken advantage of the fact that Case had holstered his gun, and the Indian had moved out from behind the log. At first he'd hugged the ground like a snake, ignoring the flesh wound in his left arm, but now, only some two to three feet from the white woman and the Ranger, he was crouching, ready to pounce on Case.

"No!" Moonflower yelled, warning Case, and Case looked up just in time to see the Comanche lunge at him.

Unable to reach his gun, but with the knife still in his hand, Case met the lunge with as much strength as he could, and both men rolled back against the tree so that Moonflower had to scramble to get out of the way.

It was too dark to see what was happening as the men bounced off the tree and disappeared into the shadows behind it. All she could hear was an occasional grunt, heavy breathing, underbrush being crushed, and now and then a garbled curse from one of the men as they rolled even farther away, ending up deeper in the underbrush. Then suddenly it was over, and everything grew quiet, except now Moonflower could hear one man breathing, but who?

She'd been crouching near some bushes, out of the way, praying to the God her father had taught her about, and she held her breath waiting. The lonely call of a nighthawk suddenly filled the air, and for a moment Moonflower wasn't sure what to do. Then the call was answered by another across the camp, and as she waited, still holding her breath, she saw Case move out from the underbrush behind the tree and stand for a minute leaning against it, the dim light from the small campfire casting faint shadows across his face.

"Moonflower?" he called softly, then raised a hand, wiping some blood from his mouth, where He Who Rides had caught him a hard one.

She let out her breath and slipped from the shadows of the bush, stumbling some as she made her way to him, and by the time Braxton emerged from the other side of the Indians' camp to check, making sure all three of He Who Rides' companions were dead, Case was holding Moonflower gently in his arms, stroking her hair as if she were the most precious thing in the world.

"He's dead?" Brax asked as he walked over to his cousin, ignoring the intimate moment Case was sharing with the woman Brax figured had stolen his heart.

Case nodded. "Only, for a minute I thought it would be me." He sighed as Moonflower untangled herself from his arms; then suddenly she realized her breasts were still bare.

"Mon Dieu!" she cried helplessly, her father's French coming to her as naturally as Case's Spanish often came to him. "What shall I do?"

Her arms covered her chest while Brax turned on his heel, went back toward the campfire, and grabbed a blanket from off the ground where one of the Indians had been lying, then on the way back he slit a hole in it with his knife. On reaching her again, he lifted the blanket, pulled it down over her head, and let it fall like a Mexican poncho.

"That should do till we get back to camp."

"But there is dirt," she complained, feeling the coarseness of it, and frowning at the smell. "And it has bugs!"

"You would rather go without?" Case asked.

She turned, looking up into his strong face. "No."

"I thought not." Case looked beyond Moonflower to where his cousin stood. "You want to just leave them here?"

Brax looked back at the bodies near the campfire, then walked past Moonflower and Case into the underbrush where He Who Rides lay, his body sprawled on its back, eyes open, staring at nothing.

"Strange, but I almost hate to see him gone," Brax

said as he reached down and shut the dead Indian's eyes. "It seemed like, if there wasn't ever anybody else to go after, there was always He Who Rides." Brax stared at the body thoughtfully. "I can remember when Aunt Heather and Uncle Cole thought he was you." He straightened, wondering who He Who Rides had come into the world as, and wondering if he would have been as savage if he'd remained with the white man. Because he was cruel, extremely cruel, and more than one tale had been reported about his tortures of the white man. Well, no one would ever know now, and it looked like his grave would be just as anonymous, because they sure as hell weren't going to have time to give the Comanche any kind of burial. "We'll leave them here," Brax finally said as he turned and joined Case and Moonflower again. "If his people don't find him, the scavengers will."

Moonflower shuddered at the thought at first, then remembered back to the look on the Comanche's face when he'd bent over her gnashing his teeth, and the sympathy for him quickly faded. She had seen mutilated women after her brothers had gotten through with them, their breasts disfigured and scarred with teeth marks, and knew what the warrior called He Who Rides had planned for her.

"Come on, let's get their horses," Brax said. "I noticed one was shod, no doubt stolen in a raid," and he headed back toward the campfire, having spotted the horses tethered close by.

Within minutes they were mounted and riding away, Brax and Case on Hickory and Compadre, while Moonflower rode beside Case on He Who Rides' big black stallion, since he wouldn't be needing it anymore, while back in the small clearing, not far from the cold ashes of the fire Brax had put out, the night scavengers were already sniffing at the lifeless bodies of He Who Rides and his companions.

Moonflower was back in her buckskin shirt and leggings again, but without the beaded band on her head this time. Case had told her they were only a few miles from his home, the Crown D, and she was nervous. Never had she been to the home of the white man before. Her life had been tepees, lodge huts, an occasional one-room cabin, and the open sky, but both Braxton and Case had assured her, as had her father, that she was sure to like it.

According to Case, they'd be stopping by his parents' ranch, since it was further north than where Braxton's family lived. Unknown to both DeMosse and his daughter, however, Case and Braxton had purposely decided on a trail that would lead them away from the line shack and corrals where Case's father broke his horses, and they did it mostly because of the men. Most of Case's father's hired hands were friendly enough, but there were always new ones to contend with, and they felt it was better not to have to worry about explaining the old man and Moonflower's presence to them.

Moonflower glanced over at Case as they rode along, trying to sort out her feelings for this man who claimed to be Texan, talked like a Mexican, yet belonged to the Rangers. Ever since the night he'd rescued her, he had seemed to act so differently toward her.

He had always been attentive before, even though she'd spurned his help more times than accepted it, and there was even that night when he'd kissed her. But now, ever since they had returned to camp after her rescue, he'd been acting almost as if she didn't even exist. Talking to her as little as possible, as well as being curt and unfriendly when he did finally say something.

Yet, ever since that night, she had tried so hard to make up to him for her earlier treatment of him. It didn't seem to be doing any good, however. And she wanted it to, too, because she'd started to admit to herself that she'd been wrong. That being a Ranger didn't make him a horrible person. That he was as human as she was, something she could no longer deny.

Maybe it was the white man's blood coming out in her, she thought as she rode along. Who knew. But whatever it was, that part of her wished he would once again be with her as he had been those first few days.

Case felt Moonflower's eyes on him, only he continued to ignore them, as he'd been doing ever since the night before last, when they'd rescued her. It wasn't that he wanted to, really. In reality, he wanted to take her and protect her . . . and yes, love her. Because he knew now just how much he did love her. He hadn't at first. Those first weeks, he'd been entranced by her lovely eyes and warm smile, yes, and had wanted to get to know her better, but it wasn't until he'd seen He Who Rides preparing to ravish her that the full impact of his feelings for her had hit him, and he'd realized just how much he cared. And when he'd held her in his arms afterward, hoping to comfort her, he'd known for sure that his feelings were even deeper than what he'd imagined.

That's why, when she'd acted so grateful, and suddenly began treating him as if he were a man rather than a vicious dog, he'd turned from her. He didn't want her gratefulness or appreciation for what he'd done. He wanted her love. It was as simple as that. And until the day when she could forget what he'd done for her and accept him for himself, and not his deed, he wanted no part of her.

Brax, riding beside Case, glanced over at his cousin, then looked over at Moonflower, and back to Case again. Fools! he thought silently to himself. Stubborn, ornery fools, and he shook his head, slowing his horse to see if DeMosse was sleeping or awake on the travois. DeMosse's eyes were open as he watched the trail behind him.

"Well, we're almost to the Crown D," Brax said, seeing the sparkle in the old man's eyes. "And the next stop is the Double K."

DeMosse nodded, rubbing a hand across his bewhiskered chin, the white beard coarse and bristly. "Good." He laughed, a low throaty chuckle. "You know, it's going to be so much fun, bon ami, to see the look on Loedicia's face when she discovers who I am." He sighed. "You did say she is widowed, oui?"

"Yeah, she's widowed." Brax answered, then studied the old man for a minute before smiling smugly and easing his horse forward again to ride beside Case once more. Damn! he thought to himself as they reined onto the worn trail that started down the back hill toward the corrals and the house at the Crown D, that old codger's still sweet on Grandma, and he too could hardly wait now until they reached the Double K to see what Grandma Dicia was going to do, while up ahead at the Crown D, Grandma Dicia, Lizette, and Heather were sitting in the parlor drinking tea and discussing the latest news Luther had brought from town the day before.

"Well, I don't care if General Taylor is calling men together to march toward the Rio Grande," Lizette said as she blew across the top of her cup, cooling her tea. "I told Bain he's fought enough. His leg still bothers him all the time and there're days he can hardly walk from the pain. I told him last night that if there's any fighting to be done, he can just let the young men do it."

Heather's violet eyes studied her sister-in-law closely as Lizette continued to find reasons why neither Bain nor Cole should go to war again. Lizette had aged so well. Maybe it was because she carried some extra pounds, and they filled out the wrinkles. Whatever it was, with her dark hair, only lightly peppered here and there with gray, she looked far younger than her almost forty-seven years, and next to her Heather felt so old. Just think, she'd be fifty in September. It hardly seemed possible. Yet, when she looked in the mirror, there was no way she couldn't see it—the crow's-feet, gray streaks in her once fiery hair.

She drew her eyes from Lizette and let her gaze rest on Grandma Dicia. Now there was a woman who didn't show her age, she thought as she listened to her grandmother take up where Lizette left off, warning them that there was no way they could avoid the fighting, then lapsing into some long-ago story about one of the past wars. A story they'd all heard half a dozen times before.

Grandma Dicia rarely wore her hair pulled back severely like most women her age, and it curled now, like a soft silver cloud about her face, making her eyes deepen to the color of wild violets. And her cheeks, not pale like so many elderly women's, wore a natural tint of pink, giving a translucent texture to her skin that even the suntan on her face couldn't hide. Far from being fragile, at ninety-one she was exceptionally strong and competent, and as she often complained, if it weren't for the arthritis in her joints, she'd join the fighting herself.

"Remember, I've shot many a rifle," she said as she ended her discourse on the new political events. "And I'd rather look down a gun sight than down its barrel."

"Don't worry, it won't come to a war, I'm sure," Heather said, joining in the conversation. Then she turned abruptly as Bessie came in. "Yes, Bessie."

"Beg pardon, Miss Heather," Bessie said as she wiped her hands on her apron and nodded toward the back of the house. "But there's horses coming down the back trail. I thought maybe you might want to call Mose."

Heather tensed. It was too early for Cole and the men. "They're not Indians?" she asked.

Bessie shrugged. "Ain't close enough yet to see for sure."

"You go get Mose," Lizette told Heather. "I'll go take a look," and both women hurried from the room, following Bessie.

"Well," Loedicia said softly to herself. "Think I'm too old, do they?" and she set her teacup down, stood up, straightening the full skirt of her rose-colored dress so her petticoats wouldn't show, and followed her granddaughters from the room.

Heather had recognized Case and Braxton before she'd even started to head for the barn to find Mose, and now she stood waiting, with Lizette beside her and Grandma Dicia a few feet behind them on the porch.

"It's about time," Loedicia said as she watched her two great-grandsons riding toward them, then her gaze moved to the rider at Case's right, and she frowned. "Wonder who the Indian woman is," she mused.

Lizette glanced back at her grandmother. "Maybe she's not Indian."

"In those clothes?" Loedicia squinted, trying to see better. "Looks like she's hauling somebody too. Wonder what those two young men have gone and gotten themselves into now," and she shook her head as she moved to the steps, making her way halfway down them, her eyes still on the rider beside Case.

Moonflower had been nervous from the moment she spotted the women standing waiting. She wanted to rein her mount up and fall back, but to do so would show cowardice, so instead she continued to ride next to Case.

"Hey, you're in luck, old man," Brax said, his gray eyes twinkling as he stared up ahead while calling back over his shoulder to DeMosse. "You won't have to wait till we get to the Double K. If I'm not mistaken, and I don't think I am, it looks like Ma and Grandma Dicia must have come calling on Aunt Heather, 'cause that sure as hell looks like Grandma Dicia standing on the back-porch steps now."

DeMosse felt his insides curl into a ball, and he reached up, wishing now he'd had time to check his beard to see if it needed any trimming first. Let's see, how long had it been since he'd seen her? Over fifty years? Brax and Case said she had white hair now. It had been so dark and curly once. He closed his eyes, trying to conjure up a picture of her, then smiled. Even after all these years he could still remember, and he straightened, then settled back again on the travois, his hands fidgeting nervously, and he bit his lip anxiously while the travois continued bumping along the dusty lane, past two corrals on one side, and a bunkhouse on the other, then jostled him around a few minutes longer before suddenly coming to a stop.

Oh how he wished he hadn't broken his damn leg and could be on his horse facing them, he thought, because he couldn't see any thing. All he could hear was laughing and people greeting one another. He heard them introduce Moonflower amid all the talking, then realized Braxton's voice was louder than the other's.

"Now, take my arm, Grandma," Brax was saying. "And when I tell you to, close your eyes."

DeMosse heard a woman's light laughter, but couldn't hear the response, if there was any. All he could do was lie there and wait.

Loedicia felt ridiculous holding Braxton's arm. He was acting as if she were senile or something.

"Okay, close your eyes," he said.

She glanced up at him, then shut her eyes and let him lead her to the back of the horse, to where he said he had a surprise for her.

"I suppose it's a bundle of pelts for that fur coat you've been promising me every year since you were twelve," she said when they reached the travois. "Or a stray dog you've rescued along with the girl."

"Hardly," Brax retorted, then suddenly stopped. "Okay, Grandma, you can open your eyes now."

Loedicia let go of his arm, straightened, then opened her eyes and stood staring at the sight of a bearded stranger lying propped up on the travois, tears glistening at the corners of his eyes as he stared back at her.

"This is my surprise?" she said, frowning.

DeMosse's eyes were intent on her face. "Hello, Loedicia."

Loedicia continued to stare. The man knew her? She squinted a little. He did look vaguely familiar, in a way. The soft brown eyes . . . "You know me?" she asked.

He smiled. "Mon Dieu, do I know you? I have loved you for over half a century, ma chérie," he answered, his voice still strong and vibrant for his age. "And if you would let me, I would love you half a century more."

Suddenly Loedicia's eyes widened in disbelief, and a hand moved to her breast to still her heart. It couldn't be, and yet . . . the slight French accent, and those brown eyes. She gasped, then found her voice.

"DeMosse?"

"Aha, see, she does remember," he said as he looked over at Brax. "Did I not tell you, m'sieur? Loedicia Locke is a woman who would never forget a man who loves her."

Loedicia could feel the heat in her face, and knew she was blushing. Something she hadn't done for years. "It's really you?" she asked again, unable to grasp the truth.

DeMosse chuckled. "The hair has lost its color, but

oui, it's me," he answered. "DeMosse Gervaise, in the flesh."

Loedicia shook her head as she stared at this apparition from out of her past.

"You do not believe me? Then ask me what happened to us after I rescued you from Quinn's cousin and we hid ourselves under the grape arbor, ma chérie," he said, and his eyes were crinkling with amusement as he saw the flush on her face deepen even more. "Ah, oui, see, she remembers only too well," he said, glancing over at Braxton again. Then he looked back at Loedicia, the laughter leaving his eyes, and they grew serious. "But here, it has been a long time, ma petite amie. I do not mean to hurt you with the reminders, only to let you know that it is really, truly me."

Loedicia was still astounded. Of all the people in the world, she thought he'd have been dead years ago. DeMosse Gervaise, rascal and wastrel. Illegitimate son of a marquess, and yet he'd outlived so many. How old was he now? Close to a hundred, she'd wager, because he'd been older than she was.

Loedicia smiled at the irony of it. "I still don't believe it," she said as she reached up, brushing a stray curl back from her forehead, and DeMosse was amazed. Except for the gray hair and a few wrinkles on her face, she was still the same lovely woman he'd fallen in love with so many years ago.

Suddenly he felt so dirty and unkempt. "Sorry I didn't have time to clean up, ma chérie, but with the broken leg . . ." He shrugged. "I was planning to do it here, so I would be presentable to you when I arrived at the ranch your great-grandson calls the Double K."

"You were going to the Double K?"

"Oui." DeMosse looked pleased with himself. "Braxton has invited my daughter and myself as houseguests, while my leg heals."

"Oh?" Loedicia looked at Braxton, who seemed to be enjoying watching the exchange between the two immensely. "You invited him?" she asked.

"Why not?"

"Why not?" She looked back at DeMosse.

"After all, Grandma," Braxton went on, "we have plenty of room now, with Blythe gone. And he can even use her special chair until his leg heals."

Oh, lovely, Loedicia thought as she stared at DeMosse Gervaise, then suddenly she laughed, as she saw the impish gleam in DeMosse's eyes that he'd never lost over the years. DeMosse hadn't changed a bit. Not at all. He was still just as much of a rogue as he'd been those long years ago, and she glanced back to where the others stood, her gaze resting on the amber-haired girl in the buckskins.

"She's really your daughter?" she asked.

DeMosse smiled. "Oui." His eyes crinkled again. "Does that surprise you, ma chérie?"

"Surprise me? Nonsense." Loedicia looked at DeMosse, then back to the young woman they'd introduced to her as Moonflower. "Nothing you've done has ever surprised me, DeMosse Gervaise," and she looked back again to the bewhiskered trapper strapped to the travois. "Now, since we were almost ready to have Luther drive us back to the Double K, why don't you join my granddaughter and me in our carriage, instead of making the trip on that uncomfortable contraption, and we can catch each other up on the past fifty years on the way home, how's that?"

"That, my dear Loedicia, is the best suggestion I've heard in a long time," and so while Braxton and Case helped DeMosse from the travois and into the big black carriage parked near the barn, Loedicia invited Moonflower to join them too.

Moonflower was reluctant at first, having been overwhelmed by the white women in their fancy clothes, as well as the size of the house, outbuildings, and just everything that was so different from the life she'd always known. Yet, riding the rest of the way over the trail through the woods alone with Braxton, since Case would be staying at the Crown D, wasn't a happy thought either. So since her father had consented to join the women in the carriage, she gave in grudgingly, and within a few minutes, after Loedicia and Lizette had retrieved their hats and handbags from the house, they all said their good-byes and Luther maneuvered the carriage down the front drive, while Braxton waved to them and took off on the trail that led behind the barn, leading DeMosse's and Moonflower's horses, minus the travois, but with the pack mule in tow, hoping to beat them to the Double K.

22

It had been a little over a week since the arrival of DeMosse Gervaise and his daughter, Moonflower, at the Double K. He Who Rides was no longer a threat on the frontier anymore—a fact that Heather and Cole thought ironic, since he'd been killed by the son they once thought He Who Rides to be. Spring was in the air with all its wildflowers, the leaves were budding green, and the nights, cool before, were now as warm as the days.

Braxton had been glad to get home, if for no other reason than to catch up on all the latest news, which took no time at all.

Blythe was now Señora de Córdoba, and although Mario still kept his villa in town, using it as an infirmary, he had helped Blythe take over the running of the lands left to her by her husband, and was well-settled at the hacienda now, along with a number of orphaned children the two had fallen in love with and brought home to stay. There were five of them, and they ranged in ages from three-year-old Miguel, with his round dark eyes and coal-black hair, to ten-year-old freckle-faced Charity, whose hair was as red as Aunt Heather's and whose parents had died of cholera at Mario's infirmary the year before.

They were quite a brood for a crippled woman to mother, so Blythe and Mario had to hire help for Rosita, who claimed she couldn't take care of Blythe and the children too.

During a long afternoon visit with his sister, Braxton had also learned that no one had heard a word from Catalina since she'd ridden away from the hacienda shortly after Antonio's death. The news had bothered him. Especially now, since Texas was part of the United States, and relations with Mexico seemed to be going downhill faster every day. He'd been hoping by now she'd have come to her senses and decided to come back. The fact that she hadn't hurt more than he liked to admit.

Brax had also learned that his sister Genée's husband, Cousin Seth, had been given a post in the new state government and was now accompanying the newly elected Senator Sam Houston to Washington, D.C., as a member of his staff, and although Genée was expecting a child in only a few months, she'd sent a message home that she was going with him. That had been some weeks back, and Brax imagined by now she was probably up in the capital getting ready to go to all the balls and soirees she'd heard her mother talk about so often. Her only problem, however, was that she was going to have to wait till her confinement was over. And knowing Genée, he wondered how on earth she was ever going to stand it.

In fact, it seemed as if babies were on the agenda everywhere lately. At least in this part of Texas. Even the Dante household wasn't immune, and he learned that Teffin and Kaelen had made Cole and Heather grandparents again, with the birth of a son, now almost two months old. His name was Jacob, only nobody ever called him Jacob. He was becoming known in all the family circles as Little Jake, and Braxton was sure he'd grow up a fighter with a nickname like that.

All in all, it looked like the family had really been busy this time while he and Case were away.

Even Pretty and Luther's boys had grown up. Dexter was one of Pa's hands now, both roping and steering, but Corbin stayed closer to the ranch yard, helping his father more, since Luther wasn't as young as he used to be. The years were slipping by fast.

"Christ, you know I'm almost thirty," Brax said one afternoon some two weeks after their arrival home, while he and Case rode Hickory and Compadre toward San Antonio. "And what the hell do I have to show for it? A horse."

"What do you want, cousin?" Case asked.

"Hell, I don't know. But there ought to be something more to life than a horse, a gun, buckskins, and a pair of boots."

"You mean like a wife?"

"Don't be funny."

"Who's being funny, amigo?" Case leaned over, patting Compadre's neck, his fingers smoothing the big horse's mane. "But a man who gets restless usually gets that way when he needs a good woman."

"I didn't say I was restless."

"You didn't have to."

"Well, I'm not." Brax took off his hat and wiped his brow, then rode along for a while with his hat off, letting the air get to his scalp and filter through his pale hair. "Just because you're starting to get flustered. Hell, why don't you just tell Moonflower how you feel about her?"

"I do not know what you are talking about."

Brax grinned. "Oh no? Then why you been coming over to the house every day? It sure as hell isn't to see me."

Case felt his face heat up. "So I wouldn't have to go hunt for horses with my father, that's why."

"Bullshit. You love running the horses."

Case straightened, then glanced over at Braxton. He never could keep anything from Brax, dammit. They'd been too close for too many years now.

"All right, so I think she's that something extra besides a gun, a horse, and boots, like you said before."

"Then why the hell don't you ask her to marry you?"

"Because the señorita doesn't want a husband. Especially me."

"What makes you think so?"

"Common sense."

"You sure don't know women, do you?"

Case straightened in the saddle, then glanced over again at Braxton. "If she is so mad for me, then why did she only start treating me as a person after I saved her from He Who Rides?"

"Because it gave her an excuse, that's why. That night

back in camp when you kissed her, did she slap your face?"

"You know I kissed her?"

"I'm not blind, you know." Brax laid the reins on Hickory's neck, maneuvering him around a deep rut in the road. "But you didn't answer—did she slap you?"

"No."

"So why don't you try it again tonight?"

"You're crazy."

"I dare you."

"Dare me?"

"Why not? I been watching the two of you the last few nights you've been over at the house. Hell, Case, she's as edgy as you are, and it sure isn't because I'm there. All you have to do is walk in the door, and she looks like she wants to die."

"Now you are being ridiculous."

They were getting closer to town, and passed a couple in a carriage. Strangers they'd never seen before.

"Wonder where they're heading," Brax mused.

Case turned in the saddle, glaring back. "Your father told me someone bought the old Sherwood place."

"Hmm, could be." Brax brought the conversation back to Moonflower. "But as I was saying, come over tonight and see if you can get Moonflower to take a walk with you. I guarantee you the lady's just waiting."

Case was sure Brax was seeing things that weren't there, but before reaching town, he'd promised his cousin that tonight, come hell or high water, he was going to give the situation his best try, and he was even going to shed his buckskins for calzoneras and a chaqueta to look more presentable.

"And if she calls me a stinking bloodthirsty Ranger one more time, just one," he said as they rode into San Antonio, heading toward the Ranger office there, "I'm going to make her eat her words, amigo," and Brax smiled inwardly, sad in a way, because he knew that by bringing together Case and Moonflower, he'd no doubt be losing a partner as well as the closest friend he'd ever had. But he was also pleased Case was going to be able to experience something he felt he'd never have in his own life.

That evening, as usual, Case arrived at the Double K shortly after the family had left the dinner table, only tonight it seemed as if they all had something to do that kept them in the house. All except Moonflower, Grandma Dicia, and DeMosse, who was still using Blythe's old chair and trying to encourage Luther to get one of those patents on it he'd heard men talk about.

Since arriving at the Double K, Lizette and Grandma Dicia had managed to talk Moonflower into wearing a dress again. The first ones she had worn were old ones that had once belonged to Blythe and Genée. Tonight she was dressed in a new dress Pretty had helped her make. DeMosse had given Braxton some pelts to trade in town, then had him buy a bolt of material, and the dress they'd made was striking with Moonflower's lovely amber hair. It was a bright blue-green watered silk. Rather fancy for ranch life, but DeMosse loved it on her, even though she did still insist on wearing the long thick braid with it, instead of leaving her hair loose.

She'd been sitting in a wicker chair at the far end of the porch, listening to her father and the old woman he was always calling "ma chérie" kibitz over a game of cards of some kind. In a way, his interest in this Loedicia Chapman was irritating to Moonflower. Her father had even trimmed his beard, cut his hair, and had Braxton buy some new clothes for him too. The first time in her life Moonflower had seen her father in anything other than his buckskins and furs.

"It isn't that I have never worn fancy clothes," he'd told Braxton the day he'd sent him to town for him. "Whenever I went east with the furs, I always took time to dress up a bit. At least when I was younger. Trouble is, the furs have been too scarce lately."

Brax had grinned. He had to admit one thing. For his age, DeMosse Gervaise was certainly well-preserved, and once cleaned up, the man actually showed some semblance of the good-looker he'd been when he was young.

Moonflower drew her gaze from her father and turned,

looking back over her shoulder toward the field north of the house, to where a rider was just emerging from the woods beyond. It had to be Case. The Ranger had been over almost every night since she and her father had arrived at the ranch.

She watched the beautiful lines of the big palomino as the stallion cantered across the field, then her gaze lifted to the rider, and she stared, frowning. Something was wrong.

It had to be Case, and yet the man on Compadre was wearing a black broad-brimmed hat edged with silver that matched his black clothes, which were also trimmed in silver, all the way down to the filigree buttons on the legs of his pants. Except for the gunbelt, he looked nothing like the man who had rescued her from the Comanche.

Moonflower watched him slow Compadre and walk him across the yard to the hitchrail, then Case dismounted and strolled over to the porch.

"Hola," he said, taking the steps two at a time, his long legs carrying him to the small table where Grandma Dicia and DeMosse were arguing over who should be winning the game.

Loedicia looked up. She'd been in the middle of a tirade against DeMosse, accusing him of padding his score. Now, as she stared up at her great-grandson, she suddenly stopped talking, and her eyes widened in surprise. It had been long time since she'd seen either Case or Braxton in anything except their buckskins.

"My heavens, who are you dressed up for?" she asked.

Case tried not to flush, and hoped if he did, Moonflower wouldn't notice. He had spotted her sitting in the chair while he was riding across the field.

"I guess I got homesick," he said, then looked around. "Everyone is busy?" he asked.

Loedicia reached up and grabbed his hand, squeezing it. "Bain's working on his books, your Aunt Liz is in the sewing room with Pretty, Luther and his boys are out back somewhere, and Brax got some sort of message and took off for town."

"Like I said,"—Case smiled back at Grandma Dicia—
"everybody's busy except you two, sí?"

"Who said we are not busy?" DeMosse retorted, and
he looked over at Loedicia.

"But then if Loedicia would just say yes and marry me,
we wouldn't have to play card games to while away the
time. Now would we?"

This time Loedicia was the one who blushed. "Pay no
attention to him, dear," she said, her eyes shifting from
DeMosse back to her grandson. "He's been asking me to
marry him ever since the day he arrived, and I don't ever
intend to say yes."

"You see," DeMosse said, the crinkles about his eyes
deepening. "Still just as stubborn as she was years ago. I
tell her I love her, oui. She tells me I am too old. Now
tell me, m'sieur, when is a man too old to love a woman?
I'll tell you when. When they are lowering him into the
grave, that is when."

Loedicia released Case's hand, her violet eyes looking
directly into DeMosse's. "You are a scoundrel, DeMosse,"
she said. "Love is more than just memories from a long
time ago."

"A long time ago?" DeMosse's eyes softened as he
looked into her face, still lovely in spite of years. "It is
not just the past that tugs at my heart, ma chérie. It is the
present also," and he reached out to take her hand.

Loedicia snatched her hand back. This was ridiculous.
They were too old to be thinking such nonsense. And
yet, she had to admit, when he looked at her the way he
was looking now, he was still able to arouse those same
old feelings in her. Feelings she thought had died with
her second husband, Roth, some thirty years before.
However, this was DeMosse, not Roth, and there lay the
difference. Even though she'd been attracted to DeMosse
those long years ago, the attraction had never developed
into love, and she was sure it wouldn't now either, because DeMosse was the same now as he had been then,
with just enough larceny in his heart so she couldn't trust
him. If not, then why was he padding his score so he could

win, after making her bet a buggy ride the next day with just the two of them if she lost?

No, Loedicia knew little had changed in the man. "Now just stop the nonsense, DeMosse Gervaise, and deal the cards and don't cheat or pad the score anymore, or you'll find yourself playing solitaire." She stopped her scolding for a second, and looked up again to her great-grandson. "Besides, Case didn't come over here to listen to us wrangling. He came to see Moonflower, didn't you, dear?" she said, and reached up, gesturing against Case's arm, pushing him toward the girl. "So go on," she said, pushing a little harder. "You know very well you didn't come to watch us fight over a game of cards."

Case moved away from the table where they were playing, and stood in the middle of the front porch, staring at Moonflower, who looked just as embarrassed as he felt. Swallowing hard, he took off his hat and walked over to her. She straightened in the chair, staring back at him curiously.

"Hello," he said.

"Hello."

"You are not busy too?" he asked.

She shrugged. "I have nothing to be busy with."

He smiled. "Bueno, then you won't mind going for a little walk."

"Where?"

"Oh . . ." He leaned back against the railing behind him. "We could walk back past the cornfield and partway up the back hill, I suppose. Or, if you want, perhaps we could go for a ride on Compadre."

"In this?" She reached down, smoothing her hands across the skirt of her dress. "I think I would rather try the walk."

"Bueno." He stood up straight again, both hands ringing the brim of his hat nervously as he waited for her to move, then he held his hand out to help her from the chair.

Her fingers were soft and warm when her hand touched his, and his own fingers quickly enfolded hers, pulling her gently to her feet, then he reluctantly released her and gestured toward the porch steps with his hat. A few minutes later they were strolling toward the back of the ranch yard, past the tree that housed Genée's old tree house, and on beyond, toward the corrals and cornfields.

So far, hardly a word had been spoken as they walked along, except to comment now and then on what a nice evening it was, and how well Moonflower's father was recuperating. But mostly they just weren't talking.

Both Case and Moonflower had been walking silently for some five minutes when suddenly Case stopped. Moonflower took a few more steps, then she too stopped, and turned, looking back at him.

"You do not wish to walk anymore?" she asked innocently.

"I do not wish to go on like we've been doing," he answered, and closed the gap between them. "This is ridiculous." He stood in the dusty trail gazing down at her. "One minute we act as if nothing is wrong, the next we act like strangers."

She stared at him, puzzled. "I am acting wrong?"

"Sí . . . we are acting wrong . . . both of us."

The sun had gone already from the horizon, and it was that short time, before darkness settled in for the night, when shadows were growing across the landscape. The smell of new earth where the corn had been planted a few days before was mingling with the pungent aroma from the cattle corrals a short distance away, and Case felt it all keenly. He reached out, took her shoulders, and gently drew her to him, waiting expectantly for her to pull away, only she didn't. Instead she just stared up at him with that strange look of bewilderment in her eyes he was so used to seeing.

"Do you not know what I want to tell you?" he said, his voice husky and strained, his Spanish accent even more pronounced, as it always was when he was nervous or excited. "I love you, querida. I guess I have for a long time, only I could not tell you because I thought you hated me."

"I do."

"You do?"

"Like I tried to tell you before," she said as she pushed herself gently back, away from him. "You are a Ranger . . . a Texan. I thank you for rescuing me from the Comanche, and because of that, I know you cannot be all bad, and I am grateful, and I will be nice to you, but to love you . . . ?"

"What's wrong with loving me?"

"Wrong with it? Everything!"

"Name one thing . . . just one."

Their eyes met, and he watched hers narrow thoughtfully while he stared at her.

"You . . . you are . . . cruel and vicious."

"When was I cruel and vicious?"

"All Rangers are cruel and vicious."

"I am not talking about all Rangers, I am talking about me, querida. When have I been cruel and vicious?"

She paused stubbornly, holding her breath for a second, then exhaled.

"See, you cannot answer me, because you know you are being foolish."

"Oh, so now I am a fool."

"I did not say that. Madre de Dios, but you are a stubborn woman." He reached out and took her by the shoulders. "Look, look at me, Moonflower, what do you see?"

Her eyes were still on his, and she was all too aware of what she saw. However, she was trying to ignore it. Trying to shut out the handsome image he made in his fancy clothes, with his mustache neatly trimmed as well as his hair, and the way his dark green eyes were shining, the silvery flecks in them staring back at her with such an intensity it was frightening. Even his mouth, half-hidden beneath the mustache, had a way of moving that made her all too conscious of what his lips could do to her, and had done once before.

"Well?" he asked again as his eyes bored into hers. "I asked you, what do you see?"

"I do not know what I see!" she blurted, and there were tears in her eyes. "I do not see the man who rides with the savage Rangers and kills women and children. I do not see the man who is like the wind, coming and going, to do as he will to those who oppose him . . . yet I know he is there."

"For a day . . . for a reason . . . when need be, sí, he is there, querida. When the wolf is at the door, a man must do what he must do. But when the wolf is gone, and the threat is over, the man is as he was before. Comprende?"

She frowned.

"Can you not understand that?" His eyes darkened solemnly as he watched her face, knowing she was totally mixed up. "You said you have brothers?"

"Yes."

"They are warriors?"

"Yes."

"Then you should know that a man's heart can be good in spite of what the world often demands of him. Only I wish you to know one thing, Moonflower Gervaise, as a Ranger and otherwise, I have never set my hand against women or children, unless they first set their hand against me. Can you understand that?"

Moonflower's topaz eyes stared directly into Case's face, and she felt her heart quicken. If only she knew what to do. Suddenly both of them were distracted as the far-off hoofbeats of a single horse could be heard, and they glanced off toward the front of the big log house to where a rider was just turning in at the front gate. It was Brax, only he didn't see them back on the trail beyond the cornfield, and slowed up by the porch first, evidently calling to Grandma Dicia.

A few seconds later he was quickly galloping toward Case and Moonflower, then reined Hickory up when he reached them.

"I figured you'd be at our place," he said, his voice breathless.

Case could tell he'd ridden Hickory hard. "What is it? What happened?"

"It's Taylor and his men, down along the border. Orders came from Hays, and we're to report to Ben McCulloch down near Matamoros."

Case frowned. "War?"

"Looks like it."

Moonflower looked over at Case. "War?"

"Sí." Case was still looking at Braxton. "How soon?"

"Soon's you get into a decent suit of clothes."

"Decent?" Moonflower looked aghast. "Today he is more decent than he has ever been before, Braxton Kolter. Why do you say he is not wearing decent clothes?"

"They aren't fighting clothes, that's why."

Her eyes grew troubled, and she looked over at Case. "You will go with him?" she asked.

"I have to."

"No." Suddenly Moonflower felt a sickening lurch in her stomach. "No."

Case looked puzzled. "No, what?"

Her lips trembled slightly. "I do not want you to go."

A sharp twinge caught in Case's chest, and his eyes softened. "Why?"

"I do not know why."

"Because she loves you, dammit," Brax cut in, hating the time they were wasting. "Now give her a kiss and a hug, we'll say good-bye to Ma and Pa, and I'll ride over to your place with you."

Case wasn't looking at Braxton now. He was looking into Moonflower's lovely golden-brown eyes. "I will meet you at the house, amigo," he said, hoping Brax would get the hint. "Por favor, give me but a minute."

Brax was still on Hickory, and he nodded. "Just don't be too long." He whirled his horse around and headed back toward the house, while Case continued staring at Moonflower. Then slowly Case reached out and cupped her chin in his hand.

"Was he right, Moonflower? Do you love me?" he asked.

Tears sprang to her eyes. "I do not know." She took a deep breath, then, "All I know is I will miss you if you go," she answered. "And I will hurt if you do not come back."

"Then you must love me."

His hand moved from her chin, and he held her whole face in his outstretched palm as he drew her to him, his free arm circling her waist.

"Was that so hard to say?" he said, his thumb gently stroking a tear from her cheek as he held her. "Would it be so hard to say 'I love you'?"

"But I do not want to love you."

"Because you think we are enemies?" He leaned forward, his lips brushing hers lightly, as if tasting a delicate wine. "Never could I be your enemy, mi querida," he whispered. "You should know that. What I fight is evil, whether it be from my people, your people, or the rest of the world. I do not fight you."

Moonflower saw the softness in his eyes, her lips still quivering from the tender kiss, and in spite of all the hate she'd been forcing herself to shower on him, she knew now it had all been for nothing. She did love him. She loved him so much that it hurt deep down inside.

"You will still go, even though I love you?" she asked.

"I have no choice."

"You will come back?"

"I will come back," and with that his hand dropped from her face, both arms went around her, and he kissed her long and hard, wishing the moment never had to end.

However, it did, and a few minutes later they joined the rest of the family back at the house, where Braxton was saying good-bye.

"And remember," Bain said after all the hugs and hand shakes were over, "we expect both of you to come home."

Case still had his arm about Moonflower. "I have already promised her," he said, then smiled as he looked over at DeMosse, who was still in the chair that had once been Blythe's. Someone had brought him down from the porch. "And remember, señor," Case reminded DeMosse, "you will keep her here until I return, sí?"

"Oui," DeMosse said, then coughed before continuing. "And I will be here too," he finished.

Loedicia glanced over at him, then to her great-grandsons. "Don't you two believe him," she retorted. "Moonflower can stay here, yes, but just as soon as he's on his feet again, we're going to send him packing back to the mountains."

"See," DeMosse said, his eyes glistening impishly. "She is a cruel, heartless woman, m'sieurs. But do not worry, I shall tame her. Now, Godspeed," and he raised a hand to wave, as the others were doing, while Brax climbed into the saddle and Case kissed Moonflower good-bye one more time. Then Case too mounted his horse, and saluting good-bye while throwing kisses to their loved ones, they rode off across the back field.

"Tell me," Case said as they cantered toward the woods and the trail that led to the Crown D. "You think DeMosse will really be here when we return?"

"I doubt it," Brax said, and he glanced back toward the house. "But it's not what you think, don't worry, Moonflower'll still be here." He turned his attention back to Case. "It's just that Mario was over earlier today to check on DeMosse, and he said DeMosse's cough's going to do him in sooner than he thinks."

"How long?"

"Three, maybe four months."

"Does Grandma Dicia know?"

"She knows. That's why she made Ma promise to let him and Moonflower stay as long as they wanted. Now, come on, let's get moving or the fight will be over with by the time we get there," and spurring their horses into a gallop, they reined them onto the trail and let the final shadows of night that had been descending quickly the last few minutes engulf them until they were lost from sight by the people they'd left behind.

Brax and Case had been riding hard for the past few hours since leaving the Crown D, where Case had changed back into his buckskins and said good-bye to his parents, and neither man had been talking much. Instead of riding into San Antonio first and dropping down the Camino Real, they had ridden directly south, planning to head straight for the Nueces River, then they'd follow it, crossing at the Real just north of the small town of Laredo. From Laredo they'd follow the Rio Grande the rest of the way to Matamoros, the whole trip running somewhere near three hundred miles. Brax slowed his horse now, with Case following suit, not wanting to wear them out the first fifty miles.

By midnight they were still some twenty or so miles north of the Nueces, but with the horses tired, and having had no sleep yet themselves, they reined up and made camp.

The next morning they were on their way again shortly before sunup, but at an easier pace this time, yet still continuing due south. Exactly a week and two days later, dusty, dirty, and eager for action, they rode up to what was left of the fort General Zachary Taylor's men had built across from Matamoros, only to discover that not only was the fighting over with for the moment, but the American troops had already crossed over into Mexico, where the army had set up headquarters, pitching the general's tent about a half-mile from the edge of town beneath a small shade tree.

After finding some Mexican boatmen to ferry them across the river, one of the first men they ran into was Sam Walker, one of their old company captains, who directed them to where Hays was staying. Now they stood before their old captain, who'd been promoted to colonel, and waited for orders.

Hays had been busy with some papers when they joined him, and Brax took time now to look around the place. The Rangers had taken over one corner of a small cantina to do business in, leaving the rest of the place for drinking, and a number of soldiers were already feeling little pain, even though it was barely past siesta time for most of the inhabitants of the town.

"Well," Hays said as he set the papers he'd signed aside and looked up at Brax and Case, "I was hoping my message might reach you two." He smiled. "Enjoy your leaves?"

Brax and Case exchanged glances.

"Weren't we supposed to?" Brax asked.

"I just wanted to make sure you were rested up, because I've got a special assignment for you." He glanced over to a nearby table and called to one of the men sitting there. "Jackson, go get McCulloch for me." Then he turned his attention back to Brax and Case. "Sit down," he said, nodding toward a couple of chairs. Then he relaxed, ordering drinks all around.

"So what's it all about, Jack?" Brax asked when they were settled in their chairs.

Jack took a deep breath and glanced over at Case. "If I remember right, you were raised in Montclava, weren't you, Case?

Case nodded hesitantly. "Sí."

"Ever been to Monterrey?"

"A few times, but that was some years back."

"Think you could still find your way around the place?"

Case shrugged. "Perhaps I could try. Why?"

Hays leaned forward eagerly. "Because General Taylor said he needs a couple of men to go into Monterrey for him and contact an American agent there. Ben and some of the men'll be heading toward Monterrey to do some scouting, and I want the two of you to go with him and infiltrate the Mexican defenses."

"Infiltrate?" Brax took off his hat. "Hell, Jack, with hair like this, somebody's bound to recognize me. I've been close to the border for too long. And besides, I sure as hell can't pass for a Mex." He ran a hand through his hair, bleached almost white from the early-summer sun.

"Don't worry about your hair. Nobody'll recognize you when we get through with you. I want a yes or no. And I happen to know you're both fluent in Spanish too, am I right?"

"Who is this agent?" Case asked.

Jack's eyes darkened thoughtfully. "Calls himself El Cougar. Taylor had a man who was supposed to rendezvous with him, but the guy's been hurt. Got in the way of a shell over at the fort. We know where, when, and how. But that doesn't do any good unless we get somebody to do it. And the general needs the information this El Cougar has if we intend to take Monterrey."

Again Brax and Case exchanged glances.

"When do we leave?" Brax asked when he finally looked back at his commanding officer.

"I was hoping you'd say that." Hays always liked it

when the men agreed without being ordered. He looked over toward the door as Jackson came back with McCulloch, a broad-faced man with boldly chiseled features and deep-set blue eyes.

"Well, well, long time no see," Ben said as he drew up a chair and sat down beside Hays. "Glad you two joined us. Jack tell you what we need?"

Brax nodded. "Only I sure as hell don't know how you're going to make me look different."

"Simple," Ben answered. "The Mexican officers just love nice black, highly polished boots."

"Aw, come on now, Ben. I'm a Ranger, remember? You wouldn't make me do something like that, would you?"

But he did, and by the next afternoon, when Brax looked at himself in the mirror, he cringed. They had saturated his hair with bootblacking, as well as his eyebrows, and it wouldn't have been so bad if it had been good-quality blacking. But the damn stuff was rancid, and smelled like the devil.

Case had all he could do to keep from laughing as he sat and watched his cousin standing before the mirror, trying to make his sticky hair look natural. They were sharing a room at the boardinghouse where Ben and his men had been staying.

It had evidently been the home of an aristocrat, with its elegant furnishings. However, it hadn't taken the Rangers long to make themselves at home, and unfortunately that meant that the expensive furniture was suffering.

Case smoothed his hands across the back of the chair he was straddling and fingered the ornate carving as he continued to watch Braxton study himself in the mirror.

"Hell, this won't work, Case," Brax exclaimed as he cocked his head sideways.

"It will if you keep in the shadows."

"And when it gets light?"

"You have a hat."

Brax glanced back and saw the hint of a smile at the corners of Case's mouth.

"I won't do it!" he suddenly said. "Dammit, I'm a

Ranger, not one of those sissy actors. I can't pretend to be what I'm not."

"Pretend? Cuernos! You won't be pretending. Except for the hair, you'll be Juan Ortega, aide and friend of Joaquín Luís de Alvarado, government courier. Just act yourself."

Brax eyed his cousin skeptically. "You think it'll work?"

"Why not? All we have to do now is find the clothes. And since the Mexicans left Matamoros in rather a hurry, I imagine there are plenty around."

Braxton turned back to the mirror, straightening his broad shoulders, and ducked just a little to get a look at the top of his once pale hair, which was now greasy and black-looking. Maybe it would work, but if it didn't, they could both be in for a hell of a rotten time. He sighed. Ah well, it couldn't be much worse than what they'd been through already over the past few years. Besides, they'd already committed themselves.

"All right, let's go," he said, reaching over to grab his hat off the bed. "We'll find out what kind of fancy clothes Ben has for us to wear. If we have to, we have to." He gestured toward the door. "After you, Señor de Alvarado."

"Ah, but no," Case said as he stood up, gesturing with his own hat. "After you, Señor Ortega."

Brax gave him a disgusted look, then hitched up his gunbelt, set his hat gently on his head, and opened the door.

Stopping for a second with the doorknob still in his hand, he looked back one more time at Case. "Now, you really think this'll work, right?" he said.

Case's eyes grew serious. "It has to work, Brax," he said, his voice solemn, all hint of humor gone. "Because if not, you and I are as good as dead," and he put his own hat on as he left the room. Braxton shut the door behind them.

The next morning, with the clothes they were to change into tucked away in their saddlebags, Brax and Case joined Ben McCulloch and the rest of his company of Rangers when they rode out of Matamoros. Not only was the Rangers' departure a cover for the two men who were to go into Monterrey, just in case there were spies in the town, but for a long time McCulloch and his men had been after a Mexican general named Antonio Canales, who, over the past few years, had become known to them as the Chaparral Fox. He and his band of men had been running forays into the Texas frontier, robbing and killing, and word was his headquarters was near Monterrey somewhere. Ben McCulloch wanted him so badly he'd have ridden to hell and back to get his hands on him. So he was glad to be heading out for any reason, even though they had almost two hundred miles to cover one way.

That first day out wasn't too bad. However, it didn't take them long to discover water was scarce, and food even scarcer. Now the real test began.

They were deep into Mexican territory some four days later, early in the evening, when Case and Brax finally stood with Ben saying good-bye. Both Rangers were wearing the Mexican clothes now, their buckskins having been shoved into their saddlebags, and Case pulled at the corners of the chaqueta he had on.

He had purposely picked black for both of them, hoping it would make them less conspicuous, and he glanced over at Brax.

They'd had to redo some of his hair, but all in all he looked pretty good, although the gray eyes were a little out of place. However, many Mexicans were of mixed blood, and Case was hoping.

"All right now," Ben said, his steely blue eyes studying both Rangers intently. "You know what you have to do. When I see you again, I expect it to be done. Taylor's giving you three weeks. If he doesn't hear from either of you by then, he'll try to send someone else in. You have the passwords, and the countersign, so good luck," and he reached out, shaking their hands, then watched the two men mount their horses and ride out, heading northwest, so they would eventually approach Monterrey from the direction of Montclava.

*　　*　　*

It was a warm afternoon, the sun hot, and Braxton was keeping his black broad-brimmed hat on just for good measure, even though he'd touched up his hair with more blacking just that morning. It had been three days since they'd ridden out of Ben McCulloch's camp. Three days in which they'd ridden northwest, then started moving south again, picking up the road down from Montclava. So far they hadn't run into any Mexican soldiers, but as Brax and Case stared ahead of them now, and on down the dusty road, they knew they didn't have long to wait, as the faint outlines of a number of horsemen could be seen up ahead, riding toward them.

"Now remember, from here on in we speak nothing but Spanish," Case reminded him.

"Don't worry, I won't forget. You just remember to call me Juan, that's all I ask," and with that Brax set his mouth grimly, his hands tightening on Hickory's reins as he continued moving forward.

Half an hour later, Brax sighed with relief as he and Case once more nudged their horses in the ribs and continued down the road. So far, so good. They'd passed the first test, having been confronted by a Mexican patrol without any problems whatsoever.

Of course Braxton had kept his hat down low over his eyes, but with his skin weathered from hours in the saddle, the whole confrontation had gone well.

As they neared the city, riding along through the rolling green countryside beneath the fortifications of the Spanish Citadel perched above the road, with the foothills of the Sierra Madre in the distance, then caught sight of the white stucco houses emerging ahead through the acacia and orange trees, their tile roofs baking in the sun, Case suddenly felt homesick. It wasn't that he didn't like his real heritage. But you couldn't grow up living one way, and then completely turn your life around and forget altogether what that life had been before.

Brax started to say something to him in English, then stopped and started in again in Spanish this time.

"Do you know where the square is?" he asked as they drew nearer the city.

Case nodded. "We turn right when we reach the road to Marin, then head toward the center of town."

"Bueno."

Their orders were to report to the marketplace, which was in the square. Once there, they were to locate a vendor selling woven baskets, then ask for a small hand-made basket to use for carrying flowers to put on the altar of the Virgin on Sunday morning. The man was to answer that he had only one basket that would do, because it had been formed by the fingers of God. In return they were to say that the Virgin would be glad to accept any gift from God, and the basket the vendor sold to them would have the address of El Cougar written on a piece of paper hidden between the woven strips at its bottom.

Brax thought it sounded rather ridiculous. But the general had been emphatic when giving them their orders. So here they were, heading for the marketplace and hoping all would go well.

Every day was market day in Monterrey, but today for some reason, perhaps because the city was overrun with soldiers, the square seemed busier than usual. At least from what Case remembered. He'd been here with Estéban de Alvarado a number of times while growing up, and had never remembered it being this busy. There were at least four vendors selling baskets, and after approaching the first two with no luck, he was almost reluctant to try the next. Still, those were the general's orders.

Since Case was more at home as a Mexican, Brax was letting him do all the preliminary work while he took care of their horses, following close behind and keeping his eyes and ears open, with one hand resting loosely near his gun. The guns were Braxton and Case's only insistence in this whole undertaking. They didn't mind all the subterfuge, but would never relinquish their Colt revolvers, hoping prayerfully the Mexicans wouldn't notice them.

Sauntering up to the dark-eyed vendor, Case lifted one of the small baskets and began to look it over carefully, then asked for the small basket, just as the general had instructed.

Expecting the same negative answer he'd been receiving, he was suddenly quite surprised when the young man selling his wares answered verbatim exactly what the general said he would.

Alert now, as well as cautious, Case finished the conversation, then bought the basket the young man offered, and walked away from the booth carrying it with him.

Not to look suspicious, since he had talked to the other vendors too, he stopped on the way to the opposite end of the square and bought a small bouquet of flowers, handing them to Braxton, then they left, disappearing down one of the narrow streets.

"Where to now?" Case asked.

"Find someplace where we won't be disturbed. We'd look stupid tearing the basket apart just after buying it."

A few minutes later, after finding a deserted alley and recovering the tiny slip of paper that had been tucked into the bottom of the basket, they mounted their horses again and headed toward the other end of town, where they finally reined up in front of a beautiful white stucco hacienda with brilliant flowers in huge flowerpots overflowing onto the stone steps.

Case was frowning as he sat astride staring at the place.

Braxton glanced over curiously. "Something wrong, cousin?"

Case took a deep breath. "I'm not sure." They were still talking in Spanish, and for a brief moment Case felt like Joaquín again. "But I think I've been here before."

"You're sure?"

"Not exactly. It's changed some. The yard's a bit different, and there used to be a fountain over there." He pointed to where there was a flower garden. "But I'm sure it's the same place."

"Well, then that's all the better, isn't it?"

"Is it?" he turned to Braxton, his face troubled. "What if they know that Joaquín de Alvarado turned traitor to Santa Anna and joined Sam Houston at San Jacinto? If so, I could be putting my head right in a noose."

"Not if the general's right and this is where El Cougar can be found. If so, he could be the only one who could keep your neck out of a noose."

"So what do I do?"

Brax sighed, relaxing in the saddle as he stared at his cousin. "I'll leave it up to you, Case," he said. "If you say we ride out, we leave. You say we stay, we stay."

Case stared at Brax for a few seconds, then looked back at the house.

"I never quit a job yet, cousin," he finally said. "Come on, let's go."

Some five minutes later they were being ushered into a small courtyard at the back of the house, where a woman stood, her back to them, as she watched a small bird cavorting around in a cage that hung from a limb overhead in one of the orange trees.

"Pardon, señorita," the servant who had ushered them in began. "But there are two gentlemen here who say they have been told to ask for the lady who will put the flowers on the Virgin's altar this Sunday. I thought perhaps I should bring them to you."

"That's fine, gracias, Rafael," the woman said as she continued watching the bird, although Braxton was certain he had seen her stiffen at the words. "Do bring them in."

"They are already here, Señorita."

"Here?" She drew her gaze from the caged bird and began to turn slowly, then froze. It couldn't be, but it was. "Joaquín?" she mumbled in disbelief.

"Catalina!" Case was astounded.

"Joaquín!"

And as Braxton stared in amazement, Case stepped forward, meeting the woman in the center of the courtyard, and Braxton watched as Case Dante stood quietly hugging Catalina de Alvarado, who had once been his sister.

23

Case's arms eased from about Catalina, and he drew back, looking at her. She had changed, and yet she hadn't. Her dark hair was just as gloriously alive, framing the same lovely face, yet her eyes held a depth of maturity that had been missing the last time he'd seen her. She was twenty-five, but seemed much older. Not in her physical looks, but in her manner.

"I can't believe my eyes," she exclaimed as she held both of Case's arms and looked up into his face. "What are you doing here? How did you find me?"

Suddenly her expression grew wary, and her hands dropped from his arms.

"You're the one who is asking for the lady to put the flowers on the Virgin's altar this Sunday?" she asked.

"Sí."

"I don't understand."

"What don't you understand?"

She glanced quickly toward where Brax stood in the shadows of the overhead balcony, hat in hand, but she didn't recognize him. Then she continued to let her eyes scan the courtyard as well as the balcony, to make sure no one else was around.

"How is it you know the passwords?" she asked, her voice hushed. "They are only known to the man who is supposed to contact me."

Case stared at her increduously. "You're El Cougar?"

She took a deep breath, then exhaled as he watched her curiously. "Why not? You named me that, didn't you?"

"But . . . El Cougar?"

"What he's trying to say is, how come someone who's always hated us stinking gringos so much suddenly decides she's on our side?" Braxton said as he sauntered toward them. This time, except for the strange hair coloring, there was no way Catalina couldn't recognize him.

"Brax?"

"Sí. Braxton Kolter, scourge of the Texas frontier and hated gringo, at your service, señorita," and he bowed low, sweeping his ornately trimmed hat in an arc that almost touched the floor, before straightening again.

Catalina's eyes narrowed irritably as she watched Braxton, then she stiffened, addressing Case, while her gaze rested on his cousin.

"Do I have to answer in front of him, Joaquín?" She looked anything but pleased to see Brax.

"Sí, I think you'd better."

"In fact there's a countersign you're supposed to give us, Señorita de Alvarado," Brax added as he stepped even closer. "Or is it señora now?"

"Why should you care?"

"I don't."

"Bueno." She looked at Case again. "I am to tell you that I have only one basket that will do, to carry the flowers in, because it was formed by the fingers of God."

"And I am to answer that the Virgin would be glad to accept any gift given by God."

"Then you're really my contact?" She shook her head. "It's incredible."

"Like I said," Brax said, his eyes intent on her face. "When did you change sides, or have you?" He was extremely alert as he looked around, then glanced back over at Case. "We could be walking into a trap, you know."

Case frowned. "Are we, Cat?"

Catalina tried to ignore Braxton's accusation. After all, he did have a right to think what he was thinking, since she had once been such a staunch defender of Mexico. But it was still irritating.

"No, you're not walking into a trap." She looked toward

the house. "But we do have to be careful. The servants are quite loyal to their country."

Braxton sneered. "So what happened to your loyalty?"

She shrugged. "Sometimes it takes a woman longer to open her eyes than it does a man, mi amigo. Perhaps because she is a woman, who knows? But come, sit down, both of you. We have to talk, and I would rather not be overheard," and she led them to the back of the courtyard, near an outside wall, where it was easy to see anyone approaching from the house. They sat down, using a couple of stone benches that had been placed there.

"So, now what, Cat?" Case asked as he watched Catalina closely.

"Now you stay until I finish getting the information your General Taylor needs, then we try to figure out a way for you to get it back to him." She sat with her hands in the lap of the rose-colored dress she was wearing, and frowned. "You see, I have almost completed a list . . . who's at the Citadel with how many men, where the redoubts are placed, and how they're fortified, as well as plans and maps showing where all the cannon are placed in every fortification around Monterrey. Only, once in your possession, you'll have to get them past the patrols."

Brax had been staring at her, his eyes intense. "You're serious, aren't you?" he said.

They were still speaking in Spanish, and it seemed so much easier to talk to her in her native tongue.

"I am quite serious."

"But you haven't told us why."

She flushed, and a sadness filled her eyes. "Let's just say I've learned what your freedom means," she answered, then suddenly straightened, her gaze moving to the far end of the courtyard, where a small commotion could be heard. "Madre de Dios, he's back!" she blurted hurriedly, then looked at Braxton and Case, hoping no one else would notice the pale eyelashes and gray eyes that didn't match Braxton's greasy black hair.

"Ah, Ricardo," she exclaimed animatedly as she stood

up and moved across the courtyard toward the man who was coming toward them. "What a surprise."

Brax saw the tall Mexican in the strange clothes that were a combination of military and civilian rake his eyes over both of them. Then the man's gaze stopped for a second on Brax before finally settling on Case again.

"Perhaps it's well I did surprise you," the man said, his voice anything but friendly.

"Oh no, mi amor, you don't understand," Catalina prated on. "This is my brother, Joaquín de Alvarado, and his friend Braxton . . ."

"Ortega," Brax cut in quickly. "Braxton Ortega," and he saw Catalina's momentary confusion, then he went on.

"Braxton, Joaquín, may I introduce to you Captain Ricardo Valencia." Catalina watched the men shake hands all around, then Valencia finally relaxed somewhat.

"Your brother, you say?"

"Sí. He came down from Montclava."

"But I thought you said he was in Texas?"

"For a while. Only for a while. You see, he too hates what the Americans are doing to our country, as I do." Catalina was trying very hard not to look nervous. "Like me, he has had enough of the gringos."

"Ah, sí. So, you are staying for a few days then, I suppose?"

Case glanced over at Catalina. "She did ask, but we wouldn't want to impose."

"Nonsense," Ricardo's eyes shifted from Case to Braxton, and Catalina saw him frown. He was staring directly at Braxton's head; however, he said nothing that made her think he had noticed anything unusual.

Instead, he insisted they freshen up for dinner, and it was during dinner that Case and Braxton discovered just who Ricardo Valencia really was. He was not only the nephew of General Gabriel Valencia, a power himself in Mexican military circles, but he was the owner of the hacienda where Catalina was staying, and the first cousin of its former owners, who had been friends of Estéban de Alvarado. On top of that, he was also a captain in General Antonio Canales' guerrillas, coming home only rarely when he got lonesome for Catalina, who, they came to the conclusion, had to be his mistress, although the word was never used.

Later that evening, after Case and Braxton had been ushered to their separate rooms for the night, Braxton made his way back down the hall and slipped into Case's room, shutting the door firmly behind him.

"Now we're really in trouble," he said as he leaned his tall muscular frame against the door for a minute, then walked over to the bed where Case was taking off his boots.

"How's that?"

"Look," and he pointed to his head. "All I have to do is put my head on a pillow just once," he said. "And the servants in this house'll know something's wrong. Cuernos! I can't sit in a chair all night to sleep."

Case studied Braxton's hair. They'd done a good job on it, as far as the blacking went, but Brax was right. The stuff had a distinct greasiness to it, and although it had colored well, and made to look like he was just a man who liked to use a great deal of pomade, all he'd have to do was rub against something, and the whole thing would be given away.

"Your bedroll," Case said as he dropped a boot on the floor. "You've still got your bedroll, haven't you?"

"Oh fine, I sleep on the hard floor on my bedroll, while you enjoy the comforts of a feather bed."

"Don't blame me. It's not my fault you were born with blond hair."

"And what about your sister?"

"She's not my sister anymore, remember?"

"Well . . . I still think of her as your sister. Anyway, she's sleeping with that jackass."

"Are you sure?"

"Am I sure? Come on, Case."

"The name's Joaquín."

"All right, Joaquín." Braxton's eyes were snapping furiously. "Jesus Cristo, don't you care?"

"And if I did? What am I supposed to do, challenge him to a duel or something?"

"Well, you don't have to act like it doesn't matter at all."

Case stood up, carried his boots to the other side of the room, and set them down near a chair, then began removing his chaqueta as he turned back toward Braxton, eyeing his cousin rather closely. Surprisingly, except for the greasy look to his hair, Brax looked rather striking as a caballero.

"So?" he asked as he tossed his chaqueta onto the chair.

"So ask her."

"Me? Why should I ask her?" He walked back to the bed and flopped down, letting out a long sigh of contentment. "I will leave that up to you my dear cousin, since you're the one who seems to care the most."

Brax gave him a disgusted look. "I hope you have nightmares," he retorted, and turned abruptly. Going to the door, he opened it, checked to make sure the hall was empty, then stepped outside. "It'd serve you right," he said, sticking his head back in for a moment, then shut the door quietly behind him and went back to his own room, where he first locked the door, then grabbed his bedroll off the chair, laid it out on the floor, and climbed in, after first messing up the bed and blowing out the candle lamp one of the servants had lit.

"Disgusting," he mumbled under his breath to himself as he tried to get comfortable on the hard floor. "I don't care how bad things were, she didn't have to resort to this," and he closed his eyes, trying to figure out, every way he could, just how Catalina could possibly have ended up where she was, doing what she was doing. It just didn't make sense, and although he managed to close his eyes, Braxton knew tonight was going to be a rough night, while down the hall in the master bedroom Catalina too knew tonight was going to be a rough night.

Catalina's gaze followed Ricardo as he moved about the room. She'd been hoping he wouldn't come back so soon. Usually he was gone one or two months at a time, but this time it had been barely two weeks, and she had so much more to do yet.

She had finally made friends with the girlfriend of one of the soldiers who was to defend the bridge to the southeast in case of attack. They were to come for dinner in three days, on the weekend, at which time she was hoping to discover whether there would be artillery or only foot soldiers to defend it. This done, her job would be complete. But now, with Ricardo here . . . Maybe he wouldn't stay too long.

She was still daydreaming over the events of the past few hours when she realized Ricardo was talking to her.

"I'm sorry. What did you say?" she asked.

He threw his uniform jacket down on a chair, his face somber. "I said, how long has your brother been friends with this . . . this Ortega, whatever his name is?"

"Braxton? For years. He lived near us in Montclava before our parents died."

"But he is a gringo, right?"

"A gringo? How ridiculous."

"Don't lie to me, my little cat," he said, his jaw clenching stubbornly. "No Mexican has gray eyes the color of Ortega's."

Catalina tried to remain calm. "Oh, that," she said as she picked up a brush and started stroking her long dark hair. "Can he help it if his mother's mother was English?"

"English?"

"Sí. Where do you think the name Braxton comes from? But his father was an Ortega."

"I see." He had already taken off his boots and now he held out his arms to her. "Querida?"

The brush froze halfway down Catalina's tresses, and her body stiffened.

"I told you before, mi amor, when I say come, it means come." His eyes narrowed. "You still hesitate?"

"At least I have that."

"Do you?" He laughed. "Your one bastion of defiance, is that it? It will do you no good, you know."

"But it is still mine."

"And I will put an end to that too someday, you will see. Now, come here," and his fingers flipped back arrogantly, with his hands still stretched out, beckoning her.

Slowly, reluctantly, Catalina set the tortoiseshell brush down on the vanity, then left the brocade vanity bench and began the long walk across the highly polished floor toward the man standing next to the ornately carved bed, the hem of her nightdress barely touching the floor as it covered her bare feet.

How many nights she'd been forced to come to him, each night hating it as much as the first. Yet knowing she had no other choice. It had been either Ricardo or the hangman's noose, and she had wanted to live.

She was almost to him, and he reached out, pulling her along more quickly, aroused now by the delightful picture she made in the sleek gown, while he wished his wife back in Mexico City was half the woman Catalina was.

"Why?" he asked as he drew her to him. "Why do you still fight me, Catalina?"

"If you don't know that, Ricardo, then you're blind."

"Do I hurt you?"

"Sí."

"How? By loving you?"

"By using me."

"Caramba! You are a stubborn woman." His hand moved up into her hair. "But such a beautiful one."

He bent down, his lips touching hers, lightly at first, then becoming more demanding with their intensity, until Catalina felt as if she were being smothered. Yet she knew to fight his assault would do her little good. All it'd get her was more of the same. So instead of fighting, she kissed him back, matching his ferocity with a pretense of liking what was happening, in spite of the fact that she hated every moment.

Later, as she settled down to sleep in the arms of the man who had rescued her from the gallows, Catalina prayed for all she was worth that he wouldn't stay long.

Her prayers were answered the next afternoon when Ricardo announced he'd be leaving the following morning. That meant he'd be gone before the weekend.

That evening, after spending a quiet day at the hacienda trying to stay out of Ricardo's way, Brax stood at the far end of the courtyard and watched the house. It was dark out already, the moon a crescent as it waned, but it felt good to be outside. Unlike the home where Blythe lived, there was a cold atmosphere inside Valencia's house that made him uncomfortable.

Case said the place had changed a good deal since he'd been here as a boy. And it wasn't just the missing fountain. There was new furniture throughout, the colors having been changed from soft browns and blue to the bold reds and golds that seemed to dominate every room.

Brax leaned back against the tree he was standing beneath and continued to watch the house. The others weren't home as yet. Case had accepted Ricardo's invitation to join him and Catalina at a fandango, but Brax had declined, saying he wasn't feeling too well. Actually the thought of spending an evening watching Ricardo treating Catalina as if he owned her held little appeal for him. Besides, he couldn't take the chance that someone might be smart enough to see through his disguise. As it was, he'd had to shave exceptionally close this morning, and was having to shave every day in this heat. Most men's whiskers seemed to grow in darker than their hair, but not his. His face was actually getting sensitive from all the shaving, and he hoped he wouldn't have to keep it up much longer. Although the thought of riding out and leaving Catalina behind was something he wasn't looking forward to either.

Brax had taken advantage of Ricardo's absence tonight, and searched for anything that looked like it might have something important in it. The only thing he had learned, however, was that Canales, otherwise known to the Rangers as the Chaparral Fox, and his guerrillas were using the small Mexican town of Reynosa, about halfway between Matamoros and Camargo, as one of their bases. The only way he learned that was by reading a letter Valencia had written to his wife, a woman named Consuelo. The letter hadn't been finished as yet, but Brax assumed it'd be finished and posted before Valencia left in the morning.

The thought of Valencia irritated him, and his jaw tightened as the jangle of harness floated back to him on the night air, and he realized they'd returned. The carriage would let them off out front, but he didn't move. The way his thoughts were running at the moment, he might just walk right up and shove his fist down Valencia's throat, because it was obvious by the looks Catalina gave the man that although she pretended to be affectionate, she was far from happy in his presence. Brax had known Catalina for too long not to be able to read the frustrated anger in her dark eyes.

He was deep in the shadows of an old orange tree, and was still watching the stucco house, when he saw Catalina step out into the courtyard, followed closely by Valencia and Case.

"I'm surprised you turned me down, Joaquín," Valencia was saying as they stopped the other side of the courtyard.

Brax saw Case shrug, then stretch and gaze about, only Case missed seeing Braxton in the shadows. "As I said, I think I can do more by staying here," Case answered. "Besides, I haven't seen Catalina for such a long time. I'd like a few more days with her."

"A flimsy reason, if you ask me, but perhaps when I return."

"When will that be?" Catalina asked.

He reached out, cupping her chin in his hand. "Miss me already, mi querida?"

Brax had all he could do to keep from killing the bastard. His hand clenched on the butt of his gun as he watched Catalina reach up and remove Ricardo's hand from her chin.

"I always miss you," she said, only her voice didn't sound too convincing. At least from where Brax stood.

He watched them talk for a little while longer, then Case went inside, leaving Catalina and Ricardo alone.

"Your brother is a strange one, mi querida," Valencia said as he watched Case disappearing inside the house. "He has the opportunity to spend the night with a beautiful woman, and he'd rather come back here and sleep in an empty bed?"

"Everyone isn't like you," Catalina reminded him. "Some men have other things on their minds."

"And you. You also have other things on your mind?"

"At the moment, sí. At the moment my feet hurt, and I'm tired."

"You won't need your feet for what I have in mind." He moved close to her. "I'll give you twenty minutes, half an hour at the most. I have a letter to finish first anyway, then I'll expect to see you upstairs. Is that clear?"

"Perfectly."

"Bueno." He drew her close, kissed her, then began to move toward the house. "Half an hour, remember," he called back over his shoulder, then disappeared inside.

Brax waited for only a moment, then straightened as Catalina turned and began to stroll toward where he was standing.

A few seconds later she reached the deep shadows beneath the orange tree, then suddenly hesitated as she saw Braxton's vague figure where he was leaning against the trunk of the tree. He saw her stiffen.

"It's me, Cat, don't be scared," he said.

She let out a sigh of relief. "Por Dios! I couldn't imagine . . ." She frowned. "You've been out here all this time?"

"Sí." He looked straight at her. "Why, Cat?" he asked as he moved toward her, then stood staring down into her face.

"Why what?"

"You know what I mean."

She bit her lip. Sí, she knew all too well what he meant, and her face flushed.

"What happened to the young woman I knew, who'd rather die than compromise what she believed to be right?" Brax went on while he stared at her. "The one woman in the whole world I knew who would never ever let a man tell her what she was or wasn't going to do. What happened to the real Catalina de Alvarado, Cat?"

"She's hiding under the name of El Cougar, but she's still there."

"Why?"

"Because she killed a man who was trying to rape her."

"What happened?"

Catalina wished she could see Brax more clearly, but it was way too dark here beneath the tree, even with the moon up.

"When I first came back to Mexico, I came straight here to see the Delgados," she began. "Only they weren't here anymore. The place was closed up, so I went to see some other friends Father had in the city. They told me the Delgados had passed away, and left the place to a distant relative, since they'd had no children."

She continued to talk as she stepped past Brax and moved deeper into the shadows beneath the tree, then she stopped and turned, leaning back against the tree trunk.

"Not wanting to go back to Montclava, I went on to Mexico City, and for a while it seemed so grand. I had heard Father speak of the Delgados' relatives, the Valencia's, who lived there. And when I looked them up, they were only too eager to welcome me into their home."

"You're talking about Ricardo Valencia?"

"I'm talking about his aunt and uncle."

"Then how . . . ?"

"I'm getting to that." She glanced toward the house, making sure Ricardo hadn't stepped outside yet, looking for her. But then, he had said half an hour. "Unfortunately Ricardo and his wife also lived with the general, since he'd been orphaned, and his uncle raised him. One evening, not long after my arrival, the Valencias had a big dinner party for the elite of Mexican society. Cabinet ministers, army officers. Anyone who was of importance was there, including one gentleman in particular who took a liking to me. Naturally the fact that he was married didn't seem to matter to him at all. Anyway, I'd been up in my room, where I'd gone to have one of the maids fix a hook on my dress that had torn loose, and after she was gone, I stayed for a minute longer to make sure my hair wasn't mussed. I shouldn't have, because after stepping out again into the hall, I was confronted near Ricardo and Consuelo's bedroom door by this same general, who shoved me inside quite unceremoniously before I even had time to scream."

She straightened and looked over to where she knew Braxton was standing, and her voice broke a bit.

"When Ricardo came in a few minutes later, my dress was half ripped off me, and General Pedro Hernandez was slumped across Ricardo's bed with a nice sharp letter opener between his ribs. It was either that or let him take what he wanted. I couldn't do that."

"And yet you let Valencia?"

"I had to, don't you see?" She had to make him understand. "When General Hernandez came after me, I didn't stop to think. I screamed, but evidently no one heard. The house is terribly big. All I knew was that I couldn't let him touch me, and I fought. I didn't kill him on purpose. He was the one who grabbed the opener, not me. His death was an accident. All I wanted to do was get away. But the gallows was very real, Brax. Ricardo helped me cover up my part in Hernandez' death, telling me that to report what he tried to do to me to the authorities would only bring terrible scandal to his uncle, who was a close friend of Hernandez,' and besides, he was convinced no one would believe me anyway. At the time, I thought he was just helping a friend. It wasn't until later that he demanded payment. To this day even Ricardo's wife doesn't know I was the one who was with the general when he died. The authorities thought it was done by an intruder. Ricardo made it look like someone had been trying to pilfer his wife's jewelry box, and the general, who'd had a little too much to drink and been given permission to lie down in the room, surprised the thief."

"What about your torn dress?"

"I hurried to my room, pulled the dress back up in place, and grabbed a thin silk shawl before the authorities arrived, then mended it later myself."

"That doesn't explain why you're still with him."

"Because it's his word against mine. You see, all he has to do is open his mouth once and I don't have a prayer."

"You were defending yourself."

"I was stealing his wife's jewels, according to the authorities. At least that's what he made it look like. There were a brooch and necklace of hers missing, thanks to Ricardo, and he still has them. It'd be so easy for him to see that the authorities find them among my things. And I don't even dare wish for his death either, because he said if and when he ever does die, he has a letter with the jewelry that would not only put the noose around my neck, but spring the trapdoor beneath it as well. No, Brax, all I can do is what I'm doing, and hope that if anything does happen to him, I can make it across the border before someone finds out where he'd hidden it."

"It isn't here?"

"I imagine it's in Mexico City, but where? Only he knows."

Brax reached out, took her hand, and drew her to him. For a moment he thought she'd protest. Instead she stared up at him, her eyes misty.

"So now you should hate me for what I've become," she said, her voice hushed.

He inhaled sharply, the sweet scent of her perfume filling his nostrils like an intoxicating drug. She looked so lovely in blue. Always had.

"That's why you became El Cougar?"

"That, and because of what I've seen over the years. I thought my country was freedom, Brax. I thought I could live as I pleased, and feel what I wanted, the way I did when I was in Texas, but I found out I couldn't. You were right, you know. You and Joaquín. I've seen people used, simply because they were expendable. I've seen cruelty beyond measure, so I fight in the only way I can, for now, and someday maybe my countrymen will also know the freedom I once knew."

Brax lifted his hand to her face, and his fingers touched her cheek. "Come with us when we leave, Cat," he begged. "You'll soon be finished here."

She shook her head. "You don't understand, this is only part of it. The rest is just as important—Matamoros, now Monterrey, they're only the beginning. I'll stay until your General Taylor marches into Mexico City."

Brax cupped her head in his hand, his fingers caressing her soft cheek, and he felt a warmth shoot through him, filling every muscular fiber of his body.

"I want to kiss you, Cat," he murmured.

She sighed. "And you're asking?"

"No, not really. I guess I never have asked you, have I?" and with that his mouth covered hers, and Brax knew, as he'd guessed long ago, why he'd never found that something else that meant more to him than just a horse, a gun, a pair of boots, and his buckskins. He'd been riding away from it every time he left home. Only the last time, she had been the one to ride away from him.

The kiss deepened, and with it went his heart, just as surely as if he had ripped it from his chest and handed it to her.

Catalina held on to Brax as if she were drowning, her lips responding to him in a way they had never answered Ricardo's, and for just a few moments she felt alive again. How many times she'd thought of Brax these past months. Remembering all the times she'd called him names, and goaded him into retaliating. Up until that last time he'd ridden away from the hacienda after kissing her good-bye. She'd never forgotten that kiss, and now the same wonderful feelings were flowing through her again, and she didn't want them to stop.

She'd been running away from that kiss for a long time, and now the running was over. Melting against him, her arms moving up around his neck, she let herself feel as she had never felt before.

After a while Brax reluctantly drew his mouth from hers, knowing they were taking a chance. That Ricardo might come looking for them.

"You know, don't you, Cat?" he said, his voice low, husky.

Her own voice was unsteady. "Know what?"

"Do I have to say it?"

"You don't have to, no. But until you do, I won't believe you."

His arm tightened about her waist. "Still stubborn, aren't you?" It was so dark, her face was just a vague shadow, yet her flesh was so close he could feel her breath on his lips. "All right, you win," he began, and was just about to open his heart to her, when Ricardo called from the balcony.

"Catalina!"

Braxton's arms tightened even more, his lips pressed against her ear. "Don't go."

"I must."

"Let someone else do it."

"There's no one—"

"Cat . . ."

She wrenched free and moved out from the shadows of the orange tree, heading toward the house, while Ricardo stood on the balcony looking down at her.

"There you are," he said, and his eyes scanned the garden curiously. "I thought perhaps you'd gone in."

"Just enjoying the night," she called back up to him, all the while hoping Braxton wouldn't lose his temper and come after her.

But he didn't. Instead Braxton stood for a long time in the courtyard, hidden deep in the shadows of the orange tree, and stared up at the window of the room he knew Catalina shared with Valencia. Then, when the light went out, angry and disgusted, not only with himself but also with the world that had done this to them, he too went inside, and on up to his own room, where he curled up again in the bedroll and tried to get some sleep.

As he'd promised, Ricardo rode out the next morning. However, it seemed like Brax was never going to get a chance to talk to Catalina alone again. Either one of the servants, or Case, or someone else was always around. And even that evening it was the same. Normally Catalina had few visitors, but tonight, for some reason, the people never seemed to stop coming until the early hours of the morning. Later, she explained to both Case and Brax that they were some of her contacts. People she couldn't entertain while Ricardo was here. That's why they'd all shown up right after he'd left.

By early Saturday evening, when she entertained a number of people at a small dinner party, along with the young couple she had planned to get her last bit of information from, Brax still hadn't had a chance to talk to her alone. So it wasn't any surprise to her when she opened her bedroom door after everyone was gone to find him standing waiting for her.

Brax had absented himself at dinner, afraid perhaps someone might get wise to who he was and the fact that his hair color was simply a disguise.

Catalina stared at him for a minute, then shut the door behind her, the light from the lamp on her vanity making shadows dance across his face.

"I presume you got your information," he said.

"Sí, I got it."

"And you had to play up to the young soldier to get it too, didn't you?"

"So?"

"So I hate it."

"You think I like it?" She flipped the inside lock on the door, then straightened and walked toward a desk to her right. Opening one of the drawers, she took out some papers and began writing on one of them.

He watched her for some time, dipping the pen into the inkwell on the desk over and over again as she wrote. Finally she set the pen down, capped the inkwell, and lifted the papers, blowing on them one at a time to dry them.

Brax walked up behind her, his hands moving to her waist, and he drew her back against him. "Is it done?" he asked, his lips against her ear.

She nodded. "For now, sí."

"Then I have something to tell you."

She turned, reaching up with her free hand, and stopped him with her fingers on his lips. "No," she said. "Don't tell me now, it would hurt too much to hear it now, por favor. For now just let me feel without knowing, sí?"

His eyes bored into hers. "You want that?"

"Sí, I want it very much."

He reached out, took the paper from her hand, and set

it on the desk behind her with the others, then lifted her up, cradling her in his arms. "You know what I'm going to do?"

Her eyes were looking into his, and she felt all warm inside. "Sí."

"You don't mind?"

"Mind?" She laughed softly, then reached up, laying her palm against his cheek as she continued to stare into his pale gray eyes that could change as quickly from anger to love, as they'd already done once since she'd come into the room, and her own eyes grew serious. "I would be pleased, Braxton Kolter," she said, her heart showing in them. "Make love to me, mi querido. At least I will have that," and as she said it, he lowered her to the bed, his mouth covering hers in a long kiss that quickly began to soothe the hurt inside her. Then slowly, reverently, he began to unfasten the back of her dress, and stripped it from her, along with her underclothes, kissing her now and then, on her lips, her throat, her breasts, while his hands continued to explore her body.

"Do you know how lovely you are?" he asked when he finally gazed down at her naked body, all tawny and golden, and his voice broke huskily.

She sighed, reaching up, and her fingers began working on the buttons of his shirt, slipping it off his shoulders. He stood up, pulling it off the rest of the way himself, while she moved to the other side of the bed, making room for him. Then, peeling the calzoneras down his muscular legs, he stood facing the bed, and Catalina held her breath. The hair on the rest of him was as blond as she knew the hair on his head was beneath the bootblacking, and she marveled at the power in his lean muscles, in spite of the scars he'd picked up along the way. He was magnificent.

She reached a hand out, and he took it, then stretched out beside her on the brocade spread, pulling her to him, his flesh prickling at the feel of her skin, soft and velvety against his.

"He has no right to you," he said, suddenly remembering whose bed they were on.

"I know." Again her hand covered his mouth. "But don't, mi querido," she begged, her eyes searching his face while she lay in his arms. "Don't spoil it for us. Don't let me hurt any more than I'm already hurting. Por favor, just let me be yours tonight without any strings attached. I beg of you."

"And that would be enough?"

"For the moment, sí. Now kiss me again, and make me forget," and moments later Catalina was lost in the wonder of Braxton's arms, remembering the past they'd once shared together, and trying to forget the future she knew would be without him, while she lived the present. And when Brax moved over her, his body claiming hers with a fervor he'd never dreamed he could have for a woman, she held on to him desperately, wishing the moment never had to end, yet knowing the wish was only a dream.

"Sí, hold me!" she begged as he entered, filling her body with all the love that had been denied them both over the years. "Hold me and make me yours, mi querido," she pleaded. And as she groaned beneath him, surrendering to Braxton what she had never surrendered to Ricardo, arching her body to meet him and letting him bring them both to a peak of pleasure that made them both fuse into one wonderful moment, carrying them beyond what normal man must feel. Neither cared that in a few hours it would be dawn. All they cared about was now, tonight. Afterward, as she lay in his arms, her head on his chest, feeling the rise and fall of him while he slept in deep contentment, Catalina prayed with all her might that someday she could be like this with him for always.

It was still dark out, but the sky was beginning to lighten off to the east, although a few stars still hung high on the horizon where darkness still clung to the sky. Catalina lay quietly, her body half-covering Braxton, who was on his back, still sleeping peacefully. Tears of joy slowly filled her eyes. She had once called him a stinking gringo. How foolish she had been then. So young and idealistic.

They had slipped under the covers sometime during

the night, and now her gaze shifted to the pillows. She frowned. Madre de Dios! they'd forgotten about the coloring on his hair. It was not only smeared all over the pillowcases, but looked like it had dried already.

Her hand moved from his chest, and she reached up, examining the smears more closely with her fingers as his eyes slowly began to open.

"Mmm! And I thought I'd been dreaming," he murmured, his arm starting to pull her hard against him, only she drew her head back, looking down into his face.

"We have a problem," she said.

His eyes were open all the way now. Still sleepy but lucid. "What's that?"

"Your hair."

He reached up quickly and touched his head. "Por Dios, I forgot," and he maneuvered in bed so he could see it too. The pillows were a mess.

There was no way they could possibly get away with pretending it wasn't there, and there was no explanation they could think of to tell the servants.

"So what do we do?" she asked.

"Hell if I know."

"We have to do something."

His eyes caught hers, and she shivered with their intensity. "We will," he said. "But until we do, we might as well make the most of it," and he drew her head down, kissing her passionately, and made love to her one more time. Only more lazily this time, savoring every moment he could before the first few rays of the sun filtered all the way into the room.

"So, have you thought of anything?" she asked afterward as she slipped from the bed and put on a wrapper one of the servants had left on the chair.

"Hell no."

"But we must think of something."

"We could burn them. It's only two pillowcases."

"And how do we explain their disappearance?"

He shrugged.

"I know," she suddenly said, and walked over to a liquor cabinet built into the far wall. "Ricardo hates to bother the servants in the middle of the night," she explained as she opened it and took out a bottle of wine. "Aha, his private stock," she said as she held the bottle up.

Instead of red as most wines were, the bottle Catalina held up was so deep in color it almost looked black.

"The Valencias are known for importing the best black-berry wines in Mexico City," she said smugly. "And Ricardo always makes sure he has a supply with him."

It took no time at all for her to bunch up the pillows, spill the wine all over them, then put more in a small goblet, tossing it right in the middle of the mess.

"There now, we can't very well keep stained sheets, now can we," she said as she studied her handiwork.

Brax laughed. He had pulled his pants back on while watching her hunt for the wine, and walked over to stand beside her.

"Clever," he said, then turned to her. "Any wine left?"

"Just enough to take the edge off the day," and she lifted it to her lips, taking a sip, then handed it to him.

Brax drained the bottle, then stared at it. "On the bed?" he asked.

"On the bed," she agreed and he tossed the bottle next to the glass, only it rolled onto the sheet.

"One more thing," she said, and went around the bed to the desk, picked up the papers she'd written out the night before, and walked over to the fireplace, where she knelt down and lifted a brick from the middle of the hearth. Reaching into the hole beneath it, she pulled out more papers, neatly wrapped in a soft piece of leather. Adding the papers she'd just taken from the desk, she stood up, handing them to Brax. "Here, these are what you and Joaquín came for."

He took them from her.

"There are two copies of each," she went on. "That way, if one doesn't get through, there's a chance the other will. How you get them there is up to you."

"Case, I mean Joaquín, said he wanted to leave this morning while most of the soldiers would be in church."

"I know. And that's another thing." She tried to keep the tremor from her voice and the tears from her eyes. "If I don't see you again before your General Taylor arrives in Monterrey, I'll leave a message here for you in the hearth."

"You won't be here to meet me?"

"You know I can't be."

He reached out, drawing her to him, and his lips found hers, kissing them lightly, sipping at them as he would sweet nectar.

"Catalina . . . Catalina, I—"

"No!" she murmured against his mouth, kissing him to stop him from uttering the words, then she drew her mouth from his. "We said no ties, remember?"

His eyes hardened as he stared at her. "When this is over—"

"Then you may tell me. But for now, we have to get you back to your room. It's barely dawn, and the servants will be up soon."

After another long kiss that tore through both their hearts with its longing, Brax gathered his clothes together, sneaked back to his own room, messed up the covers, then headed for Case's room, waking him from a deep sleep.

It was decided that each of them would carry a copy of the papers, which were first folded into narrower strips and slipped into the front of their chaquetas beneath the facing, where it was heavily embroidered, with Catalina herself doing the sewing. Then, shortly before noon, after an unsettled morning, with Catalina alternating between laughter and tears, Brax and Case bid her goodbye and rode away from the hacienda, once more heading out past the Citadel that sat majestically on its hill, helping guard the city, and moved on up the road toward Montclava.

24

The information Brax and Case had brought back to General Taylor had proved more than helpful, as had the news Ben McCulloch had given him. So instead of heading inland across the open plains, where Ben had reported little water, and even less food, with Ben's recommendation, and because Braxton and Case told him about the Chapparal Fox's hideout, the general sent a small force of infantry, early in June, upriver to Reynosa. Once there, they easily took possession of the place and set two field guns up in an unfinished church tower that overlooked most of the town.

The infantry had hoped to surprise General Canales' guerrillas there, but the Chapparal Fox had managed to elude them again. However, although it was little more than a mixture of huts and shacks, the soldiers dug in anyway, to make sure he wouldn't come back. They were still there at the beginning of July when the rest of the army finally began to move through, heading up the Rio Grande toward Camargo. Some marched, some went by boat, while Brax and Case, once more a part of Ben McCulloch's special Rangers, rode Hickory and Compadre through muck and mud along with everyone else, in one of the hottest, wettest Julys the country had seen in a long time.

One day it was nothing but mud, cold, and rain, the next heat and dust, as they made their way up along the Rio Grande, then left the river and began to drop down deeper into Mexican territory, heading straight for Monterrey. Finally, after moving through one village after another, on September 19, after being harassed by Canales' guerrillas most of the way, but being joyfully greeted and accepted by a great many of the native Mexicans, who were tired of being at the mercy of Canales, as well as the Mexican troops, the American Army, after having trudged some two hundred miles, made camp barely three miles northeast of the city. And at two o'clock the next afternoon, the siege of Monterrey began.

Five days later, on Friday, September 25, after one of the bloodiest confrontations so far, the Mexican flag was finally lowered on the Citadel, and what was left of the Mexican Army marched out of the city and down the road toward Saltillo, with a defeated General Ampudia in the lead. While behind them, the American flag was raised in its place, followed by a twenty-one-gun salute from the Bishop's Palace, on its hill a few miles away, where it overlooked the city, and the strains of "Yankee Doodle" somewhat lifted the spirits of the Americans as they plodded into the war-torn city.

Braxton and Case, tired from the fighting, and weary from lack of sleep, heard the music fading in the distance as they made their way away from the square toward the outskirts of town on foot, leading their horses over the bodies of dead Mexicans. Occasionally they'd find a man alive and call to the men behind them, who had already begun to gather up the wounded and dying from both sides. The place was a mess.

Houses and shops, once shining bright with their sun-baked walls, were now crumbling into the streets, gaping holes in their sides from being shelled, and from the advancing American Army's determination to get at the snipers inside, even if it meant blowing them up. The battle had been hard-fought, and hard-won. Now it was going to take another kind of fight to get the place cleaned up.

Brax and Case had left the men they'd been fighting with, and with McCulloch's permission were heading toward where they'd left Catalina. There was less damage in this part of town, and as the houses thinned out even more, they were finally able to mount and ride.

Unlike many of the other Rangers who, going along with orders from Taylor to Hays, had relinquished the clothes they were wearing for fringed leggings, blue or red shirts with broad-brimmed felt hats or buckskin caps, Brax and Case, because of the scouting they usually ended up doing, continued to wear the clothes they'd worn when they'd ridden down to Matamoros, with the Mexican clothes they'd worn earlier in Monterrey stuffed into their saddlebags, just in case.

The road they were on began to widen a little more now as they rode, and Brax felt a pang of regret run through him at the sight of a beautiful pecan tree he'd admired the last time they'd ridden through here. It had been heavy with Spanish moss. Now it lay at the side of the road, another victim of the cannon that had pounded down on the city, and he wondered what they'd finally find when they reached the hacienda.

A short while later, he stood looking at it. Much was still intact. However, half the northeast corner of the house was missing, and the courtyard was a shambles of rubble amid what was left of the flowers. The rest of the place, except for the disarray of the furniture left behind in what must have been a hasty retreat, was still in one piece. They had left their horses tied to the hitching post out front, and had been moving through the place from room to room, in search of anything that would let them know whether Catalina was safe or not. Now they were in the bedroom Catalina had shared with Ricardo.

"You think she got away all right?" Brax asked Case, in English now, since there was no reason for them to speak Spanish this time.

Case looked around. "At least we have found nothing that says she has not."

Case walked over toward the balcony and went on outside through the French doors, next to where the desk sat against the wall. His eyes studied the distant hills overlooking the Saltillo road, and he began wondering which direction she and Ricardo might have taken.

Suddenly he turned at an exclamation from Brax, who

was still in the room. Hurrying back inside, he found his cousin kneeling on the hearth with a letter in his hand.

"What's that?"

Brax set the brick back in place on the hearth, then stood up. "Remember when I told you she said she'd leave me a message?"

"What does it say?"

"She wants us to tell General Taylor that Ampudia got word Santa Fe fell to the Americans about a month ago, and that Kearny's sending troops south, headed for Chihuahua."

"At least that's something."

"She also says that, as of the middle of August, Santa Anna's been in command of the Mexican Army. According to Ricardo, Ampudia said Santa Anna arrived in Mexico City ten days ago, and talk is that before the month's out, he'll have the whole of Mexico back in his hands again."

"Cuernos! That's all we don't need. Anything else?"

"It seems Ricardo became rather disillusioned with Canales." Brax looked over at his cousin. "Remember when Canales sent one of his men to make a deal with Taylor to set him up as head of the government here?"

"How could I forget."

"Well, from what Cat says, Valencia wouldn't go along with his so-called deal. In fact, according to her, Ricardo accused Canales of being a traitor and left his outfit."

"You mean he deserted? Where are they now?"

Brax glanced down at the letter he was holding. "She said he talked Ampudia into sending him to Mexico City on some trumped-up errand. According to her letter, they left two days before we attacked."

"Then she's safe."

"With Valencia?"

Case saw the hard look on Braxton's face. He'd guessed a long time ago about his cousin's true feelings for Catalina. Although Brax had never come right out and admitted it, somehow Case knew the two had spent their last night at the hacienda together. Maybe it was the look in Braxton's eyes the next morning when he'd said good-bye to Catalina, or maybe it was just instinct. But he was sure he was right.

"So what now?" Case asked as he watched Brax look the letter over again just one more time, slip it into his pocket, then walk over to the liquor cabinet on the wall.

"He even took his blackberry wine," Brax said, half to himself, then turned back to his cousin. "So now we go find Ben and the others and find out if the war is still going on."

Taking one last look at the room, and the bed where he'd made love to Catalina three months before, Brax headed for the door, with Case following close behind.

It had been a little over a year since Brax had stood in the abandoned house in Monterrey and read the letter Catalina had left for him. A year filled with all the agony a war could bring to a man, and a year in which he'd heard only fleeting news of Catalina, by way of reports sent back to the troops from the elusive spy El Cougar. Neither he nor Case had ever divulged Catalina's true identity to anyone, including General Taylor. So her work went on from wherever she was, and the last message had been sent from Mexico City itself. This time to General Winfield Scott, whose command Brax and Case had joined shortly after a battle up at Saltillo.

Scott had been sent to push southward, leaving Taylor and his men to hold the northern provinces. So most of the Rangers had gone with Scott. Consequently Brax and Case had still managed to stay together. Now, here they were, still with Scott, and only some fourteen miles from Mexico City. Although when they'd first arrived, it might just as well have been a hundred miles, the way the place was fortified.

Brax and Case had been scouting for Scott, the same as they'd done for Taylor, and days ago, before even reaching here, they'd told Scott about the gun emplacements up ahead on a hill near Lake Texcoco. The Mexican Army had built a fortification three tiers high, with guns on each tier, and there wasn't a thing that could get past them without being seen. At least in the daylight.

They'd also scouted a road leading up around the same lake, and learned it was possible to reach the city from the north too. However, it would have meant approaching through Guadalupe Hidalgo, where they knew General Valencia was waiting for them. So either way was a little too risky, according to the general. As Brax sat now propped against a tree, staring off into the dusk at the road up ahead, and watched the men milling about, he sighed.

Even approaching from the south would have been impossible, because if they had circumvented Lake Chalco, they'd only have had to go through another town named Mexicaltzingo, to the north, where it was so well-garrisoned that not a flea could get through.

Besides, everywhere they'd been, everything seemed to be built on causeways. Between that and the heavy rains they'd had lately, it seemed as if they did nothing but eat and sleep mud. Everything they'd thought of seemed to be useless. Up until last night that is.

Last night Brax, Case, and one of General Worth's men, Lieutenant Colonel Duncan, had returned from another one of their reconnaissance missions. But this time they'd gone past Lake Chalco, where they'd discovered another lake. And by going past this other lake, which General Scott said had to be Lake Xochimilco, according to his maps, they had found a route directly north, traversing the area between Lake Xochimilco and the mountains to the west. Then it had moved on up through a small village, and from there the road went straight to the capital, only about ten miles away. Without any hesitation, Scott had decided that this route was the one they'd take.

Now Brax sat here, watching the men getting ready to pull out. They'd move under cover of the darkness that was soon to come, and he wished with all his heart the whole bloody mess was over, but it wasn't. Not that easily.

After several more days of mud and rain and fighting, with the Americans driving the Mexicans from the south, on up through San Agustin, all the way to Churubusco, within two and a half miles of the city, with Brax and Case right in the thick of it, Brax found himself, early one afternoon, standing in front of General Scott's tent again, with Case at his side.

"What do you think he wants now?" Case asked.

Brax frowned. "Ben didn't say."

"Well, only one way to find out, I guess. Come on," and Case gestured for Brax to go first.

Half an hour later they were leaving the general's tent, heading back toward where the rest of Ben McCulloch's Rangers were camped.

"I don't like it," Brax said as they mounted their horses. "That means I'll have to put that stupid blacking on my hair again. Christ, I don't even dare take a bath with that stuff on. I don't see why I can't just pretend to be English or something."

"Because you don't talk like an Englishman, that's why."

"Yeah, I know. And besides, I speak Spanish. All right, if I have to, I have to. But that doesn't mean I like it," and he spurred Hickory into a loping canter.

It was late the same afternoon. Brax and Case had gotten everything ready, including turning Brax's hair from its sun-bleached golden white to black again, and now Brax squinted from the heat as they headed down the road, passing American soldiers here and there, who were enjoying the good weather and quiet for a change. It was still August, and hotter than blazes; that was why Brax didn't know whether to wear his hat or not. Afraid the heat would make him sweat too much, and the sweat would start trickling down his face, bringing the boot-blackening with it.

He had consented to going through with this stupid masquerade again, but still wasn't comfortable with it. The day before, word had spread quickly through all the troops that General Scott had agreed on an armistice with Santa Anna. An armistice arranged through the British legation in Mexico City. And while the truce was on, Nicholas P. Trist, who at one time had been chief clerk in the State Department, but who was now entrusted with negotiating a peace with Mexico on America's terms, was going to try to accomplish what he'd been sent to do.

Meanwhile, however, General Scott, although not wanting his men to be aware of it, was certain Santa Anna wouldn't hold to the armistice, which stated that neither side would use the opportunity to build up forces in any way. The only problem was that in order to find out if his suspicions were true, Scott had to have someone on the inside. Since Case and Brax had done it before, and since Case had also been to Mexico City with Don Estéban when he was growing up as Joaquín, Scott's choice of the two Rangers had been a logical one.

Except for the fact that he had to put the ridiculous blacking on his hair again, Brax was really pleased with the assignment, because ever since they'd come within walking distance of Mexico City, he'd been eager to find out what was happening to Catalina. And what better way? Only Brax and Case couldn't just ride right in. Not with tensions the way they were.

In the first place, they wouldn't ride in as Americans, because even some of the men who were supposed to be granted safe conduct through the city to pick up food supplies and bank drafts Santa Anna had promised to honor for General Scott were being attacked and harassed. And if they wore Mexican uniforms, there was every possibility they'd be conscripted to fight somewhere, which would ruin their reason for being there.

So they opted to go in wearing fancy Mexican clothes again that they'd had stuffed in their saddlebags all these months. General Scott's orderlies had seen to it the clothes were presentable, and they were in their saddlebags again now, waiting for them to be put back on one more time.

As they rode along beneath the hot August sun, Brax thought over what they were going to do. There were several gates leading into the city, and each one was heavily guarded. However, they figured their best bet was to enter from the east, pretending to be new arrivals from the coast, since the American armies were now all at the western gates. That had meant either riding back to the other side of Lake Chalco again, and slipping by the three-tiered guns at Lake Texcoco after dark, which was a long ride of almost fifty miles, or heading cross-country and picking up the roadway just east of the city and about seven to eight miles beyond the mounted guns. They'd decided on the latter.

The only problem, though, was that riding cross-country meant traveling the swampy plains surrounding the city, and although it was the choice Case and Braxton had made, they knew there'd be moments they wished they hadn't. To their thinking, however, five miles through swamp and muck was better than fifty in the saddle, and by nightfall they had not only managed to leave the godforsaken area behind them without any serious mishaps, but had changed into their chaquetas and calzoneras, having stowed their worn buckskins in the saddlebags again, where the fancy Mexican clothes had been. Now all they had to do was get through the gate that guarded the eastern entrance to the city, and they were both praying silently, and hard, as they approached it.

Half an hour later, pleased with themselves, they were riding comfortably through the crowded streets of Mexico City, heading for a cantina where one of the soldiers at the gate said they might be able to find lodgings for the night.

When they had first reached the gate, Brax had been afraid they were going to have trouble. However, after mentioning that they'd come to visit General Valencia, and his nephew Ricardo Valencia, the names suddenly brought a reversal for them, and the guards, at first hostile, let them pass with no more questions, even giving them directions to the general's house.

"Maybe we just ought to head there tonight," Brax said, in Spanish now, since they were inside the city.

Case frowned as he maneuvered Compadre around a group of soldiers who seemed to be enjoying their respite from battle. "I doubt that would be a good idea." He looked thoughtful. "They might get suspicious if we arrived this late," so with Brax agreeing, they continued heading for the cantina.

By the next afternoon, after spending the night at the

cantina, which was anything but elaborate, especially with so many refugees from the outskirts in the city, Case and Brax mounted their horses again and headed through the busy streets toward the address the guard had given them. It was close to an hour after starting out that they finally slowed their horses and dismounted in front of an impressive house that reminded both of them of the de Léons' hacienda back home.

The drive out front had been placed between two thick walls, with an arch overhead, and the yard was landscaped with a number of large trees shading it. Brilliant flowers bloomed everywhere.

"Well, the Valencias live in style," Brax said as they dismounted, then tied their horses to the hitching posts near the steps.

Case frowned. "What if Ricardo and the general aren't here?"

"So much the better. I think I'd rather talk to the wives anyway rather than them. Especially Ricardo's wife."

"You think she'll know where Catalina is? Just because she was with Ricardo up north . . ."

"You know, women are funny that way, cousin," Brax said, smirking. "How much you want to bet she knows all about her husband's affairs, and knows exactly where Catalina is?"

They'd started walking up the steps now and Case glanced over at Braxton. "Well, if she does, let's both hope that she's been understanding, or we could find ourselves in even more trouble," and he watched Braxton's eyes suddenly look worried.

However, Consuelo Valencia was not at home, according to the servants. Nor was the wife of General Gabriel Valencia. Both women had been sent, by their husbands, to a city in the northwest, called Queratera, where they'd be safe from the fighting.

"However, Señorita de Alvarado is in residence," the servant offered a bit dubiously. "If she might be of help."

Brax and Case exchanged surprised glances, and in a few minutes were being led from the marble-floored foyer through the large impressive house.

The general's home was even more elegant than Brax had imagined it would be, and he let his eyes take in everything as they passed through room after room of elaborate furniture enhanced by paintings, sculptures, and gilded accessories. Gabriel Valencia was evidently a man of means, and Brax was reminded of the rumors that had been filtering into the American camps about how Valencia had been coveting Santa Anna's political position for some time now, and Brax thought how ironic it was that the spy known as El Cougar should be ensconced in the man's very own house.

A few minutes after being escorted into the drawing room, Brax stood staring out one of the windows into the lovely garden at the back of the place, while Case paced the floor behind him. Then suddenly Brax tensed as he heard Case greet his sister, and knew the two were no doubt hugging each other. He turned slowly, and stopped, his eyes on the woman he hadn't seen for so long.

She hadn't changed, not a bit, except to become more lovely. At least to him.

Catalina drew back from Case and studied him closely. She hadn't seen Brax as yet.

"Braxton . . . he is alive?" she asked.

Case smiled, and nodded toward the windows, then watched her eyes light up as they fell on his cousin.

"Brax?"

Brax tried to smile. "In the flesh."

He was reluctant to get any closer to her in front of Case, but Catalina didn't seem to care. She flung herself at him, her arms locking around his neck.

"I was hoping," she murmured as she gazed up into his face.

He looked down at her, and suddenly his whole resolve not to let Case know how he really felt about her flew out the window. Lowering his head, he covered her mouth with his and gave her a slow, passionate kiss that seemed to burn itself right through both of them. It had been so long.

Brax finally drew his head back, his gray eyes warm and tender. "I've been so worried."

"You think I haven't?" She reached up, touching a spot near his hairline. "Soon perhaps you won't have to resort to this." She turned to gaze back at Case. "I presume the two of you are here on your own this time, since you haven't used any passwords."

"A little of both," Case answered as he walked across the room, with its gilt-edged paintings and elaborately carved furniture. "We were sent into the city to find out if Santa Anna's keeping to his promise not to build up his defenses during the armistice."

"So you came here?"

"Why not?"

"After all," Brax said as he released her, "if anyone would know, it'd be you."

"Then why didn't your general just go through our regular channels? I'd have gotten the information for him."

"Let's face it. There are places you can't go this time, Cat," Case said. "Besides, I don't know if you realize it or not, but I think someone's getting too close to you. The last contact you sent out didn't make it. They found his body floating in one of the causeways between here and our lines."

She looked aghast. "No, I didn't know."

Brax's eyes darkened. "You think maybe Ricardo?"

"Perhaps. I don't think so, though." She looked worried. "Maybe the two of you shouldn't be here. I never dreamed . . ." She wrung her hands worriedly, then hesitated, thinking, the crimson dress she had on making her look pale. "If it is Ricardo . . ."

"If what is me?" Ricardo asked from the doorway, and all three whirled, surprised to see Ricardo Valencia standing there, the gold buttons blending with the fancy gold embroidery that bordered the red bib and red cuffs on his blue uniform. He had evidently left his shako in the foyer, and Brax couldn't get over the difference between his polished appearance today and the well-worn uniform he'd had on when they'd last seen him.

"Oh, it must have been you," Catalina said, saving the moment for them all as she moved away from Brax and

Case and took Ricardo's arm, ushering him the rest of the way into the room, "I thought you were with your uncle's troops, but Joaquín and Braxton said they were sure they'd caught a glimpse of you this morning on the street."

"I see." Ricardo's dark eyes shifted from Case to Brax, and back to Case again. "You seem to appear in the strangest places, Señor de Alvarado," he said as he stared at Case, and Catalina felt him squeeze her hand slightly where it rested on his arm. "How is it the two of you are here, and wearing civilian clothes, while our city is under siege?"

"Luck, I guess. Just plain luck," Case answered, trying to be nonchalant about the whole thing. "You see, I'm afraid I'm a bit of a coward, Captain," he continued, hoping to look the part of a dandy. "But I just can't see myself dying in order to try to keep a piece of land someone else wants, when there's such a great big world out there to live in."

Ricardo's eyes narrowed, his strong jaw tensing. "I presume that's the reason you refused my invitation to fight with us up north, am I right?"

"I guess, perhaps." Case looked over at Brax. "Would you say that was the reason, amigo?" he asked.

Brax tried to keep his anger at this pompous ass from showing as he watched the way Ricardo held Catalina close to him. "That, and the fact that we like living," he answered, forcing himself to go along with Case. "You see, Captain, if we had joined you there, then we might not be standing here now, now would we?"

"And you are here. Why?" Ricardo asked.

"To see my sister."

"And to enjoy your uncle's hospitality, if he'll have us," Braxton said, boldly ignoring the fact that he and Case had just informed the captain that they were cowards.

A slight smile played about Ricardo's mouth. "Well, one thing I'll say for the two of you. You may be cowards when it comes to putting your lives on the line, but you certainly do have an incredible amount of nerve."

They stood in the parlor for some time while Braxton

and Case made up a number of stories about their adventures over the past year, while trying to keep out of the fighting, and what one didn't think of, the other did. By the time General Valencia himself joined them, shortly after lunch, Ricardo had come to the conclusion that no one in the heart of Mexico City, or anywhere else, for that matter, had anything to fear from either Braxton Ortega or Joaquín de Alvarado, and he introduced them to his uncle without any qualms whatsoever. Even though he did wish someone would tell Señor Ortega how ridiculous his hair looked with all that heavy pomade on it.

Greasy hair was the least of Braxton's worries, however. Right now, the only thing he was afraid of was that General Gabriel Valencia would possibly recognize him. Because now, as he shook hands with the man, Brax suddenly realized he'd been only a few feet from the general during one of the battles some days before. There was no mistaking the man. The face, the uniform he wore, with its pale blue silk sash, had stood out among those of the plain soldiers.

Evidently either the general's memory was short or he'd actually looked right through Brax instead of at him. Either that or the change of hair color did what it was supposed to do. Fortunately, whichever, the general didn't seem to have the slightest suspicion Brax and Case weren't what they claimed to be. And he even made sure they could attend his little dinner party that evening, then offered to find some more presentable clothes for them to wear while they were his houseguests, since they'd been traveling so light.

It was shortly before the guests were due to arrive when the general informed them that since his wife was gone, Catalina would act as hostess for the evening. The statement had started Brax wondering if the general knew about Catalina and Ricardo. Was that why she hadn't been sent away with the other women? If so, the general didn't seem too concerned about the situation. But then who knew, maybe he had a mistress of his own somewhere in the city.

Later that evening, Brax stood outside the courtyard

and watched Catalina excusing the men from the dinner table so they could retire to the drawing room for a glass of wine and to puff on their cigarittos. A custom that had become quite prevalent in Mexico during the past few years.

Brax had excused himself a few minutes earlier, when the chili pepper in the meat sauce had plunged right through his stomach like a bullet ricocheting off a rock, and he had been just outside now, on his way back in, when he'd seen them all starting to get up from their chairs. Only he certainly didn't feel like going with them, just to sit around listening to a bunch of men trying to figure out a way to win the war. Not with Catalina around. He'd leave the spy part of it up to Case this time. So instead of coming back in, he was waiting until the men, including Ricardo, left. When they were all gone, he stepped back into the dining room.

"Cat?" It was the first he'd caught her alone since they arrived.

Catalina whirled around. She'd been the only woman in attendance tonight, and now she hurried over to Brax, motioning for him to be quiet, then she grabbed his hand, pulling him back outside into the garden, hoping they could reach the shadows before the servants came in to clear away the dishes.

"Shhh . . ." she cautioned him as she continued dragging him as far from the house as she could, then she stopped and faced him. "Do you have any idea at all of how glad I am to see you?" she asked.

It was dark out, and he couldn't see her face, but her voice told him so much. "I was afraid something had happened to you," she went on. "And I think if it had, I should die."

His eyes grew misty. "Now, may I tell you?" he asked.

Catalina knew what he meant, only it still wasn't the time. First he had to know, and she couldn't tell him here in the garden.

"Later tonight," she answered, her eyes looking deeply into his. "Ricardo said he has to get back to his troops tonight, and we can find time to be alone somehow."

He reached out, taking her hand, only she cautioned him, squeezing his hand affectionately. "Not here," she said. "Here we have to be very careful. The general expects me to be loyal to Ricardo. I was fortunate this afternoon that one of the servants didn't come in. Now, go back in there and pretend you just came back. If you don't, they'll begin to wonder. Now, go, hurry, until later," and she watched him reluctantly return to the dining room, then Brax went on into the general's library, where he found himself a comfortable seat in one of the corners and listened intently to the other men, who were already in a heated discussion about Santa Anna's bungling.

This in itself was a surprise to Brax. He had thought all of Mexico was unconditionally behind Santa Anna. Now, suddenly, to discover there were those, even in the president's own army, who thought so little of the man, was somewhat of a shock. All during the rest of the evening, the talk was centered on the fact that Santa Anna was calling for Valencia's court-martial for his defeat at Contreras, and the only thing keeping Santa Anna from demanding it was Valencia's political power. It seemed Valencia was too close, not only to Santa Anna's own cabinet, but to the president's friends as well. Even tonight, many of Santa Anna's best generals, including generals Vizcayno and Torres, were at General Gabriel Valencia's, enjoying his hospitality.

By the time the evening was over, with Ricardo naturally being the last to leave, Braxton and Case, after listening quietly to all the military talk, while continuing to play the parts of apathetic bystanders, realized General Scott had been right. Not only was Santa Anna expecting the hostilities to resume, but according to his generals, he was looking forward to it by smuggling more and more cannons into the city, as well as men and ammunition.

"So who goes to tell Scott?" Case asked later, as they stood alone in the drawing room, while the general left to say good-bye to his guests and Ricardo went to look for Catalina.

Brax walked over to one of the back windows and looked out into the garden just in time to catch a glimpse of Ricardo and Catalina disappearing into the shadows beneath a pepper tree.

He tensed. "This time I'll let you go," he answered.

"Don't do me any favors."

"I'm doing me a favor this time," Brax said as he turned back toward his cousin. "You can get in and out of the city better than I can. Besides, I have some unfinshed business here."

"What do I tell Scott?"

"Tell him the job's not over yet, until we can give him names of places."

"You think we'll get them?"

"Why not? Surely the general knows, and staying in the same house with him, how can we miss?"

Case looked skeptical. "I don't know, Brax . . ."

"You've got to talk him into letting us stay as long as it takes." Brax's gray eyes darkened. "I can't just ride out and leave her again, Case," he said, trying to keep his voice low. "I just can't. Not yet."

"I know." Case laid a hand on his shoulder. "I've known for a long time, it's just that I hope you know what you're doing."

"Don't worry. I do." Brax glanced back out the window toward the garden. "You don't have to come back, you know. Not if you don't want to, because I have a feeling when I leave here this time, it won't be alone."

Case watched his cousin closely, as Brax caught sight of Ricardo and Catalina again when they stepped out of the shadows and headed for the house, and he hoped Brax wasn't going to be digging his own grave. Yet, he knew if Brax was, he'd be right there beside him, because if there was any way at all the general would let him, he'd be back.

The guests had been gone for well over an hour, Case and Braxton had been shown to their rooms already, the lamps downstairs were out, as well as the lamp in Brax's room, and he stood just inside the door, ready to open it cautiously.

Catalina had promised while they were in the garden earlier that they'd have time alone tonight, but it had been so late when the discussion in the salon had broken up, and even later when Ricardo left. Even the general had insisted on being overly friendly. Consequently, they hadn't been able to find even one moment to be alone together.

Well, that wasn't going to stop Brax. He had watched, so that he knew which room was Catalina's, and since it had been close to an hour already since the household retired, he was sure he could locate it again, even in the dark.

He was just ready to ease the door open a crack, to make certain no one was in the hall, when a slight noise made him freeze, and he felt the door begin to inch toward him. Startled, he stepped quietly back, then waited and watched as the door continued opening, and a vague figure, resembling a filmy ghost, slipped inside, then the door closed quickly behind it.

"Brax?" Catalina called out softly.

He'd been holding his breath, and exhaled. "Cat?"

A hand flew to her throat, and she jumped, startled, not expecting him to be so close.

"Por Dios, you frightened me."

He reached out, pulling her into his arms. "What do you think you did to me? I thought maybe it was the general."

"Hardly."

His lips found hers in the darkened room, and the kiss was long and sweet.

"I told you we would have time alone," she whispered.

His arms tightened around her. "So now I'll tell you," he began again.

Again she stopped him. "No, come," and she took his hand, pulling him to the bed, where she made him sit down, then she stood before him, looking down into his face. The moon coming in through the window was casting shadows across it, and she thought he'd never looked handsomer. Oh, he'd aged a little perhaps. After all, he was almost thirty. "Now first, I will tell you," she said, her voice husky, dark eyes warm with love.

"Tell me what?"

She reached out, holding his face in her hands, and she moved closer, so she was standing between his legs, the scent of her filling his nostrils, and bringing with it so many memories.

"You and I . . . we have a daughter, mi querido," she murmured, and saw the puzzled expression in his gray eyes. "She was born March 16 of this year."

Brax couldn't find his voice, let alone any words to put to it, even if he could talk. All he could do was stare at her.

"Sí, she's yours," Catalina explained, keeping her voice barely a whisper. "Ricardo thought it was his, and that the baby didn't live, but a couple where we were staying at the time helped me."

He swallowed hard, reaching up, and took her hands from his face, holding them in his own, which were trembling. "Where is she?" he asked.

"Here in Mexico City."

"But you said . . ."

"Sí. She is still with the people who helped me. I had them bring her here so I could be with her. Tomorrow we will go see her, but we'll have to be very careful."

"I really have a daughter?"

"Sí."

"What does she look like?"

"Her father. That's why I didn't dare let Ricardo see her. He was away at the time, for a few days. When she was born, and I saw all the blond hair, I knew he'd never believe she was his. So I explained to the people where we had stayed for a few days that Ricardo was forcing me to stay with him. Thank God they felt sorry for me. You see, he was forcing them to take us in, and they too had little love for him. So we buried some rocks in a box, told him the child was born dead, and they left her with friends until we were gone." Her eyes suddenly glistened with tears. "Only I couldn't leave her there, mi amor, and I paid one of my contacts here in the city to go back and have them bring her here."

"Her name?"

"I call her my little Texas because she is so much like you."

"That's no name for a girl."

"It is for ours, because she is like Texas, beautiful."

He pulled her closer, looking up into her face. "Now may I tell you?" he asked, and his voice was breathless, full of emotion.

She kissed him lightly. "Sí, now you may tell me."

"I love you, Catalina de Alvarado. I love you with all my heart," and without thinking, he pulled her even closer against him and began to fall back on the bed.

"Madre de Dios!" she blurted as she struggled against him, pulling back, yet trying to hold her voice down to a whisper. "Not again, mi querido. Tonight there'd be no wine with which to stain the covers."

His arms were still around her as he realized what she meant, and carefully, yet deliberately, he eased his hold, then grabbed her hand and led her across the darkened room to where he'd spread his bedroll earlier. He gestured dramatically.

"After you, mi querida."

She squeezed his hand, then while she lowered herself to the bedroll, he locked the door, stripped off his chaqueta, boots, and calzoneras to join her, and while Case lay in the big bed in the next room, dreaming of the day when he'd be able to return to Texas and show Moonflower how much he loved her, Braxton once more made love to Catalina, this time promising himself that he wouldn't leave Mexico without her.

The next morning Case left early, using the excuse that he wanted to see some of the sights, and the general made sure to caution him not to get too near any of the fortifications. Actually Case was sure he could move through the gates of the city quite easily, after the little resistance that first night. And promising to be back before dark if at all possible, he rode off on Compadre, while Brax and Catalina watched from the veranda of the white stucco house.

After their lovemaking the night before, while Catalina lay in Braxton's arms enjoying the secure feeling they gave her, she told him that she was sure Ricardo had the jewelry and letter she'd told him about the year before in a safe downstairs in the library, behind a picture of the Madonna that hung beside the fireplace.

She'd discovered the safe quite accidentally only few days before. She'd been heading for the drawing room, when she saw Ricardo disappear into the library, and curious, wondering what he was up to, she had furtively watched him pull the picture aside, open the safe, and put something inside.

However, it was not only too high for her to even try to reach, but impossible for her to attempt to open. Now, all Brax had to do was figure a way to open the safe, walk out with its contents, and leave the city with Catalina and the baby without being caught. An easy task if there hadn't been a war going on. But what seemed like an impossible one now.

However, first things first, and later that morning, after the general had left to go to an appointment somewhere with one of the cabinet members, Brax and Catalina soon left the house themselves, he riding Hickory, she riding sidesaddle on a lovely black horse Ricardo had bought for her after what he thought was the loss of their baby.

Not quite an hour after riding out through the magnificent arch heralding the driveway that led from the general's fine hacienda, Catalina and Brax were entering a small stucco house near the southwestern end of town, not far from the Garita del Niño Perdido, one of the well-fortified gates to the city. It was a two-room hut, barely big enough to straighten up in, at least for Braxton. But although the place was small, it was as neat as its occupants could make it under the circumstances.

Situated on one of the back alleys, it wasn't much use to the soldiers, so was ideal for its present use. Catalina greeted the couple inside enthusiastically, introducing them to Braxton as Señor and Señora Martinez. Only she was more used to calling them Hernando and Juanita.

Brax greeted them rather hesitantly, his eyes not on the two middle-aged people, but on the tiny baby Juanita was cuddling on her lap. The little girl was wearing a white dress made from the same material as the woman's blouse, her small bare feet sticking out from beneath it, and for a moment Brax could hardly speak as he stared hard at the dainty little thing, with her tawny skin, pale hair like unruly wisps on top her head, and big dark eyes. Catalina tossed her riding crop aside and hurried over to take the baby from the woman, and a lump jumped into Braxton's throat.

"Wait, let me," he said, finally finding his voice, and Catalina turned, a smile on her face as Brax walked toward her and the baby.

Reaching out, Brax held his hand palm-up, then watched closely as the child poked at his fingers, trying to pull his big hand to her mouth.

"Look, she likes me," he exclaimed.

"She shall love you, just like her mother does," Catalina said. "Give her time," and with a smile on his face, Brax lifted the baby into his arms. He held her close, kissed her, and it felt so good to be together, that they spent just a little over an hour in the small hut, playing with the baby and talking, until Catalina suddenly remembered Ricardo had said he'd be back in the early afternoon.

"And I don't want him to get suspicious."

So after some reluctant good-byes, Brax took one more long look at the baby, who had finally fallen asleep in her little wooden cradle, and they rode away from the hut, heading back again to General Valencia's.

For the next few days, while Braxton racked his brain trying to think of a way to get into the safe in the library, Case returned with General Scott's blessing, and Brax and Case continued, with Catalina's help, to feed information to General Scott outside the city. They told him about the placement of soldiers, guns, and if they could, the general feelings of everyone, about the way Santa Anna was running things. Finally, one day almost two weeks after the armistice had been called, Case, who had ridden out early that morning, planning as usual to leave the city just long enough to meet his contact, then ride back in again as if he'd just been enjoying the sights, arrived back earlier than usual.

"Something's up," he told Brax and Catalina, who were just finishing lunch and getting ready to go see their daughter. "Scott's ordered us out." Brax had told Case about the baby the first night he'd returned, and although Case had been surprised, he seemed to have accepted it as a natural course of events.

Brax stood up. "I can't leave. Things aren't settled yet. What about the baby?"

"It'll have to wait."

"The hell it will."

Case's jaw tightened as he gazed about to make sure they weren't being overheard. "Orders are orders, Brax," he said. "Besides, they've put new cannon up, and doubled the guard on the gates. We'll be lucky if we can even get back out now."

Catalina looked puzzled. "What do you think happened?"

"Negotiations probably broke down. Quién sabe? One thing for sure, though, if Scott says we go back, we go back."

Brax didn't like it. That meant he had to leave Catalina and the baby here. "Damn!" he blurted, then felt Catalina's hand on his arm as she too stood up.

"No, don't be angry, mi querido. Just go," she said, her dark eyes pleading with him. "I shall be all right, and so will the baby. God will protect us. And I'll be waiting here when you ride back in."

"But there's no guarantee."

"There never is, not on life, querido," she said quickly. "But there are still things I can do from here. Remember, there are still those here who are on our side."

"But to leave you?"

"I will be fine."

He stared at her for a long time, then his jaw set in determination. "All right, I'll go because I have to, but if anything happens to you . . ."

"Shhh," she murmured softly. "Someone will hear.

Come, let's get your things," and within ten minutes'
time Brax and Case were once more on the crowded
streets of Mexico City, heading back toward the gate of
San Lazaro. By late afternoon, after talking their way
through the gates with the use of the names of various
Mexican generals spicing their conversation, they made
their way into the swampy causeway that separated the
roads leading to Mexico City, and headed back to join
their outfit again, as the general had ordered.

It was just a little before dark, and Catalina was nervous as she stepped from the carriage, then told Hernando
to take both carriage and horse around to the back of the
general's house. For the past few days she'd done nothing but move from room to room in the big house,
listening to the sounds of battle in the distance as the
fighting got closer and closer.

It had been a week since Brax and Case had left, and
she hadn't seen much of Ricardo lately either. Or the
general for that matter. She assumed they were either
fighting alongside their men, even though Santa Anna had
tried to relieve the general of his command, or else the
general was still somewhere in the city trying to usurp
Santa Anna's power, while Ricardo did the fighting. Whichever it was, they certainly weren't here, and she was
glad, because as soon as the sounds of battle started,
she'd had Hernando and Juanita join her here with the
baby.

Now, as she made her way into the house, she grimaced. They hadn't had any fresh food for days, the
baby needed milk, and everyone was off fighting or hiding behind barred doors. It was as if the whole world had
suddenly stopped living, except for the soldiers. They
were all over the place. Even the servants had disappeared one by one, and she imagined they too had either
gone to join the fighting or were hiding somewhere,
afraid to fight.

She stood for a second on the veranda and stared off to
the west, where the cannon echoed through the city,
rumbling across the buildings and trees like thunder,

accompanied by faint rifle shots. The fighting was getting even closer.

Quickly she opened the door and entered, heading straight for the drawing room, where she knew Juanita should be with the baby. Suddenly she froze. Juanita wasn't in the drawing room, but Ricardo was. He was sitting in one of the fancy overstuffed chairs a few feet from the fireplace, and he was leaning back all too relaxed, staring directly at her, the smoke from a cigaritto trailing just above his head.

"Well, well, so, you decided to return," he said, his eyes hardening as he continued to lounge comfortably in the chair.

Catalina watched him closely. He might look relaxed, but she could tell by the look on his handsomely chiseled features that he was anything but relaxed. Taking a deep breath, she strolled toward him, trying to keep her legs from trembling.

"I thought you were with your men."

He took a drag off the cigaritto, blowing the smoke out in a long stream, his eyes still on her. "I was," he answered. "Until we were cut down, and they all scattered."

"You deserted?"

"Deserted? Me? Hardly. But someone had to report to what's left of the government here."

"We heard the British consul tried to negotiate again with the Americans."

"Which was a laugh. But then I didn't come here to talk about the fighting. I came to see you."

"I see. In the middle of a battle you come to see me. Why?"

"Because I heard a rumor I didn't like. Only when I got here I discovered it wasn't a rumor." His eyes bristled furiously. "Whose is she, Catalina?" he suddenly asked.

She tensed, but didn't answer.

He smashed his cigaritto out in a dish on the table beside his chair, then stood up and walked toward her.

"I asked you, whose child is she?"

Catalina was breathing heavily, trying to control her anger as well as her fear. "Where's Juanita?"

"Don't worry. She'll live."

"What did you do to her?"

"Never mind what I did to her."

"If you've hurt her . . ."

"I should have killed her!"

"Swine!"

He grabbed her wrist. "Oh, I see, now I am a swine. Since when, mi querida?"

Her dark eyes narrowed, and his fingers dug into her wrists.

"Since the day you forced yourself on me."

"I gave you love."

"Love? Ha! You don't know the meaning of the word. You flaunt me in front of your wife." His eyes darkened viciously. "You think Consuelo doesn't know? She knows, and it's breaking her heart."

"Who's the father?"

"A gringo! A beautiful, wonderful Texan whose boots you aren't fit to lick."

He was still holding her wrist with his left hand, and she let out a soft cry as he raised his free hand to smash her across the face.

"Do that, and you're dead," Brax yelled from the doorway.

Taken by surprise, Catalina whirled, wrenching free, as Ricardo stared incredulously at the vague outline of a buckskin-clad man in the doorway.

Gun in hand, and taking his hat from his head, Braxton stepped from the shadows, and purposely let the last faint rays of the setting sun catch in his pale blond hair, no longer darkened from the bootblacking. He heard Ricardo gasp, his eyes widening in surprise.

"You?"

"Sí, me," Brax shot back, and he put his hat back on, moving closer, grabbing Catalina with his free hand and maneuvering her behind him to shield her. "So now you know who the Texan is."

"Bastardo!" Ricardo's face was livid.

Braxton's gun was still leveled on him. "I'd watch what I was saying if I were you," he warned.

Catalina peeked out from behind him. "How did you know to come?"

"The garitas have all been taken, and I happened to spot Ricardo here taking off when we hit his artillery, and his men started scattering. I had a feeling by the direction he was heading that he wasn't planning to get reinforcements."

Ricardo's eyes were blazing. "How did you get this far?"

"Wouldn't you like to know. The point is, we'll have the whole city by morning."

"And you think that'll help you?" Ricardo laughed. "Even if you kill me, señor, whatever your name really is, the authorities, American as well as Mexican, will prosecute your puta here for murder."

"Not if they don't have any evidence. Come on," and he waved the gun at Ricardo, motioning for him to move.

With the gun at the captain's back, Brax made him leave the drawing room, with Catalina following, and they headed for the library, where Brax reached up with his free hand, swung the picture of the Madonna on the far wall out, and revealed the safe Catalina had told him was there.

Ricardo's jaw set stubbornly. He wasn't about to give in. He'd planned everything too carefully. He'd planned to come back to get Catalina, they'd join Santa Anna when he evacuated the city, and he'd take the evidence with him to wherever they ended up, then life would go on as before in spite of the war. But now . . . he wasn't about to let it all end like this. Catalina was his. She didn't belong to this goddamned gringo.

"You think I will open it?" he said, his voice harsh, the fire of his anger making it crack as he spoke. "I would die first, and you will never get it open," and with that, he moved quickly, his hand snaking out to slap at Braxton's gun.

Brax, bracing himself against the blow, took a step

backward, catching Ricardo's left arm, and Brax spun him around as Catalina dove out of the way. Then, seconds later, she watched, horrified, from where she was crouched behind a chair, as the two men fought for the gun that was still in Braxton's hand.

Suddenly a shot rang out and Catalina held her breath as both men seemed to hesitate momentarily, as if stopped by some unnatural force, then slowly she saw Ricardo's eyes widen, then close, and he slumped to the ground at Braxton's feet.

"Damn!" Brax exclaimed as he stared down at the crumpled body. "Now we have no choice."

"What's that?" Catalina was creeping out from behind the chair.

"We'll have to burn it."

"Burn the house?"

"Sí. The marble and stucco won't burn, but the rest of it will. These walls . . ." He grabbed a poker from the fireplace and smashed the wall beside the safe. It was wood. "The safe is solid, but not fireproof, and even though the jewelry would still be inside, any papers would be charred to a crisp from the heat."

"Are you sure?"

"I'm certain. Now, we don't have much time. Your General Valencia or someone else might show up. So grab whatever you have to, and I'll take care of this, then we'll go get the baby."

"We don't have to go get her. She's upstairs."

"Here?"

"Sí, with Juanita."

"That's better yet. Now, are there any horses here?"

"Just the old carriage horse. The army took the rest. They said she wasn't worth it."

"Bueno, then here's what you do."

Some ten minutes later, Braxton rode away from general Valencia's hacienda with his daughter in his arms and Catalina riding beside him on the old carriage horse, while behind them, in the general's library, flames were already making their way up the draperies and creeping across the floor where he'd spilled whale oil from the lamp, to help its progress.

Catalina had given Hernando and Juanita a choice of coming with them if they wanted. But weary from the upheaval their lives had been in the past few months, and afraid of what the coming events might bring, they opted to sneak out of the city and go back to the farm they'd once lived in, wishing the two young lovers good luck.

We're going to need it too, Brax thought as he drew rein for a second and started back at the hacienda, making sure the fire had caught.

Minutes later, after he and Catalina made sure the orange glow was beginning to color the night sky, they turned their attention once more back to the baby and the best route to take from the city, then dug their horses in the ribs, heading toward where Brax was sure he could reach the American lines with the least trouble, and without endangering their lives any more than he had to. All around them while they rode, the sporadic rifle fire became scarcer and scarcer as darkness fell over the city.

By the next morning, when he, Catalina, and the baby finally reached the safety of General Scott's tent, a few miles from the front lines, it was all over. White flags were going up all over Mexico City. Santa Anna had surrendered. The Americans had won.

Brax sat in a quiet corner in the ballroom of his sister's hacienda with his daughter on his lap while he watched the couples dancing, then he glanced over to where Blythe and Catalina were talking. Strange how the years had changed people, he thought. Even him.

If anyone had told him ten years ago that by March of 1848 he'd be married to Catalina and have a beautiful daughter, with another baby on the way, he'd have said they were crazy. Yet, here he was. His gaze moved to the thickening waistline of his wife as his hands toyed with the baby's fine hair. He'd never been quite so proud in all his life as when the village priest had married them back in Mexico City, right after the surrender.

Now that was all behind them, they were living at the

Double K while they built a place of their own, and here they were at Case and Moonflower's wedding. It had taken the four of them months to get home from Mexico after he and Case had finally been released by the army, because they'd had to come overland, not having enough money for passage on any ships. They'd arrived just a little over a month ago, making plans for the wedding as soon as they reached San Antonio.

Naturally, Blythe and Mario had been delighted, insisting the wedding should take place here in the chapel, and Brax drew his gaze from Catalina again, letting it fall on the bride and groom, who had eyes only for each other as they twirled about the dance floor. They were lucky, so lucky. Or was it more than that?

All the fighting, the years of violence, they'd all been through, and yet the only one who hadn't come out of it unscathed was his father, who still limped from the leg wound he'd suffered during the war for independence.

And then there was Moonflower's father, although DeMosse hadn't been a casualty of war. He'd become a casualty of life, just as they all would be someday.

Brax straightened, a strange warm feeling running through him. It was good just to be alive, and he looked down at little Texas, as they still called her. She'd be a year old in a few days. God had been good to him, so good.

Suddenly he turned, glancing back toward the ballroom door, where a commotion was going on. Then he sat up even straighter as he caught a word here and there.

"Ratified . . . the whole thing . . . just came through on the wires from New Orleans. . . ."

By the time he got up from his chair, maneuvering the baby around in his arms, and made his way through the crowd that was forming, the music had stopped, and started up again, playing "Yankee Doodle," and everyone was shouting and carrying on like it was the end of the war all over again.

"What is it? What happened?" he asked when he reached Blythe.

Blythe's gray eyes caught her brother's, and she looked from him to Catalina, then back again.

"One of the men just rode out from town. They got word that the Mexicans have ceded California, New Mexico, and everything north of the Rio Grande. We got what we wanted, Brax. It's been signed, ratified, and it's official."

Brax took a deep breath, then glanced around at his mother and father, talking excitedly to Aunt Heather and Uncle Cole, and to Teffin and Kaelen, who were trying to keep their daughter, Loedicia, who was almost nine now, from making too much noise. They'd promised her she wouldn't have to stay home with her two-year-old brother if she behaved. Then he thought of Genée and Seth, and their young son Michael, who were all still in Washington, and how excited they must be, being a part of it all.

He frowned, looking around. "Where's Grandma Dicia?" he asked.

Blythe's hand flew to her breast. "Oh dear, I almost forgot. She got tired a little while ago, and Mario helped her upstairs so she could lie down on our bed. She likes it in our room, where the breeze can reach her from the portico." Blythe reached out and put her hand on her brother's arm. "Go tell her," she said. "She'll be so glad to hear."

He looked at Catalina. "You coming too?"

"I will wait here." She smiled. "With the baby," and she reached out her arms.

Brax put little Tex in Catalina's arms, kissed the baby on the cheek, then left the ballroom, heading for the foyer at the front of the house, where the stairs were, while up in the master bedroom Loedicia lay on the bed, her eyes closed.

She was tired. So tired. Funny how just moving could be such a chore at times, she thought. Lizette had thought perhaps she shouldn't come today, that it'd be too much for her. But pooh! As long as Loedicia Chapman had a breath in her body, she wasn't about to miss a wedding. Especially this one. She had promised DeMosse. And it had been so pretty too. Moonflower had looked just lovely in the white lace dress with its long train and frothy veil.

Opening her eyes, she stared up at the ceiling and smiled, the music and noise from downstairs floating in through the open French doors. What a wonderful day it had been, to be here with her family like this. A noise caught her attention, and she turned, looking toward the door.

Brax stuck his head in. "Good, you're not asleep." He opened the door wider, and she sat up on the edge of the bed, smiling.

"You know, I think I might have dozed off at that," she said. "Up to a few minutes ago."

He strolled over to the bed and sat down beside her. "How do you feel?"

"What do you mean, how do I feel? I feel fine. A little tired perhaps. After all, wait till you're ninety-three."

"Ninety-two, Grandma. You won't be ninety-three for a few days yet."

"Oh pooh, who counts days. It's the years that are important, aren't they?"

"Are you sure you're all right?" he asked again when he saw her start to stand up, then hesitate. "You look a little pale."

Her hand covered his, and he frowned. For the first time he could ever remember, Grandma Dicia's hand felt cold.

"I've been staying out of the sun too long, I guess." Her violet eyes warmed softly, and she took a deep breath. "Maybe . . . you don't suppose, dear, you could just sort of help me out onto the balcony, do you?" She hated having to ask him for help like this. "It's just that sometimes these old legs of mine don't want to do what I want them to anymore, and the sun would feel so good. I could maybe sit on Blythe's lounge chair for a while."

Brax stood up. Only instead of helping her, he bent down and lifted her into his arms.

"I said help me, not carry me," she said, protesting as he headed for the French doors.

He stopped. "Now look, Grandma, if I want to carry you, I'll carry you, understand? Besides, I'm bigger than you are."

She pressed her hand against his shirtfront, trying to look stern. Then her eyes softened, the muscular feel of him reminding her of when she'd been young and Brax's great-grandfather had carried her like this. She smiled sheepishly.

"Well, all right then, on with it," she said, her voice warm with affection, and his arms tightened around her as he maneuvered them both through the French doors and out onto the balcony.

Grandma Dicia had lost a little weight over the past year, and her skin had wrinkled more because of it, but there was still that air of calm beauty about her that had always fascinated Brax when he was growing up. She never seemed to age. Not the way other women did. Her hair was whiter, her skin softer, but her eyes always twinkled, laughter falling so easily from her lips. And yet she had a way of making everyone sit up and take notice when she was around. Some folks said she was feisty, others often referred to her as stubborn and independent. He'd always thought of her as a lady.

He set her down on the lounge chair where Blythe usually sat in the evenings before going to bed, then made sure she was comfortable. There was a roof over the balcony, but still the afternoon sun felt warmer out here, and the scent from the flowering vines that graced the veranda below was as strong on the air as the noise from all the celebrating.

Brax winced as he sensed she was struggling to get her breath.

"Grandma?"

She breathed in deeply, finally getting air into her lungs. "It's nothing . . . I'm fine," she assured him.

"Maybe I ought to call someone, Mario . . ."

"Good heavens, no. I'm all right. Just a little tired, that's all. Now"—her eyes crinkled as she patted the chair beside her—"Sit right down here and tell me what all the commotion and hollering is all about downstairs. I'm sure it has nothing to do with the wedding."

He sat down, but continued watching her closely. "Well, somebody from town rode out with the news that Mexico finally decided to give us all the land Polk asked for," he said. "California, New Mexico, and everything north of the Rio Grande, all the way to the Pacific Ocean."

"Oh my!" Loedicia looked pleased, and suddenly there were tears in her eyes. "Do you know what this means?" She shook her head. "No, you wouldn't, how could you." She reached over and took his hand, holding it tightly. For some reason it was becoming a little harder for her to talk, and she knew that holding his hand would give her more strength. "You know, a long time ago Mr. Jefferson told your great-grandfather he had a dream about this country," she said. "He told him that someday this country would stretch out all the way beyond the rivers and mountains, from one ocean to the other. And now his dream's come true."

"You mean Great-Grandpa Quinn really knew President Jefferson?"

"Good heavens yes, and George too, and Ben Franklin, and Daniel Boone. I told you all about them, didn't I?"

He squeezed her hand affectionately. "I always thought you were just making it all up, Grandma," he said. "You know, trying to think of exciting stories to entertain a little boy with."

"Oh my, no." Her eyes grew serious. "Your Great-Grandpa Quinn was quite an important man in his day. The son of an earl, you know."

"Yes, I know."

"That's not why I loved him, though. You understand that." A faraway look crept into her eyes, and even though her voice faltered shakily, her hand still held his firmly. "I loved him because . . ." She paused a moment, as if thinking back, then glanced over at Brax. "You know, I really don't know why I loved him, but then, how do any of us know why we love? I guess it's something we just do, like with your Great-Grandpa Roth and me too."

She was still holding his hand, and it continued giving her strength, although there were moments when she felt so strange, almost as if she were floating. Was this what death was like? She thought for a moment. Then brushed the thought aside as she concentrated once more on Brax, where he sat beside her.

"You don't remember much about your Great-Grandpa Roth, do you?" she said.

He felt a pang of hurt inside. "I know he died because of me."

"Nonsense!" She drew her gaze from Braxton's face, and stared off toward the late-afternoon sky, with its lavender clouds shrouded in pink and gold, as if she were trying to see into the past. "He died because he loved you. That's the way he was." She looked back over at Brax. "You used to follow him around like a little shadow."

Suddenly her eyes widened, and he knew she was having difficulty breathing again.

"Grandma, are you sure you're all right?"

She coughed.

He started to get up. "I'll go get Mario."

"No!" Her voice was barely a whisper, her fingers tightening on his hand, keeping him in the chair. "I don't want anyone else. I want you, dear. Let me do this my way, please."

"But . . ."

"Please, Brax, humor an old lady."

He lifted her hand, and held it in both of his. "You're not old."

"Now who's the dreamer?" She sighed wearily. "You're as bad as DeMosse—you know that, don't you? Trying to make me feel young again." She took another deep breath, and he frowned. "I wish DeMosse could have lived awhile longer," she said, and her free hand moved up slowly. She laid it on her breast. "At least until the war was over, and the wedding. He'd have been so pleased, and proud."

"You loved him too, didn't you?"

She looked directly at him, her eyes veiled with tears. "You know, in a way, I guess I loved them all. And now, God willing, maybe, just maybe, I shall finally get to see them again. Do you suppose?"

His face paled. "No, Grandma."

"Hush," she said, her voice faint. "What more is there for me here, dear? And I'm so tired."

"Please . . . let me get someone . . ."

"No . . ." Her fingers tightened even harder on his hand. She just wouldn't let go, and he didn't have the heart to pry her hand loose. "I don't want a big fuss. I only want you, dear," she went on. "You've always had a special place in my heart. You know that, don't you? So did your mother. I guess because you both seemed to need me more. Like your Great-Uncle Heath."

Brax reached out and touched her forehead. Her breathing was so shallow now, and her skin cold, yet dry, even in the heat of the afternoon. She was dying, he was sure of it, and yet her hand was holding his so tightly, as if he were her last hold on life.

Tears filled his eyes, and he drew her hand to his cheek. "Please, Grandma, you can't," he whispered, his gray eyes searching her fragile face. "What would we do without you?"

"But don't you see, I've seen it all, dear. There's no reason for me to stay. It's been such a long time." She sighed, closed her eyes for a moment, then opened them again and looked at him, her eyes crinkling in the corners the way they usually did when she was squinting to see something. "Do you know how long I've been without Quinn and Roth? And now DeMosse too . . . Too long. So let me go, dear, please. Let me go. Just sit here and hold my hand for a little while, though, because I'm a wee bit frightened. I never died before, you know, although God did promise . . . and Jesus . . ."

"Grandma . . ." The tears were streaming down his rugged face now, and he sucked in a sob.

"Hush, and listen," she interrupted. "I want you to do something for me, will you, dear?"

"What?"

There were tears in her own eyes too now, and he had to lean close in order to hear.

"I was here when the first shots were fired at Lexington, Brax, did you know that?" she said, her voice shaking, unsteady. "I was here when this country first came to life, when it first cried out for freedom, and I helped your grandfather fight for it too. Now, I'm still here when the last shot is fired in Mexico, stretching this country from one sea to another, just as Tom Jefferson said. But now it's your turn, dear. You, and the others. Take care of this country, Braxton. Take care of what you've fought for, so that those who went before you can be proud."

"I will, Grandma."

"You have a heritage, you know," she went on, as if she were speaking not just to him, but to all of them. "A violent one at times, yes, but one that's also filled with love. So do the others. Only I want you to promise me one thing, dear. A promise only you can keep." Her fingers tightened on his again. "Make them understand that it's up to them now, Brax, and you too. For whatever you become, whatever this country becomes, will be the heritage you leave to your children, and theirs after them. So do them proud."

He swallowed hard. "I promise."

"Good." Her voice was husky, breaking on every word. "Now I can go." She tried to smile, but didn't have the strength, and instead exhaled wearily. Then, slowly, hesitantly, her eyes closed. At first he thought she was just resting again, but suddenly he realized she was no longer breathing. A lump came into his throat and he stared at her for a long time, wanting to bring her back. Wanting her to open her eyes for just one last moment, one last soft kiss, one last word of comfort. But it was too late, and he knew it, as her fingers slowly eased on his hand, the strength in them gone.

"Good-bye, Grandma," he whispered. Yet he still sat there holding her hand and staring at her for such a long time. This quiet lovely lady who had meant so much to all of them. Then slowly, tears still in his eyes, he reached out and laid her limp hand beside the other on her breast as he studied her face. She was so still, her skin like porcelain. Yet there was a faint smile on her lips, and he wondered. Was she with them now? Could she see him?

Taking a deep breath, he stood up, and gazed down at her for a moment longer, then slowly turned and strolled to the railing that bordered the portico, where he stood looking off toward the western hills. She was right, he thought. She'd seen it all, from one beginning to the new one they were now facing, and now she'd left it all to them. What a legacy. What a gift. So precious.

He looked back one more time at her frail figure lying on Blythe's lounge chair, then listened to the noise of the celebrating downstairs, and he sighed.

"I promise, Grandma," he whispered tearfully again, his deep voice barely audible as he glanced out once more to the hills beyond the walls of the hacienda. "I promise you that none of them shall ever forget, not as long as there's a breath in my body," and he straightened proudly, walked back over to where she lay still in death, bent down, kissed her wrinkled cheek one last time, then left the portico, moving through the master bedroom, and heading on downstairs to tell the rest of her family that Loedicia Aldrich Locksley Chapman, that tremendous little lady who was not only responsible for all of them being here but also had in her own inimitable way helped mold and shape their lives, had finally found her rest.